Killing Time

by

KJ Waters

Book 3 in the *Stealing Time* Series

A Blondie Books Novel

Killing Time Published by Blondie Books

Visit my website at kjwaters.com/ for links and more information.

Cover design by Blondie's Custom Book Covers and Jody Smyers Photography (jodysmyersphotography.com). Photography by Jody Smyers Photography.

ISBN: eBook: 978-0-9862508-7-3
        Paperback: 978-0-9862508-5-9

Created in the United States of America

Subscribe to my newsletter here: www.kjwaters.com/newsletter to receive exclusive excerpts from my novels plus, advanced notice of sales and giveaways, and previews of future books. You will also receive special deals, exclusive offers, and updates on my writing.

Stealing Time, Book 1 in the Stealing Time series.
Shattering Time, Book 2 in the Stealing Time series.
Blow – A Short Story, short story during hurricane Ivan.
Tornado Alley, a short story anthology published with Caprock Writers' and Illustrators' Alliance in 2020.
Killing Time, Book 3 in the Stealing Time series.

Coming Soon:
Fracturing Time: Book 4 in the *Stealing Time* series
Blondie's Diner. Book 1 in the *Blondie's Diner* series

Killing Time

by

KJ Waters

This book is dedicated to

My brilliant, loving parents who sacrificed so much

to make our lives peaceful and happy.

Prologue

Shattering Time

Ronnie Andrews collapsed on the hard packed earth, forcing air to escape from her lungs in a loud whoosh. As her blood soaked into the dirt floor, a peaceful coldness swept through her body, originating in her gut and spreading to her limbs. A shadow in the corner of the room demanded her attention. The Grim Reaper stretched to his full height and folded her in his skeletal embrace. Ronnie did not resist. This time, she welcomed his caress.

A noise nearby startled her eyes open. She'd forgotten about the fallen man only a few feet away. His dark eyes locked on hers and she felt the sharp edges of his soul hardened by warrior training. They were tinged with selfish, unmasked evil. Ronnie recognized him, not from this life, but from her own. The realization tore through her soul, sent gooseflesh across her skin, and destroyed the peace that settled in her bones as life faded away. Ronnie imprinted this notion, and despite the chaos of the moment, she pulled the knowledge deep into her psyche to absorb its meaning in another time and place. Hatred ebbed and flowed between them until his spark went out and she was left alone looking into his cold, dead eyes. His life force dissipated like magician's smoke, leaving an unexpected feeling of surprise, relief, and unease. To her horror, Death grasped the man and pulled him close, holding them both in an abhorrent, intimate grip. Ronnie tried to push away, but her body was no longer under her control.

Morris, in old-fashioned clothes, knelt on her left side. In a flash there was another man in modern dress on her right. Over four hundred years separated them, yet they were connected to her somehow through time. They uttered equivalent words, one spoken with an English tongue, the other with American. Both merging into one solid man with dramatic implications for her past, present, and future. A bloodcurdling scream resonated across the abyss as her soul was ripped loose, and the reverberations echoed for eternity through every cell in her body.

This terrifying, electrifying, and excruciating millisecond changed her profoundly, but she would not fathom the meaning until the message was received at the other end of time. Fate loosened the grip of Death's bony fingers and for the fourth time she returned to her present life...inexplicably.

"CODE BLUE," a nurse called out. "Room 227, CODE BLUE." The intercom blared, and Ronnie trembled as her world shattered. Was she dying again? Would this be her fifth time, or only the fourth? How did one lose count of how many times they had met the Dark Angel?

Chapter 1

Sunny Skies Turn Gray

Wednesday, September 8, 2004, just north of Orlando, Florida

Ronnie Andrews pushed the grocery cart down the aisle, the wonky wheel pulling the cart to the left, trying its best to derail the buoyant feelings bubbling up inside her. She felt so free, so alive. Apparently, almost dying did that to you.

It was Ronnie's second day sprung from the joint (the hospital) and a decent meal was at the top of her list of things to accomplish with her new lease on life. With a spring in her step, she sashayed down the next aisle. Her inner voice urged moderation, to save her energy for more important things. Ronnie was halfway down the lane before she realized what was wrong. The shelves were nearly bare. She grabbed the only six-pack of toilet paper that remained, super ultra-luxury, like the last-picked rich girl at the schoolyard game of tag.

Bummer, since the contents of her refrigerator sat rotting in a trash bag in her garage, with the power out for the last five days. She'd already restocked the damn thing three times since moving here almost a month ago. Hurricane Charley had led the welcoming party only three days after she'd moved from out of state, and a few weeks ago she'd moved into her first home.

Hurricane Frances had run wild over the land last weekend, likely stalling all the trucks sent to resupply battered Central Florida. It would be slim pickings until the roads were all cleared, and normalcy could return. Ronnie longed for normalcy. The entire summer had been fraught with turmoil. From here on out it should be easy breezy as she settled into her new house and new job.

"No worries, I'll make something amazing with what's left," Ronnie mumbled to herself, glancing at the cart's contents—pickles, peanut butter, sundae topping but no ice cream, and a box of raisins. "Oh, who am I kidding? This is pointless."

On her way to the register, she found a carton of eggs and a lone wedge of twelve-dollar cheese, hopefully not too weird-tasting. She passed on the stray olive loaf at the meat counter.

Undeterred, she turned the corner, ready to pay for her meager supplies, and was greeted by a huge line. The buoyant mood slipped a little and Ronnie pulled it up like an errant sock, hoping to salvage the day.

An elderly lady smiled at her, shaking her head. "You have about as interesting a selection of crap as I do."

Ronnie laughed, noticing what was in her cart. "I see you're going to have jelly sardine sandwiches tonight!"

The woman smiled and shook her head. "How can there be a line with so little to buy here?"

Ronnie glanced around, shocked at how many people were there.

The woman reached for a pack of gum, tossing it in her cart. "Did you hear the weather forecast? Another storm is coming. They'd better get something here or we're all going to starve to death. It's not like we can go hunt for our dinners." She shook her head and pressed her lips together in disapproval.

The smile fell from Ronnie's face. "Another storm? Are you sure? We've already had two major hurricanes. Isn't that enough for a decade or two?"

"This one has already set major records. They call it Ivan, and I'm nicknaming him Ivan the Terrible. Can you believe it? It's supposed to be worse than Charley and Frances. I'm not going to have any trees left! I've already lost two."

Fear coalesced inside Ronnie's brain, turning it to mush. "I just moved here a few weeks ago from Virginia. I've got rather bad timing. I hope your house is okay."

She nodded. "Piss poor timing, sweetie. Luckily, it just messed up the yard. My begonia bed is destroyed."

Ronnie had been lucky. She'd only had slight roof damage. "I didn't hear about Ivan. My power's been out, and I just got out of the hospital."

"Oh dear, well you look fresh as a daisy. Just be ready. Ivan is going to hit Florida. Now we wait and see if it's like Charley, fast and dirty, or Frances, a long, hard screw." She winked. "If I were you, I'd move back to Virginia where you came from. Florida is being punished for something. I don't know what, but we have to repent or be sacrificed."

"I'm tempted to do just that." Ronnie considered driving back to her mom's for a while. Her new friend checked out and waved. Ronnie paid for her meager supplies and rushed her cart out to the car, all buoyant thoughts rained out. Should she head north? Her mom could take care of her while she recovered. A crushing, oppressive wave of nausea mixed with the hot humidity of the parking lot washed over her. She could not go back to her old life in Virginia. She needed to face what was happening here. Was the woman right about Florida being punished for something in its past? Was she being punished for a wrong choice of her own? Ronnie took a few deep breaths.

A few minutes later, Ronnie's new lease on life was delivering a painful dose of reality. She turned on the radio, impatient for the ads to be over. Orlando's rush hour was full of angry, sweaty people honking their horns in an attempt to force traffic to move again. The pocket opened, inching them all along, until it stopped suddenly. Ronnie had to slam on the breaks to avoid hitting the car in front of her, causing a new cacophony of horns rising like the crescendo in a symphony.

The carton of eggs she'd carefully placed on the passenger seat smashed to the floor, much like her day. Ronnie reached down to salvage what she could as the honking continued. Traffic moved ahead, leaving a huge gap between her and the car in front. A man drove by giving her the finger.

"That was totally unnecessary, sir!" Ronnie yelled.

Finally, the commercials were over and Terry James, the local TV weatherman, was back on the radio. "The latest track of Ivan shows the potential for landfall in Florida a pretty good certainty. We are still watching this one closely because it is breaking records with every news cycle."

Ronnie turned up the volume so she wouldn't miss a single word.

"On September third, as we were preparing for Hurricane Frances, Ivan set the record for the most southerly location for the formation of a major hurricane. Within six hours it set another unprecedented record for the most southerly location for a Category 4 hurricane. Today it is approaching Jamaica as a strong Category 4. There is a lot of warm water for it to strengthen further on its northerly journey towards the Sunshine State."

"Crap!" Ronnie smacked the steering wheel, realizing it was now covered with sticky, raw egg.

Terry continued, "As has been characteristic this summer, the wind shear is absent, allowing perfect conditions for strengthening. I see Ivan reaching Category 5 over the next few days." Terry signed off and the station picked up its regular programming.

As she took the exit off I-4, a few splatters of rain smacked her windshield, making her heart leap into her throat. Ronnie drove the last few minutes to her house, contemplating the uncanny bad luck of moving to Florida during the worst hurricane season in decades.

On Friday, she would be a Florida resident for one month, and in that time two major hurricanes had devastated a huge swath of Florida. One from the Gulf Coast and the other from the Atlantic, marking a huge 'X' with her house as the intersection of the two. It couldn't have been better executed if it had been planned.

Ronnie tamped down the panic. The storms, as bad as they were, were nothing compared to what happened to her while they raged. Inexplicably, the hurricanes carried her back in time to horrific conditions, ultimately leading inevitably to her death in various gruesome ways.

Fighting tears, Ronnie pulled into her driveway just as the sky was about to open up. She grabbed the groceries and dashed the ten feet to her covered porch, the smell of rain permeating her nostrils.

What a contrast. When she'd left the house, optimism had been high. Now she felt trodden upon. Everything Ronnie had found comfort in before she'd moved here had been overturned, rummaged through, and stepped on, leaving her feeling alone, damaged, and unsure of everything she thought she knew about the world.

Chapter 2

Trust Your Gut

Ronnie unlocked the door, and a meowing, white blur ran towards her, then stopped, flattening its ears against its skull. A clap of thunder echoed across the hardwood floor. The cat followed Ronnie to the kitchen, where she tossed the broken eggs and washed her hands.

She scooped up her white Persian cat, Fluffy, and clutched the terrified animal to her chest, petting her soft fur. "It's okay, Fluffy. Everything will be okay." Letting the words soak into her own frazzled soul. Would it be okay?

Ronnie reached for the TV remote, clicked on Channel 13, hoping for more information. Terry James, the lead weatherman, was in front of the green screen, excitedly giving fair warning to whoever would listen. He was showing the cone of uncertainty for the likely path of the storm. Orlando was dead center, but most of Florida was as well because the storm was still so far away. The radar depicted its looming red circulation churning in the Caribbean, poised to hit Jamaica and Cuba.

"Damn it. When is this going to stop?" she demanded.

Terry James shrugged as if in response. "Florida can't seem to get a break. We will watch this storm closely as it develops. The warm sea temperatures make it ripe for further development. This year is proving to be one of the most severe in decades. Stay with Channel 13 for updates on this evolving situation."

Ronnie clicked the TV off and paced across the living room, trying to tamp down the panic that was threatening to push her blood pressure to near bursting. Fluffy sensed her distress and rubbed against her face, purring into her ear. Ronnie buried her face in the soft, white fur. "Fluffy, I will not be so stupid this time. I am leaving town no matter what!"

During Hurricane Frances, she'd tried to head north to her mom's house in Virginia, but fate had intervened. Fate or her boyfriend Jeffrey. He hadn't exactly been her ally in the effort to get ahead of the storm. Instead, he had been more interested in getting laid than letting her evacuate, and it had almost killed her. This time she'd not let anything get in her way. Screw Jeffrey and whatever he had in mind. Screw work, screw anything that put her in the path of another killer storm.

Thunder crashed again and Fluffy jumped from her lap and ran to her favorite hiding place, under her bed. Ronnie wished she had somewhere to hide. It felt like an oppressive weight was closing in on her, the open portal to another place and time looming overhead to take her away to a more dangerous and deadly one.

She tried to shake the feelings of doom and gloom and walked to the kitchen to put away the groceries. The torrential rain out her back window made her pity her neighbors who had so much damage to their properties. What havoc would this thunderstorm bring to their already soaked homes? Ronnie felt lucky to have a roof over her head and a meal in her own home. Even a weird haphazard one was a blessing. Despite her anger towards Jeffrey, he had come through, swiftly hiring a crew to repair her roof before she'd been released from the hospital.

Ronnie put away the cold foods, barely filling one shelf in the fridge. She would give anything to have a few quiet weeks to recover. If she were to believe the doctor, her mother, and Jeffrey, the time traveling was not real. According to her mom, the visions were just a manifestation of her broken mind brought on by the stress of moving, and a rare disease called Korsakoff syndrome. The doctors still had no logical explanation on how she'd contracted it, but the lack of thiamine in her blood immediately after the episode had led them to that diagnosis. Never mind the typical patient was a severe alcoholic with years of abuse, not a healthy person who rarely drank.

Ronnie unpacked the other sad grocery bag full of weird, desperate purchases. She knew to the core of her being that she had traveled back in time, not just once, but four distinct times and places. Once during Hurricane Charley, and three times during Hurricane Frances, leaving Ronnie's psyche as tattered as the trees in her neighborhood.

The only person who believed that she'd time traveled was her best friend Steph. Jeffrey barely listened to her, claiming she was crazy. Now, when she needed to sort through her experiences and make sense of them, he shut her down, showing anger, mistrust, and jealousy. The initial dream of being a happy couple heading towards marriage that had enticed her to move was fading quickly. Out of self-preservation she needed to sort through what she wanted out of their relationship, if anything.

Ronnie grabbed a paper plate and made a cheese sandwich, hoping the *Époisses* cheese wasn't the only one left for a reason. She tore open the package and was assaulted by a strong bacon-foot smell. "Ugh." Without many choices, she hacked off a chunk of the cheese and set it on top of a piece of bread, popping it in her toaster oven. Maybe melting it would add to its appeal. When it was done, she plated it. and sat at the small kitchen table.

Ronnie examined these new and frightening feelings about ending it with Jeffrey, holding them between her fingers as if testing the quality of silk. Deep in the pit of her stomach, she recoiled, and her mind tried to pull her off topic to avoid the pain. What was it that made her so sad? The thought of ending a long-term relationship was emotional, but there was something more to this soul-clenching feeling. It reminded her of the despair she felt when her father passed away five years ago.

The dark, angry feelings reemerged, throwing her right back to the difficult months after he was gone. His death made her feel like something precious had been stolen. Without him her life would never be the same, and the gaping wound from the loss would never heal.

Ronnie took a bite of the sandwich and focused on the warm, sharp flavor, tempered by the bread, setting aside the sad, dark emotions for just a moment of respite. Thunder clapped, but this time farther away, and Fluffy returned to her lap ready for comfort, and her own dinner soon.

Jeffrey Brennan had appeared out of nowhere and swept her off her feet while she was recovering from the loss of her father. Nothing would replace her dad, but having a strong man, much like her father, love her, truly love her, helped piece her heart back together and made her feel whole again. Would leaving Jeffrey drop her back into that depression?

A flash of anger tore through her. She was stronger than that. She hated there was even a single doubt about her ability to stand on her own. Perhaps this was the type of thing you got used to in pieces, like dipping into the cold lake, inch by inch, eventually getting used to the chill.

Somehow it felt like everything was coming full circle now. She'd briefly heard her father's voice the last two times she'd slipped between this time and space and the other. Was that her mind finding another respite, or had he been somewhere in the ether as she transferred between worlds?

The last words he'd spoken to her echoed in her mind—*trust your gut*. What did her gut say about Jeffrey? Last month it told her to move to Florida to be with him, despite her inner voice telling her that there might be a reason he moved away from their life together in the first place. What did her intuition say now?

A kernel of an idea tore through her sad, foggy mood. Before Frances hit, her new boss, Mike Walsh, asked her to go to Puerto Rico to meet a new client. A glimmer of sunshine poked through her cloudy thoughts. That would solve two problems. First, it would remove her from the path of Hurricane Ivan. Second, it would get her away from Jeffrey and allow her to sort through these feelings.

She looked at her phone and opened her contacts, clicking through until she saw Mike's number. A thrill coursed through her unexpectedly. His bright blue eyes smiled in her mind, and she knew this was what her gut was telling her to do. Mike wouldn't have an opinion either way about her time traveling because he knew nothing about it. He only knew about her illness, since he'd been there in the hospital. It would be helpful because he would let her rest when she needed.

Ronnie's phone buzzed in her hand, and she nearly dropped it. It was Jeffrey intruding on her thoughts. She let it ring to voice mail and walked over to the get-well flowers Mike had sent. Ronnie lifted the vase to smell their fresh, happy scent. A warmth spread from her chest to her limbs, and with it a calming wave of energy pulsed through her body. This idea just felt right.

Her logical mind interceded with the ugly fact she'd have to travel all the way to Puerto Rico, but she pushed it aside and lifted the note Mike had sent with the flowers and read it for the umpteenth time.

Ronnie,
Welcome home. I hope these flowers cheer you as you recover. Please don't worry about work. We're thinking about you as you heal and welcome you back

when you feel ready.
With affection, Mike.

"I feel ready, Mike," she said and chuckled at the possibilities of exactly what she might be ready for with this decision. It was much more appealing than spending time with non-believers. Instead, she could find answers to some very troubling questions about Mike and how he might be connected to her through the past.

After her first time travel episode, she'd had a vague sense that Mike was tied to Mathias, the man who had saved her. The way she'd returned this last time was unmistakable. The shattered image filled her mind of Morris on one side holding her hand in the year 1588, and Mike holding the other hand in the present. Both images merged into one excruciating moment, one extraordinary melding of times, the contrast of modern, sterile, white walls with roughly hewn wood and blood-soaked earthen floors. Merging two men, one her new lover and the other her new boss. Both looked at her with such tenderness. Were these men connected through time and deeply entangled with her soul, her very essence?

What did it mean for her future? In a weird and unexpected way, it felt right and true as anything in her life. Ronnie put the dish in the sink and retired to the couch, letting the memory flood her thoughts. The passion she'd shared with Morris made her breath quicken. He had been so tender and loving until he'd taken her with animalistic abandon. The feelings she had as they lay together afterward were so different than any intimacy she'd shared with Jeffrey. Sex had always been good with her boyfriend, but she'd never felt more connected to another human being than she had with Morris.

Ronnie would follow her father's advice and trust her gut. This was something that needed exploring. It had to be significant. The alternative was the story Jeffrey and her mother told her. She was falling off the deep end, and that was much too horrible to contemplate. Ronnie chose to believe everything she'd been through had meaning, not just mental illness with a jumble of weird thoughts. Maybe this trip would answer some pressing questions about Mike. A smile spread across her lips with the decision made.

Chapter 3

Honey Brown Pools of Anger

Ronnie grabbed the suitcase from the guest room and plopped it on her bed. She'd packed it and moved temporarily to sleep in the guest room during Frances so Steph and her boyfriend Nick could sleep in the master suite.

She pulled out a t-shirt and shorts and added them to her drawers. Under the last remaining item there was a small baggie. Ronnie picked it up and cringed at the red blood along the inside of the bag.

"Oh my God! I forgot about this!" So much had happened since she'd stuck this in her suitcase.

The baggie contained a rose gold watch, her birthday present from Jeffrey last month. During Hurricane Frances, Ronnie had worn the watch, hoping it would... She wasn't sure what she'd been hoping, but it was the only thing that went back in time with her.

That trip, Ronnie had landed in a little girl's body infected with the bubonic plague. To force her return as a massive fire approached, she'd had to slit her wrists to avoid being burned to death. It had been a terrible choice, in a terrible situation.

Oh God, this could change everything. If the blood showed bubonic plague, it would prove without a doubt she'd traveled and would dispute her mother's claims that it was all in her head. Not even Jeffrey could debunk that evidence.

The doorbell rang, startling Ronnie. She shoved the watch in her pocket and nearly tripped on Fluffy retreating to her hiding place. Ronnie opened the door, half expecting Mike's perfect smile to greet her.

"Ronnie," the man said, but he was too caramel-blond and too slight in build to be Mike. Jeffrey smiled then kissed her on the cheek as he passed. "Hey, babe, how are you feeling today?"

Her excitement dissipated, and annoyance grew in its place. "You never said you were coming by, Jeffrey."

"Babe, I called but it went straight to voice mail. I wanted to see how my favorite hot blonde was doing." Jeffrey reached out to hug her, but she dodged it.

Was she ready to break it off with him? A twinge of panic clouded her thoughts. "I'm freaking out about Ivan. They say it'll hit Florida." Her heart skipped a beat, and both panicked thoughts dueled for dominance.

"It's still a long way off, Ronnie. It will probably hit Florida but could easily head towards the panhandle or Miami and not even affect us here in Central Florida." Jeffrey reached out to hold her hand and she pulled away. His touch made her cringe.

"True." She stuck her hand in her pocket, feeling the watch that had warmed with her body temperature. She imagined the bubonic plague bacteria flourishing with the heat and fought the urge to wash her hands immediately.

His expression shifted from concern to excitement. "Do you know how infrequently a hurricane makes landfall in the United States, much less three times in the same summer? This is incredible! It's a once-in-a-lifetime opportunity, Ronnie." His excitement was the polar opposite of her feelings of dread and fear. Jeffrey's eyes were alight with passion. "I can get my experiment underway. I have made so much progress already. I may even move closer to landfall if it will miss us here."

Ronnie stared at him, shocked he could be so clueless. Everything was always about *him*. She embraced the anger that had been growing for months.

Jeffrey continued, oblivious to her change in mood. "Why don't you spend the night at my house tonight, Ronnie? I've got power. I don't have any water yet, but I've got power. Funny how basic necessities seemed so unimportant after the last storm when I had both." He laughed.

"It's amazing what you take for granted, Jeffrey," Ronnie quipped, not expecting him to pick up on it.

Jeffrey honed in on the bouquet on the coffee table. He nodded at it. "Who sent those?" His mouth was a thin line.

"Mike." She stifled a smile.

The note was still in the arrangement, but he didn't reach for it.

Ronnie used the change of topic to drop her news. "As thrilled as you are about Hurricane Ivan, I'm thinking about getting out of town. I cannot be here for another storm."

A look of sympathy crossed his handsome features. "Babe, are you strong enough for that? I don't want you to overdo it. The doc said to take it easy for a few weeks."

"I know. But I'm telling you now, I am NOT staying here if Ivan is even glancing this way." She took a deep breath, steeling herself for his resistance. If Ronnie reached the point of no return and let her emotions take over, he would explode. She swallowed the biting words that begged to be let loose.

"Babe, I can fly you up to your mom's, but I'd have to leave the next day so I don't miss the storm."

Ronnie thought of being stuck with her mom for days on end while she assessed her mental health. It would probably topple her already tentative grasp on reality. "I've been toying with the idea of heading to Puerto Rico." She inwardly braced for his reaction.

"Puerto Rico? With Mike?" His face reddened as he lost the battle to control his anger. "Ronnie, that is the stupidest thing you've ever said." He sat on the couch. "Sit.

Let's talk about this, Ron." He patted the cushion next to him.

Ronnie crossed her arms and stood her ground, looking down at him. "There's not much to talk about, really."

Jeffrey pursed his lips, a sure sign an outburst was building. "Why? For Christ's sake, this is a really dumb idea. Let's just go to your mom's. Maybe she can help sort some of this medical stuff out."

"Listen, there is no way you're carting me off to my mom's to be psychoanalyzed and pitied." Ronnie shook her head but tamped down her angry tone to keep his in check. "It's for work, and I will not be caught here in another storm. Last time you kept me from leaving town. I won't have it this time."

His eyes were wide, showing a mixture of anger and shock. "What the hell? I didn't keep you from leaving. We just had no idea that it would be such a traffic jam with all the evacuations."

"Sure, manipulate the facts like you always do. I let you seduce me into staying the night when everything inside of me screamed to leave. Why did you shut off my alarm?"

Jeffrey blinked and squinted.

"Instead of getting me up early, you let me sleep. You even admitted you watched the news covering the traffic. You purposefully waited until it was too late so I would have to stay."

"That is totally NOT what happened, Ronnie." He said it with conviction, even bluster, but the nervous glance towards the bedroom gave something away.

As much as she tried to hold it in, there was too much to be said. "You, sir, are full of shit. This time I am looking out for myself, not being sucked into your damn manipulation. I will NOT be here for Ivan. I don't care what you say to keep me here. I am not going to take that risk."

He stood now, all attempts to control his anger gone. "Full of shit! You're crazy. How dare you talk to me like that."

Ronnie recoiled at his anger, even though she'd expected it. It echoed something stuck in her subconscious. Fear spread through her blood like the germs festering in her pocket.

"I'm not going to let you go, Ronnie," Jeffrey said through clenched teeth.

She took a step out of his reach and fought back tears of frustration, grasping at the one thing she could control in the wild and reckless life Florida had forced upon her. The kernel of the idea of escaping to Puerto Rico popped into reality. She was going.

"This is because of Mike, isn't it?" He nodded at the flowers, his voice still civil, but an angry set to his mouth gave away what was coming. "Is he pressuring you to go? That bastard."

"No, of course he isn't. He doesn't even know."

Jeffrey stood glaring down at her with hands on his hips. "That makes it an even stupider choice. Why would you, just out of the hospital, go all the way to the Caribbean with him, when we could go to your mom's?"

"I'm just going to present the software and come back." She bit back her anger.

"Would you be going if he wasn't offering *champagne in first class*?" He spat the words Mike had said to her on her first day of work, when Jeffrey had walked in on them.

"I'd have gone no matter who hired me, Jeffrey, because it is required for my job. You can't control everything I do." Ronnie looked up at him, embracing the blossoming resistance to anything he suggested.

"You don't have to travel thousands of miles the week after you almost died. You should be taking time off and resting." He shook his head, bouncing a few stray curls on the top of his otherwise closely cropped hair. "You shouldn't even be working right now."

Ronnie slowly shook her head, not trusting his motives. Of course, he wanted her here under his thumb, and away from Mike.

"You can't tell me that he is not a factor in your decision to go. I'm not buying it, Ronnie. Tell me again why he was at the hospital when I showed up."

"Don't, Jeffrey. We've already been through this." She took another step towards the front door, away from his aggression. "I'm going because it's my job, because I can't take another storm. I'm getting away from you and my mom, who think I'm crazy." It was almost laughable that Jeffrey and her mom agreed on something, except it aligned them both against her when she needed them the most.

"Don't avoid my questions. Why was he there by your side at the hospital, Ron?" His jaw muscle tensed. "I still don't understand why he, of all people, just happened to live a few blocks from where the Jeep broke down. It's too convenient. For Christ's sake, he was there at the hospital staring down at you like you're fucking Sleeping Beauty. "

"Real cute! But since I was unconscious when it all happened, you should be asking Steph how it all played out. I had nothing to do with any of the decisions, and I shouldn't have to be grilled about it. You should be grateful he was there to help, Jeffrey. God knows you were nowhere to be found. We all might have been killed. A frigging tree fell on Nick's Jeep while we were waiting for him to come back, you know."

"Damn it. You bitch." He looked away and a change of expression gave away how truly upset he was, and he balled up his fists. She had hit a nerve with her accusation about him not being there to save her. "I am NOT grateful that the meathead is moving in on you. I'm still furious that at your weakest moment you woke up to see him and not me." He grunted. "I am not grateful for that."

"I'm a bitch now? Why, because I don't just bend to your will? If you'd not spazzed out when my friends came over, we wouldn't have needed Mike's help."

"How the hell did Steph know where Mike lived? It doesn't add up, Ronnie." Jeffrey made a noise akin to a snort and crossed his arms.

"When I first moved here, Mike sent me a note with his address so I could contact him when the phones were out. You saw the note yourself. Steph remembered his address and thank God for that. God knows you were useless."

The angry lines intensified around his eyes. "Look, Ronnie, I am sorry I wasn't there for you. I couldn't bear to be with Steph and her entourage. I was pissed that you invited them over. I thought we were going to be alone."

Ronnie's thoughts roiled around, marinating in the anger and fury. More than anything, she needed to escape the dooming diagnosis that she was losing her mind. As much as she hated the time traveling, it was so much better than the thought of a slow spiral into mental illness. It was too terrifying to contemplate.

"Ronnie, I asked you a question." He interrupted her panicked thoughts.

"What?" Fluffy rubbed her ankle, still wanting her dinner, and Ronnie reached down to pet her.

"Why do you think Mike would be interested in you? Can he see how you're losing your grip on reality?" Pure vehemence laced his words.

Ronnie eyed the flowers, then confronted him, not dodging his piercing stare. Instead, she dove into the honey brown pools of anger and stood up to the fury building. "This isn't about Mike. I don't know what the hell Puerto Rico holds for me, but what won't happen is me submitting to Ivan." Ronnie added another blow. "Or, for that matter, you."

Jeffrey's face flushed red. He was not used to anyone standing up to him. His reaction gave her strength to pull the trigger.

Chapter 4

Crazy

The dam broke and Jeffrey's fury released in a tirade. For once Ronnie stood firm, allowing the anger to flow around her, instead of through her. She wasn't letting the torrent of bitter accusations seep in. Instead, she stared at a pulsing vein on his forehead and finally couldn't keep a snicker from escaping. These fights used to nearly destroy her. She hated making him so angry. Now she realized she didn't care. Nothing would deter her from going to Puerto Rico.

"Is something funny?" Jeffrey sneered.

"You. For God's sake, why should I have to stand here and listen to you throw a hissy fit? I'm a grown-ass woman. I can make my own decisions. Yelling at me doesn't change my mind—it makes me resent you."

Jeffrey's eyebrows nearly touched, and she could almost see his mind spinning. He was accustomed to running these arguments for his own gain. "He is such a manipulating tool, Ronnie." The snark in his voice relayed his seething hatred for Mike. "Can't you see that? The meathead is trying to get you alone." He shook his head and tapped his fingers on his thigh.

"Wrong. This is why he hired me, to persuade customers to use our systems. Mike is just doing his job. Your jealousy is really showing. Jeff, your eyes are turning green."

He flashed her an angry look. "I can't let you go, Ronnie. It's for your own good."

"*Can't let me go?* Here is what you can't do, Jeffrey Brennan. You can't tell me what to do. If I *friggin'* want to go to Puerto Rico, I'm going to Puerto Rico. End of story!" Ronnie marveled at how his insistence had sealed the deal.

Jeffrey took a few steps closer. "Ronnie, this is not a joke. This isn't me being jealous. It may be a matter of life and death. What happens if you have another episode? Your doctor would never allow you to travel so far so soon after your hospitalization. How can you think this is smart?"

"Jeffrey, there will not be another episode." Ronnie felt he was the connection to the time traveling and somehow this part of Florida. Why else would two storms cross paths directly over her? Why else would this happen right after she moved here? Ronnie needed to escape Florida, at least temporarily, and get away from Jeffrey permanently. Then all would be well. She felt it in her bones.

"Ronnie, there is no way you can know that. How can you go there after all you've been through? Less than a week ago you died. *You fucking died.* We don't even know if Ivan will hit here!"

"I will be fine, Jeffrey. I feel strong. I'm just helping negotiate a deal and then I'll come back. It's not like I'm going to trek across the island or anything." She leaned over and picked up Fluffy, holding her close.

"Ronnie, it's crazy to take this risk on a whim based on your emotions! You'll be so far from your doctor or, for that matter, any US hospital." Jeffrey put his hand on her shoulder.

Ronnie shrugged it off, knowing she was getting away from the devil she knew, and he was standing right in front of her. She'd rather take her chance with lovely lady fate and the possibilities with something new, something better.

"It is my risk, Jeffrey."

"Ronnie, you aren't in a good place to make decisions like this. Your grasp on reality is thin. Your mom confirms this—she's an expert after all. I need to step in and make this decision for you. It's for your own protection."

His final tactic released a cold tendril sliding down her back, raising the hairs on her arms. A deep, visceral reaction took over. In his eyes she saw cold, calculating, raw intelligence and something else that scared her. An overpowering memory resurfaced, but like a rat, it wasn't ready to be caught and slipped out of her grasp, leaving her feeling chilled to the bone.

"If I have to get a doctor to hold you here, I will." Jeffrey stepped towards her, and she retreated, wanting nothing more than to escape this feeling.

"Do you know what I think, Jeffrey?"

"I'm not sure it even matters," he spat. "You're not going to listen to reason."

"I am done with you. I'm sick of you calling me crazy, manipulating me, getting angry and loud so you can get your way." Ronnie took a step towards him.

Jeffrey held up his hands. "Me being manipulating? This is more proof that you're mentally unstable. It's Mike who is pressuring you to..."

"Jeffrey, shut the hell up and let me talk, for once."

Fluffy hissed and swiped a paw at Jeffrey before jumping out of her grasp.

"God, Ronnie, you've changed. How can you...?"

She surprised him by pushing him to sit on the couch. She had the element of surprise and would take full advantage of it. And for once he let her.

"You have bossed me around for the last time, you son of a bitch. I am not crazy—I traveled back in time. I don't know if you're connected to it or not, but I don't give a shit what you think." She stomped her foot. "If you had supported me through this, we might have been okay, maybe. I don't know. But making me think I'm crazy? That is a huge betrayal and I'm not putting up with it."

Jeffrey opened his mouth to respond, and she stepped closer, wagging her finger in his face.

"Nope, I'm not done. You have put my friends down for a year. You've cheated on me. You sorry sack of shit."

Jeffrey wore a look of utter shock, mouth opened and eyes wide. "More lies that Steph told you, no doubt."

"Steph has never lied to me. You lie all the time. I cannot stay with someone who puts his needs over mine. Like the night before Frances, you just wanted to get laid and you got your way, risking my life and safety by keeping me from leaving. Who does that? That is the ultimate unforgivable act."

"I did no such thing. You wanted it as badly as I did, Ronnie. You can't put that on me." His face was growing redder by the minute.

She racked her brain for every wrong he'd done her. This was her chance to spit fire before she kicked him out. "Who else have you slept with, Jeffrey? Steph told me she saw you out to dinner with some ho bag when I was still in Virginia."

His mouth was a thin line, and he nearly growled his next words. "I was out with Hannah, Ronnie. The chick in the lab next to me. We were talking business, and it wasn't for pleasure."

"I call bullshit on every word you've ever uttered to me, Jeffrey. If you are capable of love, you would be looking out for me, not your damn libido. I needed all my friends with me as the hurricane approached. What did you do, you sucky-ass boyfriend?"

He stood and glared down at her now.

Ronnie wasn't cowed. "You demand in a hissy fit that I ask them to leave, as if you are more important than my abject terror of another time travel episode. As usual, Jeffrey is the most important person in the room. What about me? When do we cover that? Steph has been the *only one* helping me through the most horrific thing I've ever encountered in my life. Oh right, you think I'm just crazy, that I imagined the whole thing." She waved her hand dismissively.

"Well, you are acting crazy right now, Ronnie. You have to admit." Jeffrey took her arm and led her to the couch. "Why don't you sit down and let me get you something to drink."

Ronnie jerked her arm out of his grip. "I'm not falling for your bullshit anymore, Jeffrey. You'll get me drunk, have sex with me, and leave me alone and terrified yet again. Just like you did when I first got here in Florida, threatening to leave me alone when Hurricane Charley was about to hit."

He softened his tone, as if talking to a small child. "I didn't leave you, Ronnie, you came to my lab. Remember?"

"If you remember correctly, you told me you couldn't be with me, but then at the last minute you changed your plans. It wasn't about my birthday. It was about *you*, Jeffrey. It's always about you!"

"How can you say that? I had your favorite dinner, a beautiful watch, the works." He looked dejected now, his puffed-up chest deflated, panic in his eyes.

"I can say it because I know you better than anyone on this planet, Jeffrey, and it is always about what *you* want. You bluster and fuss until you get your way. You get loudest when I won't bend to your will. Well, you know what? I'm going to Puerto Rico with Mike and there is nothing you can do about it."

"Sure as hell there is something I can do about it." Jeffrey's voice was menacing now.

A snake of fear crawled up her spine. "I want you to leave." She said it calmly, firmly, and with a tone that she hoped conveyed no argument.

His expression changed from icy to something she'd rarely seen in the time she'd known him—surprise. She'd never once ended a fight with him. The pure force of his personality would be released, and she'd bend to his will. This time he would be robbed of that victory.

"What?" He reached for her arm. "I'm not done, Ronnie." He took a breath to continue.

Ronnie jerked her arm out of his grip and marched to the front door before he could say another word. "You're done if I say you are." Ronnie pulled the door open. "And don't ever come back here. Don't call me, don't text me."

His eyes narrowed and they almost glowed with anger. Then something caught their attention. A man stood just outside the door. For the second time tonight, she thought it was Mike, but realized it was the FedEx man, his shirt logo a dead giveaway.

"Miss Andrews? I have a package for you. Can you sign here?" He held a clipboard out.

Ronnie stared in surprise. "Just one minute. My guest was leaving." She turned to Jeffrey, who looked equally surprised.

In a huff, Jeffrey walked out the door, rudely pushing past the FedEx guy. He turned halfway down her driveway and said, "Ronnie, you will regret this."

Ronnie calmly waved, hiding the shaking that had begun deep in her gut.

"You okay, Miss Andrews?" The FedEx guy glanced back at Jeffrey, who stepped into his car. "You need me to stay another minute until he leaves?"

"Yes, that would be really nice if you could," Ronnie said, letting down her façade of steely strength. She covered her quivering mouth, then signed for the package. Jeffrey drove off, squealing his tires.

"You gonna be okay?" the FedEx guy asked gently.

"I'm fine. He will go home and probably call me to give me an earful." She tried to smile, but the corners of her mouth turned down. "Nice thing about that is I can just not answer the phone."

He handed her the package, and they both looked at her driveway. There was no sign of Jeffrey's baby blue Mercedes. "If you say so." He waved goodbye. "You stay safe, Miss Andrews."

"You too." Ronnie locked the door behind him and pressed her forehead against the cool metal. She hugged the package to her chest and finally realized what she was holding. It was from her mother and contained one of the most valuable commodities on Earth, at least to Ronnie.

Chapter 5

Psychic Troubles

Ronnie felt a tumultuous swirl of competing emotions as it hit her. She'd just broken up with Jeffrey! Her legs felt weak as she returned to the couch, then closed her eyes and took a few deep breaths, focusing on letting out the terror Jeffrey had incited. Would he be back to stop her from leaving? Would this push him over the edge, making him redouble his efforts to control her? Surely he couldn't commit her—he had no authority over her. She forced out another exhale. Jeffrey would not get the chance. Steph would be here soon and maybe she could spend the night at her house.

Her attention shifted to the package, and she eagerly tore open the box, surprised to find a leather-bound book with intricate embossing. It reminded her of riding horses at Girl Scout camp. She held it to her nose and took a deep breath, reliving the freedom she'd felt on a horse.

This volume held a different kind of freedom. One that gave her a precious gift. A glimpse of the free, uninhibited thoughts of her father. Hopefully, this volume would answer some questions. Her mom had been quite mysterious about what it contained, only saying it might give her answers about her recent brush with death.

She cracked it open. On the first page a date was scrawled in the neat, fluid cursive of her father's hand, *Volume 12, January 1998*. A thrill ran up her spine, and in her mind, she felt his strong, firm hand on her shoulder. She reached up to grasp that hand from the past and squeezed it.

Ronnie flipped the page and read his first entry. It didn't contain any precursory text explaining the purpose of the journal. Volume twelve implied eleven other gems awaiting her. Her father had been meticulous about keeping a daily log of his life, but her mom had never offered any up before. Ronnie suddenly craved to read every word he had ever written. She steeled herself for an emotional ride reading her father's journal entries from two years before he died.

January 28, 1998

It is odd how just overnight my mood has shifted from optimism about the project to a near hopelessness. I have poured more than 26 years into this project and have made extensive breakthroughs, yet today I feel hopeless at any completion. I have hit a brick wall in the research and there has been almost no progress in nearly two years.

My lab partner, Dr. Steinblat, is encouraging me to hire a young graduate who may be able to look at my research with fresh eyes. I am beginning to take this to heart and have started my search for such a person. Perhaps that would give me the breakthrough I need to further the study.

Ronnie's dad had been a scientist, but she didn't know anything about what project he'd been working on with Steinblat. Her dad had died of a heart condition. Did this melancholy lead to his premature death? She read on, skimming through pages full of scientific formulas, scribbled notes that were way above her head, then stopped on a page with actual words.

March 12, 1998

Steinblat is unwilling to further my studies and we have decided to work independently on our own projects. It is adding to my fatigue on this research, and it feels like abandonment. He has not outrightly said he has lost faith in the project but instead has made outside factors the reason for his shift. The lab director is in agreement, and we have begun autonomous grant writing projects to further our individual causes. It saddens me greatly to go our separate ways, but as things often do in my studies, they morph into failures and disappointments.

I do not hold a grudge against my good friend Steinblat. He has given his all to my vision. It is only fair to allow him the freedom to pursue his own studies and break free from the clipping of his wings with my dead-end project. This has furthered my efforts into seeking a new protégé who may breathe fresh life into my work, and perhaps make the breakthrough that has eluded me.

Ronnie could feel his pain through her father's words. She hadn't noticed a shift in his demeanor, but at the time, she'd been a sophomore in college and had been caught up in her own world at the University of Virginia. She tried to remember her interactions with her father over spring break. Was this around the time he seemed to shrink and wither? She had thought it was just regular aging and maybe stress, but she vaguely remembered starting to see her dad in a new light. His vigorousness was waning, and for once he was beginning to look his age.

Ronnie read a few more pages until she was interrupted by Fluffy, who gave her the *feed me now* look. What was so urgent that her mom had sent this journal now? Was it merely that his work wasn't going well, and he had felt abandoned? Her mom could have just told her that. There had to be much more in this volume. She stood and stretched, setting the book down on the table next to the flowers. This would need a quiet afternoon and some coffee.

"Poor kitty, I'm so sorry." Ronnie stood and fed the cat her long-awaited dinner.

Fluffy purred happily and scarfed down her food.

Ronnie's cell phone rang, and anger flashed through her, expecting Jeffrey needling her. To her delight, it was Steph calling.

"Luv, are you ready? I've got a surprise for you." Her chipper Scottish brogue was comforting.

"Wow, surprises, I can't wait." Ronnie stifled a yawn. What she really wanted was to spend the evening with her dad's journal, but she feigned excitement for her best friend's sake. "What do you have planned for me?"

"You will see. I'll be there in fifteen minutes. Bring your courage. This may prove to be either ridiculous or deeply troubling." Steph played it up by whispering the last few words.

Ronnie laughed at her playfulness. It was precisely what she needed. "Should I wear a suit of armor or clown shoes?"

Steph laughed. "Both!" Steph hung up.

Ronnie chose a pair of cut off jean shorts, leather flip-flops, and the American Idiot tour shirt her college roommate had sent for her birthday. Surely that would be appropriate for anything Steph had planned.

She washed her face and added light makeup, singing, "Wake Me up When September Ends."

Steph knocked on her door a few minutes later and maintained the playful mystery. Ronnie held back her news about Jeffrey, not wanting to interrupt the adventure Steph had put so much work into. They drove to a part of town Ronnie hadn't seen before.

"God, you're quiet, Ronnie. Are you alright?" Steph glanced at her as she drove.

"I'm tired. And there is so much on my mind, Steph."

"Let me guess, Jeffrey?" Steph glanced at her, eyes flashing blue to match her royal blue capris.

"Well, that and I was just reading my dad's journal. Remember I told you about my weird conversation with my mom the other day? She won't tell me what this journal has to do with what happened to me during the storms. I'm supposed to call her when I'm done reading it."

"It's not like your mom to be so cagey about anything. What do you think it means?" They turned down a partially abandoned street then continued into a residential neighborhood.

"Not sure. My dad was really depressed but I never knew it. The journal was written when I was in college, so I wasn't around. I don't remember him being down about much. He was always glad to see me when I got home."

"Oh, that sounds heavy, Ronnie. Let me know when you figure it out. It's weird that she just doesn't come out and say you're crazy. She's a social worker for God's sake. It's what we all expect from her."

Ronnie tamped down the hurt over the last conversation with her mom. She'd given zero credence about her going back in time. Ronnie was convinced that the Korsakoff symptoms were a reaction to the time traveling, not, as her mom thought, the cause of hallucinations about the events. At least Steph was willing to give her theory the benefit of the doubt.

Steph glanced at her, a twinge of worry crossing her pretty face. "Okay, do you remember hearing about my friend Phillipa?" They pulled up to a small stucco house. Phillipa and Steph worked together, and they'd become fast friends in the office in the same company Ronnie worked in.

"Yeah. Is this the surprise?"

"Nope, she will be our tour guide to the surprise's location." Steph beamed, then turned off the car and opened the door.

"Oh God. Steph, what have you done?" Ronnie exited Steph's Jeep Liberty and felt the hot humidity soak into her skin as they approached the house. The front door was painted a powerful red.

The door flung open and Phillipa stepped out onto the stoop, her long, beaded braids tied up in a colorful scarf, her mahogany skin beautifully contrasted against the white peasant blouse. She hugged Steph and smiled at Ronnie.

"Ronnie, it is incredible to finally meet you. I've heard so much about you," Phillipa said, holding her hand out.

Ronnie shook it and glanced at Steph, wondering how much she'd shared with Phillipa. "I've heard only great things about you, Phillipa." Ronnie fumbled into a sideways hug as Phillipa caught her off guard.

Phillipa stepped away and jingled her key ring with a purple rabbit's foot and various dangling mementos in silver and bronze that extended down eight inches. "We must get going. I don't want to miss our appointment."

"Appointment?" Ronnie's mood shifted from her father's gloom to a new kind of dread mixed with excitement. "What have you two concocted here?"

Steph and Phillipa laughed and walked towards the golden-brown Dodge Dart parked in the driveway.

"Wow, what year is this car?" Ronnie was impressed with the impeccable restoration.

"This old thang?" Phillipa smiled as she sat in the driver's seat. "1967. My husband is an old car buff."

Ronnie opened the heavy door and sat down on the neat, firm back seat.

Phillipa adjusted the driver seat and turned to Steph. "I think we should tell Ronnie where we're going. She needs to get her mind ready for this." Phillipa turned around to look at Ronnie in the back seat.

"You're probably right." Steph took a deep breath and let it out dramatically. "Ronnie, Phillipa is taking us to her psychic." She pressed her lips together, waiting for Ronnie's reaction.

A stabbing fear tore through Ronnie. "Oh, God."

Phillipa laughed. "Yeah, baby, Steph said you would react that way, but we both think it may help. She's been super mysterious about it. Something about a new boss and a weird feeling that you are connected in a past life or something."

"Past life?" Ronnie met Steph's intense look.

"Or something." Steph lifted her eyebrows and lowered her chin, that Ronnie read as *I didn't tell her your secrets*. "Let's go ask some questions. I think you should do this alone, Ronnie, but we will be just outside the door. We will be here for you."

Ronnie looked through the greenery of Phillipa's yard, shaking her head. "Steph, won't you go in with me?"

"Ronnie, I can't. I just cannae." Steph did not need to explain that she was Catholic and wasn't able to delve into the dark arts.

"If you need me, I'm here," Phillipa said. "But you're gonna love Ini. She is so wise." Phillipa smiled. "And I swear to you on my life that she is not full of crap. I can see you're skeptical."

"Maybe." Ronnie sat on her hands and dove deep in thought as they drove fifteen minutes to a small, quiet neighborhood in Winter Park. They all exited the Dodge Dart and Ronnie tried to swallow a lump in her throat. Visions of Madam Zangari's dark living room in eighteenth-century London fostered a new fear. That encounter had brought bloodshed and begun the downhill spiral leading to her first demise.

Steph grabbed her hand as they walked the short way up to the door of the small ranch-style home. In the window was an orange neon *Psychic* sign. "It's gonna be worth it, Ronnie. I can feel it."

Ronnie's legs shook with each step. "I hope so, Steph."

Phillipa was ahead of them and rapped on the storm door. Ronnie saw clear images of a bear standing before her in the dark from her last trip back. A deep, visceral fear tore through her, forcing her to step off the stoop. Steph pulled her back up the single step and squeezed her hand.

Ronnie hadn't ever truly believed in psychics, but certainly that opinion had changed when the old Native woman N'auhtuck's vision had come true within the hour. Ronnie heard the strange words back in 1583 sharing her premonition about the lightning strike and events that followed. She would need to put her trust in this process, if for no other reason than to get some answers about Mike, her father, and everything else she'd been through in the last month since the time traveling had begun.

Chapter 6

Who Is Dis Man?

Ini opened the door and beamed at Phillipa. "Sista, pleased to see you," she said in a musical Jamaican accent. "I see yuh bring yuh friends dis time."

Ini stepped aside and let them in her home, for that was what it was. The rich, spicy smell of incense wafted around the room and caused a smoky visage. A soothing, comfortable feeling crept into Ronnie's bones, and she relaxed a bit.

"Tea? Coffee?" Ini offered and both Steph and Phillipa declined. Ronnie did as well. "What brings you here today, chile?" Ini said to Phillipa, glancing at all three women.

"This one here." Phillipa tilted her head towards Ronnie.

Ini smiled and squeezed Ronnie's arm. "Yeah, you're di one that have mi thinkin' hard."

"Me?" Ronnie wanted to pull from her gentle grip, but manners kept her in place. A tendril of energy entered her arm, worming its way up her shoulder into her mind, sparking it with energy and soulfully deep questions. It surprised her how much credence she was already giving this woman. "I do need help sorting things out." Ronnie glanced at Steph, who smiled uncomfortably. Steph was really bothered by being in this house. "Steph, you go wait in the car. I'll update you later." Ronnie smiled at Ini. "I'm ready."

As she and Ini started down the hall, Phillipa handed Steph the rabbit's foot and the string of keys and baubles, and Steph left the house.

"Come dis way, please." Ini gestured ahead of her. "I can feel yuh anxiety." Ini's brown eyes showed care and concern. She spoke to Phillipa next. "What a happen with yuh frien'? 'Ar vibe salt, mon." There was no menace in the unfamiliar words, but it added a layer of intrigue.

Phillipa smiled and responded, "Yeah, she's not feeling too lucky right now, so she may just give you a chance, Ini."

Ini laughed and continued walking down the hall. She pushed open a bedroom door and Ronnie entered. Ini followed and shut it behind her. In the center of the room was a small round table with a hurricane lamp covered in golden glass panes. The walls were covered in a dark purple foil paper that reflected the flickering candle.

Ronnie's guts were in turmoil. She couldn't squander this opportunity.

"Please, sit down an' relax." Ini sat across from her on a low wooden stool. A flickering candle on the glass table made every square inch of the room alive with movement.

Ronnie took a deep breath and tried to calm her nerves. Like Steph said, this could end in great discoveries or complete disappointment.

"Before we begin, can I tell yuh what I'm feelin'?" Ini said, a dark look passing across her lively features, adding years to her face.

Ronnie had thought she was in her twenties, but with the smile gone, she looked older, perhaps her forties? "Please. I'd love that."

"A feel someting coming right off yuh skin 'ere." Her hands hovered over Ronnie's. "Someting bigga dan di two of us, bigga dan dis house. Bigga dan anyting dat evah walk in my shop before."

Ronnie looked away, unable to meet her gaze. Ini's calmness was gone, and in its place was anger. The corners of her mouth turned down, emphasizing how affected she was.

"Well, girl, talk! Di trut', now." Ini leaned towards Ronnie, her eyebrows drawn together.

"The truth? I'd be happy to share it if I understood the truth. What do you want to know?" Ronnie swallowed hard, her nerves drying out her mouth.

"Who is di man," she tapped the table, "dat doin' deez tings to yuh? Dat carryin' yuh to places you don' want to be?"

"Man? Do you mean Morris?" Ronnie asked.

"Di man is..." She stood and paced the room and, in a flash, turned around, her batik skirt flowing out from her hips and around her thighs until it settled. "A bad man. 'Im always been a bad man. 'Im a ginnal."

Morris did not fit that description. "A bad man? Do you mean now in this time or in the past?" Ronnie didn't understand her anger. Was she mad at Ronnie or this man?

"Yes, bot' in dis moment as well as every time you 'an 'im deal. He always ruins you. Every moment, every time, every touch is like di kiss of deat'." She sat down on the stool and the air she stirred made the candle flicker wildly, reflecting the unsettling conversation.

Ronnie wanted to answer quickly, but instead, she held back and let Ini's words soak into her like a drop of water into a sugar cube, dissolving every conceived notion of how this meeting would go. "I'm not sure what you mean."

"You know di man. Everywhere yuh go, he's there. 'Im destroyin' yuh peace, 'im changin' yuh path prematurely."

Ini's dark eyes bored into her soul and planted a seed of thought that grew in her mind. A warrior dancing before a fire. One who forced her to do a wicked deed in another time and place. Another man standing in a courtroom speaking against her, forcing her to use every mental tool to save her life. Ini had cut straight to the heart of the matter. It completely spooked her.

"I... yes..." Ronnie wanted to tell her there had been a man that fit this description each time she'd gone back, but something was tugging at her memory. Something set deep in her psyche that was trying to surface. "I hope you can help me sort through it all." Wishing now she'd said yes to tea or coffee, as her throat was bone-dry.

"Dis is why we are togetha. To discovah the trut' about dis. And also, to stop dis man from destroyin' more dan *your* worl'." Ini crossed her arms, her mouth a thin line, making Ronnie's nerves so taut you could play a tune on them. "Come on, spit it out, girl," Ini said, her expression softening, and she reached out to touch her hand. "I get emotional when people bring big tings fa mi to help dem wid. Please, I am here to help yuh, not frighten yuh."

Ronnie relaxed a notch and took a moment to gather her thoughts. Despite the number of times she retold this story, she had not yet come up with a decent way to start her strange tale. "Ini, I'm terrified of what has happened. I have to figure out how to make this stop or I'm sure it is going to kill me one way or the other."

"Tek yuh time, chile. We will fin' yuh salvation togetha." Ini smiled sweetly, giving Ronnie a smidge of her confidence back.

"During the last two hurricanes I traveled back in time. I don't have any idea how it happened, but it did." Ronnie watched Ini's expression change from nearly blank to a heavy squint, as if her eyes couldn't believe what her ears heard.

"Yuh mean yuh travel back in time?"

"Well, I think so anyway." Ronnie detailed her time travels and the harrowing events that had brought her here, a place she'd also never expected to be.

Ini listened carefully and finally stood and walked to a corner cabinet built into the room, pulled out a bottle of rum, and poured two drams, returning in a flourish of batik to the table. "Drink dis."

Ronnie knocked back the rum in a single uncharacteristic gulp and set the glass down on the table in unison with Ini.

"How what yuh tellin' mi have anything to do with di man I jus' describe to you? What yuh tink about what I tell yuh about 'im actions?" Ini dipped her finger in the dram and swiped the remaining rum and delivered it to her mouth.

"I was shocked, Ini, because I had feelings of another man, a good one that I encounter each time I have traveled. I hadn't ever thought about the bad one you describe until now."

"Okay den, tell me about dis good man. Maybe it will lead us to di same crossroads where we will fin' di dark one."

Ronnie focused on her feelings towards Mathias, and the overwhelming connection she felt with Morris in early America. "Both men I felt an instant attraction to, and an unexplained trust that shouldn't have been there in any normal situation."

"Dere's more. Tell me." Ini tapped the table.

"When I returned the last time during Hurricane Frances, something went wrong. During the transfer, I was in two places and two times simultaneously. Morris was on one side of me in my moment of dying in early America, and Mike, my boss, was on my other side in the hospital. Every other time I returned it was like I'd been asleep, then would wake up back in Florida. This time I was in both places at the same time and my soul was leaving my body in both places at that moment."

"Tell about di boss man," Ini said, leaning forward to soak in every detail Ronnie conveyed.

Ronnie couldn't help but smile in describing Mike. "He was there when I woke up. He helped me get to the hospital while I was unconscious."

"Unconscious, but in anotha worl', eh?" Ini asked.

"Yes, exactly. I was living in another time and my body was here, but my consciousness was not."

"Go on. Dis Mike is a good man. Do you have di same feelings about 'im like you had for Morris and Mathias?" Ini's eyes were nearly glowing, and Ronnie could see the gears turning inside. She was putting all this together, not with skepticism as everyone else had shown her, but with a different energy, stronger even than Steph, who was always on her side.

"I'm beginning to. It wasn't as strong as with the men back in time, but the shattering moment really impressed upon me that there must be a connection. Oh my God, Ini. I just remembered something." Ronnie took a deep breath and let out some of the pent-up stress. "When I saw Mike right after my first time traveling, I had this overwhelming feeling that he and Mathias were the same person."

"Oh, see, dis is big stuff. Di puzzle pieces dem comin' togetha nicely. Tell me about any otha man dat take on dis same role of a good man at otha times."

Ronnie thought through the other times she'd traveled. First was Mathias in London during Hurricane Charley. During Hurricane Frances she had gone back several times. First was after the shipwreck off the coast of Florida with a man who called her baby. The image of his crew cut, and sunburned face swam in her mind, and she flinched at the memory of what had happened to him.

Ronnie focused on Ini's anxiously awaiting face. "The time with a shipwreck, there was a good man. He had said a man named George sabotaged the mast of our boat and lied about the weather forecast. We were stranded off the coast of Florida during a storm."

Ini's eyes grew wider. "So, a bad man in dat time." She smacked the table with her palm.

"Yes, there was. Let me think. Next, I went to the Fire of London and a little boy had helped me try to escape the fire." The boy had been so kind waiting for her, risking his life to help save her. "He was definitely the good one."

"Aha, yes. I see a pattern, Ronnie. Tink now." She tapped the table. "Was dere a bad one dere, too?"

That threw Ronnie off track because there had not been anyone in particular that stood out. Her father in that time had not helped her escape but he wasn't doing it out of malice. "The only one that could be considered evil was the cousin who trapped us in the inn."

"'Im trap yuh and make di fire burn yuh up?" She shook her head in disgust. "Das an evil act. Okay, di nex' time, where were you and what kinda people yuh meet?" Ini asked enthusiastically.

"I'm not sure if he was the evil one though. He didn't know the fire was coming when he nailed the window and door shut. The next time I met Morris was in early America and we had this instant connection." Ronnie could feel the blush rising up her neck, remembering the heat they'd shared.

"With di good man, right? So, who was the evil one dat yuh met? Maybe he's di one I felt so strongly when I see yuh?"

"They called him Wahab." Ronnie shuddered, remembering the last time she'd looked into his cold, dead eyes. "He was without a doubt evil. How did you feel his presence when you first met me?"

"He's still wit' you, Ronnie. A part of 'im spirit still clingin' to yuh." Ini shook her head and stood again, refilled their drams, and left the bottle of rum on the small table between them.

"Oh God, really?" Ronnie felt a shiver up her spine and reflexively took the dram and emptied it, hoping it would bring some warmth to the remaining chill Wahab left in her mind. "How is that possible?"

"Ronnie, tell me dis. Di moment yuh leave dat place, where was Wahab?"

A stab of fear ran through Ronnie's heart. "He was right next to me, Ini. We were both dying on the floor, and we locked eyes."

Ini wiped a trickle of sweat that ran down her forehead. "Pure evil. I feel him strongly. Yuh bring back some o' 'im spirit with you. I felt the evil oozin' off of you the minute I touch yuh."

Ronnie had to force herself to breathe. A deep, visceral reaction shocked her to the core as goosebumps rose along her arms. "Can you help remove it, Ini? Please, you have to get him off me." Ronnie wiped at her arms as if that would break Wahab loose.

"You have Mike, your boss, here in dis time representing di good man. Who yuh tink represents di bad man in yuh life now?" Ini asked urgently.

"I don't know," Ronnie said instinctively, but in a burst, the memory she had suppressed with Jeffrey was broken loose and poured forth into her mind unabated, as if it had been waiting for this moment to present itself. She closed her eyes and held up her hand to silence Ini in case it would interrupt the feelings.

Her mind relived that intense moment on the dirt floor of Morris's cabin where her blood mingled with Wahab's. She forced another breath, not realizing she'd been holding it. In the second her eyes locked with Wahab's, just before the shattering, she had realized a great truth. Something she'd locked away because of its magnitude and the pain it would cause. A sharp stabbing in her heart made her clutch her chest at the realization. Tears rolled down her cheeks.

Ini grabbed her hand and squeezed it. "Breathe, Ronnie! Yuh turnin' blue, chile."

Ronnie inhaled deeply and the image fell away, the dark, haunting thought clear as day now. Wahab was the dark side of Jeffrey's soul. Her boyfriend for the last year and a half was the evil that Ini had been describing. In a flash, she saw the same evil in Jack, another dark side of Jeffrey, from her first time traveling. Ronnie opened her eyes, or maybe they'd been open but lost in the memories. She'd been sleeping with the enemy, tied to him through time, encountering him on each trip back.

Ini was by her side, pushing her blonde locks out of her face. Ronnie wrapped her arms around Ini's waist.

"Jeffrey is the evil one, Ini." And the pain of the words hit her like a tsunami.

"Who is dis man?" Ini asked again.

Ronnie tapped the empty dram and waited until the fire in her belly was stoked before telling Ini about Jeffrey, and how he may be connected to her troubles.

Chapter 7

Ghost in the Machine

Ronnie wiped her eyes and took a deep breath. It did little to calm the terror that had broken loose with the revelation that Jeffrey was the evil Ini had felt. "How can I be in a relationship with someone who represents such evil, Ini?" Fear poked around the edges of Ronnie's heart, making it beat faster. "I still can't completely see it. We've had a lot of wonderful moments."

"'Im powerful, the kinda man dat makes you feel someting dat probably not dere. People like 'm is master at manipulation. It easy fi dem to make yuh believe anything dem want yuh to believe." Ini handed her a Kleenex and Ronnie used it.

A tsunami of emotions flowed over Ronnie. Memories of their intimacy and what she had thought were genuine feelings of love. Steph had always accused her of being naive about him. Had she been right all along? Her ego told her this whole thing was bullshit. Her logic pieced all of his bad behavior together into a straitjacket of manipulation and abuse.

"Ini, I have a lot of questions for you. You can sense that something really strange is going on, can't you?"

Ini cracked a wide smile. "Dat may be di understatement o' the year. Of course, dere is a deep, dark magic dat I don't understand 'ere. Tell mi more."

Ronnie took a deep breath, not sure where to begin. "I can say this to you because you believe in things that a lot of people don't." Ronnie paused, her courage growing.

Ini's eyebrows knitted together, but she restrained herself, which was a surprise given how everyone else had reacted to that particular confession.

"My mom thinks I'm crazy. Jeffrey does too. Steph wants to believe me, but I can see doubt in her face. I mean this is some weird stuff. I just need someone to listen and help me think this through from a different perspective."

Ini flipped the dreadlocks behind her shoulder and cocked her head to the side. "I can see it spillin' outta yuh. Just let it fly into dis space so we can examine it togetha. Start at the beginnin'." She waved her hands in a circle.

The cinching in her gut loosened a tad and Ronnie took a deep breath. "Jeffrey works at a cloud weather lab and had to work the night of Hurricane Charley. It was also my birthday and he invited me to spend the night away from the storm. He gave me a watch."

She looked at her wrist, remembering that she still needed to get it tested for the plague. She'd keep that tidbit to herself for now.

"Just as Charley was reaching its peak, I went back in time to London in the 1800s. I met a man named Mathias who tried to help me." Ronnie remembered the last moment she'd seen Mathias, and the intense sadness returned. She could feel the corners of her mouth turn down, but she refused to let her emotions keep her from telling the story. Ronnie continued with the broad brush of what had taken place over the last few months. Near the end of her telling, she couldn't keep it together.

Ini reached out to touch her hand. "So how yuh manage fi get back to dis time?"

"I died. I frigging died and that brought me back to Jeffrey's lab," Ronnie blurted, and she could feel her face go hot with the memory.

"*Death*' brings yuh back!" Ini stood and let out a stream of unfamiliar Jamaican words. "Den durin' Hurricane Frances? Di same?"

"Yes, the same thing. I died each time I came back."

"Blouse an' skirt!" Ini slapped the table, making the candle dance wildly. Ini's eyes were wide, but she didn't have the look of disbelief. She looked at her intently and nodded. "Gowan." She sat back down, looking at her intensely.

"During Frances, I returned to my house and was able to talk to Steph and tell her what happened. Later, after I'd been asleep for a while, I went back again to the sixteenth century. This time I was in Colonial America in 1588. I woke in a grave where the people surrounding me thought I'd risen from the dead. Morris protected me from the crowd and in a lot of ways reminded me of Mathias."

Every time it had ended with her death, but she had taken control of the situation twice now and she was afraid of the consequences. Ini's dark eyes were even darker now, as if she knew what Ronnie couldn't say.

Ini spoke in a deeper voice with an incredulous timber, "I feel your pain. I feel anger, and I feel sadness. But yuh keepin' someting from me...what is it?"

Ronnie swallowed hard. Steph believed suicide was a mortal sin. What would Ini think? "The last two times I took my own life to force me to return. Before you react, let me just say I didn't know what else to do and I knew that dying seemed to bring me back to my own time. So that's what I chose. Do you think there will be consequences for that choice?" Ronnie shook her head. "I killed myself, but not in the true sense. I did it to return to my own life."

Ini took a deep breath and cocked her head to the side. "You did what you had to do. Nothin' nuh wrong with doin' wha' yuh have do fi save yuh life. Dat is survival. Yuh jus' have to do wha' yuh gut tell yuh."

Her father had said nearly the same words. A pang of fear forced its way in the competing emotions. "Ini, I don't know how to make this stop. The hurricanes just keep coming."

"Yuh evah go back when no storm not happenin'?" Ini leaned towards Ronnie.

"No, I seem to be fine until there is a hurricane."

"What about durin' a thunderstorm?" Ini asked.

"No, never."

"Every time it happens yuh was in the same place with di same people nearby?"

Ini's dark, inquisitive eyes shone in the light.

Ronnie paused. "The first time I was with Jeffrey at his lab. The second time I was at my house with Steph, her brother Ian, and her boyfriend Nick."

"Where was Jeffrey the second time?" Ini asked.

"We were together before the storm hit, but he left. He was mad I invited them over. That's what is so weird. During both storms I was in two different locations, with totally different people. The only thing that was the same was the fact that a hurricane was nearing its peak."

Ini shook her head, making the dreadlocks come alive again. "Mi nevah hear anyting like dis before. I can feel a little o' what yuh been through. Dere is a tangled web with di thread from yuh past and from yuh future."

Ronnie's eyes opened wide. "My future?"

Ini smiled. "Dere are otha realms dat we can dabble in. I don' fully understan' it, but I tend to believe in past lives. Dere's always a man who wi' help yuh and anotha man who wi' harm yuh."

"Yes." Ronnie felt that same connection with Mike. Could he be one of the future connections?

Ini asked, "Who is di bad man from di firs' time you go back?"

Ronnie sat up straight. "Jack Ingram. He was my brother in that time."

"Yuh brotha. Okay. Past lives yuh deal with di same people in each life, but they might be in a different role. It could be yuh fahtha one time, maybe yuh brotha di nex'. Maybe is jus' a close frien'. Di same pattern is here in dis life wit' di same people. Dere's a good man, a bad one, and dere may be othas."

She knew Ini was trying to wrap up their time together, but before she left, she wanted to address another concern. "There's one other thing that happened with the time traveling." Ronnie paused, reading Ini's eager expression.

"Gwan." Ini nodded.

Ronnie picked up a tissue and blew her nose. "A few times when I traveled there was another voice in between the past and returning here. Like the in between worlds in its own space and time." Ronnie's mouth trembled and she took a minute to get her voice back from the tightening of emotion.

Ini leaned in towards her. "Girl, yuh full o' intrigue."

Ronnie shook her head, wishing she was back to a rather boring existence, before all of this started. "It was my father's voice. He passed away five years ago, and I've not had any, um..." Ronnie struggled for the words, "contact with him. I mean I miss him terribly and think about him a lot, but this was..." She wiped away a tear. "This was my dad talking to me. Comforting me after I'd left the Fire of London and before I'd returned to Florida."

Ini's eyes reflected the candle that was still. "Tell me 'bout it."

It was so freeing to just expose her deepest thoughts and have someone listen to her, really understanding what she'd been through. "He was talking to me. I heard his voice. I felt his hand on my shoulder. I felt his presence and he said to trust my gut."

"Dis is the nethaworl', chile. When yuh in between sleep an' wake, there's a openin' to otha worl's. Das where yuh talkin' to yuh father. 'Im may be in spirit form. Was he connected to yuh travels?"

Ronnie wiped her eyes. "So, you think I actually spoke with my father?"

"Yes, absolutely."

Tears flowed. Ronnie had been so deprived of her father's presence, so desperate to feel the connection with him. "What does this mean? Why is he talking to me here, Ini?"

Ini reached out and touched Ronnie's hand, closed her eyes, and sat like that for a minute. Ronnie felt the same energy snaking up her arm into her mind and nearly felt the sparks coming off her brain from Ini rummaging around in there.

Finally, she spoke. "'Im involve in this. I don' know how, but he's a part of yuh traveling. Maybe 'im feel responsible for yuh trials with the past?" she said quietly, but with utter conviction.

"My father is involved with the *time traveling*?" Ronnie repeated incredulously.

Ini nodded. "Yes, he is…"

"Are you sure? How could he be involved in this? He's not around anymore."

"Chile, he's at the center of dis. I know is true, but I don' know why."

Ronnie pulled out of her grip and sat back, her mind whirling, emotions on hold while the world reset on a different axis point. "My dad is at the center?" Her own words sounded wooden. Was this why her mom had sent the journal? Ronnie shook her head, not wanting to believe it. Was he the reason she was going through all this? Was he there just out of reach? If she could tap into his voice somehow, he could help unravel this mess, like pulling on the loose string.

Chapter 8

Sweat

Thursday, September 9, 2004

Mike Walsh stepped into the garage and searched for his work gloves. For the second time this month, he had to clean up just about every damn leaf in Maitland that blew into his yard. During Hurricane Charley, a camphor tree had flattened his shed completely. This time his trees had survived, despite three days of howling winds Hurricane Frances had thrown at them. The pool, however, was again filled with a green mass of Florida's abundance.

Mike turned on his iPod, cranked up "The Reason" by Hoobastank, grabbed a bottled water, and got to work, bobbing his head to the beat. He didn't mind hard labor, something the Marines helped you learn quickly. The trick was to think about something you love and soon enough it would be done. Sweat trickled down his back, soaking into his shirt. Central Florida was delivering its usual ninety-plus degrees with about the same humidity. But Mike didn't mind it despite growing up in Upstate New York. Plus, working up a sweat paid off some of the penance for his misdeeds.

For the first time in eons, Mike felt a glimmer of hope. This notion grew as the image of Ronnie's smile kept him company. She had entered his life a month ago as a new hire, and initially he only saw a professional woman with raw intelligence, elegance, and the most adorable dimples that only appeared when she flashed a smile. Mike never expected to develop feelings for her. Hell, he'd had a million chances with other women, but none of them captured his interest, and he'd dodged all the flirtatious invitations over the years.

What was it about Ronnie that pulled him in with a powerful magnetic force? He couldn't deny it. There was a quality about her that no other woman he'd ever met possessed. Beyond her outward beauty, there was an essence about her that was genuine, playful, and inescapable. Ronnie didn't need fancy nails, gobs of makeup, or designer clothes to be noticed. She just radiated *life*. There was nothing more satisfying in the world than to make her laugh, to make that spark fly. And the dimples didn't hurt either.

Mike scraped the rake across the lawn, imagining her eyes full of playful innocence, suddenly shifting to a stormy fire that drew him in and made him want to get lost in her passion. All of this made more intense when Mike was unwittingly shoved into the role of rescuer. Now he couldn't get her out of his head.

If someone had told him a year ago that he'd be wandering out in the middle of a hurricane, he'd have told them to shove it. Yet when a stranger had knocked on his door asking for help, he'd been more than happy to oblige. It had been like one of those disaster movies, with the forces of Mother Nature roaring through the scene, boiling everyone down to their core persona.

Watching Ronnie in the hospital later had given him a chance to soak in her remarkable beauty. Her finely curved cheeks and blonde hair spilling across the pillow made her look like Sleeping Beauty. "What the hell, Walsh? Pull yourself together." Mike was mortified at his ridiculous sappiness. Did he just imagine her as a helpless damsel in distress? It was so unlike him to romanticize any part of his life. Over the last five years, he'd been the master of his emotions. Now he was full of soft, squishy thoughts. More evidence that he was turning into a blubbering idiot. He took a swig of the water and set it back down.

Mike tried to block out Ronnie's terrified scream just before she'd coded. His heart blasted against his chest, and he paused in his work to take a sip of water. As hard as it had been, it brought to the surface the feelings he'd been denying. Steph and Nick left to get some food, and Mike was alone by her hospital bed. Her eyes opened and her entire being lit up. Ronnie was close to death without the energy to put on a mask, and one glimpse at his ugly mug and she'd radiated such joy. In that moment, Mike felt they'd known each other for decades, even lifetimes. It was as if their souls had touched and it had left him eager for more, changing him permanently. Soaked in the absolute terror of her death, the protective walls had dissolved and reformed into a new, solid structure able to withstand the seeds of doubt, and the risk of being destroyed again. Much like the houses that were destroyed in the storm but would be rebuilt with tougher materials to withstand the next one.

"Ah, God damn it, you're a chump, Walsh." Mike had managed to push everyone else away, not willing to have his heart melon-balled out of him again. With one glance, Ronnie had sparked hope. Acting on it was an entirely different story. She may never give him the chance. But nonetheless, it was groundbreaking.

Mike grabbed a huge branch partially attached to a tree and twisted it to no avail. Finally, an excuse to use the chainsaw. In the garage, he topped off the gas and returned to the branch, pulled the cord, and held it up like a WWE fighter, letting it roar. He laughed at how stupid he'd become. But love could do that to you. Make you coo coo loco. He cut the branch into smaller pieces, setting them in a neat stack on the lawn.

His mind returned to his new obsession. As terrible as that night had been, it had brought him closer to her circle of friends. Steph, her best friend, was a perky Scot who truly loved Ronnie. It had been hard to watch her suffer while they were all unsure of Ronnie's fate. Steph's boyfriend, Nick, was gentle and kind, but a scrapper. No way Nick would have let him refuse to help when he knocked on his door that night. A momentary queasiness took over at the thought of what might have happened if Nick had not found his house. It had been a miracle that they'd been nearby when the Jeep broke down.

Mike finished the water and flipped the empty bottle across the yard into the half-opened trash bag, nearly making the shot, but at the last second it bounced off the edge of the bag.

Only one small thing stood in his way. Jeffrey Brennan, Ronnie's asshole boyfriend. The pulse in his temple pounded. He'd only met Jeffrey twice, and both times the pencil-neck made sure he knew that Ronnie was off limits. He talked big, but guys like that always assumed you wouldn't call their bluff. Mike was prepared to not only call his bluff but beat the living hell out of him if it came to protecting Ronnie.

He put his back into the work, releasing the pent-up anger at the mere thought of his pretty boy looks and too perfect hair. Jeffrey had somehow charmed his way into her life. Ronnie may be fooled by his bullshit, but Mike saw right through him. Jeffrey Brennan was the typical rich boy, selfish and arrogant to the core. A shitty, unscrupulous man. Mike imagined Jeffrey's hand clutching Ronnie's sleeve and used the chainsaw to cut it off, then chastised himself for being such a miserable, violent cuss.

When finished cutting up the branches, Mike sat down on the patio with the glorious Florida sun baking into his skin, sweat freely dripping off his nose. He downed another water and got lost in the shiny blonde, flowing hair and blue, sparkly eyes. Tossing the crumpled water bottle in the nearby trash bag, Mike decided to tackle the pool. He pulled out his headphones and dumped water on his head to cool off, then heard his cell phone ringing.

The musical voice of Ronnie Andrews glided over his ears, forcing his mouth to smile uncontrollably, and ridiculously wide.

"Hey, how are you?" Mike sat on the patio chair and focused all his attention on her voice, imagining how her lips formed the words.

"Good, I'm good," Ronnie said tentatively.

"Are you feeling okay?" A momentary flash of fear struck him. Was she calling because something was wrong?

"Oh, yeah, much better. Thanks for asking. I wanted to tell you I was feeling well enough to join you on your trip to Puerto Rico." Her voice quavered at the end, as if she were unsure of her choice.

"Seriously? Aren't you still recovering? I mean really it's only been a few days, Ronnie." His heart skipped a beat. He'd been hoping for this for weeks, but was now the right time?

"No, I feel good. How soon were you leaving? I'm hoping to get out of town before Ivan approaches and messes everything up." Her voice was a musical delight, full of curves and playful tones.

"Ivan? Oh, Ronnie, I don't blame you. But we're leaving Saturday. I don't think you want to go that soon, do you?" The smile fell off his face and was replaced with worry about her illness and recovery.

"This weekend?" She paused and a muffled voice sounded like Charlie Brown's parents in the background. She came back on the line. "Perfect, I'll be ready. Is it too late to make my flight reservations?"

"No, it should be easy. I'll get Ciel on it in the morning." A rush of adrenalin coursed through his veins, excitement growing at the prospect of having time with Ronnie, twinged with worry about her health. Was she strong enough for this?

"Can't wait, Mike." Ronnie's voice was electric, and this excited him more than the prospect of anything else in the world. Was she starting to feel something for him?

"This is a big opportunity for us. Frank has been working on this client for a long time, showing what our systems can do to dramatically improve healthcare outcomes for the island. Carlos is finally ready to present it to the board of directors." Mike softened his tone to convey his affection. "Ronnie, you have no idea how happy this makes me. I promise you'll get plenty of rest. I'll make sure you're not overworked."

"Thank you. I'm excited. Do you think we can get in the water? It's always been my cure-all."

Did he imagine the returned affection? "We have all day Sunday for a dip in the Caribbean."

"Then it's a deal. I'm so excited. I really need a change of scenery. I can't handle another storm, and I just thought it would be good for me to get away." Ronnie's voice carried her smile and the resulting show of the precious dimples.

"You're sure you're up for this? You can join us on our next trip in a month or two."

"No, you're pitching the software, right? I'd like to be involved at the very beginning. I'm excited to meet Carlos and his team."

Mike stood, adrenaline coursing through his veins, making him restless. "We've got Carlos on the verge of a yes. You can be part of that last push to get them to sign. As long as you're sure."

"I am. Gotta go. Let me know when Ciel has my flight times."

"Will do. Rest up, Ronnie. This is going to be a memorable trip." He waited for her goodbye and hung up.

A rustling in the corner of his yard caught his attention. Billy Nemish, his best friend, charged toward a pile of leaves, kicking a green cloud into the air. Mike ran over to tackle him before he could launch another half hour of yard work into an airborne mess.

"Billy, you asshole!" Mike yelled before colliding with the six-foot-four former West Virginia University football kicker.

The two men crashed to the ground, laughing.

Mike ground his elbow into Billy's chest as he got up. "Dude, you're the largest child I've ever seen!" He offered his hand to help him stand.

"Oh God." Billy rubbed his chest and bent over, catching his breath, laughing. "Why did you have to do that, Mike, my man?"

Mike laughed and handed him the rake. "Dumbass, get busy tidying those piles back up or I'll do worse. I'm not doing this again."

Billy good-naturedly picked up the rake and returned the leaves to the pile. "How else am I going to compete for your attention?" He stopped raking and gave Mike his best roguish grin. "What's cooking with Ronnie, anyway?"

"Man, you're such a Nosey Nellie," Mike quipped.

Billy was an open book, but Mike had learned to keep the book closed on his personal life. Unfortunately, Billy had a habit of revealing Mike's deepest, darkest secrets to near strangers without a single thought.

"She's going to Puerto Rico with me, man." Mike unsuccessfully tried to stifle his smile.

"Seriously?" Billy bent over and threw a large stick at Mike, trying to catch him off guard.

Mike snatched it out of the air and threw it right back at Billy's head. With lightning-fast reflexes, Billy used the rake as a bat, sending the stick high and long over the fence. They heard a splash, and Mike guessed it had landed in his neighbor's pool. He prayed no one was in it.

"Dude, seriously, you're like a bull in a China shop." Mike shook his head, preparing to apologize to the neighbors if he heard anything from that side of the fence. Thankfully, there was only silence.

Billy made bull horns out of his index fingers and swiped the ground with his foot. Mike couldn't help but laugh at Billy's perpetual antics. He was the perfect friend, always playfully keeping him from taking life too seriously. These skills had been pure gold when Billy had pulled him out of a deep depression after they'd first moved to Florida. Billy had stuck by his side during the worst moments of his life when no one else had. Mike pretended to hold up a blanket and Billy charged it.

"So, Puerto Rico, eh? Does that mean you're going to see her in a bikini?" Billy wagged his eyebrows suggestively. "Or better yet, out of one?"

Mike laughed. "Jeez, Billy, you have a one-track mind." But the mere suggestion did bring up images of that possibility. Her bright eyes sparkling in a white suit, perfectly lean, tanned legs. "Seriously, I'd given up hope that she'd ever go on the trip after what happened in the hospital."

"I forgot about that. What made her change her mind?"

"Ivan," Mike said. A pang of fear presented itself, and a disaster of epic proportions ran through his mind if her health deteriorated while they were there.

"The storm that is freaking out all the weathermen?" Billy asked. He rested his hands on the rake and looked puzzled. "That isn't coming here, is it?"

"Who knows? But it is the impetus for her getting out of here." Mike raised one shoulder and let it drop.

"Thank God for Ivan then, eh?" Billy's booming laugh echoed around the yard.

"Yeah, I just hope she's strong enough for the trip. It's a long-ass flight there, then a car ride down the length of the island to the south coast."

"What could go wrong?" Billy lobbed a small stick at him, and this time Mike whacked it with the rake, sending it into his own pool.

"Everything. Or nothing." Mike shook his head, hoping for the best. At the very least he'd get her away from stupid fucking Jeffrey Brennan.

Chapter 9

Dinner with Scots

Thursday, September 9, 2004

Ronnie inhaled deeply, smelling the shepherd's pie Steph gently placed in front of her. Steph's hand was covered in a Scottish kitsch, over-the-top sheep's head oven mitt. The meal was a little heavy for Florida's September heat, but in Scotland, where Steph grew up, September was the perfect time to begin fattening up for winter. Steph always served the pies in the cutest sheep tins, adding to the Scottishness of the experience, making Ronnie feel like she was getting a big cozy hug from her grandmother.

Ronnie waited for Ian, Steph's younger brother, to crack open the top of the pie and release the first steamy curlicue before she shared her big news. Steph's mum, as they called her, had sent Ian to Florida hoping his older sis could rehabilitate him. Mum had grown tired of Ian's antics fueled by drinking and hanging out with his Glasgow mates.

"Steph, thank you for letting me stay here for a few days," Ronnie blurted, hoping to take over the conversation. "I have big news on several fronts."

Steph leaned forward in her seat and responded in the same excited tone, "Anytime, luv. Do tell!"

Ronnie mimicked Ian's movements, wanting to be a proper Scot showing the honor she felt for the meal, and opened her pie with the tip of her fork, savoring the deep, rich aroma that escaped. "I didn't want to just blurt it out, Steph. This news deserves your full attention."

"You've got it now, Ronnie," Steph said.

Ian piped in, mouth full of the hot, steamy goodness, "Out with it, lassie."

"It has been one hell of a day." Ronnie knew she was about to lose control of the conversation when Ian and Steph reacted to her news.

Ian took a breath and started with gusto, "Me too. I met this stunner last night and after a hot, sticky night I realized that I slept with her sister last week."

Steph glared at him. "Ian, hold your whisht."

Ian looked dejected and returned to his pie.

"Ian, you're going to like this news, too. I just can't decide what to tell you first."

Ian rushed in before Steph could respond, "Tell us what Steph will like the most." He shot an apologetic look at Steph.

"Okay, that's an easy one. Are you sure I shouldn't save that one for last?" Ronnie teased.

Steph gave her the stink eye and tapped the table. "Stop messing with us and just tell us already, Ronnie."

"Well, yesterday Jeffrey visited, and we had a little conversation about the impending storm and a few other things." Ronnie watched Steph's face closely.

"And..." Steph was losing patience, but this was totally worth dragging out.

"After a long talk about what he thought I should do, and how he thought I should act, and how he thought I was crazy..." Ronnie caught her breath, reliving a bit of the anger she'd felt about his manipulative ways. "I told him what I thought he should do with his advice." She extended the dramatic pause a tad longer than necessary. "I broke up with him, Steph," she said, releasing a gush of sadness she hadn't realized was waiting behind the words.

The look on Steph's face was a mixture of utter shock and disbelief, with a halo of happiness growing with every second. "Stop messing with me. We were together last night. You didn't say a thing."

"Steph, I didn't want to ruin your surprise. This deserves its own moment." Ronnie cleared the emotion from her throat.

Ian jumped up and hugged Ronnie. "Tell us everything. What did he do? Did he go mental? How did you end it?"

Ronnie took a deep breath and soaked in her friends' excitement. It made her sad since she'd had high hopes for their relationship. She had to get used to the thought of life without Jeffery, and there were a lot of good things to that, but it also came with sadness and loss. "He came over and was so excited about Ivan approaching and what that meant for his research. He was going on and on and it just hit me. The man is so selfish. With all that I've been through with these storms, his only thoughts were about his research. I mean, I get it. It's a big deal but have a little sensitivity for Christ's sake." Ronnie felt her face go hot.

Ian took her hand and squeezed it. "I knew that guy was an effing asshat from the start. Ronnie, you need me to go skelp his arse?"

"Oh, come on," Steph laughed. "He would snap you in half, Ian. You're a toy compared to him."

"Not if I take Mike with me." Ian winked at Ronnie.

She laughed, knowing Ian and Steph were solidly on Team Mike. "I just couldn't take it anymore. I should've listened to you when we first started dating, but there's just something about him that got to me."

Steph made one of her familiar Scottish noises. "Och, no! He's just a pretty package wrapped around..."

Ian interjected, "A jobby."

Ronnie laughed. It felt good to tell them and to hear the positive side of it.

"So, what did he do, luv? Did he throw things? Did he have a fit?" Steph followed the same train of thought that Ian had started.

"He was mad. He pretty much wasn't allowed to talk because the FedEx guy showed up and that's the next amazing piece of news that I have to tell you!" Ronnie said, clapping her hands.

"Lemme guess." Ian smacked the table. "You've pumped the FedEx man!"

Ronnie laughed again. "Better than that. I'm going to Puerto Rico with Mike."

Steph stood up, making her chair fall over dramatically, clattering as it impacted the floor. "Ronnie, oh my gosh. As happy as that makes me, you just got out of the hospital."

Ian righted her chair and Steph sat back down.

"I know, Steph, but this is perfect. I've left Jeffrey. He won't be in my hair, and to tell you the truth, I don't like the looks of Ivan. If that storm hits, I just can't be here. I just can't go through another storm."

Ian patted her hand. "I get ya, lass. I'm not keen on these storms either."

"Two major hurricanes in a month. I'm not going to be here when number three hits," Ronnie said. "I need to get out of Florida. I need to get away from Jeffrey. I don't want to give him the chance to come over and try to sweet talk me or sex me up or anything." She looked from Ian to Steph. "Can you take care of Fluffy while I'm gone? Maybe get my mail and water the plants?"

"Sure, luv, I'd be happy to. I'm worried about you, though. Are you strong enough for this?"

Ronnie was touched by her friend's concern. "I feel great. It should only be a couple of days."

"Oh my gosh. When are you leaving?" Steph asked.

"Well, that's what is making me panic a little. Mike and Frank are leaving in two days!"

The smile fell from Steph's face. "Ronnie, I don't know about this. I understand you want to get away, but you've just been through this terrible ordeal. You've got Korsakoff syndrome."

Ronnie shook her head. "The biggest component of this right now is my mental health. I need a clean break and a reset, Steph." Ronnie was not going to let Steph's fears enhance her own. "And technically I don't have Korsakoff anymore. That is just the state I was in at my worst. My doctor said I can return to my normal activities as long as I felt well. I do."

Ian looked puzzled. "Korsakoff? What the hell is that? Sounds like a fancy Danish pastry."

She looked at Ian. "The doctors told me my vitamin B1 levels were really low after I woke up. The condition is called Korsakoff syndrome, but it only describes the lack of that vitamin in the blood. It's really only something you see in drunks who only drink their meals. It's not something I have anymore."

Ian shook his head. "You're no a drunk. Why would you have that? What are the symptoms?"

"Ian, I don't know. I think it must be caused by the time traveling. They say it can cause memory gaps, and short-term hallucinations. Now can you understand why I want to go, right?"

Ian nodded enthusiastically. "I'm working on not using so many sweary words, but fuck yeah, I get it. Just to get away from Jeffrey the asshat is a big enough reason to leave."

Ronnie nodded. "Yes! Maybe I can solve all my problems with this trip, Steph." She ticked off the reasons on her fingers as she spoke. "First, Jeffrey won't be there. Second, I'm going to try to do an amazing presentation and show Mike I am a good fit for this job." She looked at Ian, who was keeping count with her. "Three, avoid Hurricane Ivan. You all might get blasted by that storm, but I'm not going to be here to enjoy any of that fun."

Steph clapped her hands. "Oh my God, that storm better not hit here. It is a huge, devastating monster. It's taking aim at Jamaica and looks like it will be a Category 5 when it hits." Steph's eyebrows nearly touched. "I will take care of Fluffy. It will keep me from missing Hamish so much." Steph looked up at the ceiling and Ian crossed himself. Steph's cat, Hamish, had died during an accident during Hurricane Charley. "But I want you to rest. Don't be out partying. Once Ivan passes, hurricane season will be over for this year, and you can be done with all this turmoil. If you have any trouble, Mike will look after you." The worry lifted a smidge off Steph's expression.

Ronnie hadn't expected the comment about Mike. "Why do you say it like that?"

"He is into you, Ronnie. You didn't see what I saw in the hospital. I've never seen a more tender look on a man's face in my life."

"On whose face? Mike's?"

"Ronnie, when you were lying in that hospital bed, he looked at you with more than friendship. There is no mistaking it."

"You never told me that before." Ronnie's feelings for Mike had grown a lot already. Maybe he did want to go out with her.

Ian leaned back in his chair and crossed his arms. "I wanted to go and bide with you at the hospital too, Ronnie. Steph, you know I looked at Ronnie this same way. How could you ignore such an important moment in my life?"

Steph said what Ronnie was thinking. "You were not looking at her with compassion or tenderness. You were looking at her with the horn dog eyes."

"Stephanie. I'm appalled at your false accusations!" He faked indignance but there was humor underlying his scowl. "No, seriously, Ronnie, you know that I care about you."

"I know but that's never going to lead to anything, Ian. You know that."

Ian gave Ronnie puppy dog eyes.

"You're not my type."

Ian was taking it personally now. "What type is that? Scottish?"

Ronnie played along, but she knew he was only half serious. "I like you better as a friend."

Ian grabbed his chest. "Oh, Stephanie, she's put me in the *friend* zone. This is the worst!" Ian fell off his chair and writhed in anguish.

Steph kicked him and he hopped back up. "Cut the dramatics, Ian. Oh shoot, Ronnie, you realize you're flying out on September eleventh?"

Ronnie felt a gut punch of panic and impending doom. "I'm not even going to think about it. No wonder Mike said it would be easy to get a last-minute flight."

"Okay," Steph said. "It's settled. You go enjoy your trip and I think we're going to have a grand time here with Hurricane Ivan."

Ian made a face and his Scottish noise. "Och, no, Stephanie, you're going to have to get some more Glenfiddich. That was the highlight of the last hurricane because from the moment we had our spirits everything went to shite." He looked at Ronnie. "Not to take anything away from you, but it was probably the most terrifying day of my life to see you like that, just unconscious." He turned away, visibly shaken. She'd never seen him show much emotion other than a desire for half-naked women.

"I know, I'm sorry I worried you, Ian." When Ian had been worrying about her, she wasn't even here. She was suffering early America and all the dangers it entailed. "I have one more thing to tell you!" Ronnie grabbed Steph's arm. "Remember the watch?"

Steph looked puzzled. "What about it?"

"I'm going to send it off to be tested!" Ronnie looked from Steph to Ian, but neither of them seemed to understand the significance.

"Do you remember when I came back from the 1600s, I had the watch on? It was covered in blood from the little girl's body I'd landed in?"

Ian shook his head. "Wait, slow down. What little girl's body were you in?"

"Ian, when I go back in time, I land in someone else's body. That time I went to a girl infected with the plague." She turned to Steph. "Don't you see? If a lab can find bubonic plague, I will have solid proof that I time traveled!"

Steph stood up. "Holy hell, Ronnie, how could I have forgotten about the watch?" She hugged Ronnie tightly.

"I pretty much died in the hospital that night. The watch wasn't your first priority."

Steph pulled away. "When will you have the results back?"

"Soon, I think it will take a week at the most." She laughed. "I'm not crazy, you guys, I swear, and this will prove it!"

"Will you be back from Puerto Rico by then?" she asked. "If not, I can get your mail and call you with the results. Ronnie, this is brilliant!"

"Yeah, I can't wait to tell my mom that I'm not friggin' crazy. Jeffrey too."

They continued the meal and talked about ordinary things while Ini's terrifying words about the evil one rolled around in her mind. She knew she'd done the right thing by breaking up with Jeffrey. His threat at putting her away loomed large. At least she'd be out of his reach in Puerto Rico, and Mike would be there by her side, just in case. She pushed aside the even more chilling discovery at Ini's and hoped the evil one wouldn't reach into her current world.

Ronnie and Steph cleared away the dishes and Ian excused himself. Ronnie took up her position as dishwasher as they talked more.

"I have another item for your checklist, Ronnie," Steph said with a playful tone. "Now you're free, you need to think about maybe running around with Mike. You're going to be on a tropical island with him for a couple of days."

Ronnie listened to her friend's advice but tried not to get her hopes up. She'd been through so much lately. The last thing she needed was more complications. "We'll see. I don't want to deal with any man right now." The underlying fear of something happening to her, and by the extension of her time traveling horrors, Jeffrey coming after Mike, was a scary possibility. Would she be better off on her own? Or would she need his help to defeat the evil she'd brought to her own life?

Ian walked into the kitchen and chimed in, "Stephanie, you know she should just save herself for me. There's no reason she should get tangled up with a big man like Mike. No good could come from that."

Ronnie laughed. "You're jealous of Mike?"

Ian looked mad. "I am. But I'll still be here for you when you return. You'll see I'm worthy. I'm volunteering my services to keep an eye on Jeffrey."

"What ridiculous thing are you cooking up, Ian?" Ronnie examined Steph's face to see if she knew what Ian was up to.

Steph put her hands on her hips. "Listen, clothead. You are not getting involved in anything. Jeffrey is much smarter than you and there's nothing that you could do but make that situation worse."

Ian shook his head "Naw. I'm going to make myself useful. There is one thing that I am good at, Stephanie, something that you don't even know about."

"Oh, I know about it, Ian. It's why you ended up here in my house, ya wee eegit." She shook her head, making her blonde curls bounce.

Ian crossed his arms. "Never ye mind." He looked at Ronnie with steely eyes and she knew that he was not going to butt out. But maybe he would drum up something useful. Ian turned to his sister. "Stephanie, I need to meet Nemish. Can ye drop me off?"

"I can." Steph dried her hands. "Be back in a minute, luv."

Steph and Ian left Ronnie with her tumbling thoughts.

Chapter 10

Call Your Mom

September 10, 2004

Ronnie dug in the couch cushions searching for the TV remote. Fluffy had a habit of playing with it and it would end up in odd places. The tropical update would be on in ten minutes with up any new information on the storms. Part of her was hoping for failure so she wouldn't have to hear any bad news about Ivan descending on Florida. "Ah ha!" She reached for the remote.

The doorbell rang, startling her out from under the couch. Ronnie had called for reinforcements in a complete panic over the fact she was leaving in the morning.

Steph engulfed her in a brief hug and pecked her cheek. "Luv, let's get to work!" She walked towards Ronnie's bedroom. "What are you going to wear for the presentation?"

Ronnie followed her into the bedroom. Steph was a bundle of fire, ready to help. Her whirlwind of activity was comforting. It dampened down the fears that were running through her mind. Was she ready for this? Doubts about her stamina mixed in with fears of heading to the heart of the tropics made her wonder why the heck she'd agreed to this. No, check that. She hadn't agreed to it—she'd created it. Too late now, they'd already bought the tickets. Plus, the thought of staying here was just as terrifying with Jeffrey's storm brewing as well as Hurricane Ivan's. Ronnie had managed to avoid him so far by staying over at Steph's the last two nights.

"Thank you for dropping everything and coming over."

Steph stopped digging in her dresser and turned to look at her. "No big deal, Ron." A book on the dresser caught her attention. "What's this?" She ran her fingers over the engraved leather.

"It's my dad's journal. My mom sent it to me. Why she waited five years, I dunno."

Steph cracked it open and looked inside, examining her father's neat, tidy script. "It's like a time capsule. This is incredible." She sat on the bed and flipped through a few more pages. "So, what's the big mystery about it? Why did your mom send it now?"

"I have no idea. I've been reading through it and there's some information there, but it's very sketchy. I don't know why my mom is being so cagey about it."

"We are running out of time. Pick out your first day's worth of clothes while you talk. Do you need to wear a suit for this? Or can you be a little more casual since it's Puerto Rico?"

"I have no idea." Ronnie pushed through her closet, wondering if anything had gotten lost in the move.

"You could call Mike and ask him," Steph said absently, turning another page.

Ronnie stared at her as if she had three heads. "Seriously. You want me to call my new boss and ask him about my clothing choices? Have you lost your mind?" She laughed.

"Okay. You're right, that's ridiculous. He's a man anyway. He won't care what you're wearing as long as you don't look like a scrap heap."

"I'll just bring my best suit and a casual thing or two and hope that works." Ronnie flicked through her suits hung neatly on hangers. Tropical temps would rule out all her winter work clothes. Her favorite summer suit was a simple Evan Picone that fit her well and was a lightweight fabric. She didn't want to wear something wild and floral. She had never been to Puerto Rico to know the customs and wanted to play it safe with business attire. She hung that suit on her windowsill. "Can you read me the part with the little bookmark?"

"Okay." After reading for a while, Steph stopped. "Ronnie. He's hiring a new intern. What year was this?"

"1998," Ronnie answered.

"Okay, so I wonder where that guy is now. Maybe we can find him and ask some questions."

"Oh my God, Steph, you're brilliant. We could find out what happened the night he went into a coma."

"What was your dad working on?" Steph's eyes were wide.

Ronnie held up a white blouse to the suit and turned to Steph. "I don't even know. He hasn't really said much about it except his first experiments had completely failed and his lab partner gave up on it. He seemed so down about it too."

Steph said, "Awww, that's sad."

"I know." Ronnie sat next to her on the bed. "That really bothers me. I never saw my dad as depressed, but in here he just sounds so, so heavy."

Steph stuck out her lower lip and cocked her head to the side.

"I was in college, and I really wish I'd been able to talk to him about his work stuff, but he never shared it with me, and I didn't ever think to ask. I was too self-absorbed with my college activities."

Steph put an arm around her. "Don't beat yourself up. That's what everyone in their twenties does. You're trying to figure out who you are. If your dad wanted to talk to you about it, he would have. Don't put that on yourself."

Ronnie wiped away a tear. If she'd had any idea that he would have been gone from her life at such a young age, she'd have spent every minute with him. "I just miss him."

"It's okay to be sad. Every little girl loves her dad. There is just something about a dad and his daughter. It's such a special relationship."

"You're right. Keep reading." Ronnie tapped the page. "Maybe we'll find out something else."

Steph continued to read from the journal while Ronnie picked out a light blue blouse and a matching patterned skirt. She found a couple of casual things, hoping to be able to go running or maybe do something fun. Mike had promised a day at the beach. She rummaged through her swim gear and debated about bringing her flippers and snorkel, but there wouldn't be room in the suitcase.

"Listen, Ronnie, why don't we just call your mom and ask her what you're supposed to find out from this journal?"

"It is so weird, Steph, I agree. Why didn't she just come out and tell me what's on her mind?"

"I mean, you can read the rest of this. There's like a hundred more pages of his tiny scientist script. Or you can call her and cut to the chase already." Steph smiled. She was always good at getting to the heart of the matter.

"I was planning on reading the whole thing before I called my mom."

"Why? Just ask her what's going on. Maybe she knows the name of the guy that your dad hired, and we can hunt him down and get the full scoop."

"That's a great idea. I guess I figured if my mom wanted, she would have already told me." Ronnie grabbed a few pairs of underwear and tossed them in the pile of things she was taking.

Steph set the book down on the bed. "Maybe she just wanted to share a part of your dad and didn't want to broach the subject unless you were interested."

Ronnie laughed. "Unless I was interested? This is my dad. Of course I'm interested."

"Yeah, but you know your mom. Maybe she doesn't want to put any more pressure on you with all you're dealing with. Maybe she's just broaching the subject, opening the door for you to ask questions."

Ronnie sat next to her friend. "I never thought about it like that."

Steph stood and grabbed Ronnie's phone off the table by the bedside. "Okay, luv, call her."

Ronnie took the phone and looked at it, panic rising.

"Take a deep breath," Steph said soothingly. "Shoulders back, head up, and dial her number."

Ronnie had to laugh at Steph's stage directions, but it did help. Steph pushed the autodial for her mom and smiled.

The phone rang and Ronnie shot Steph a panicked look. Her mom picked up on the first ring. "Mom. Hi." Ronnie tried to sound confident and normal. It came out in a squeak.

"Ronnie how are you feeling?" her mother asked.

"I'm doing really well. I feel good."

"It's so good to hear from you. Did you get your dad's journal?" Her mom sounded relaxed. It was a good time to broach the subject.

"I did, and it's been very interesting reading it, but there's a lot of words and not a lot of plot." Ronnie smiled at Steph, who silently laughed, slapping her knee.

"Yes, I know, honey. I wanted you to have it. I thought it would be special to have something that meant a lot to him." Her mom's voice trailed off, making it clear there was a lot more to say, but she was being careful with her, just like Steph had predicted.

"Yeah. Mom, I really appreciate that. Are you trying to tell me something with this?"

Her mom paused and sniffed. "Oh, Veronica, there is. I haven't been completely honest with you about what happened with your dad's death."

Ronnie's heart sank and Steph mouthed "Veronica" and pulled her over to the bed to sit down.

"Mom, I want you to know Steph is here, too. Do you mind if I put you on speaker?"

"Are you sure you want to talk about this with Steph right there?" Her mother sounded worried.

Steph leaned close to the phone. "Hi, Mrs. Andrews."

"I don't mind. Steph was the one who suggested I call you instead of guessing about all of this." Ronnie pressed the speaker button.

"Hello, Stephanie, how are you?" Her mom sounded stressed, her voice rising. "I don't mind sharing this with Steph there. As long as you're ready for the repercussions. It's kind of a big deal, honey, and I feel guilty for not telling you all this time. The problem was it was never confirmed. It was just a suspicion. The doctors had no real information."

Ronnie's cheeks were on fire and Steph's eyes were wide with surprise. "Mom, what are you talking about? What happened with Dad?" Was her mom crying? "What happened, Mom?"

Her voice was shaky now. "Yes. Veronica, what happened to you and the reason I sent the journal are connected. You probably can tell what I'm getting at by reading the tone of your father's writing."

"Yes." Ronnie felt queasy and she braced herself for bad news. "I've just read enough to find out Dad was very depressed. He was having trouble with that experiment he'd been working on for so long and Steinblat had left him. I got that whole part. What else though?"

"Sweetie." She sniffed again. "Your father was working on an important experiment. He ended up...I don't even know how to say this." She paused. "One day a few years after this journal was written, he told a similar story...almost identical to yours, sweetie. I just couldn't believe it. I mean, he seemed like such a stable man."

Steph's eyes were wide, and she mouthed *oh my God*.

"Wait, Mom, are you saying Dad time traveled?" Ronnie's heart leapt to her throat.

"I don't know if he did or not. He said something to that effect. The experiments had been very hard on him. I think he was exhausted from years of trying to prove his theory. He showed signs of manic behavior. I feel like maybe there was a bipolar element."

Ronnie rolled her eyes. "Mom, stop adding your psychology stuff to everything. Was he bipolar, or did he actually discover something? He'd be manic if everything went great or if he ran into trouble. You can't call that manic if it's not brain chemicals causing it."

"Veronica, really, are you telling me you believe he discovered time travel?" Her mom's voice was mocking. Steph shook her head and went to grab a box of tissues, anticipating Ronnie's breakdown.

"Absolutely. I've gone back in time, too, Mom. I'm not bipolar. Neither was Dad."

Her mom's tone turned more clinical. "Well, this is my point. Let me finish telling you what happened with your father and then maybe we can get you some help."

Ronnie's anger rose. "I don't need any *help*, Mom. I just need to find out what's going on. Why are you being like this?"

"Listen, let me just tell you everything before you become defensive. It's been bothering me since he passed away."

"Tell me, Mom."

Steph's expression showed the shock that Ronnie felt.

Chapter 11

Pull the Plug

Mrs. Andrews continued, "Well, your father…" She paused again, trying to form the words. "Your father was busy. I hardly saw him the months leading up to this because he was working night and day. You can't fault me for thinking he was manic. You didn't see it because you were off at school, and I was so alone. He couldn't tell me because of the nondisclosure agreements, which really upset me at the time because he'd always shared everything with me." Her mom's voice was wavering, and the cadence of her words sped up. "About eight months after he was in that manic phase, he was very depressed again. I guess they'd run into some hurdles with the experiments. He seemed to not be quite as coherent. When he spoke, there was a little bit of a disconnect in the ideas he was talking about and the words he was using."

"Mom, stop being such a social worker. Just tell me what he said and what happened."

"Okay. Okay. It's hard for me to separate the two because I really feel that the result was a mental health issue." Her mom continued, "The day that your father died, he…he had been up all night and he'd come home talking frantically of time travel, and that it existed, that he had gone somewhere. He just would not stop talking about it. Didn't really make a lot of sense."

"Mom, this is huge. I can't believe you didn't tell me this before," Ronnie said, hurt clouding her thoughts. Steph hugged her and leaned her head on Ronnie's shoulder.

"Well, your dad is not here now, so he's in no danger of prosecution. Nor am I. I never signed any nondisclosures. The experiments ended after your father passed, and it took the lab until recently to give me the journals back. When you told me of your time traveling, whether it's real or not, I just thought it would be helpful for you to see for yourself through your father's journal. I'm still having trouble coming to terms with the fact that there is a bizarre connection between you and your father, and I can't understand how or why." She sniffed. "Plus, I guess I was protecting him. I didn't want you and your brother to think badly of him."

Steph leaned towards the phone and asked, "Mrs. Andrews, where did he say he went?"

"I don't know for sure. He didn't want to give me too many details because it was in his contract to not talk about it. All he would say is it was a miracle that it finally had worked. To me it just proved my theory about Ronald's mental breakdown. Later that night, he went back into the lab, planning on doing another experiment, and the next morning he had not come home, which wasn't completely unusual. Around that time, he would stay up all night and then come home for breakfast and shower, maybe sleep a while, and go back to the lab. This time he didn't come home."

Ronnie's heart was breaking. If only her mom had believed in her dad, he may still be alive. "So, what happened?"

Her mom blew her nose, and her voice was shaky. "He was unresponsive. They had discovered his body in the lab and called 911. He was breathing and his heart was beating, but there was no response. So, they took him to the hospital, and he was there for quite a while. They did every test they could think of. There was no evidence of him having any issues except for heart disease."

"What did the tests show, Mom?"

"There were no detectable drugs in his system. There were no strange changes to his blood chemistry. They found no microorganisms that had attacked his body. He just wouldn't wake up. He was in a coma."

Steph grabbed Ronnie's arm. "Oh my God."

Ronnie's mind was racing. A terrible thought struck her. "Mom, what if he was in a coma because his mind was back in time?"

"Veronica, do you really believe this whole time travel thing? That's the stuff of movies."

"He was your husband. Do you think he spent his life's work on something that wasn't even possible?"

"Veronica, I work in the world of realities. I work in the world of science-based research."

"So did Dad. He was a physicist. This wasn't some science fiction book where you have to suspend your disbelief to enjoy the plot. This was the man you married. You have to believe in him."

"No, Ronnie. He was crossing over into psychosis. There is no such thing as time traveling. I'd spoken to Steinblat years ago and he said it was all a pipe dream. The concepts were based on a science that didn't exist. The theory was solid until you got to the one element needed to make it work. Steinblat said he pulled out of the project when their experiments showed it was not possible."

Ronnie held the phone away from her and shook her head, nearly numb with her mom's words. "Mom, he was an expert at the scientific method. How can you put more credence in Steinblat's word than your own husband's?"

"I don't doubt his work, Ronnie. I doubt his lucidity. I doubt that he ever went back in time. I think he wanted it to work so badly he had a psychotic break borne out of mental illness, sleep deprivation, or some other cause. I feel like he had gone off the deep end. I still do. But I can't grasp how this reaches forward to you after all this time and pulls you into the same thing."

Ronnie took a deep breath, hoping to hold back her anger. "Why didn't you ever tell me about any of this when I came out to say goodbye to Dad?"

"I called you and David to come out and..."

Ronnie cut her off. "Yes, Mom. You told me he had a heart issue. Was there ever a heart issue? Did David know about any of this?"

Her mom exhaled. "Your brother doesn't know any more than you do, honey. I need to get this off my chest. In performing the tests, they found he had a few blocked arteries that required surgery. He was on the edge of a heart attack."

"So that part was true?" Ronnie was relieved that it wasn't all lies.

"Yes, he needed surgery, but they wouldn't perform open heart surgery on someone in a coma. Especially for an unknown cause. We waited and waited for him to wake up. Do you remember?"

"Yes, I do. Did they ever find a reason for his coma?"

"No. It didn't add up. There was no brain injury. There was no reason for him to be out like that."

Steph whispered, "I know why. He was back in time." Steph's eyes showed such sadness and it hit Ronnie. He'd been back in time when all of this had been happening. It was exactly what had happened to her when Steph had been trying to get her to the hospital.

Her mom was crying now as she said the next part, her voice high and shaky. "Finally, the stress of being in a coma took its toll and he had the heart attack. After that, I made the choice to pull the plug. He wasn't coming back. He told me that he did not want to be a vegetable."

Ronnie burst out crying and tears fell down Steph's cheeks. "Mom, I can't believe you did that!" Ronnie shook with anger and fear of being that helpless. Her mom could have done the same to her—ending her life if she were stuck back in time.

"Honey, I'm so sorry I didn't tell you. I just didn't feel like it was going to help you deal with his death, knowing he had such a difficult psychotic break at the end. We knew your dad was already gone. There had been no brain activity for a month after the heart attack."

Ronnie's heart shattered. "You don't *understand*, Mom. That's what happened to me when I was back in time. I was in a coma and Steph took me to the hospital. I was back in time too, just like Dad, but my body stayed here."

"No, you have to come to terms with this. Your father was mentally ill. He had depression, then a manic state with psychosis."

"Mom, everything I went through is mirroring exactly what Dad went through."

"No, Ronnie. *You* don't understand because you're in it. You're going through the same disease process as your father, except now they've found the Korsakoff as a cause. We never had that evidence with your father. No one thought to look for that."

Ronnie did not know what to say. There was no convincing her mom that she wasn't batshit crazy. Ronnie was crying so hard she couldn't speak.

Steph took the phone. "Mrs. Andrews, I just wanted to tell you I was there with Ronnie when she had her episode. She showed no signs of depression, psychosis, or manic behavior. We were all hanging out together during the storm. Ronnie is not having a psychotic break."

Mrs. Andrews paused and finally said, "Maybe you didn't see it, Stephanie. I know Ronnie better than anyone, and her stories of time travel don't add up. They don't even match history. The United French Colonies, the Fire of London, the Lost Colony? Its psychosis based on her active imagination."

Steph's tone hardened. "Ronnie is as stable as any person I've ever met. She is not mentally ill. I took Ronnie's lifeless body to the hospital in the middle of a hurricane. The circumstances were identical to what happened to Dr. Andrews. She was in a coma for no real reason. Then when she came back, she told us everywhere she'd been and everything that had happened to her."

Ronnie snatched the phone back. "Mom, listen. I want to know everything that happened with Dad. What was the last thing you two talked about before he went into the coma?"

"We were talking about this bloody experiment. It took over his whole life."

"But, Mom, why do you doubt him? Why did you doubt he wasn't actually inventing time travel?"

"Now, Veronica, really, there is no such thing as time travel. How can you think that this would be true?"

"I didn't before it happened to me. Now I've gone back four times, there is no doubt in my mind. It's not about believing it. I actually time traveled, Mom."

Her mom's tone softened, as if she were talking to her as a child. "I understand everything that you said, and I think you believe it is one hundred percent true. But listen to your story. That is what I hear in the hospital all the time. People come up with these delusions. Maybe there's a seizure that you and your father both had that made you think this happened. He had a lesion in his brain. He had a lesion just like you do."

Ronnie smacked her leg. "Wait, he did? Maybe the time traveling causes a brain injury. Either way, it doesn't mean it's mental illness. It doesn't mean it's a seizure. What if it's *actually true*? What if we both actually went back in time?"

Her mom sniffed. "I can't believe it, honey. I just can't."

"Why, Mom? Why can't you believe us?"

"Because if that's true, I killed your father."

Ronnie dropped the phone and burst into tears. Steph scrambled to the floor and picked it up, handing it back to Ronnie.

"What do you mean you killed Dr. Andrews?" Steph asked, seeing Ronnie couldn't talk through her sobbing.

"Please put my daughter back on," Mrs. Andrews said in an angry voice.

"I'm here, Mom."

"Ronnie, I don't mean that I actually killed your father, but if he was back in time and I pulled the plug on him…" It was her mom's turn to cry. She talked through the emotions, her voice squeaking out the words. "We could have done the surgery and found a way to get him back. I should have gone to the lab and had them look into ways to help him. My mind was too sure of what caused it. Now, with you having the same symptoms, I'm faced with the same problem. Either I'm losing my daughter to disease from her father's bad genes, or she is really going back in time that will probably kill her from damage to her brain."

"I get it. Mom, you don't want to feel guilty about it, but look at the reality of the situation. We have both had the same experiences and I have come back to tell you the same story without knowing what happened to Dad. I had no idea what he'd been through."

"I know. I've spent so many years sure of what I knew about Ron's death, and now you're casting doubt on it. I have to process this."

Ronnie felt the same frustration every time she spoke to her mom.

"Veronica, please understand, I'm a social worker. Of course I feel that's what's causing this. Can't you see that side of it?"

"I can, Mom, I understand, and you also don't want to feel like you've destroyed your husband. Just don't destroy your daughter as well." Ronnie paused, but her mom didn't respond.

Steph grabbed Ronnie's arm. "Ask her about the lab assistant."

"Mom, do you know the name of the lab assistant Dad hired?"

Ronnie's mom paused, thinking. "No, I can look through his papers though. I'm sure I have it somewhere."

"Please, it would be extremely helpful. We can ask what happened and see if they discontinued the research after Dad's accident."

"I will, Ronnie. I'll see if I can find the guy who ran the lab too. He should have the paperwork."

"I love you, Mom."

"Love you too, honey."

Ronnie hung up the phone.

Steph hugged her. "Ronnie. I don't even know what to make of that conversation."

"I do. My father went back in time. What if this is some kind of weird disease that makes you time travel? I mean, I know I went back. I have zero doubt about it. I just hope the watch can prove it's true."

"Where is it?" Steph asked and walked towards her dresser and opened the top drawer. She must have remembered what she told her at dinner.

"It's in a baggie underneath my bras."

Steph held it up and examined it. "Gross."

"Yes, gross, but what if this can prove my sanity and my dad's?" She wiped a tear. "I can't believe she pulled the plug on him. That is so heartbreaking. All those years I could have been with him. If she'd only believed in him."

"You can't look at it like that. Your mom had no idea."

Ronnie shook her head. "No, that is not true. My mom had every idea. Dad told her what was happening, and she didn't trust what he was saying. Just like she doesn't trust me."

Steph sat next to her on the bed and put her arm around her shoulder, holding the bloody baggie between them. Ronnie took it out of her hand and turned it over.

Steph said into her hair, "Look, your mom is going through her own filter. My question is not, *Did your dad go back*? I feel like he did, but *how*? How did he go back? How are you going back? What is the connection? Why did you come back, and he didn't?"

Ronnie pulled away. "You're right. I never thought of that."

"Didn't you talk to him in between times?"

Ronnie almost quit breathing. "I did. I need to talk to him. Maybe he is still back in time somewhere."

"Damn, Ronnie, don't you see? That's another layer of evidence. Your dad is in there somewhere. Maybe his body is gone, but his spirit or whatever is still there!"

"Where, Steph?"

"I don't know. But he could be alive in spirit at least."

Ronnie turned away. "Unless that is just evidence that I really am crazy."

Steph shook her head. "Did you tell your mom you spoke to your dad?"

"No, she made me feel like a nutcase before I could. Oh my God, Steph. My dad could be alive. I am going to find him and get him back."

They sat quietly together for a few minutes while Ronnie relived the conversation she'd had with her dad.

"It was incredible to hear his voice after so long. He told me to trust my gut."

"I can only imagine after five years of being away from him. Trust your gut. What was the context?"

"Nothing, just to listen to what my heart says, maybe to not be pulled down by doubts. Steph, Ini said that my dad was definitely connected to this. I just need to find out how."

"While you're in Puerto Rico, you can comb through your dad's journal and deal with all of this. Your dad's word may answer a lot of your questions."

"This gives me hope. I need to get my dad's other journals."

"Call your mom back and ask her for all of them."

"How about we do it tomorrow? I don't think I can handle talking to my mom right now."

Steph took her hand and squeezed it. "Listen, do not be angry at your mom. She did the best she could. There is no reason she would want anything to happen to your father. They were close."

"I know. She meant well. I wonder if I can bring Dad back, though."

Steph shook her head, making her blonde curls bounce. "Two months ago, we'd have said there was no way on God's green Earth that anyone could time travel, and now look at us. We're talking about it as if it's real and as if your father has done it as well. Is it some kind of disease you guys have? Or is there something else?"

"I don't know. Steph, if there is any way to talk to my dad again, he will be able to clear this all up." Ronnie looked down at her hands and realized she was holding the watch. "I meant to take this in yesterday, but I didn't want to come back here in case Jeffrey was waiting for me. Can you take it to Questlabs and get it tested? I've already arranged it. I just never took it over to them."

"Yes, I can do that. That would give your mother some hard evidence anyway. Ian and I can start looking into who worked at your dad's lab. Can you write down what you know and leave me your mother's number? We can at least get that part started."

"You are the best, Steph." Ronnie hugged her friend, and for the first time in years, the desperate weight of sadness surrounding her father's passing lifted. Growing anger towards her mom released a little bit and she set a new goal to find her father.

Chapter 12

Off to Witch City

Saturday, September 11, 2004

Ronnie hugged Steph as they stood outside the Orlando airport. "Don't forget to take the watch in and then look for the lab results. Take care of Fluffy for me."

"I will, luv. Don't do too much. I know you. You're going to be exhausted. Just be sure to slow down."

Steph knew her too well. "Okay, Mom, I'll go to bed on time." Ronnie waved and grabbed her rolling suitcase and suit bag and walked into the airport. A blast of cold air brought goosebumps along her arms.

She recognized his broad shoulders immediately. The fears fell away. Mike would make sure everything went smoothly today. Standing next to Mike was Frank Coleman, shorter and equally muscular, with his mahogany skin set off beautifully against his tan suit.

Frank's handsome face lit up when he saw Ronnie. "There she is." His smile was electric. She'd forgotten for a second that Frank was joining them. She relaxed a smidge. This would keep it professional, which was good. She needed time to sort through her feelings about her dad and the bombshell her mom had tossed at her last night. She also needed to study Mike and see if there was any connection to her past travels.

"Hi, Frank, great to see you." Ronnie side-hugged him. Had she been too friendly? She'd never seen Frank outside of work.

He didn't seem to mind. He hugged her and laughed. "The gang's all here."

"I'm here reporting for duty, bright and shiny, ready for Puerto Rico!"

"You're gonna love it there," Frank said. "It's gorgeous. The people are chill."

Mike was ahead of them at the counter, getting his boarding pass. He glanced back and nodded, then motioned that he'd meet them at the gate.

"Mike was telling me something about taking tomorrow to get out on the water." Ronnie watched Mike walk away, not at all disappointed at the view.

Frank smiled. "He told me we had to because it was what sealed the deal to get you to come with us."

"Really? I guess it was. I love the water and I've never seen the Caribbean before."

They got their tickets and made small talk as they headed to the gate. Ronnie grabbed a coffee and returned to find a hushed silence in the terminal. The unfamiliar sounds of Orlando International Airport faded away as everyone focused on the television screen showing the first plane hitting the Twin Towers. All of the news coverage was focused on reliving the terrible wound America had suffered three years ago.

Not a single person in the terminal broke the silence—even the small children sensed the intensity of the moment, despite the hubbub a few moments ago. Her fellow travelers joined in taking an impromptu moment of silence. A deep well of sadness tore through Ronnie as she remembered the tragedy of a close friend who'd lost her father that day. It still haunted her family, wondering if he could have been one of the people who'd jumped to avoid the flames.

Ronnie wiped away a tear and prayed quietly for all of those who had lost a loved one that day, and for Americans who had lost a sense of peace forever.

Frank took her hand, and it soothed her a little. Mike looked out the window, blinking away the evidence of his emotions. They sat in solidarity with the rest of the terminal. Ronnie felt an unexpected unity with her coworkers and the strangers that filled the room. Was this happening throughout the country? She hoped it would always bring Americans together. In a moment when the terrorists were trying to tear the country apart, it had had the opposite effect on the American spirit.

Soon they were in the queue for the flight. Frank had upgraded to first class in the same row as Ronnie and Mike. They were all in somber moods. She wondered if either man had been directly affected by the attacks but thought if they wanted to share it, they would have.

Ronnie was one of the first to board the 737 to Puerto Rico, followed by Mike and Frank. She watched the other passengers board and found it comforting to see several familiar faces who had shared the 9/11 experience. It was peculiar to feel such a kindred spirit with so many strangers, especially on an airplane, where most people kept their distance from each other in such close quarters. The plane took off and Ronnie was lost in the scenery of the stunning Florida coastline, aqua waters, and boats dotting the deeper blues of the ocean.

Ronnie tried to read the book she'd bought but just kept rereading the same sentence over and over. She wadded up the first-class blanket and wedged it between the window and her head, letting her mind rest. She was heading to a good place. The sadness of the day dissipated and in its place a burgeoning excitement grew. Tomorrow she would swim in the Caribbean! The fears and worries that Florida had brought were falling away, and her thoughts were shifting to a new beginning.

If Steph was right, Mike was definitely interested in her. Everything she'd learned about him so far from Steph and her own experience had been exceptional. She could feel Mike's presence almost akin to heat coming off his body. Were their spirits mingling in this quiet, contemplative moment? Was he thinking about her too?

Ronnie opened her eyes to see if that rang true. Mike turned and smiled, changing his body position to point his knees towards her. "Hey, you doing okay?" His voice was smooth as silk, filled with a tenderness that brought tears to her eyes.

"Yeah, I'm good." And she meant it. For the first time since she'd moved to Florida, she felt good.

Was she an idiot for contemplating a workplace romance, especially after just ending it with Jeffrey? She smiled, taking in his strong jaw, bright blue eyes, and eager smile, then laid her head down again, breaking the connection before she gave away her feelings. Mike Walsh was ridiculously attractive while not being the man-slut that plagued so many good-looking guys. But was she the type to cross the boundaries of a workplace attraction? Normally, she would give a hard pass on that drama, but Mike had the potential to be *the one*. She couldn't pass on finding her person, even if it meant being destroyed if it didn't work out. She was a sucker for love. Besides, it was a whole lot easier to get a good job than to find a good man.

When they landed, Frank and Ronnie made their way to baggage claim while Mike rented the car. They had several hours to drive from San Juan to Guayama. Ronnie rejected Frank's offer to sit in the front seat, trying to imagine his long, thick legs folded up in the back seat. Plus, she didn't want the copilot job, having no sense of direction what-so-ever.

As Mike wrestled with the San Juan traffic, Frank held up a brochure on Guayama. The front showed a map of Puerto Rico with a dot marking the coastal city in the bottom right section of the island. "Check this out. Guayama was founded in 1736 by Matías de Abadía. It is called la Ciudad del Guamani," he badly mispronounced each word, "Spanish for the city of Guamani."

Ronnie abandoned the lazy view out the window and turned towards Frank. Fear in the pit of her stomach overwhelmed her and she forced it to calm down.

Frank continued, "Or el Pueblo de los Brujos, the Witch City."

Mike glanced at Frank. "Intriguing...City of Witches!"

Frank turned around to look at her with an expression of excitement that quickly turned to puzzlement. "Ronnie, are you okay?"

Ronnie was shaky, almost nauseous. Her past travels were haunting her here. The first time she'd traveled, Mathias Stohl had risked everything to help her escape the accusations of being a witch. This was hitting way too close to home. She took a few breaths to calm down, but the raw emotions from the day, coupled with the terribly inconvenient coincidence, tore through her. The panic attack reached a crescendo. This was all a mistake. She should not have left Florida. She should have gone to her mother's and spent the next few weeks combing through her father's journals.

Mike leaned back and touched her arm. "Ronnie."

His fingers were like an electric shock on her skin, and she pulled away, looking at him in surprise. "Can we stop for a second, Mike?"

Mike, unaware of her freaking out, pondered the request.

Frank shot her a worried glance. "Better stop the car, Mike. Ronnie, are you going to be sick? Pull over here." Frank pointed to a scenic lookout and small parking lot on the side of the highway. Mike obeyed, shooting a worried glance back at her.

Mike stepped out of the car and opened her door, offering a hand to help her out. Ronnie took it but couldn't meet his eyes. She was mortified that she couldn't just quietly deal with this in the back seat while they covered the miles. Her body's reaction was overwhelming.

"I just need some air." Ronnie walked a few steps away, taking deep gulps of the wet, humid air. It was hotter outside than it had been in the car, increasing her queasy feeling. She should've stayed put.

Witch City bounced around in her mind, and she felt the noose tightening around her throat from Jack's betrayal in 1752. She wanted it all to go away. Couldn't she just have a calm day? She looked up at the bright, sunny sky and the beautiful flowers and trees all around her. "Deep breath...let it out." It was the mantra her mom had taught her to calm down. The thought of her mom abandoning her father, leaving him lost in time, put her over the edge.

Mike followed her. "Are you okay? Did we make a mistake bringing you here so soon after your hospitalization?" He echoed her worries perfectly.

"No, I'm okay. Just give me a minute." She turned to see Frank's concerned look over the top of the rental car. "I'm so sorry. Can you guys go back in the car or something? I just need a few minutes."

Mike and Frank obliged, disappearing back into the car. If she puked, she did not want an audience. Ronnie felt Mathias's presence on the island. Instinctively she glanced back at Mike. His expression mirrored Mathias's precisely down to the furrow between his eyebrows. She remembered the words Ini had spoken. Mike was Mathias in that time and space. Squeezing her eyes shut, she tried to ignore the image of Mathias's big brown eyes stoked with worry and sadness as she was hanged by the neck.

Was that a bunch of crazy talk from a psychic, or was she speaking the truth, seeing something beyond this earthly plane? Was Mike here to help get Jeffrey out of her life? Was he Mathias reincarnated, or just representing the man in this realm? She studied his face behind the car window, and he lowered the window, surprising her. With the barrier between them removed, it exposed the raw connection they shared. She felt weak and squatted down to keep from fainting, breaking the eye contact that sent her over the edge.

"You alright, Ronnie?" Mike's voice pierced her soul. Ronnie closed her eyes from the intensity of the déjà vu. Was it confirmation that something otherworldly was happening between them, leaving her with no other explanation except what Ini had put forth? She ignored the image of her mother tapping her head, reminding her she was nuts like her dad.

She might just be crazy. It felt like Mike was willing her to be well...and it was working. Ronnie stood, testing her newfound strength, and started towards the car. "I'm sorry, I just got a bit carsick."

Mike got out of the car and walked towards her. "You need to sit in front. That will help."

"No, Mike, thank you. I am going to try to sleep. The back seat will be much more comfortable." She climbed in the back seat and smiled at Frank. "Dude, I'm okay, really."

Frank smiled good-naturedly and Mike said, "Just let me know if you need to stop again, Ronnie. I'll do my best, but these roads are getting narrower with the mountains ahead." He pointed to the map on the dash.

"Thanks." Ronnie settled into the back seat. "I'm sorry."

Frank held up the brochure and said, "Let me finish reading about witch cities and what else we can expect in Guayama."

Ronnie held her hand up. "Can we not?"

Mike turned to look back, surprised at her reaction.

Frank smiled. "Sure, sure, sure."

Ronnie wadded up her summer sweater and leaned up against the window of the car. She tried to close her eyes, but thoughts of her father's struggles, whatever they may have been, mixed with thoughts of Mathias and all he had done to help her. Was he okay? She fought the stress and tried to get her mind to calm down. Would Mike be worse off for knowing her like all the men who had tried to help her back in time? Morris had likely been murdered by the Natives. Mathias had been shot and stabbed. Guilt flushed over her. Would Mike be left in a similar place, damaged, reeling from his sacrifices to help her? Reliving all these terrible things would get her barfing in the mountains if she wasn't careful.

She tried to hold back tears but failed. Hopefully, Mike or Frank would not turn around and see her crying. Then they would want to know why, and she couldn't explain anything to them.

Finally, she fell asleep. She woke up with a start as they were pulling into the hotel. The National Suites sign loomed among the palm trees.

"Are you ready for some dinner?" Mike asked, glancing at her.

"No, guys, I think I'm going to go to bed. I'm not feeling a hundred percent."

Mike's brows met. "I know you've been through a lot this month."

"I'm okay. I think it's just the traveling and the emotional impact of September Eleventh. Why the hell did we fly today of all days?"

"I know." Mike grabbed her suitcase from the trunk and Frank pulled his own out. "I thought that was pretty weird myself, but with Ivan lurking nearby, we had to get out while we could. Are you up for going out on the water tomorrow? Did you see it when we were landing?"

Ronnie's eyes had been glued to the shimmering turquoise Caribbean. "It's absolutely gorgeous. Let's make a day of it, but please, Mike, can you let me sleep in?"

"Sure. That's no problem. Get a good rest. Have some dinner and we'll see you in the morning. Okay?"

They checked into their rooms and Ronnie was grateful they were not on the same floor. She needed to feel like she wasn't going to be bothered tonight. She needed a quiet evening, a good sleep, and time to sort through all the emotions the day had brought out.

In her room she dumped her stuff on one bed and flopped down on the other bed, exhausted. She wallowed in her emotions for a while, hoping it would pass so she could order food and get to sleep.

The big presentation would have to wait, although she toyed with the idea of working tomorrow instead of having fun. Her inner child stomped her foot. *How dare you bring me to the tropics and keep me in a dark, dank hotel room. We are going tomorrow, no matter what!* Ronnie also listened to the adult telling her to wash off the germs of the day and brush her teeth. She took a quick shower and hung up her nicer clothes, then ordered a sandwich from room service. Her hair was still wet when she crawled into bed, feeling like a drowned little rat. Would she be strong enough to do everything she needed here? Or would she fall apart and be a total disaster? After eating, Ronnie fell asleep with the worries gnawing at her peace.

Chapter 13

Pause in the Plans

Saturday, September 11, 2004

Jeffrey Brennan answered his cell phone. "Yes?"

"Jeffrey, Dr. Vasu would like to schedule a meeting with you first thing in the morning." It was Kathy, Dr. Vasu's secretary.

"On a Sunday? Do you know what it's about, Miss Adorableness?"

Kathy tittered. "I'm not supposed to say, you know that."

"Please, I'll throw in a back rub if you just give me a topic." His voice oozed charm.

"You know I can't resist you, Jeffrey." Her voice lowered. "It's about the Homeland Security guys. That's why they're doing it on a weekend. They're going to conduct a search. Please don't let on that you know."

"Of course not." Heat flushed Jeffrey's face, and he loosened his collar. "Gotta dash, sweetie. I'll catch up with you later."

"Okay, hun. See you in the morning." If a voice could smile, Kathy's was beaming.

Jeffrey shoved the small laptop into its case, then wadded up the cord. Fury was building, ready to burst. Between Ronnie dumping him and refusing to talk it out, and the potential for Homeland Security breathing down his neck, everything was going to shit.

A search of his office wouldn't reveal much, but this was the new federal agency set up after September eleventh. He didn't know much about them, or what their reach would be. It was new territory. It was not good news, especially if you were sitting on a mind-blowing discovery, one that might be seen as a danger to the world.

His initial hope was that Hannah Volpe's cloud seeding work was creating the pulse, but the timing of the pulses was too precisely aligned with his own experiments. If she pointed the finger at him for paying to steer the last two storms, he would go down fast. Even if she hadn't, they'd be asking questions, probing into his research, searching his hard drives. He'd been smart about compartmentalizing everything into a few devices so he could stash them if necessary. He'd just hoped it hadn't been necessary.

There hadn't been time to even crack the surface of the treasure trove of data he'd collected last weekend during his multi-day experiment. Now, any work on it would have to be postponed until they were off the trail.

If they'd been able to pinpoint where the pulses were coming from, it would show they were right next door to his girlfriend's house. Well, technically, ex-girlfriend. Hopefully they wouldn't put those two things together.

It was time to give the project a rest anyway. Ronnie had almost died from his last round of experiments. He had pushed it too far, getting greedy by sending her back so many different times. She needed time to recover while he crunched the data he'd gathered. The lesion in Ronnie's brain would be the type of thing that could destroy any hope of moving forward on human testing of his time travel device. At the very least, it would alter the usability on human subjects. Some of the damage could be explained by his mistake during Ronnie's transit back to her body. Stupid rookie error. If he could just get a better handle on the immense power needed to fuel TOTO, the time travel device. His power capture disks were functional, but clunky and not without their own set of problems.

So many things had gone wrong that night. Despite his best efforts to keep everything in a controlled environment, he was forced to break all manner of scientific principles, chasing Ronnie and her entourage through the hurricane and finally reconnecting in the hospital to bring her back before the storm's power dissipated. When it came right down to it, Steph had caused Ronnie's injury. If she'd just left her in the house, he would have been able to reconnect her in time. That was where most of the damage had occurred. Precisely why he hadn't wanted others around that night.

Jeffrey finished packing the remaining research materials into his duffel bag. He needed to store all this off-site somewhere. He'd have to keep his nose clean at least for a little while. Hurricane season was winding down, and after Ivan passed, there would be all winter to crunch the numbers and write up his research.

He glanced around the room, looking for anything else he'd need to stash. He zipped up the bag and slung it over his shoulder, then stepped out of his lab, locking the door behind him. To his surprise, Hannah Volpe was locking up the lab next to his. He took in the curves of her body pressed against the white silk blouse, with a necklace hanging between her breasts and disappearing under the shirt. She shot him an angry look.

"Hello, Hannah, how are you this lovely day?" Jeffrey braced for her anger.

"Can I have a word with you in private?" She crossed her arms across her ample chest.

"In a bit of a rush. You can accompany me to my car. Piss poor timing." He shot her an apologetic look.

A little crease formed between her eyes as they narrowed in on him. He walked to the stairwell, skipping the elevator. Hannah followed closely behind, her heels clicking on the linoleum.

"To what do I owe the pleasure of your company?" Jeffery glanced back at her, hoping she'd pick another time to have this chat.

"Did Vasu ask you to a mysterious meeting in the morning?" She looked pissed.

"Yeah, what gives? What kind of weird shit are you experimenting on in there,

Hannah?"

She gave him the side eye. "I know you're up to something, Jeffrey. Why exactly are you paying me to steer the storms?"

"Hannah, darling, you *know* what I'm working on. The entire lab *knows* what I'm working on. Power, baby." He smiled charmingly and opened the stairwell door, not holding it for her.

She must have run the last few steps to catch the door because it jerked open, and she called up at him. "So why weren't you here during Frances? After all the work to get the storm in your exact location..."

Jeffrey leaned over the railing, calling down at her. "Oh, I get it. You don't think I've been grateful enough for your help. Seriously, I'm an ass. I get so excited that your storm steering is so well perfected that I forget to properly thank you. I'm free tonight if you want to reconvene. Right now, I need to be somewhere."

Hannah's angry voice echoed around the stairwell. "God you're an arrogant son of a bitch, aren't you?"

"I've been told that before." Jeffrey sprinted up the flight of stairs to the main level.

Hannah raised her voice and yelled after him, but the words trailed off as the exit door slammed. "Dr. Vasu told me you're working on a side project. What exactly is *that*, Jeffrey?"

Jeffrey smiled and answered to the breeze that greeted him. "Just a remnant from my grad school days." Why was she asking so many questions?

Hannah surprised him by bursting through the door and chasing after him. He was almost to his car when Hannah's wide eyes showed a glimmer of fear. "Dr. Vasu said you thought the pulse was from my lab. My work is just looking at data. There is nothing I'm doing to create electrical energy spikes."

Jeffrey smiled. "Hannah, honey, I never said that. Dr. Vasu is just needling you to find out why his lab is under scrutiny again." He opened the trunk and tossed the duffle bag in then slammed it shut.

She stood between him and the driver's door. "Jeffrey, damn it, you know the energy I use does not coincide with the timing of these pulses. You know I seed days ahead of time and steer with tiny drones. They don't create unexplained anomalies."

"Are you sure? I mean, it's all new research, right?"

"Jeffrey, I saw the data on the pulse. Its pattern has never been recorded before. They want to make sure there is nothing dangerous about it. I mean, what if it's terrorism?"

Jeffrey immediately thought of Ronnie's brain scan. "That is a pretty scary thought. I sure hope they get to the bottom of it. But here is the deal. I paid you to guide in the last two storms. I also paid you to keep your mouth shut. So, I think you better keep that in check. I'm not threatening you, but don't think for a second that I don't have a contingency plan if you should turn on me."

Hannah glowered at him. "Jeffrey, I'm going to find out what you're up to if it takes ruining us both."

Jeffrey cupped her chin, and she swatted his hand away. "Hannah, I think you better watch the threats you're throwing around. You forget, if I go down, you go down with me, and my contingency plan may include throwing you under the bus for all the death and destruction your storm steering caused the Orlando area. It's entirely possible there would be criminal charges. I mean, think how pissed Disney will be when they learn you've altered the path of Hurricane Charley for cold hard cash. They haven't shut down the entire park since they opened until that storm. That's at least a substantial civil suit."

Hannah bit her lip and looked away.

"I don't make deals without backup plans in case something goes awry. Who knows? I may have documents that show you're connected to a Russian terrorist group paying you to destroy American assets."

Her face crumpled a little and Jeffrey had the distinct feeling Hannah was regretting ever meeting him.

"Some people make the biggest mistakes when they get cocky about their talents and abilities. Don't let that be you, Hannah. We have a great working relationship. Let's not panic and ruin it. You give me what I want, and I give you seed money for your project."

Her anger fell away, and she took on a slightly less aggressive tone. "That's exactly what I'm going to do as long as Dr. Vasu doesn't block me. I'm going to the Caribbean where the conditions are perfect for furthering my research. This phenomenon may not happen for another decade."

"That's wonderful. Seriously, though. I have to leave right now. Ronnie is waiting for me. I don't want to be late."

She squinted suspiciously. "Why the rush?"

"I forgot we were meeting. I'm really late. Listen, do not talk about your storm steering. Only seeding, got it?" Jeffrey glanced at his watch. "I have just enough time to get there, if you would kindly get out of my way."

She rolled her eyes. "I know, you've made this very clear." She stepped away from the car. "I understand what my parameters are, but I need to get something out of this research. I'm so frustrated that after two amazing successes of steering hurricanes I can't even talk about it. I need to separate from this lab, and from you, and prove the technology works so I don't lose my grants."

Jeffrey unlocked his car and turned to her. "Baby, I am your grants. I wish you the best of luck. Please be safe."

Hannah shook her head. "Is that your way of saying don't let the door hit you in the ass? You're impossible."

Jeffrey sat down in the driver's seat and smiled. "I've got something that can hit you in the ass if you're interested. Send me a postcard from the islands." He started the car.

Hannah's mouth dropped open in shock.

Jeffrey rolled down the window. "Your work is impressive, Hannah. Don't let your emotions cloud your judgement, though. We have a good thing going here. Gotta dash." Jeffrey glanced in the rearview mirror. Hannah stood in the middle of the parking lot watching him leave, her hands on her hips. He sped off north of the city, trying not let the panic overtake him. "Be good, Hannah."

At his condo he sprinted up the stairs and unlocked his door, rummaged through the closet, and pulled out the keg-sized TOTO. If the Feds suspected him, they could watch the videotape of the elevator and the parking garage. Damn it, he could have it erased, but all of these actions left a trail and a potential witness.

Jeffrey's mind raced as he shoved TOTO in a tall laundry bag, stuffing a sheet over it so it looked like laundry overflowing. The water was still out from Frances. A laundromat trip was totally plausible cover. He found his treasured journal, running his fingers over the embossed leather and carefully wrapped in in a towel to protect it. He shoved it in a bag, along with a few disks, a notebook, and stuffed them under the sheet. A quick check around his apartment for anything else associated with his experiments revealed nothing. Jeffrey awkwardly carried the bag to the elevator.

Chapter 14

Spies

September 11, 2004

Steph drove through the traffic light heading towards city center of Winter Park and glanced over at her little brother. "Ian, I just want you to know I actually have enjoyed having you around."

Ian's face lit up and the sun flashed in his blue-gray eyes. "Stephanie, are you feeling aw'right? That's so unlike you to be nice after all the crabbing and bitching since I got here."

Steph smiled, not letting his negativity break the mood. "I know, but luv, it's hard to have a little brother. You haven't grown up that much since we lived at home. After being in America for so many years, it is really nice to have family with me here. And I can see that you're trying to change."

"I am, Stephanie. One of my favorite people, hottest girl I've ever met, almost died right in front of me. I mean, she was like limp and floppy. That changes a man."

"I know, Ian. I wish you wouldn't talk about her like that. Ronnie is a great person—she's not just a conquest." If she could change one thing about her brother, it would be his view of women.

"But don't you see, Stephanie? She's both amazing and," he held his hands out and squeezed the air as if testing melons at the grocery store, "and amazing. That's why she gets my motor revving." The smile lit up his face.

Was he actually in love with Ronnie? "Gross. She's my best friend, ya wee man-whore." Steph smacked his arm.

Ian pulled away, taking away the worst of the blow, and laughed. "A wee part of it is my mates back home think it's funny. It's mostly taking the piss, messing about, you know? Hanging around you and Nick, I'm learning that my Glaswegian mates are immature and probably never gonna get shagged by quality. You've been a good influence on me."

"Ian, you don't understand, there just aren't so many people that are like that here."

"Naw, that is nae true." Ian wagged his finger. "Look at Billy. He's exactly like me. He's just a lot taller and American." Ian smiled victoriously, reminding her of days gone by when he'd been just a bairn.

"Yes. I suppose there are still some men like that around. It is not necessarily a good thing."

"Oh, he's harmless, Stephanie."

"No, Ian. Both of you are not harmless to unsuspecting females." A blue Mercedes sped past her. "Oh my God. That is Jeffrey's car, isn't it?"

Ian craned his neck as she caught up to him. "There he is. That's Jeffrey right there!"

Steph slowed down, not wanting to be seen.

"Follow him!" Ian called out.

"No, I will not!" But she was following him, nonetheless. They were on the same road.

Ian persisted. "Don't lie, you are totally suspicious of him too."

"He is a total sleekit bastard." Without realizing it, she followed Jeffrey as he turned left onto Maitland Avenue North.

Ian continued to prod her. "You know you want to find out what he is up to, to save your wee friendie from his treachery."

"Ronnie ended it with him, and he will be out of her life. We shouldn't butt in." She didn't fully believe that but didn't want him getting mixed up with the likes of Jeffrey. He was dangerous.

"What makes you think he will be out of her life? He's not going to let her break it off. You know he'll do something to either get her back or..." Ian made finger quotes. "'Get her back.'"

"Oh my God. He's taking the ramp. Should I follow him?"

"Hell yeah, you should." Ian grabbed the wheel.

Steph smacked his hand off. "Stop that."

"Look, let's just follow him for a few turns, see where he is going. You never know where it might lead." Ian rubbed his hands together and chuckled.

"What about Billy?" Steph glanced at Ian, not at all liking the gleam in his eyes.

"Billy will totally understand. He knows what is up with hawbag Jeffrey. Hopefully this'll give him some scoop." Ian flipped open his phone and began texting Billy.

Ian whooped, making Steph glance over at his phone. A picture of a bikini-clad woman filled his screen.

She loved her brother, faults and all, but this was revolting. It was nice to have him back in her life, and this time he was on her terms, which meant no drinking, no whoring around, and no hanging out with the ne'er-do-wells from Glasgow that were doing nothing but ruining his potential for a future. The hideous tattoo on his forearm said it all. It was a naked lady on a motorcycle. The corruption had already happened to her dear brother. Maybe she could turn him around. She just needed to get him to stay longer and find a normal girl to date. Who knew?

They continued following Jeffrey up Highway 17 North until he pulled off at the Sanford exit towards Eleventh Street.

Ian was giddy with excitement. "What a lucky find! We're like the spies in all those Bond movies. And look, I believe this is a first. You've listened to me!" He beamed, thoroughly enjoying the moment.

"Yeah, my subconscious listened. I didn't want to." Steph laughed.

"You're in trouble, lass. I know your weakness and it's Ronnie."

Steph smiled, but then thought about it. Ian was right. She'd do anything for Ronnie. He was right about Jeffrey, too. He'd been so angry when they broke up and even more when Ronnie had left with Mike. She had played a few of his voice mails for her. Who knew what he would do now? "Hopefully Jeffrey'll just leave her alone, but he is unhinged right now."

The smile left Ian's face. "What do you mean? Why does that sound like the plot to a horror film?"

"I don't know. From the moment they started going out, I felt there was something more sinister going on with their relationship. I've always wondered if he faked loving her. Or if he was just using her for another reason, and not in the way *you* use women. He stuck around, but never quite seemed to be all in like a man in love would be. Like anyone with Ronnie *should* be."

He squinted and pressed his lips together, chewing on her words. "Go on."

"It's like a sixth sense. I've always felt weird about Jeffrey from the beginning. It's put a wedge between us. After a year of telling her my feelings, she's finally pushed him away. It was so hard to see them together because I just knew he would hurt her, damage her in ways other men were just not capable of doing."

Ian's gobsmacked look surprised her.

Steph continued, "Now we will just have to wait and see what he does. Hopefully he'll disappear and let her be, but I don't know. My intuition is telling me there's a lot more to this."

"Did yee, aye?" Ian's anger was palpable, with his arms crossed and his face scrunched. "Well, even better reason to find something we can use against him. I just hope he's taking us somewhere interesting."

They sat in silence while following the blue Mercedes, hoping he was lost in thought and not aware of their car constantly behind him.

Finally, Ian broke the silence. "Damn this city center is shite. Almost as bad as Glasgow."

Steph stayed a few cars behind and nearly lost him at a light.

"Aghhh, I need to make sure he doesn't see us. I'm no good at being sneaky, Ian."

"Let me drive, Steph."

"Hell no, Ian. You'd probably get arrested for driving without a license and crashing into something."

"Nae, yer wrong about me. I'd only have to get used to driving on the wrong side of the road."

"My point exactly."

Ian pointed to the left. "He turned up there. I'll keep an eye on him and you just try not to be noticed."

"Okay." Adrenalin coursed through Steph's veins. She followed as Jeffrey pulled into a self-storage business. "I cannae follow him in there. He'll see me!"

"Turn here." Ian pointed right and they turned into an apartment complex that abutted the property. Steph parked in a space where they could see Jeffrey's car. He walked into the office. A few minutes later he came out holding a key and got into his car. They watched him drive out of view.

"Now what?" Steph asked.

"He has to come around the back. Wait until we see him drive past. Then we can move."

"Ian, he will see us."

"Nae, he won't think to look around. And even if he does, do you actually think that self-absorbed prick knows what your car looks like?"

"Naw."

They watched Jeffrey drive past on a long, narrow road to the side of the storage units. When he turned down a far row, Steph backed out of the spot and weaved around the apartment parking lot until they were closer.

"Now what? We can't see him," Steph said, frustrated.

"Stay here." Ian opened the door and walked briskly between two apartment buildings and disappeared. Steph felt stupid for going along with this idea. She shook her head and leaned it against the steering wheel. "Why do I listen to this eejit?"

Steph lifted her head and was horrified to see Ian hopping the fence to the storage units. He was surprisingly agile—the fence must have been nine or ten feet tall.

"Naw, Ian! What the hell are you doing?" Steph whispered and watched him walk quickly down the aisle on the opposite side of where Jeffrey was. Steph's heart beat out of her chest. What would Jeffrey do if he spotted Ian? "Damn it, Ian, get back here!" Steph continued her panicked thoughts. Would he just be mad and act like an ass, or would he become dangerous?

Then Jeffrey drove away, not glancing in her direction. Where was Ian? Steph dug in her pocket for her phone. But before she could dial his number, he jumped the fence and walked back towards her.

Ian was beaming as he approached the car. "Got it." He held up his phone.

"Got what?"

"Picture of the unit. He's unloading a bunch of stuff. Do you think he took anything of Ronnie's? I mean, he probably has a key to her house."

Steph shook her head. "Why would he do that?"

"Stephanie, it's Jeffrey. Why does he do half the ornery shite he does? Why else would he be hiding something way out here? We're like an hour north of his flat in Winter Park."

"What did you see?"

Ian smiled then rubbed the sweat off his upper lip. "Some huge thing covered in a tarp. Looked like a keg. Then he unloaded a duffle bag, some boxes full of papers. What I don't get is why he'd bring that all the way out here. It's not enough to rent an entire storage unit."

"Maybe he is coming back later with more stuff?" Steph said, but it didn't add up. Why rent a place so far from home?

"Nae idea."

Steph patted Ian on the back. "You're not a completely useless clothead."

Ian smiled triumphantly. "Let's go into the office and gather more intel."

"What, are you a detective now?" Steph shook her head, but she appreciated Ian's help. She was not cut out for being a spy. They drove out of the apartment complex to the office.

Ian jumped out of the car, then spoke to her over the roof. "Just let me do the talking, okay?" A woman entered the building and Ian stood outside the car. "Wait until she is done."

Steph stood awkwardly waiting where Ian took up a more casual stance leaning against the hood of her car. When the woman exited, Ian smiled and nodded at her. They walked into the office and stepped up to the counter.

The clerk greeted them. "Hello, how may I help you, sir?"

Ian glanced at Steph and gave her a nearly imperceptible head shake that she read as *don't talk, ye blathering eejit*. Steph crossed her arms but kept quiet.

"We just moved here and I'm wondering how it all works. We're from Scotland and we don't really have this kind of place." Ian feigned innocence.

The clerk smiled. "Welcome to Florida. I thought I caught an accent there."

Ian smiled and spoke again, accentuating his brogue. "Aye, laddy, ge'on wi'it."

The man looked puzzled. "Yes, well, we have a move-in special. The first month is free. It's forty-five dollars a month after that for the large unit."

"Aye, how is it secured?"

"There are cameras on each aisle, and you'll have a key. We are a secure facility."

"Is it a padlock and key or do you have locks built into the frame?"

The clerk cocked his head as if that was an unusual question. "Yes, keyed entry. You can access your unit twenty-four hours a day. You will need to put in the code after 8:00 and before 8:00 in the morning to get past the gate. We lock it up overnight for your security."

Ian turned to Steph. "That's grand. So, a month free. Do I get to pick the unit location?"

"As long as it's available, yes."

"Great, let me speak to my sister and we'll get back to yee." Ian glanced at Steph. "Do you have a card?"

The man pointed to the cards on the counter then added, "So weird we've had three inquiries all bunched up. The lady just before you asked a lot of similar questions. Most people call instead of stop in."

Ian smiled and glanced back towards the parking lot. "That lady before us?"

"Yeah, what's up with that?" The clerk was about Ian's age, and he relaxed.

Ian leaned into it. "She was kind of hot." Ian smiled at Steph, who smacked his arm. "Did you get her name?"

The clerk laughed. "I did. And her number." He scrunched up his nose. "For the rental."

Ian poured on the charm. "I could totally hit that."

The clerk looked both ways, as if checking to be sure the supervisor wasn't nearby. "I think she was stalking the guy who came in before her. I bet she was an ex or something."

Steph perked up. The person in before her was Jeffrey. "The guy in the blue Mercedes?"

"Yeah, she came in just after he left and asked about getting the unit next to his."

"Really? Did you give it to her?" Steph asked.

"I mean, I wanted to. That one was occupied, but the one directly behind it was free. I hope she doesn't cause any trouble."

Steph tried to remember what she looked like. Brown hair, pretty face, and a long chin. She looked a little like a brunette version of the *Sex in the City* actress, Jessica something.

"Who knows? There are a lot of psychos out there, eh?" Ian said.

"Yes, hopefully just a crush or something." The clerk looked worried.

Ian shoved the card in his pocket. "See ya."

The clerk waved and Ian opened the door for Steph and waited until they were outside. "Someone else following dear Jeffrey. That is sketchy as fuck."

"Yes, and something is familiar about her. I can't tell if I've seen her before or if she just looks like an actress from TV."

"She's got a nice rack. I don't remember seeing that before." Ian laughed.

Steph glared at him. "You're more likely to remember her breasts than her face? You can't be that shallow, can ye?"

"Aye, I can, and you know it."

Steph shook her head and tried to tamp down her anger. "Ian, this is serious. Someone else is following Jeffrey around town too. Who do you think would want to do that? Another girlfriend? A paid private investigator?"

"Dinnea, but if she was willing to put her name on a contract, she's probably a real person or someone with fake ID. No one would be that dumb if they were up to nae good."

"True. Were we dumb to show our faces in there? Do you think they've got cameras in the lobby?"

"Just above the front desk and catching everything out in the parking lot. They have a camera on each row, but there are enough ways to get around that."

A brief twinge of panic rose, making Steph glare at Ian again. "What are you cooking up, you wee clothead? Don't you go breaking the law just to see what Jeffrey is up to. He is not worth your freedom."

"Aye, but Ronnie is. Let's just let sleeping dogs lie, and I'll let you know when they wake up."

They drove in silence for the next fifteen minutes while Steph wracked her brain trying to remember where she'd seen that woman before. Worry grew about her little brother getting pulled into something he couldn't handle. He was her responsibility now, and this was taking a dangerous turn.

Chapter 15

Dip in the Pool for Breakfast

Sunday, September 12, 2004

Ronnie slept soundly and woke at 8:59 a.m. She stretched and lazed in bed, grateful there was no place she had to be yet. Finally, she clicked on the TV and scrounged for her phone. She'd forgotten to plug it in last night. A text message from Jeffrey flashed on the screen. Stress bubbled back up when she read it.

Let me know you are there safely. Check your email. I need to talk to you. The anger in his text was almost palpable.

The last thing she wanted was to talk to him. She'd already said everything she had wanted to.

Jeffrey's second text read, R, *check your email. I've sent you some information about Mike you need to know.*

Ronnie threw the phone down on the bed. "No, you can't invade my peace here, Jeffrey. Leave me alone." Ronnie left the phone on the bed and fought back tears. She missed the good times they'd had. She missed his kisses and loving, but none of that was worth the pain he caused her. She would not miss his manipulating bullshit. What she needed was a long swim with the sunshine soaking into her skin.

Ronnie dug in her suitcase for the aqua bikini and swim goggles. She put her hair up and brushed her teeth, then put on a pair of shorts and a t-shirt and grabbed her room key card. Excitement bubbled up.

Ronnie took the elevator down and walked through the enormous lobby, marveling at the sun shining through the atrium, the plethora of plants soaking in the rays. She found the door to the pool and opened it, hoping no one would be out there. The hot, humid air caressed her skin and coaxed her towards the pool. Ronnie dumped her stuff on a chair and approached the edge of the water, excited she had it to herself. The pool had an infinity edge overlooking the ocean a hundred feet below, displaying her favorite colors, turquoise blue with dark sapphire edges.

Ronnie made a beeline for the water, shedding her clothes as she went, tossing them on the chair. The edges of her sadness broke and fell away, dissipating into the cool, clear water. She would heal and life would return to a new normal.

Ronnie leaned back, her arms against the side of the pool, letting the sun work its magic on her spirits, caressing her skin in gentle, warm waves. She took a deep breath and slowly let out all this stress, letting her mind fill with joyfulness. Jeffrey was not allowed here. Neither were her mom's secrets. This was her private bubble of therapy. Sun and water had always been her tonic.

Ronnie cleared her mind and closed her eyes. A vision of her as a young child with fogged up goggles playing Marco Polo with her dad in the neighborhood pool. In her soft, comfortable place, she called out, "Marco."

A man's voice returned, "Ronnie, there you are."

Ronnie's eyes flew open. She shaded her eyes to see Mike's smiling face.

"Good morning." Mike's deep voice cut through the Zen. "Frank insisted it was you walking through the lobby, but I didn't think you'd be up yet."

Part of her was happy to see Mike. The other part was protective of her quiet contemplation. "Hey there, good morning." A shyness crept over her. He'd caught her off guard and half naked.

"Frank and I were going to go rent a Boston Whaler today." Mike pulled up a chair and sat, casually looking down at her.

"What?" She stared at his legs, trying not to look up into the bright sun. A thick cord of muscle defined his calves, broadening into thick, muscular legs. She was uncomfortable looking at his flip-flop-clad feet. It seemed too intimate. He should be clad in work shoes. He was her boss after all.

"There is a dock down there." He pointed towards the ocean. "We don't have to leave yet, but I was thinking about grabbing sandwiches and getting out on the water. Are you up for it?" Mike's smile nearly glowed in the bright sun.

"I am totally up for it." This might be her only chance to swim in the Caribbean on this trip. Nothing soothed her soul more than the ocean.

"Great, we can go around eleven if that works for you."

"What time is it?" she asked.

He looked at his watch. The fine hairs on his arm were shining golden brown in the sunlight, which was surprising since his hair was so dark. "It's 9:15. You have plenty of time. Get your swimming in and then we'll go."

"That sounds great, Mike. Thanks."

Mike stood and leaned over the railing, scanning the water. "Look at this day. It's spectacular." He glanced back at her.

Ronnie tried not to notice how well he filled out the polo shirt, or the shorts for that matter.

"Ronnie, I promise this will be fun. We'll make it lighthearted, no talk about work or storms, okay?"

He had read her mind. A warm glow from more than the morning sun crept over her. "That's exactly what I need."

Mike smiled and looked back over the water. "We've escaped Ivan. He can't get us here, right?"

"Nope, certainly he can't." She soaked in the 'we' of the sentence and felt his protectiveness.

"Ivan passed by a few days ago so we're out of the danger zone there too. The rest of this trip will be easy breezy," he said, and she really wanted to believe him.

"We deserve a nice, calm day, don't we?"

"Hell yeah we do. Enjoy the pool. I'll see you at eleven in the lobby." He plucked the polo from his skin.

"Bye." Ronnie listened to his flip-flops clicking as he walked away. She closed her eyes and soaked in the sun for another couple of minutes and then began her laps.

Her excitement grew as she swam—the thought of a glorious day on the water with Mike. But she was glad Frank would be there too. It needed to be just a relaxed day full of watery fun. Frank's presence would keep it right there.

Twenty minutes later, Ronnie grabbed a towel from the shelf near the pool and returned to her room. Today she was eager to explore her feelings for Mike and look for clues about his possible connection to Mathias, Morris, and her past.

Back in her room, Ronnie combed her hair into a high, tight ponytail, adding a bit of conditioner to get through the tangles. The swim, restful sleep, and sunshine had worked wonders on her funk, and she tried not to admit that the sunny prospect of Mike's company all day added a spring in her step.

Ronnie hoped Frank would be just as playful and fun as he was in the office. There would be no talk of pulling plugs, hurricanes, ex-boyfriends, witches, or work for that matter. She grabbed a small bag with a towel, goggles, and a bottled water.

The elevator doors opened to the lobby, and she immediately saw Mike nearby wearing a Buffalo Bills baseball cap. His smile broadened as she approached, buoying the bubble of excitement that was growing inside her. He drank the last sip and tossed the cup into the trash can as he walked towards her.

"You look fresh as a daisy," Frank said, smiling.

She hadn't even seen Frank. "Morning, Frank. It's only the contrast to how I looked yesterday."

"Let's go have some fun," Mike said, dangling a paper bag in front of her. "This is our lunch."

Frank held up a six-pack of beer. "And this is *my* lunch." They all laughed.

Mike led them out to the back patio, where a hotel worker was waiting with a golf cart. Mike motioned for her to sit in front while he and Frank sat in the back facing backwards. The driver made small talk as they drove down the winding hill lined with oleander and rose bushes to the dock. Ronnie was drawn to the shimmering ocean dotted with boats full of people enjoying the glorious Caribbean weather.

They all thanked the driver. Mike announced, "You guys go ahead. I'll go sign the paperwork for the boat."

Frank walked with her down the pathway to the dock. "I'm glad you could come with us. How are you feeling?"

"Much better. I slept like a log. How was dinner last night?"

Frank chuckled. "Dinner was nice. They had a reggae band and it was very mellow, other than some chick sending Mike shots."

"Ha, seriously?" Ronnie laughed. "Did he meet her?"

Frank glanced at Mike at the small hut on the other side of the dock. "Was a little weird. She waved and next time we turned around she was gone." Frank shook his head. "Other than that, it was fine. I mean why didn't anyone send me free drinks?" His bright smile showed his teasing.

Frank led them to the Boston Whaler, a small motorboat with a broad blue Bimini providing shade to the back half of the boat.

Ronnie's excitement doubled. "We're going to swim, right?"

"That's the plan. I may just read. I'm not much of a swimmer. Mike was glad you could join us so he'd not have to go it alone. I mean, if he's gonna drown, what can I do for him but toss him a beer? Am I right?"

"Hey, Gilligan and Mary Ann!" Mike walked towards the boat, carrying several white shopping bags and a Styrofoam cooler.

Frank laughed, "Nope, I'm the Professor. You must be Skipper, the dumbass."

"I'm just glad you didn't call me Ginger," Mike quipped, setting the cooler down on the bench.

Ronnie laughed, enjoying their banter. "I'm totally okay being Mary Ann. Ginger is too Hollywood for me."

Mike handed her the paper bag. "For you, Mary Ann."

She peeked inside and found a chocolate chip muffin. "Thanks, that looks great."

"I got you both presents!" Mike's smile beamed in the bright sun. He was full of mirth. Mike reached in a plastic bag and handed each of them a big, fluffy towel.

Ronnie opened hers up to reveal a huge palm tree with *Puerto Rico* written on it in bold cursive letters. The background was as blue as the ocean behind her. Frank's was yellow with the same palm tree and writing.

"Aw, you the man, Mike!" Frank punched his arm.

"Thanks." She felt a bit uncomfortable accepting a gift from him, but at least he had gotten Frank one too. It certainly would be better than the hotel towel she had brought. Frank folded his towel and put it on the bench next to him.

Mike pulled another towel out of the bag. It was the same one as theirs but with a white background. "Hey, it's all they had, but they're pretty nice, huh?"

"So fluffy. That was thoughtful of you." Ronnie wadded up the towel and put it under her arm.

"A memento of our first of many trips here."

Mike held her gaze, mesmerizing her for a few seconds until she lost her nerve and looked away. He did get her heart beating fast.

"Frank, these are for the cooler." Mike handed him a plastic bag of cold drinks.

Frank took the lid off and filled the cooler, adding his beer, then Mike added a bag of ice on top.

Mike turned to her. "Ronnie, you should go and get your snorkeling gear, unless you brought your own. I wasn't sure what size to get you for the flippers."

"Okay, be right back."

As Ronnie made her way to the shack, the men's voices carried across the dock. Frank asked, "This water is choppy. You sure you're up for this, Mike?"

"Never doubt the Skipper! It's just a three-hour tour, a three-hour tour." Mike sang the rest of the *Gilligan's Island* theme song and Frank chimed in, making Ronnie glance back and laugh. Mike saluted her with his towel.

It was a tad weird to be going on this excursion with Mike and Frank. It was the kind of thing you did with your boyfriend, or a group of friends, not your boss and a coworker you barely knew.

The man working at the shack, a native Puerto Rican, smiled as she approached. He reached back into the pile of gear and fished out her size mask, snorkel, and fins. She paid the man and thanked him.

Just as she was turning away to leave, he stopped her. "Don't go too far out." His accent was thick and exotic, enhancing the warning to his words.

"Why not?" A pang of worry crowded in. She needed a peaceful day.

"Ivan blew by just a few days ago. The whole Caribbean is like a big bathtub still rocking the storm waves. Be careful out there."

Ronnie looked up at the sky that belied his claims. Not a single cloud in the entire expanse. "Okay, we will be very careful. Thanks." A brief flash of the shipwreck in her time travels shot a pang of panic through her gut. A storm brewing out at sea had caused the shipwreck. Would this day turn to horror like every one of her time travels? She shoved aside these worries, not allowing fear, panic, and dread to ruin the potential for a break from all she'd dealt with in Florida.

Dread followed her back to the boat. Mike and Frank were already aboard. She had to wait for a wave to pass so she could board it. Mike took her snorkel gear and her hand, helping her on board.

"Sorry about the waves, Ronnie. It's always rougher in the harbor, where they have so many things to bounce off."

Frank plopped himself in the back corner of the boat and smiled.

Mike teased, "Frankie, you going to barf, ya landlubber?"

"Nope," Frank said but wasn't very convincing. He looked worriedly at the water.

Chapter 16

Aqua Blue Waters

Ronnie settled into the seat at the front of the boat as Mike backed it out of the dock and steered towards a series of small islands.

"Frank, buddy, give this to Ronnie." Mike handed him a bottle of sunscreen.

Frank stood and took a few steps towards her.

Ronnie reached out and grabbed the bottle. "Thanks."

As Frank returned to his seat, Mike asked, "So, Frank, how do you like it, fast or slow?"

"How I like it with my wife, or how I want you to drive the damn boat?" Frank acted indignant but winked at Ronnie.

Mike shoved the throttle forward. The boat sped up and bounced off the waves, catching Frank off guard, which was Mike's purpose. Frank teetered towards his seat, taking a swipe at Mike's shoulder on the way. Mike was laughing with tears running down his face. Frank laughed, too. Ronnie had no choice but to join in. This was exactly what she needed.

The ocean was rough, bouncing them around as Mike cut his way through the waves towards the islands. For a brief moment they were airborne, and a rush of adrenalin burst forth, making her laugh. This was the happiest she'd felt in a long time. Ronnie glanced back at the dock, leaving her worries on shore. She imagined the gray shapes standing on the pier, wringing worried hands, their tattered, ghastly clothes flapping in the breeze.

Mike motioned for her to sit next to Frank, but she shook her head. She was enjoying the wind in her hair and the sun on her back. The water was her favorite color, turquoise, with fleeting, dark shapes below the surface, either fish or seaweed, deepening the shade to an equally gorgeous greenish blue. She could feel the panic and the desperation evaporate away in the sunlight like the saltwater spray on her cheeks.

Mike's dark curls were waving in the wind, and his t-shirt pressed against his chest like a second skin. Frank looked not quite so green, and he gave her a blazing smile. She smiled back and returned her gaze to the scenery ahead of them. This was medicine for her soul. If she could just stop getting palpitations whenever she glanced at Mike.

Mike yelled over the motor, "We're almost there."

Ronnie's excitement grew as she dipped her hand in the sea, testing the temperature. It was perfect, about eighty-two degrees. Anything cooler would strip away your body heat quickly.

Mike slowed the craft down to a spot about twenty yards offshore, in a calm spot, the waves blocked by the island. He turned them into the wind and lifted the back bench, pulling out an anchor, pitching it overboard, making a delightful plunk as it hit the water.

Ronnie opened the net bag holding her snorkeling gear and laid it out on the bench, then pulled off her tank top and shorts and applied the sunscreen.

"Jeez, Frank, they are never going to fit your feet!" Mike held up Frank's flipper. "These are made for kids."

Frank grabbed it. "Shut it, Mike. Just because I don't have size thirteen Sasquatch feet doesn't mean mine are small."

"Dude, you're almost my height. How the hell do you walk on those pegs?" Mike laughed while pulling off his shirt, sliding it over the steering wheel and tying it underneath to keep it in place.

Mike was in impeccable shape. Long hours at the gym were evident with defined muscles Ronnie didn't even know existed.

"Man, what the hell is this? I'm an old guy. How can I even compete with that?" Frank smacked Mike's abs, leaving a red mark.

Instead of leaning into the compliment and flexing or something equally meatheadish, Mike looked embarrassed. "Frank, you're in amazing shape, and I bet when you were my age you could have kicked my ass." Mike pointed at Frank's feet. "Oh wait...not with those little infant feet."

Frank couldn't help but crack a smile. "My tiny infant feet will kick your ass now, Michael J. Schwarzenegger." Frank laughed and halfheartedly swiped his foot at Mike, who deftly dodged the blow.

Catching the playful mood, Ronnie picked up the sunscreen and yelled, "Hey, Mike, think fast!" Hoping to catch him off guard, she chucked the sunscreen directly at his face.

Mike caught it with quick reflexes and said, "Oh, it's going to be like that, huh?" He lunged at her. Ronnie snagged the snorkel and mask and did a front flip off the bow of the boat into the glorious water, letting out a yelp as her sun-warmed skin instantly cooled, waking up every nerve in her body. All thoughts of dark and tattered fears waving bye on the dock were banished from this blissful refuge. Water had always renewed her soul, and saltwater was the additional tonic mixed with playful friends to lift her spirits back to her usual happy place.

Ronnie flitted along the bottom using a dolphin kick and realized her flippers were still on the bench. She came up for air to find the two men watching her. "Ha, in yo face, Mr. Bossman."

Mike stood on the bow. With the sunlight shining behind him, it was hard to see his expression, but she could hear him laughing.

Frank slapped Mike on the back. "Mr. Bossman!"

Ronnie slid on the mask and adjusted the snorkel while treading water. The black rubber had heated up and instantly fogged with the cooler water. She wished she had her small bottle of baby shampoo. It had been a staple when she'd played underwater hockey with her college friends. A small, thin film on the inside of the glass would keep it from fogging up for the hour and a half she'd play, as long as she was careful to not rinse it off.

Ronnie caught Mike glancing at her as he was putting on lotion, and he looked away, embarrassed, tugging at his board shorts. Frank was out of view. She spat on her finger and rubbed it on the glass and returned it, then slid her head under the surface. The chill of her sun-warmed hair under the cool water made her shiver as she swam to the sandy bottom about ten feet down, marveling at how clear the view was. The last time she'd snorkeled had been in Virginia Beach, clouded by nearby Chesapeake Bay runoff.

A giant splash scared her, but she soon realized it was only Mike jumping in. His fin drifted downward. She caught it an inch before it hit the bottom, then swam back to him.

"Sir." Ronnie imitated her best British accent. "I do believe you dropped this."

The mask was on his forehead, and he was trying to adjust the snorkel to reach his mouth.

Ronnie called out, "Hey, Frank, toss me my flippers if you don't mind."

Frank leaned over and grabbed them from the bench. He tossed them near her.

"Thanks. C'mon in and join us." Ronnie slipped the left flipper on, holding the right one under her arm. Frank stood up with all his gear on, looking like a penguin in Miami, out of place and uncomfortable.

Mike called out, "Get in here, old man! Roll in backwards if you don't want to lose your mask."

Frank slapped the flippers as he walked towards the ladder at the back of the boat. Mike and Ronnie swam to the ladder where Frank was heading.

Mike flipped the ladder down. "Frank, it'll be easier for you to come down facing me."

Frank awkwardly put his foot on the first step, then dropped into the aqua sea, holding onto his mask, then swam a few strokes and his mask fogged up. "I can't see!" He was in a panic.

Ronnie swam to his side and grabbed his hand and brought him to the safety of the ladder. "Here, hold onto this."

Frank yanked off the mask and handed it to her.

Ronnie dipped the mask underwater and shook it, then held it to Frank's face.

Mike treaded water a few feet away. "Frank, I thought you said you've snorkeled before."

Frank's mouth was tight. "Yes, but from shore, not from a damn boat!"

"Let's get going. I see a lot of fish down there." Mike's hair was darker, and curls broke out where it wasn't flattened by the mask's rubber strap. Realizing they weren't swimming, he lifted the mask, revealing eyes almost the same color as the turquoise water.

Ronnie pulled the strap over Frank's head. "Please, Frank."

Frank rolled his eyes.

Mike called out, "Put your mask back on and let's go."

Ronnie stayed with Frank while he adjusted it, then pulled the mouthpiece into position. "You ready?"

Frank adjusted the mask. "Yeah, don't go too far, please."

Ronnie held his hand, and they swam together. Frank lifted his head, accidentally angling the snorkel directly into a swell, inhaling a mouthful of water.

Ronnie took his arm as he lifted the mask, coughing uncontrollably.

Mike came to the other side and held his arm. "Frank, you drowning, old man?"

When he could breathe normally again, he nodded towards the Boston Whaler. "I will be on the damn boat."

Ronnie tried to salvage the moment. "No, Frank, let me teach you, please."

Mike helped him to the ladder.

Ronnie spoke in a soothing tone. "Frank, you had your head at the wrong angle. You have to look down at the bottom."

Frank turned to Mike and spoke confidentially. "She said that I need to look at her bottom. How is that gonna help?"

Mike smiled, then glanced tentatively at Ronnie. "Uh, no, she didn't."

"Frank, seriously, stop that!" She gave him the evil eye, scrunching up her face to make her look more serious. "If you look at the bottom, your head is in position. Watch me." She showed the proper head position with the snorkel pointed up at the sky. She came back to the surface. "See?" She glanced at Mike, hoping for encouragement. "Now watch me again. This is what you were doing." She stuck her face below the surface, looking at the horizon with her chin forward. The snorkel dipped under the waterline. "Your head tipped up, pushing the end of the snorkel underwater."

Frank shook his head. "But the water is so choppy. It's only going to get in there again."

"Not if you look down," Ronnie urged. "Try it."

Frank put his face underwater and took a tentative breath and jerked his face out, coughing again. "Damn, Ronnie, you think if I drink the entire ocean it's gonna make it shallower for you two?" Frank pulled off his flippers and flung them into the boat, then stepped on the first rung. "Nope, I'm going to enjoy a cold one and watch you fools drown. I'll call the Coast Guard when I can't see either of you." He winked at Ronnie.

"Aw, Frank, don't be a party pooper!" Mike said. "C'mon."

"No, you guys go enjoy yourselves. I've got a good book and a six-pack I have to get started on." He glanced around. "Yo, Mike, can you put up the shady thing for me?" he said, pointing to the Bimini.

"Sure, hang on."

Ronnie moved out of the way so Mike could reach the ladder.

Mike turned, gripped the railing, and pulled off the flippers. "I'll be right back." He flashed a smile. "Would you hold these?"

Ronnie took the flippers from him, noting they still held his body heat. Damn, why did Frank have to bag out on them? She didn't want to be tempted to be too chummy with Mike, yet.

Mike climbed out. Ronnie was close enough to get an eyeful of flexing chest, shoulder, and ab muscles. Then took a deep breath and dunked under the surface before her face revealed what her mind was thinking. The image was implanted in her mind permanently. A rush of adrenalin coursed through her veins, making her burn through oxygen quickly, forcing a quick resurface for air. Mike was putting up the bright blue Bimini, stretching to fasten it. Bulging, tan muscles filled her view.

Mike grabbed a beer out of the cooler and held it up, offering it to her. "No thanks!" she said, maybe a bit too loudly.

He handed it to Frank and cracked one open for himself. He clinked Frank's bottle and talked to him for a minute while he finished his beer, but Ronnie couldn't make out the words. He patted Frank on the shoulder then a second later jumped into the water and swam over to Ronnie. She could smell the beer fresh on his breath and imagined tasting it on his lips.

Mike held something up out of the water. "Here, I brought you something."

It was a disposable underwater camera. "Thanks." Ronnie handed him the flippers then held up the camera and snapped a picture of Mike smiling with his mask and snorkel on. She slipped the strap over her wrist. "What a great idea. That was so nice of you."

"I promised a relaxing day. How am I doing so far?" His tone softened, and she imagined it was because Frank was not in earshot.

"Superb. You and Frank are hilarious. Thank you for setting all of this up. What a spectacular place."

"I've been coming to Puerto Rico for a while now, but never got a day to play. You gave us an excuse to finally do it. Thank you, Ronnie." Tenderness coated his voice.

Ronnie soaked it in. Steph was right—he was definitely into her. "You give me this perfect day and then thank me?" She laughed. "Ridiculous!"

Mike grinned. "What's ridiculous is you tried to knock my head off with that sunscreen."

Her cheeks were hurting from smiling, with the mask pressing down on her face. "Wicked fast reflexes there. Were you a wide receiver or something?"

"No way. Those guys were tiny and fast. I was a linebacker. I got to sack the arrogant quarterback."

Something splashed in the distance and Ronnie pulled the mask down to look along the waterline. Hovering near the surface were several tiny squid. "Mike, look!" She pointed.

Mike stuck his face underwater. "Wow, I think those are reef squid."

"They're so cute!" Ronnie ducked underwater and swam towards the closest one, but it kept its distance, always about ten feet away. The creature was about a foot long with tentacles and large eyes watching her every move.

Mike was next to her, keeping pace. Ahead, a dark shape appeared as they approached, revealing a huge rock covered in coral with an endless commotion of fish and other sea creatures. Ronnie dove, pulling the camera out, and snapped a few pictures. A large blue tang, just like Dory, nibbled algae off the coral. A larger fish swam by, startled by her presence. Ronnie smiled, making water enter her mask. The fish's lips looked like they were outlined with blue lipstick, where the rest of its body was green and pink.

Ronnie ran out of air and returned to the surface, where Mike was watching with his face in the water.

She let the mouthpiece fall out of her mouth. "You gotta go down there, Mike. It is amazing! You won't believe the colors when you get closer." He followed her down, and she snapped pictures of him pointing at various fish. Mike looked funny with the mask pushing on his upper lip, making his mouth misshapen.

He tapped on her shoulder and pointed at a squid not far away. This time she could see shades of green, purple, blue, and pink, almost flashing as his fins rippled, keeping him in place. She snapped a picture.

They surfaced. "Did you get it?" Mike asked excitedly.

"I think so."

"Let's go around the other side." He swam down around the reef and Ronnie followed then swam by his side, feeling the heat coming off his body where her shoulder was close to his. An enormous, dark shape swam towards them and veered off, likely as startled as they were. Panic that they were confronting a shark tore at her nerves. The screams of the man attacked by the shark in her time travels echoed in her mind.

Mike grabbed her arm, pulling her behind him. They watched it swim by. It was enormous and black with a huge mouth frowning at them. They came up for air. "Oh my God! That was amazing." Mike let the snorkel drop out of his mouth.

"What the heck was that?" Ronnie pointed down at the reef, her heart still beating a mile a minute.

"Grouper, and at least six feet long. Let's follow Black Betty." He smiled, already naming their quarry.

They gave chase and caught up to Black Betty swimming around another coral monolith. They tried to keep up, but it outswam them and disappeared out of sight in the distance.

At the surface, Mike's eyes lit up. "It scared me to death. I was sure it was a shark or something coming to eat us!"

"I know, right? That was crazy. Mike, it was bigger than you!" She held up the camera. "That would have been a great shot."

Mike grinned. "Now it's just another big fish story no one will believe."

Ronnie laughed and ducked back underwater, not wanting to miss another shot.

They enjoyed the afternoon, exploring the reefs nearby, never getting too far away from the boat. After about forty-five minutes, Mike surfaced. "Ronnie, you look like that parrotfish." Mike's expression showed mirth.

"I do?"

"Yeah, your lips are blue. I think we need to get you in the sun for a bit."

Ronnie had been shivering for ten minutes but didn't want to get out yet. They swam back to the boat. She hated leaving the beauty of the sea, but she was freezing her butt off. Mike held her flippers as she ascended the ladder and he handed both sets to her before climbing up. Frank was asleep in the shade with a book in his lap.

Mike pressed his finger to his lips, borrowing the camera dangling from her wrist. He took a few pictures before kicking Frank's foot, waking him.

"What!?" Frank shot up, dumping the book on the deck, giving Mike an excellent shot. Then he turned around and snapped a shot of Ronnie, catching her off guard.

"Beautiful!" Mike broke out in a smile, then handed her the camera.

Ronnie pointed to the bench near Frank. "Sit next to your buddy. Let's get one for your office." Ronnie snapped the two friends smiling and Frank gave her a thumbs-up.

Mike grabbed a fresh beer and offered her one. Ronnie declined and instead he handed her an iced tea. "You ready to eat yet?"

Frank held his hand out, and Mike filled it with his sandwich.

"No, I'll wait till my teeth are no longer chattering." Ronnie spread the towel Mike had given her on the bow of the boat and lay face down, letting the sun soak warmth back into her cold flesh. Mike excitedly told Frank about their grouper sighting.

Frank lifted his sunglasses and squinted suspiciously at Mike. "I don't know, man. That sounds like a fish tale to me. Ronnie, do you vouch for this clown?"

Ronnie nodded. "Oh yeah, that thing was bigger than Mike, absolutely."

Frank held up his hand. "I'd have crapped my pants. No doubt."

Ronnie smiled and closed her eyes, tuning out the friendly banter between her shipmates. She was mesmerized by the healing rays of the sun penetrating her soul, massaging her nerves to total relaxation, the gentle waves rocking the boat like a cradle. This excursion had been precisely what she needed today.

Chapter 17

Never See Them Coming

Jeffrey Brennan shifted in his chair while locking eyes with Dr. Vasu, the head of the cloud weather lab. A trickle of sweat snaked down his back but he ignored it, confident in his well mastered skill to appear calm and collected while his insides wanted to scream in panic. It was easy really. You just believed the lie you were telling. He was a believer and focused everything on Dr. Vasu as he spoke.

"Jeffrey, I'm sure news has made its way around the lab that more of the unexplained pulses were detected during Hurricane Frances."

Jeffrey nodded intently. "That's pretty interesting. Don't you think, Dr. Vasu?" Another strategy was to distract, dodge, and weave. "What do you think is causing these strange pulses?"

"I find it fascinating, yes, but I've not looked into it enough to form an opinion of the cause. Jeffrey, I understand you were not here during the last storm. Where were you conducting your research?"

He'd already practiced his responses. Dr. Vasu was a highly intelligent man, but he had no spontaneity, offering the advantage of predictability. Unfortunately, Homeland Security would be much more skilled. "I was home during the storm. I was hoping to do another round of experiments, but during Hurricane Charley, one of my power capture disks was shattered, so I wasn't able to start the experiment. I'm really quite pissed about it."

"I had expected you to make great strides during a storm of such long duration. I'm disappointed you weren't able to further your research."

"You mentioned plural pulses. How many were detected this time?" Jeffrey leaned forward, resting his elbows on his knees as if he couldn't wait to hear the answer. Of course, he knew precisely how many pulses there were.

"They're pinpointing. It looks as if they're not willing to share that information. They would like to interview our staff again."

"Think they'll tell us anything? I'm dying to know what this is all about. Where in the lab was it? I mean, why else would they be interviewing us again?"

Dr. Vasu sat back in his chair, steepling his fingers, looking over his hands at him, probably not quite sure what to make of this new chipper Jeffrey. "Well, we shall see.

I've been asked to keep you up here until they call you. You may make yourself comfortable just outside my door."

"Of course. I probably won't be much help since I was red-shirted for Frances. This interview won't be too long. I am thinking about going mobile for Ivan. I have a lot to do before that beast comes ashore."

"I don't know." Dr. Vasu nodded as Jeffrey's cue to get out.

"I'll be out here." Jeffrey waved politely and stepped out the door into the waiting room. There were ten people waiting nervously for their turn. He leaned in close and whispered to Dr. Vasu's secretary, Kathy, otherwise known as Miss Adorableness, "Hey there, sweetie. Don't forget. I owe you that back rub."

Kathy blushed deeply, then whispered, "I definitely will not forget." She waved him to a seat nearby.

"Coffee?" Jeffrey smiled winningly at her.

Kathy leapt up, eager to please him. "Cream and sugar?"

"Nope, black, just like my heart." Jeffrey poured on the charm.

Kathy tittered while pouring coffee into one of her personal mugs. "Black like your heart."

He took it from her, grazing her chubby fingers. "You are a delight." The mug had flowers forming a heart around the picture of her cat. "Aw, Mr. Paws, right?"

She cocked her head to the side. "No, this one is Miss Paws. Turns out he's a *she*!" Kathy laughed just a bit too loud.

Jeffrey smiled. "How long am I stuck here? These guys going through everyone pretty quickly?"

"They've been in there with Hannah for quite a while." Kathy crinkled her nose. She was not a fan of Hannah since Dr. Vasu couldn't take his eyes off her sweater meat.

Jeffrey sipped his coffee and gathered his thoughts, hoping to glean whatever he could from the Homeland Security agents. Hopefully, they'd tire of his golden retrieveresque demeanor and move along. He suspected they were keeping everyone up in the management offices so they could search their labs unfettered.

Hannah was probably trying to explain what her research was about. She'd overexplain, trying to sound smart, and if it was a man with a heartbeat, she'd have to throw in a few flirty moves to distract him.

Fifteen minutes later, Hannah was escorted out of an office by a tall, humorless man. They walked through the lobby and towards the elevators. Hannah squinted a faux smile as she passed, conveying the un-funness of her interview. The agent exuded seriousness and professionalism. He was here to do his job, not get a hand job from Hannah. Too bad for her. Hopefully Hannah had squirmed a little, but they'd likely not find anything in her lab. She had legitimate research, and as she'd said, her storm steering was all done well in advance of any of the pulses.

"Dr. Jeffrey Brennan?" a wiry, dark-haired man called out.

Jeffrey stood and walked towards him.

"This way, Dr. Brennan. Thank you for joining me today. I'm Agent Ferguson." He motioned towards the guest seat. Ferguson was quite tall, well over his own six feet.

"Good morning, Agent Ferguson. Nice to meet you."

The agent closed the door and sat next to Jeffrey in the second chair instead of behind the desk. Classic move to make the subject feel more comfortable, more on equal footing. Jeffrey knew better.

"We are talking to everyone here in the lab this morning to gather information for a case we are building," Ferguson said with a preciseness of diction that belied his training.

"A case, how interesting. Does this have to do with those weird pulses that happened during Charley?" Jeffrey imitated the tone of his best friend from college, a demeanor that could only be described as bouncy.

"Yes. Can you tell me where you were during Hurricane Frances? My report says you were off-site from the hours of 10:00 a.m. Friday, September third, through Monday at midnight, September fifth."

"I was at home, hunkered down for the storm, seriously pissed that I was pulled off my experimentation. One of my power disks busted during Charley. Kept me from getting in the game this round."

The agent made a note on the spiral notebook in his lap. "Dr. Brennan, what is your role here at the lab?" His eyebrows rose, waiting for the answer.

Jeffrey soaked in his confidence. This guy was a few clicks down on the IQ scale, easily handled. "I'll put it in terms you will understand. I'm looking at ways to store energy from weather events to provide power to areas affected by electrical outages."

"Fascinating. Can you outline the nature of the experiments you're conducting for this research?"

Jeffrey outlined the materials he used, and the processes, using the most technical language possible.

Agent Ferguson nodded. "If I were some simple noob, I'd have not understood a word of that. I guess my agency is lucky to have my expertise in physics. How do you capture the power, Dr. Brennan?"

Jeffrey smiled. He'd underestimated Ferguson. "How the hell did you choose to work for a new government agency instead of making the big bucks in industry?"

Ferguson smiled and shook his head. "How do you know I don't make the big bucks?"

"For one, your cheap shoes and off-the-rack wool suit." Jeffrey smiled coolly.

"Now why would I waste my good clothes on a job like this? I've had to chase down criminals in these bad boys." Ferguson rested his ankle on his knee, showing off the shoe in question. "What you don't see is the sneaker sole inside." He tapped his temple and nodded.

Jeffrey laughed. "You got me there, agent."

"Can you detail for me the electronic aspects of your research? I'm assessing if your methodology would be the cause of the pulses we are looking into. But before you walk me through that, tell me something, Dr. Brennan. Are there any projects you're working on outside the scope of the lab's directives?"

A twinge of panic hit his heart, but he dampened it by shifting positions. Dr. Vasu must have told him about his side research. "I have permission to go outside my usual parameters as long as I provide my own materials and don't tax the resources of the lab."

"What is the nature of this research?" Ferguson leaned forward just slightly towards him, giving away the importance of his answer.

"I mentioned it already. In pursuit of a power capture device, I've created polymer disks that absorb energy. They suck right now. Turns out when you study hurricanes, they often destroy your equipment." He laughed, observing Ferguson's body language.

"I would love to see one of these disks, Dr. Brennan. I'm very curious about your work."

Jeffrey blinked lazily and smiled. "I wish I could. I think you'd find them truly unique, but I have scrapped that design and I'm hoping to purchase new disks this week. I can share my new designs. God, I'm so pissed these damn things broke. Do you know how many hours of storm research I could have had during Frances?"

"I believe you have written abstracts on what you hope to accomplish with your projects, within the lab's directive and outside of it. I will need you to share those with me."

Jeffrey nodded. "Sure, that's no problem." He feigned the roommate's demeanor, but some of the luster was waning.

Ferguson nodded. "What material will you use for the new disks?"

"A new polymer, but I don't think it has the same properties as the other disks. I just need something sturdier."

Ferguson laughed. "You're making me glad I didn't go into research. I had a summer internship at a lab and all we did was wait around for things to fail. Was a total waste of time."

"I know. That is the worse part of the job. I guess you chose something faster paced. Catching bad guys. That's gotta be a rush."

"It is. There is something very rewarding about outsmarting the intellectually elite. That's mostly who I deal with. They always think they're the smartest guy..." he tipped his head to the side, "or gal in the room. My little secret is they never see it coming." A smile spread across his lips.

Was this Ferguson's way of telling him he knew something? Or was he just an asshole to everyone who came in here? "You love that element of surprise. I can see that in your eyes. Maybe I should get into law enforcement. I think that would be a blast."

Ferguson nodded slowly, maintaining eye contact. Jeffrey felt the man was looking directly into his soul. "So, when can I inspect your lab?"

The smile dropped off Jeffrey's face, betraying his chipper words. He hoped Ferguson didn't pick up on the disconnect. "Let's do it. I can show you the prototype of the first disks I developed. They were a complete flop, but they make great paperweights." Jeffrey stood and stretched. "Come on, let's do this."

Ferguson stood and followed Jeffrey out the door to the elevator. Jeffrey redoubled his effort at being bouncy and eagerly headed towards the elevator. He held the door for the agent, who watched him closely. A brief glimmer of Ferguson's *I got you* expression returned but disappeared as quickly. Was he just being paranoid?

Jeffrey pushed the button to the basement and turned towards Ferguson. "So, we have a pool going about the pulses. How many were there? What part of the lab did they come from?"

"If I were at liberty to tell you, I would. But I am not." Ferguson smiled and they were interrupted by the ding notifying their arrival.

Jeffrey strode towards his lab and unlocked the door, holding it open for the agent to enter. Ferguson's eagle eyes were soaking in every detail.

"Does this bring back memories of your undergrad labs?" Jeffrey asked, trying to appear as much of an open book as possible.

"Hell no, I went to Rensselaer Polytechnic Institute. They didn't call it RIP for nothing. We definitely did not have swanky labs like this."

"RIP." Jeffrey laughed. "I've heard of RPI. It's like the redheaded stepchild of MIT. Science and math minus all the bullshit social science classes."

"Precisely."

Jeffrey opened a drawer and pulled out one of the early models of the disks, then handed it to Ferguson. "This is the most expensive paperweight in this lab."

Ferguson held it up, allowing the light to shine through it. Lavender and cobalt swirls tightened near the center, making the pattern look like a mini universe. "Where do you get your seed money, Dr. Brennan?"

"Government grants, mostly. I've put a little of my own capital into this project, but it's like a snowball. Once you get the first grant, it rolls along nicely until you have some exceptional cash coming in."

"I'd like to see your proposals. Perhaps that will dive into the science more. Surely you explain the methods and purpose in a lot of detail to pursue the grant."

"I do. I'll have Kathy print those off for you. She's Dr. Vasu's secretary." Jeffrey sat on the edge of his desk, waiting for the barrage of questions.

Instead, Ferguson was quiet as he opened drawers, pulled out file folders, and lifted equipment. Finally, after a half hour of this methodical search, he spoke. "I'm going to send in my forensic guys this afternoon. We'll need your passwords."

"Passwords to what? My computer?" Jeffrey asked. This computer was clean, but he naturally bristled at the invasion. "You have a warrant? Or is this a voluntary situation?"

"Warrant? No, we're just looking into the cause of the pulse," Ferguson said. "I'm under the assumption right now that the pulses are being caused unknowingly by a local scientist."

"Right, that makes sense. But since I was offline this round, why would you need to see my computer? I was at home and everything was shut off here."

"Were they operating during Hurricane Charley? I understand you were here for that storm."

"I was, yes. I'll check with Vasu, if you don't mind. This is proprietary information. I don't think he is keen on letting Feds just poke around in there."

"Dr. Brennan, you mentioned government grants? I'm the government exercising the right to examine where the money is being used."

Jeffrey smiled, knowing this was total bullshit. "I'm not sure it works like that, Ferguson."

"I don't think you understand the purpose of Homeland Security. We have an unusual set of powers to prevent situations like September Eleventh. They don't always follow the traditional rules." He smiled and handed Jeffrey a pad of paper. "Passwords."

"I'm going to check with my boss on this one. Not that I don't trust you, just that the government isn't always on the up and up with its citizens."

"I totally understand." Ferguson waved towards the phone sitting on Jeffrey's desk.

Jeffrey dialed Kathy's number. "Kathy, did Dr. Vasu say it was okay to share passwords with...?"

Kathy interrupted him. "I'm putting you through to Dr. Vasu."

Jeffrey waited for his boss to pick up. "Jeffrey, I understand you have concerns."

"I just want to be sure I'm following your wishes, Dr. Vasu." He glanced at Ferguson, who was studying him intently. "They want keys to my office and passwords to my computer. Are you authorizing this? Did they sign a nondisclosure agreement? My stuff is protected, and I've put in for a patent, but it's not come through yet."

"We have to cooperate fully. I'm sure they're just looking for anything that can lead to the origins of the pulse. Please, allow them whatever access they need."

Jeffery turned away from Ferguson. "Are you sure you're okay with this, Dr. Vasu? Did you consult with legal?"

"I have. They assure me cooperating is in our best interest," Dr. Vasu said with utter confidence.

Jeffrey cupped the phone, lowering his voice. "I don't like the government in our files. How do we know they're legit?"

"Don't be paranoid, Jeffrey. Let the men have access. They'll be done soon enough."

"I want you to make note that I am cooperating but with concerns," Jeffrey said, turning back around to eyeball Ferguson.

"Fair enough. Please, I have an employee in here that needs to know what is going on." Dr. Vasu was losing patience.

Jeffrey hung up and watched Ferguson carefully, hoping he'd reveal something with his body language. He was well schooled in hiding his thoughts. Jeffrey could learn a thing or two from him. "Okay, the boss trusts you. I don't, but it's his lab."

Ferguson handed him the pad and Jeffrey scrawled the computer password on it. He purposefully did not offer the password-protected documents, but surely if they were any good at what they did, they could open those. No worries, this computer held only the files that wouldn't interfere with his freedom.

"Should I take the day off? Or will I have some time to get work done before your guys show up?"

"You're welcome to stay as we do our work. That way you'll be available to address any issues that may arise."

"Great. That can at least make this day not a total waste of time." Jeffrey wished he could just walk out of here and head home, but it may be useful to watch the progress and monitor any reactions or findings.

Ferguson pulled a small communications device out of his pocket and spoke a single phrase. "Green light."

A few minutes later, a team of agents entered the lab. In a matter of minutes, they'd copied Jeffrey's hard drive and handed it to Agent Ferguson.

"Thank you for your time, Dr. Brennan. I hope you sort through your issues on polymers and move forward with your grants."

"Thank you. Kathy will have all the specs of my grants and side project." He smiled coolly as Ferguson left. Jeffrey approached the man working on his computer, hoping to watch, but one of the agents blocked his way.

"Sir, please allow me access to the locked file cabinet in the back of the lab."

Jeffrey pulled out his keys, glancing back at the computer, worry growing.

Chapter 18

Deathly Discovery

Sunday, September 12, 2004, 5:00 p.m.

Ronnie stood under the shower in her hotel room reliving the adventures of the day, resisting the next item on her agenda. In an hour, they would meet the client for dinner. For now, every cell in her body permeated peace and tranquility brought about by the perfect day with Mike and Frank on the crystal-clear waters.

Watery, bathing suit-y images of Mike swirled around in her mind as the suds begrudgingly washed the sea off her skin and hair. Her imagination had Mike joining her in the shower, pressing that perfect chest against hers, transforming into new, invigorating feelings. Shower spray caressed her skin and she imagined throwing her arms around Mike's thick neck and planting a kiss on those full, ready lips.

Ronnie had not been disciplined enough to feel out whether he was connected to her past. She needed this unstructured, unencumbered time to just be. It would be easier when there was no snorkel stuffed in Mike's mouth as well.

She stepped out of the shower and wrapped a towel around her body, twisted another one around her hair, then wiped a steam-free circle on the mirror. Her cheeks were pink. Too much sun, or too much thinking naughty thoughts about Mike?

Ronnie combed her hair and relived the moment Mike had taken off his shirt, marveling at how telling it had been. He had been hesitant, waiting until the last moment to disrobe before they swam.

When he'd caught her checking him out from the water, his reaction had been so raw, so genuine, not full of pride or insecurity. Instead, he'd smiled and lost his nerve and looked away, making some comment to Frank. She had expected him to flex his arm or do some other buff dude thing joking around. Instead, he'd been vulnerable. And that made him even more attractive. Any doubts that had plagued her about coming here were fading away.

Ronnie smoothed leave-in conditioner through her locks and contemplated makeup. She usually didn't wear much, but since this was a business meeting and she wanted Carlos to not think she was young and naive, she'd have to do something. Settling on mascara, foundation to tamp down the pink, and a little neutral eye color for a polished, understated look. Mike had warned her about Carlos Munoz's forward, chauvinistic ways, so she was ready for his advances, if that was what he had in mind.

The hotel phone bleeped, startling Ronnie. It was probably Mike looking for an ETA. "Hello."

"Ron." It was Jeffrey's aggressive voice. "How are you doing?"

Ronnie inhaled sharply. "What is up with the fifty texts, Jeffery? We're done. Leave it alone." Her anger boiled up at this intrusion.

"Did you read my email?" Jeffrey's bluster faded to concern.

The question caught her off guard. "No, I'm trying to de-stress here, Jeffery." She knew she should hang up.

"Please, Ronnie, I'm not trying to bother you. I'm trying to protect you from Mike. I found out more on him. He is really dangerous. Promise me you won't be alone with him."

She rolled her eyes. "What the hell is wrong with you?"

"I'm dead serious. You have to see the pictures to believe it. Open your damn email, and for God's sake open your eyes. He is extremely dangerous."

"Jeff, you really have outdone yourself. He's my freakin' boss. He isn't dangerous." Ronnie's anger rose.

"I wish you hadn't gone." His voice was hard, angry. "Please, promise me you will look at the email. He beat her to death, Ronnie."

She wanted to hang up and yell, "Get lost, Jeffrey." Instead, she took the bait, knowing she would most definitely regret it. "Beat who to death? Aren't we being a bit dramatic?"

"See for yourself. Open your email. I'll wait." His voice was a mixture of panic and smugness, something pretty hard to pull off unless you were Jeffrey damn Brennan.

"You are unbelievable!" Ronnie slammed the receiver down and tried to blow it off. Jeffrey's words replayed in her mind. He beat her to death? Who? Curiosity overcame her as she opened the laptop and found the email from Jeffrey.

> Ronnie, please don't be alone with Mike. He beat his fiancée to death. I knew something was off about him from the second I met him. I'm enclosing an article from his hometown newspaper that covered the story. He must have had a hell of a good lawyer to not be rotting in jail right now. Did you ever ask him why he moved to Florida? Just get home as soon as you can, and I can help you find another job. You just can't be working for a man like this.

"Damn it, Jeffrey!" Ronnie's anger fumed. He was not going to ruin this trip, ruin what she'd started with Mike. He'd find her a new job? What a controlling ass. She clicked on the image and waited for the slow hotel dial-up Internet to catch up with the large file. A quarter of an inch at a time it revealed its horrible picture. The first few inches showed *The Democrat and Chronicle*, Rochester, New York, March 5, 1999.

The blood drained from her face as the headline appeared, "Domestic Violence Turns into a Murder Investigation."

"Oh my God." Ronnie steeled herself for the next segment. As the image loaded, it slowly tore down her hopes and dreams. On the left was a picture of a man being arrested. It was definitely Mike. His hair was shorter, but it was him. The picture on the right was of a pretty woman with dark, haunting eyes. Jeffrey wasn't messing around. This was damning evidence, and from a trusted source, the Rochester paper.

Once the body of the article loaded, she read it, her heart pounding in her throat. "Local man, Michael Walsh, suspected in the death of his fiancée, Kelly Escobar. Evidence at their shared home led to Walsh's arrest. Camera crews captured the bloody scene at Walsh's home in the 800 block of Guinevere Drive." In the left column there was a small image of blood-streaked shower walls and a covered body lying crumpled in the shower. "Walsh had a blood alcohol level well above the legal limit. The image (above left) of his arrest shows blood on his right hand." The image continued to load, and Ronnie slammed her hand on the table. "Come on already! Crappy Internet!"

Another image loaded and it was revolting. Kelly's bruised and battered face, with blood caked in her hair. Her long lashes and fine bone structure belying her beauty.

"We are awaiting the coroner's report to build the case against Walsh, a US Marine. Fourteen percent of all homicides against women are due to domestic violence, and thirty percent of women report some form of domestic abuse at some time in their life." The article listed other prominent domestic violence cases.

Ronnie tried to look away from the beaten and bruised image, but she couldn't. Sweat collected under her bra. The phone rang again, making her jump. Ronnie shut the lid of the laptop, wanting to hide what she had just seen, to make it go away forever.

"Jeffrey, leave me alone!" Ronnie yelled into the phone.

"Oh, um." It was Mike. "Hey, we're down in the lobby. Come on down when you're ready."

Ronnie's mind froze. How the hell could she go to dinner after seeing Mike's handiwork on that poor woman? "Okay."

Ronnie hung up the phone and stared blankly at it. Two images of Mike battled it out in her mind. The blue-eyed snorkeler with a sexy smile, and the version from the newspaper capable of beating someone to death. Could it be the same person? It was hard to put them together. The angry Mike with no conscience, no humanity. That wasn't the man she knew. He was funny, engaging, handsome, and professional. Not a monster who could kill someone with his bare hands. Which one was the real Mike? He was certainly strong enough to beat someone to death. A flash of the shirtless Mike she had just seen with his hands around a lifeless woman's throat added to the terror that grew inside her.

"Oh God, I'm shaking." She held her hands out in front of her as proof. "Crap."

She flung off the towel and got dressed, not paying much attention to what she was doing. How the hell was she going to spend the evening with Mike? And impress Carlos and his team?

"Oh God, this is going to be a friggin' disaster." Ronnie slipped on wedge sandals and looked in the mirror. The floral skirt and white top hugged her curves. Originally that was what she was going for, but now it seemed too much. She tore through the closet but didn't find anything more suitable for a business dinner.

Ronnie held her head in her hands, and she forced a few deep breaths. All the magic from the afternoon dissipated into thin air. Could she feign illness and stay home? Her mind went back to the image of Kelly Escobar's face and felt each blow that marred her beauty and stole her life.

Her cell phone buzzed, and Ronnie absentmindedly picked it up. It was a text from Jeffrey. *Stay away from him.*

"I can't." Ronnie whispered. She grabbed her purse and room key and left her room, trying to push it all down before she saw Mike. "Keep it together, Andrews."

Chapter 19

Carlos and Chaos

Sunday, September 12, 2004, 6:00 p.m.

Mike glanced at his watch. Carlos was already at the restaurant waiting for them.

"She'll be here soon," Frank consoled. "Women take forever to get ready. If you had a wife, you'd know that."

"I don't need a wife, Frank, I have you." Mike blew him a kiss.

Frank's expression shifted from puzzled to laughing. "Oh no, don't you..."

The elevator dinged, and Ronnie stepped off, startling them. The glow from the day on the water had added a bronze tone to her skin, and the white shirt enhanced this effect.

"Hey, there you are." Relieved, Mike stepped towards her.

Ronnie smiled at Frank and turned to Mike. Her face hardened, and if he were being paranoid, he would have sworn she winced.

"Hi." Ronnie dodged Mike and strode towards Frank.

"There's Ronnie. Let's get moving." Frank walked out of the lobby doors and Ronnie followed.

Mike struggled to catch her eye, but Ronnie sped up and spoke to Frank. Was she regretting what they'd started today? *Don't be paranoid, she's just nervous.* They strolled through the parking lot to the car and still Ronnie wouldn't look at him. Frank moved to the passenger side, giving Mike a chance to talk to her alone.

"You okay, Ronnie?"

She rounded towards him, her mouth a tight line. "Yes." Then she grabbed the door handle and paused, waiting for him to unlock it.

"What is it, Ronnie? You nervous about meeting Carlos?" Mike reached out and caught her arm.

Ronnie jerked out of his grasp and looked startled.

Mike held his hands up. "Whoa, what's going on here?"

Ronnie stole a glance towards Frank. "I'm just edgy." She crossed her arms. Her eyes were wide, and her mouth was open slightly, as if needing extra oxygen in case she had to run away.

Mike eased his approach. "You feeling okay?"

Frank tapped the roof of the Jeep. "We are going to be late. Let's catch up in the car, okay?"

Mike hit the fob, and Ronnie sat in the back seat. It was clear something had unsettled her. Had he done something earlier to upset her?

Mike slid into the driver's seat and twisted around to face Ronnie. She forced a smile. He reassured her. "Dinner will be fine. There is nothing to be nervous about."

Frank, unaware of anything amiss, looked back at her too. "You nervous, Ronnie? After your fearlessness in those choppy waves, I can't believe anything would faze you."

Ronnie's expression changed, and she smiled at Frank. "I'm not so much nervous. Just had an upsetting call, that's all. I'll be fine."

"Okay. Mike, drive the damn car, we are going to be late." Frank shook his head and stared forward.

Mike watched Ronnie for another second, but she wouldn't look at him. "I hope everything is okay."

She nodded slightly but her expression remained neutral. But when she spoke to Frank, her face lit up. Ronnie had been playful, even flirty in the water. Maybe it was just as she said, an upsetting call.

The hostess showed them to a private room in the back. Carlos stood and waved them over as soon as he saw Mike. Carlos was a good-looking man, about five-nine, stocky, with a bit of a belly and a slightly receding hairline.

"Mike, *buenos noches.*" Carlos shook Mike's hand like he meant it. Mike and Frank had built up a rapport with Carlos over the last year and there was an unspoken connection built on respect.

Carlos hugged Frank, who had met Carlos's family on one of his longer trips and he'd made a friend for life.

"Carlos Munoz, I'd like you to meet Ronnie Andrews. She's the newest addition to our team."

Carlos's eyes widened. "Ronnie Andrews." He took her hand, then kissed it. "What an absolute pleasure to meet you. I've heard great things about you."

"Mr. Munoz, it is my pleasure." Ronnie was professional and handled herself gracefully. Her smile was natural, but not overly friendly. She was setting her boundaries with Carlos, which was an excellent sign. Carlos was a notorious flirt, with rumors flying around about more than one mistress on the island.

"No, please, I insist you call me Carlos." Carlos took Ronnie's elbow and manhandled her away from the others.

Ronnie would be fine, but it still was annoying that Carlos hadn't even settled into the meal before stealing her attention. Mike didn't blame him. Ronnie was stunning, sleek, and slender, her hair shinning, with the recessed lighting making it look like spun gold. She stole a glance at him but instead of the warmth he expected, it was laced with the cold, hard stare she'd shown him in the hotel lobby.

The man standing near Mike was chatting about his family. Mike had already forgotten his name. Was it Manuel? "How nice to have three kids. That must keep you busy." He'd always had trouble with names, but tonight his mind was on Ronnie and not in the way he'd hoped. Had the day out on the water been too much for her? She was still in a delicate state from her ordeal during Frances. He'd have to keep this short so she could get some rest. After all, they were presenting in the morning. She'd need her energy.

Carlos pointed to a seat at the round table in the center of the room. "Mike, please, sit here across from me. Ronnie..." Carlos pulled out the chair next to him. "I need to get to know you better." Ronnie finally met his eyes and bit her lips. Her façade was cracking. The blood in Mike's veins turned to ice. Why did she have the expression of a traumatized animal?

Frank was to his left, and the other men sat in the remaining chairs. Carlos commanded the conversation, shepherding it adeptly from sports to family then around to insisting that they retire after dinner to the roof for cigars. A few times Mike felt Ronnie's eyes on him, but the vibe coming across the table wasn't of wanton lust as he'd hoped.

Carlos whispered something in Ronnie's ear, and she snickered, flashing those magical dimples, her face alight with the light he had craved. A pang of jealousy sparked through him. He tamped it down.

Mike enjoyed the rich, colorful meal and Manuel's equally vibrant stories about island life. When the servers cleared the table for dessert, Ronnie excused herself. Mike ordered a bourbon on the rocks and watched anxiously for her return, hoping she wasn't feeling sick.

Frank noticed his uneasiness and cocked his head, questioning.

Mike mouthed, *Ronnie.*

Frank shrugged his shoulders and went on chatting to the man on his left.

When Ronnie returned, Mike sighed in relief. Carlos had been watching for her return as well, and that made him nervous.

"Gentlemen," Carlos turned to Ronnie, "and lovely lady, let us retreat to the cigar bar upstairs to shift our meeting to the business at hand."

Everyone stood and followed Carlos up a flight of stairs to the open rooftop lounge. Lush tropical plants in colorful pots the size of grown men lined the rooftop, separated the tables, and provided a modicum of privacy for big deals to be made.

They were shown to a table in the back corner, with plenty of space for privacy. Carlos held Ronnie's chair and pushed it in gentlemanly behind her. She was glowing with his attention and obviously feeling well enough to continue the evening. Carlos sat next to her at the head of the table, with Ronnie to his right. The other two men crowded in and sat near Ronnie. Frank sat next to Carlos, and Mike took the last seat to Frank's right.

Ronnie mesmerized Carlos and his men. They hung on every word, laughed enthusiastically, and couldn't take their eyes off her. Ronnie had come alive with the attention and was in her element, polished, professional, charming, and lively. Mike was out of earshot and couldn't hear most of what they were saying, with the wind carrying the sounds out to sea, but knew she'd exceeded all his expectations for her role in sealing the deal. Hell, she was doing a better job than he could have.

Mike sipped his bourbon and drank in the situation, glad to be unencumbered with small talk. Ronnie had always come across as confident, but on the shy side.

Tonight, she had every man at the table eating out of her hand. Almost every man. Mike could hear wisps of a story from her last job. She was sparkling, commanding the table effortlessly. The men roared with laughter at the conclusion of her recounting. What made her so captivating was the spark of personality and her attentiveness to their needs. She was subtle, connected, generous, and mesmerizing. As he'd predicted, Carlos had fallen under her spell, and he was leaning towards her, almost pawing her as he begged for another story.

A pretty waitress in a low-cut floral dress presented the cigars on a small intricately ornate silver platter. She instinctively knew the pecking order, serving Carlos first, then gliding around the table to Mike, skipping the other men. Her dark eyes shone in the low light, and wind picked up her long ponytail of glossy, black hair. She held the tray out to Mike, leaning over enticingly.

Mike chose a fat Cuban and lifted one of the heavy chrome lighters. "Thank you."

As the waitress presented the tray to Frank, she coyly smiled at Mike, batting her eyelashes. He smiled and toked on the cigar, displaying his appreciation, blowing it skyward. It was a beautiful night, and the liquor was working at taming the troubles. The ocean breeze snatched the smoke and pulled it up into the luminous night sky.

The waitress made her way to everyone, pausing finally near Carlos, all the while stealing glances at him. Mike basked in the warmth of someone's attention, but preferred Ronnie's eyes on him. They were not. Carlos shared his cigar with Ronnie, and she cautiously took a draw and blew out the smoke. Her new entourage, egging her on. The smirk on Carlos's face expressed it all. Ronnie was sealing the deal, and not just for the business side of things.

The serenity of the night evaporated. He'd warned Ronnie about Carlos back when they'd first met just after Hurricane Charley. Why hadn't he thought to remind her earlier today? Ah yes, the truce on all things stressful. If he could just catch her eye.

Ronnie returned the cigar to Carlos, who leaned in conspiratorially and whispered something to her. Ronnie's head tipped back as she laughed. Mike's jealousy triggered again. He wanted to be the one making her laugh. Ronnie was playing the work game with the client as the most interesting man in the room.

The nagging worry resurfaced, and no amount of cigar smoke or booze was going to displace it. Something had changed between them, and that scared him. Mike had had no expectations when they'd come on the trip. Hopes for a deepening friendship, but despite wanting more, he had not expected it. He certainly didn't want to lose the sparks they'd lit on the boat and when they'd been alone in the water.

Frank was deep in conversation with the man across from him but shifted topics and pulled Mike into the conversation. "Manuel, you should have seen the Skipper out on the water today." Frank laughed and patted Mike on the back. "This man is a maniac behind the wheel. He nearly tossed me on the floor within minutes of hitting the waves."

Manuel laughed. "Sounds like the sea was a bit rough."

"Frank likes it rough," Mike laughed. "Until we ask him to snorkel. Then he is scared shitless."

Frank laughed. "Hey, I know my limits. I'm an excellent swimmer, I swear. Just not when the waves are trying to drown me. Hell no."

Manuel shook his head. "It's hurricane season. There are some tropical waves out there making our seas a bit rough. You should come back in January. No tourists, calm seas."

"We will be in the thick of this install by then, so it's a deal, Manuel," Frank said.

"Sir, would you like another drink?" The waitress smiled and batted her thick, dark lashes.

"I'm good, thank you," Mike answered.

She leaned in closer and whispered, "It's on me, if you like."

Mike smiled. "No, no. I'm driving my staff back to the hotel. I need to be sober."

"Oh." She cocked her head to the side. "I get off at 11:00. Which hotel? I could meet you in the lounge."

Mike's eyes widened. "That is such a wonderful offer. But I'm sorry. I have to be up early." He smiled to soften the blow but did not want to encourage her.

She smiled and nodded, then slipped a piece of paper in his hand, then left, swinging her hips as she walked away. Mike slipped the paper in his pocket and looked around for Ronnie. She was not there.

Frank leaned towards him and whispered, "What was that about?"

"Oh, she offered to buy me a drink, and meet me..." Mike flicked his hand, dismissing it.

Frank turned to Manuel. "I swear, some hot chick buys Mike a drink every damn time we go out. What about me? Am I chopped liver?"

Manuel laughed and patted Frank on the shoulder. "Puerto Rican women are suckers for tall blue-eyed devils. They just can't help themselves."

"Maybe, but it happens in Florida, too. This man is a chick magnet." Frank clapped him on the back. "You'd think he'd be married by now with all that attention."

Embarrassed, Mike quickly changed the subject. "Hell no, Frank. I see them eying you, too. It's that hard outer shell that scares 'em off, though." Mike glanced around, realizing Carlos's chair was empty as well. "Where is Ronnie?"

Frank looked around and shrugged, continuing the conversation with Manuel. Alarm bells rang. What if Ronnie was feeling ill? Mike pulled out his phone and texted her. Maybe her nausea had returned, boosted by the cigar smoke. After five minutes she'd not answered, Mike stood and made his way down the stairs to the restrooms. He asked a woman to check and see if anyone was in there, but she said it was empty. Then he checked the men's room to see if Carlos was there. Nope.

Ronnie would have mentioned something to Frank if she were going to be awhile. Anger peppered through the competing worry. Carlos had her cornered somewhere, no doubt. He'd seen it in the past, especially with Carlos's minions fawning over Ronnie, fueling his need to conquer her to prove his machismo.

Mike excused himself and retreated down the stairs, then stepped inside the dining room. Maybe they'd ordered dessert, if she wanted a break from the cigar smoke. No sign of either of them in the dining room. Mike made his way downstairs, planning on checking the parking lot. His mind flashed an image of Ronnie stepping into a car with Carlos, then he shook it off. Ronnie would not cross the line with Carlos—she was too professional for that. Any attention she gave him came from a work-oriented place.

Near the restrooms, there was a door that led to a stairwell. Voices carried up the steps and Mike bolted down two at a time, hoping to find her. At the bottom of the stairwell, a couple was talking closely together. The man was built like Carlos, and he'd cornered the woman. She was attempting to get past him.

"Carlos, please, I want to go back upstairs," the woman said.

"Carlos?" Mike called out.

The man turned around and stepped away from the wall. "Mike, I was just getting to know Ronnie a little better. Glad you could join us."

Ronnie quickly started up the steps, flashing Mike a look of anger and shock. She shook her head. "No, Carlos, I'm done here."

"You okay, Ronnie?" She was almost eye level, standing on the step above him. She exhaled and looked away. "Yup."

It was obvious Carlos had crossed the line with her. All professional courtesy was out the window.

Mike turned back to Carlos. "What the hell is going on here?"

Carlos held his hands up. "Now, now, don't be alarmed. I was just talking to her."

Mike turned to Ronnie. "Just talking? Here in the dark stairwell?"

Ronnie shook her head. "I'm done talking, Carlos." Her tone worried him.

"Ronnie, I'm going to have a few words with Mr. Munoz. You're welcome to join us or..."

Ronnie paused at the top of the landing and shook her head. Her eyes narrowed and lips set in a firm line.

Mike turned back to Carlos. "I will only say this once. Man to man. Ronnie is off limits."

Carlos smiled, his mustache spreading wide with the gesture. "How can any man resist her? God made beauty to be enjoyed, Michael. You cannot resist her charms, either. Admit it. I saw your eyes on her all night."

Mike lowered his chin and narrowed his eyes. "How about this? Don't ever corner her at the bottom of a fucking stairwell again." He knew his anger was taking over now, and he was pushing the limit for respecting the client, but Carlos had already thrown all of that out the window.

"I am sorry. I can see you are possessive of her. Ronnie didn't mention she was taken, Mike. You have to understand, I cannot help myself when you bring such a creature before me. It is my duty as a man to respond to her charms."

Mike took a step closer, clenching his fists. "Carlos, women are not yours to conquer. Ronnie is not yours to respond to."

Carlos shook his head. "If she didn't want to be down here with me, she could have walked away at any time."

Mike tamped down the urge to punch Carlos in his smug little face. Instead, he leaned closer and looked down at him. "She is my employee and has a right to come to a business meeting without being hit on."

"If she wants me, what am I to do?" Carlos held his hands out and shrugged.

Mike pressed his hand into Carlos's chest, pinning him against the wall. "You will have me to deal with if you so much as whisper in her ear."

"Now, now." Carlos pushed Mike away and readjusted his shirt. "No need to lay hands on me." His words were smooth, but the message had gotten through. He nervously glanced up the stairs and back at Mike. "If she doesn't call my driver to come pick her up, I will leave her be. If she does, it is out of my hands." Carlos pushed past him and started up the stairs.

Mike spun around towards him "Call your driver?"

Carlos stood a few steps up, looking down at Mike. "Yes, he can bring her to my condo down the street." Then he turned and continued up the steps.

Mike nearly leapt to the landing and stood in front of him, blocking his way. "You are crossing the line, Carlos. She isn't here to share your bed."

"Let's allow Miss Andrews to decide for herself. After all, she is not your wife. Is she your girlfriend? She didn't say she was dating anyone."

Mike lost it and gripped the front of Carlos's shirt, lifting it to his chin. He wanted to tell him she was his, but it would be a lie. Despite how much he wanted it to be true. "You so much as touch her, I will..." Mike caught himself before he demolished any chance of a deal. He let go and smoothed down Carlos's shirt. "I'm just telling you to leave her alone. She is in a vulnerable state. Don't take advantage of that."

Carlos smiled. "I like delicate females. They're..."

Before Carlos could finish his sentence, Mike pulled his arm back to punch him, then instead, opened his hand and pushed him. Carlos stumbled on the top step of the next landing and sat down hard on the steps. Mike leaned over Carlos and pointed his finger in his face. "Watch yourself, Carlos. Don't trip up or you'll be dealing with me." Then stormed up the stairs and back to the outside lounge.

The humid air hit him, snapping him out of his angry stupor. He forced the snarl into a neutral expression and returned to the table. Ronnie followed him, walking towards the table, her eyes wide and questioning. At least she was looking at him now.

Mike let the anger show briefly, and he shook his head. "Well, fellows, we need to get going." Mike stood. Ronnie and Frank did as well.

"Please," Manuel urged. "Let's sit and talk until Carlos returns. He should be here to say his goodbyes."

Mike turned to Manuel and lowered his voice. "I think Carlos has said entirely enough tonight."

Manuel stared back until a spark of understanding changed his expression. "Very well then, we shall be sure and let him know." Manuel shook his head.

Mike let the mask of calm drop, revealing the anger seething below.

Ronnie followed Mike's lead. "Yes, it's getting late. Could you give this to Carlos?" Ronnie clasped Manuel's hand, leaving something in it, then she walked away and waved to the other men. "Good night, everyone. It was a pleasure getting to know you."

Frank said his goodbyes and waited until they'd made it to the stairs, then grabbed Mike's arm. "Hey, what the hell was that about? You're snubbing Carlos? Mike, do you understand the culture here? It's all about showing respect."

Mike glanced at Ronnie. "Do you want to respond to that, Ronnie?"

Frank furrowed his eyebrows and took a step closer to Ronnie. "What is it? You not feeling well?"

Carlos appeared from the stairwell and approached Frank. "Gentlemen, Ronnie, don't leave. The night is young."

Mike clenched his fists, and Carlos stepped backwards away from them.

Frank shot an angry glance at Mike and approached Carlos. "Look, sorry, Carlos, we would like to stay, but Ronnie is recovering from..." He stopped mid-sentence and glanced at Ronnie, not wanting to share too much. "We need to hit the hay."

Mike inwardly groaned at Frank's choice of words and turned his back on both of them, ushering Ronnie ahead as they made their way down the steps. Frank followed behind, utterly confused.

"Mike, seriously, I've never known you to be so rude. This is our biggest client. Why are you...?"

Mike interrupted him. "Frank, shut it. We will talk when we get to the car. This is not our usual situation."

Frank shot him a steely glance as they silently made their way to the car.

Chapter 20

More Than Sack-Worthy

Mike clicked the fob to unlock the Jeep. "Frank, can you sit in back?"

Frank looked confused. "I can."

Ronnie shook her head. "It's okay, Mike, really. Frank, you sit up front. I'm fine."

Frank sat in the back seat, settling in. Ronnie opened the passenger car door and looked over the roof at Mike, then shut the door, leaving Frank alone to ponder what the hell was going on.

"Thanks for saving me back there." Her words were laced with defeat and underlying anger.

"What did he say to you?" Mike wanted to scream and cause a ruckus, but he was taking cues from her quieter approach.

"He..." She bit her lips, as if not wanting to share. "The bastard handed me his card, asking me to call him. He would send his driver to pick me up so I could join him for a nightcap."

"Hmmmm." Mike exhaled the statement, trying to keep his temper in check.

"Mike, I've had guys hit on me before, but he was so aggressive. I declined and tried to leave but you see how he blocked me."

Frank tapped on the window and looked up at Mike. "Man, it's hot in here."

Mike responded by locking the door so Frank couldn't get out. He banged on the window in protest and then realized something bigger was happening outside the car.

"I'm so sorry, Ronnie. I knew he was a dog. I just thought at a business meeting he'd show you the respect you deserve."

"Yeah, American men are much more subtle." She looked away, grimacing. "I'm just glad you came when you did. No harm, no foul."

"Major harm, major foul on his part though." Mike looked away, not liking the vehemence soaking into his words. He reset the tone. "Men here are machismo. I think he felt challenged because his friends were eating out of your hands."

Ronnie shook her head. "What did you say to him?" Her expression was tentative, almost afraid of his answer.

Mike looked away and took a deep breath. "Not enough. Damn Carlos. I know this puts you in a difficult situation. Do you want me to do the presentation tomorrow?"

"Oh hell no." She looked angry. "Why would you do that? You hired me to be your marketing guru. Don't deprive me of my job because Carlos doesn't know the boundaries of decency. It's like being punished twice for being a female."

Her words punched him in the gut, like he so desperately wanted to do to Carlos. "I didn't mean that at all. You're gonna kick ass. I just wanted to offer in case you needed that. I'll do whatever you want, Ronnie."

"I want to be lead tomorrow. Just leave it be, Mike. I'm fine. It's fine." Her tone was angry, but it shifted from Carlos to him.

"Your call. I'll be right there and so will Frank."

She opened the car door and sat down, turning to say something to Frank he couldn't hear. Mike took a second to formulate what to say to Frank. He took a deep breath and forced out some of the pure vehemence at Carlos for destroying this deal for Ronnie and his team. Then opened the car door and sat down.

Frank was silent, probably sensing something big was happening. He must have known by their abrupt departure what Carlos had done.

Mike put the car in reverse and made their way back to the hotel.

Frank waited ten minutes, God bless him, then said, "Anyone care to tell me what the hell is going on? Or will I have to ask Carlos tomorrow?"

Yeah, he *knew*. "Frank, remember what I predicted last time we were here?"

"That the Red Sox would win the series?"

Mike chuckled. Frank was the best. "Yeah. They still might do it."

Ronnie looked out the window silently, but then turned to Frank. "Carlos cornered me and slid his hand up my skirt after he offered a limo ride for me to join him at his apartment down the street."

Mike almost slammed on the brakes. "He what?"

Frank said what Mike was thinking but with much more class. "Damn, Carlos, you are dead meat."

Ronnie twisted to face Frank in the back seat. "Yeah, and he got a good handful of my ass while he was up there. I hope you could see the slap mark on his face when you spoke to him, Mike."

Mike's anger boiled over, but he kept his mouth shut, only by the grace of God, and instead grit his teeth, biting back the anger.

"Surely you didn't let him get away with that? Mike, you had words with him?"

Mike looked in the rearview mirror. "Oh, I had words. Threatening, angry words." He looked at Ronnie. "But I had no idea he actually assaulted you."

Frank threw out an uncharacteristic, "That *motherfucker*."

Ronnie eyed Mike, fear painted in her tight lipped, eyes-wide expression.

Mike slapped the steering wheel. "He actually grabbed you? That fucking asshole!"

Ronnie cringed. "Settle down. I handled it. He won't try that again. But damn, Mike, I'm not some helpless female. I can handle myself. I just wasn't expecting him to be so forward."

Frank leaned towards the front seat. "Ronnie, one thing I've learned about men here in Puerto Rico is their attitudes are very different towards women."

"I see that now," Ronnie said curtly.

Frank cleared his throat. "Um...how do I say this?"

Ronnie turned around to face Frank again.

"When he offered you his cigar, Ronnie…" Frank paused, searching for his words. "It was likely understood that you would, ah..."

Mike stole a glance at Ronnie's face as she took in what Frank said.

Understanding transformed her features and her jaw dropped. "Oh my God!" Ronnie slammed her hand on the console. "Frank, seriously?"

"Yeah, it's a phallic symbol and I am assuming you toking on that bad boy was as good as a yes. Sorry to be so blunt."

Mike's blood was boiling and he white-knuckled the steering wheel, taming the instinct to punch something.

"I'm not saying you did it for that reason. I'm telling you what Carlos likely thought."

"Damn it!" Mike said. "This is a disaster. Guys, I totally understand if you want to just go home. Do we want to present tomorrow? Is this thing shot to hell, Frank?"

Ronnie's eyes were tearing up, and Mike softened his tone.

"Ronnie, seriously, this is not your fault. Carlos was way out of bounds. He essentially screwed up this whole deal tonight."

Frank shook his head. "No way. We were sent here to do a job. Sell the software. We can't leave without trying."

"Ronnie, your call," Mike said, eying her.

"I'm embarrassed. No, scratch that. I'm mortified. But there is no way I'm going to let Carlos intimidate me out of doing my job. I'm sorry this has gone so badly tonight." She struggled for the next words or struggled to get a hold of her emotions. "I'm presenting tomorrow. No further discussion needed."

"Ronnie." Frank leaned forward, straining against the seatbelt. "This is a big deal. Carlos disrespected you tonight, in a huge way. Do you mind me asking if he offered to sign the deal if you slept with him?"

Mike turned around. "Frank, for God's sake!"

"I'm sorry, Ronnie. I am not prying—it's important for our company. If he did, we need to handle it differently. If he was just being a horny asshole, that's different. Did he put conditions on the contract?"

Mike took his eyes from the wheel to see Ronnie shaking her head. "No, thank God. I'd have really been pissed if he'd said that."

"Okay, that is a relief. A small one. He still sexually assaulted you. He's gonna hear from our HR department. So now we make the call to continue as planned. Ronnie, you can show him what you're made of."

Ronnie smiled.

Damn, Frank was invaluable. He was giving her the control she needed while keeping her dignity. Why hadn't *he* thought of that? Instead, Mike had only made it worse by yelling and making her feel more helpless.

"Damn right I will. He has no idea I have a brain along with my other assets." Her attention was fully on Frank and for once Mike was okay with that.

Frank laughed. "Oh, yeah, your *ass-etts*. I see what you did there!" Frank pointed and winked.

Mike kept his pie hole shut. Frank was pulling her out of the scared mode and prepping her for conquering this. That man needed a raise.

Frank leaned forward. "You get in there and tear it up, Ronnie. Let him know you are a hell of a lot more than just sack-worthy. You're gonna hand him his sorry ass on a platter, but not until you've sealed the deal!"

Ronnie nodded enthusiastically. "That's right! Carlos Munoz is going to see my real worth tomorrow morning over his smug little mustache."

Frank cooed, "A force to be reckoned with."

Mike watched her transform. The scared look was shifting to something else. He wasn't sure what, but it beat seeing her looking terrified every time he glanced her way.

Frank reached out and tapped Ronnie's shoulder. "Okay, here is a bit of advice from a wise old man, Ronnie. Practice your presentation and imagine Carlos is sitting right in front of you. Look him in the eyes. Practice until you can do that without flinching. Then you'll nail it for the real thing."

Ronnie smiled. "Brilliant, Frank. Thank you."

Frank gripped Ronnie's headrest. "Mike and I will be there if you forget anything. If it helps, look at me most of the time and I'll send you kick-ass vibes."

Ronnie reached out and covered Frank's hand. "You are wonderful, Frank. Thank you."

Mike stole a glance at Frank in the rearview mirror. He made eye contact and nodded, hoping it conveyed his appreciation. Mike knew his anger, fueled by jealousy, would have beaten down her confidence, ruining their chances of making the deal. Instead, Frank's understanding of both the Puerto Rican culture and what Ronnie needed had saved the entire night. And along with it all of their hard work to get Carlos to the table.

Chapter 21

Lioness in for the Kill

Monday, September 13, 2004

Wind whipped through Ronnie's hair. Panic rose and she looked behind her. A dark figure spread a menacing shadow across the damp grass. She ran, not sure where to go, but facing him was not a choice. Whoever was following her was holding a knife. The light from her lantern glinted off the metal gripped in his hand. Her mind screamed out to hide, but logic told her that would just leave her trapped. Ronnie blew out the lantern and sprinted into the darkness, away from the frightening figure. Icy wind tore at her cape, flipping it over her shoulder. She pulled it back in place and ran towards the sound of the sea, keeping the wind in her face, hoping it would offer the protection of drowning out the sound of her footsteps down the gravel path.

The roaring of the ocean was loud now, the salty scent stronger. Ronnie made her way down a path cut in the grass, barely visible in the low light of the moon through the clouds. It descended downwards and she hoped it would hide her from her pursuer. The path narrowed and brought her down a steep cliff, heading towards the ocean. Behind her, the sound of footsteps crunching on the gravel path above urged her on. Ronnie stumbled on a loose stone, nearly falling to her knees. If she lost her footing, she would fall to her death. Ronnie tried not to look down at the crashing waves, but they drew her in like a magnet. She risked another glance behind her. The man was closer now, close enough to see his beard and old-fashioned clothes. Her foot caught on a root, and she reached out for anything that could save her.

Ronnie's hands came away empty, only a cliff face to reach out to. She tumbled to the ground, the impact jarring her, and to her horror, gravity pulled her down and her momentum threw her over the edge, down the face of the cliff.

An incessant beeping pulled her away from a horrible death. Ronnie's eyes snapped open, and relief flooded through her groggy mind as she fumbled to find the unfamiliar clock radio's off switch. She sat on the edge of the bed, blood still coursing through her veins. It had felt so real. Under different circumstances she would dismiss it as her vivid imagination. Her time traveling had put this in a new light. Gut instinct told her it was another piece of the puzzle that had plagued her since she'd moved to Florida.

Ronnie leaned over to the side table and picked up her journal, then spent a few minutes capturing the details of the man's face, the feelings she'd had, and the location before it slipped away.

Today was the presentation to Carlos Munoz and his team and the entire reason they'd traveled to Puerto Rico. Ronnie clicked on the TV and was comforted by the familiar faces of Charles Gibson and Diane Sawyer giving her a piece of home she needed. It was also a welcome distraction to keep her mind from reliving her interactions with Carlos last night. She opened a protein bar and nibbled on it. It would have to do for breakfast. She needed time to practice.

First, she headed to the bathroom and spoke to the shower walls, glad no one was there to hear how cray cray she sounded. She quickly got ready, putting on her makeup and fixing her hair.

Ronnie went to the wardrobe to choose her clothes. It was a big day and she needed to look professional but toned down on the sexy. Today she would start again, this time focusing on the software, and without getting rattled. Doubts crowded in. Carlos would not take that away from her. She imagined if she failed, Carlos would swoop in and offer to convince his board of directors, but only if she slept with him. No way in hell she'd give him the chance. She had to deliver a polished, professional, convincing talk. Damn Carlos for making this so much more difficult.

She tried not to think about Mike's anger, his willingness to beat the hell out of Carlos. He'd instructed her to look at him if she got nervous. That would make her lose her nerve even more than slimy Carlos. She'd look at Frank, and the other faces in the room, before she'd look to Mike.

Ronnie had brought her power suit, the one Jeffrey had given her, and wished she'd listened to Steph and chosen a different one. She did not want Jeffrey's energy in the mix. It was already crowded enough in her mind with Carlos, Mike, and her dad fumbling around in her brain. It *was* her most expensive suit. Why Jeffrey had chosen beige was beyond her, but typical of him to not even know she preferred blues and grays to the brown family. Still, it was tailored and spoke of her competence. When presenting to a man who only looked at you for your sexuality, you needed every tool in your arsenal.

Deep in her thoughts, she tuned out *Good Morning America*'s chatter until she heard familiar words, ones that induced panic deep into her soul. "Hurricane Ivan is approaching the Florida Gulf Coast. Pensacola Beach is preparing for this monster storm." The video showed waves attacking the shore with all the beachfront stores and homes boarded up. "New Orleans is extremely vulnerable to flooding. We have civil engineers assessing the levees. The trajectory may be the fatal blow for this city, as a worst-case scenario."

Ronnie was relieved it had missed Orlando. There would be less cleanup, and Steph and Ian wouldn't have to suffer through another storm. They spoke a little more about Ivan and Ronnie switched to the Weather Channel. It was two minutes before seven and she just caught the end of the tropical update.

Stephanie Abrams was on the beach with her hair blowing around. "Winds are picking up here along the Florida coast. The National Weather Service is calling for high potential for tornadoes tonight as the storm makes landfall."

Ronnie felt panic rising in sympathy. "Get out while you can!"

Stephanie ended her coverage and tossed the ball to Paul Goodloe. Ronnie sat transfixed on the end of the bed when they showed a map of the Caribbean.

Paul's voice carried over the graphic. "We've been watching this tropical wave for a while now, and it's been very weak due to Hurricane Ivan's wind shear. Today we see some development as it is approaching Puerto Rico. We will keep an eye on this as it develops." The image showed a time lapse of a clump of clouds that blew up dramatically in a matter of hours, approaching Puerto Rico.

Ronnie opened the curtains, expecting to see the sunny skies she'd been welcomed with since her arrival. The familiar banded clouds were forming along the horizon. Gloomy shadows of an approaching storm had taken over her happy corner of the island.

"Shoot." Ronnie looked back at the TV, but they'd moved on to covering weather around the US. Ronnie felt sweat gathering on her freshly washed skin.

An overwhelming feeling of doom crept over her, but she had no choice but to tuck that away. Everything had to be swept out of her mind to make room for her part of the pitch. It had to be perfect. This was her first true test on the job, and she wanted to impress Mike. Her heart sank as the bloody face of Kelly Escobar popped in her mind again, crushing her confidence. Maybe they could leave tonight, and she would be away from Mike's past. She had no energy to panic—that could be well tended to after she was finished. One elephant at a time. She took a bite out of this one, focusing on Carlos and his team.

Ronnie opened the laptop, ignoring yet another email from Jeffrey, and clicked on her presentation. She set the laptop on the desk near the TV and ran through each slide, watching herself in the mirror as she did. The first time she stumbled, but then worked through it twice more with perfect precision.

Then she ran through it once more, imagining Carlos and his senior management team in front of her. That version went badly. Very badly. She practiced one more time, violent images of Mike and Kelly distracting her, Frank supporting her, and Carlos trying to grope her or being mad that she resisted him. Just a few days ago when she'd left Florida, she'd felt prepared for anything. Now, she was not ready for any of this, most especially the cold, hard truth that Mike might be a murderer.

Ronnie lay back on the bed, covering her eyes, breathing deeply, imagining everything going perfectly. She could push away the distractions and conquer this. It was trivial compared to what she'd been through back in time. This was just a measly fifteen-minute presentation.

Ronnie packed up her things and left her room, heading down to the lobby. Mike and Frank looked fresh in their suits and ready to go.

Frank was chipper. "I'm heading out as soon as this is over. We're flying to Kansas for a wedding."

"Kansas, who the hell lives in Kansas?" Mike asked.

"Cousin. He's on his second marriage, but it's going to be an absolute bomb wedding."

Mike nodded, then turned his attention to her. "You ready for this, Ronnie?"

"I am." She avoided looking at Mike so the constant debate over who he was would not continue playing in her mind, like a bad movie.

Frank smiled. "Ronnie, you're going to wipe the floor with Carlos and his sleezy womanizing ways."

She laughed as they made their way to the garage. "Hope so."

Ronnie spent the ride taking deep breaths, trying to calm down, going through the presentation in her mind, telling herself that it was going to go well. Mike and Frank joked around and showed no signs of nervousness. They'd done this enough times it probably didn't faze them in the least. Of course, neither of them had slapped the decision-maker across the face the night before a major presentation. They got out of the car and made their way up to the conference room.

A receptionist greeted them and one of the board members escorted them to the conference room on the top floor. Carlos sat at the head of the table and smiled when they arrived, raking his eyes over her like he was inspecting fresh meat. Everything she'd practiced fell out of her brain like a dropped file folder, hitting the plush velvet carpet on the boardroom floor.

Instead of crawling back in her mind's scaredy place, she stepped forward and held out her hand. "Mr. Munoz, good morning."

Carlos stood and smiled, but not the beaming confidence she'd imagined. He looked uneasy, as if taken off guard by her direct approach. "Miss Andrews, I must insist you call me Carlos. I trust you slept comfortably." The mustache lifted at the edges as he gripped her hand and pulled her closer, his offer from the night before reflecting in his body language.

"Slept great, Carlos. You?"

"Was a bit lonely..." Carlos said, mischief showing in his eyes.

Mike stepped forward and intervened. "Hey, give it a rest, Carlos. Let the woman be. She's not interested in your..." Mike's expression hardened, his brows nearly touching his eyes.

Frank shook Carlos's hand, but the only thing he offered was a cutting look. Then Frank moved on to the other men in the room, pouring on the charm, then glanced at her, giving her the thumbs-up.

As the men made small talk waiting for the rest of the meeting attendants to file into the room, Ronnie imagined the first two slides and went through them in her mind. Carlos's dark eyes were watching her with interest as he talked to Manuel.

Ronnie approached the breakfast bar set up at the end of the room. This was a perfect location outside of Carlos's line of vision. She poured a cup of coffee she had no intention of drinking and slowly stirred it, absorbing the feeling of excitement and congeniality as everyone greeted each other.

Mike stood next to her and poured a cup and snagged a pastry. "You ready?"

"Oh yeah, I'm a lioness ready for the kill," Ronnie said, as much for herself as her boss, believing it for the moment. In her final perfect-world practice session, she ate them all with bloody abandon. In other versions, she'd been the antelope struggling to free herself from their jaws. She tossed that version aside and smiled confidently.

Carlos's voice carried over the din of friendly greetings. "I would like to call this meeting to order." He remained standing as the rest of the group settled themselves in their respective seats. Ronnie took hers between Mike and Frank and felt well protected. But soon she'd have to leave to fend for herself.

They made their introductions again for the new staff members in the room. Mike squeezed her arm. As if to test her resolve, she looked Carlos dead in the eyes, shifting in her mind away from the creepy man from last night to a customer she was going to win over. This wasn't about him. This was about her successfully showing her worth. He would not steal that victory from her.

Carlos commanded the attention of the room. "Thank you for meeting with us today. We graciously welcome you to Puerto Rico and are eager to hear more about your proposal." Carlos nodded at Mike. "I will yield the floor to you, Mike. Please, everyone, give a warm welcome to Mike Walsh, Ronnie Andrews, and Frank Coleman."

Mike moved to the front of the room just under the screen. He was looking dapper in a well-tailored suit, nicely showing off his broad shoulders and thick biceps pressing against the material, unwilling to hide in the expensive fabric. Biceps that were powerful and completely capable of bloody violence. Ronnie abandoned that line of thought since it would result in her demise.

Mike commanded the room, confidently setting the stage for her part. "Thank you, Mr. Munoz. I want to thank you all for such a gracious welcome. We are enchanted by your island."

Ronnie watched Mike work the room, hoping someday she'd be that confident, that smooth. As he spoke, he connected with each person, focusing on everyone individually. The board members relaxed and listened intently. All except Carlos, who met her gaze with a seductive smile. Ronnie tensed, and for a second, she lost her nerve, returning her eyes to Mike. Her brain snapped to focus, drowning out her thoughts of rapists and murderers.

Mike paused to make sure everyone was focused on him. "I'm excited to bring our new product to you. Feel free to ask any questions you have at the end of the presentation. Please let me introduce Ronnie Andrews. She's our newest employee, so go easy on her. She's still learning the material, but she's got a great mind."

Movement from Carlos caught her eye and he leaned into the man next to him. She could read his lips. "And a great ass." Both men laughed.

Mike's eyes widened for a second, urging her to join him at the front of the room. Ronnie stood and was momentarily blinded as the blood rushed to lower extremities. Nerves dried out her mouth and she saw a flash of utter failure. She joined Mike, nearly tripping on the cord for the projector. She stood staring at the faces, gathering her confidence around her like a thick, cozy blanket and channeling her inner lioness.

She started with her prepared line. "What a pleasure to be here in Guayama with you all today. I'd like to start with an overview of our product." She clicked on the laptop in front of her and the presentation came to life. Thanks to the practice, her autopilot took over, so her portion of the presentation went off without a hitch. In her mind, and quite possibly in real life, she even surprised Carlos. His expression shifted from suave seductor to interested client.

When she was done, Mike took a step forward. "Nice job," he whispered. Then Ronnie returned to her seat, feeling her cheeks flush, not remembering a single word uttered by the rest of her team.

One bite of the elephant chewed and swallowed. Next would be getting out of Puerto Rico and away from creepy Carlos, sketchy Mike, and the possibility of a brewing storm.

The meeting concluded with questions from Carlos and his team. Mike and Frank handled those gracefully. A wave of relief washed over her. Despite fears of totally screwing up, it had gone pretty well. Carlos stood in front of the group and asked for his team to wrap up the questions, then spoke briefly about his impressions and concluded with a remark to the team to consider signing the contract.

When he was finished, Carlos approached. "You are very impressive. Brains and beauty." He smiled cordially, the smug seductor gone for now. "Mike was right about you. You add a lot to the project."

Ronnie was careful to keep it professional, wary of what he'd say next. "Thank you, Carlos."

Carlos looked up at Mike and smiled. "You were right, she has a great mind."

Mike patted Ronnie's back. "She is everything I said she was. Smart, quick on the draw, and eager to learn."

Ronnie felt the heat rising in her cheeks. "Thank you. I'm excited to be part of the project."

Carlos leaned in towards her, slightly turning away from Mike. "We would like to take you out to dinner to celebrate and discuss more details." Carlos didn't wait for an answer. "We have this magnificent authentic Puerto Rican place we need to take you to."

Mike glanced at Ronnie. "Let me discuss it with the team, Carlos."

"Mike, you can't be so American. Here we enjoy the victory and cement the relationship over a fine wine, then dessert, and make future plans. This is our way. You must join us."

Mike shook his head. "I think..."

Frank read Mike's body language and intervened before things blew up. "I'm heading out tonight, and Ronnie is recovering from an illness." Frank raised his eyebrows at Ronnie.

Mike nodded and rubbed his chin. "Right, right."

Carlos patted Mike on the back. "Nonsense. It's a perfect night for dinner. We celebrate! I promise to not keep you out too late." Carlos lowered his voice and looked at Ronnie. "Unless, of course, you want to."

Mike and Frank exchanged a glance and Frank shook his head, as if warning Mike to keep a cool head. A few other attendees interrupted their conversation. Mike and Frank were occupied with their questions.

Carlos turned to Ronnie, pulling her aside. "I am sorry about how we ended things last night. Please forgive my boorish behavior. I simply mistook your Americanisms for forwardness and near insistence that I pursue you." The last bit was said in a bit of a question, as if he was searching for a yes this time.

Ronnie nipped it in the bud. "I'm flattered, but I'm also glad you see it was nothing more than naive politeness on my part."

"You must forgive me, there is just something about you. But I was wrong to..." He cocked his head to the side and smiled, then leaned in closer to whisper. "You must accept that I deeply regret my behavior."

Ronnie tried to read his expression. Most likely he regretted making Mike and

Frank angry, and worse, he had to explain to his buddies that he hadn't bagged the blonde.

Mike returned to Ronnie and introduced her to another board member, leaving Frank alone with Carlos. Mike's eyes were steely. Did he just clench his fist? Ronnie looked away before she saw more of the anger brewing.

It was becoming more difficult to smile through this day. Sure, the hard part was over, she had not totally choked, but her presence was causing friction, and that was never good for business. She should have stayed home. Ivan had missed Orlando after all. The easy flow with Mike was over, thanks to meddling Jeffrey. Frank was leaving and she'd have to spend the next few days with Mike, Carlos, and the men who had joined them at the restaurant.

Chapter 22

The Envelope

Carlos turned to Frank. "What will I tell my team? They are expecting dinner to celebrate."

Carlos pulled Frank aside and a heated discussion ensued. Mike eyed Frank, then turned his attention to Ronnie, softening his tone. "You killed it, Ronnie. Great job."

Ronnie looked away, uncomfortable with his praise, but glad it had gone so well. "Thank you. I'm glad it's over. It could have gone so badly."

Mike smiled and shook his head, eyes squinting with sincerity. "No, really, most people would have cracked under that situation. I'm glad you insisted on doing it. You showed us all what you're made of. I think Carlos sees you differently now. As much as someone like that can."

Ronnie let the mask slip and shot an angry glance at Carlos. Frank happened to be looking at her, and he mouthed, *Don't worry.*

Mike watched the exchange. "God bless Frank. I'd have just punched Carlos in the face and thrown this all out the window. He saved this whole shitshow."

Ronnie cringed at his choice of words, but it was a relief he had taken Carlos's bad behavior seriously. "What are we going to do about dinner? I really didn't need any more of Carlos."

Mike leaned in close. "Frank will handle it. He knows I'd…" he lowered his voice to a whisper, "fucking kill him if he tried anything again."

Ronnie inhaled sharply, staring into his face. Were these the eyes of a murderer? The words matched, but she still struggled with the Mr. Nice Guy Mike she had been introduced to a month ago. A firmly planted impression enhanced by Steph's ringing endorsement of his character and reputation.

The rest of Carlos's team approached and shook their hands.

Manuel was the first to approach her, while another man spoke to Mike. "Beautiful job. We are excited to be working with you."

"Thank you so much, Manuel. We are excited as well." Ronnie smiled and nodded.

Manuel took her elbow and moved her to a quieter corner of the board room. "I am sorry for how things turned out last night. Mr. Munoz explained what happened."

Ronnie was surprised at his confession. "What did he say?"

Manuel glanced at Carlos, who was still in a heated discussion with Frank. "Just that you stopped him in the stairwell and..." Manuel smiled, looking down at her. "Mr. Walsh interrupted you."

"Is *that* what he said?" Was he implying that she had wanted to *continue?*

"Yes, he wanted me to give this to you." He slipped an envelope into Ronnie's hand. "Please, accept it as a gesture of affection and respect."

Ronnie slid it into her suit pocket. She tried to read more from Manuel's expression, but he was cagey.

"He knows Mr. Walsh is your boss and, understandably, he is protective of you. Just know Mr. Munoz will respect your wishes but will not be brushed aside if there is any lingering interest outside of the workplace."

Ronnie's cheeks burned. "Let me be really clear. If Carlos thinks I'm up for another round of grab ass, he is sadly mistaken." Ronnie kept her voice low. "You can tell him to never try that again, or he will deeply regret it."

Manuel's head jolted back, as if struck in the face. "Miss Andrews, I..." He stared at her, but a colleague stuck out his hand.

"Miss Andrews, it's so great to be working with you. I know the island can really use this technology to improve health care outcomes for our people. I'm excited to learn more about how the software will integrate with our current systems. Will you be joining us tomorrow? Mr. Munoz said you'd be here for a few days."

"Yes, we can begin sorting out the details in the morning." She glanced at Mike, slight panic rising. They'd planned to stay a few days to begin working out the requirements and upgrades necessary for their software to track outcomes and collect data to build a database of best practices.

Ronnie met other important board members, and everyone made small talk about the ideas presented and how to proceed. Finally, Ronnie was able to step away and made a beeline for the restroom. She shut the stall door, pulled out the envelope, and opened it. It was a handwritten note with exquisite script.

Dearest Ronnie,

My most humble apologies for my behavior last night. I was overcome with desire for you. I feel for your position, not wanting your coworkers to know of our mutual interest. With this in mind, I have purchased a plane ticket for you to return on Sunday, giving us the weekend to explore. I can easily make the request of your time, or any other excuse you would like to make for a later return. Perhaps you will say you just want some time to explore the island?

I promise to make it worth your while. I have powerful connections, limitless resources, and an abundance of energy to make it a deeply memorable experience.

Affectionately, Carlos

Anger flared, then doubled when she saw what was behind the letter. The return ticket to Orlando on Sunday. Carlos's business card was paper clipped to the ticket with his personal cell scrawled in the same cursive script.

Ronnie's hands shook with fury. Mutual interest? *So, he thinks I want to sleep with him?* Tears of anger dampened her lashes and she wanted to scream. Instead, she dug her fingernails into her palm and whispered a stream of obscenities, one possibly inspired by Frank.

The bathroom door opened and someone else entered. Ronnie took a few deep breaths, calming down enough to not have her head spinning as she left the restroom.

∞

Ronnie stood in the hot sun watching Frank gather his things. They'd left the meeting and driven straight to the small local airport. Frank had made excuses for their inability to join Carlos for dinner, out of respect for Ronnie, and promised a rain check next month when they returned.

"Hey, buddy," Mike said as he shook Frank's hand. "Have a safe trip home."

"Will do, man. Just wish you two were heading back too." Frank turned to Ronnie. "Hope it all goes well." He side-hugged Ronnie.

"Sure thing, Frank. Fly safe and hold down the fort for us." Mike shaded his eyes from the bright light.

"Ronnie, I hope you can feel good about the presentation. You really knocked it out of the park." Frank's expression shifted to anger. "I'm so sorry about Carlos. He will be dealt with. Don't you worry, Ronnie."

"Thank you, Frank. We are going to miss you!" It was sinking in that she would be totally alone with Mike. Her heart sped up a notch.

Frank picked up his small leather suitcase and suit bag and walked away, then turned and waved.

"We'll see you in a few days." Mike waved.

Ronnie sat down in the passenger seat and waited for Mike to open the driver's door.

"Where do you want to eat? We need to celebrate your victory." He glanced over, his smile beaming.

Ronnie shrugged.

"Hey, what's wrong? You really were impressive, Ronnie. Seriously, especially after the added pressure of what Carlos did, you killed it."

Ronnie smiled. "Yeah, I'm so glad it's over."

Mike started the car but stayed parked. "So why do you seem so subdued? You should be bouncing off the walls."

"Mike..." She lost her nerve. How could she tell him about the plane tickets and sordid note from Carlos? He would freak out.

"I get it." He filled in for her. "We are supposed to go and work in their facility tomorrow. I don't think Carlos is going to be there. He runs the entire hospital system. I'm sure he doesn't have time to be involved at this level. We can make sure he's not around. Or I can go talk to him."

A new burst of panic bubbled in her chest. "Oh, no, I don't think you should talk to him again. You almost wrung his neck."

Mike laughed. "I'm sorry, that's a bad thing? The only way Carlos will ever change is if someone scares him out of his bad behavior."

Ronnie was thankful Mike and Frank hadn't swept it under the rug. "I just think for your job's sake you better not be talking to Carlos."

Mike bared his teeth and growled. "I think we should get some food and not think about god damned Carlos for a bit."

Ronnie laughed, not wanting to, but it was nice to have someone mirror her exact feelings. "Lunch it is."

A comfortable quiet settled in the car. It gave her the chance to think things through. If it felt like a good time to tell him about the plane tickets, she'd do it. Otherwise, she still had the option to keep it to herself. Could he handle it, or would he fly into a murderous rage? She watched him closely as he drove through traffic, still trying to piece together Kelly's death and Mike's alleged involvement. Anything Jeffrey told her was suspect, but the article had been damning. His response to Carlos told her rage was inside him, lurking. A voice in her mind defended him. He was protecting her, and to echo his words, was that a bad thing?

Ten minutes later, Mike stopped at an Americanized sports bar. "Can we just have a little taste of home? I've had a bit too much Puerto Rico for today." Mike smiled.

"Works for me. I can definitely eat a burger."

The hostess showed them to a table near the bar and they both had a good view of the TV showing a baseball game. Red Sox at the Yankees Stadium. Mike ordered two beers, looking at her to be sure that was okay. "We're celebrating, remember?"

"Yes, Sam Adams, please."

"Ah, cold brewski, baseball, apple pie, and Orlando not being battered by Ivan. All the simple pleasures in life." Mike smiled, showing his blood pressure was capable of returning to normal.

"Mike, I am sorry all of this crap happened. I know this client is really important to you. If I'd just stayed home, none of this would have happened." Guilt mixed into her tangled emotions.

Mike's eyebrows bunched and he leaned forward. "Don't you dare apologize. This isn't your fault. It's about a machismo man who thinks he can do whatever he pleases, no matter the consequences. I knew he was a dog. But, Ronnie, his utter disrespect for you, for me, and for Frank, is what pissed me off."

Ronnie bit her lips and sat back against the booth. "But Mike..."

"But nothing. You do not apologize for this, Ronnie. I'm serious. I just feel horrible I didn't prevent it. I mean, it isn't like I didn't know he was into pretty women."

Ronnie picked at the seam on the chrome edging of the table. "Mike, how could you prevent it?"

Mike looked out the window, his scowl deepening the lines on his face. "I could have warned him ahead of time. Carlos is one of those guys who takes what he wants and throws it away. He doesn't realize the hurt he causes. The damage to..."

The waiter returned with their beers.

Mike thanked him then held his up. "To Ronnie! Bravo for rising above the situation to show professionalism in the worst of circumstances. You are truly remarkable!"

Ronnie held up her glass and clinked his. "Thank you, Mike. I appreciate that. I am glad of how things went this morning."

Mike smiled, but his eyes remained angry. Cold, hard steel showed through the blue. "I want you to promise me something."

"What?"

"If Carlos does anything, even so much as smile inappropriately, you let me know."

"Anything?" Ronnie asked, her heart racing now. She couldn't agree and not tell him about the envelope.

"I'm serious. Carlos will not harass you in any way. You deserve respect. If he so much as blinks wrong at you, I want to know. I'll pull both of us off this client so fast. Frank can finish up without us. There is no reason you should be subjected to that kind of bullshit. I will not tolerate..." He cracked his knuckles and bunched up his lips. It was the lippy version of the snarl he'd showed in the car.

Ronnie steeled herself for the proverbial poo hitting the fan. "So, I should probably share the envelope Manuel gave me after the meeting?"

Mike looked at her, his scowl deepening. "The *what?*"

Ronnie pulled it out of her pocket and set it on the table between them. "Wasn't sure what to do with this. I didn't have time to tell you guys about it in the car."

Mike's expression darkened. He picked up the proffered shitstorm and pulled the contents out just as the waiter showed up to take their food order.

"Can you give us a minute?" Ronnie piped in, irked at the interruption.

Mike scanned the papers and returned his attention to her. "What did he say when he gave this to you?"

"Manuel apologized for what happened last night. Then said Carlos told him what happened, that I stopped him in the stairwell, and you interrupted us. He said Carlos understood I had to be careful around my coworkers."

Mike's eyes widened. "What the...!?"

"Yeah, the bastard. I told Manuel if Carlos thought I was up for another round of grab ass, he would regret it."

Mike's jaw went slack. "You badass."

She tapped the papers. "Read it."

"Are these plane tickets. Seriously?" Mike raised his voice, almost yelling.

Ronnie looked around to see if anyone noticed. "Shhhh."

Mike unfolded the note and read it. When he was finished, he closed his eyes and took a deep breath then let it out, looking like he'd rather be releasing a stream of obscenities more wicked than her own. He gulped half of the beer and looked out the window.

She could almost hear his brain explode.

"Wow," he finally said, looking back at her. "So, what are you gonna do with *that?*" He set the letter and ticket on the table and pushed them back towards her.

Ronnie's temper took over. Did Mike think she wanted this? "I've no idea. What an arrogant piece of shit. Carlos stopped *me*, not the other way around. He gave me a hotel room key. I'm so pissed. Do you think he told Manuel a lie about what happened, or is this his way of further manipulating me into agreeing? It's almost like he doesn't even care if I'm into him or not, it's only about what he wants."

"So, you're not going to take him up on that exciting weekend?" Mike said it neutrally.

Ronnie examined his face and leaned towards him, stabbing her finger at him, making him flinch. "What? Are you freaking kidding me?"

A tiny smile broke free. "Of course I am. What the hell, Ronnie?"

Ronnie shook her head. "This is beyond aggressive. The man bought a plane ticket and offered a number of excuses so I can stay longer. Is he a sociopath, totally unaware of other people's feelings? Does he even understand how damn insulting this is, like I wanted him so badly and he was being polite offering to serve my needs? Arrrgggghh." Ronnie slammed her hand on the table, tipping her beer. She caught it just before it spilled, then took a big swig. "God damned bastard."

Mike's eyes widened. "I am so sorry, Ronnie. Seriously, I knew he'd be into you, but if I'd had any idea he would be this forward, I'd have intervened somehow. Now I just want to fucking wring his little neck." His hands mimicked the motion.

There it was again, the murderous element poking free of the mask. The man had a temper, there was no denying that. But was he a killer? It still didn't feel right, but wasn't that what every neighbor said about the murderer next door?

Mike noticed the change in her expression. "Carlos has to be put in his place." Mike took another long swallow of his beer.

The waiter hovered nearby. Ronnie nodded for him to come over.

"Hey. Sorry, are you guys ready to order?" he asked.

"Sorry about that. Just an important moment. Burger for me. French fries." Ronnie glanced at the TV while Mike ordered. Red Sox hit a home run!

Mike bit both lips and shook his head, looking at her. "I'm going to call Carlos and tell him to fucking shove these tickets up his..."

Ronnie reached out and grabbed his arm. "Hey, hey. No, you're not going to say a friggin' word."

His face was flushed again. "What are we supposed to do tomorrow when we go into the office? I'm not going to be able to control myself, Ronnie. I'm going to want to fucking kill him."

Ronnie released his arm, as if it had been on fire.

Mike gripped his beer in one hand. "Ronnie, I'm sorry, I just don't understand guys like that. I can't imagine pursuing someone with such aggressiveness." He turned his head to the side and mouthed, "Fuck," slamming his hand on the table. If this had been a cartoon, steam would have been coming out of his ears. "As your boss, I have to do something. As your friend, I'm going to listen to what you want. But bottom line, Carlos needs his head bashed in to teach him a lesson."

"It is not your place to do any bashing, Mike. Seriously, listen to you. You sound scary." She'd meant it as a joke, but she couldn't control her features. Surely he could see her fear. She'd never been good at hiding her emotions.

If only Frank had stayed. He'd have smoothed this over. Now neither of them could face Carlos without jeopardizing the project.

"What do you want to do, Ronnie? I hate that you're in this situation." Mike's expression softened a little.

"I don't know. I don't want to abandon the work. We came out here to sell the software. We did. Now we have to get started on it. We have to, Mike. That's what we were hired to do."

Mike shook his head. "They did not hire you to have some *sato cabrón* make sexual advances."

Ronnie didn't know the words, but they sounded appropriate for Carlos. "WWFD?"

Mike scowled at her. "WWFD?"

"What would Frank do?"

Mike snorted. "Hell if I know. I am not half the man Frank is, that is for damn sure."

They continued the meal, both lost in their thoughts. Finally, after Mike paid the bill, they returned to the car.

"Ronnie, I want you to take the rest of the day off. You came here fresh from the hospital. You need to get some rest. Let's plan on heading to the office in the morning. I'm going to get Frank on the phone and beg him to lay down the law. Carlos is not allowed to be there tomorrow. He'll do it in a way that saves face when we show up. I bet good money Carlos wasn't planning on being there anyway."

"Okay. What if Carlos is there, though? Will you strangle him to death?" Ronnie immediately regretted her words, and visions of Kelly Escobar clouded her vision for a minute.

"I promise, I will control myself. Carlos will leave after I have a few words with him. I plan on doing some deep meditations tonight and getting into a calm state of mind impenetrable by even Carlos." His words were topped off with a smile that faded into a sneer.

"I guess that's the best we can do. Deep meditations, though?"

"Also known as golf." He smiled, shaking his head. "Ronnie, I'm not built for this. Marines are trained to take action. The fact that he's my biggest client ties my hands in a way that adds to the frustration."

Ronnie looked down at her hands in her lap and imagined them tied together, leaving her helpless.

He didn't seem to notice her change in thoughts. "Right-o." He parked the car in the hotel parking garage. "I am going to say goodnight. Be ready about 8:00. We can meet for breakfast and regroup."

"Goodnight," Ronnie said as they went their separate ways, realizing it was only two in the afternoon. She welcomed the evening off and would make good use of it.

Chapter 23

Over the Edge

Tuesday, September 14, 2004

In the morning, Ronnie got ready and went down to the breakfast area, hoping to have a quick bite before they left for the office. Dread permeated every cell in her body. Today would not go well. Mike was going to blow up the client they'd been courting for over a year. Where was Frank when you needed him?

National Suites served breakfast in the atrium surrounded by tropical plants and a small koi pond. The atmosphere was free, open, and full of life, a stark contrast to the confinement of the hotel room she'd been cooped up in since yesterday afternoon and regrets roaming through her mind. As she scanned the selection of hot breakfast items under the sneeze shield, Mike appeared next to her.

Ronnie jumped. "Oh my God, you scared me."

He smiled, looking much better than he had last night. The gray shadows of fury had dissipated, replaced with pink sunburned cheeks, making his eyes appear even brighter than usual. "Morning. How are you today?"

Ronnie, still leery about the fury lurking just below the surface, smiled. "I'm good. You're looking very...pink."

"Pink?" Mike's eyebrows nearly touched, then he smiled. "Oh, sunburned. Yeah, I played a round of golf yesterday to let off some steam. Forgot the sunscreen."

"Sounds fun." Ronnie scooped fried potatoes on her plate, adding a sausage link and fruit salad.

"What did you do last night?" He filled his plate then walked with her towards the coffee station.

"Just relaxed. I debated about swimming, but I decided to just take it easy. I mostly just watched bad TV and went to bed good and early."

They filled porcelain mugs with coffee and found a table near the bar area. It seemed like the entire hotel had shown up for breakfast.

"How are you feeling about today?" Mike leaned towards her.

Ronnie wanted to have breakfast alone, but how could you tell your boss to get lost? Maybe it would be helpful to get their plan in place if Carlos was there. "I'm good. Just a bit worried about what is going to happen this morning."

"Yeah, me too. I'm glad I decompressed yesterday. I think I can do this, if Carlos can just keep from saying anything that's going to set me off. He has a way of politely sliding a knife into my gut."

Ronnie frowned, not at all enjoying the violent image.

A shadow flickered in Mike's eyes, reminiscent of the outburst yesterday. "Carlos knows my weakness."

"He does? What's your weakness?"

He ran his fingers through his hair, looking away, then met her gaze. "You." His expression changed from anger to an embarrassed smile.

Ronnie leaned back in the chair, examining his face. "What? I don't understand." Heat rose in her cheeks.

Mike let out a sigh of frustration. "Just what I said. *You're* my weakness. Carlos enjoys this little game because he knows I have feelings for you."

Ronnie suddenly felt out of breath. A few days ago, this would have sent her emotions soaring as high as the top of the eight-story atrium. Now it stoked fear.

Mike's pink cheeks reddened. "I figured you knew. We had such a great day out on the water." Ronnie's icy heart melted a tiny bit with his embarrassed, shy expression. "I don't know what to say except I'm sorry. I hate that he is playing games with you, especially with me as the pawn."

"Don't apologize. It's not your fault." Ronnie echoed the words he'd given her yesterday.

Mike took a sip of his coffee. "I should have couched my feelings around him better. It does not excuse *his* behavior though. To him it's just a pissing contest, with you as the prize."

"That's a hideous thought." Ronnie laughed uncomfortably. "I don't want to be that kind of prize. I'm a person, you know, not a trophy to be peed on."

Mike set the mug down, spilling it. He mopped up the liquid with a napkin. "Tell that to Carlos. Women were invented to stoke his ego, nothing else."

Ronnie leaned back in the chair, gathering her hair in a ponytail and letting it drop. "Damn, I told you I shouldn't have come here."

Ronnie looked away, not wanting the intensity developing at her breakfast table. The TV in the bar caught her eye, with a ticker at the bottom of the screen grabbing her attention: *Tropical storm warning issued for Puerto Rico.*

"Oh my God!" Ronnie shot up and walked closer to the TV to hear what the man in front of the weather map was saying.

Mike followed her. "What's *'Oh my God?'*"

Numbly Ronnie nodded at the TV. "Tropical storm warning for Puerto Rico." Her voice squeaked out the last words.

The TV reporter delivered the news that caved in her world. "A tropical wave formed over the Antilles. Overnight it strengthened further and is expected to become a tropical storm and possibly gain enough strength to reach hurricane status overnight."

Ronnie felt sick.

When the station moved to other news, Mike said, "Really, Mother Nature is going to get into the mix again? We left Florida to get the hell away from that."

Ronnie pulled her hair off her neck again. "Oh my God, Mike. This was not supposed to happen."

He ran his fingers through his hair. "Ronnie, let me call Ciel and see if we can get an earlier flight out of here."

"Could you?"

He pulled out his cell phone. There was no service in the breakfast area. "As soon as I can get a signal, I'll call her."

Ronnie remembered little from the rest of the breakfast. Her mind was in a complete panic, rolling around with the possibility that she may go back in time. She may also not survive the weekend.

"Hey." Mike returned and accompanied her to refill their coffee cups. "The good news is this may solve our other problem." His eyes twinkled.

"What's that?"

"Carlos. If we fly home, we don't have to see his damn face today." Mike laughed, then stifled it, seeing her stressed out expression.

They walked together in silence to the lobby where cell service was stronger. Ronnie sat on a bench while Mike called his secretary, walking across the lobby to get some privacy. Mike punched the air in anger and turned around so she couldn't see his expression. Her heart sank. She needed to get the hell off this island and somewhere safe...pronto. Mike turned back around, making eye contact with her, and shook his head.

She texted Steph then Ian. *Everything has gone to hell. I need to talk to you.*

The image of a murdering Mike rolled around with stressful, stormy thoughts wrestling for control. She hated Jeffrey for telling her about Kelly and saw it for precisely what it was, Jeffrey manipulating her. Despite knowing that, it was impossible to get the image of her battered face out of her mind. Her hatred grew, knowing Jeffrey was right about the storms hitting Puerto Rico.

A full-on panic blossomed silently inside her. Frank was gone. If they couldn't get a flight out, she would be stuck here alone with Mike for the storm. She felt hot and stifled an urge to run, releasing the pent-up energy from this stress. Instead, she sat as if glued to the bench.

She should have left with Frank and grabbed a flight off the island, anywhere but here. Mike's voice carried across the lobby, likely Ciel taking the brunt of his frustrations.

The kaleidoscope twisted once again, forcing the beads to fall into a different position, showing Mike in a different light. Was he the good man she was connected to in the past? Or was Jeffrey rightly accusing him of violence? If he were guilty of harming Kelly, how could he be walking free? Was it just an accident?

If she could catch a flight to Virginia and stay with her mom, she could dive into the mystery surrounding her father's death. Could she convince her mom that she'd actually time traveled? Had her father too? She could look for her dad's lab assistant. He would know what project they'd been working on and maybe even what had taken place that fateful day.

These worries were stacked among the more pressing ones making her mind swirl and her blood pressure rise. Was she doomed in her own time as she had been each time she'd been transported back in time? Would the Korsakoff syndrome damage her further, leaving her in a coma? Was that what had happened to her father?

Mike slid the phone in his pocket and started towards her, shaking his head. When he was closer, he said, "Nope, no dice. Ciel had us on a flight out this afternoon for just a few minutes, but now it's canceled too. Everything is canceling. It looks like they're preparing to close the airport, sending half full planes elsewhere to avoid the storm damage."

"No! They're closing the airport! How can they do that? We'll be trapped on this island!" She stood facing Mike, taking in every worried line on his face.

"They're not letting incoming flights land and those are the planes we need to leave." Mike sat on a nearby bench, his arms resting on his knees. Ronnie joined him on the bench. "If we can't get out now, we may be stuck here for the rest of the week or longer." Mike ran his fingers through his hair, triggering a memory, but Ronnie was not able to focus on it.

"Well, what do we do now?"

Mike shook his head. "I think our only real choice is to hunker down here. It's not supposed to be a very big storm." He must have noticed the panic in her expression, for he changed to a softer, more soothing tone and leaned towards her. "Ronnie, it should be okay. The hotel is built well. We can just stay in the interior rooms away from the windows."

She tried to talk, but her voice was choked with emotion.

Mike continued, "We can just shut the door and protect ourselves."

Ronnie cleared her throat and finally squeaked out, "Yeah." She felt an inward crashing, as if the structure of her life had fallen like Jenga pieces, clattering to the floor. Mike shifted in his seat towards her, concern written all over his face. Maybe even more than concern considering the deep groove between his brows, evidencing downright worry.

Chapter 24

Monet-Level Painter

Steph's legs were lazily draped over her boyfriend, Nick Sharer's lap. Nick sipped his coffee then gently set it down on the table. "Any word from Ronnie?"

She frowned. "She texted me Sunday after swimming with Mike. She was on cloud nine."

A low chuckle escaped his lips. "So why are you frowning? Isn't that what you wanted from her? To get over Jeffrey and start something with Mike?"

She poked his ribs and he attempted to block her, instead grabbed her hand and held it against his stomach. Steph took full advantage, exploring the abs evident under the t-shirt. "Of course it is. I just have this sixth sense that something is about to hit the fan."

Nick rolled his eyes. "Wumman, can't you ever just be happy and relax about your friend?"

Steph was surprised by this comment. "Nick, you know she's been through absolute hell lately."

He picked up her hand and kissed it. "I know. I saw it firsthand during Frances, but now she's off on an island retreat with a studly Marine. She's going to be fine, Steph. Just have faith."

Steph slipped her arm around his waist. "My faith is strong but so is my intuition. I feel something big in the works and I don't like it."

Nick held her face for a long kiss and then released her, leaving her breathless. "Focus on the feelings I give you, baby. Ronnie can handle herself. Plus, she's in Mike's capable hands."

"True." She leaned in, eager for more, but his words rolled around as they shifted to lying prone on the couch, his hands caressing her curves.

"You are looking more ravishable than ever in that sundress, Miss McKay."

She'd chosen it this morning thinking of this moment, knowing he liked the little blue flowers that reflected the same shade in her eyes.

Their relationship had begun the night Hurricane Charley hit, after years of flirty friendship. Timing had never been their friend, with her always in a relationship, usually a bad one, when he was single and vice versa. They'd finally both been free when she'd asked him over when Ronnie had left to be with Jeffrey during Charley.

Nick kissed her again, holding her hands in his, pinning them to the couch as he pursued her hungrily with sultry, full-lipped passion. Did he know this drove her wild? The thought that if he wanted to, he could just overpower her, but part of his strength was his gentleness with her. That control mixed with deep passion, the delightful show of power without using it made her lose it.

Nick pulled away from the kiss, but kept her hands pinned. "Hey now. I just had a delicious thought. Ian is gone! Can we make good use of this rare moment without the pest nearby?"

"We sure can."

He released her and stood up, retaking her hand and pulling her through the kitchen to the master bedroom. Steph floated behind him, anticipating his advances. Nick shut the door and came up behind her, kissing the back of her neck, sending shivers down her spine. He unzipped the back of her dress. "May I, madame?"

"Please, please." The last word melted away as his lips met the skin at the nape of her neck, plucking up gooseflesh over her entire body. He unhooked her bra and she stepped out of her dress, leaving it in a puddle on the floor.

He knelt on the floor and hugged her legs then pulled away, looking up at her. "May I?" A small, sexy smile took over his full lips.

She wasn't sure exactly what he was asking but didn't care a whit. "Yes, please, baby."

Nick slid off her white cotton panties and added them to the pile growing on the floor. Steph realized she was still clutching her bra to her chest and let it drop, adding to the mosaic of discarded clothes, eager to add his to the mix. She reached for his shirt, and he let her pull it off in one smooth motion.

Steph ran her hands over his gym-buffed chest and shoulders. Nick gently walked her back to the bed until she was sitting on the edge looking up at him. He knelt again and palmed each foot, pushing her to lie on the bed.

Nick planted kisses on her knee and worked up her inner thigh. She watched his every move, her hands on his shoulders and in his hair. It was the art of the tease, and Nick was a Monet-level artist.

Steph heard noises of the front door opening, and Ian called out to her. There was nothing on Earth she needed to hear other than Nick coaxing her along.

A loud knock on her door made her sit up. Nick was unperturbed and pressed harder into her flesh. "Hey, Stephanie, Ronnie's tryin' to get aholt a yee. You in there?" He opened the door and stopped dead.

"Ian!" Steph yelled, expecting him to run off.

"Get yee some, Nick, atta boy," Ian said and then ran away when Nick stood up and rushed him, slamming the door.

"Little prick," Nick said under his breath. "Why does he just bust into your room then stare? He knows you're his sister, right?"

Steph was furious. "I'm sorry, he's a disgusting pig. I don't even know how we are related." She opened the bathroom door and grabbed her robe and put it on.

Nick followed her into the bathroom and kissed her. "I cannot wait to continue where we left off, baby."

He slid his hand under the robe. Steph grabbed his shoulders to stay upright as he worked his magic, bringing her to a quick climax with adept fingers. He kissed her moans and pressed deeper as he finished her off with another intense release.

"Mmmmmm, you make me ravenous," Nick whispered in her ear.

Ian's voice carried through the bathroom door. "Steph, did you hear what I said? You need to call Ronnie."

Nick barged out of the bathroom and chased Ian into his room. Steph laughed. It was unusual for Nick to get mad, but Ian was pushing the wrong buttons today.

"Okay, luv," Steph yelled after the two men and rummaged around for the phone somewhere in her purse. There were several messages from Ronnie. She dialed her number and took the phone back into her bedroom. Nick was putting on his shirt and sat next to her, kissing on her ear. "Babe, lock the door next time."

Nick shook his head, shooting anger towards the pest. "I will not forget."

Ronnie answered on the second ring.

Chapter 25

Hurricane Jeanne Pops By

Ronnie sat with Mike in the National Suites lobby, feeling like the world was collapsing in on her.

Mike turned to her. "Can I ask you something?"

Not trusting her voice, Ronnie nodded.

"What happened during the last storm? You had some health issues that put you in a coma. Could you share more of what I might need to do to help you or how to prevent that from happening?" His mouth was set in a thin line and Ronnie felt his worries mounting alongside hers.

"Oh, God." Ronnie turned away, embarrassed at the tears that stung her eyes. That fear tossed aside the rest of the worries into the heap she was already toiling with. She turned back to him and explored his deep blue eyes, hoping to find answers. Which Mike would be there for her? Her version or Jeffrey's newly planted one? She desperately needed the Mike that was made in the mold of Mathias or Morris, the men who had helped her in the past.

Full on panic returned. Ronnie stood and took a few steps away and then turned back to him.

"Mike, I can't stay here. Can't we just go to the airport and try to find a way out? Any flight out, anything? Please! I can't be here!"

Mike stood, shaking his head. "Ronnie, you don't understand. By the time we get there, the airport will be closed to any outgoing flights."

A twinge of pain stabbed above her eyes, serving as a stark reminder that her brain may not ever be the same. Ronnie shook her head. "No, we have to go. Mike!"

"Ronnie, we only have the small commuter airport. It's not like San Juan where they have a slew of airlines. There is no way out. They're closing it up at 2:00 today. You understand? They're pulling all the planes in and securing the facility for the storm. I am not risking driving back to San Juan. We just don't have enough time, especially with the rain already starting." He nodded towards the window.

Ronnie tried to tamp down the panic, but it escaped. "No, I'm not going to stay here. Give me the keys. I'm going anyway."

"No. Ronnie, the outer bands of that storm are already here, right offshore. You saw the roads we took coming down here. We cannot just drive up to San Juan. Please just trust me on this."

The words 'trust me' seeped into her thoughts and she held on tight to the sentiment. She had no choice but to put her trust in him.

Mike stood looking down at her. "Ronnie, it's going to be okay. We will get through this together, I promise." He reached out to hug her, but she stepped out of his reach. He seemed to shrink at the rejection.

Ronnie wanted to believe him, but the nagging doubt from Jeffrey's voice crept in, exactly as he would have wanted it to. Her cell phone buzzed, and she pulled it from her purse and answered. She mouthed to Mike, "It's Steph."

He nodded.

"Hey, Steph. I'm here with Mike." Ronnie turned away.

"Luv, you texted me. Is everything okay?" She sounded chipper.

"No, nothing is okay. Steph, a tropical storm is about to hit. We don't have time to catch a flight out of here."

Mike watched her intently, then interrupted, "Be right back." And he walked to the front desk.

"How can that be? Ronnie, you're a friggin' storm magnet." Steph shuffled the phone and then it sounded like she was on speaker.

"Didn't you see it on the Weather Channel?" Ronnie's head was buzzing with the adrenalin faucet open wide.

There was a long pause. "Ronnie, are you joshing me?"

"No, this is not a joke." Ronnie paced in the lobby.

"But you went there to get away from all of this stress. Wait, I've got the news on now. Oh God, Ronnie, they're saying up to twenty inches of rain with this storm!"

"No!" Ronnie had to force herself to breathe. "Steph, this is not what I signed up for."

"I know, luv. Do you remember what the docs said? You cannot travel again—it could result in permanent brain damage." Her voice was shaking now. "You have to get out of there!"

Ronnie crumpled down on a bench. "They're shutting down the airport, so they have time to prepare. There is no way to get out of here."

"Och, I dinnae like the sound of that. If they're prepping the airports, they must know something you don't. A small storm wouldn't cause that much panic."

"Maybe they're just being cautious? Steph, the hotel is right on the water!"

"It is! You left Florida to get away from all of this!" Steph echoed Ronnie's words.

"Did I tell you what Jeffrey sent me?" She knew she hadn't had a chance to tell her yet. Ronnie looked around, making sure Mike wasn't returning.

"Jeffrey? Is he still bothering you? What is that snake up to now?"

"He sent me an article on Mike from five years ago." She didn't want the words to be spoken, but she had to say them. "There is a newspaper article that claims Mike killed his fiancée. Supposedly beat her, Steph."

"Nooooo! Ronnie, that is bullshit!" Steph said, the incredulous tone shifting to anger.

"I saw it myself. They had a picture of Mike and this woman before she'd been beaten." The horrible image would never leave her mind. "And after."

"If he killed her, how the hell has he spent the last five years in Florida instead of rotting in jail?" Steph echoed what Ronnie had been struggling with.

"I don't know. He had a good lawyer? Jeffrey could be totally full of shit. But I don't know how he could have faked the picture."

"So now your only ally there to help you through this is possibly a murderer? An abuser?" Steph said incredulously.

"Pretty much. I'm about to explode with stress, Steph. What if I go back again? I'm going to be stuck here *with him*."

"But, Ronnie, I just don't see Mike being violent. I don't see him hurting someone." Doubt was palpable in her voice.

Ronnie clung to this. "I know, I'm having a lot of trouble putting those two pieces together. But you know he was in the Marines. We don't know what happened there. Post-traumatic stress or something." Ronnie watched the flickering lightning reflecting off the mounting waves down below.

"Seriously, have you ever seen him lose his temper?" Steph asked. "All these years and no one has seen any signs of it?"

"I have seen him angry. Some crazy crap going on here. The man we're trying to pitch to..." Ronnie didn't want to go through all of this but continued out of respect for Steph. "Carlos Munoz," she spat out his name, "groped me during our dinner meeting. Mike almost beat the crap out of him right there in the restaurant."

"Oh my God, no! What happened?"

"The man cornered me in a stairwell, then reached up my skirt and grabbed my ass. Mike came looking for me and gave Carlos a piece of his mind."

"Oh my God. Ronnie. I told you how Mike feels about you. He is protective, angered that someone took advantage of you. You have to be happy he showed up and put Carlos in his place."

"Yeah, I agree, but you never really know about someone, do you?"

Steph's tone changed to anger. "Yeah, like Jeffrey. Who would have known...?"

Ronnie could almost hear Steph's eyes rolling.

Her friend launched another round of support for Mike. "Look, you can't think like that. It's Mike Walsh. He's been the knight in shining armor ever since you met him." She paused. "Plus—oh, Ian is here."

Ian's deeper voice chimed in, and it struck Ronnie how similar they sounded. "Aye, you okay over there in Rico, Ron?"

Ian's playful banter was usually an annoyance. Today she welcomed it. "Hey, Ian, how you doing?"

"Steph, can I tell her about...?" Ian said excitedly.

Steph interrupted him. "Haud yer wheesht, I need to tell her something before Mike comes back." She paused then continued. Ronnie could hear Ian talking to Nick in the background, but Steph must have taken it off speaker phone. "You really have no choice. You're not but a week out from your last hospital stay. Don't you dare go through this alone, Ronnie." Her tone had shifted to anger. "And don't try to leave. Mike is right, it's much safer there in the hotel. Hunker down and ride it out there."

"I know that is my dilemma. I need his help." Her ears almost rang with adrenaline coursing through her blood. "But I'm afraid."

"Look, Jeffrey is a thousand miles away. If he is behind your time traveling, he certainly cannot be orchestrating anything from here. Most likely you have a bad night and some flooding to deal with, then you're back home and all is well."

"I know, Steph, but we both thought that during Frances. How could Jeffrey be involved when he wasn't even around, but yet it happened anyway? Whether Jeffrey is causing it or not, storms damage me. Whether I travel or not, it may still hurt my brain."

"He's a sneaky wanker," Ian said. "Let me tell her!"

"Just a minute, Ian." Ronnie could hear a door shut. "Ronnie, the odds of something happening during this storm are really slim. Jeffrey is so far away. We've seen him here."

She paused and Ronnie chimed in.

"Steph, what if the time traveling doesn't have anything to do with him? I know you think he's involved, but isn't it possible that my dad traveled too? That it has more to do with Dad's research, or his genes that are causing this? I keep talking to him during my travels. My mom said he had similar experiences. Could I be going through a mental issue? Or a genetic one that makes me time travel during storms?"

"I dunno, Ron. My intuition is usually dead on and I've not trusted Jeffrey since the beginning. And don't listen to your mom, you are not going through a mental issue. This is real, Ronnie, I know it. I don't really know what to make of your father's problems."

Ronnie turned around and scanned the lobby for Mike. He was talking animatedly with the woman at the front desk. "You remember what Ini said? My dad was definitely involved. It's frustrating that I only have a few pieces of the puzzle. How could both Jeffrey and my dad be connected to my time traveling?" She hoped Mike wouldn't return. She needed Steph's advice.

"Look," Steph said, "all I know for sure is Jeffrey is somehow involved. I've no idea what your dad has to do with this, if anything, but I do know you are not crazy."

"Well, Jeffrey is sketchy and selfish. But that doesn't mean he is behind this. I mean, he wanted me to go with him to my mom's away from the storms. If he were sending me back, wouldn't he want me to stay in Florida and have another go at it?"

Steph was adamant. "I wonder if your near-death situation scared him off it. What if he...?" Ian banged on the door. "Oh, right." Ronnie heard the door squeak open. "Here, Ian wants to tell you something."

The phone shuffled for a few seconds then Ian's voice was louder. He must have the phone off speaker. "I've been following your big, geeky fanny. He has a secret storage unit about an hour away."

"Ian, really? You've followed Jeffrey around?" Ian had kept his promise. "Where is it? And what is in there, Ian?"

"Sanford. I don't bloody know what's in there, but I cannae wait to..." He stopped abruptly. "Naw, I'll have to tell you more when you're home. I don't want anything in the universe to conspire against my plans. Steph's taught me when I open my big mouth it always makes things fall apart. This time I'm going to show some self-control."

Ronnie had to laugh despite her stress. "You of all people are showing self-control? Your mum was right to send you to stay with your sister."

"Aye, she was. I know, I'm really stretching for you." He chuckled. "It's not all I'm stretching for you."

"Ian, gross. Keep up the sleuthing. I do appreciate you looking into Jeffrey for me. But for God's sake, be careful. He could be dangerous."

Mike left the front desk and was making his way back to her.

"Hey, he's back," Ronnie whispered. "Write down the address where we are." Ronnie gave her the hotel address. "If you don't hear from me for a while, don't worry, we probably won't have cell service and I won't be able to call." She waved to Mike.

"Okay, luv. Let me speak with him," Steph asked.

Ronnie whispered, "Why, what are you going to say?"

"Just hello. Come on, luv, hand him your phone," Steph coaxed.

"Steph wants to talk to you." Ronnie offered her phone to Mike.

Mike took it, and Ronnie inwardly begged Steph to behave. "Hey, Steph, I guess Ronnie told you we're stuck here for a while." He smiled reassuringly, not taking his eyes off Ronnie.

Mike paused as Steph responded, but Ronnie couldn't hear her.

"Yeah, well, I do have one question. What happened to Ronnie during Frances and what can I do to prevent it?"

He looked out the window, watching a couple walk into the building, then turned around and took a few steps away from her. Would Steph ask about Kelly? He would explode if he knew Jeffrey was poking into his past.

Mike glanced back at her then asked, "Ahhuh, and when did you decide to go to the hospital?" He paused, listening to her response. Ronnie tried not to notice the bunched-up bicep stretching the fabric of his dress shirt. A strong, solid man capable of keeping her safe. Equally capable of doing bad things.

Mike wandered out of earshot, then glanced back at her, fully engrossed in what Steph was saying. He nodded then said something she couldn't hear. It made her uneasy to be discussed as if she weren't even there.

Mike came back and made eye contact. "Right, no, for sure. I know she is precious." He smiled, shaking his head. "I know, Steph. I'm your guy. She will be well taken care of. You don't have to threaten me. We have the same mission, Steph." Mike laughed, showing even, white teeth. "You too, Ian." He shook his head. "I certainly will not...listen to you, Ian." He laughed again. "Bye." Then handed her phone back.

Ronnie put the phone to her ear. "Steph, so what was all that about?" It was Ronnie's turn to walk away from Mike.

"Mike is a doll," Steph said. "I just can't see him hurting you, Ronnie. I'm going to put Ian on the case. Turns out the little terrier is good at digging things up. If there is anything out there about Mike and his fiancée, he's gonna find the truth."

"What did you tell him, Steph? You didn't say anything I'm going to have trouble explaining?"

"Of course not. Why would I do that? I just told him how you were during the hurricane and what the docs said at the hospital. Unknown cause, but it was good we got you to the hospital when we did, given what happened."

"Okay, thank goodness. I hope Ian can clear some of this up. See if Jeffrey is totally full of shit, or if there is something to this whole thing." Ronnie looked back at Mike, who was talking on his phone with his back towards her.

Steph continued. "Keep in mind that anything Jeffrey says is likely bullshit. He could teach a master's class in deceit. Mike isn't a murderer. But I am a little worried about you. If you get into trouble, I feel like Mike's the guy to keep you safe."

Mike slipped his phone into his pocket, then shot her a worried glance, returning to the bench, and sat worriedly picking his calluses.

"Okay, Steph. I gotta go. Take care of Fluffy for me. Give her an extra squeeze."

"Will do. Be careful, Ron. Love you," Steph said affectionately.

"Love you too, Steph." Ronnie hung up and pocketed her phone, returning to sit next to Mike. "So? What did she say?"

"Oh my God. They're a pair, huh?" Mike smiled but it didn't make it to his eyes. "Steph just told me what she thought was happening when you were out, and you felt so cold and clammy. She said she finally panicked and took you to the hospital. Despite it being super dangerous, she thinks it may have saved your life. But equally could have ended it as well."

"And...?"

"And that I shouldn't hesitate to get you to a hospital if I'm at all worried, but I better damn well not crash or get stuck like she and Nick did because I," he pointed to his chest, "wouldn't bloody be there to rescue us." He laughed again.

Ronnie smiled. That sounded just like Steph. "What did Ian say?"

Mike let out one telling 'ha' and shook his head. "That kid has it bad for you. That's all I'm going to say about that."

"Oh God." Ronnie shook her head. "You have to tell me what he said, Mike."

"In his own unique way, he told me to not make any moves on you because he had dibs."

Ronnie laughed out loud. "Oh, he never gives up, God bless him. Ian has it bad for every female."

Mike smiled and shook his head. "I know. But he is a good kid. Funny as hell. The accent just adds to his wit."

"Yeah, he is a good kid. Misguided, but he's a gem. Steph'll straighten him out. What did they tell you at the front desk?"

Mike shook his head. "No help whatsoever. I guess they're waiting for instructions from corporate." He looked sympathetic, and then looked out the window.

"Well, that's supremely helpful."

"Nope. Ronnie, this is an international company. I'm sure they're well prepared for hurricanes. Everything is going to be okay. We can ride out the storm safely right here." He nodded towards the breakfast area in the lobby. "I told Carlos and company we deeply regret canceling. Come on, let's grab a cup of coffee. They've got the Weather Channel on."

Chapter 26

Beriberi Scared

Mike followed Ronnie to the other side of the lobby, where the breakfast buffet had been cleared, leaving just a coffee station. After they poured the coffee, Mike ushered her to a table in front of the TV. He could sense the fear wafting off her.

After a few minutes of ads, the Weather Channel was back covering the tropics, showing the radar. "Hurricane Ivan is battering the Gulf Coast today. Pensacola braces for the worst." Images of palm trees bending to Mother Nature as if paying homage to her power. "A severe outbreak of tornadoes is forecast for the Gulf Coast."

Tornadoes were the exuberant offspring of a hurricane. Would they pop up here? The hotel would be sturdy enough as long as tornadoes didn't come into play. Finally, the Weather Channel showed radar of the Caribbean. Ronnie gripped her coffee cup, giving the Styrofoam a run for its money. She wouldn't make eye contact with him, likely lost in her own dark thoughts. The outer bands of the storm were already covering the eastern part of Puerto Rico.

Paul Goodloe sat calmly at the Weather Channel desk tearing their world apart with his words. "We now have a defined eye of the storm. This one popped up quickly from a tropical wave to now a named storm. Hurricane Jeanne."

They exchanged glances.

Ronnie's eyes widened. "Crap."

The reporter continued. "We can expect up to twenty-six inches of rain in some places with this storm. The mountains of Puerto Rico will affect the strength of Jeanne, likely reducing the wind speeds by the time it runs over the island. Along with the rainfall, we can expect mudslides, flooding, damage to property, and likely lives lost."

Paul continued with the expected path of Jeanne heading through Hispaniola. "Puerto Rico should begin feeling the effects of this storm in the next hour. Warnings were issued earlier in the day."

Mike watched her face closely. "You okay?"

"Nope." Ronnie shook her head, making the cascade of blonde waves shimmy across her shoulders.

Ronnie's sculpted cheek bones nicely framed her expressive eyes. Right now, they looked terrified.

"The hotel is sturdy," he tried to reassure her. "We should be fine."

She inhaled sharply, then looked away, batting away tears. "I'd give anything to get off this island. Are you sure we can't get a flight out?"

"That is not gonna happen, I'm sorry to say."

She shook her head, pulling her hair into a ponytail and letting it drop, revealing the nape of her neck. "What do you think we should do then?" Ronnie clutched her Styrofoam cup as if it were her life preserver.

"I think I should be nearby in case you have issues." Mike wanted to reach out and touch her hand, but she'd been skittish the last day or so.

Ronnie kept her eyes on the disaster unfolding on TV and didn't reply, likely reliving her other storm ordeals.

"We should really start preparing. Should I come to your room?"

Was he being paranoid, or did she just flash a look of abject fear? Her gaze returned to the coffee, but her mouth was tight.

Ronnie frowned. "I don't know, Mike. I just don't know."

He would have to push her along gently. Mike longed to have more time alone with her, but not like this. It was a terrifying responsibility to have someone else's life in your hands. He tried to read her thoughts.

Ronnie looked nervous, then stood up and poured another cup of coffee, taking her time to doctor it with cream and sugar. Her face was turned away so he couldn't try to read her thoughts.

Mike chuckled at the clever phrase *WWFD?* Frank wasn't entangled in a mire of emotions about damsels in distress. He didn't have to worry about splaying his heart open to someone after being a hermit for half a decade. What *would* Frank do? He channeled Frank's easy smile and good-natured humor. What they needed to do was get ready to be stuck in the room for the storm. The fear plainly showing in her eyes the last few days had him off his game. What had happened to the playful spark between them? It had dissipated so quickly, and now she was in fight-or-flight mode fearing for her life. It was impossible for him to separate the new storm fears from the moment she'd changed towards him after the 'upsetting phone call,' as she had put it.

Ronnie wouldn't glance over, which said a hell of a lot. Maybe it was the whole Carlos thing making her even more skittish. He didn't blame her. It was no wonder women were afraid of men when predators like Carlos were roaming loose damaging their trust in the world.

Mike tamped down the anger that had been ever present since he'd found them in the stairwell, rekindled by the plane tickets and egomaniacal note. He ground his teeth and turned back towards the TV, whispering under his breath, "God damned fucking Carlos."

Ronnie returned and set the cup down. She smiled, keeping her lips closed, and looked like she'd come to a decision.

They watched another segment of the forecast and when it returned to the Midwest, she turned to him and sighed. "Yeah, I don't know how else to do it. If I'm in a coma, I'm not going to be able to text you to come help me, am I?"

"Look, Ronnie, I get it. I'm your boss and this whole Carlos thing has you feeling more vulnerable around me or any guy. It's totally understandable. I'm pissed off that he treated you like that. How any man could be so callous about women is beyond me." He tried to catch her eye, but she continued to hold court with her coffee. "I just want you to know I am *not* Carlos. I would only be there in case you needed me. There are two rooms in your suite. You could kick me out of the interior room, and I can stay in the bedroom area. Or vice versa. I don't really care."

Ronnie cocked her head, looking at him, her eyes squinting. He could feel her digesting his words, deciding if she could trust him. What had happened to the Ronnie he'd seen in the ocean the other day? She'd been falling for him. He had felt the energy coming off her skin. Now, she was wary. What had he done to make her so cautious? It had to be more than Carlos's aggressive behavior. She'd been aloof in the ride to the restaurant before it even happened.

"It's totally up to you, Ronnie. I just want you to know I will be a perfect gentleman. I'm here to protect you, nothing more."

A corner of her mouth lifted, and she shook her head. "I don't really have a choice, Mike. I'm terrified to be alone after what happened during the last two storms."

"I know. But don't spend any energy worrying about how I'm going to act. I'm going to be one hundred percent there for you like I was during Frances."

Ronnie bit both her lips and sat back away from him, still not answering.

"Is there something else worrying you? You do seem a little different lately."

She sat up a little straighter and her eyes opened wider. "I do?"

"Yeah. We seemed so close in the water. But now you seem afraid of me, or something...anyway." Mike watched her closely, hoping she'd give him a reason for the change.

Ronnie blew out a deep breath and shook her head. Then stood and crossed her arms. "I'm freezing. Let's get up to the room. I don't like talking in the lobby with a damn storm ready to murder us."

Mike stood and offered his suit jacket.

She refused it and briskly walked to the elevators, her shoulders hunched, then turned, waiting for him to catch up. "I guess you should go get your stuff. Is that okay? Can you come to my room in an hour?" She didn't look happy about the position she was in.

"Only if you're okay with it. I don't know how else to help you." He wished she was excited for the excuse to spend the night together. Now she was resigned to it because there were no other satisfactory alternatives. Worse yet, he was sworn to brotherly care instead of throwing caution to the wind.

They both stepped onto the elevator. When the doors opened to her floor she said, "Just come to my room when you've grabbed your stuff."

"Great." Mike held the door as it tried to close. "What room?"

She called out a number and he watched her go.

∞

An hour later Mike stood at her door, pausing to calm down before knocking. He wanted to put her at ease, and the frantic packing and calling the front desk to get more information had gotten his nerves going. They were preparing to close the lobby area and send everyone to their rooms. It wouldn't help knowing how serious it was getting.

He knocked and Ronnie opened the door then disappeared. Mike followed her into the room. It smelled like her, and he was surprised at what that did to him. There was no way he could keep his eyes off the lithe lines of her legs and small tan feet with pink painted toes. She'd changed out of her suit and was wearing a loose, white t-shirt and beige shorts, both enhancing her tan, smooth skin.

Ronnie sat on the couch, glued to the TV watching the Weather Channel. It was the same information they'd already provided. "Hey. If you want to put your stuff in the closet, that's fine." She waved towards the small closet near the bathroom but didn't look at him.

Mike set the large paper bag of supplies on the desk, then opened the closet. He hung up the suit bag and tossed his duffel on the floor, then turned to assess the situation. Would she completely fall apart? Her strength this morning ruled that out—she was not a paper tiger. Would she be angry, scared, or distant? Probably all of the above. It was understandable.

"I called the front desk again." Mike sat in the desk chair and swiveled it towards her. "They're providing food and fresh linens tonight so they can let their kitchen and housekeeping staff head home, leaving a skeleton crew."

Ronnie glanced at him, but her eyes weren't registering what he was saying. "Okay."

Mike waited for her to say more, say anything, but she remained quiet, occupied. He held back his instinctual desire to hug her.

"We needed some food in case we are here for the next few days. I hate the thought of relying on National Suites. Who knows if they'll have enough?"

She nodded almost imperceptibly but kept her eyes on the TV.

"So, I got us some food." He waited for it to register.

"Oh." Finally, she unglued her eyes from the unfolding disaster and looked at him. "Yup."

Ronnie focused on him now. "What did you get?"

Mike smiled, finally getting a smidgen of the attention he wanted from her. He stood and handed her two large grocery bags.

She set one on her lap and opened it. "Wow, look at you. So prepared." She set each item on the coffee table. Soon it was covered with batteries, flashlights, salads, a wedge of cheddar, crackers, a package of small cereal boxes, a few chocolate bars, iced teas, diet Cokes, and a jar of peanut butter.

He took the refrigerated items and put them in the fridge. "Turkey and roast beef. These bad boys ought to last us a while." Each was a foot-long double-stuffed.

Ronnie's manners took over. "Mike, you are Mr. Prepared, aren't you? Thank you so much for doing that."

Thank you, Mrs. Andrews, for teaching your daughter manners, even in difficult circumstances. Kelly would have bit his head off.

"Plus, there are two extra sandwiches and the cooler we used on the boat. I've got a twelve-pack of waters and ice in my room. I can run up and get it if the power goes out, just couldn't carry it all with my luggage."

A smile broke through the stress. "Mike, you thought of everything, didn't you?"

"I hope so. You hungry? We can eat soon if you like."

She shook her head, then stood up and paced back and forth. "I'm not hungry. Go ahead and eat if you need to."

"No, we can eat together when you're ready."

Ronnie twisted something between her fingers, fidgeting. "Back in the lobby you asked what you need to do to help me." She bit her lip.

"Yeah, and you delicately slapped that down and asked to leave the island." Mike chuckled.

Ronnie shook her head. "I wish we could. But now that we're stuck here, I need to talk to you about a few things."

"Right." Mike realized she'd been nervous about this. Maybe she'd calm down once she got it out.

The panicked look was still there. "The doctors don't really know a whole lot except in the hospital I suffered from Korsakoff syndrome." She hesitated, then looked at him. "Also known as beriberi."

Mike's eyes widened. "Why does that make me think of pirates? Ronnie, what the heck is Korsakoff syndrome?"

Ronnie bit her lips again.

Mike leaned in towards her. "And why are you pausing as if you aren't sure if you want to tell me everything?" He shook his head. "Stakes are high. We may be in a similar situation as last time. You have to tell me everything so I can help you."

Ronnie stood and paced across the room. "Korsakoff is a thiamine deficiency that severe alcoholics get because all they ingest is booze. I assure you I am well-fed and not an alcoholic."

Mike nodded, smiling. "Well, I already know that."

Ronnie's voice shook. "I guess the one thing that helps after I come back is to eat foods rich in thiamine." She pursed her lips, acknowledging that wasn't very helpful.

Mike looked at her blankly. "*Come back?* From where?"

Ronnie inhaled sharply. "I mean if I wake up."

"*If?*" His voice rose. "You're not going to think like that, Ronnie. You're going to wake up, and if I have anything to say about it, you're not going to get that sick again. I'll make sure of it."

Ronnie watched him carefully.

Mike waited for her to respond. When she didn't, he prodded. "What are you not telling me, Ronnie? How serious is this? What causes it?"

Her expression crumpled and she looked like she was about to cry. "Aren't you good at cutting right to the chase?"

Mike smiled. "One of my many skills."

Ronnie's hands dropped to her lap. "I think the storms are causing it. It happened the first time during Hurricane Charley, then you saw me during Frances. That storm lasted for days so I..." She fought to control her emotions, "got really sick." Her delicate brows nearly touched, and she squinted.

"Is that why you freaked out a little bit when we first met at the bookstore, right after Charley?"

"Yeah."

"Makes sense. What about the storms cause this though? I've never heard of anyone actually getting sick from bad weather, other than aching joints." Mike ducked in the bathroom, grabbed the box of Kleenex out of the holder, and tossed it to her.

She deftly caught it. "I really don't know."

Mike tamped down his frustration. "You're obviously not telling me a lot, but I get it. I'm your boss and we aren't close like that. I do want you to trust me though." He scraped his fingers through his hair. "Your life may depend on it."

Ronnie looked down at her fidgeting hands and shook her head.

"Can you at least tell me what I should do if you go into a coma? I mean, if you're passed out and I'm the only one that can talk to the doctors, what do I tell them? They won't have access to your medical records."

"Get a doctor, I guess." Her words were feeble now.

Mike inhaled and let it out slowly. "You're gonna have to give me more than that. Please, I know this is awkward. You can trust me. I'm here to help you."

She stood and paced back and forth then turned to him. "You're right. There is one thing the doctors were pretty clear about. There is a lesion on my brain. They urged me to not relapse because it could cause permanent damage." She looked scared, her eyes were wide, and she screwed up her mouth to the side as if to say, *Sorry for the terrifying news.*

"Well shit. I don't like the sound of that." A thrumming in his temple demonstrated the rise in blood pressure. Her life really was in danger. Damn.

"Just keep me comfortable, Mike."

"Okay. I can do that. At what point should I get help? I mean..." He shook his head. "I saw you in the hospital. What did they do for you last time that helped wake you up?"

Ronnie reached for a book on the table next to the couch and ran her fingers over the embossing. It was an old leather journal. Then she looked up at him. "I don't know what woke me up." Her eyes said differently, but there was still doubt there. "I'll need thiamine when I wake up."

"I will get you to eat." The words sounded helpful, but how the hell could he make good on it? "I wish I had a better idea what you'll need. I'm trained in first aid. I can help you for small stuff, but I've no idea when you're going to need more help." Mike replayed what Steph had told him, about her feeling clammy and cold. If the phones were out, how would he get help without leaving her alone in the room? Despite his desire to remain calm, Mike felt the pressure mounting.

Chapter 27

Hurricane Prep

Tuesday, September 14, 2004, 6:00 p.m.

The phone rang. Ronnie stood and crossed the small room. "Hello."

A woman with a thick Puerto Rican accent spoke. "*Hola, senorita.* We are calling all of the rooms to come to the lobby and get our hurricane care packages."

"Sure. I have two rooms. Do we need to send two people down?" Ronnie eyed Mike, who looked puzzled.

"No, ma'am, just bring your room keys and we'll log it in. Your schedule time is in an hour."

"Great, thanks!" Ronnie hung up. "They're giving out hurricane care packages in the lobby in an hour. We just need to have one of us bring down our room keys."

"I'll go down and get it. Give me your key." He dug in his pocket and pulled out his own room key.

Ronnie nodded, *Sure*, then rummaged around in her suit jacket hanging in the wardrobe in the other room and pulled out the key card and handed it to Mike.

Mike set it on the table, then rummaged through his duffel bag and pulled something out. "I bought a map. The good news about our location is there are no tall trees to fall on the hotel up on the fifth floor. The bad news is we are facing the ocean, so we get the full brunt of the storm. It's not expected to be too wicked, but certainly there's potential damage of flying debris and driving wind."

"They said there will be twenty-six inches of rain in some places," Ronnie blurted. Her stomach roiled with stress.

"That will complicate things a lot." He spread out the map on the small coffee table near the couch then sat down.

Ronnie sat next to him.

"You know what that's going to do to this terrain." Mike tapped the map, indicating the mountainous region between where they were in the southeast corner of the island and San Juan in the north. "There will be mudslides. Ronnie, I'm worried we're going to be stuck here for a long time if we don't get out before all the rain trickles down from the mountains."

"Really? Why do you say that?" Ronnie had to force herself to breathe.

"When the storm drops several inches per hour, the roads are gonna be washed away. We are going to be stuck down here for weeks until they can rebuild infrastructure, rebuild missing sections of roads, and repair the power lines. If they get the airport up and running, we can fly out, but if that is hampered, or the roads are blocked to that airport..."

"You can't be serious?" Ronnie felt like crying. Her eyes fixated on his large, meaty hands, and against her will she imagined them around her neck. She suddenly felt lightheaded and leaned back against the couch. "What do you think we should do?"

Mike turned towards her. His expression of sympathy matched the tone of his voice. "If the storm is really bad, though, we need to have a backup plan. We will need to get ahead of the rain that will be coming down the mountains for a few days after the storm passes."

"Okay."

Mike flipped the map open, laying it on the coffee table. "If you need a doctor and the roads aren't too bad, we can leave as soon as the winds die down." He leaned back against the couch and pressed his lips together.

"Where is the nearest hospital?" Ronnie inhaled deeply and let out some of the building panic. Was she really going to be stuck in this damn room with him? The image of Mike as her attractive boss vacillated with the view Jeffrey had planted.

"Not sure." Mike stood and pulled the hotel directory off the desk and brought it back to the couch. He flipped through the pages and found the medical center listings. Then found it on the map. "Not too far." He marked it on the map. "You okay with this game plan?"

Ronnie pulled her knees to her chest, curling up in the corner of the couch. She was definitely not okay with this but understood they couldn't stay here for months. "In concept I think it is a good, solid plan."

Mike sighed, letting out a stream of air, possibly inspired by her own. "If you're not feeling poorly, we should leave in the morning and drive farther away from where the mountains are going to dump the water. If we can get out from under that deluge, it will be easier to get out once the airport reopens. I just want to be sure you are on board in case something happens." Mike ran his fingers through his hair.

"Well, if something happens to me, get me to that hospital." She tapped the map.

"Will do. Ronnie, it's going to be okay." Mike pressed his lips together in a partial smile and patted her knee.

Ronnie cringed at his touch but tried to hide it. She looked at the map again and tapped the middle. "Mike, did you see the path of Jeanne?"

He pulled his eyes from the Weather Channel. "Yeah."

"Look here." Ronnie pointed at the map. "The storm will hit worse here." She pointed to the upper right quadrant of the island. "The western side isn't expected to get as much rain. Should we try to go west instead of north?"

"Well, aren't you a smartie." His smile was affectionate. "Yeah, I think that may give us the best shot. We take 53 then," he pointed at the map, "all the way to Ponce. Do you think that's far enough?"

"Who knows? This part will be tricky through the mountains." She pointed where

52 started north.

"It'll be all about the timing," Mike said, smiling. "And luck."

"I wish we could start driving now, not wait till morning, adding all that rain to the mix." It was feeling like one stress too many clogging her mind. Ronnie paced the room, then sat down in the office chair next to the couch, feeling overwhelmed.

"Are you okay?" Mike's voice softened.

"Yeah, maybe I need to eat something. This stress is making me feel funny."

"Let's stuff you full of thiamine to head off any trouble." Mike smiled. "I need to head down soon to get the supplies. Why don't you snack on something until I get back? Maybe they'll give us a hot meal. Or at least dinner of some sort."

"Hand me the crackers and peanut butter."

Mike passed the crackers and jar to her. "I'll be right back."

Ronnie walked past the couch into the bedroom to the window. The curtains were drawn, and she pulled them open to look out onto the ocean view. Dark clouds nearly black as night roiled and toiled in the sky. Rain dotted the window, and a low, dense fogbank hovered offshore, obscuring the horizon, clouding the view that had been picture perfect until today. She wished Mike hadn't splurged on the ocean view room for her now. With clouds blocking out any sun leaving an ominous, eerie feeling in the room. A gust of wind splattered raindrops against the pane and startled her. She retreated to the interior room, closing the bedroom door, doing her best to let go of the dread that lingered in the air like the fogbank outside.

Ronnie stuffed a few crackers in her mouth, fear nearly closing off her airway. She cracked open a bottled iced tea and took a big swig. If she were in dire straits, the hotel would not have the resources to help her. She picked up her cell phone and called her mom, wanting to at least tell her where she was and to not worry if they were out of touch for a while.

The answering machine picked up and Ronnie left a voice mail. Then Ronnie called her brother David. Again, there was no answer, but she left a voice mail and felt a smidge better hearing his voice. Would he know more about what their father had been working on? She would have to check with him when this was over.

She replayed Steph's version of Mike—that lessened her panic a bit. A lingering flash of Kelly's bloody shower spiked her with adrenaline. Ronnie shoved that little beast back under the bed for now, but the worry grew. She would be stuck in this room with Mike for at least tonight, maybe longer. At the very least it would be awkward. At the worst it would be dangerous.

Mike took longer than she'd expected, and when she'd had enough to eat, she put the food away. Then paced the room, finally deciding to find the bedding for the pull out couch. She'd sleep in the bedroom area and lock the door that separated it from the living room. He could have the fold out couch. That would leave him access to the bathroom that was just outside of the bedroom door. Could she fall asleep with Mike in the next room?

A knock on the door startled her out of her thoughts. She swung the door open, and Mike stepped into the room, hands full of towels and a large grocery bag. She took the towels from him and put them in the bathroom.

Mike opened the bag and set everything out on the table. "They've given us candles, a small flashlight, some sandwiches for tonight, and these." He held out a few lame breakfast bars. "There is a curfew at 8:00 and we are instructed to stay in our rooms."

"Okay. Did they tell you anything about what happens tomorrow?" She grabbed the food and helped stock the refrigerator.

"Not really. I got the distinct feeling they were still waiting for more information from corporate. They all seemed a little spooked."

"Spooked?"

"Yeah, Ivan just passed through here and they were not eager for another big storm to come a-knocking."

"Shoot. What happens if the power goes out?" Ronnie had hoped for more preparedness.

He nodded at the candles and flashlights. "Light 'em up."

"Open flames? Is that a good idea?" She imagined the candles tipping over and setting the entire hotel on fire.

"Just told us to be safe."

They ate the sandwiches and talked of other things. Ronnie was thankful for the reprieve from stressful topics—storms, Carlos, and her illness.

At ten, Ronnie could barely keep her eyes open. "Do you mind if I sleep in there?" Ronnie nodded at the bedroom.

"Not at all. I'll be happy to sleep on the fold out." He patted the couch he was sitting on. "You go get some rest. Tomorrow will be here before we know it. I'll let you sleep in late unless something is going on."

"Mike, I really appreciate you being here," Ronnie said. "I'm going to get ready for bed and settle in."

A few minutes later, Ronnie slid under the covers, hoping she'd be too tired to let the swirl of emotions roll around too much. She ran her fingers over her father's journal on the bedside table, imagining her father nearby, his protection wrapping around her as she slept. Then she slid it in the bedside table drawer, wanting to protect it from the raging storm outside.

"Good night, Dad."

Chapter 28

Cracking Good Time

Wednesday, September 15, 2004

A loud *bang* startled Ronnie out of a deep sleep. Her foggy mind translated the sound into a gunshot, but she tossed out that explanation once she switched on the flashlight the hotel had provided and shined it around the room. Her heart was thumping wildly.

Mike knocked on the door. "Ronnie, you okay?"

Ronnie opened the door and glanced around the room. "Yeah, did you hear that noise?"

Mike looked sleepy, but otherwise wore the same t-shirt and shorts he'd been in earlier. "Yeah. Did something hit the window?" He walked to the window and pulled aside the curtain.

A spider-like fracture in the center of the window spread slowly, making another cracking noise.

"Shit."

"Mike, oh my God!" Ronnie instinctively stepped away.

"We're on the fifth floor. How did something hit all the way up here?" Mike pulled the curtain closed. "Let's get your stuff out of here before that cracks all the way."

"Sure." Ronnie opened the small wardrobe and handed Mike the hanging clothes. She opened the drawers and shoved everything into the suitcase, including all of the loose things on the desk. Mike returned and grabbed the still-opened suitcase, carrying it into the other room. Ronnie looked around for anything that remained. She grabbed the cell phone cord and her shoes and walked around the sofa bed to the closet near the front door, depositing the items next to Mike's things.

Mike shut the bedroom door and turned to her awkwardly. "You dropped this."

Ronnie's face felt hot. She snatched her bra from his hand and shoved it in the bag. "Sorry about that."

Mike's eyes lit up, reminding her of their budding attraction in the turquoise waters only a few days ago. A million years had passed since that moment. Everything had changed.

He laughed. "Don't mind at all."

"Pillows!" Ronnie dashed back into the bedroom and gathered two pillows from the bed and returned for the comforters. The couch was now a bed taking up most of the open space in the room. Mike was talking on the phone. Ronnie stood awkwardly, holding the comforter, feeling like she'd invaded his space.

Mike hung up the phone. "Just telling the front desk. They said to move into this room and stay put. They'll send up someone if they can in the morning. Sounded unlikely." He pulled the pillow off the bed and straightened the sheets. "Here, you take the bed. I'll sleep on the floor."

Ronnie hesitated, not happy with the turn of events. This took away any barrier between them. A terrible thought crept in, wedging between panic and fear. Would Mike accidentally kill her in his sleep, like the soldier killing his family instead of the imagined enemy? Ronnie glanced back at the room she'd left, longing for that modicum of privacy and veil of protection the flimsy hotel door offered.

"Seriously, Ronnie. Let's get back to sleep. Take the bed." Mike sat on the floor against the wall, fluffing the pillow he'd been using.

Ronnie pulled the flimsy blanket off the bed and handed it to Mike, then tossed the comforter to him. "Here, you take one to sleep on for cushion."

Mike caught it and laid it out on the floor, smoothing out the edges. "Thanks."

"Damn, that scared me to death. What do you think caused it?" Ronnie sat on the bed clutching the pillow.

"No idea, but could be a palm frond, a bird. Anything that is picked up by the wind. Do you mind if I turn the TV on for a few minutes? I just want to see what's going on out there. We will probably lose power soon. It may be our last chance."

"Sure, I need to calm down a bit before I can sleep anyway." She glanced back at the bed, feeling very out of sorts. How could she lie down on a bed that was still warm from his body?

They watched the weather as tiredness crept back in. She counted her blessings. They still had power and she hadn't gone back in time. Small victories. Maybe this would be uneventful, and they could get home in the next day or so. She let these thoughts comfort her as she drifted off to sleep. She woke briefly when Mike clicked the TV off.

∞

Ronnie woke before Mike. The power was still on, but not for long. The Puerto Rican authorities had decided to shut power off to protect the power grid and prevent electrocutions. She'd heard the news coverage before falling asleep. Quietly she grabbed her suitcase and took it into the bathroom, locked the door, and took a shower. When she was finished, she stared at her reflection in the foggy mirror hiding her features. Was this how her mind would function if the lesion expanded and destroyed her memory? The panicked thoughts would do her no good. Ronnie combed her hair and put on a little makeup. The eye of the storm would be approaching around noon today if the predictions were right. The hotel was to the east of the eye, giving them the strongest quadrant of Jeanne, and a likelihood of spawning tornadoes. A ball of tension grew in her stomach. Ronnie closed her eyes and prayed fervently. *Please don't let me travel today!*

She shut off the bathroom light and quietly returned to the bed, but Mike was a light sleeper and woke.

"Good morning, sunshine." A sleepy smile spread across his face.

She'd hoped he'd stay asleep so she could have a moment alone. "Hey, how was the floor?"

"Magnificent. Beats sleeping in a mud puddle. Been there, done that."

Mike sat up and stretched his thick, muscular arms. He was utterly adorable with his sleepy expression. Ronnie looked away, putting forth the battered Kelly to dissuade the closeness that was trying to rekindle between them.

"Let me get you some thiamine for breakfast! I have an excellent recipe." Mike laughed. "Crackers?" He stood and picked up the box. "Yup, lots in here. Can I interest you in either a wedge of cheese or peanut butter for your gourmet breakfast?"

"Sure." Ronnie tore off the sheets and transformed the bed back into a couch. Mike was busy preparing a plate of cheese and crackers. Mike reached into the fridge and grabbed two waters and a bunch of grapes he rinsed in the small sink near the fridge.

"So, how are you this morning? Feeling okay?" Mike asked, watching her out of the corner of his eye.

"I feel good." She clicked on the TV and hushed him, as the tropical update was front and center. The weather geeks were covering it around the clock between Ivan and Jeanne dueling for attention. Ronnie turned to Mike. "What is going on outside, can you tell?"

Mike slowly opened the bedroom door a crack, then walked in and looked out the window. "Damn, Ronnie, come look at this."

She walked into the room expecting to see broken glass. It had held. She walked closer and looked down. The ocean was an angry monster, the waves battering the deep grooves carved into the side of the cliff. "Look how high the tide is. The beach is completely underwater!" Ronnie imagined the shack where she'd rented the snorkel gear. It must be washed away.

"Yeah, the worst hasn't even come onshore yet." Mike shook his head.

The clouds were boiling, angry, and flashing with lightning. Rain pelted the window.

"Let's get away from here. If it goes, we'll get cut up for sure." He stepped back into the bedroom and shut the door behind her. "Why don't you eat up? I'm going to grab a shower before the power goes out."

"Okay." Ronnie relaxed her fists and shook out her hands.

"Your breakfast is on the desk. Go ahead and get that thiamine drip started." Mike pointed at the plate.

Ronnie tried to soak in his calmness, but it was of no use. The terror grew as she balanced the paper plate on her lap and watched weather coverage with the foreboding warnings for the island, then showed the utter destruction Ivan had caused in Pensacola.

Ronnie forced herself to eat, eying the candles the management had given them in case the power went out. She patted the flashlight in her pocket, making sure it was nearby as well. A few minutes later Mike burst forth from the bathroom, letting out a billowing of steam. A towel was wrapped around his waist, and his thick chest muscles and abs glistened in the low light.

"Sorry, forgot my clothes." Mike clutched the towel and turned away, uncomfortable with his intrusion.

Ronnie soaked in the perfect sculpture of his shoulders and deep groove down his back. As he bent over to grab his suitcase, a thick, muscular thigh escaped the gap in the towel, cut by the tan line. Bulging muscle flexed as he stood back up. The image of his near nakedness remained after he closed the door. Damn, why did he have to have a sketchy past? She could easily devour him.

Dueling emotions set Ronnie over the edge. Was Mike a murderer? Was he the man she met in the past every time she went back? Tears squeezed out of her eyes. Would she live another day? Would her brain be totally destroyed? A buzzing in her head ramped the fear up a few notches and she covered her face, blocking out the light.

Ronnie heard the bathroom door open. Mike wore a black USMC t-shirt and Army green cargo shorts. She watched him carefully as he dug in his bag, pulling out a pair of socks, and bent low to pick up his running shoes. If she could have hand-made the perfect-looking guy, it would be Mike Walsh. Only she'd have to pull out the angry rage lurking inside. Damn it.

Mike looked up and smiled, aware of her eyes on him. "Thought I'd go business casual today, seeing as we're gonna be sweating once the power goes out."

Ronnie took clandestine glances, remembering the naked flesh from a few minutes ago.

Mike crossed the distance between them and sat on the couch, making her recoil against the corner. "Geez, you're jumpy. You okay?"

Ronnie's cell phone buzzed. It may be her mom or brother calling back. Ronnie stood and pulled the phone out of her pocket, turning her back to Mike. It was Jeffrey's number. A text message appeared. *Where are you, R?* His annoyed tone oozed through the words.

Then another text message appeared as she watched.

For your sake I hope you're not with Mike.

Ronnie felt the panic swirl out of control. She wanted to scream at the top of her lungs, but she tamped it down enough to pace back and forth.

"You okay?" He stood and took a step closer.

"No, I am not okay. I..."

"What happened?" Mike asked softly.

The phone lit up again. "Jeffrey texted instructions." Ronnie pressed her lips together, not hiding her anger.

Mike looked puzzled. "What instructions?"

She read the latest text out loud, not realizing a new one had appeared. "All in caps, 'YOU NEED TO GET AWAY FROM HIM!'" Ronnie slammed the flip phone shut and panicked. She'd not meant to read *that* aloud.

"Who? *Me?*" It was Mike's turn to be angry. "Does Jeffrey really want you to be alone now after what you've been through the last few storms? Is he that big of an asshole to put his jealousy over your safety?" Mike scowled.

Another text came in. Ronnie opened the phone again and looked at it. Mike leaned closer and read the words as she did. "He beat her up." Ronnie slammed the phone shut and felt the heat creep up her cheeks.

Mike's expression darkened. "Beat her up? What is Jeffrey talking about?" His mouth was a straight line, and she imagined his mind exploding with rage.

Ronnie stood and took a few steps away from him. Would he snap? Was this the moment she would discover the two Mikes merging into one, and not in the good way connecting to Mathias?

"Ronnie, what the hell is Jeffrey talking about?" Mike cracked his knuckles, waiting for her to explain.

She stood paralyzed. What could she say?

"Look, we are going to be stuck together probably for days. You need to be honest with me, Ronnie. What is Jeffrey talking about? Who beat *who* up?"

"You're telling me to be honest with you?" All the stresses spilled out as her pressure valve opened. "Why don't you be honest with me about your past? What happened five years ago, Mike?"

"Five years ago?" Mike glared at her. "Why the...?" He looked at the wall, running his hands through his hair, and faced her, looking a smidge calmer. "You tell *me*? What happened five years ago, Ronnie?"

Anger and mistrust bubbled forth. Then a truly horrifying feeling took over. Black tendrils wrapped around her soul, pulling her back. "Oh my God." A wave of familiar nausea pulled at her. Ronnie covered her mouth.

Mike reached out to touch her arm. "Are you okay?"

Ronnie jerked away. "Why the hell am I stuck here with you, of all people!?"

Mike's expression shifted from worry to anger. "What the hell do you mean by *that?*"

Ronnie ran to the bathroom, pushing against her stomach, hoping to quell the queasiness. Just then the power went out and they were plunged into darkness. A low light from the curtains that faced the lobby let in just enough light to see his shadowy form approach her, inducing sheer panic. "Noooo!" Ronnie reached in her pocket and pulled out the flashlight as she pushed the bathroom door open.

Mike grabbed her arm, turning her around to face him. She jerked her arm free. "Look, Ronnie, *talk* to me. What bullshit is Jeffrey telling you? Why are you afraid of me?"

Ronnie felt too anxious to couch it, to soften it, and it burst forth out of her in the worst possible way. "What happened to Kelly? Was she afraid to stay with you, too?"

Pain immediately registered in his eyes, his mouth opened in shock.

What was lurking in his past? She stood her ground, taking in every nuance of his body language, ready to run into the bathroom and lock the door if he made a move towards her. Mike would lie about Kelly, but maybe she could read enough of the subtle cues to know more.

Chapter 29

Fight and Flight

Ronnie waited for Mike to say something…anything that would explain Kelly's death.

Mike's expression fell and a flash of pain flickered in his eyes. Then he took a step back as if punched in the gut. "What about Kelly?" He crowded her against the wall near the refrigerator.

Ronnie held up her hands. She couldn't breathe. "Mike, you're scaring me. Step back, please."

Mike held his hands up, as if showing he wasn't going to pull her head off…yet.

"Ronnie, this is…" Mike took a step backwards, then sat in the desk chair halfway across the room and leaned forward, elbows on his knees. He ran his fingers through his hair, and this time Ronnie recognized it. That was what Mathias did when he was stressing.

Mike's expression shifted, this time to something she'd never seen before. His mouth turned down as if he was going to cry. Mike Walsh, United States Marine, ready to cry?

The muscle in his jaw tensed. "How the hell do you know about Kelly?" His eyes were wide and vulnerable. Surprise and hurt vacillated to intense anger.

Ronnie eyed the bathroom, inching closer, not sure what he would do next—cry or lash out. His vulnerability, before it had been covered with anger, pulled at her heart.

"What do you know about Kelly?" Mike asked again, his patience wearing thin.

Ronnie spit it out without wordsmithing to make it sound better than it was. "Jeffrey said you killed her. He sent me an article." She reached behind her to grab the doorknob to the bathroom.

"An article?"

Fear choked off logic. The image of Kelly's battered face flashed in her mind, mixing in with nausea, overwhelming her.

"From where?" Mike demanded.

"From the one in Rochester." She watched intently, waiting for the explosion.

Every muscle in Mike's body tensed. "Ffffffffuck…" Mike stood and in one lithe and deadly movement, he drew his fist back and slammed it into the wall.

This was the picture of a man who would hurt someone in the heat of passion.

Terrified now, Ronnie stepped into the bathroom and slammed the door shut, locking it in a panic, her heart beating out of her chest.

Mike pounded on the door. "Ronnie, please just listen."

Ronnie dropped the flashlight on the floor, the beam bouncing off the white tile. She knelt near the toilet with her head in her hands, gasping for air, holding back the nausea. The feeling was creeping over her again. She lifted the toilet seat. This was it. She was going back in time! Ronnie tried desperately to anchor herself to this place, but she'd been through this enough to know there was no stopping it. She clung to the toilet and an enormous pressure pushed her to the floor. A foggy mist crept under the door.

"No!" Ronnie screamed. She did not want to leave now. In the heat of the moment Mike would speak from his heart while it was still raw, before he could smooth it with logic and nuance. To her horror, she'd seen a glimpse of the murderous rage that killed Kelly. She had her proof, but it was too late. This door wouldn't hold a powerful man like Mike. She slid onto the floor near the bathtub.

The door handle jiggled. "Ronnie, please just let me tell you what happened that night."

Terror overwhelmed her thoughts. A familiar wrenching on her soul ripped her apart, separating her body from her mind. The buzzing was so loud she could no longer hear Mike's voice. The pounding on the door synced with the drumming of her heartbeat. Ronnie floated to the ceiling, where she could see her still form splayed on the floor.

Within seconds, Mike had jimmied the lock and was at her side. "Ronnie, please..." Mike knelt next to her. Would he hit her? Ronnie was surprised when he showed tenderness, smoothing the hair off her face. His knuckles were bleeding. She saw it so clearly before she shot up towards the heavens. Would she ever know what had happened to Kelly?

Her attention was pulled to a new reality as Mike drifted out of sight. Would she find Mathias? Stars, or maybe just pinpoints of light, flew past, her hair whipped behind. Would she be able to survive this? Would she return damaged forever, or not at all, like her father?

Finally, unable to force a cohesive thought, Ronnie floated as if in utero, surrounded by a noise-dampening liquidity and warmth. Blackness crept in and covered her in a cool mist, not quite comforting, but not painful. Had she always been surrounded by inky night? In this nowhere-land she reached out to her father. It was hard to focus on a single thought, but after what seemed like hours, she gathered mental energy and forced her mind to call out.

"Dad, are you there?" She listened for a response, but the deathly silence felt like an empty void.

Just as she was giving up hope, his voice entered her mind. "Ronnie, you're back! I was hoping you'd not have to suffer through this again."

Relief rocked her to the core. She wasn't alone in the darkness. "Dad, oh my God, you're here!"

"Yes, Ronnie. I am always here. You're just learning to tune me in now. I'm so grateful for these fleeting moments with you. I've missed you beyond words."

"Me too, Dad." She was surprised at how childish she sounded. "Why is this happening to me?" Maybe the question she couldn't get answered in her own time and place would be answerable here.

"It is my fault, Ronnie. I caused this…" Her dad paused. Ronnie inserted a throat-clearing sound, but there was no throat since he was speaking to her in her mind. "But it makes no sense that you would be affected by it."

"Dad, how did you cause this? What is happening? How do I make it stop?" Another reality burst forth and interrupted the precious time with her dad.

Ronnie landed hard on dry-packed earth. Her mind screamed out for her dad, but he was no longer there. Her first breath was choked with a fine, dry grit. Fear coalesced around her like the cloud of dust that settled in her lungs. She tried to cough but she wasn't firmly planted in the new body yet. Every time she'd traveled, it had not ended well. In fact, the only way it ever ended was through her death.

Chapter 30

Wide-Open Terror

Ronnie felt the heat of a harsh sun on her face as she struggled for breath. An ominous shadow blocked the beating rays, providing a reprieve. A man, breathing hard and fast just above her, struck fear deep into her gut. A tear landed on her cheek, and for a split second she thought she was in the grave in Morris's time. That idea was immediately dashed when the man spoke unfamiliar words, delivered with pure hatred. He knelt next to her and grabbed the hair on top of her head, jerking her head backward. Fear coalesced into terror, and if she could have forced her voice box to eke out a sound, it would have been a bloodcurdling scream.

Bang! A loud noise reverberated through her skull, one similar to the sound that had woken her earlier. He released her hair as he fell backward. The blinding light, no longer blocked, forced her eyes shut. The acrid scent of gunpowder gave away the source of the sound.

Events were happening faster than she could process. Terror coursed through her veins, and she held her breath, waiting for another shot to end her life in this plane, almost welcoming it.

Instead, she heard hoofbeats, and a man yelled out, "ROSE!"

A shadowy figure approached, her eyes struggling with the brightness.

The man shook her shoulder. "Rose, I plumb thought you were gone." He knelt next to her and wiped at her forehead.

The sounds of metal clinking and a snort from a horse filled in what her eyes couldn't make out.

"We gotta go, Rose. Can you stand up?"

Words couldn't form. Her tongue was stiff and immovable in her mouth.

"We're about to be overrun. Do you think you can get up on my saddle?" The man helped her to sit, then before she was ready, he pulled her to a standing position and shoved her up on the horse. She swung her leg over the saddle and uncoordinatedly sat.

Ronnie forced her arms and legs to respond, but they were unruly. The man settled into the saddle, struggling to place his other foot in the stirrup as the horse, likely protesting two riders, turned in a circle, lifting his head, pulling on the reins. On the ground below them, a puddle of dark liquid pooled around a shirtless man. To her horror, it was a Native bleeding profusely into the grass.

"Help him?" Ronnie asked, wondering why he would leave someone dying.

"The injun? He was scalping you, Rose. So, I shot him." The man did the work for her, gaining control of the horse while gripping tightly around her waist. He spurred the animal to a frantic pace, glancing back every so often. Her mind was struggling to keep up with what was going on. She'd nearly been scalped and left for dead.

Ronnie, or rather Ronnie in Rose's body, 'woke' to this new world. A rough start indeed. Every inch of her flesh felt bruised and battered. No body part hurt more than the rest. Was that a good thing? Ronnie impatiently waited as her mind gained control of Rose's body.

"Keep yourself on the horse, Rose. I know you're hurting, but I have to..." He turned and fired the pistol, startling Ronnie out of her stupor.

Her ears rang, and she glanced around to see another Native on the ground. Adrenalin coursed through her newly found brain and did wonders to speed up the process of taking control. She gripped the horn of the saddle for all she was worth, one hand digging into the mane for good measure. The dead man's horse galloped, but finally stopped and turned, making its way back to the rider, who lay still on the ground.

Ronnie scanned the vast wide-open prairie and saw no other riders. "Is that the only one?"

"There is always more. Always." The man's stubbly face brushed against her cheek as he turned the horse and scanned the horizon, stopping to confirm there were no others in pursuit, yet. Behind them stretched miles and miles of grassland that disappeared up a hill. But anyone or anything could be just over the next berm.

"Hold on. We're going to get our money's worth out of Smokey here." The man spurred the horse and held her tight. There wasn't room for both of them on the saddle and he sat just behind it. If the horn hadn't been so prominent, she would have moved forward onto the horse's neck. He had the stirrups that helped him hold on with her wedged in front, but it was precarious. If the animal did a quick turn, they'd both tumble.

Ronnie leaned forward into the wind and gripped the saddle with her thighs, using every complaining muscle in her body to stay on. Ahead was a dugout cut into the side of a hill. The horse saw it and broadened its stride, recognizing the target now.

By the time they approached the small building, Ronnie was thoroughly exhausted, covered in dirt and sweat. The man stopped the horse and helped her dismount. He was tall with a dirty face, black cowboy hat, and a fierce expression in his dark brown eyes.

"Rose, we are in a pickle. I'm just going to run in and see if there is anyone here. Them injuns will likely find this place and we need to be long gone when they do." He led her to the entryway of the roughly made dugout and plopped her on a stone wall in front of the structure, then unlatched the door and stepped in. Ronnie turned her attention to the horse, who stood nearby panting from exertion. The horse scanned the grassy landscape, pulling Ronnie's eyes along the horizon. She prayed no one would be tearing through the grass in their direction.

Her legs were shaking but she scolded herself, as the gray, glistening animal had done all the work. Something tickled her forehead and she wiped at it. Her hand came away covered in blood. A split second later and she'd have been scalped. Thank God the man prevented it. She didn't even know his name. This new reality was already delivering a gut punch.

The man burst forth from the small structure, startling her.

"Not a damn one of them is here." His hands were full of gear. He handed her two wool blankets. "Roll these for me, Rose, please." The man took the rest of what he was holding and shoved it haphazardly in the saddle bag as Smokey kept watch on the land.

Ronnie shook one blanket and folded it in half, then rolled it in a long, skinny roll, remembering what she'd seen in Westerns. He took it from her and attached it to the back of the saddle with a leather loop. She rolled the second blanket, and he added it to the loop.

"Rose, go and water Smokey here." He patted the horse's rump and pointed around to the back of the dugout. "We're gonna need more outta him shortly."

Ronnie took the reins. Smokey watched her closely as they made their way up the hill. Did the horse suspect the truth, that she was no longer Rose? She patted his neck and prayed the watering hole wasn't too far away and that she'd be the only one there. They crested the hill and Smokey pulled her along, down the other side towards a small stream set in a copse of trees. Ronnie let him free to wander knee-deep into the meager flow of water.

The horse seemed to relax, but Ronnie's nerves were taut. Nearly being scalped would do that to a person. Being alone and unarmed with angry Natives roaming around didn't help the fun factor a bit. The memory of the Native in her last time travel episode tore through any last hope of calming down. Ini had said she'd felt his evil presence through time. He was clinging to her still. Was he here in this time period?

Kneeling down by the water, she caught her reflection, confirming the mark from the Native. She dipped her finger in the water and wiped at the crusted blood along her hairline, then washed her face and hands. Tiny cuts stung her fingers. What had happened to Rose when she entered her body? Did she die? Or was she sent back to another place like she had been? "Sorry, Rose! I wish I could make it stop."

Ronnie stretched, then gasped as a sharp pain along her ribs let her know there was damage. Whatever had happened before she'd come into this body had been brutal. Every muscle in this body was resisting her movements.

Smokey lifted his head and snorted. A brief flash of panic urged her to hide in the mesquite shrubs lining the stream. A split second later she heard hoofbeats. Smokey heard it too and lifted his head from the water to listen intently, then whinnied. A return nicker sounded, and a second later five men on horseback broke through the shrubs.

Ronnie crouched out of sight, willing her heart to slow down. It took every ounce of control to not run away. Were these companions of the Natives her rescuer had killed? What would they do if they discovered her? Smokey moved towards the other horses, who were carrying riders. Or were they part of her rescuer's party? A new worry occurred to her. If they were, would they notice she was not Rose?

"Where the hell is Clayton?" A man in a green leather vest dismounted and patted Smokey's neck.

"Jere Miah, help get him down," a mustached man barked from his horse, pointing behind him. Jere Miah helped the injured man slide off the saddle, then the rider jumped down and supported him to the water's edge.

The rest of the men dismounted and let their mounts drink while they cooled off on the bank. Ronnie took in every detail of their dress and speech and tried to assess what time period it was. Natives were an issue before 1900, which matched their dress and the use of horses.

"Max, come on, man, wake up." The sandy-haired man gripped the injured man's shoulders and shook gently, trying to rouse him. The man with the mustache, splashed water in his face.

"Hey, stop that," Max sputtered, waking suddenly.

Ronnie peeked through the bushes to get a better look. All of the men were in old-fashioned clothes with white long sleeve shirts and vests of different colored leather and suede, and all were strapped with pistols. Their clothes mimicked what she'd seen in Western movies, but the hats were not the typical cowboy style. Instead, they had smaller brims, much like a bowler hat curled up around the edges.

Mustache pointed at the injured man. "Max shoulda been trampled to death after what he pulled back there. Gary, surely you can see that."

Gary stood behind Max and grabbed his shoulders, in a way protecting him from Mustache's anger. Max looked like he'd been knocked out in a boxing ring, unsure of his surroundings. Gary shook his head. "I don't think he was trying to get away rightly. I think he just got turned around, Ben."

"Gary, what makes you say that?" Mustached Ben responded, taking an aggressive step towards Max.

Gary was unperturbed despite the angry tone. He shook his head as he dipped his hat in the water, filling it and clapping it back on his head before responding. Water ran down his back, darkening the vest. "He's just not the type of man to do that. Max needs the money as much as any of us."

"Max's foolishness allowed the Comanche to kidnap her. They'll either scalp her, leave her for dead, or take her for ransom. How is Jeb going to pay us for that?"

"We may find her yet, Ben. Clayton was tearing off after 'em when I last saw." Gary grabbed his horse's reins and moved him off the bank where he was munching grass and led him into the water. The horse bent his head low and drank.

Max caught sight of Ronnie hiding in the bushes. "Hey, you." He pointed, giving away her precarious hiding spot.

That caught everyone's attention.

Gary walked towards her. "Rose? Oh, my Lord, what a sight to see. Are you okay?"

She stood now, revealing her hiding spot, and glanced back towards the house, hoping Clayton would appear from the dugout. When he didn't, Ronnie took a step towards them. "Yes, I think so."

Ben walked briskly towards her. "What the hell were you thinking? Why did you ride off without us? You trying to run away again, Rose?"

Ronnie took a step back. "No." Her mind whirled. What had Rose done before she'd landed in her body? By the angered expressions on their faces, she'd gone against their wishes.

Ben turned to Max. "Were you taking her away?"

Max looked as dumbfounded as Ronnie felt. "No, absolutely not."

Ben interceded. "Look, I'm sure there is a perfectly good explanation. Sadly, whatever the hell you were doing almost got us all killed. We may yet pay the price. Where is Clayton?"

As if summoned by his words, Clayton appeared around the corner and signaled for the group to join him.

Ben glared at her, then gave Max the same angry look. "We will talk about this later."

The men gathered their horses, and Gary filled Max's canteen and handed it to him. They all walked towards Clayton, taking the heat off her for now.

Ronnie turned to Max. "What happened?"

Max teetered but steadied himself. "I just had a fall and..." He tousled his hair that dripped down his face. Noticing he held his hat in hand, he clapped it on his head and looked at the other men. "Far as I can recall, I was nearly trampled to death by a herd of buffalo. Then I woke up here in this stream."

Gary grabbed Max's arm, leading him up the hill, his horse's reins in hand. Ronnie turned to grab Smokey's reins and walked near Gary and Max. Another horse sans rider followed behind, loping up the embankment, not wanting to be left behind.

Clayton, his body language showing tension and fear, came down the hill so they could hear him. "Injuns are likely to be here soon. We killed two racing back here. Come on, boys, we need to beat feet, and fast."

Alarm spread through the group. Several mounted their horses. Gary and Max walked briskly, and Ronnie followed behind.

Max turned to her. "Rose." He tipped his hat.

"Max, I'm glad you're okay." Ronnie liked the way he said her new name. Something about him felt familiar. Was Max her Mathias in this time? She needed an ally, most especially one with broad shoulders and a well-muscled frame, made more obvious with his wet clothes plastered to his body.

A million questions clouded her mind. What was Mike doing back in Puerto Rico? Was he hurting her? Was he panicking? Would he get help? There was no time to ruminate on any of them. They ransacked the house, gathering their things, and left the area in a matter of minutes. Ronnie was back on Clayton's horse, leading the group towards the setting sun. Before them stretched wide-open grasslands, and absolutely nothing else. The landscape was nearly featureless all the way to the horizon, with wide-open mass of short mesquite trees and endless waves of tall grasses blowing in the wind.

Without any distractions, Ronnie was left to gather her worries around her for comfort. Would they ride through the night, or stop to make camp? Would the Comanche find and kill them? Would they realize she was not Rose? Her mind wandered from this reality to the past, wondering what Mike was thinking about her absence. Scratch that, this was the past. Mike was waiting for her in the future. She'd missed her chance to hear his confession or tease out the truth about Kelly's death. By the time she would return, if she in fact would go back this time, the element of surprise would be gone. She would miss the chance to read his body language and learn how Kelly died. Would he lie or tell her what had happened?

Chapter 31

Ian's Confession

Wednesday, September 15, 2004

Steph woke after a fitful night of dreams about trying to get to Ronnie. Anxiety overtook her desire to sleep in, and worries piled on top of worries. Would Ronnie time travel during this storm? Would she be okay? Was Mike a murderer? Finally, giving up on sleep, Steph stretched and decided to get breakfast and go to church.

She padded out to the kitchen and prepared a pot of coffee. Ian's door was closed. At least he was home. He'd been out the last two nights with Billy, whoring around. Ian had better damn well be alone in there. She had made it clear he wasn't allowed to bring the skanks into her house.

While she liked Billy, she worried that he may not be a good influence on her brother. Was he the same type of blathering eejit that got him thrown in jail in Glasgow, wee men drinking too much and carrying on at all hours of the day and night? At least Billy had a decent job, unlike the ne'er-do-wells Ian hung out with back home.

Steph opened the front door and grabbed the paper. It felt cool in her hands. The heat of summer was finally fading into more reasonable temperatures. The aroma of the brew tweaked her appetite. It would have to be a quick breakfast then off to visit with God. Church always made her feel refreshed and alive. Steph made jelly toast and poured a cup of coffee then sat down to read the paper, enjoying her Sunday morning ritual.

A few minutes later, Ian walked towards her. He was up much too early.

"Get any new diseases last night?"

Ian looked remarkably awake and fresh. Something was up. "Nary a single wee germie." He hugged her then went to the kitchen to pour a cup of coffee.

"Ian, I'm going to kirk. Maybe yee should join me and wash away your sins." This was the first time she'd seen him before noon since he'd arrived. He wasn't even hungover. Steph eyed him suspiciously. "What did Billy say about this whole *Mike's a murderer* situation?"

"I got the full scoop. Plus, Billy and I had another kind of adventure last night

But you'll have to make ma breakfast to hear more."

"Naw, this can't wait. What happened to Mike's fiancée?"

"Bloody hell. This Jeffrey arsehole is a right bastard. Billy told me the whole situation." He blinked, wide-eyed, then rubbed his eyes. "Please, Stephanie, I'm famished. I'd love some eggs, tomato, and toast." He nodded towards the stove. "I hae a right tale 'bout our big fanny Jeffrey."

Steph followed him into the kitchen, her curiosity piqued. What could these two knuckleheads be up to? "What do you know about Jeffrey?"

"Eggs, tomato, toast." Ian looked smug. He had something to tell, and he knew information about Jeffrey was worth the bargain.

"Ian, I'm no gonna lift a finger until ye tell me what you're playing about." She crossed her arms, glaring at him.

"Naw." He crossed his arms too, mimicking her defiance. "This is too good to not get ma breakfast first."

"Och, Ian. You're not gonna push me around."

"Two words, Stephanie. FBI," he said, holding up two fingers.

"That's three letters, ya numpty." She eyed her little brother. "The FBI?" Now he was just playing games with her. The wee gomerel and his childish new friendie playing spies. "Is Mike's situation connected to the FBI?"

"Stephanie, the eggs and I'll tell ye about what we found at Jeffrey's crackin' condo." He used the same description she had in the car on Friday night.

Her defiance fell to the floor, shattering. "What in the bloody hell are you talking about? You and Billy were at Jeffrey's?"

"Ah, now I have yer attention. Eggs." Ian smiled and stretched as if he had all the time in the world.

Steph lit the stove, her mind swirling with relief that whatever Ian had been messing around with didn't find him sitting in a jail cell. Most likely he'd added the FBI just to get the breakfast. It was 9:15. Making it to church would depend on what kind of story Ian told.

Within a few minutes, Steph plated Ian's bribery meal and sat down next to him. "Spill the beans, Ian."

Ian sank his fork into the fried egg and dunked a strip of toast into the yolk that oozed out.

"Salt, please." Ian smiled, toying with her.

She passed him the salt, slamming it on the table. "Ian!"

"Hold yer knickers, woman." Ian took another bite, watching her closely. "Billy and I came up with a plan on Friday night when we were making friends with the wee lassies. Billy sells flats, right?"

"Go on." If he had been in Jeffrey's flat, that was breaking and entering. This was serious.

Ian talked around the bite of toast. "Well, I mentioned where Jeffrey's flat was..." He swallowed and sipped his coffee. "A tiny glass of orange juice would be fab." Ian lifted his chin towards the fridge.

Steph crammed down her annoyance as she went to the kitchen and poured the brat his juice, hoping he would get to the bloody point before she choked it out of him.

Ian sipped the juice, smiling sweetly. "Thank you, luv. Saturday evening Billy had an appointment to show a flat in the same building. Get this. It was three down from Jeffrey's." Ian's eyes were wide.

Maybe she really did not want to hear the rest of this. "How do you break in when he's there, Ian? He's likely to shoot you, or at least beat the crap out of you."

"Jeffrey is out of town. He's not been there for a few days. Billy let me in while he tidied up for the appointment and turns out it was vacant." Ian saw her puzzlement. "Billy's condo, not Jeffrey's."

"Och, Ian, I know."

"Stephanie, you know why wee Stevie is still locked up at Bar L?" His face lost the playful smile. Bar L was the nickname of the prison in Glasgow.

"I certainly do. Breaking and entering while he was blootered. Get to the point, Ian, or I'll wring your little neck."

Ian smiled, but his demeanor changed to a more serious tone. "I was dead sober this time. Made all the difference."

"Ian, please. What did you find out about Mike?"

Ian updated her on the entire Kelly situation Billy shared with him. Then told her about his time at the crackin' condo.

∞

Ian was excited to get back to the pure adrenaline rush of his favorite Glaswegian pastime.

Billy gave him a salute. "Dude, are you sure you're not going to kill yourself? Because I will totally lose my client and about thirty grand." He laughed, but it faded as the truth of his words hit home.

"If I fall, you're welcome to go back home and act like nothing happened. I promise my ghost will not haunt you." Ian opened the slider and scoped out the situation on the veranda.

"Well, that's a relief," Billy said halfheartedly. "Good luck, man. I'm not gonna watch. I can't even..." Billy covered his mouth as he glanced down the five stories to the road below.

"Lighten up. Don't you have faith in me, Billy?" Ian slapped him on the back, making Billy even more uneasy.

Billy nodded. "I do. What if it's locked, man? You'll have to climb back." Billy glanced at the sky. "What if that storm comes and you have to return in the rain?"

They'd waited until it was after midnight. Directly across was another building under construction, so there wouldn't be any witnesses from that side. The biggest obstacle would be the three verandas he'd have to climb across. They'd scoped it out carefully. There was a single lady and her dog in the first veranda, and a couple at the second one, and Jeffrey's after that.

The first veranda was closed up tight, blinds drawn and lights out. Either they were asleep or not home. The hardest part would be the six feet to cross to the next veranda. The fall would kill him for sure. Challenge accepted. He always worked best under life-and-death circumstances. Forcing his gaze forward and not at what would cause his untimely demise, Ian climbed over the railing and imagined every step, playing it out in his mind like a movie. A support beam stuck out two feet, so he would have somewhere to jump. The first one would be the hardest.

Ian closed his eyes and said a wee prayer. Then a burst of adrenalin surged, and he rode it across the gap, landing one foot on the beam. He gripped the railing, and in a quick motion stepped over it, crossing in front of the sliding glass door. Ian steadied himself and listened for any movement inside. He'd not considered all the plants blocking the railing. A siren sounded off in the distance, urging him forward. Had someone seen him and called the police?

Ian perched on the edge and scoped out the next balcony, relieved the dog wasn't barking his head off. The next condo had the blinds open, but the lights were off. "Shit."

There didn't seem to be movement inside. Hopefully, they were asleep. *Now or never.* He jumped, one foot landing and sliding. In a panic he reached out for the railing and climbed over, quickly crossing the other side. A small dog appeared, barking frantically.

Damn it, they'd mixed up the flats—this was the one with the dog. Ian climbed over the railing and jumped to the next balcony, heart beating rapidly. One more to Jeffrey's unit. Ian ducked behind tall plants just as someone let the dog out. "Haylee, hush."

Hopefully, the cloak of night and the tall plants would block the woman's view of him. If anyone were awake in the flat, they'd see his arse pressed against the glass.

The dog continued to bark, and the woman said, "What is it, girl?" Finally, the sound of the slider closing, and dampened barking, indicated he was in the clear.

In a flash, Ian ran in front of the window, then climbed the railing and eyeballed the next target. A rumble of thunder in the distance urged him on. This would be nearly impossible in the rain. The next one was Jeffrey's. At least the dipshit wasn't home, and he had nae pets. Ian jumped, grabbed the railing, and climbed over, ducking behind Jeffrey's grill in case anyone was watching from the veranda he'd just crossed. He heard nothing but street traffic from the opposite side of the building.

Ian patted his pocket and felt the tools of his trade. Jeffrey would never know he'd been there. This time he was stealing information, not items to fence, making his retreat considerably easier. The sliding glass door lock was crap and thank blessed Mary there was nae security bar holding the door closed. Like most people, Jeffrey figured no one would be stupid enough to climb across and risk their life. Jeffrey had not figured on Ian McKay. A white shield on the glass noted the alarm system, which was a friendly reminder to address that pronto. The cheap plastic contacts at the top of the slider confirmed their presence. Bah, nae problem.

Ian pulled the packet of tools and black gloves out of his pocket, feeling like Tom Cruise in *Mission Impossible*. In less than a minute he'd jimmied the lock but didn't open the door. First, he had to find the alarm pad. Jeffrey's curtains were open, and he peeked inside, hoping the telltale flashing light would give away its location. Either way it would be close to the door. Likely this would trip the alarm, which would drastically cut into his time to search. Damn it, he was hoping to not leave any evidence that he'd been there.

He debated about using the glass cutters. Given the circumstance, it was a necessary evil. Damn Jeffrey for having an alarm. In two minutes flat, he'd made quick work of the glass and released one side of the plastic contact, then taped both sides of the contacts together. Next, he'd have to secure the motion detector. *Thank you, Stevie, for the education. Sorry for your sacrifice.* At least he was using his skills for good this time. What would Stephanie say? She'd likely forgive him if it turned up anything useful. A nagging doubt surfaced. What if he couldn't disarm the motion detector? Would the system function like the ones in Scotland? Shit. He held up the tiny mirror, looking for the telltale red light of the motion detector.

Chapter 32

Dingus

The long, dry grasses and rolling hills blurred past as Ronnie clung to Smokey's mane. Ronnie shared Clayton's horse and was constantly jostled by his movements that never seemed to sync with hers. Her already battered body exhausted quickly, eventually numbing her mind to the constant assault. Eventually the land flattened out to parched grasslands, providing a clear view of the horizon in every direction.

The men were deep in their own thoughts and made little effort to speak, pulling on Ronnie's already frayed nerves. She pondered Rose's situation, which had suddenly become her own, and wondered why she'd been left alone to be nearly scalped. From what Jere Miah said, Rose had run off and put them all in this situation.

In her more lucid moments, which were becoming sporadic, Ronnie studied the men and their gear. Her best estimate was late 1800s. Their dress and weapons strapped on every man and horse were much more modern than she'd seen in her previous travels. It all reminded her of the old Westerns and the TV show *Bonanza* she'd watched in reruns as a kid.

When the pace slowed, Clayton slowed down to let Max catch up. He looked shell-shocked, with a wide-eyed expression, his hat casting a shadow from the urgent sun.

"Max, you should drink. You're looking a bit worn out."

Without words, almost zombie-like, Max reached back and grabbed the canteen, absently sipping from it, then capped it and retied it to the saddle. He said something to Clayton, but his words whipped away in the wind.

"Max, snap out of it, we're falling behind." Clayton led their horse close to Max's and leaned over to smack the animal's rump, causing it to jolt forward. Thankfully, this sparked some motion on Max's part to keep the pace.

Jere Miah slowed his horse to talk to Clayton. Anger oozed off him like the sweat dripping onto his shirt. A brutality emanated from his every pore. "How did you find Rose?"

Clayton turned to Jere Miah. His words were concise, but they showed something else—respect. "Mighty close to being too late. Once the herd broke up, I found them a half mile away. Looked like the injun's horse had been caught in a 'dog hole but it hadn't deterred him. I suppose he thought she were dead and no good for ransom.

171

Sure looked that way to me, too. But thankfully I got there just in time to murder the son of a bitch and save her hide. Shot 'im dead as he was fixing to scalp her." Clayton shook his head.

Ronnie's mind leapt to that moment, replaying her arrival, adding Clayton's description. Her blood ran cold. The tear that had fallen on her cheek had not been one mourning her loss. It had been sweat from the effort of the Comanche's final act, one of pure hatred and violence. He was a millisecond from scalping her, likely in revenge for all the horrible things her people had done to the Natives. Fear coalesced in her throat and her eyes watered. Would that be her fate in this life, to be brutally murdered?

Max was watching her as if waiting for a response.

Her mind played back his words. She'd heard him speak but just hadn't paid attention. "Really, I don't remember..." Ronnie met Max's eyes. She was caught there, lost in his gaze. Neither of them could look away. A thrill of adrenalin coursed through her body as she saw something there that gave her hope. Was this the good guy she encountered every time she traveled? Was this Mathias or Morris but in a different window of time? The sparks flew between them for a drop of endless time.

Jere Miah interrupted the moment, punctuating his terse words with rapid blinks. "We're nearly there."

Annoyed at the interruption, Ronnie braved a question and immediately regretted it. "Where are we going?"

Jere Miah's tone said it all—he'd had enough of this excursion, and she was the cause of his ire. "Takin' you back. We'd not be in this scramble if'n you'd stayed with your man." His eyes narrowed. "Speed it up, fellas, watering hole ain't far from here." Jere Miah rode off ahead, glancing back with an expression of disgust.

Her cheeks felt hot, and the spell was broken. Ronnie felt terrible for putting everyone in this situation. Of course, she knew it wasn't her doing, but Rose's. Clayton urged their horse back to the front and they rode silently. Ronnie felt Natives' eyes all around and feared they would attack at any second.

Clayton nudged her to face forward, growing annoyed with her constant shifting.

∞

An hour later, with the horses watered, they returned to their mounts and continued their trek across the plains. An eerie feeling of déjà vu struck her, and she explored its origins. On her previous trip back, she'd arrived in the body of a woman who was being buried. Everyone who had seen her rise from the grave thought she was devil spawn. Ronnie's gut tightened, remembering the vicious anger directed at her. Morris had stood by her side, but she'd decided to run away to spare him.

Her choice had caused a cascade of horrible events leading to the destruction of the entire town. Would this play out the same way? She'd finally been able to research the names, confirming her suspicion that she had been part of the ill-fated Lost Colony of Roanoke Island off the coast of what would later be North Carolina. It still remained one of America's earliest mysteries. When the governor returned to the island a few years later, he found everyone, and everything, gone. The only thing that remained was a carving in a nearby tree with the words *Croatan* marked on the trunk.

She'd not found anything showing Morris had survived the brutal Native attack that sent her back to her own time. As she'd left that body and returned to her own in Florida, her entire world shattered, both worlds in fact, nearly killing her. When she left this time, would she return to Puerto Rico in the same near-death state? Her mind wandered along the stretches of time she'd visited and settled on each horrible ending. She'd been torn away from, what felt like, her soul mate at the hands of an evil man. Would that pattern repeat here? She dreaded that moment, but the knowledge that she had some control of when she returned gave her a small amount of relief. She could take her own life and force the return.

Soon the sun grew tired and lay along the soft plains, ready for a long night's rest. They stopped to make camp. The stars above spoke of another time and place, for they shone in such abundance it hardly looked like the night sky she knew. It made her think of summers during her childhood, playing hide-and-seek in the dark with her brother, David, and their friends in the neighborhood.

By all appearances, these men had slept out in the open air too many times to count. Each man knew his role. They unsaddled horses, gathered fuel, and set up camp. Ronnie wondered what they could possibly use for a fire, since there was not a tree in sight.

Feeling useless, she approached Max, encouraged by his smile. "Can I help you with anything?"

Max squinted with the last of the sun in his eyes as it readied to dip beyond the horizon.

"No, I've got it." Max lifted the saddle off the horse and Ronnie removed the blanket, then followed him to the camp. He was the only one who made an effort to be pleasant. The other men gave her no more than a snort when she came near.

Max set the saddle down and Ronnie handed him the horse blanket. The other men had laid them flat lengthwise to the fire, creating a spoke pattern with the fire at the center and the saddle at the end away from the fire. Max did the same but took the extra step of curling the ends of the blanket up at the edges with small rocks. Ronnie knelt and helped him.

"Why are you doing that?" Ronnie nodded at the rock in his hand.

"Bath tubbing," Max responded to her puzzled look. "It helps keep bugs off while I'm sleeping."

Ben approached and kicked the ground, sending sandy soil onto Max's blanket. "Stop that tomfoolery and help us settle in."

Max stood looking eye to eye with Ben, squaring his shoulders. "What would you like me to do?" They were about equal height, both taller than the other men and solidly built.

"Carry your weight around here, boy. Just take care of the camp duties you did last night." Ben lifted his chin and tilted his head towards the horses.

Max turned on his heel and walked to Gary, who was hobbling the horses.

Ben shot Ronnie an angry look. "I hope you appreciate Clayton saving you from that savage. By the sound of it, it was a real close call." He shook his head and looked grave. "Dumb as dirt to leave our camp, Rose. Don't get that inkling again, you hear?"

"I won't." Ronnie was shamed, as if she were a young child again, not fully understanding her sins.

"Sit right there near the fire so Jere Miah can keep an eye on you." Ben pointed at a blanket. "I don't mean to be harsh to you on account of your tumultuous day. But if we're all going to get back alive, you need to follow some rules." Ben spoke sternly, counting on his fingers with each point he made. "First, do not leave camp unattended. Do not make loud noises. All our lives are at stake here. The noise carries across the plains, and they'll be on us in no time." He flattened down his mustache.

"I can do that. I would hate to put anyone in harm's way." It had been Rose who'd angered him, but she felt the burden of his words heavy on her shoulders.

"If you'd not been so foolish this morning, we'd be back in town with our bellies full of vittles. Instead, we have another night out here." Ben placed a big hand on the back of his neck and Ronnie flinched, afraid he would strike her. His anger softened when he noticed the tears forming in her eyes. "Perhaps you didn't know the dangers Texas delivers. But your gumption to leave Jeb is what got us all into this mess. I don't need to tell you what could happen, for it almost did—scalped and left to rot in the grass. Don't let them get ahold of you again, Rose. And for heaven's sake, don't get us all killed because of *your* carelessness. Do I make myself clear?"

Ronnie nodded. "I won't." A trickle of fear edged back in with the clear and present danger.

"Good. Now you get comfortable, and Jere Miah will get some food and coffee going shortly."

Jere Miah blinked rapidly and nodded, his mouth tight in disapproval. The unevenness of his ears gave him a young, comical look, but hard steel shone in his eyes, providing a disturbing contrast, like the killer clown in a horror movie. Not so funny. She watched him build the fire with dark, oddly shaped kindling He was older than she'd initially thought, likely in his late twenties. He'd obviously seen hard times in his life.

Ronnie took Max's advice, building a perimeter, propping the blanket up with small stones and sticks, hoping the bugs would stay away. Jere Miah got the fire blazing using dry grass as the final ingredient. "Jere Miah, what are you using for firewood there? I didn't see a branch anywhere around."

He kicked a loose chip with his boot to shove it under the others in the pile under the flames. "Ma'am, we use dried buffalo chips. They're all over these parts."

"Poop?" she asked.

Jere Miah blinked in rapid succession, giving the impression of an absentminded professor. His instant response belied that impression. "Well, I don't know what *poop* is, but it's droppings from the buffalo."

The only odor was smoke and a slight scent of burning grass. "I didn't know you could use that as fuel."

"Yes, ma'am. It's quite plentiful. As you can see, there are no trees anywhere. Back in Missouri, we have a mite larger selection of wood to use, but around here we take what nature gives us."

"Glad for it. The temperature is dropping fast." Ronnie scooted closer to the fire and held out her hands, soaking in the heat from the flames. The warmth of the day was dissipating into the cloudless sky. It would be a cool night and she hoped the horse blanket would be warm enough. Did someone have a rolled blanket for her?

Jere Miah nodded as he set a pot on the flames and emptied a nearby canteen into it. Soon the other men gathered around the fire and ate from their saddlebags while waiting for Jere Miah to finish cooking dinner. When the water boiled, he emptied a dark substance into it from a small burlap sack. The scent of strong coffee gave away the contents. In another pot, Jere Miah emptied several cans of beans and stirred it with a knife.

Gary approached from the darkness and handed Jere Miah a bundle wrapped in leather. It was a huge chunk of meat from an injured bison they'd encountered at the watering hole.

Max handed her a biscuit, and she bit into it, nearly breaking a tooth. "Careful, it's hardtack." Max smiled.

Ronnie held it awkwardly while she watched the men gather around the fire and settle in for the night. Clayton approached and held out a blanket and small leather pouch. Inside was a comb, a cloth, and some hardtack of her own. The sun had set, and the only light was from the fire that threw shadows all around, adding an unsettling, ethereal feel to the camp. The horses were nearby, as evidenced by the occasional snort. When the coffee boiled and sat for a spell, the men dipped tin cups in the pot, coming away with grounds sticking to the edges.

The men were quiet but finally Gary spoke up. "Look, we're almost home. Let's be grateful that Rose is okay, and we didn't lose Max."

Jere Miah added another few chips to the fire from a pile nearby. "I'm grateful. I just want to be back in my own bed." He glanced at Ben as he spoke, and the other men turned their heads to see what Ben's response was.

Ben set down the tin cup he was holding and turned sharply towards Jere Miah. "Look here, dingus, the only reason we are out here is because of you. This whole plan was cockamamie to start with."

"Ben, I don't rightly appreciate your use of the word dingus." He glanced at Ronnie. "Not in front of the lady."

Ben stood and walked the few steps to stand behind Jere Miah. "Why don't you tell the men the reason I call you dingus?" Ben gripped Jere Miah by the neck and shoved his head down, making him spill coffee on his pants.

Jere Miah stood and faced Ben. He was a few inches shorter. "There is no need for this, Ben. Uncle Macy asked me to find her, and you know it. Don't get all sore with me because it's gone to hell in a handbasket."

Ronnie felt her cheeks blush. "I am sorry for any trouble I caused you all." She glanced around the campfire at the worn faces.

Ben ignored her, cleared his throat, and turned to Jere Miah. "Hold your hand up, dingus."

Jere Miah shook his head and shot Ben an angry glance. "No, I will not oblige."

Ben leaned over and grabbed his shoulder. "Hold your left hand up. Imma tell the gang here why I call you dingus."

Jere Miah held both his hands up. "Dad burnit."

Ben nudged the middle finger on Jere Miah's left hand. "Look here, fellas. Dingus and I were in the Confederate Army a few years back, as you all know."

In the low light, just barely visible, the last knuckle of his index finger was missing, and a violent scar was visible.

"Dingus here was shot. But not by murdering Union scum, mind you. He earned this name fair and square by blowing off his goll-durn finger cleaning his pistol." Ben tossed the hand forward and Jere Miah pulled it close to his chest, cradling it.

Ronnie looked around at the dirty, stubbly faces. Clayton was chuckling, showing white teeth in the low light, eyes shining in the glow of the fire. The other faces were smiling. All except Max. His eyes were huge as he glanced from Ben to Jere Miah. He seemed to deflate as he exhaled.

"What's a' matter, Max? You queasy all of a sudden?" Ben asked.

"Yeah, I'm not liking the image of so much blood," Max said, clearly shaken by the story.

"Just keep this image in mind as you listen to young Jere Miah here. He is a first-class dingus, and his judgment is represented nicely by that story. Next time he talks about some half-witted scheme, walk away. No, don't walk, run as fast as you can in the opposite direction."

Clayton and Gary laughed again. Jere Miah glared around the campfire, silencing the men. He blinked rapidly and returned his gaze to Ben. "You're unconscionable."

The men laughed louder, and Gary slapped Jere Miah on the back. "Dingus, don't cry, man."

Jere Miah pulled out his revolver and pointed it at Gary's left eye. "You will not call me dingus, you hear." He pointed the gun at the other men. "None of you's." He punctuated his words with a succession of rapid blinking. He followed Ben as he took his place on the empty blanket.

The men good-naturedly held their hands up and mumbled they wouldn't. Gary chimed in, "Settle down, Jere Miah. This whole goat rope is going to be over soon. Tomorrow morning, we will deliver Rose and be done with this unfortunate situation. We'll all be toasting their merry reunion and be on our way."

Jere Miah glared at Ben and shook his head, then stabbed the hunk of meat in the pan and turned it over. The meat glistened in the low light, singed nicely from the flames sealing in the juices.

Max caught Ronnie's eye and pressed his lips together.

Max cleared his throat. "What if Rose doesn't want to go back? You all know he's a son of a bitch. For Christ's sake, he's already struck her."

Ronnie's heart lifted from the grim conversation and saw the potential for an ally. All eyes were on Max now.

Ben focused his anger on Max. "You want Rose for yourself, old Max?"

Max touched her hand, signaling her to keep quiet. "Clayton filled me in on the situation with Jeb." Max turned to study her face, then looked around the campfire at each man. "You all know she lost the baby when he threw her down the stairs." Max's gaze shifted to Ben. "Or is your loyalty more to a wife-beater than Rose or that poor baby?"

Ronnie was going back to an abusive relationship. No wonder Rose had run away from Jeb. Had she been trying to end her life by throwing herself in harm's way?

Would they turn on Max now?

The men exchanged glances. Ben spoke up. "No one is changing these plans. Rose will be in the care of Uncle Macy, and he will deal with her situation as he sees fit." He made eye contact with each man. "None of you will interfere. Do you understand?" The men nodded and Ronnie's heart sank. Her chances for escaping were evaporating before her eyes.

Jere Miah stirred the beans and ladled the food into tin cups, setting them in the dirt in front of him. He stabbed the meat, lifting it out of the pan to check its progress, then set it back down, moving the pan next to the cups. He sliced the long slab into bite-size pieces and dropped the chunks into the cups. Gary passed the food to his left, and Clayton to his right, reaching everyone around the fire.

Ronnie took her cup and waited for it to cool, half listening to their conversation while lost in her own frightening thoughts. Would Jeb beat her like Jack had when she'd first time travelled to London? When that thought saturated into her already frayed nerves, Ronnie's mind ruminated back to Puerto Rico. Was she unconscious on the floor with Mike hovering over her lifeless body? Was he responsible for killing Kelly?

Finally, the day caught up with her, and her mind numbed. She took a tentative bite of the hot, lumpy food. It reminded her of the gruel she'd been served in the London prison with the fingernail in it. It smelled good, and she was hungry enough to eat it regardless of how bad it was. Ben set the hardtack in the cup to soften it up. Ronnie copied him and was glad for it. There were only so many beans she wanted in her system, but the hardtack softened nicely and did enough to fill her belly. The meat was tough, but flavorful. Soon she was too sleepy to keep her eyes open and lay back, gathering the blanket around her. Max reached over and made sure her feet were covered.

It was a small comfort to hear the male voices telling stories around the fire as she drifted off to sleep. At least they offered protection from Natives, if not from the violent man named Jeb. Just before she dozed off, she said a prayer for their safety.

Chapter 33

Snake Bite

Ronnie was running along a cliff, holding her cloak tightly to her chin. Wind was blowing intensely at her back, urgently pushing her along, sucking away any remaining warmth her cloak attempted to hold close to her body. She glanced behind her, and hair whipped in her face, blocking the already limited view in the fog. What was chasing her? Whatever it was grunted like a hungry animal, spiking the fear that was already growing. Her foot caught on a root, and she stumbled forward, reaching, clawing at the cliff face, but to no avail. The rock she clutched fell with her over the side of the precipice, wind pulling at her cloak and billowing it into the air behind her. Noises that didn't belong tore through space and time and she woke with a start. A man crouched down near her and was shaking her shoulder.

The edges of consciousness overtook Ronnie's dream and it occurred to her that it was the same one that had been plaguing her for a while now.

The man said, "Rose, it's time to go."

Her world caved in, and she fully woke to her new reality. She was back in time, and this would be the day she was reunited with Jeb, Rose's abusive husband.

Max smiled. "Sleepyhead, wakey," he teased. She sat up with a start, looking straight into his dark, liquid eyes. "Easy now, Rose. Let me help you."

Ronnie was mesmerized, feeling like she was peering into his soul. Ronnie recognized a flash of home, a glimpse of someone she'd known for centuries. Did Max feel it too? He held her gaze and reached for her hand, grasping it and pulling her closer. It was impossible to look away, for what she saw in his expression was so familiar. She searched her memory of what it felt to be close to Mathias. This was different. She examined every nuance of the feelings that were stirred in her heart and asked it if Morris were here in this man. Again, it was different, but very similar. In different circumstances she would have eased forward and kissed him, but here and now, there were too many eyes watching. Ronnie's breath quickened and she looked away, losing her nerve. Max helped her stand and kept his hand cupping her elbow with a comforting touch. She wanted to deepen the intimacy, but they were not alone.

Ben walked towards them. "Max, get her ready to leave. The sun is gonna be upon us shortly."

Max's hand moved to the small of her back and she felt she may die a little if he lost contact with her. Damn, she was being dramatic. *Pull yourself together, Andrews.* Ben leaned down to pick up her blanket and walked towards his horse, rolling it as he did, and she turned her attention back to Max.

Clayton walked toward Ben and pointed at her, shaking his head. They stopped talking as she approached.

Ben cleared his throat. "Clayton needs a break from carrying you."

"Max, she's riding with you?" Ben barked.

She hid her smile.

Max responded, "No problem." Then he turned to her. "I'm not the horseman Clayton is, but I'll do my best for you."

Ronnie glanced around to see if any of her meager belongings were left behind. Someone had packed them for her. Jere Miah was spreading the remains of the fire and kicked dirt over the rest of it. The other men were mounted on their horses waiting for them.

Max cupped his hands and waited for her to mount the horse.

She smiled at him. "Thank you for riding me today." Then rubbed her brow, hiding her embarrassment, realizing too late how raunchy it sounded.

Max blinked in surprise, then he smiled. "At your service, ma'am." She hoisted herself up on the horse, grabbing the pommel, and settled in the saddle. Max stepped in the stirrup and Ronnie watched the muscles of his shoulders bunch as he mounted the horse and tried to quell the naughty thoughts coursing through her mind, ashamed of her Freudian slip.

An idea grew stronger as they rode through the dry western landscape. Her worries about its success grew as well. Ronnie knew one thing for certain—she was not going back to Jeb. Her return would be a disaster. The only abuse she'd ever endured was at Jack Ingram's hand in her first trip back in time. That small taste was enough to spur her on, unwilling to allow anyone to have the opportunity to hurt her again. What Jack had delivered was nothing compared to what a man could do to a woman. She clung to the idea that Rose had to be running from something pretty horrible to risk being scalped by a Native.

Max had shed light, so these men knew exactly what they were doing when they returned her to Jeb. They had no conscience and plainly were in it for the money. Ronnie would have to create an opportunity to escape or die trying.

As they rode, Max increased his grip around her waist. Instead of making her nervous about the possessive way he held her, she relished the energy it gave her. She felt alive, powerful, and not alone in this world.

Ronnie glanced back, catching a smile that warmed her to the core. There was something about Max she wanted to dive deep into, like the shimmering Caribbean she'd enjoyed with Mike before everything went to hell. Was Ini right? Was this the man who connected her to this time period? Would he help her escape or at least look the other way and give her a head start? Settling into the ride, Ronnie's mind began to wander. As a kid, she'd loved watching reruns of *Bonanza*, enjoying the adventure of the wide-open land waiting to be explored coupled with the simplicity of only needing a horse and a few supplies out on the range. Watching Little Joe wasn't half bad either.

∞

Ronnie's ruminations were interrupted by the horse stopping dead in its tracks, causing her to fall over his neck, giving her an excellent view of the enormous rattlesnake coiled on the ground in front of them, tail raised and rattling in warning. Max tried to maneuver around it, but the horse was paralyzed with fear.

Max whistled and spurred their mount, but the rattler coiled and struck out, just barely missing its foreleg. The horse whinnied and reared up. Ronnie gripped the horse's mane, leaning forward, pulling free from Max's grip, who fell in the unexpected melee and landed squarely on his ass. The horse nearly missed Max's head but was coordinated enough to scramble at the last second and instead crushed his hand. Ronnie heard the crunch of bones and reached for the reins, pulling the horse away from further trampling him. Max cried out in pain and scrambled away from the coiling snake, readying for another strike.

Ronnie eyed the wide-open landscape and the men who continued to ride on, oblivious to their plight. She debated for a split second about spurring the horse and escaping. Jere Miah turned and called out to the other riders.

Her attention returned to Max. The rattler was ready to strike. Before she could cry out, Max grabbed a nearby rock in his good hand and thwarted the snake's strike at the last second, then he rolled and scrambled to his feet, stepping away from the snake. It was enraged and followed him, startling the already terrified horse into near frenzy. It reared up again, this time dumping Ronnie on the solid, dusty ground, knocking the air out of her lungs, dashing her hopes of any escape with or without Max.

Ronnie struggled to fill her lungs but realized there were more pressing concerns. She'd lost sight of the snake and scrambled to her feet, terrified that it would strike at any second. It coiled and launched itself towards her arm and she braced for the impact. Instead of pain, the crack of a gunshot tore through the air. The snake writhed on the ground, headless, blood oozing out of the stump. Ronnie watched the life force of the beast soak into the dry, sandy soil and had to turn away when Max stabbed the snake's body with his knife and held it up.

"Got 'im!" Max said, a rush of adrenalin making his face redden. "Wow, look at this! It's almost as tall as you!" He held it up to her, making Ronnie step back away. It was nearly five feet long and was still twitching.

Max's horse was spooked and ran at breakneck speed across the grassland. The other men made their way back to Max and Ronnie on horseback.

Gary rushed over and pointed at the snake still attached to Max's knife. "That's a keeper. Gonna make us a fine meal tonight. Nice work." Gary clapped Max on the back, then noticed how he held his hand close to his body. "Max, were you struck?"

Max shook his head. "No, my horse clipped me, after she dumped me on the ground." He held out his left hand and the bones stuck out at a problematic angle.

Ronnie turned away, nauseated at the deformity. "Oh God, Max."

Ben called out as he approached, leading his horse by the reins, "Max, every Native in twenty miles was just alerted to our presence."

Jere Miah dismounted and walked over to them, letting his horse roam free. Blinking in between each word he said, "Thrown from your mount? You've gotta be joking." He glared at Max. "Your ineptitude will get us all killed, Max."

"The beasts have conspired against me." Max's voice was laced with anger. "My mount lost his nerve and dumped us. I'd like to see you do better under the circumstances, dingus."

Jere Miah blanched at the unwanted nickname and took a few rapid steps to close the distance between them. "I've had about enough of you. I've about half a mind to murder you right here in this patch of dirt."

Max took a step back, holding up the knife-stabbed snake to fend off the aggressive Jere Miah. "What the fuck is wrong with you, man?" Max jutted his jaw, putting the dead snake between them.

Gary helped Ronnie to her feet and glared at Jere Miah. "Now listen here, you fools. We are not here to kill each other. We have a job to do."

Jere Miah ignored Gary. "And please, by all means, tell me why I shouldn't tan his hide when he fires a weapon, drawing attention to our whereabouts." He shook his head and stepped closer to Max, pushing against Gary's hand. "He already put us in a bad spot yesterday with his incompetent horsemanship when we encountered the Comanche. He nearly got us all killed. Now he insults me and disrespects a woman with foul language?"

Max turned around to her and said, "I am sorry for using such foul language. I guess my rough manners have offended you. I do apologize, Rose." He turned back to Jere Miah. "As for you..." Max lifted the knife, still heavy with the snake, and snapped it like a whip, hitting Jere Miah squarely in the mouth and splashing fresh blood on Jere Miah's boots. "You will keep your half-assed opinion to yourself, or I'll treat you like I did this serpent."

And that was that. It took all the men to pull Max and Jere Miah apart. Ronnie eyed her horse, who was still panting from his panicked run. Could she mount the beast and ride off while they were distracted?

Jere Miah emerged wiping the blood from his mouth with the back of his hand, the split on his lip a black line in the red mess that was smeared on his chin. He reached for his sidearm, but Ben stopped him from drawing it.

Jere Miah said, "He has to go, Frank." Jere Miah glanced around at the other men.

Frank? Ronnie looked at the faces that showed surprise. Had they noticed the slip? Or was their shock due to Max's actions?

Max shot her a glance and shook his head, then grabbed the reins and awkwardly mounted his horse, protecting his broken hand. "Rose, I'm very sorry you had to risk your life with a venomous animal." He nodded at Jere Miah. "Let's just hope he won't bite you with his bloody mouth." Max spurred the animal and rode off in the direction they had been heading.

Jere Miah reached for his pistol, but Ben, or was it Frank, stopped him, struggling and kicking up a cloud of dirt that merged with the billowing cloud from Max's dramatic exit. Finally, Max was far enough away that Jere Miah conceded defeat, but bloodlust clouded his eyes.

Jere Miah picked up the snake that Max had unceremoniously dropped on the ground and flung it as far as he could. "If I ever see him again, he is dead."

"Now, now," Ben said, leading him towards his horse, "he's gone. There is nothing to get sore about anymore." Ben turned to Gary, nodding at her. "Can she ride with you?"

"Yes, sir." Gary motioned her towards his horse.

The pain of the fall hit her, now that the tense confrontation was over. All she wanted to do was sit and nurse her minor wounds, not be jostled to death riding with another man towards an unknown fate.

Gary offered a hand to mount his horse. Her only thoughts were of Max. Would he end up shot between the eyes? In that burst of energy between the two men, her hopes of escaping evaporated, like dust in the wind.

Chapter 34

Chili con Carne and Yellow Fever Dreams

Ronnie grew annoyed at the constant dirt blasting her face as they rode. Clayton, Gary, Ben, and Jere Miah pulled handkerchiefs over their faces and tipped their heads, letting the brim of the bowler hat take the brunt of the blast. No wonder Jere Miah blinked constantly. The air was dry, the sand was fine, and no one had invented sunglasses yet. Ronnie kept her eyes closed and her head down, not having the luxury of any gear to help ease the suffering.

After an hour, they stopped at a natural spring surrounded by a copse of trees. Leery of an ambush, they circled the area, hoping to flush out any would-be attackers. Two deer leapt from the bushes and scattered down the creek and away from them. Gary helped Ronnie off the horse, his hand rough and strong, then he made his way down to the water to make sure it was safe.

When the all clear sounded, the men dismounted and allowed the horses to drink and munch on the deep dark grasses that clustered around the stream.

Gary made small talk with the men. Ronnie knelt down and scrubbed her face in the clear, cool water. The heat emanating from the raw, sunburned skin on her face enhanced the chill of the water. Where was Max? Had he stopped to water his horse or kept riding ahead of them?

Soon it was time to ride again. Gary was leaner than Max, giving her a bit more room, but still it was uncomfortable. Gary lacked the rhythm Max had on the horse. Somehow Max had an innate sense of how to move together with the horse's gait. With Gary it was a constant jostle, adding to her exhaustion, making her less coordinated as they rode.

Ronnie mulled over her options. When could she escape and avoid a reunion with Jeb? She glanced at Ben and Jere Miah, who rode side by side, talking animatedly.

Jere Miah's posture carried an edge of anger, accentuated by the set of his mouth and narrowed eyes. Max would get the hard end of that anger if they ever met again. She inwardly chuckled, remembering how he had used the snake to bridge the gap

Gary had tried to make between them. It had been so unexpected. Max must have known the reaction he would elicit from Jere Miah. In a time where men wore guns and could use them in the heat of passion, it was a bold and incredibly dangerous move. Max had been lucky he'd survived the exchange but would not be so lucky the next time they met.

Jere Miah called out at first sight of the town. From this distance it looked like a small shadow on the horizon, but as they got closer, Ronnie could make out the varying heights of the buildings. Her guts rumbled with stress, making her wish she was not on a horse jostling everything around. Surely Jeb would punish her for leaving him. She mulled over her exit plan she'd already used in two previous time travels— death by suicide. She'd need an opportunity but what could she use? A pistol? She had more to learn, as Ini's theories were still untested. Did Jeb represent the evil one who had plagued her every time she'd gone back? Did he fill the role of Wahab or Jack in a different realm? Maybe Jeffrey with a more violent streak? She had no idea how to prove any of this, but gathering the evidence was crucial to her goal of sorting through this mess. If Ini was right, she needed to break the pattern so she would not have to have it repeat the pattern in her own lifetime.

The horses sensed the proximity of a reprieve and picked up the pace. Her head was aching now, and her muscles were exhausted.

Despite the heat dissipating as the sun set, sweat rolled down her back, soaking into her already filthy beige dress. Uncomfortable undergarments poked into her sides, and she imagined what weird version of stays she wore this time. Dirt encrusted every square inch of the dress, and likely coated her hair and the filthy cap covering the top of her head. It would take a fair amount of scrubbing to make her presentable. Would they deliver her like this to Jeb? Or would she have a chance to clean up, and possibly escape?

The sun was low in the sky as they approached the town. As the men slowed their pace, the animals grouped closer together. Ronnie could hear only snippets of their conversations. Darkness may buy her some time, to postpone the inevitable return to Jeb. So far, the men here hadn't been friendly, but they'd not harmed her.

They rode through the main street of the small town that was a dead ringer for any Western movie set. Ronnie eyed the few people walking on the sidewalk, wondering if they could help her, until they stopped in front of a building. A small hand-painted sign, *Silver Star*, hung above the swinging doors.

"Welcome back to Sterling City, boys," Gary said as he dismounted. He reached up to help Ronnie down, grabbing under her armpits and setting her gently on the ground.

"Thank you, Gary." Ronnie was warmed by his smile. "Is Jeb here?" she asked.

"Oh no, ma'am, we are just wetting our whistle. Jeb isn't far and we will send for him once we arrive at Macy's house." Gary changed his friendly expression to one of concern, his eyebrows meeting, and the corners of his mouth turned down. "Are you nervous about your untimely reunion? If you don't mind me askin'."

"Yes, I am afraid he is going to hurt me," Ronnie answered honestly but played it up a little, hoping to pull on his heartstrings.

"I don't know the man. I'm just hired to help get the job done," Gary smiled as he held the swinging door open for her.

The Silver Star was bustling with men drinking, playing cards, and flirting with women who were dressed up in brightly colored, low-cut gowns. Smoke hung in the air, as did the strong stench of cigar and body odor.

"How far away is Macy from here, Gary?"

"Not so far that we couldn't get there tonight if we wanted to. If'n I had my druthers, I'd sleep in this fine establishment in the upper chambers and get an early start. But as I'm not running this expedition, Ben will have to make that call."

"I'd rather stay here. I don't like the idea of night riding with the Comanche out there. I've seen them up close and personal and would like to pass on another encounter." Ronnie shook her head.

"I understand your sentiment, Rose. I do." Gary led her to a small table in the back of the saloon and held a chair for her.

Jere Miah and Ben sat with Clayton at a different table across the room. It was nice to have Gary to herself, for he was friendly and comforting, unlike the other surly men in the party.

Small talk filled in the time until they ordered the food. Ronnie got up the courage to broach the subject plaguing her. "Where do you think Max is right now?"

Gary looked surprised at her question. "Heck, I suspect he hightailed it back home. He doesn't live far from here. We all reside in the general vicinity of Sterling City." He scanned the room for Ben and Jere Miah and relaxed his expression. "Max really surprised me today. After Jere Miah's warning about calling him dingus, he must have known that it would set him off. What goes through a man's mind is a mystery to me sometimes. Jere Miah's killed men for less than calling him an unwelcome nickname. But the snake incident?" He glanced back at the subject of the conversation. "He was plumb lucky Ben intervened. He could have shot him in the back, and no one would have thought twice about it. We all know better than to anger those boys."

Jere Miah was speaking heatedly with Ben, his face taking on a reddish hue. Was he having the same conversation with Ben and Clayton? Ben glanced at her, leaning away from his dinner companion to nod at her. Ronnie returned the gesture. When Jere Miah turned to see who Ben was acknowledging, a chill ran up her spine. Jere Miah blinked rapidly and pursed his lips, with Max's handiwork bunching awkwardly with the action. She could feel his anger spreading across the room to her table. Jere Miah turned back around and downed the glass of liquor in front of him.

Gary laughed, having witnessed the exchange. "Spitting mad still. That man has a temper, as you can see." He sat back in his chair, allowing space for the server to set their plates down in front of them. Ronnie had asked for the special, not wanting to risk any of the other choices. A steaming bowl of chili con carne, beans with meat, wafted its delicious aroma. It didn't resemble the dish she'd had in modern times. Simply beef, beans, and red peppers in a sauce, it didn't have many ingredients, but it tasted fantastic.

Gary's meal was a simple piece of steak with coleslaw.

"Gary, tell me about yourself. How did you end up here?" She had no expectation about his answer but was relaxing into the meal and was curious about him.

He finished chewing a bite of steak and sat back in his chair. "Aren't you a funny gal? I don't think anyone has ever asked me such a thing, especially not a young woman." He wiped his mouth and thought for a second, then responded, "I'm originally from Tennessee. I suspect you detected a bit of my home state in my voice."

Ronnie hadn't, but nodded agreeably, wanting to hear more.

"I was born in Lawrence County. Are you familiar with it?" Gary shoveled the coleslaw into his mouth, waiting for her to answer.

"Oh, no, I've only been to Memphis on a layover to Tucson." She realized her mistake and hoped he wouldn't ask questions. There was no Memphis airport in these times, and she had no idea what the word layover would mean to him. Or Tucson for that matter.

He was too eager to tell the highlights of his story and didn't seem to notice her error, thankfully. "We decided to move to Texas when I was eleven. My father had the unfortunate happenstance to contract yellow fever on the way. He died in Alexandria, Louisiana." He said it without emotion in his voice, as if he'd come to terms with it, but Ronnie saw the shine of emotion in his eyes. "This left my mother with the five of us with no home, without a dollar to our names."

"Oh my gosh, Gary, what did you all do? What terrible luck."

He paused to take a sip of whiskey and gather his thoughts. "Hard times, you know?" he finally responded. "It was honestly a terrible time. A lone woman stranded in that situation. We had no money to give Papa a proper goodbye. He's buried in an unmarked grave there. I keep meaning to go back and pay my respects."

"How did you end up here in Texas?" Ronnie felt for him, but her heart felt heavy for his mother. Five children depending on her for survival while stranded in a strange place. Ronnie felt a similar desperation, with no money, no power or influence, and stuck in a strange place and time. At least she didn't have the responsibility for five children.

"It was not easy but the six of us worked picking cotton for a planter in Alexandria until we had enough money to continue on our original path to Texas. We finally placed our feet on Texas soil when I was twelve. My brothers ranged from eight to sixteen. We aimed to buy a tract of land in Sabine County, and rightly did so in time, as we earned enough. I ended up in Sterling City shortly after the war, after Mama passed away. God rest her soul."

"Amen," Ronnie said. "What a difficult start to your life, Gary. I'm so sorry you all had to live through that."

He pressed his lips together in a sad smile. "My story is a mild version of the hardships life brings. I'm very fortunate to have survived the war, especially after all we have had to endure." He cleared his throat and glanced over at Jere Miah and Ben. "Those two have seen the harder side of life. Ole Jere Miah joined the war when he had just turned fifteen years of age. He has seen the atrocities of it up close and personal. In fact, he joined up on account of Union soldiers torturing his stepfather trying to get information about Quantrill."

"That is a rough beginning. The war has nearly destroyed the country, hasn't it?" Ronnie didn't know who Quantrill was but was afraid to show her ignorance on the subject. Jere Miah sat quietly now with Ben as they both ate their meals. He looked to be in his mid-twenties and Ben a few years older than that. If he was in the Civil

War at fifteen, it had to be somewhere in the 1870s.

"Those two have seen," he chuckled, "and caused atrocities that would curl your hair. I'd be a fool to cross them. I still can't fathom why Max would break rank and make an enemy of such a pair. Plus, riding away, abandoning his share for all the work he put in. I don't know him well, but he is a trusted man in their circles. Now he will likely be gunned down by the likes of these two, once we deliver you back to your family."

Ronnie blanched at that. The words 'her family' sounded so loving and safe. Jeb was likely neither of those things. "I'd rather not go back there, Gary. I think I'm better off away from Jeb."

"Miss, I don't need to get involved in your matrimonial spats, I really don't. I'm here to return you as those fellas have contracted me to assist. I'll likely part ways with you after tonight and let them continue on to Macy's." Gary pushed away his nearly empty plate.

Something about his tone had changed. Did he feel he'd gotten too friendly with her and regretted it?

Gary continued, "I'm merely a hired hand as a buffer against the Natives out in the prairie. Two men won't get far in these parts if them injuns want to harm you. It's a lot like being around bears, not that we have them in these parts. But out in the wild acres of Tennessee, the black bear rules. If you're in a big group, they won't bother you. If you're off alone, you may be their dinner." He picked up the whiskey glass and emptied it. "Same with the red man. In a group, you're likely to not even know they're around. But like you experienced, once you're alone, they see the opportunity to capture for ransom, or just outright kill you. You're damned lucky Clayton saved you. He said you were fixin' to be scalped. Damn injuns must have thought you were too scrawny to ransom off." He laughed and picked up his hat, clapping it on his head.

"Too scrawny?" Ronnie laughed but sensed Gary's unease. This was his way of politely shutting the door on helping her. She may have no choice but to meet Jeb and deal with the consequences. She'd have to suffer the damage until she could take matters into her own hands.

On every time travel situation she'd faced, the only way back to her own time had been death. It may put her through hell, but she could handle a hell of a lot more than she'd ever given herself credit for before all of her time traveling. Despite what anyone else thought of her, she was proving to be hard as nails. Not completely without moments of bawling her head off, but you could handle only so much before you cracked and let the emotions leak out.

Chapter 35

Skip to the Loo

Ronnie knew time was running out. She'd have to make a move soon to escape before they regrouped. She stood and smiled. "I'm going to freshen up, Gary."

Gary looked puzzled, but then seemed to sort out her meaning. "Don't be too long, you hear?"

Ronnie looked around for the most logical place for the bathroom. A waitress walked by carrying a tray of dishes. "Ma'am, where is your restroom?"

The woman looked Ronnie up and down. "I don't take you for a woman of the variety to be in need of rest." Anger peppered her words.

Ronnie felt her cheeks burn and regretted her choice of words. "I'm sorry, I just need to use the lavatory."

The woman studied Ronnie's face and her expression softened. "Now aren't you Mrs. McIntyre, Jeb's wife?" The lines in her face cracked as she smiled.

"Yes, I guess I am," Ronnie said, making the leap from her use of Jeb's name.

"I'm surprised you didn't recognize me. I'm Jeb's cousin Minnie. He's been looking for you."

Ronnie's stomach lurched. Now that she was back in town, more people would recognize Rose and know of her transgressions.

"Cousin Minnie. Of course, it's wonderful to see you again." Ronnie crossed her legs and made a face. "I'd love to catch up, but I need to use the loo."

Minnie squinted and shook her head. "You best get back home to your husband." She nodded her head to the right through a set of double doors. "You know where the necessary is, dear, just down that hall. I'll send someone along to let Jeb know you're back. He will be so relieved to know you're safe."

"No, really, you don't have to do that. I'm with Ben and Jere Miah. They're taking me back as soon as we're done eating."

Minnie eyed her skeptically. "Oh? Seems an unlikely story. Don't mind if I send word to my cousin. Either way, he will be relieved his dear wife is back."

Ronnie's panic upped a notch. Even better reason to get the hell away from here. She turned and stepped through the doors as Minnie frowned. Halfway down the hallway, a large sign above the door indicated the WC, water closet. A foul odor assaulted her senses, making her eyes water. Indoor plumbing of the late 1800s was severely lacking, although it was a vast improvement from a chamber pot or outhouse. The room was tiny and, other than the smell, not too different from a modern bathroom. A small metal basin sink, and a pitcher of water were on the right and an off-center commode to her left, with a window in between. The commode was a plank of finer wood with an off-center hole and a metal bowl set inside. Weird but efficient. Ronnie peeked out the half-opened window. It led to an alley behind the restaurant. A breeze from the window picked up another odor and Ronnie looked around for its source, curiosity piqued. A small pail of yellowish liquid sat on the floor near the commode. Inside the liquid was a stick wrapped with rags. A strong odor of vinegar mingled in with the poo smells. A revolting thought distracted her from her escape. Did they use the gross rag instead of toilet paper? Ronnie's stomach turned. Did all the patrons share this vinegar-soaked rag to wipe? There was nothing else available.

Pondering this revolting modernity, Ronnie stepped on the commode bench and ducked through the window, dropping onto the ground. A cloud of dirt billowed out and was immediately caught up by the wind. Her foot tangled in a tumbleweed two feet around and she was glad of the boots that covered her ankles. It took some effort, but finally she disentangled it from her skirts, eager to get far away from her captors.

A low light along the horizon lingered from the sun that had already set. Darkness would nicely mask her escape. A narrow alley separated the restaurant from the back of the stores on the next street over. Ronnie glanced behind her then ran towards the alley.

"Hey, you!" a man called out.

It was Clayton and he gave chase.

"Crap!" Ronnie ran across the street and dodged a carriage, narrowly escaping. A flash of memory from the first few seconds in 1752, where she'd been struck by a carriage, spurred her on. Clayton was held up by the carriage and Ronnie took advantage of his blocked view to dodge between the storefronts to an alley on the edge of town. She sprinted towards a huge barn behind a row of houses, gasping to catch her breath.

The animals reacted to her intrusion. A horse in the closest stall neighed. Ronnie startled and stepped away from the door, then ran down the center aisle, hoping to hide somewhere before Clayton barged in and grabbed her. Would the animals give away her hiding spot? The barn was huge with dozens of stalls. Ronnie finally found an empty one and ducked inside, pulling the half door shut behind her. She squatted down in the hay in the back corner, panting to catch her breath, hoping the shadows concealed her presence.

A man's voice called out in a loud whisper, "Rose! Are you in here?"

Ronnie tried to quell her panic and looked around for a better place to hide. If she left this stall, Clayton would see her.

The intruder made his way quietly through the barn while agitated animals stomped and shuffled, marking his progress. He called out again, "Rose, where are you?"

Ronnie held her breath as he approached. *Please keep going!*

A man peeked into the stall. "Rose?"

Ronnie sat stock-still, hoping he wouldn't see her in the low light. A shadowy figure stepped in the stall and carefully shut the door behind him. Why was he being so quiet and careful?

He whispered again, "Rose? Is that you?"

The voice was much deeper than Clayton's. Ronnie stifled a scream, but then noticed his left hand was wrapped with a strip of linen, the same material as his shirt.

"Max?" Ronnie stood and hugged him. "Oh my God, what are you doing here?" A wave of relief washed over her.

Max smiled. "Rose, I was hoping you'd be brave and make a break for it. I saw you enter the restaurant and then kept a lookout for you in case you managed to separate from them."

"You were here all along? Oh my God, I'm so glad. I had no idea what I was going to do next. I thought you were Clayton." Ronnie smoothed down her hair, suddenly conscious of her appearance.

"I think you lost him. He ran down the street after someone dressed like you." Max pulled her down to sit in the hay next to him. "Are you okay? Those men didn't hurt you after I ran off, did they?"

"No, but Jere Miah nearly shot you in the back. You're lucky Ben stopped him. From what I hear, Jere Miah is ruthless and deadly with a weapon."

Max shook his head. "You could say that with confidence. I know his reputation. It's why I made that scene and left."

"You fell off the horse on purpose?" Ronnie was surprised.

"No, Rose. But I saw the opportunity to get away and return to help you escape the fate of rejoining Jeb." He looked down at his bandaged hand. "They told me what Jeb did to you, Rose. I just couldn't let him hurt you again." His eyes shone in the low light.

"What did they tell you?" Ronnie wiped her hands on her skirt.

Max's mouth was a thin line, and he shook his head. "That you lost the baby last spring after Jeb pushed you down the stairs. You show up in town with bruises on your wrists, and one time a black eye." The emotion showed on his face, and he looked away. "No way in hell I was going to let them collect the reward for returning you to a man like that." The set of his mouth said it all—he was pissed. "Sometimes men get angry, and we hit things, but we should never take that anger out on a woman. Ever."

Ronnie couldn't help but think of Mike punching the wall. "Thank you, Max. You're risking a lot to help me. How is your hand?"

"Been better, no doubt." Max held it up and winced when he tried to wave it.

"Broken?" Ronnie resisted the urge to touch it.

"Multiple breaks. I've not been to the blacksmith yet. He apparently is the one to set the bones." He grimaced. "That should be fun. But I didn't want the distraction since I knew you'd be arriving. And here you are."

Ronnie settled next to him in the hay. "I'm so sorry." Her stomach turned with the thought of the blacksmith setting bones with no meds to numb the pain other than booze. Then it struck her. The pattern was consistent in this time period. Max had risked everything to help her. It mirrored what Mathias had done for her in 1752, and what Morris had done to protect her from the mob and the Natives in 1588. Max was repeating the pattern. Their efforts had only delayed her death and caused their own downfall.

Max jutted his chin out. "Why are you looking at me like that? I'm telling you about broken bones and you're smiling."

Ronnie laughed. "Sorry."

"It's okay, I guess I did go on a bit too long on a gory subject. Please forgive me, Rose." His voice softened as he said her name. Not *her* name exactly, but the one he thought was hers. "You remind me of somebody."

Max mirrored her thoughts. His mannerisms and speech reminded her of someone too, but she couldn't quite place it. "Who do I remind you of?"

He shook his head. "Not anyone that you would know. There's something about you, though. I feel like I've known you longer. I mean, we really just met, haven't we?" His expression had changed from serious to almost a shyness around the edges of his words.

Ronnie laughed out of discomfort, but also out of the excitement of knowing he had a similar feeling. "Thank you for taking the risk for me, Max." She leaned in and kissed him gently on the lips.

Max pulled back with his eyes wide, then blinked a few times, before pressing his lips to hers.

If she'd had any doubt about their connection, the kiss confirmed everything she'd known deep in her soul. Something inside her changed, melted with the veil of intimacy now broken.

Max shifted positions, cupping her cheek with his good hand. Finally, after a few minutes, he pulled away. "I'm sorry, I didn't mean to..."

Ronnie pressed a finger to his lips. "Don't be sorry. I'm the one who kissed you."

Max's grin grew to a huge smile. "Well, you got me there."

Ronnie kissed him again, catching the last word on her lips, enjoying the taste of him, the feel of his mouth on hers. Was this Morris in a different time? Mathias perhaps? She pulled away and laid her head on his chest and he stroked her hair.

"Well, that is an interesting development." A little chuckle accompanied his words. "Do you ever wonder why we are here?"

Ronnie enjoyed the rumble of his voice against her ear. "I do often." Ronnie had been asking that question for two months now. Why was she back in time? What did it mean? Ronnie replayed Ini's terrifying words about the bad man and that the evil was wafting off him. Was Jeb this man here in this time, or was it Jere Miah? Either way, she had Max alone and some time to kill.

Ronnie kissed his chin and followed up with a kiss on his mouth. Max wrapped his arm around her and rolled her to rest on the hay. The kiss deepened, and she could taste his passion, and feel his muscular body pressed against her.

After a minute of bliss, Max pulled away and sat up. "I hate to stop that loveliness, but we have to get ahead of our circumstances." He stood and peeked over the stall door.

She'd completely forgotten about Clayton. "He must not have seen me, but they've gotta be looking for me by now."

Max held up his hand, shushing her. Then stood and glanced over the stall door.

The gentle clip clop sound of horse's hooves echoed just outside their stall. She curled up in the darkest corner and Max joined her.

Ronnie moved in front of Max. If anyone was going to get shot, it would be her.

The low rumble of a man's voice carried over the stall. He sang in a deep baritone, "The wealthy and proud may talk as they like, but they'll have to give in to the Eight Hour Strike, hmm, hmmm."

Max looked at her with wide eyes.

Chapter 36

Buttercup

The man opened the stall door next to them and led the horse in, then promptly strode out. "Be right back, Buttercup. I need to fetch some water for you."

Ronnie watched in disbelief as Max snuck into the next stall and returned a moment later leading an elegant palomino with a long silver mane.

Max whispered, "Rose, our free ride has arrived."

Ronnie walked alongside Max and Buttercup out to the back of the barn. The horse eyed them both but didn't protest. He opened the door and looked around the corner. This side faced the wide-open plains.

"Climb up there, Rose."

Fear choked off any resistance and Ronnie used the plank in the stall to ascend the saddle.

A skinny, graying man cried out to them, scaring her as she arranged her skirts. "Howdy, y'all, I'll be right with you."

Ronnie stared at Max, puzzled, and he grinned. "He must think we're here to stable our horse!" Then he waved at the old man. "No rush, old-timer." Max motioned for her to wait as he peered outside. "Hold on to your knickers, Rose, we're making a break for it." He led Buttercup to the side of the barn and handed her the reins. "I'll be right back. Just need to get my noble steed."

Ronnie patted Buttercup's neck, hoping she'd not make any noise that would draw attention from the stable hand or, for that matter, Ben and his crew.

Max arrived on horseback just as the man shrieked, "Hey, you varmint, come back here." The old man chased them for a few paces and gave up.

Max spurred his horse, and Ronnie and Buttercup followed, making their way along the back edge of town, out towards the parched, dusty plains. Hours ago, she'd been desperate to be out of the driving wind. Now it was their salvation. In the dim light of the moon, Max looked magnificent on the towering black horse, his broad shoulders squared and his entire body agile and powerful. They were heading out of town into the dangers of the black, inky night.

"What are our plans, Max?" Ronnie knew their options were limited. They could encounter Natives or find the murderous Jere Miah.

Max waited for her to catch up. "Should we risk riding in the dark to the next town, or hide here someplace?"

"Don't you live nearby? Can't we stay there?" she appealed, not wanting to risk the Natives.

Max turned and shook his head. "Ah..." He scanned the sky, now nearly invisible with no sign of the moon. "We wouldn't last long. They all know where I live."

Max pulled the reins, fighting his mount as it resisted heading out into the blackness.

The horse's hesitation spooked Ronnie. He knew as well as she did the dangers out on the prairie at night. "As much as I hate the idea of riding out there with unknown bands of Natives waiting to ambush us, I don't think it's safe to stay here. Max, Jere Miah will kill you on the spot."

"Yeah, my vote is to take our chances out there." He nodded away from town.

The barn was no longer visible, other than a low light from the lantern shining through the window. "How far is the next town?"

"About an hour ride, maybe more. Entirely possible we get twisted around and not run into anywhere to stop until dawn. We don't have good choices, Rose." Max gained control of his horse. "Are we in agreement then? Head out and risk the devil we don't know?"

Ronnie glanced back at Sterling City, now barely visible. "Yes, the devil we know is determined to find us both."

Max led them away from the security of civilization, and they settled into the ride. He made no attempt at conversation and Ronnie was glad of that, not wanting to draw attention.

The wind was relentless, and the blowing dirt felt like an unremitting barrage of tiny needles. Her eyes stung, and her face was raw, already sunburned and sandblasted. Buttercup politely followed Max, and it suited Ronnie. She could close her eyes and hunch over to keep warm. Temperatures dropped rapidly with the sun no longer warming the land, and she started to second-guess this plan. After an hour, Buttercup's gait changed, and warning bells rang in her head. Were there Natives lying in wait nearby?

"Where are they in such a hurry to get to?" Ronnie's voice cracked.

"Not certain," Max replied, then slowed his horse down to wait for her. "Are you okay?"

"I'm freezing and tired of the blowing dirt." Buttercup caught up and they were side by side.

"Here, take my vest. It'll help a little." Max unbuttoned it and handed it across to her.

"Thank you." Ronnie tied the reins around the pommel and slid the vest on. It was enormous, but his body heat lingered on the leather, warming her considerably. Something solid weighed on the left side, and Ronnie slid her hand into the chest pocket. She pulled out a heavy engraved pocket watch and quickly returned it, patting it gently to be sure it was properly stowed.

Max glanced down as she picked up the reins again. "Hey, do you see that? There is an outbuilding ahead."

"That must be what the animals were reacting to." She sat up now, urging Buttercup forward. What was the etiquette out here? Did you knock on the door and ask to sleep in the barn? Or did you just explain in the morning?

They heard the barking before they could see the dogs, but after a minute, two labs were wagging their tails, welcoming them—one jet-black, the other brown with some white splotches. Buttercup lowered her nose to say hello, while Max's horse was anxious and jumpy, pulling away from the hounds' attention.

With their presence announced by the dogs, they should let the owners know they were on the property. A new worry wormed its way in. What if they knew Rose or Jeb? Was this Uncle Macy's place? This could be a godsend, or a catastrophe.

Max turned to her. "I don't want to be deceitful, but we should probably give them fictitious names, in case they know of your escape."

Ronnie nodded.

Max leaned in close. "Great, just go with what I say."

"Okay." Rose was already her fake name. What was one more falsity?

Max led them to a two-story house and dismounted. Then he gently tapped on the front door. There were so many ways this could go awry. She scanned the night sky, wishing the dogs hadn't forced their hand.

"I suppose we have to let them know we're here. Don't need them worrying about horse thieves or anything." Max knocked on the door while the dogs sniffed his feet, and he patted their heads. He helped Ronnie down from Buttercup and rounded to the door.

Candlelight marked the owner's progress toward them. A tall heavyset man opened the door, gripping a candlestick that he carefully shielded from the wind. He was clad only in long underwear and boots.

"Howdy, sir." The man bowed to Max, then noticed Ronnie. "Ma'am."

Max took off his hat and clasped it to his chest. "Sir, I'm Billy and this is my bride…" Max glanced back at Ronnie, smiling. "Melissa. Is there any chance we could take respite in your barn for the night?"

Chapter 37

Refugees

The man spun around and yelled, "Maggie, we'se got us some fella and his wife needing some vittles!"

Max insisted, "Oh, no, we couldn't impose like that, sir. Please, we just need to stretch out in your barn for the night."

"No, if you've been traveling this late into the evening, you require some nourishments. You've happened upon the right place. Maggie's sausage is the finest around. I can see you have been through a rough patch." He nodded at Max's hand.

"Sir, I don't wish to sound ungrateful, but we couldn't put you out like that." Max glanced back at Ronnie and grinned. "We made it this far without encountering Natives. I expect that's all the luck we require."

"Now that's a bit of the dev'l right there." The man gestured towards a woman approaching from the back of the home. "Please come in and meet my better half, Maggie."

The woman wore a simple dress, and she patted down her hair as she shuffled towards them, beaming. She extended her hand. "So awfully glad to meet you!"

Max took her hand and kissed it. "A pleasure to make your acquaintance, ma'am," Max crooned. "I'm Billy English and this here is my lovely wife, Melissa."

Maggie blushed and held her hand to her bosom. "Such fine manners, Mr. English."

Ronnie stepped closer and bowed her head. "It's a pleasure to meet you."

Maggie nodded. "Welcome to our humble home. Please join us while we break bread."

Max stood on the stoop as Maggie stepped inside the house. "We had no intention of waking you, but your dogs noticed our approach, and we didn't want to worry you. We just wanted to get out of the wind for a spell and would be most obliged to take respite in your barn for the night."

Maggie tied an apron around her midriff. "Don't you be silly. We have this big ole house. You have to get some food in your bellies and sleep in comfort. Then you can set on your way when the sun is up, and the passage is safer." She cast a glance at Ronnie, then looked away, her smile fading. "Sunrise is only a few hours off. You both must be exhausted."

"We wouldn't hear of it, sir, ma'am," Max said. "Just your barn. It's much too late to bother you with making us a meal and putting us up."

"You can call me Lawrence, none of this *sir* stuff. I'm just an ole rancher. Maggie is a fine cook, and when the cooler temps roll in, we get little company out here. We wouldn't hear of you sleeping in the barn like a dirty ole animal." He grinned and then realized he was in his long underwear. "And these are my drawers. Let me do something about that. Just give me a minute."

To Ronnie's surprise, Lawrence swept past her and grabbed Buttercup's reins, then whistled loudly, suppressing the animal's startlement by clutching the halter. Max's horse was munching the sparse grass nearby but glanced up at the sound. A young teenager stepped out of the barn carrying a lantern, looking sleepy and a tad annoyed.

"Boy, please water and stable their horses," Lawrence barked, his tone stern.

Max called out, "Please leave the saddles on. We need to be off in a few hours."

"Yes, sir." The boy grabbed both horses by the reins and led them into the barn as Lawrence ushered Ronnie and Max into the house.

"I'll be right back." Lawrence hurried out of the kitchen towards the back of the house, carrying the candle to light the way.

Maggie lit the candles at the massive wooden table in the heart of the kitchen. "Make yourselves comfortable. I just need to run to the larder." Maggie tapped on the table. "Please sit here. I will be right back."

Max sat next to Ronnie and smirked. "Well, lookie here, we got us a home-cooked breakfast and a warm bed to slumber in, honey." Max's eyes were shimmering in the candlelight.

Ronnie enjoyed the break from the wind, reveling in the prospect of falling asleep in an actual bed rather than on the ground. She lingered on the image of his big, warm body spooning her as she slept. "Yes, we sure do."

Max's gaze remained on hers, making her think he was having the same thoughts. Then she leaned in. "Are we safe here? Do you recognize these people?"

Max shook his head as Maggie returned, bearing a basket of food. Within minutes, she was rattling pots and pans in a flurry to whip up a meal.

"Maggie, you are a godsend. What can we do to help?"

"Don't even think of lifting a finger. Right quick, I can boil you some eggs. We have cornbread leftovers from supper and the finest sausage west of the Mississippi."

"That sounds like a feast for a king, Maggie," Max declared. "Woo-wee, we landed in the right stretch of dirt, didn't we, Melissa?" He chuckled.

"Boy howdy, we sure did!" Ronnie wished they'd just settled in the barn and taken their chances, but the boy sleeping out there would have sounded the alarm anyway. Had they set him up out there to protect the livestock from rustlers or Natives?

Maggie poured coffee and offered it to Max. "Billy, I had noticed your injured hand. How did you come to such an injury? Golly."

Max shook his head dramatically and glanced at Ronnie, then back at Maggie. "Well, old Midnight lost his mind when a rattler nearly got him. He threw me to the ground, and in the confusion, he clipped me!" Max held up his fist and looked strained.

Lawrence returned, dressed in dungarees and a cotton shirt. He sat next to Max at the table. "What you require is a respectable blacksmith. My son had a wagon run over his leg and the blacksmith put it back together. He can't walk just right, but it healed well enough to work his land. Few choices out here when your leg's broke."

Ronnie grimaced. "Did they give him anything for the pain?"

Lawrence shook his head. "Not much more than the spirits we had on hand. I held him down. They had such a time resetting the bones back together on account of the muscles pulling on either side."

Maggie added, "Praise the Lord he fainted so they could finish the job. It took five of us to help." She dabbed her eyes with a cloth. "Bones grinding. That's a sound you can't rightly get out of your head, you know?"

"That is awful. I'm glad your son healed up so well." Max clutched his injured hand. "Let's hope this is a fair bit easier to manage than a leg."

"It has to be. No large muscles to draw the bones too far out of alignment," Maggie replied. "How many pieces of sausage are you good for, Billy?"

Ronnie cringed at the awkward segue way.

Lawrence answered for him, "The size of this ole fellow, I'd say get him at least a dozen."

Max grinned, catching Ronnie's eye. She stifled a yawn and watched Maggie at the stove.

Lawrence clapped Max on the back. "So, the price of your breakfast is a good ole-fashioned chewing of the fat. Tell me your news from whence you came."

Max's smile diminished, and he reached under the table and took her hand. "Melissa's mother's health is failing. We are on our way back home."

Maggie set a pitcher of cream between them, then set a cup of coffee in front of Ronnie. "I'm so sorry to learn about your mother. Where are you from, dear?"

Ronnie, caught off guard, shot a panicked glance at Max.

Max was quick to answer. "It's painful for Melissa to talk about her ma, it's such a shock. The letter was dated a few weeks back, so we are eager to get our journey started."

Maggie watched Ronnie intently. Did she suspect something? A shudder of dread hit Ronnie hard. She was no good at lying. The topic drifted to more mundane talk of their ranch and what old man winter would bring. Maggie bustled around the kitchen and, after a bit, brought a platter of eggs, sausage, and hot buttered cornbread to the table. Maggie's demeanor was more muted now as she passed around plates, and the mood seemed to shift. Lawrence was blind to it, but Max noticed it. He shot her an unsettled look.

Maggie sat next to Ronnie, passing the platters as they listened to the men talk of colts and breeding. There was nothing Ronnie could contribute without giving away her ignorance on both topics. Other than horseback riding camp, Ronnie had little experience caring for animals.

After a few minutes, Maggie turned to Ronnie and cocked her head. Her face registered something other than the friendliness she'd displayed thus far. "You look so much like a girl I used to see around town, Melissa. Do you have a sister?"

Ronnie felt her cheeks go hot. "No, I don't."

Maggie pressed her lips together and shook her head. "You're the spittin' image of that McIntyre girl. What's her name, Pa?" Maggie grabbed Lawrence's wrist.

Lawrence glanced at Ronnie. "Who? Maggie, your eyes are failing you quicker than a dove's wings after it's been shot clean out of the sky." He leaned in on his elbows and examined Ronnie closer. "No, that girl has much lighter hair and has got to be ten years younger than Melissa. Plus, she's hitched to that other fella."

Ronnie laughed, attempting to camouflage her alarm. "I do hear that a lot. People tell me I look like someone they know."

Maggie smiled with her lips, but the wheels were turning behind the cold eyes.

Max interceded. "Melissa and I are newlyweds. We are on our honeymoon looking at land in Sterling City. I don't see how she can rightly be two women at once, do you?" He tapped Lawrence's arm and chuckled with the ease of a clean conscience. Man, he was good at this pretending stuff. Ronnie lost her nerve and nearly blurted out all her sins to Maggie, with the cold, hard look she delivered.

Lawrence scolded, "No, Ma, you're mixed up. This gal is Billy's wife. Don't go on about this and badger them no more, you hear?"

Maggie raised her chin defiantly. "What you don't realize, because you're a homebody ole goat, is that Rose has run off. Some claim the Indians got her. Now her spitting image shows up at our doorstep with a fine-looking fella in the middle of the night. Tell me, husband, you don't see the remarkable coincidence?"

Max squeezed her hand under the table and shot her a look, raising his eyebrows. Ronnie read it as *keep your cool.*

Lawrence looked from Max to Ronnie and back and flapped his napkin at Maggie, rejecting the suggestion. "Eat up, you two. We won't be passing any judgments on you young 'uns. Ma, we won't be sticking our noses where they don't belong. I may be a homebody ole goat, but I know how to let folks live free from suspicion."

Maggie shoveled a bite of sausage in her mouth and huffed, appearing to settle into her temporary defeat, but Ronnie could see the strong will in the set of her shoulders. And that meant trouble.

Max smiled at Maggie then shot her a look of calm confidence that was a major contrast to how she felt. Ronnie suddenly wanted to take her chances out in the chilly wind again.

They made small talk, but the elephant in the room hogged all the delicious food and sucked out any passion in the conversation. Lawrence was lively as ever, but the suspicious eyes of Maggie lingered on her every move, making her performance stale, especially compared to Max's suave transitions and confident demeanor.

Ronnie pushed the half empty plate away and stretched dramatically. "I can hardly keep my eyes open. Billy, darlin', I think I'm going to fall asleep right here at the table."

Max smiled, and a look of honest affection was impossible to disguise. "Me too, honey. It has been a pleasure getting to know you all." Max had emptied his plate several times, refilled by Maggie's watchful attentiveness.

Maggie stood. "Just give me a few minutes to prepare your room. Why don't you have another cup of coffee? Pa, will you help me with the trunk?"

Lawrence stood and stepped into the next room, wiping his mouth as he waited for Maggie to join him. They whispered as they walked towards the back staircase.

Ronnie glanced at the door, then at Max. "Should we just go?"

Max clasped her hand, pulling her close as they whispered. "No, I think Maggie is suspicious, but what can they do? It's the middle of the night. We will just sleep a few hours and leave before dawn."

Lawrence sat back down at the table and finished the last bite of cornbread on his plate. "Mighty glad you stopped in."

Before Max or Ronnie could respond, Maggie called out, "Melissa, will you help me prepare your room? I can show you where everything is."

Ronnie stole a panicked glance at Max, who nodded. Ronnie turned to Maggie. "My pleasure."

"Please follow me." Maggie waited for Ronnie to accompany her, holding one of the candles from the table.

Butterflies rolled around in Ronnie's stomach, making her feel queasy. Ronnie stood, leaving the protection of Max's subterfuge. Maggie led her through a large living room. "You have such a lovely home."

Maggie ignored her and continued rapidly down the length of the house, passing several rooms decorated with sparse, functional decor. At the back of the residence, they climbed a narrow staircase, making a turn to the next level halfway up. The painted wooden steps were worn, leaving streaks of oak peeking through.

They passed a few vacant rooms and stopped at the end of the hall, where Maggie stepped inside and turned around. Ronnie followed but halted upon seeing her indignant expression.

Maggie walked past her and shut the door. "Now listen here, missy." She crossed her arms over her ample bosom. "What are you trying to pull?"

"Pull, ma'am?" Ronnie played it cool, but her cheeks blazed.

Maggie narrowed her eyes. "Jeb is out searching for you and you're roaming around the plains with some strange man getting all cozy." She pressed her lips together and narrowed her eyes. "That's just not the Christian thing to do."

Without the suave Max to bail her out, Ronnie had to make a choice. Her honesty broke through, hoping to win on her sympathies as a woman. "Maggie, the Christian thing to do? Jeb pushed me down the stairs and murdered my first child. Jeb made me lose the baby. He punished me when I was sick. I just couldn't stay with a man like that." Ronnie spoke candidly, adding the empathy she'd felt for Rose.

The steel in Maggie's eyes softened. "Child, are you speaking the truth?"

"I am telling you the absolute truth." Ronnie was weak in the knees and leaned against the bed, wanting to sit down, but didn't feel the freedom to do so.

"You were with child? Oh!" Maggie's lips quivered, and she dabbed at her nose with a lace hankie she drew from her sleeve.

Ronnie pushed it further, channeling Rose's predicament. "Do you have any idea how hard it was to stay as long as I did? I struggled to talk to other women about it, but they just advised me to take my lot in life and be at peace with it. God's will and all."

Maggie sat down hard on a chair against the wall. "The poor babe." She rubbed her eyes and blew her nose ungraciously. "My daughter had a stillborn babe a few months ago. Mary finally disclosed to me that her husband had punched her in the belly a few times to teach her a lesson. He pressured her to keep working through her last few weeks of the pregnancy." Maggie sobbed. "Broke my heart to learn that she suffered through a stillbirth because of her husband's cruelty. I had three stillborn before my first child survived, later to be taken by yellow fever on her fifth birthday."

Ronnie put her hand on Maggie's shoulder. "I'm so sorry. I just couldn't stand it anymore."

Maggie stood and covered her mouth. Her eyes were enormous. "Oh, my stars."

"What is it?" Ronnie took her elbow to steady her.

"Oh my." This time she stared at Ronnie with dread in her eyes. "Lawrence sent for Jeb when he was getting dressed."

"Jeb? What?" Ronnie felt like the air was knocked from her lungs. "Why did you...?" The wave of nausea struck her hard. She perched on the bed. "How long ago, Maggie?"

"Just as you settled in for supper." Maggie sat back down, sounding thoroughly distressed.

Ronnie took a deep breath. "How far away is he?"

"Not so far. If he were home, they should be here real soon." She shook her head and dried more tears.

"Maggie, Jeb will beat me senseless for leaving him. The men they're with will kill..." Ronnie stopped herself from saying Max at the last second. "Billy. They're cutthroat villains, Maggie. You've given us both a death sentence."

Maggie rose and hugged her. "I had no idea, Rose. I just didn't know he was hurting you."

Ronnie pulled away from her embrace and opened the bedroom door, rushing out. Would there be time to escape?

Chapter 38

Showdown

Ronnie bolted down the stairs, retracing her steps, barely able to see without Maggie's candle. "Max! Max!" She raced through the other rooms and smacked into him as she entered the kitchen.

Max held her shoulder. His eyes were wide in alarm. "What is it?"

"They sent for Jeb when we first arrived. He will be here any minute. No!" Ronnie pointed behind him.

Lawrence seized the shotgun over the doorjamb and growled. "You can't rightly show up in the middle of the night with someone else's wife and not expect me to sound the alarm." He underscored his point with the barrel of the gun.

Max stepped in front of Ronnie, shielding her. "There is no need to bear arms against us, Lawrence. I will not let Jeb hurt her again. You're gonna have to make a choice. Either let us pass or shoot me now."

Maggie rushed in, clutching her handkerchief to her mouth. "Pa, please. Don't do this."

Lawrence's eyebrows shot up. "Maggie, Rose ran away from Jeb. Plain and simple. We can't just let her leave with this fella." He lowered the barrel but kept the weapon in both hands. "Jeb is on his way. Let's let sleeping dogs lie."

Maggie walked between Lawrence and Max, spreading her arms to defend them. "Jeb's abused her, Pa. She lost the baby because of him, just like with Mary."

Lawrence shook his head. "Look at them, Maggie. As plain as the nose on your face, these two are in love. She's stepped out on her man. Jeb will sort this out and you will not interfere."

Distracted by Maggie, Lawrence didn't notice Max lunging towards the shotgun. They wrestled for a moment, but Max tore the shotgun out of his grip and bolted towards the exit. "Come on, Rose." He opened the door and pointed the weapon at their hosts. "Thank you for the hospitality. We could have done without the cowardly backstabbing."

Ronnie sprinted towards the barn and turned as the dogs barked their warning. A voice called out, but Ronnie ignored it. If they could leave before Jeb arrived, it would get Maggie and Lawrence out of the middle of this whole goat rope and maybe even save Max.

As Ronnie reached the barn door, a voice called out, "Howdy, Rose." She spun around to watch three riders approaching on horseback.

Max pointed the shotgun at them as the man in the center with dark, stringy hair crooned, "My dear devoted wife." Ben and Jere Miah flanked him.

Ronnie gasped, "Jeb."

Max stood his ground and smirked. "Mighty snakelike to slither over here with these two pieces of shit. Rose, come back over here." Max slowly backed towards the house, ascending the stairs, not taking his eyes off the men. Jere Miah's hand was inching towards his revolver.

Ronnie was frozen in place, eyes glued to Jere Miah, certain a shot would ring out any second.

The spell was broken when Maggie cried out, "Rose, dear, come back inside. I'm sure we can work this out, boys." Maggie stood in front of Max on the stoop, wringing the handkerchief in her hands.

Ronnie ran over to the door and Maggie ushered them in. Lawrence blocked the entrance, but Max pushed past him and held it for Maggie and Ronnie to enter, then he barred the door behind them.

"Stay out of this, Lawrence. I don't need you or the missus hurt. Rose, run upstairs. I'll hold them down here while we chat." Max's tone was urgent.

"Please, Max, just let me go with them. I don't want any of you hurt. Your life is worth more than this. Jere Miah will kill you if he comes in here. You know that."

Max jutted out his jaw, then said, "No, Rose, I won't allow that monster to lay a hand on you. It isn't right. Men don't hurt their women. It's not how it's supposed to be. They protect them with their lives."

A banging on the door made everyone turn. Maggie pulled Ronnie's sleeve. "Rose, come upstairs. He is right. We need to get out of the way in case they start something." Maggie grabbed her hand and pulled Ronnie up the stairs.

Max's voice, strained with the stress, called out, "Lawrence, no, don't let them in. Please, stay out of this."

At the top of the stairs, Ronnie hesitated, wanting to end this escalating situation.

"Rose, come in here!" The older woman ushered Ronnie into the closest bedroom. "You can hide up there." She pushed Ronnie into a closet. "There is a trapdoor. Pull down the ladder so you can climb into the attic."

"I don't want to hide, Maggie. I can't put you in the crosshairs. I should surrender to them."

Pain showed in Maggie's eyes. "Rose, don't you see, he will punish you for leaving. You may not survive his brutality. You've shamed him."

"Why did you have to call for Jeb? We could have ridden away." Ronnie fought back tears.

Maggie ignored her and yanked the string fixed to the ceiling. The candle flickered, nearly going out, but it corrected itself. She set it down on the bedside table and used two hands to pull down the narrow ladder leading to the attic. "Now, Rose, get on up there and stop talking nonsense."

The chilly air from the night spilled down around them. "Maggie, you go first. I want you out of the fray."

Steely eyes met hers. "I will not hide. They won't get past me, Rose. If I could have done the same for my Mary, I would have."

"These men are merciless. You haven't seen what I have. Jere Miah will kill Max. None of you should be in danger because of me."

Gunfire echoed through the upstairs, and the sharp stench of gunpowder was heavy in the air. Ronnie's heart practically stopped. She flew out of the bedroom towards the stairs.

"Max, are you okay?"

Maggie ran out of the room. "Rose, get on up there. I got you into this situation— you need to allow me to sort it out."

Max was at the halfway point of the landing, with a fresh bullet hole in the wall next to him. His eyes were wide. "Rose, do as Maggie says. They're coming up here one way or another." He glanced backward, then clambered up the remaining steps towards her. "Maggie, you have ammo up here? I'm going to need it."

Maggie pointed to the bedroom at the end of the hall. "Under the bed in a wooden box. I'll keep her safe, don't you worry." She turned to Ronnie. "You cannot go back to him. Rose, you just can't." Maggie grabbed Ronnie's hand.

Indecision plagued Ronnie. She needed a way out of this. She followed Maggie into the guest room as Max rushed to fetch the ammunition. Then Ronnie broke free and bolted to the stairwell, surprising Maggie. "It is between me and Jeb. None of the rest of you should be dragged into it."

Ronnie dashed down the stairs and through the house towards the kitchen, searching around for Lawrence, Jeb, and the other men. It was quiet, other than Maggie yelling after her. She eyed the front door, wondering if she could just run away, but Max would still be in the line of fire.

A man called out as she approached the door. "Rose, darlin'." It was Jeb.

Startled, Ronnie faced him, letting loose her anger. "Don't you *Rose darlin'* me!"

"Rose, don't." Jeb moved closer, forcing her retreat. "You can't run away from me. You are my wife. You *belong* to me."

His soft tone confused her. This was not the Jeb she'd expected. "I don't belong with a man who would hurt me or my baby."

Jeb's mouth curved down, and he glanced away, surprising her with the expression of regret. "Rose, you know that was a mishap. You stumbled over your skirts and fell down. I've never laid a hand on you in my life." Jeb lunged at her, seizing her wrist before she could pull away. The irony of his words hit her hard.

Ronnie jerked her hand up, trying to break free, but he kept a steady grasp. "Ouch, get off me."

He dragged her towards the door. "No, you are leaving with me now, Rose, where we can talk in private. I already had to pull Macy's nephews into this." His uneven teeth were bared. Coupled with the greasy hair, it made him look like a drowned rat. "You've cost me more than I care to account in money, time, and reputation. You will pay me back with your hide." Jeb punctuated his words by jerking her arm painfully behind her, reaching with one hand for the door.

"Leave her be." Maggie's voice hailed from the entrance to the kitchen.

"This doesn't concern you, missus. I'm very grateful that you provided my errant wife sustenance while she waited upon my arrival." Jeb's sweet tone returned, but he continued to hold on to her tightly.

Ronnie struggled to free herself. "Let go of me, Jeb. This is no way to treat me." Out of the corner of her eye, she saw movement, a blur running through the living room.

Maggie followed her gaze, watching the figure disappear around the corner. It was either Ben or Jere Miah heading towards Max! "Boys, I don't want you upstairs."

Ronnie's heart sank.

Maggie shook her finger. "Jeb, don't you leave with her until we have words." Then turned on her heel and strode briskly after whoever was making his way up the stairs.

"Max!" Ronnie yelled at the ceiling. "Max, they're coming for you!"

Jeb twisted her elbow. "Hush, you've done enough damage. Let those boys reunite with their friend." Jeb shoved Ronnie out onto the stoop, then pushed her down the steps. Ben was standing nearby, guarding the door. That meant Jere Miah was heading upstairs.

She couldn't breathe. Fear choked off her diaphragm.

Jeb whistled for his horse, and when it didn't come, he called out, "I'll be obliged to have our horses now. On account that we are fixin' to head back home."

A gunshot rang out in the night, then another one, spooking Ben's horse. He controlled it.

Ronnie cried out, "No, Max!"

Ben peered up at the second-story window. Ronnie followed his gaze. The window was open, and the white curtain reflected the candlelight.

Ben paused, then thundered, "Jere Miah! Holler at me out the window if'n you're alright."

The curtain flapped in the breeze as the only response. Ben scrambled to the door. Ronnie tried to as well, but Jeb stopped her.

"No, Rose, we're heading out of here." He nodded towards Lawrence, who was leading Buttercup out of the barn.

Ronnie pulled away. "Jeb, let me go. I need to see if Max is okay."

Lawrence handed the reins to Jeb. "That fella she's with needs a lesson taught as well. He's got some attachment to your woman that should be addressed."

Jeb glanced at Ronnie, tightening his grip. "Is that so? I may need to have words with him, then."

Ronnie interrupted. "Don't you dare. He's done nothing wrong." Then she turned to Lawrence. "Did you hear the gunshot? Maggie is upstairs with Max and Jere Miah."

Lawrence's expression fell, and he ran into the house. "Maggie, where are you?"

Jeb glanced up towards the window as several voices rang out. He drew his pistol from the holster. "Mount that animal, Rose."

"You wouldn't dare shoot me, Jeb." Ronnie ran back to the house, not caring if he pulled the trigger.

Jeb closed the short distance between them in a heartbeat and grabbed her arm, holding the pistol in her face. "Mount that mare, Rose, we are leaving now."

Ronnie struggled out of his grip, but he overpowered her. She mounted Buttercup at gunpoint and watched Jeb gracefully hop on his bay without taking the gun off her. "Don't you want to know what happened to them?"

Jeb ignored her question and grabbed the reins out of her hands and led both away from the ranch into the dark landscape.

Ronnie yelled, "Max! Are you okay?" Tears streaked down her face. They made it past a copse of trees before she pulled herself together. "Jeb, you have no concern for those people up in that house? Not even curiosity about the outcome?"

"There wasn't supposed to be any bloodshed. Those boys should not be in the middle of this to begin with." He dismounted and approached Buttercup, still holding the reins. Ronnie realized in the low light of the rising moon that there was a shed nearby.

Then Jeb jerked her off the mare, helping her to stand upright. In a single motion, he carried her to a small wooden shed. Jeb kicked the door open and unceremoniously dumped her on the floor. Before she could scramble to her feet, the door shut, cutting off any remaining light. A strong smell of smoke assaulted her, but it lacked the heat of a fire. Was this a smokehouse? The pitch darkness closed in on her and she banged on the door, trying to open it. It was latched from the outside and she shoved against it in vain. "Jeb, don't leave me here!"

The sound of retreating hoofbeats rang out.

"Help, get me out of here!" Finally, Ronnie dropped to her knees and cried. Would Jeb murder Max? Was Maggie caught in the crossfire? Everything was caving in on her, like it did each time she travelled backward in time. Regrets flew around in the darkness, and she wished she'd not fought what fate was trying to take her towards— the evil one. Would she need to find him in her own time, and deal with him to make these time travel disasters end?

Chapter 39

Key to His Heart

Sweat lined Ian's latex gloves. This was the make-or-break moment. If he missed something when the slider was opened, an alarm would sound. Police would show up, even if he disarmed it. An investigation would be triggered, and the rich asshole would find out someone had broken in.

Ian kissed the St. Dominic Savio charm, the patron saint of juvenile delinquents, that hung around his neck and gently slid the door open. He braced for chaos but was met with silence. The contacts stayed together, and the alarm didn't sound. "Yessss!" The next challenge—did Jeffrey splurge on the motion detector? If he did, it wasn't lined up properly between the back and front doors. Ian crept around the perimeter of Jeffrey's place, still leery of a misplaced motion detector, but there were no red lights. Either the batteries were dead, or he'd not troubled to buy it. *Big mistake, Mr. Asshole Brennan.*

Ian quietly scoped out the layout, judging the potential for hidden secrets. It was identical to the flat Billy was sitting in a few doors down. Two bedrooms, one loo, this one furnished sparse and modern. Most likely place to strike gold would be the office. Ian quickly rifled through the filing cabinet, then turned his scrutiny to the tidy desk. He carefully replaced everything he'd touched. The top drawer was locked, but it was pure crap like the sliding glass door, and he jimmied it open, then quickly scanned it. Ian gently detached the entire drawer and flickered the flashlight in the opening. A metallic object was wedged in the back.

"Oh yeah, come to papa." Ian reached into the narrow space, but his hand was too thick. A pencil quickly withdrew the item. "Bingo!" He crammed the key in his pocket, then replaced the drawer, relocking it. His triumph was short-lived. One reason he was so good at being a thief in Glasgow was his excellent hearing and crack intuition. Stevie called it a sixth sense. Unless he was wasted. This time he was dead sober.

Ian crept across the living room to the front door. No doubt, someone was out in the corridor. Ian peeked through the peephole and nearly shit his trousers. At least three men were outside dressed in black, a bold, gold *FBI* embroidered on their chest pockets. *Feds! Shit.*

In a flash, Ian was out on the balcony and shut the slider behind him. Wind, kicked up by the approaching storm, cooled the perspiration that had broken out all over his body. He debated hiding behind the grill, but he'd be snagged sure as shit. His heart stopped when a light inside the condo turned on. They were inside! In a split second he was on the next veranda over with the dog owner. Thankfully, the wee beastie was silent. He leapt to the next veranda, fear fueling his escape. If he were outside anywhere, they'd see him, unless he hid behind plants.

Lightning flashed, and a few drops of rain pelted his scalp. "Damn it!" Ian, fueled by terror, crossed the remaining distance to the flat where Billy was nervously waiting.

∞

Steph glared at her baby brother. "Ian! How can you be so bloody *schtupid*? You're gonna end up in jail." She grabbed the dish towel and hit him with it. "What the hell were you thinking?"

"You're missing the forest for the trees, lass. I have this." He held up a key.

"No!" Steph snatched it out of his hand. "Is this for the storage unit?"

"I dinnea ken, but I'm guessing so." Ian beamed.

Steph returned the key. "Where was it?"

"Hiding very well. It's definitely a huge, smelly secret. Best part is I kept the FBI from discovering it! Me, Stephanie! Little ole me kept whatever is in there from the fucking Feds!"

Steph felt her face go hot. "How do you know it was the FBI and not the police?"

"They weren't police. They had black jackets with an FBI emblem on the chest."

"The big question is, what has Jeffrey gotten into that the Federal Bureau of Investigation is searching his place?" Steph pushed aside her breakfast, losing her appetite. "Ian, the FBI is nothing to mess with. What if they'd arrested you?"

"Stephanie, they had no idea I was there. It's actually a good thing."

Steph leaned forward, glowering at her daring, stupid sibling. "A good thing?" Her blood pressure rose. "How am I supposed to tell Mum you've ended up in the federal penitentiary? Ian!" She stood and raised her palm to pretend to smack him.

Ian flinched. "Come on. Their search hid mine. He will just assume they searched the unit." He chuckled. "Plus, I'm no a little kid. You can't thrash me into behaving."

Steph sat back down and glared at Ian. His eyes were clear, not the usual bloodshot. He'd actually laid off the booze for a night. He hadn't even stayed out late. "Ian, do you swear on the Holy Bible that you are telling me everything?"

Ian's blue eyes grew wide. "What? Why do I need to do that?"

"Okay, ya wee gomerel, tell me what you left out. I need to learn everything so I can be prepared."

Ian grinned. "How do you always do that?" Ian's eyes showed guilt, and she dreaded what he would reveal next. "Yeah, okay, I may have lifted a few other things."

"Ian McKay! He'll know someone was there!"

"Duh. He'd already know because the key would be gone. Now the Feds covered up for me." He beamed.

"What did you take?" Worry and anger overwhelmed her mind. This was problematic.

Ian let out a protracted sigh. "I discovered a stash of dirty pics of Ronnie. He must have snapped them when she was asleep." He grinned but looked sheepish. "Come on, the dipshit was the perv for taking them. Just let me enjoy the spoils of plunder."

Relief washed over her. "That's it? You swear you didn't take anything else?"

"No. God, no. Jeffrey is a pretentious prick. Anything of his would carry his asswipe spirit and shatter my happiness for nicking it."

"Give me the pictures, Ian. I cannae have you invading Ronnie's privacy like that."

His smile collapsed. "No, I earned those. Plus…" The grin returned. "The truth of the matter is I saved Ronnie's honor. Those Feds would totally have seen Ronnie naked, passed them around, and probably each kept one or two. This way I've protected her honor."

A blend of relief, irritation, and dread took away her caustic remark. "The pictures, Ian, or you are sleeping outside tonight."

Ian frowned, forming lines around his mouth. Smoking was aging him quickly.

Undeterred, Steph continued, "If Jeffrey realizes someone broke in and stole the photographs of Ronnie, the first person he would think of is you. You've been a perv towards her from the second you met her. He knows that."

"So. What does that matter?"

"Ian, Jeffrey Brennan is dangerous. Remember Ronnie's warning?"

"I do. He doesn't scare me." Ian crossed his arms.

"Ian." Steph squeezed his shoulder. "He will find your dirty little secrets and," she snapped her fingers, "just like that you're deported and in jail. Breaking and entering is a felony. You've got to use your brain, even when you're sober."

"He won't. He will never know I was there." Ian smirked, but there was fear in his expression too. "The Feds made certain of that."

"Ian, we are dealing with a dangerous man with limitless resources. Don't poke the bear. We have to be smart about this. I can't deal with you being locked up. I just can't." Steph held back tears.

He squeezed her hand. "Stephanie, dinnae worry about me. Billy and I are only going there to see what Jeffrey is hiding."

"Hell no. You're not going with Billy. He's as dumb as you are. Jesus, Mary, and Joseph, please protect this eejit." Steph looked at the ceiling.

Ian's eyebrows knitted together. "Billy *was* worthless. He's petrified, just like you are. He's not a lawbreaker. He just appreciates women like I do."

Steph pinched his arm.

He jerked back. "Stephanie, I'm a grown man, stop pinching me as if I'm a we'an."

"Get your breakfast gone and we'll go there today before anything else happens. If the FBI knows about the storage shed, they may already have taken what's inside. If not, we'll find out what he's so eager to hide."

Ian's eyes lit up. "Really? You'd do that for me, Stephanie?"

"Absolutely not. I'm doing this for Ronnie. I'm doing it to find out what the scoundrel is up to. When we know, we've got leverage if this thing goes south on us."

"Leverage, what do ya mean?" Ian cocked his head, reminding her of Ginger, their parent's cocker spaniel.

"If Jeffrey comes after Ronnie, we will have information to use against him. If the Feds come after you, we've got leverage for a plea deal."

"Plea deal? For what?" Ian looked thoroughly confused.

"For you, dumb clothead. If you get caught up in Jeffrey's mess, you can use it against Jeffrey, then maybe they'll let you go because they'll realize you're on their side."

"Oh, smart wee lassie. You might be right. Genius, because no one ever would suspect you of committing a crime. You look so innocent. Hey, wear some shorty-shorts in case there is a man to sweet talk while I steal the goods."

Steph smacked his arm. "I don't own any short-shorts, you eejit. I do, however, have a low-cut blouse that may serve the same purpose." Steph inwardly grimaced. Instead of going to church, she was now drawn into Ian's scheme. Hopefully, there was something useful in the storage unit.

Chapter 40

Smokehouse Blues

Ronnie pulled herself together and stood. Was Max alive? The time traveling pattern was clear—Max was in danger for one reason alone. He had helped her. She could not let Max die because he'd chosen to protect her.

Ronnie felt blindly in the dark, hunting for a window, and in the process broke a spider web with her face. "Ahhhhh!" Ronnie panicked. "Get it off, gross!" She clawed at it, stumbled, and landed hard on her hands and knees. "Damn it." Rubbing her bruised shin, she sensed something trapped in her dress and she wrenched it loose. It was a piece of kindling, a stout stick about two inches thick, cut to burn readily. Ronnie crawled around, searching for an escape, gripping the kindling.

Her shin throbbed, but she recognized it would be the least of her injuries if she didn't break out of this shed. The thought of Jeb's fists smashing her face spurred her on.

A tickle along her neck set off a panic attack. "Noooo!" She killed the spider and wildly shook out her hair, then rubbed her face, ears, and neck free of the web, imagining an army of arachnids.

An exhaustive search revealed the shed had no windows. Her only escape was the latched door. A sliver of light peeked through the crack where the door and shed met. Jamming the kindling into the gap, she torqued it, driving with all her might. The door didn't budge, but the shed wall acquiesced a little with her struggles. The night sky was now visible through the crevice.

Ronnie used every ounce of strength to twist the strip of wood next to the door. A piece broke loose, and she reached through, lifted the latch, and opened the door, scraping her fist in the process.

Fresh air filled her lungs, but movement to her left struck dread into her heart. She froze. A slight glimmer along the horizon provided the only light, and she labored to see what lay beyond. Was it a coyote? A person? It stood silently observing her. She willed it to be Buttercup grazing nearby, or better yet, Max coming to collect her. Her subconscious told her otherwise.

Ronnie's heart thudded a quickening tempo in her ears. Had she just imagined it? Panic overwhelmed her rationale, and she scrambled back inside the shed. Her former

211

prison now a refuge. To her abject horror, her movement provoked a flurry of activity. Shadowy figures surrounded the shed, and Ronnie stifled a scream.

Instinct took over, and she grasped what remained of the door and held it closed. In her mind, she counted the number of figures she'd seen in the split second before she ran. It was more than four. They were silent. Jeb or Ben would have cried out.

Childhood nightmares of hideous beasts chasing her in the night flooded her mind. These horrors were more welcome here in the dark than the reports of what the Natives would do to her.

A deep, reassuring voice whispered in a Native tongue. She imagined he was cajoling her to let them in. Perhaps they were speaking to each other, but it inspired renewed feats of concentration to maintain the separation between them. She clung to the door, gripping it closed.

The Native pried her fingers away, freeing the door. Ronnie fell backward on her butt, defenseless. Five Natives stared down at her, backlit by the first faint light of the coming dawn illuminating their shapes, her frightened imagination superimposing the image of the aliens from *Close Encounters of the Third Kind,* with the light from the spaceship casting shadows towards her.

They had every right to despise her, to loathe what her people had done to them. One man extended a hand to help her up. She accepted it and stood face-to-face with an enormous Native, well over six feet tall, and muscular as a bodybuilder. The others, perhaps sensing her panic, retreated a few steps away. Buttercup and another horse snorted in agitation. Were they stealing the horses from the ranch?

Her mind raced. Would they know English? "Hello, my name is Ronnie."

"Ron-eee," the huge man echoed, nodding as he did. His hand traveled to his heart. "Kwa-na."

A flicker of hope grew. If they spoke English, maybe they could help her. The fact they didn't scalp her on the spot was a good sign.

"I am pleased to meet you." She scanned the Natives, all men and all observing her closely. To say she was intimidated was a tremendous understatement.

Kwa-na looked her up and down. "Slave?"

Ronnie shook her head. "No. I'm..." In a way, Rose was enslaved by her abusive husband, but that wasn't the same. Not even close. "I am free, but not well treated."

Kwa-na spoke rapidly, while using hand signals. He pointed at her face and hands. Ronnie glanced down and realized her entire body was covered in soot from the smokehouse. Was her face covered too? Would they treat her better if they assumed she was a slave?

As he spoke, Ronnie absorbed every nuance of Kwa-na's appearance and speech in the low light. He was shirtless in buckskins and moccasins, looking lithe and dangerous. His hair plaited on both sides, and his high cheekbones belied his wisdom. Another man strode forward and spoke, but it was with a gentle disposition, although still incomprehensible. Kwa-na gestured with his hand in a curving forward motion, then pointed to her while nodding. He seemed to be asking if she would accompany them. To her astonishment, they were inquisitive, but not aggressive, as she had expected. If they were going to harm her, they'd not be standing around chatting.

It would be the experience of a lifetime to live among the Natives even for a short time. But the horror stories told around the campfire gave her pause. Plus, she had to know what happened to Max.

"My friend is in trouble back there." Ronnie pointed towards the house. They couldn't understand her—their faces showed it plainly. It didn't stop her from trying.

The sun was rising, allowing her to see more of their dress and expressions. Ronnie seared it into her memory. Feeling more confident, she stepped away from the shed towards the ranch.

"I need to help Max."

Kwa-na stepped aside and spoke to his men. Then turned to her. "You come." He made the same waving motion with his hand as if parting the land as they moved southward.

"You come," Ronnie retorted, asking if they would join her. Could they create a disturbance so she could escape with Max? What alternative did she have? They could have just grabbed her and ridden off.

Kwa-na didn't speak but accompanied her. Her stride was quick and clumsy compared to his silent, catlike step, as he chose his footing carefully.

Was she leading Kwa-na to slaughter? Was she bringing terror to Lawrence and Maggie? How many more lives would be destroyed because of her? Ronnie stopped behind a shrub, listening for any voices. It was silent, which heightened her concern.

Sunrise was shining as if a beacon off Lawrence's house. A horse was grazing nearby, but the fact it was roaming loose gave her a sense of impending doom. Her loyalty to Max urged her on. That and the fear of how the Natives would treat her when they realized she was white.

The chill of the air sucked the warmth from her body and butterflies danced in her belly, forcing nausea to rise. What would she find up there? Should she run away and risk being captured by Jeb? Doubt made her slow the pace. She approached the horse and stepped next to it, shielding her from being seen from the house. Was this Ben's mount? Kwa-na grabbed the reins and led the animal along with them, masking their approach.

Ronnie ran to the side of the house, then crept towards the back, her boots crunching on the parched earth. Kwa-na was leading the horse back through the brush to the shed. Three horses? Would they attack to get the rest?

A murmur of male voices carried from the back of the house. Ronnie snuck around towards the sounds, but no one was there. A few birds startled upon seeing her and flew away.

Suddenly the rear door burst open, and Lawrence stepped out backward, pulling a man by the armpits, his boots dragging over the threshold. Ronnie's heart leapt into her throat, and she suppressed a yelp, then crouched back behind the house. The man he was carrying was bloodied, but his face was obscured by Lawrence's big frame. Lawrence muttered something Ronnie couldn't make out. The crunch of wheels on the dry, parched ground and the jumble of tack startled her. She glanced around the corner again and saw Ben guiding a team of horses and a wagon from the barn on the opposite side of the house. He disembarked and strolled towards Lawrence.

Ronnie wracked her brain, trying to recall what boots Max had worn. What color pants did he wear? She closed her eyes and tears tumbled down her face. Was he just injured, and they were taking him to a doctor? She braved another glance and watched Ben help Lawrence load the body into the bed of the wagon. Lawrence started back to the house. Streaks of wetness ran down his face as if he'd been crying.

Ronnie's heart sank. Maggie was nowhere to be seen. Why else would Lawrence be crying? Where was everybody else? Jeb? Jere Miah? Ben stood near the body and shook his head, then turned and followed Lawrence up the steps. It was deathly silent. Ronnie risked it and rushed to get a closer look at the body in the wagon. A tarp covered the body, confirming whoever was under it was no longer alive. Ronnie lifted a corner to expose dark hair matted with blood. It was Max. "Oh my God." Ronnie covered him back up. Tears stung her eyes.

The door opened and Ronnie jumped off the wagon and hid behind it, inching her way towards the horses. Ben and Lawrence awkwardly carried another body and hoisted it to the wagon, making it rock with the added burden. Ronnie crept past the animals, who eyed her but thankfully kept quiet. She balked, needing to run, but didn't want to be caught.

Ben spoke. "Dingus, you had to go and get your revenge. Now look at you." He coughed. "Why the hell did we take on this job? It was supposed to be easy money. Help a friend…"

Ben clutched his hat to his chest, then turned to Lawrence, who stood dumbstruck nearby.

Ben's deep voice continued, "My condolences, Lawrence, I know Jere Miah wasn't aware she was up there with 'em. I wish it were me and not your missus. I truly do."

Ronnie clamped a hand over her mouth. Maggie *was* dead too. That only left Jeb. Would they go back inside for another body? She glanced around, now terrified that Jeb could be nearby.

Ben turned and walked towards the porch, and Lawrence followed, looking shell-shocked. A waft of freshly murdered men, real or imagined, overcame her, inducing an uncontrolled panic. Ronnie sprinted away from the ghastly scene. What would she do now? There was no one to help her. Max and Maggie had died to protect her. She leaned against the house, forcing down the bile that threatened to rise. The dogs discovered her and barked, giving away her presence.

Ben called out, "Rose, is that you?"

In full panic, Ronnie sprinted back towards the front of the house, the dogs chasing behind.

"Rose, where did you come from?" he called after her, slowly walking around the wagon, but then he noticed her sprinting and he followed suit. "You left with Jeb…Rose, get back here!" He followed her around to the front yard, then stopped short and drew his sidearm. "Lord have mercy. Injuns. Lawrence, grab the rifle!"

Ronnie sprinted in the direction of the shed. A cloud of dirt rose from the earth, then out of the brush, Kwa-na rode towards her on horseback. He reached down and grabbed her arm, pulling her up in one smooth motion and setting her in front of him on the horse.

A shot rang out. "Rose, no, don't let them kidnap you again!" Ben ran towards them, pistol drawn. Another shot sounded as Kwa-na pulled the reins, moving the horse momentarily to face Ben as he worked around the stump of a dead tree.

Searing pain tore through her ribs and she involuntarily slumped forward. Kwa-na wrapped his arm around her and dismounted, landing hard on the ground, then he smacked the horse, who ran directly at Ben, blocking further gunfire as Kwa-na ran towards the shed, holding her limp body. Ronnie's side was sticky with blood. Kwa-na carried her behind the shed, laying her gently on the ground.

Kwa-na tore her skirts and pressed the fabric against the bullet hole, making Ronnie yell out in pain. He pressed hard against her wound. One of Kwa-na's men barked something, and the rest of the party rode off. Kwa-na's horse was wandering nearby, and he whistled to the animal. In response, it trotted closer. Kwa-na waved it off and the horse ran a few hundred yards and then stopped and lowered its head, grazing.

Ronnie closed her eyes, and the Native caressed her hair off her forehead. He spoke to her in soft Native words that in her delirium translated into her father's voice.

"Ronnie, you are gaining strength in this sphere and in your own life. Trust your gut and you will wander to the right realm and undo what has been set askew. Find Jason Korbin. He will have the answers you are seeking."

Ronnie reached out to touch her dad's face and it morphed back into Kwa-na's. "Thank you." She caressed his cheek and suddenly was pulled upward like a puppet on a string, her arms and legs flailing below her. She could see Kwa-na's large form bent over her and Ben making his way on foot a distance away. Then everything was cloaked in blackness. Ronnie flew to the in-between space, her father's words, clear and strong, still echoing in her mind.

Chapter 41

Return

Ronnie faded in and out of consciousness, belatedly realizing the agonizing pain had ceased. The air was no longer choking with the grit and dryness she'd become used to over the last few days. Humid air rushed past her as she fell, plunging through space and time. Would she shatter on impact? Would she wake up dying in the hospital, or not wake up at all? The transition grew dark, and she curled into the fetal position, with the fleeting thought that she was in an embryonic state before being birthed. Ronnie drifted into a quasi-trance, free of discomfort, but worry growing. Was she dead?

Suddenly and painfully, Ronnie landed in a violent splash. The shock knocked her unconscious.

When her rational mind gripped this latest reality, an uneasiness filled the void. Was she unconscious because Jeb had beaten her senseless? Or was she sleeping by a fire with Kwa-na? Would they treat her horribly as Jere Miah and Ben had predicted? Or was she just dead, leaving her body for heaven…or hell?

A whisper nearby startled her, and she replayed the words. Ronnie reached out to touch Kwa-na's face again, then jerked her hand away, finally piecing it together. She was back in Florida with Mike. Ronnie inhaled sharply and rolled away, but the toilet blocked her movement.

"Ronnie! Thank God you're awake." Mike's voice affirmed his fear.

"Mike?" Ronnie's head was reeling, and she squeezed her eyes shut, not ready for the transition to her own time. Too many demons were waiting for her here.

Worry permeated every nuance of Mike's being. "Oh my God, you scared the absolute hell out of me. Are you okay?"

Ronnie assessed her body. Her hand grazed where the bullet had pierced her chest, expecting excruciating pain. There was none. She was whole again and was in Puerto Rico, not Florida!

"Jesus, Ronnie, can you answer me?" Mike shook her shoulder. His expression brought it all flooding back. He'd been furious when she'd revealed she knew how Kelly died.

Would Mike choke her in a murderous rage like he had Kelly? "No, please no,

Mike, don't hurt me!" She sounded weak and pitiful. That scared her. The doctors warned another episode could kill her. Her ears buzzed with the overwhelming fear of dying, either through Mike's hands or from her body's response to another time travel episode.

Mike sat away from her. "Hurt you? Ronnie, I could never..."

The room was dark with a little light from a candle glowing in the other room. Shadows flitted across his face in a macabre dance of benign and horrific expressions.

"Ronnie, you know I could never hurt you, right? I want to help you, please..." His voice choked off with emotion. "You need a doctor." His mouth crumpled. Fear, not rage, was written on his perfect features.

Her panic tamped down a notch. "No, don't get a doctor. Please, I'm okay."

"You had another episode. I've already called the front desk, but the sons of bitches haven't sent the doc up yet."

Heat crept up her cheeks. "How long was I out?"

"God, I don't know." Mike checked his watch. "Maybe an hour. I lost track of time." His eyes were intense. "We need to get some food in you pronto."

Kelly Escobar's broken face appeared in her mind, making her gasp, then she rolled away. "Mike, please don't." Tears stung her eyes. She'd already seen the devil in Jeffrey, Jere Miah, and Jeb. Were all men born of evil, or was that her skittish, thiamine-deficient mind playing games with her? Was Mike the connection through time, or was he a scary fiancée murderer?

A loud crashing sound caught their attention, and Ronnie remembered the raging storm, bringing her energy down another few notches.

Mike jumped up, jerking the hotel door open. "Shit!" Then he returned, bringing back cooler, wetter air. His face was pale.

"What?" Her ears buzzed now with the stress. A visceral inward tugging broke inside her, and an uncontrollable shaking started.

"Please, Ronnie, don't..." Mike grabbed her wrist and took her pulse, brushing her forehead with the back of his hand. "I need to move you. You're going into shock!"

Ronnie's heart raced. Mike's meaty hand clutched her arm. She jerked away. "Shock? Are you positive?"

"Hey, Ronnie. Jeez, let me help you for God's sake." Mike bent down to pick her up.

"No!" Ronnie pulled away. "Get off me!"

Mike sat back on his heels, palms up in an expression of defeat. "I'm *not* going to hurt you. I need to elevate your feet. You're going into shock, Ronnie." His tone held no anger. Instead, it was laced with tenderness and concern.

Gnats flew wildly around her vision and Ronnie squeezed her eyes shut, but not before she saw the deep lines of exhaustion worn prominently on his face. "Okay. Okay."

Mike carried her to the sitting area and gently settled her on the floor, picking up her legs and elevating them to the couch. Then, in a blur, he returned with a blanket and covered her up. His voice was farther away. "I need a doctor NOW! Room 527." Mike took on the same menacing tone he had just before he'd punched the wall.

Ronnie shut her eyes and focused on the shaking that started deep in her gut.

"My friend is going into shock. I need a fucking doctor NOW!" Mike spoke into the phone. "Ronnie has a condition that could kill her... Twenty-eight-year-old female, Korsakoff syndrome. K-O-R-S-A-K-O-F-F."

Mike's terror-filled eyes never left her. He must have seen the Dark Angel circling her head.

Mike slammed the phone down. "Fucking useless!" He knelt next to her and tucked the blanket around her. "How do you feel?"

Ronnie slurred out the words, "In a time warp."

Mike bit his lips. "You're shaking. Cold? Or...?"

"Uh," was all Ronnie could manage.

Mike held her wrist, checking her pulse. Ronnie drifted off to sleep for what seemed like days. A peaceful, lush meadow was all around, and a monarch butterfly floated past her. Ronnie startled awake at the sound of his voice.

"Here's my concern. If you're in shock, you shouldn't eat or drink. If you're having a thiamine drop, you need food. What sounds right to you, Ron?"

The shaking had quieted a little and a deep gnawing in her stomach answered the question.

"Ronnie." Mike placed his hand on her forehead, panic clear in the short, clipped tone.

"Food," Ronnie eked out.

"Did you feel like this the first time?" Mike moved one section of hair out of her eyes.

"No. But I did in the hospital," Ronnie said with tremendous effort.

"Shit." Mike reached across her and snagged the cracker box. "I hope this is the right decision." He handed her one cracker. "Sit up so you don't choke. Do you need help?"

Ronnie nodded, hating being so vulnerable.

Mike gently lifted her up to a sitting position, moving her feet at the same time. He took her pulse again.

Ronnie settled against the couch, relaxing her arm in his grip. "I'm okay." Was the single cracker in her hand her lifeline? The shivering had slowed with the warmth of the blanket. "What was that noise?"

Mike shook his head, glancing away. "Just some glass breaking in the lobby. Don't worry about that. We should be okay here."

"Glass breaking?" Ronnie tried to recall what the lobby looked like. "Must have been a lot of glass."

"Eat." Mike pushed her hand towards her face. "You look a lot better than you did ten minutes ago." Mike watched her intently. "Pulse not so rapid, too. Eat." His tone softened.

Ronnie took a tiny morsel of the cracker and chewed.

Mike twisted the top off a water and pressed it into her free hand. "Wash it down. The sooner you get some in your system, the better you'll feel." His voice was urgent.

Was there an inkling of evil there? Devastatingly gorgeous eyes flashed a concerned blue at her. Half of her wanted to run far, far away. Unfortunately, the legs weren't ready for such things. The other half wanted all of him. That thought made her queasy.

Ronnie ate. As much as she despised Jeffrey, he was right about coming to Puerto Rico. Every instinct to save herself had done nothing to accomplish that. She shoveled crackers in her mouth, annoyed at all the chewing. Thiamine needed to be in her system pronto. He needed to *not* be a friggin' murderer. The memory flooded back of her time with Morris, and a hard flash of Max in the 1800s overwhelmed her. She used that memory to compare Mike to Max, and while the physical resemblance was there, something about the demeanor of Max was familiar. A few strange things he said as well. Was that Mike in another life? Was she connected to him in ways beyond this realm?

Ronnie opened one eye as Mike shifted to the floor across from her, giving her some space. She got an eyeful of his flexing muscles. No doubt Mike was eye candy. Was he a good kisser? A wave of nausea hit her hard. Ronnie sprinted to the bathroom just in time to slam the door in his face. Again.

"You okay?" Mike called through the door.

Ronnie threw up all the hard work of her cracker chewing. When she didn't answer, Mike shoved the door open, and she kicked it closed, not wanting to share this horrid moment with anyone, especially not him.

"I'm getting the doctor," Mike yelled through the door.

"No, don't leave me alone!" Ronnie took a few calming breaths, then brushed her teeth. Feeling a profound need to lie down, she opened the door and Mike took her elbow and led her through the living room.

She lay on her side, stretching out on the couch. "It's going to look like I'm dead, but I'm just going to rest for a minute."

"You're not planning on dying, are you?" Mike attempted to be lighthearted, but the twist of his mouth showed his regret. He handed her the blanket.

She spread it over her legs. "Does anyone truly plan on dying?"

"I didn't, that's for sure." He sat against the wall and shook his head.

What a weird comment. *Didn't plan on dying.* Why didn't he say *I don't* plan on dying? God, she hadn't either, but it kept happening every friggin' storm.

"Thought you were going to close your eyes." His face looked less pinched, and that restored a modicum of calm in her.

Food was the cure. But barfing was not a suitable response. Did any thiamine get into her system? Ronnie willed the nausea to pass, forcing her body to relax. He'd not murdered her yet, so there was that. She tried to tune out the roaring of the storm just a few feet away.

In less than a minute, Ronnie was dreaming of riding Buttercup in a field next to Kwa-na, glancing at the other Natives, trying to read their expressions.

Chapter 42

What Happened That Night?

Mike kept a close eye on Ronnie sleeping on the couch, peering at his watch every minute or so. He knew rest was necessary, but how long would it take for her to crash without the thiamine?

He lightly shook her shoulder. "Sorry to wake you. I think you should eat more." Mike was surprised at how worried he sounded. Hell, he *was* terrified she would pass out again, but he needed to convey calm to her.

Startled, her eyes were wide. Did he detect a sliver of fear? Unsure if it was from his presence, or fear of the illness, he concluded it was likely both. She probably thought he had beaten Kelly to death.

Ronnie sat up, stretched, then reached for the crackers, taking a small bite. She no longer had a grayish-white hue—more of her natural coloring had returned.

Relief washed over him. "Feel better?"

She nodded. "How long was I asleep?" Her thick lashes brushed her cheeks as she blinked awake.

"Fifteen minutes."

"That's it? Seemed like a lifetime." Ronnie lay her head back down and closed her eyes.

He shifted closer. "Keep your eyes shut. I want to check your pulse again. You look stronger, not so pale."

"I do? Good." She spoke around the crackers.

Mike counted the heartbeats, ticking down the time, marveling at how slim her wrist was. As he calculated the numbers, he studied her face. Despite her illness, she was ridiculously beautiful. With her eyes closed, it offered free rein to take in the full, pink lips, sculpted cheekbones, and her delicate jaw that made her eyes seem even bigger.

As if on cue, they popped open and displayed the oversized irises that gave her an almost otherworldly beauty. He momentarily got lost in their gray majesty glowing in the candlelight, a deep, angry ocean with twinges of blue from the couch.

"Dr. Walsh, what is your diagnosis?"

Mike chuckled. She'd caught him off guard. If he weren't careful, he'd fall head over heels and be completely useless. "My patient is looking better. Not out of the woods. Eat more, please."

The gray-blue oceans squinted as she delivered another cracker to her perfect lips.

Her improvement allowed a new worry to blossom. The sound outside the room had been a portion of the atrium crashing fifteen stories into the lobby. Had they been struck by a tornado? What other damage had it caused? National Suites would have to evacuate when the building deteriorated from the rain pouring in and more glass started falling into the lobby. Damn, it would also mean that the storm was wreaking havoc on the rest of the island, filling up the hospitals.

He eyed the curtain that covered the glass, making up the fourth wall of their room. It would not be safe to stay here as the winds whipped up inside the hotel. Something could easily get picked up and shatter that glass. Who had designed such an unstable structure near the shore on a Caribbean Island? He'd downplayed the damage to Ronnie, but at some point, it would be inevitable. As soon as she was stable, they would have to leave. He would hate to do it, but they would need to drive to a hospital before all the MRIs were overbooked.

"You okay?" Mike felt like a broken record asking the same questions, but it was a changing situation.

"Yeah. How much do you suppose I need to eat?" The strength in her voice was gone for now.

"I don't know. Do you want a protein bar or something more substantial?" She would need it for the drive to the hospital.

"What about the food they gave us earlier?" She sat up. "What kind of sandwich was it?"

"Peanut butter, I think." He walked to the fridge and snagged one of the bags.

"Sounds good."

Mike handed her the wrapped sandwich out of the bag. "An apple, too."

"Fancy." Ronnie removed the plastic wrap from the sandwich and took a bite, then made a face. "What the hell is that?" She spoke around the food and removed the top piece of bread. "Mike, seriously?"

He leaned down to examine the pinkish spread with distinctive red splotches. "Oh, that's a Puerto Rican sandwich. I had one the other day. Spam, Cheez Whiz, and red peppers. It sounds horrible, but it was pretty damn good."

"Seriously?" She ate more and analyzed it. "It's delicious."

He tossed the bag with the apple in it, and it landed next to her.

"You eat too, Mike. You'll need your strength for all the sitting we're going to do." She smirked. An excellent sign.

"Nope, I'm gonna keep my girlish figure and watch you cram your face some more." He sat back in the office chair where he could give her space.

"Tell me whilst I chew, what happened to Kelly?" It came out in a neutral tone, but she couldn't hide the steel in her expression.

Well shit. Mike shoved down the fury. He deliberately chose his words, stalling by rubbing his scraped knuckle where he'd jabbed the wall.

Ronnie ate more and eyed him, stress turning her mouth down.

Mike started at the calmest place possible. "Kelly and I were engaged. She was everything to me. We had so many plans, so many dreams, all cut short that day."

Ronnie's eyes held a mixture of curiosity and mistrust.

His anger flared, knowing what she was thinking, knowing what that stupid newspaper had accused him of doing to Kelly. "What Jeffrey showed you were sensationalist lies." Mike groaned in revulsion and forced back the vicious hatred at how he'd been treated by the media, and worse yet, how his hometown had betrayed him. He drew a deep breath, attempting to calm down so she could hear his words, not his anger. "Ronnie, she did die in the shower, just as that damn rag said. But she didn't die by my hands. She had epilepsy."

Ronnie squinted and her head tilted in surprise. Was she blinking back tears? "She did?"

"Yeah." Mike was overwhelmed with emotion, but he continued. "We had a fight that night. I was given a promotion, but it meant we had to move to Florida. She didn't want to leave her family, and I was being a selfish ass." Mike assessed her reaction, but she remained neutral, probably sussing out if he were full of shit or not. "Kelly was happy about the promotion, but she was afraid of losing the help her parents could provide if we stayed in Rochester. She couldn't drive because of her condition, and they were always there for her. Her sister, too. They were so good to her, supporting her where I couldn't."

"So how did she die, Mike?" The challenge was out of her words, and her tone had softened.

Mike attempted to continue, but his emotions took over. He steepled his fingers, trying to hide behind his hands and compose himself. Then he shrugged one shoulder and covered his face, unable to stem the tears. He looked up at the ceiling. No point in hiding the overpowering grief. "We were fighting about the move, and I lost my temper."

Ronnie drew her knees to her chest and curled into a ball.

Mike sat up and leaned towards her, making her flinch. "No, God no. Shit, Ronnie, don't think that about me. I just punched the wall. I could never hit Kelly. I could never take my anger out on a woman. Ever."

Her eyes were wide, and she inhaled sharply.

"Ronnie, I loved Kelly with everything I am. Losing her like that was the most horrific moment of my life. Not far behind was what the papers reported about me." He angrily wiped away tears.

Finally, he continued as Ronnie watched him closely. What exactly had Jeffrey told her, the damn manipulative snake?

"She reacted like you did when I punched the wall. I have a temper, as you saw, but I would never hurt her...or you. We'd been drinking, and she stepped backward and lost her balance. Kelly hit her head on the edge of the bedside table. I will never forget the sound of it. It was horrifying. I got her ice. It was only a little blood and a knot on the back of her head. She seemed to be okay. After, we watched a movie... She seemed fine."

Ronnie wiped a tear, and her mouth tightened with emotion.

Mike continued. "I fell asleep. I can't forgive myself for that. While I was out, she died in the shower." Against his will, he let out a sob. It had been bottled up for so long, there was no way to suppress it. The remorse and the terrible loss overwhelmed him nearly as much as it had at the time. The wound opened wide—the sorrow and regret flowed out in his ridiculous tears.

Mike wanted to get it all out now, so she knew the whole truth, the full story, so they'd not have to discuss this again. He spoke, not even wiping the tears now, but let them fall with the raw emotion of reliving the moment.

"I woke up to use the bathroom a few hours later and heard the shower running. I knew she'd been in there when I'd fallen asleep. The impact with the table must have triggered an epileptic seizure and she..." His words choked off.

Ronnie yanked out a tissue and chucked the Kleenex box at him, then dried her tears. "I am just so sorry, Mike."

He wiped his eyes. "I heard nothing. Her seizure made it look like she'd been battered. The media interviewed a cop on the scene, and he was convinced I'd beat her. For Christ's sake, he was merciless. I guess its what cops see most of the time. I don't blame the guy, but I'll never forgive him for talking to the stupid paper. My hand was bloody. My blood alcohol was high enough they suspected I'd beat the hell out of her and forgotten."

The anger in Ronnie's eyes had diminished, and hopefully the lies Jeffrey had told were falling away, her mistrust along with it.

"The medical examiner told a different story along with the forensic expert I brought in to explain the injuries. Her cause of death was drowning." Mike swallowed a sob. "She drowned because I wasn't there for her. I will never forgive myself for falling asleep." He'd stifled the guilt down for years now. There had been no reason to relive the incredible pain, knowing he could have prevented her death.

Ronnie blinked at the tears gathering. "Mike, I'm so sorry. It must have been hard to go through that, then to have everyone accuse you of hurting her." Ronnie looked drained, but her pinkish tones still played on her cheeks. "No wonder you were so pissed when I let it fly that I knew."

Mike shook his head, shoving the anguish back down, pulling himself together. After all, he was a damn US Marine. They were not blubbering idiots. "Pissed doesn't even describe my feelings about that pencil neck."

"Jeffrey emailed me the article and told me to never be alone with you."

He turned towards her, biting his tongue, wanting to spew a lengthy string of foul-mouthed, highly expressive words describing Jeffrey Brennan, but controlled himself. The last thing he needed was to scare her more or get her agitated in her delicate state.

Ronnie watched him intently, as if she'd dropped a bombshell and he'd ignored it. "What was that?"

Ronnie uncurled her legs. "I said we broke up before I left." A look of disgust crossed her face, but then it smoothed out.

Mike let that soak in for a few heartbeats. "Wait, you broke up with Jeffrey? You two are done?" A smile formed unexpectedly at the corners of his mouth.

"Yup. You'd have been proud of me, Mike." She smiled now, lighting up her entire being. "For the first time, I stood firm against Jeffrey's rant, letting all of his anger flow around me. For once, I didn't care what he said. He threw his usual torrent of bullshit at me, manipulation, guilt, and insults, and I told him to get the hell out."

Mike laughed. "Really? Damn, I wish I'd been there."

Her eyes sparked with excitement. That was a good sign. "When I told him I was leaving to come here, he lost it. That's what prompted me to dump his sorry ass. Jeffrey acted like he owned me, like I had no choice but to listen to him. Like I was crazy." Ronnie held the Kleenex up to her mouth, probably reliving the moment. "Thankfully, the FedEx guy showed up and got him out of my house before it was too heated."

"When did he tell you about Kelly? I mean, you're pretty brave to leave with me, especially having just gotten out of the hospital."

Her brows furrowed. "While we were flying here. He texted me a million times to read the email he sent, which I ignored. I thought he was trying to get me back. Then, after we had that lovely day in the ocean, I picked up the phone, thinking it was you. He insisted I open the email so I would know who I was dealing with." She shot him a sympathetic glance. "He must have looked into your past after I left, but he didn't waste any time sharing the newspaper article with me."

Mike felt the fury rise and tried to contain it but stood up and paced the room. "The damn asshole. Stirring up all of this. Look how much he's upset you. He knows you're still recovering."

Ronnie drew the blanket over her knees, looking wary of him again.

"I'm sorry, Ronnie." Mike held up his hands, then sat back down. "It infuriates me. He's such a tool, a manipulating sack of shit, to put you through that."

"And _you_." She shook her head.

"What did you ever see in him, Ronnie? He must be able to put on the charm, but I sure as hell don't see it."

Ronnie wrinkled her nose and shook her head. "Of course you don't. He hated you from the second you met, Mike. It's no surprise he tried to keep us apart. He certainly couldn't let you 'champaign and first class' me like you promised when he walked in on us on my first day of work."

"Jeffrey was such a prick that day, wanting to make sure I knew he was your boyfriend." He packed down the pure hatred and fury for her sake. It hadn't lessened those feelings any, though.

"Operative word," Ronnie made finger quotes, "'was'! Anyway, thank you for telling me what happened that night with Kelly. What a terrible loss." She wiped her eyes again and sighed. "I'm so sorry this got stirred up by the asshat. Jeez, like you already didn't hate him enough."

Mike released a protracted exhale.

"So, you never had a trial?" Her eyes were wide now.

"No, the district attorney was trying to build a case, but once they saw the coroner's report, he dropped it, despite the media incessantly covering it on the news. My lawyer forced them to clear my name by printing a new story. You can find the coroner's report in _The Democrat and Chronicle_ if you Google my name."

"Is that why you moved to Florida?"

Mike pressed into his eyes and wiped away the remaining tears. "If I tell you, will you stuff your pretty face with thiamine?" He nodded at the sandwich.

Ronnie laughed. She dutifully took another bite. "So, Florida?"

"Yeah, Florida." Mike smiled. "Keep eating and I'll keep talking."

She shoved another bite in her mouth, and he nodded.

"Thank God for Billy. He kept me sane through everything. He hauled me out of the pit of hell and talked me into moving with him to Florida. He applied for a job and surprised me by coming over with a car full of boxes. We packed up my place and left right after Kelly's memorial service. Billy's been down here with me ever since."

Ronnie shook her head. "Wow, you can't ask for a better friend than that, can you?"

"Steph and Billy are alike in that way, right?" He smiled, relieved that they'd gotten over that hurdle.

A knock startled them both. Ronnie dragged the blanket up to her chin. Mike opened the door, letting in a wall of wind, making the candle on the table flicker.

A man stood there, soaking wet. A National Suites name tag was pinned to his white short-sleeved shirt. "Good evening, sir, I'm Dr. Acosta. You called the front desk asking for me?"

Mike nodded. "Yes."

The doctor continued. "We will have to evacuate pretty quickly, but I wanted to assess your concerns. Then we must..." The force of the storm dipped through the broken atrium glass and swirled, flinging a huge palm frond against his leg. Before Mike could react, another whirling gust sprayed against the door, sounding like more than just rain. Shards of glass lay on the carpet by the doctor's feet. Mike's attention was drawn up when the doctor grabbed the side of his neck and his knees buckled.

"Doc, you okay?" Mike caught him while pulling him into the room. He gently set Dr. Acosta in the desk chair.

Ronnie jumped up and closed the door, blocking the wind. "I didn't realize how bad it had gotten out there."

"Ma'am." The doctor nodded at Ronnie as Mike hovered nearby in case he teetered off the chair.

"You're bleeding." Ronnie pointed to a stream of red liquid pouring down his calf.

Mike ducked into the restroom, grabbed a washcloth, and handed it to the doctor. The doctor stared at it as if it were a loaf of bread.

Chapter 43

Goggles

Ronnie pressed the washcloth into the wound on the doctor's calf. Stuff scattered on the carpet near his feet looked like broken ice. Ronnie poked one massive piece with her finger. It was a shard of glass, about an inch long and a half inch thick.

Mike bent low to speak face-to-face with him. "Doc, how are you doing?"

The doctor touched his neck and struggled to speak.

"Hey, Dr. Acosta. How many fingers am I holding up?"

Dr. Acosta glanced woozily at Mike. "*Sí, señor*, you have many, many fingers." Then rambled off something incomprehensible in Spanish. Mike caught him just as he slid off the chair.

"Doc, there is a shard of glass puncturing your neck," Mike blurted.

Ronnie looked down at the doctor. Buried in the side of his neck was a three-inch-wide chunk of glass. Blood gushed out of the wound down the back of his shirt.

"Shit, Ronnie, get me a towel."

Ronnie ran to the bathroom and grabbed one of the extra towels. Mike rolled the man on his side and examined the injury. Arterial blood kept the beat of his pulse, spraying out of his neck, soaking into the carpet.

Ronnie squatted down to help. "Oh God, he's really hurt."

Mike wadded up the towel and pressed it around the glass. "It's from the atrium!"

Ronnie watched in horror as the blood rapidly soaked into the towel.

Mike shook his shoulder. "Doc, are you awake?" His eyes were closed, and Mike tapped his cheek. "Dr. Acosta."

Ronnie stepped back away, sitting on the couch. "Mike, is he alive?" Her stomach lurched.

Mike pressed into the carotid artery and searched for a pulse. A faint beating answered the issue. "Yes."

"Pull out the glass, Mike."

"No, we should leave it. It may stem a larger bleed."

Mike pulled the flashlight from his pocket and clicked it on. He lifted one eyelid and flicked the beam, but the doctor's pupil didn't react. He lifted the other lid and repeated the action.

"Damn."

"Well, that's not good."

Mike searched for the man's pulse again, then leaned his cheek near the doctor's mouth. "He's not breathing."

Ronnie felt sick. "Oh God, is he dead?" Smaller cuts along his exposed skin were oozing now.

"'Fraid so, Ronnie." He squatted back on his heels and shook his head.

Ronnie absently wiped the blood from her hands onto the washcloth, trying not to be sick. "So, he's really dead?" Ronnie's vision blurred as the tears swamped her eyes.

"He definitely is." Mike opened the door a crack and closed it. The wind came in gusts. "We need to get out of here. The atrium will become a death trap as it continues to collapse."

Ronnie peeked through the crack in the curtains, looking out to the lobby. "Mike, is this glass going to protect us or become a major liability?"

"Liability. We can't stay in the bedroom. The full brunt of the hurricane is blasting the cracked window, and we can't stay here." He glanced at the dead doctor. "We could stay in the bathroom, but I don't want us to be trapped up here. It will take too long for the rescuers to find us." He shook his head. "Are you strong enough to go downstairs?"

She sat back down, eying the dead man. "Yeah, we certainly don't need to hang out here."

"Pack your stuff. We need to time it between bands of the storm." Mike gathered the food from the fridge and shoved it in his duffel.

The blood transfixed her, coagulating around the doctor. Her stomach roiled at the sight.

Mike covered him with the towel, blotting out the horrid details of his death. "Ronnie, we need to leave before the hotel deteriorates any more."

"Mike, I gotta lie down. Just give me a minute."

"Okay. Close your eyes and gather your strength. Don't even think about him."

Ronnie took deep breaths and forced her shaking muscles to relax, willing the adrenalin to filter out and reserve that energy for later.

"Mind if I gather your things?"

"Please, that would be great." Ronnie thought through the embarrassing items she'd left out but remembered her rapid cleanup before he'd arrived.

He buzzed around the room, placing her loose things on top of the suitcase, then disappeared into the bathroom.

"Eat this, Ronnie." He tossed her a protein bar.

She shoved it in her pocket. "I'm kind of nauseous."

Mike filled his cargo shorts pockets with waters, a few protein bars, and a package of crackers. He unwrapped the sandwich and ate the whole thing in two bites. Then roamed through the rooms, checking for anything left behind. "Alright, let's just talk through what we're going to do. I need you to take that blanket and cover your head and body with it. It should protect you from any falling glass."

"I can do that. What about you?" Fear piled in, competing with the horror of Dr.

Acosta's untimely death. Would something fall on them? Would she have enough energy to make it downstairs without crashing? What then?

Mike opened his suitcase and pulled out the baseball cap he'd worn on the boat. God, that seemed like years ago. He pulled out a pair of sunglasses. "I'm good."

"That's it? That's all you have?"

"I'm fine. Do you have glasses?"

Ronnie snorted. "I have my goggles."

"Where?" He was serious. "They'll protect your eyes from rain and debris."

"Outer pocket of my suitcase."

Mike pulled the goggles out, then tossed them to her.

Ronnie slid the goggles on. They still smelled of the ocean. "It's like I'm dressing up for a play or something."

Mike stood and peeked out of the glass wall overlooking the lobby, then opened the door and studied the scene.

"You ready? The wind seems to have died down a tad."

Ronnie felt sick.

His tone softened. "It's gonna be alright. We'll get out of here. We just need to make it quickly to the staircase. There won't be anything flying around in there."

"Okay. Are you sure?"

"It is made of concrete so we should be safe." Mike examined the map plastered to the hotel door. "Let's see, it's about thirty paces to the stairwell on this side." He pointed to his right. "On the other side…fifteen." Mike turned towards her. "Once we make it to the stairs, we should be alright. We have to stay out of the center section of the lobby where the atrium is falling. The rest is protected."

Ronnie brightened at that. "It doesn't sound too hard."

Mike smiled. "Nope. It's going to be okay." He ducked into the bathroom and removed his cap, flopped a hand towel over his head, and replaced the hat. "I'm ready."

"Nice, now we both look stupid." She pulled the goggles over her eyes, then covered her head with the blanket.

"Whenever you're up to it, Ronnie."

As long as she didn't glance at the doctor, she could keep it together. "What's the plan when we get to the lobby?"

"They need to know about the doc." He glanced at the body. "I feel horrible for his family."

Ronnie said a quick prayer for them all. Then took a deep breath and didn't like the shakiness evident there. Panic rose again, alarmed at her precarious state. Where would they go next?

He offered his hand. "Madam."

"We make a great pair." What if she crashed like she had after Hurricane Frances? Even then, she'd almost died with a full hospital at her beck and call.

The smile left Mike's face. "Grab your stuff and let's get out of here before another rain band hits."

Ronnie knelt in front of her bag and gently put the things he'd gathered inside, trying to control the fear and dread. As soon as they left the room, she'd have nowhere to lie down if she fell apart.

Mike opened the door and assessed the situation. "Ready?"

Ronnie stood on shaky legs and blew out the candle. She gathered the blanket over her head. "Ready as I'll ever be."

Mike slung the duffel bag strap over his shoulder and picked up the other bags, gathering them in one hand, the hang-up bags draped over his arm. She glanced around the room, worrying that she'd forgotten something, but didn't have the energy to look thoroughly like she normally would.

They ran towards the stairwell, with Mike on the outer side closest to the railing. The hurricane had invaded the building. Wind and rain whipped around. A scream from the lobby tore through her like a physical blow. A plastic bag swirled as if caught in a tornado, hovering at eye level five stories up. It was a hauntingly terrifying scene.

Mike grabbed her elbow, pulling her along, swung the stairwell door open, and they stepped inside. He smiled and wiped a leaf off her cheek. "You okay?"

"Yeah, that was wild." She held up the wet blanket. "I can't make it down the stairs with this stupid thing." The air was calm in the stairwell. Such a contrast to the noise and chaos right outside the door.

Mike grabbed it, wadding it under his arm. "Careful, you're dripping. We don't have too far to go. Just keep it together, Ronnie." Mike took her elbow as they made their way down the stairs.

"Where will we go?" Ronnie asked.

Mike shoved the sunglasses in his pocket. The emergency lights were still on but fading as the battery power drained. "Who knows? The doctor said we'd have to evacuate soon. I wonder if we will have to cram into the conference rooms."

"Or maybe a hotel nearby?" Ronnie's legs wobbled with each step. He matched his steps to hers as they continued down to the lobby, her rolling suitcase occasionally hitting the railing.

"Yeah. Problem is, if this entire hotel evacuates, the other hotels will all be full."

Ronnie fought through the weariness and sat on the top step on the second-floor landing. The wind whipped up her worry.

"You alright?"

"Weak." She wondered how far the hospital was from here, and if the roads would be passable. She sat for a few minutes, then they continued down to the lobby level.

Mike listened at the door before cracking it open. "The elevator has a covered section. We should be okay." Mike's expression lightened. "I don't think you'll need your protective layer." He nodded at the blanket under his arm. "Ready?" he asked, his hand on the door handle.

"Yeah." Ronnie pulled the goggles over her eyes again and Mike pulled his cap low, leaving the sunglasses in his pocket.

Damp, humid air engulfed her, and an occasional spray of rain whipped towards them, but it was free of blowing glass or damaging debris. Mike took her by the arm and led her to the office. Two men sat huddled around a desk.

Mike set down the luggage and stepped into the small room. "Hey, we're in room 527."

"Hello, sir. Everything okay?" One man stood and nodded at them. His name tag read *Manager.*

"Well, not exactly. We called earlier asking for the doctor to check out my friend here." Mike nodded towards Ronnie.

"Yes, has she been checked out?" the manager said, almost defensively.

"No, actually, Dr. Acosta..." Mike glanced at Ronnie and shook his head. "He's dead."

"Excuse me?" The manager walked towards them. "Dead?"

Ronnie spoke up. "Yeah, a huge piece of glass cut him pretty badly and he bled out in a few minutes. He's still up there."

"Dr. Acosta is gone?" The manager made the sign of the cross. "No..." He eyed his coworker, mouth agape.

"She still needs help. Is there another doctor on staff that can examine her?" Mike turned around, worry lines showing between his brows.

"Sir, he was the only doctor on staff." He wiped his eyes and pressed his lips together. "There is no way to find anyone in this chaos."

"Are you evacuating the hotel?" Mike asked while slicking water out of his eyes.

The manager spoke through his grief. "Our instructions are to evacuate to the three hotels nearby. We're sorting through which patrons go to which hotels. We should have it done within the hour. There are only three shuttles, so it will have to be coordinated. We'll need to get everyone downstairs into the ballrooms where they can be protected while we wait."

Mike helped Ronnie into a chair. "You okay?"

The room was spinning, and Ronnie leaned over, trying to make the spots dancing around her vision go away. Male voices blended into the storm raging outside, and she lost track of the words.

Chapter 44

Out in the Storm

Mike turned back to the hotel manager, imagining every guest in the hotel crammed into a ballroom while tornadoes bandied about.

The manager shook his head. "Your best bet is to get her to the hospital, sir. There are so many injured here, and without our doctor, we won't be able to tend to any of them."

"How far away are we talking?" Mike asked.

The clerk opened a drawer in his desk and pulled out a pamphlet. He offered it to Mike. "I have this from the community medical center. It is ten minutes away."

"Is that just a doctor's office? I don't want to get all the way out there and find it closed." Mike stepped closer to take the pamphlet from him. "I can't be driving around out there lost in the storm with her like this." His pulse beat in his temples.

"No, you're right, that's probably closed right now." The manager took the pamphlet back and opened a file cabinet.

Ronnie slumped off the chair and slipped to the floor in the cramped office, bumping against Mike's leg.

Mike caught her and set her on the floor, tugging the goggles off so he could get a better look at her. They tangled in her hair, the blonde strands gripping tight. Her forehead was clammy again. Was she going into shock? "Damn it, wake up, Ronnie!" He raised her feet and settled them on the chair.

Ronnie woke up confused.

"You fainted, Ron." Mike watched her intently.

Her eyes were closed, but she surprised him when she whispered, "I need food." Her voice was weak.

"Sure." Mike rose and drew out a package of peanut butter crackers from his pocket. "Can I sit you up now? Once we get to the car, you can lie down again."

She nodded.

Mike gently set her back in the office chair. He knelt near her, making certain she'd not topple over again. He opened the crackers and raised one to her mouth. "Ronnie, I hate to say it, but we have to go to the hospital."

Her face crumpled. "How far?"

"It's not far, it's only a twenty-minute drive. I think." Mike glanced at the manager, and he nodded.

Ronnie's eyes opened. "In a hurricane?"

"A tropical storm, maybe," Mike corrected.

She closed her eyes and exhaled sharply. "Remember the last time I went out in a hurricane?"

"Yeah, I do. But I got you to the hospital safe and sound. We should be okay. Just need to go right now before things get worse out there." He smoothed her hair off her face, pulling the goggles out of her hair and shoving them in his pocket.

The two employees spoke in rapid Spanish, then the manager switched to English. "Sir, with all the rain, many of the roads will be flooded. You should take the mountain pass to the hospital." He took the map and followed with his finger. "It's only a few minutes longer."

"Okay, that sounds good. Can you mark it for me?" Mike tapped the map.

The manager grabbed a Sharpie and marked the road from the National Suites to the emergency room, making a detour up a mountain, well above the floodwaters.

Mike folded the map and crammed it into his back pocket. "Thank you so much."

"Mike?" Ronnie tugged on his sleeve.

"Yeah?"

"Where is the car? Is it in the outside parking area?" Her mouth crumpled, and she struggled with her emotions.

"No, it's in the covered garage. I'll bring it closer."

She shook her head. "No. I need to stay with you."

A twinge of alarm surged through his chest. She was scared, and that meant she was close to crashing. "I'm not leaving you."

The manager motioned to his clerk, who squeezed past them. A second later he returned, and they loaded Ronnie into a wheelchair, covering her with the blanket for protection. Mike set the duffel bag on her lap and balanced Ronnie's rolling suitcase on the left handle of the wheelchair and picked up the hanging bags, flinging them over his shoulder. The manager let them through the back hallway and held the door open for them. "The elevator is out, of course, but you can use the ramp to find your car."

"Thank you." Ronnie sounded shaky.

Mike shook his hand. "Thank you for your recommendations."

"Yes, you're very welcome. Feel better, miss."

Ronnie waved.

"Here we go. You ready for a wild ride, Ronnie?"

"Yeah. Woo." She raised her fist and then adjusted the blanket to cover up to her neck. It was breezy but there was no debris blowing around.

Mike pushed her up the ramp to the third level, breaking a full sweat with the workout. It was good to be moving again after so much lounging about. He spotted the Jeep and helped Ronnie inside, then piled their gear into the trunk, then sat in the driver's seat.

"Ready, Freddy?" Mike glanced over at her.

She smiled. "Ready as I'll ever be. Let's beat the floodwaters, Mr. Walsh." Then she tossed the blanket in the back seat.

"Do you mind if I crank up that air conditioning?" Mike asked.

She shook her head.

"Eat those crackers. I don't want you to keep crashing." Mike turned the engine over and cranked up the AC. He hesitated, staring at her, and she finally took the hint by cramming a cracker in her mouth.

"I'll make a deal with you. If I promise to not crash, you do the same." She scrunched up her nose playfully.

"Deal." Mike opened the map and pointed to the hospital. "This is where we're going. Can you follow along and make sure I don't miss *that* turn?"

Ronnie took the map and flattened it out on her lap.

"You need anything?" His worry was quashed for now. It was strange how she seemed fine for a while then she totally fell apart. At least there were good moments before she crashed. Maybe the thiamine was working.

"Nope, I'm good."

Mike turned down the parking lot ramp, adrenalin spurring him on, hoping he was making the right decision about leaving, about taking the mountain pass. There were risks with that route as well.

As they left the safety of the garage, the storm shoved them around like a toy. Ronnie sat up and clutched the handle on the roof.

"Relax if you can. You'll need to save your energy, Ronnie. I got this." As Mike made the first turn, the wheels hydroplaned on the slick pavement. "Sorry, the roads are covered in leaves and mud. Hard to keep traction."

Ronnie redoubled her grip as he proceeded. The wind pummeled the SUV, and occasional leaves and small branches splatted the windshield. Mike swerved into the opposite lane to dodge a downed tree.

Ronnie pulled out another cracker, glancing at the map. "You're just going to stay on this street until we turn onto the mountain road. Turn left at the next intersection. It'll be a while." She popped the cracker in her mouth.

"Alrighty." Mike attempted a chipper tone, hiding his apprehension. The left turn brought them to a long winding ridge. It was difficult to see farther than a few feet ahead of them. As the elevation increased, the treetops were parallel to the car on the passenger side. Mike had to focus intently on the road, trying not to think about how far down they'd fall if he made a mistake. Mud covered the lane in front of him and the wheels fought to maintain traction. A low rumbling vibration caught his attention.

Ronnie turned to him. "Do you hear that, Mike?"

The noise intensified, and Mike stopped, craning his neck to look up the cliff. "Shit!" He jammed the Jeep in reverse as a murky shadow slid down towards them. "Mudslide. Ronnie, hold on."

A roaring drowned out any other sound as metric tons of earth and rock forced the Jeep closer to the edge of the precipice. Mike tried to back out of the avalanche, but it overtook the Jeep, engulfing it in mud.

"Oh my God, Mike!" Ronnie yelled.

Mike reached out to pull her tight, protecting her as the vehicle was slammed on the driver's side, forcing it through the guardrail, down to the depths below. Time seemed to slow down as every loose object in the Jeep was airborne. Ronnie screamed as the windshield cracked, allowing the mud, rocks, and leaves to ooze over the dashboard. They rolled in a deathly dance with gravity.

Chapter 45

River Rescue

Impact jarred every bone in Ronnie's body.

∞

Intense pain blocked out her other senses, but a sound drew her out of the confusion. When the noise suddenly stopped, she realized it was of her own making. An ice-cold sensation covered her feet and was rising rapidly to her waist. Was she paralyzed? Thoroughly awake now, Ronnie took in the damage. The roof was crushed, the windshield cracked, and the destroyed rear window was letting in a torrent of frigid water that was rising at an alarming rate. They'd fallen all the way down to the river!

A horrible grinding sound, metal against rock, followed by movement, sent a rush of strength through her muscles. The Jeep was rotating in the river with the full power of the current against the car. Her window was holding it at bay, but for how long? The current lifted the vehicle, forcing Ronnie to grip the seat until it rocked to a stop, lying on the driver's side. Mike's unconscious form dipped underwater as the Jeep filled, submersing him completely. He still didn't move.

Ronnie shook him. "Mike, Mike!" When he didn't respond, she reached for his seatbelt, fumbling with numb fingers. Frantically she searched for the button, and it released. Then she unbuckled her own seatbelt and lifted Mike's face out of the murky water, just as the river forced another rotation, flipping the Jeep upright again, slamming her hard against the passenger door. Her teeth slammed together with the impact. Mike was still unconscious.

"Mike, wake up!" Ronnie shook him, panic rising. The car turned clockwise and jammed against a rock, wedging it in place. This new position created a plume over the windshield, leaving a gap as the river diverted around them, creating an opportunity to escape. Ronnie crawled to the back seat and kicked out the rest of the rear window. She reached between the driver's door and Mike's seat, lowering his chair, and Mike along with it.

Ronnie reached under his arms and tugged, pulling him into the back seat, grateful for the buoyancy offered by the half-filled car. Would the current pull Mike from her grip and drown them in a matter of seconds?

Her lifeguard training kicked in and Ronnie slipped her right arm under Mike's t-shirt, gripping under his armpit. His head had to stay above water, or he would drown. Ronnie kicked against the rear seat to position their entry into the water. The Jeep jerked to the right. Her window of opportunity was running out.

Something caught, impeding Mike's movement. "Crap, what the hell are you caught on, Mike?" He still didn't respond. Ronnie grabbed his waistband, pulling hard, but still, his leg was caught. Moving down his body towards the impingement, she positioned his chin up, straightening the spine to keep his face above water. The seatbelt was wrapped around his foot. Ronnie freed it and felt her way up his body, pushing his butt and the small of his back up so his midsection stayed near the surface, keeping his head above the waterline. This was not how she'd imagined feeling him up. He was supposed to be awake for that.

Ronnie paused, taking one last chance to check his breathing before abandoning the car for the river. She'd not checked his airway or pulse. Was he alive? Full of fear, she leaned close, placing her cheek near his mouth. A tickle of warm breath brushed against her cheek. He was breathing! Thank God! Blood oozed from an injury to his temple. Would the movement paralyze him? Better paralyzed than drowned. Ronnie repositioned her arm under his shirt, across his thick chest, and gripped under his armpit. For the first time, she wished he was a smaller man.

The Jeep shifted again, raising the flood to the bottom of the window, but that was a blessing, for now Mike floated on the surface, allowing her to push against the rear headrest and swim to exit the rear window. Water rushed around them. The pocket of calm was disappearing as the car shifted to the right, pulled downstream by the raging floodwaters.

She arranged their entry position to prevent Mike from being torn out of her control. Spots danced in her vision. Was she about to faint? The river was impatient and tore them loose from the rear window. Ronnie redoubled her grip around Mike's chest, using every ounce of strength to keep both their heads above water, pushing her hip into his back and using her free arm and legs to sidestroke.

Something struck her back and caused her to dip underwater, pulling Mike under as well. Ronnie fought desperately to break free, but an immense tree shot past them. With Mike firmly in her grip, Ronnie rolled over to disentangle them from the branches, one catching in her hair.

Finally, Ronnie broke the surface and greedily gulped for air, ignoring the dancing spots in her eyes. This was not the time to pass out! Mike's airway was clear, his head cradled between her arm and chest. The tree was now ahead of her, and she swam towards it, until the river snaked to the left, jamming the trunk on the far bank, forcing them to the left, entangling her feet in the branches. Using every ounce of energy, she kicked free while the current washed them to the shallows. Ronnie scrambled to stand and dragged Mike further toward the bank, away from the raging rapids.

Ronnie caught her breath and scoped out the best way to get him to higher ground. Behind her was a sharp incline gouged out by the river, but to her left the land rose gently. She lifted him by his armpits and dragged him backward up the embankment, until she tripped, and all of his weight landed on her, pinning her to the ground. Ronnie gasped for air, gathering her strength, and checked his breathing, ignoring something jamming into her lower back. Was this how she was going to die? Crushed under Mike's dead weight, making Jeffrey's fear of *death by Mike* come true? "Mike, wake up!" She smacked his chest, but he did not move.

Ronnie bent her leg and pressed against the embankment, using her last remaining strength to roll Mike off her, finally succeeding enough to pull her leg free. She knelt next to him, fighting back tears and gasping with the effort. How the tables had turned. When she was strong enough, she stood and dragged him up the incline. The deep grooves made by his running shoes filled immediately from the unrelenting storm.

A huge, canopied tree was nearby, and she pulled Mike under it, leaning his back against the massive trunk. She didn't want to lay him flat for fear of him drowning. He already had water in his lungs from several submergences.

A tremendous crack of thunder overhead made her jump and stabbed a new level of fear in her heart. What if lightning struck the tree? How long until the river flooded this area? Mountains rose steeply on either side. Could she move him up the mountain? Ronnie fought back tears, knowing she would have to leave him to save herself.

Ronnie glanced at his lifeless body lying still in the grass, praying it wouldn't come to that. *Did his eyes just flutter?* She shook his shoulder. "Mike, you awake?"

Mike groaned, then sat up and coughed violently.

Ronnie knelt next to him, her heart beating out of her chest. "Thank God you're back!"

He sputtered in between coughing, "Oh…head hurts so much."

"Mike, you scared me to death!"

When he tried to stand up, she pushed him back down. "No you don't, mister. Lie right there while I check you out." Ronnie bent over him. "Look at me, Mike." He obeyed, and she examined his head. "You got a nasty gash on your temple."

"No duh." Mike touched the wound gently. His eyes widened when his fingers came away coated in blood. "What the hell happened?" Anger laced his words.

"Mudslide." Ronnie glanced towards the water, searching for evidence of the crash. "Do you know your name?"

"I do. Do you know *your* name?" he responded in an angry tone.

She persisted. "What is it?"

"Michael William Walsh." He punctuated the words with another coughing fit. When he caught his breath, a glimmer of hope washed over her. He was lucid. "What day is it?"

Mike shook his head. "I know what *damn* day it is. Um…Wednesday, August fifteenth, 2004. I know we're in Puerto Rico and we are heading to the hospital."

"Close enough, thank God."

"Why are we sitting under a tree, Ronnie?" His tone softened now. "In the rain."

"We crashed into the river."

"We what?" Mike sat up but didn't stand. "Holy shit, Ronnie, are you okay?" He reached over to remove a clump of leaves stuck to her arm.

"I think so. The bigger question is, are *you* okay? You've been out for at least ten minutes."

"Shit, really?" He glanced around, confusion apparent. "Where is the Jeep?" Before she could stop him, he stood up and staggered towards the riverbank.

Ronnie followed, afraid he'd fall into the water. There was no way she had the strength to rescue him again. She grabbed his elbow and steadied him. "In the river."

Mike scanned the raging flood. "Where?" He turned to her, waiting for an answer. She pointed downstream. "Gone."

"*Gone?*" His tone was accusing. He followed her gaze at the mass of debris spinning by in an uncoordinated rush downstream. The Jeep was nowhere to be seen. "So, we're stranded in the mountains, no car, nothing but the clothes on our backs?"

Emotions overcame her, and tears stung her eyes. "Yeah, I guess so. But you're alive, Mike. I didn't have that guarantee a few minutes ago."

An expression of compassion overtook the anger. Mike folded her in his arms and kissed the top of her head.

Ronnie hugged him back. Overwhelming relief washed over her. He was alive. He was okay. Without thinking, she kissed him, releasing a flood of emotions. Relief, gratitude, and something else she'd not expected—passion. His lips tasted of the river, and they were strong and supple.

Mike pulled away, eyes wide in surprise. Then he strengthened his hold on her, nearly lifting her off the ground, and he returned the kiss with equal passion. Ronnie wrapped her arms around his neck and held on, getting lost in a swirl of tender passion. Mike broke the seal of her lips with his tongue, as if not wanting to scare her, but urged a renewed need from the depths of her soul.

She melted into him, feeling a desire she'd not expected. Their wet bodies became one as she explored this exciting, unfamiliar territory, pushing out the terror and thinking only of tasting his mouth. His eager passion released an urgent, animalistic need she'd last released on Morris just before she'd returned. Mike eagerly slid his hands over the curves of her ribs and hips.

Ronnie slid her hands up to his chest, pressing into the muddy t-shirt plastered against his skin. She gripped solid muscle and leaned in to find that eager tongue, imagining what else it could do to her. Another deafening crack of thunder made them both jump, and Ronnie stepped away, regretting the loss of his body heat as it dissipated.

Mike reached out to hold her hand and smiled. "Wasn't expecting that. Thank you."

Ronnie couldn't stifle the smile. "I wasn't either." Across the bank, a wall of mud tumbled down the mountain, moving with it smaller trees and rocks, then splashed into the river, bringing their plight crashing to reality. "Oh my God, Mike, all our stuff is in that river. My ID, passport...money."

Mike tapped his back pockets. "Shit. My wallet too." His eyes were wide. "I don't remember leaving the car. How did we get here?"

Ronnie let out a sigh. "You're damn lucky I was a lifeguard."

Mike cocked his head to the side. "What...?"

"And you're lucky I was strong enough to drag your huge ass up the embankment, too. Dang, how much do you weigh?"

He stared at her, not fully comprehending. "About two-ten."

"Eighty-five pounds more than me, holy shit. No wonder I struggled." Ronnie shook her head.

"What are you talking about?" Mike squinted, looking thoroughly confused.

"Let me spell it out for you, Michael William Walsh. We were driving up there," she nodded at the mountain on the opposite bank, "when a mudslide crashed into the Jeep and it pushed us off the road, and we tumbled into the river. On the way down it smashed out windows and totaled the Jeep."

Mike's jaw went slack, and he looked dazed.

"You were unconscious. I pulled you out, swam like hell, and somehow made it to shore. But not before a tree nearly drowned us."

Mike blanched. "Wait. You're not joking?" He glanced back at the river. "Ronnie, I'm supposed to be protecting you and..." He wiped the rain from his eyes.

"Yeah, I saved the big ole Marine. Stick that in your pipe and smoke it." She cocked her hip and smiled.

Mike bit his lips and shook his head, overcome with emotion. "Damn, I am so sorry. It wasn't supposed to happen like this. You're not supposed to save my useless ass."

"It's a colossal blow to your manhood, I know. But I can only hope you'll recover, eventually." Ronnie kissed his hand, still in her grip. "It wasn't all hard work. I managed to give you quite a wedgie trying to get you free."

Mike laughed and drew her close. "Holy shit, you're gonna get it." And he hugged her tight, poking his fingers into her ribs. She squirmed, enjoying the solidness of his conscious flesh a lot more than the dead weight from a few minutes ago.

She pulled away, fighting the urge to soak in more of his body heat and passion. "Dude, we need to move to higher ground. We can have regrets after we're safe and dry."

Mike smiled, shaking his head. "You're a goddamned badass, Ronnie. You know that?"

Ronnie smiled. "Just get us out of this mess, Mike. I'll even let you be the hero this time."

Mike's eyebrows nearly touched. "How the hell did you swim hauling me in the middle of *that?*" He nodded at the rapids, congested with entire trees, branches, and trash.

"Massive dumb luck and a little skill," she laughed.

Mike pressed his forehead against hers, looking into her eyes. "Thank you, Ronnie. I owe you my life."

Ronnie resisted the urge to devour him again. "I guess we're even now, eh?"

He laughed. "I guess so, my little badass."

Ronnie kissed him, exerting some control, then tore away. "For the record, I was totally okay with owing you for the rest of *my* life."

Mike's smile morphed into a frown. "How are you feeling? Does anything hurt?"

"I'm fine, Mike, you're the one who got knocked out."

"We crashed down a hundred feet or more. Before we hike up the mountain, I need to be sure you're not hurt." He nodded to the beastly incline. Mike stared into her eyes, then touched her neck. "Adrenalin can keep you from feeling pain. Anything hurt here?"

"No."

"Lift your arms to the side," he barked.

She obeyed.

"Turn around."

Mike pressed into her spine, between her shoulder blades and down. "Any pain?"

"Nope."

He then gripped the top of her pelvis and squeezed. "Now?"

"Nothing hurts." She slicked the rain out of her eyes.

Mike turned her to face him. "Lift one leg...now the other. Can you touch your toes?"

She followed his instructions until he was satisfied.

"You're lucky, nothing skeletal." Mike winced.

"Let me look at your bashed-in head."

He cringed at her choice of words but bent over so she could examine it.

Ronnie pressed into the injury, and he jerked away. "Ow."

"Sorry. That is a nasty gash, Mike. Do you feel okay?"

He nodded. "So far so good."

Ronnie grabbed his shoulder and turned him, enjoying the solidness under her fingers. Pressing down his spine, she marveled at the broad groove of muscle on each side. She resisted the urge to grab his butt and wondered if he'd used the same restraint, then copied his instructions and he halfheartedly followed along.

"Okay, let's tackle the mountain." Mike kissed her hand, then walked away, looking up the precipitous hill, scoping out the scene.

The shaking started deep in her gut, and it scared her. Did she have any energy left? What if she couldn't climb up the hill? What would a few hours out in the rain do to her already tapped energy?

Mike returned. "It's gonna be a hell of a climb. Are you up for this?"

Ronnie nodded. "Do you have anything in your pockets?"

Mike's eyebrows met, then he realized what she meant and searched. "Yeah, a water and this." He pulled out a squished protein bar.

"Oh, thank God. Let's save it for later. It may be our dinner."

He shoved them back in his pocket. "Just let me know if you're feeling weird and we can stop to rest. I don't want to overtax your system, but we can't stay here. That river is going to rise fast, and we have to be out of here."

Ronnie eyed the steep incline and felt the shaking again, trying to brush away the near-death experience. Was she just shivering? They should have died in that river. "Yeah, piece of cake."

Chapter 46

Contingency Plans

Jeffrey dialed the number for the third time. The phone buzzed, and he held his breath. "Please, just answer the damn phone."

A woman's voice spoke in rapid Spanish, then when he said hello, she switched to English. "National Suites Guayama, how may I help you?" It was not a recording. It was a woman who sounded like she'd been through hell.

"Hello, my name is Jeffrey Brennan. I am looking for one of your guests."

"What is the name, sir?" she asked politely with a Puerto Rican accent.

"Ronnie Andrews." What would he say to her? Would he cuss her out for hanging up on him or tell her how much he missed her?

"Sir, we sustained damage from a tropical storm. We checked out most of our guests and sent them to other hotels. Let me see which one she was transferred to. It's going to take me a few minutes to go through our list. May I put you on hold?"

"Yes." He expected to hear elevator music or an ad for the hotel while he waited, but the line was silent. A million scenarios raced through his head. Had she and Mike left before the storm started? Was she somewhere else enjoying the carnal pleasures with that meathead? His jaw clenched, and he forced the thought out of his head.

The woman's voice interrupted his controlled exhale. "The only information I have is she is no longer here. I can leave a message for her at the front desk in case she returns."

"I'm confused. Did she check out?"

"I'm sorry, sir, there is no record of her checking out. All our guests were instructed to evacuate to another facility. If a guest left without taking the shuttle, they will not be on our list. She is unaccounted for at this time."

"Unaccounted for? That is not acceptable. I need to know where she is." Worry seeped through the anger.

"I'm sorry, sir, this is out of our control." She sounded eager to get back to her magazine or whatever she did when the hotel was closed.

"Can you check on another guest for me?"

"Certainly. What is the name?"

"Mike Walsh. He was traveling with Ronnie."

"Hold please." Jeffrey paced around the room, tapping his fingers on his thigh. Then threw his pencil across the room. It slammed into the sliding glass window with a thunk and fell to the floor.

After a few agonizing minutes, she returned. "I'm sorry, sir. He is not on our lists. If you do hear from Mr. Walsh, please ask him to contact the hotel security or local police as soon as possible." She sounded serious.

Interesting, he could use this. "I will deliver the message. Can I give him any more information about why they need to talk to him?"

"I don't know other than Mr. Walsh was the last person to speak to our hotel physician." Her voice was emotional. "Is there anything else I can do for you, sir?"

"Is the doctor dead?"

"Sir." Her voice shook, and she paused, composing herself. "He is no longer with us. We need to make a report to the authorities, and we were hoping to get a statement from the witness."

"The witness? You mean Mike? You should know that he is accused of killing someone else. Are the authorities out looking for him?"

"I don't know why they would be. We are in the middle of an emergency situation." She was losing patience.

"Please, may I talk to the hotel manager? I'd like to convey some relevant information about Mike Walsh. It's urgent."

"Yes...I...um..." The phone shuffled, then she came back on. "Hold please."

A deep male voice laden with a Puerto Rican accent picked up the line. "*Hola, señor?*"

"Yes," Jeffrey replied.

"I am the head of security of National Suites Guayama. How may I help you?"

"Thank you for taking my call. I hear Mike Walsh is wanted for questioning for the murder of one of your physicians." Jeffrey didn't mind planting a seed that may grow to be useful.

"Sir, while it is true he is wanted for questioning, we don't...ah..." The man cleared his throat. "What information do you have?"

"I was calling to track down my girlfriend, Ronnie Andrews. She is there with Mr. Walsh on business. Mike killed his fiancée, and I worry he has a disturbed attachment to Ronnie and will do her harm. Do you know where they are?"

"Thank you for the information, sir. What is your name?"

"Jeffrey Brennan. I'm afraid for her life if he's already murdered the doctor... He is really dangerous."

"I was there when Mr. Walsh brought your girlfriend down. She's a tall blonde lady?" the man asked.

"Yes, so you saw her?"

"I did. Now that I think about it, she was really out of it. I wonder if she was drugged or something."

"Seriously? Did you call the police?" Jeffrey sat down now, focusing all his attention on the call.

"No, sir, you realize we are in the middle of an emergency weather situation. We evacuated the entire facility due to tornado damage. They left together a few hours ago. Now that you mention it, they both had blood on their clothes."

"Sir, did they say where they were headed?"

"*Si, señor*, they were going to the hospital. She passed out right in the office. Either she is sick or drugged—she was loopy."

"You're sure they didn't go to another hotel?"

"I don't know. They got directions to the nearest hospital. I'm guessing that is where they went. That's all I know."

"Thank you. Will you put my information in your notes to the authorities? I hope they will pursue him. Just in case, can you tell me where the other guests relocated to? I'll call over there just to be sure."

"Those who didn't leave on their own were shuttled to nearby hotels." He rattled off the names.

Jeffrey grabbed a pen and jotted down the information.

"Thank you." He called the other hotels, but she was not there. "Where the hell are you, Ronnie?" Was the pressure making Mike crack? Shit, was Ronnie in trouble? Worry jumbled his thoughts. Mike would either be getting too cozy with her or wrapping his meaty fingers around her neck, and he couldn't do a damn thing to stop either scenario.

Jeffrey opened his laptop, then typed the c prompt code that brought up a classified tracking application.

"Where the hell are you, Ronnie?"

He typed in commands until a map of the world popped up, then zoomed in, looking for the red blinking dot. Finally, it showed up in the southeastern corner of Puerto Rico.

"What the hell?" He wrote down the coordinates and dropped in the satellite imagery overlay. He blinked, not trusting what he saw. The storm must be screwing up the feed. It looked like Ronnie was in a river ten or more miles west of the hotel. "What the absolute…?"

He clicked on the refresh button. Something was definitely screwed up. The computer initiated the signal search again, hopefully recalibrating her location with the satellite overlay. Once he relocated the red blinking dot, it had moved north ever so slightly. No doubt it was an active feed. He typed more commands to show nearby buildings. Was she at the hospital? Still, she shouldn't be so close to a river in this storm.

He zoomed in, scanning for any nearby buildings, roads, or other signs of civilization. There was nothing but a solitary gas station, and even that was a half mile up the mountain from where she was. He zoomed back in and checked the coordinates again. She was on the move. In dismay, he glared at the screen, breathing hard. Her movement was too slow for a vehicle. Was she on foot out in the storm? "This doesn't make sense. Ronnie, why aren't you sheltering in place?"

He watched it carefully, then pulled up a Google map, trying to sort out what was in that area of Puerto Rico.

Jeffrey slammed the desk, making the mouse jump off the pad. "Why the hell are you in the absolute fucking middle of nowhere?" He'd cultivated her far too long to lose her like this. Especially at the hands of Mike fucking Walsh. "I should never have let you go." The words rattled around in his mind. He'd tried to talk with Ronnie before she'd left, but she wasn't home. She wouldn't answer her phone.

Jeffrey paced the room, forcing down the alarm that, if he let run wild, would tie his brain in knots, leading to bad decisions. He made a beeline to the closet. On the floor, behind the suitcase, he hauled out a black backpack and tossed it on the bed, rummaged around, and drew out a cell phone. He dialed a number.

A man grumbled, "Hello."

"Sarge, Jeffrey Brennan here."

The man's deep voice almost growled in response. "Jeff, man, long time no..." He let it trail off.

"Yeah, long time no fuckery. Are you up for some now?" Jeffrey was glad he'd answered. It meant he was between jobs.

"Always up for fuckery. What flavor?" Sarge sounded hungover.

Jeffrey laughed. "I knew you'd be ready for something. How does rescuing a damsel in distress sound to you?"

"Lame. What else you got?" Sarge barked.

"Aw, you don't want to fly to the Caribbean in a hurricane? It could be dangerous and likely end in a windfall of cash."

Sarge cleared his throat. "Now you're talking. Tell me where and when."

His eagerness was intoxicating. "I'll be there this evening. You got the next few days free?"

"What size windfall are we talking?" Sarge sounded more awake now.

"Double last time. Crew of five? Let me shoot you a proposal and you can tell me what your expenses will be. Then call me when you've sorted the details. This has to be clean." A surge of energy coursed through his brain, sparking a million ideas.

Sarge cleared his throat. Jeffrey imagined him sitting up now, eager to jump on this. "Clean is my middle name. Use the underground. I don't want tracing."

"Done. I'll be in touch." Jeffrey hung up.

He glanced at the tracking application. The red dot was still moving, and from the satellite overlay, it looked like she was climbing a mountain. He wrote the coordinates and consulted the map.

Jeffrey shook his head. "God damn it, Ronnie, now I have to pull you out of a fucking hurricane, again. Why can't you just listen to me for once?"

Jeffrey packed a bag and called his boss, leaving a message.

"Dr. Vasu, this is Jeffrey. I have a family emergency I need to deal with and need to take a few days off to address it. I'll be in touch."

**

Jeffrey held his breath as he showed the ID to the TSA agent. The man likely sniffed Jeffrey's lying nature, but the ID was kosher. Not in every way, but in the way that mattered today. The man straightened his boarding pass and eyed him again but returned his license and papers. "Have a nice day, Mr. Korbin."

Jeffrey nodded and continued through screening, then grabbed a coffee and sat comfortably at the gate, watching who approached. Would Ferguson's men follow him, or had his trail grown cold? They'd asked him to not travel for a few weeks, but there were ways around that. A man sat a few seats down and pulled out a tattered paper. Was he a Fed? Jeffrey watched him out of the corner of his eye until he stood and left.

Soon the loudspeaker called the sections to board. He was one of the first to be seated, which gave him a great view of his fellow passengers. No one looked overly suspicious. Most were tourists leaving Florida loaded with Disney gear. Good riddance. They were the clueless hoards clogging up the highways and restaurants, making his life more difficult, despite the fact he was forty minutes north of Orlando.

His mind wandered to Ronnie, and a nagging doubt crept in. It was weird how the hurricane formed so quickly right offshore in Puerto Rico. Hannah was not too far away from there in the Virgin Islands. Was it possible that she was seeding this storm, or even steering it? She'd been spitting mad when they'd spoken last. Would she do something like that out of spite? God only knew. Women were weird like that, always creating drama when there really didn't need to be any. Take Ronnie for instance. Why couldn't she just quietly listen about Mike? There was no reason to hang up when he'd pointed out the cold, raw truth. Maybe slightly manipulated truth, but seriously, calm the fuck down and just listen.

Now he had to create contingency plans and leave the state when they were watching him closely. At least he had a connecting flight that would reveal anyone who was following him. He'd done his best to cover his tracks, walking to Starbucks near his condo then slipping out the back and through the next few high-rises to lose any tails. Then a cab to the airport and voila, no one the wiser.

The stewards went through the safety protocols and the plane took off. Jeffrey settled into the flight, ticking through his mind what needed to be done. First stop Naval Air Station Oceana in Virginia Beach to catch up with an old friend. They'd meet with his crew and sort through the best way to end Mike's career, save Ronnie, and get her back on continental US soil and back under his control. Hurricane Jeanne provided both alarming challenges and opportunities to cover their tracks. Jeffrey closed his eyes and forced his will onto the universe. This *had* to go well. Hopefully, Ronnie had already become leery of Mike and kept her distance. She was stubborn, and hot as hell. Mike would pour on the charm. Would she resist? Would she confront him about Kelly? The whole plan may fall apart if she did. He'd chosen the most effective clippings out there. There were others that shed a different light on the man.

Chapter 47

Climbing the Mountain

Ronnie shivered uncontrollably, her teeth chattering like one of those gag toys. Could someone shiver to death? Was that a thing? At least they were moving, and she'd not had another collapse. Were they stuck in an endless loop of fertile mountain landscape? Had her thiamine levels recovered enough, or was she just running on adrenalin? Would she go into shock, and they'd die on this damn mountainside? Her worries rolled around in her head, distracting her from the burn in her thighs and calves from the constant climb.

What she wouldn't give for a raincoat and hiking boots.

Mike broke through the shrubs and young trees, creating a path for them, occasionally holding a branch out of the way to let her pass. After ten minutes of rough terrain, the low-lying shrubs cleared, presenting the new challenges of a steeper incline. The torrential rain only allowed about ten feet of visibility, making it impossible to tell how much farther they had to go. Even once they reached the top, there were no guarantees of shelter.

Mike stopped, holding his hand out to signal her to hold still. He was listening, but for what? The only sound Ronnie heard was the rain battering the trees and rocks.

Ronnie eyed his full lips, now pursed, and relived their kiss, mortified at how aggressive she'd been. Where the hell had that come from? A blend of relief and attraction? Would she have reacted that way with Jeffrey even earlier in their relationship? No way, she'd always been passive with him. Was it the connection to Mike through time from her past travels, or past lives, as Ini had described it, or something else? It left her wanting more, and it wasn't just to get warm from his body heat.

He took her hand and helped her across a rivulet of rainwater blocking their path. The earth had been washed away, leaving only slippery rocks. He turned to find the next section of territory to tackle.

Ronnie took a step towards him and slipped, scraping her knee, drawing blood. "Crap!"

He helped her to her feet. "You okay?" Mike knelt to see the damage. "Scraped and bleeding. Come sit down." He meandered to an outcropping of rocks and motioned for her to sit on top while he examined her knee at eye level. Then he tore a strip about a foot long from his shirt and tied it around her knee, stopping the bleeding with the pressure of the makeshift bandage. "Shoot, sorry about that. That should hold it." He kissed the top of her knee.

"Thanks. You sure are handy with that first aid training."

"Yup. You okay to keep going, or do you want to rest for a few minutes?" His t-shirt was plastered against his body, showing every cut of muscle.

She looked away. "How much daylight do we have left?"

He glanced at his watch, making the muscles in his forearm flex. "About an hour with this thick cloud cover."

Ronnie shook her head. "Damn. Do you need to rest?"

"I'm fine. I guess we could just chill here for a while, enjoy the view?" He motioned to the vines, fallen trees, shrubs, and rain pouring in a seemingly endless torrent.

Ronnie chuckled. "You sure you're okay? Less than an hour ago you were unconscious." She motioned to the bloody spot on his head.

"Oh, that," he said rolling his eyes as if she were being dramatic. "You must not know that I am indestructible."

"What?" She loved that he could be playful now, with all the chaos and uncertainty surrounding them. "You are not indestructible. You would have died if I hadn't rescued you."

"No." Mike shook his head. "If you hadn't interfered, I'd have lazily backstroked to shore, saving a baby alligator on the way."

She laughed, harder than she should have, but his lighthearted banter was so unexpected. "So, what's our plan?"

"I'm not stopping until we find a dry spot to spend the night." He bent down to check her bandage. It was still tight. She'd forgotten about her skinned knee. "We should clean that up before too long."

"With what?" They had nothing with them.

"You forget, I am a Marine and I've got skills, baby!" He playfully squeezed just above her knee, making her jump.

"In that vast array of skills, do you have any tools to make it stop raining?"

Mike shook his head. "I'm just glad it's not thirty degrees and snowing. We could sleep out in this if we had to." He looked around. "Mudslides, hypothermia, and chupacabra are all big risks. I'll be happier when we're at the top of this mountain."

"Chupacabra? What the hell is that?"

"The name translates to *goat sucker*." Mike had a glint in his eye. Was he teasing?

"Ew. That sounds hideous." She held out her arms, and he lifted her off the rock and set her in front of him. She resisted the urge to kiss him. Instead, Ronnie stepped over a fallen tree and nearly lost her shoe in the mud.

"Not many people have seen one. It's the Puerto Rican version of our bigfoot. It's left unexplained, blood-drained animals around the island." He wiped his face clear of the rain.

"Really, you're not kidding?"

"Cross my heart. Goat-sucking monsters roaming the wilderness searching for ravishing young beauties to drink their blood." He grabbed her arm and pretended to bite her wrist.

Ronnie jerked her hand away, not liking the image of a horrible beast sucking her blood while she slept. She smacked his shoulder. "Let's get somewhere safer."

Mike cringed and gave her a wicked smile.

As they picked their way through the uneven footing, Ronnie noticed the vine-covered trees that created an endless array of hiding places for red-eyed goat suckers. "How big are they supposed to be?"

Mike held his hand three feet off the ground. "Yea high."

They were in a desperate situation. Where would they sleep? Would there be anyone on the top of this mountain to help them? They walked in silence for a while, the rain making it impossible to carry on any conversation as they climbed single file.

Mike had gotten farther ahead of her and stopped at the beginning of a clearing. He waited for her to catch up.

"Look." He pointed up. Above their heads was a power line. He slicked the rain out of his eyes again. "We're going to follow the wires. It's gotta lead somewhere useful."

"Let's just hope it's not fifteen miles away!"

"The land is evening out. We are near the top." He squinted, or was he wincing? "You okay? You look like you're struggling."

"Just a little shaky. I can't tell if it's shivering or…"

Mike folded her in his arms. "God, you *are* shaking."

Ronnie wrapped her arms around him, soaking in his warmth, laying her cheek against his chest.

"I'm hoping there's shelter up there. We need to get you out of this weather."

Ronnie's legs felt weak. Stopping gave her the chance to consider the toll this was taking on her.

Mike sensed her distress. "Do you need to rest?" He walked her over to a tree that had been blown over by the hurricane. She sat and put her head between her knees, fighting the feeling she was going to faint. She did an internal inventory. There was no pain, other than the scraped knee and burning muscles from the climb.

"Ronnie, what can I do?" The panic in his voice was palpable.

Ronnie shielded her eyes from the rain and looked at him. "I just need a minute."

Mike reached into his pocket and pulled out the bottle of water. "Take a few sips of this."

Ronnie opened the bottle. A huge clap of thunder made them both jump.

"Shit, that scared me to death." Mike smiled. He pushed a strand of hair out of her eyes.

"Yeah, I just need to rest a minute. I'll be okay." She sipped the water.

"Hey, sit tight. The electrical wires disappear up ahead. It may be a house or something. I'll be right back."

"Okay, don't be gone long."

"I won't." He climbed up out of sight.

Alone now, her mind started wandering back to the chupacabra creeping up the hill behind her. Lightning lit up the lowering clouds, reminding her of the fading daylight, punctuated by a low, rumbling thunder that lasted a full minute. Another flash allowed her to see a form jogging towards her. It was Mike.

"Ronnie, great news! It's not far. Come on!"

"Really? What did you find?" Ronnie stood shakily, and he took her hand.

"A building." Mike was out of breath.

"Oh my God, seriously?" Relief washed over her.

"There's a road and some sort of building. Not far."

"Shoot, as long as we can get out of the rain. You look a hot mess, Mike." Dark shadows were visible under his eyes.

"I'm fine, Ronnie. Let's just get you out of the storm."

They walked slowly in lockstep. Ronnie was glad the ground was nearly flat. Her legs and back were exhausted.

He held her hand to his chest. "Ronnie, I'm so sorry I got you into this. I wish we'd stayed at the hotel." Mike scratched above his eyebrow, then bit his lips.

"Don't do that, Mike. We didn't know this would happen." Ronnie squeezed his hand.

"Yeah, it was my job to protect you, and I certainly failed at that. For God's sake, you had to pull me from the river." He shook his head. "It was a huge risk leaving. I put your life in danger."

"We decided this together. Don't put that burden on yourself."

"We could have died." He stopped and held her hands. "It's my fault we were in an accident."

She melted at his confessed sins. "Mike, it's my fault we had to leave the hotel. You were just trying to get me to the hospital."

"No, I pushed us to leave. I'm so sorry, Ronnie. I will make this up to you. You deserve so much better than this."

Ronnie wrapped her arms around his neck and held him close. "You've already made it up to me."

Mike pulled away, about to say something, and Ronnie pressed her finger against his lips, then kissed him. He lifted her off the ground and kissed her back, squeezing her tight. His biceps and pecs tightened, pressing harder against her.

Mike set her down. "Oh, sorry, I didn't mean to squish you. I didn't hurt you, did I?"

Ronnie laughed. "No."

He took her hand again. "Good, let's get you out of the rain, Ronnie."

She squeezed his hand. "How does your head feel?"

"Like dog shit." He smiled.

"You look like dog shit." He would have two black eyes by morning, she was sure of that.

In the distance, the vague outline of a building became clearer through the rain. Ronnie wondered how they'd get inside.

Chapter 48

Convenient

Daylight was fading fast as they traversed the final hundred yards to the building. Mike turned to Ronnie and lifted his chin towards their destination. "I didn't want to get your hopes up, but I think it's a gas station."

Why wouldn't she be excited about a gas station? It seemed like a weird thing to say, but shelter was shelter. She wasn't going to be picky. Her worries fell away as they walked towards the building, gas pumps more visible as they got closer. Ronnie was chilled to the bone, colder now than she had been all day. With relief in sight, her mind allowed the full discomfort through the veil of consciousness.

Wind whipped towards them, forcing her eyes closed as the incessant rain battered her face. When her vision cleared, the plate-glass window revealed it was more than a gas station. It was a convenience store! "What luck!" Ronnie ran the last twenty yards, splashing in the puddles. Mike jogged to catch up. She stopped under the eaves and hugged him. "Mike, this is a miracle!"

Mike hugged her, then turned to the front door. "It's all going to be locked up tight," Mike said.

Ronnie tried the door anyway, eager to get out of the storm.

"Let's check the back door."

Ronnie followed him around the garage to the back, her shoes sinking into the mud. The back door was locked.

Mike walked a few paces away and searched around for a rock. "Breaking and entering it is."

She followed him as he scoped out the best place to break in. "Sorry to the owners, but I'd definitely call this an emergency." At the back of the garage, they found a door with a window. "Wish me luck!"

"Luck!" Ronnie stood away as he did the deed.

It took a few tries, but the window acquiesced. Mike used the rock to remove the shards at the bottom and then reached in and unlocked the door. "Yes!"

Mike opened the door and let her go in first. The musty odor of tires and oil was a welcome scent, for it translated into safety.

"Thank you, God!" Ronnie twirled around in the empty bay. In the second bay was an old, battered Chevy pickup truck.

A violent crash made Ronnie jump. Mike was already working on the door that separated the garage from the convenience store. It was a cheap wooden door that didn't stand a chance against his two hundred plus pounds. He broke it down quickly with his shoulder.

"Safe and dry. Check. I'm going to see if the phone works and call for help. Then we can get some food," Mike said as they walked down a dark corridor, passing a few closed doors.

Ronnie opened one and found a cramped bathroom with a tiny window, letting in a little light. The room held only a toilet, sink, and filth, but it was a lot better than the raging storm and the woods. "Hey, I'm going to use the restroom."

Mike stopped. "I'll go check it out. Come find me when you're done."

Ronnie closed the bathroom door behind her. Her reflection stared back, but it looked more like a woman raised by wolves. Sticks were caught in her hair plastered to her head. A mud streak down her cheek and coating of river water finished the look. She cranked on the tap, rinsed her face, and washed her hands and arms, slicking the swampy river stench off.

Avoiding her reflection, she opened the door and walked into the convenience store, noticing a flashlight shining near the front entrance. Rows and rows of snacks and toiletries made her nearly giddy. "Mike, oh my God, look at all this!"

"Over here, Ronnie! Bad news is the phones are out. Good news is they've got clothes!"

"No way!"

She followed his voice to the front of the store with a display of souvenir t-shirts and bathing suits. A flashlight sat on top of the clothes rack so they could see in the fading light, despite the meager light from the plate-glass window at the front of the store.

"You need to get into some dry clothes. Here, drink this." He handed her a bottle of water.

"Such excellent service, thank you." Ronnie cracked the bottle open and drank half. "It's not even lukewarm yet."

"Nope, and they've got booze too!" He grinned at her over the rack.

"Shut up! We hit the jackpot!"

"Yeah, we did. What a relief to find this place. Damn lucky."

Mike held up a t-shirt in front of her, checking the length. "You a small or a medium?"

"It depends on if there are shorts for me to wear." She turned to the other rack of clothes and sifted through them. "Bathing suits." She selected her size and grabbed an extra-large white t-shirt with *Puerto Rico* in bold rainbow letters across the front. "Hey, Mike, they've got your towel."

He was chugging a water and stopped to glance in her direction. "Hey, look at that, it's the one I gave you on the boat. I guess you were meant to have that!"

"Ha, yeah. I guess so." She took it off the hanger and then walked down the aisles, hoping there was shampoo and soap.

Mike followed her, lighting the way. "I tried to call for help, but the phones are down. I feel terrible that we broke into this guy's store, so I left him a note. I hope he'll call me so I can pay for any damages."

Ronnie would have done the same thing if she'd thought of it. "That was smart. I don't like taking his stuff either, but if we can pay him back, I won't feel so bad. It is an emergency, after all."

"Yeah, he's probably a hardworking guy. I'd hate to add to his hardship with the storm and all the other damage the island is dealing with. He'll probably lose some inventory with the power out." He stopped and held something out to her. "Hey, I got this one for you." Mike handed her another flashlight.

"Thanks. I'm gonna get washed up. I smell like a fish tank."

He laughed. "So do I. I guess I better do the same."

"There is a miniature sink in the bathroom."

Mike shook his head. "I saw a hose out back. I think I'll use that. No way my big head is going to fit in a tiny sink."

Ronnie laughed, almost giddy now with relief. She found the shampoo, soap, and a comb and returned to the tiny, gross bathroom to wash up. She stripped off the wet, muddy clothes and set them on the windowsill, realizing she could see Mike through the glass. He was peeling off his shirt, and she turned away, wanting to give him the privacy he thought he had. The image of his sculpted chest and abs, topped by broad shoulders, made her slightly dizzy. Damn, he was well made. She snuck another glance as he removed his filthy shorts then turned away, not wanting to be too creepy.

In the cabinet above the toilet were disinfectant and paper towels. She took a minute to spray the entire bathroom and quickly cleaned up as much as possible. Then started her own disinfecting with soap and shampoo, scrubbing her hair and face, then worked her way down, focusing on the gash on her knee and other cuts and scrapes on her arms and legs.

When she was finished, she wrapped the towel around her body. Then she washed her dirty clothes with the shampoo, placing them near the window to dry. A very dirty puddle covered the floor now, and she carefully stepped over it, taking her clean clothes with her.

She stepped into the hallway. "Mike, where are you?"

"Out here preparing a feast. You okay?"

"Yes, be right there." She set the flashlight on the floor and hung the t-shirt on the door handle, then pulled the tags off the bikini and slipped on the bottoms.

As she stood up, a figure approached. "You okay, Ronnie?" Mike called out. He surprised her and was only a few steps away.

Ronnie covered her chest and yelled, "Mike, what are you doing? I'm getting dressed!"

Mike turned around. "Oh God, I'm sorry, Ronnie. I thought you called out because you needed something. I couldn't hear your response, so I came to see…"

"See my boobs? Damn, Mike." She slid on the oversized t-shirt, skipping the bikini top for speed.

"I didn't think you were naked in the hallway. I really am sorry." Then he walked back to the garage. "I'll be over here skulking if you need me."

Ronnie could feel her cheeks go hot. She was both mortified and a bit excited, hoping he liked what he'd seen, for he'd definitely gotten an eyeful. Smiling, she rinsed her sneakers in the sink full of soapy water and squeezed them as dry as she could, then wrapped her hair in the towel and dried her locks and ran the comb through the tangles. When she was done, she returned to Mike.

Mike was clearing off the counter near the cash register and laying out paper plates, napkins, and food still in the wrappers. He looked fresh, clad in navy trunks and aqua t-shirt with the same logo as hers.

Mike pulled out a folding chair he must have scavenged from the back room. "Madam, welcome to *Chez Miguel*. May I take your drink order, *s'il vous plaît?*" He sounded like the announcer from *SpongeBob*.

Ronnie laughed. "*Merci beaucoups.* I shall have a water and a..."

Mike interrupted, "Oh, how rude of me. Let me tell you what we have, mademoiselle." He listed about ten drinks then paused. "Plus a mystery beverage called blah blah something in Spanish."

"I'll take one of the blah blah things." She was grateful he was offering them a distraction from her earlier embarrassment.

"At your service." Mike bowed and walked to the drink coolers in the back and returned a minute later carrying three drinks. He set them down on the counter. "It turns out it's not blah blah blah. It's called a pitorro, and apparently is also known as..." He held the bottle up for her to read. "Puerto Rican moonshine."

"Oh, you don't say. That sounds like it may have medicinal benefits."

"Most definitely. Would you like the fruity blend or coffee and hazelnut?"

She tapped the coconut pineapple bottle, and he opened it and set it on the counter in front of her, then opened the coffee hazelnut one and held it up. "Cheers, to a romantic dinner of spam and cheese sticks."

Ronnie laughed and lifted her pitorro and clinked his bottle. "Cheers to surviving multiple near-death experiences...together!"

A shadow crossed his sunny expression, but he hid it by sipping his drink. She wondered if he was still punishing himself for leaving the hotel.

"Not bad at all. This tastes like a great way to get FUBAR."

She tried her drink, and it was sweet, creamy, and had a bite of booze after it went down. "Delish! Do we really have spam and cheese sticks for dinner? And what is FUBAR?"

He smiled devilishly. "No, I have something better, but it's still cooking. FUBAR...fucked up beyond all recognition."

Ronnie laughed and glanced around for something he could have been cooking on, but since the power was out, it seemed unlikely.

"I'll be right back, mademoiselle." He took his pitorro and disappeared for a minute, then returned with a huge smile. "One hot meal for one hot lady." Mike set a steaming paper plate in front of her with two burritos and a plastic packet of salsa, sour cream, and hot sauce. He put a similar plate across from her, then went around to the cash register side of the counter and sat on a stool opposite her. "Dinner is served!" He set the flashlight on its end facing the ceiling, offering just enough light to see the food and the light reflecting off his eyes.

"Mike, you are hilarious! How did you manage to heat these up?"

"You know I was a Marine, right? I've got mad skills." He couldn't help but smile, looking proud of the surprise.

"A meal fit for a queen stranded on the isle of Puerto Rico." Ronnie's stomach growled, insisting manners be damned and begging her to just eat the feast in front of her. She was grateful to be warm and dry.

"Don't forget the pineapple dish." He pushed a can of pineapple chunks towards her. "I can make it flambé if you like."

"Ha, I'm good, thank you." She stood and leaned over the counter to kiss him, eager to feel his lips on hers again. He tasted of chocolate hazelnut, and she put her hand on his cheek, wanting to feel more of him. His skin was fresh and clean, and she lingered with the kiss, this time outlining his lips with her tongue, then deepening the kiss. In the process, she knocked over the flashlight, spilling her drink.

Mike reacted quickly and rescued both items, laughing. "An apt reward for my efforts, m'lady."

"I'm such a dork, sorry." She sat back down and lifted her boozy beverage, not at all minding the fire burning in her belly.

"There is not a single dorky bone in that body. You're elegant, graceful, and absolutely lovely."

She glowed with his praise. "Gracefully slipping and bashing my knee."

"No, Ronnie. Gracefully saving my life, saving *our* lives, being strong and a pure pleasure to be around even in the worst of times."

She soaked that in, enjoying his view of her. "Mike, you are incredible. I'd never have made it up that hill without your strength and optimism. And teasing about chupacabras. That was an excellent motivator to get me moving, so we'd not end up sleeping outside tonight." She laughed. "Did you make that up?"

"No, that's all true. It is a Puerto Rican legend. But there are none here, so no worries." He leaned towards her, a glazed expression in his eyes.

"You okay, Mike? You're pretty banged up." A worry stabbed at her. "How is your head?"

"It hurts, but not bad."

"You're gonna have some really sporty black eyes tomorrow."

"Damn, that ought to improve my look immensely." He smiled, looking sleepy.

They laughed and made small talk about what they wished was here in the convenience store as they ate the meal, drinking a few more Puerto Rican moonshines.

In a natural pause, Mike picked up her hand. "We will need to clean your knee with antiseptic. I don't want it getting infected."

Ronnie raised her drink. "That should be loads of fun."

Mike shook his head. "It may sucketh greatly, but better now to prevent a nasty germ. Who knows what might be in the floodwaters?"

"True. You're going to have to let me tend to your injuries, too. Do you think you have a concussion?"

Mike nodded "Yeah, I probably do."

"What is the protocol for treating that?" What if he needed medical help?

"The best thing for a concussion is rest. I'll probably sleep like the dead tonight."
He smirked, but it struck a chord, changing the relaxed mood.

They were in trouble and there was no way to call for help. "Mike, do I need to
wake you up? I mean, are you supposed to go to sleep with a concussion?"

"If you are awake, just shake me and if I don't respond, rouse me." Mike grinned,
but a flash of worry shadowed his eyes.

"But what if you don't wake up? What the hell do I do then?" Fear snaked through
her veins.

He picked up on her worry. "We both need to be seen by a doctor at some point.
How long was I out?"

"I don't know. It all happened so fast. Probably about ten or fifteen minutes." She
took a bite of the burrito.

Mike glanced away. And that worried her more than anything. He was having
doubts as well.

"Mike, we don't know the extent of your injuries. Sometimes it takes a while for
you to know."

"Ronnie, I'd not be so charming now if I were badly hurt, would I?" He tried to
play it off. "Let me sleep as long as I need to tomorrow. I may have trouble staying
asleep."

She nodded. "Okay, if you do, wake me up. I'll keep you company."

Mike shook his head. "You need your rest too. All you've been through in the last
twenty-four hours."

"Well, our plans are very light tomorrow." Her worry lingered. Mike had been so
good to her.

Mike smiled, but it was obvious he was running out of energy. Ronnie studied his
face as he ate. When the smile dropped, he looked like death warmed over. He could
be in a coma tomorrow if his brain swelled. Ronnie's pulse quickened with the
possibilities that the next few hours could bring.

Chapter 49

Are you Crazy?

Mike was entertained by Ronnie's rapid expression changes, enhanced by the Puerto Rican moonshine. The booze enhanced her playfulness, and he reveled in the teasing banter and animated expressions.

"Should we see if that car in the garage works? Maybe we can start it up. Then we could try for the hospital tomorrow, and if you're worse, I will at least have an exit plan."

"Outstanding idea. Why didn't I think of that?" Maybe the moonshine was dulling his mind. Or maybe Ronnie was right, he was exhibiting signs of a brain injury. His pulse quickened, and he could feel every beat of his heart thrumming in his temple. Best switch to water.

"You're excused from having great ideas until you get some rest." She smiled.

Mike ran his fingers over the top of her hand. "How are you feeling?"

"Pretty good considering how I felt after Hurricane Frances." Ronnie shook her head. "Steph says I almost died."

"I was there. You coded, Ronnie. It was terrifying." Mike ran his hand across through his hair. "I never want to see that again."

"Well, I'm not planning on it." A small smile crossed her lips, and she shifted to a look he'd not seen before. Her eyes danced back and forth between his. She was studying him.

"What?" He wanted to climb in her mind and answer the questions she was having about him. At least she knew the Kelly situation and thank God he'd been able to tell her before his mind turned to mush. "You are sussing out whether I can revive you from a code blue with what we got here?" He spread his arms wide and looked around the store. "I mean, I'm pretty handy, but I don't have paddles to shock your heart."

Ronnie tossed her head back, laughing, flashing the dimples he'd missed during the serious part of their conversations. "No, just grateful for all you've done. You really saved our butts during Frances. And again here."

Mike looked down at his hands and touched the cut from punching the wall, regretting so much over the last twenty-four hours. "Ronnie, I didn't. I put our lives at risk. We just as easily could have died in that mudslide. Just dumb luck we didn't."

Ronnie shook her head and leaned towards him, mischief in her eyes. "Hey. My name isn't dumb luck."

Mike laughed, despite the pain it caused rippling through the muscles in his face. "No, you're right. Your name is badass. You deserve one hundred percent of the credit. It's just the crash, Ronnie. You know how close we came to not making it. It gives me chills." He rubbed his arms.

"I'm just glad we are here pretty much intact." Ronnie looked away now, and the shining rays of light from her boisterous mood faded.

He mourned the loss. He wanted to kiss her, craving the touch of her soft lips, eager to arouse the animal she'd shown him by the river. But that would be for another day when he could give her his full attention.

"You were magnificent. Ronnie, you're my hero." He leaned back and smiled. "I never needed a hero before, but if I ever do again, I want it to be you."

Ronnie cocked her head and smiled, her hair falling over her shoulder. "Me too. But we have to make a truce. I'd like to get to the point where neither of us needs rescuing. Can't we just have a calm, happy existence?"

He lifted his water bottle, content with that plan. "Cheers to that!" She'd been through enough with the storms, the health issues, Christ, even breaking up with that damn pencil neck. An overwhelming weariness crept up from deep in his bones, forcing a yawn. "Let's get this wound care started so we can sleep."

"Aye, captain." Ronnie mock saluted him.

Mike stood up and stretched. "Let's find the first aid section, if they have one." He walked around the counter and offered his arm. "Madam." She took it and they wandered down a few aisles until they found gauze pads, Band-aids, and antiseptic, many with Spanish labels.

"Bingo." Mike took them off the shelf and handed Ronnie a bottle of Advil and medical tape. "Pretty decent selection. Thank God."

"Yeah. What a godsend." Her face was wooden now. He surmised she wasn't looking forward to her knee being debrided. "Where are we going to sleep?"

"In the magnificent, luxurious accommodations of Shell Station number twenty-seven's floor." He imitated Robin Leach's voice that had the desired result of making the dimples reappear.

"Yay," Ronnie responded lamely. "I don't think it will matter. I'm exhausted."

"Same." Mike set everything down on the counter. "You can torture me first and then maybe drink another liquid courage."

"Okay, I'll take you up on that."

Mike returned to the cooler and brought her back a different flavor, cracked it open, and set it next to the supplies. He returned behind the counter and sat across from her, elbows on the table, leaning towards her, pointing at his head. "Start here."

"Hold still." Ronnie teased as she opened the antiseptic and soaked the gauze pad. "Tell me about your family while I do this."

"Okay, you're going to shrink my head while you clean it. Wonderful." Mike smiled playfully until the gauze touched his temple. "Oooofft." Mike winced but leaned into her administrations, hoping she'd be done quickly. "Can we talk about Kelly? Now that we are calmer, I want to answer any lingering questions you have." Jeffrey had done major damage to their budding relationship, and he wanted to undo what he could.

"Okay."

"I just want to help you see the entire situation, so you don't have doubts about me."

Ronnie nodded and moved to cleaning a scrape along his jaw.

Mike waited until Ronnie moved to another spot. "I felt responsible for Kelly's death. The same way I feel responsible for getting you into this situation." He pulled away, examining her expression.

Ronnie's mouth turned down, and she looked sad. Sad was better than scared. "Mike, things happen that are not your fault."

"I know, but it doesn't mean I can't do a better job at avoiding dangers. Kelly paid the ultimate price. I can't let anything happen to you."

Ronnie sat back away from him, absorbing his words, then took a deep breath. "I see how this is weighing on you. I told you we should leave though. You didn't make this decision alone."

"I know. You have to understand my guilt about Kelly. If I'd not fallen asleep, if I'd not hit the wall, if..." Mike stopped before his words broke with emotions.

"If I'd not moved to Florida, if I'd not gotten some strange disease during storms, if Steph hadn't taken me to the hospital..." Ronnie raised her voice at the end. "Life is full of *ifs*, Mike. We cannot spend our lives wishing we'd made different choices. We have to make the best decisions we can with the information we have. I understand how you feel about Kelly. You've healed over the last five years from that tragedy, but it will always be a part of who you are."

Mike took Ronnie's hand, pausing her administrations. "Ronnie, I caused Kelly's death. You know what happened."

"Bullshit." Ronnie pulled her hand free. "Epilepsy caused Kelly's death. You didn't give her the disease, just like you didn't cause my Korsakoff's."

Mike crossed his arms over his chest and shook his head, looking away. These were Billy's words too, but he knew better. "My carelessness caused Kelly to fall and hit her head. My carelessness caused us to leave the hotel and put our lives on the line."

"You have to change the narrative that you've done something horrible. You haven't. You had no idea she would die that night. If you'd known, you would have done everything to stop it. I know it. You know it. Stop beating yourself up about it. Same with the mudslide. If you'd known it would happen, neither of us would have taken that risk. But we didn't know. You didn't know."

Mike shook his head, fighting back the emotions that had overwhelmed him five years ago. This had brought it to the surface, nearly as raw as it had been then.

Ronnie touched his face and turned his gaze back to her. "You're human. You make mistakes. But you have to forgive yourself." Her eyes were intense, and she spoke harshly. "Cut Mike Walsh a little slack. He's a great guy with a big heart."

Mike loathed self-pity, but it was there, and Ronnie had earned the right to see him in this vulnerable state. "I hear he's a selfish bastard."

"Nope, he'd give you the shirt off his back. He'd take care of you fiercely no matter what challenges there were." She bit her lower lip, maybe keeping it from quivering.

"But would he fall asleep?" His words sounded bitter. They'd been bitter for years.

"I hope he sleeps but isn't hard to wake up." She smiled, cocking her head playfully.

Mike gave her the side eye.

"I'd trust him with my life."

Mike's composure crumpled for an instant, but his resolve returned, like a well-practiced friend helping him tamp down the overwhelming feelings of regret. "Thank you for saying that, Ronnie. It means a lot to me." He reached out and took her hand and kissed it. "I will do anything to protect you, to make you feel safe. I just wish we'd stayed at the hotel."

Tears gathered in her eyes, and Ronnie leaned in to kiss him. Mike didn't want to be a sappy sad sack. But most women wouldn't even know about his past. Ronnie had jumped that hurdle with grace and compassion. Their kiss was tender and sweet. He pulled away, not wanting to let it get too far. "Clean my wounds, woman, so I can return the favor."

Ronnie smiled and dabbed the antiseptic on the gauze and cleaned up a cut on his forearm. Neither of them spoke. Mike was grateful for the space to replay her words, letting them soak into the cracks in his armor. He enjoyed the irony that Jeffrey's ploy to keep them apart had done the opposite. He felt closer to her than even Kelly in their first few months together. Sharing the worst part of his soul had broken down the walls he'd built after her death. From their first lunch together, he'd known Ronnie may just be someone he could re-enter the world with. He'd been locked in purgatory, punishing himself while trying to deal with the guilt and self-abuse.

This beautiful, passionate woman had set him free from the pain and forced it out of his heart like letting the air out of a balloon, releasing the pressure. He touched around the edges of the hurt over Kelly but didn't have to dive into it completely. Then it struck him. He watched Ronnie as she moved to the scrape along his forearm. He'd punched the wall and Kelly had died, but this time Ronnie had woken up. She was alive, and he had another chance at love. This was his second chance at living. A wave of dizziness overwhelmed him, and he closed his eyes, lost in the irony of their twisted fate. Ronnie had done what he couldn't for Kelly—she'd saved him from drowning.

Ronnie was gentle but proficient, not afraid to scrape with her fingernail to remove a fleck of dirt or a line of dried blood. Mike studied her face, wondering what was behind her set jaw. Was she replaying their conversations? Was she planning their next steps? Was she utterly exhausted and letting her mind focus on the task at hand?

"Okay." She smiled playfully. "Can we see if you need attention under that fresh white shirt?"

Mike smiled. "Yeah, probably have some scrapes on my back." He stood, turned around, and pulled off his shirt. He glanced backward and was surprised by her expression. She quickly masked it, but it was unmistakable. She wanted him, and that instantly cleared his foggy head.

Ronnie gently ran her hands over his shoulders, then walked away, but he realized she was coming around to his side of the counter.

"How does it look?" Mike asked as she approached in the nearly see-through white shirt, her curves pressing tauntingly against the fabric. He could have that shirt off in a millisecond.

Ronnie didn't answer with words, but her hands said everything he'd wanted to hear, sliding over his shoulders, following his lats down where they cut along his ribs. Mike was silent, enjoying the seduction, as he revealed more of his flesh for her to examine and purify.

"Better sit down so I can tend to your wounds." Ronnie reached behind her to grab the gauze and antiseptic. The hem of the shirt was tantalizingly close to revealing the bikini bottoms.

He sat backward in the chair, exposing his back to her, aroused despite the pain from debriding his wounds. She'd given him plenty to be distracted by with that one long caress.

Ronnie broke the silence when she was finished. "Turn around, Mr. Walsh."

He stood, crowding her against the counter, but didn't go in for a kiss like every fiber of his being wanted. This needed to be on her terms, and he would be patient.

Her eyes locked on his, then she playfully pushed him, his chest burning where her hands had been. "Sit."

Mike looked up at her, then he spread his arms wide and sat up straight. "Madam, I am all yours."

Chapter 50

Floating Down the River

Mike was surprised when Ronnie straddled his lap and sat down, kissing him as she had by the river, with intense passion. He succumbed to her deep kisses, and he mustered every ounce of control, with his body urging him to throw her on the counter and take her right there. Instead, he placed his hands around her waist and felt her ribs expand and contract as she breathed hard. The things she could do with that limber tongue had him melting in a puddle of desire. She pulled away, craving in her eyes.

"Your mouth seems to be free of injury. Shall I check the rest of you?" Ronnie grinned and stood up.

Mike was panting and tried to act cool, but there was only one thought racing through his mind. He was quiet, hoping to not make a wrong move and break the mood.

Ronnie stood between his legs, leaning close to clean a scrape on his upper pectoral muscle, and he gently touched her legs, just below the hem. Her skin was smooth, warm, and firm under his fingers. He struggled to slow his breathing, but with her so close, so full of sexual power, he couldn't tame it. "Sorry, I seem to be out of breath. Don't exactly know why."

"Must be the pain. I'm sorry if I'm hurting you, Mike." Ronnie smiled devilishly.

"I have no pain, m'lady."

"Do you need me to look over your legs?" She sat on the counter, leaning forward towards him, just out of reach. The shirt hiked up high on her legs. Her confidence was intoxicating.

"Nope, I got it."

Ronnie stood and handed over the tools of germ killing. "Alright then. I'm going to use the restroom before you torture me." She slipped past him and walked away. Her slender, tan legs were bare to mid-thigh. He snapped out of the lustful fog and dabbed the gauze on the many cuts and scrapes along his shins and knees, reveling how she'd felt in his arms.

Ronnie returned and sat in the chair across the counter from him, looking anxious. "I'm ready." She held out her hands, and he looked them over.

"You washed these with soap?"

She nodded.

"You probably don't need this stuff on 'em." He patted the counter. "Sit up here so I can get to your knee."

Ronnie crawled over the counter and sat on the edge near him, dangling her legs over the side. The muscles in her face were tense.

"Tell me about *your* family, Ronnie." He knew she just wanted to get this over with. He tried to ignore how the t-shirt hiked up higher on her legs, revealing toned, tan flesh he'd already discretely inspected on the boat.

She hesitated as he started then shook the discomfort and continued. "My mom and brother live in Virginia Beach. My dad passed away five years ago. About the same time Kelly died."

"I'm sorry."

Ronnie's mouth crumpled. "Yeah, it was horrible. I just found out last week that my mom took him off life support. I didn't know that until she..." Ronnie looked away, blinking away tears.

"Oh wow, I'm so sorry." Mike could see the pain in her expression.

Ronnie nodded and took a minute to compose herself. "Oh my God, Mike!" She almost stood up, but he put his hand on her other knee, holding her in place.

"What?"

"Damn, I'm so dumb!" Her face reddened, which was hard to do in the low light of the flashlight. "My dad's journal!"

Mike stared blankly at her.

"I brought it and now it's floating down that river!" She pointed towards the front of the store.

"Are you sure you packed it? I didn't see it when I grabbed your things." Mike tore the gauze out of the package and soaked it in antiseptic.

"Wait." Ronnie looked away, as if visualizing the hotel room. "No! I'm even stupider than I thought. I left it in the hotel!"

"Are you sure?"

She rose and paced. "Yeah, I put it in the drawer next to the bed. I got worried if there was a leak it would be ruined. I meant to grab it before we left, but I was so out of it after that doc died, right in front of us. My stupidity saved it!" She shook her head. "You didn't grab it, did you?"

"No. Damn, we will have to go back, or call them and ask to send it to you. What luck!"

"Yeah, that is probably my most precious possession. I shouldn't have brought it with me, but my mom sent it just before I left, hinting that it may hold the answers to my situation."

Mike patted the counter, and Ronnie sat back down. "Your situation?"

Ronnie shook her head. "Yeah, she thinks my dad had similar symptoms of Korsakoff's before he died."

"Wow, seriously? Is that what he died of?" He held both her knees and listened intently.

"I always thought it was heart issues, but my mom just confessed last week that there was a lot more to it." She bit her full lower lip. "She sent the journal so I could hear it in his own words. I haven't gotten very far yet. Apparently, he kept a series of journals about his work and life."

"What a gift! How bittersweet. Did you find anything out?" Mike returned to cleaning her knee.

"I learned about his failed experiments. His lab partner lost faith in the concept and decided to work on other things. Ouch."

"Sorry. Hold the flashlight so I can see." Mike cracked open a bottle of water and set it next to her. "Keep talking. I'm just going to grab a bucket." He stood and returned with a small trash can. He pulled out the empty liner and set the can under her foot.

She shined the flashlight on her knee, and Mike adjusted its angle.

"My dad sounded so depressed. I never saw that side of him—he was always so upbeat."

As she spoke, he poured the entire bottle of water over her scrape, the trash can catching the runoff. "This is gonna hurt." Then he cracked open another bottle and repeated it, sliding his thumb over the wound as the water washed out the smaller particles. "Keep talking. Just going to hold this over your scrape for a minute." Then he picked up the gauze pad.

Ronnie tensed as he pressed the gauze into her cut. "Last I read, my dad was about to hire a new assistant who could breathe life into the project with some fresh ideas."

"Yeah, did he hire someone?" Mike looked up at her, happy to see her getting into the conversation and not just focusing on what he was doing.

"Uh huh, a guy named Jason Korbin. I'm hoping to find him when I get back and see if he can tell me more about my father's experiment and his mental state."

Mike picked up the tweezers, and she took a deep breath as he dug into the knee, fishing out a tiny chunk of silica. "That's an outstanding idea. I can help if you like. I'm good with the ole computer." He smiled.

"Ha. Of course you are. You're vice president of Information Technology." She seemed to brighten at that until he dug in for the next fleck of silica shining in the beam of light. "I'm hoping this Jason guy had some brilliant ideas about how to make his experiment work."

"That sounds promising." Mike looked up from the bloody knee. Shadows played across her face. "What did your dad do?"

"He was an experimental physicist. A lot of the journal is formulas. Just looks like chicken scratch to me."

"Impressive. Do you know what the experiments were about?" Mike dug out the next piece, holding her shin so she wouldn't kick him.

"Owwww!"

"Sorry, take a sip of your moonshine. This may be awhile." Mike waited while she took a swig.

"Not really. I probably wouldn't have understood it even if he said what it was. Much to my father's chagrin, physics just wasn't my thing in college."

"Yeah." Mike listened intently, grateful she was sharing so much with him. Kelly had been very closed off about her family struggles. She'd grown protective of her parents, as much as they'd done for her with all her medical issues.

Ronnie continued, "He always told me as a kid..." She flinched as he dug for another fleck. "...your best discoveries happened after an enormous setback. Like a dance, one step forward, two steps back."

"Yeah, sounds like us. Is this our discovery after that setback?"

Ronnie smiled. "Oh, I hope so." She reached out and played with the curls on top of his head. "They bounce so nicely. Ever let it grow out?"

Mike laughed. "My mom loved it longer when I was a kid. Her hair was poker-straight. Once I joined the Marines, I've always kept it short."

"I like it short on the sides, but this..." She ran her fingers through the longer section on top. "I love."

"Then I shall keep it." The feel of her hands running across his scalp was heavenly. He refocused, hoping to get through the last few pieces he could see before his eyes stopped focusing.

"My dad came up with the idea after my great-aunt's funeral in the 50s. He'd been in an accident, and when he was recovering, it just came to him. He'd spent his entire life on this project, and it was cut short when he died."

He expected her expression to be sad, but instead she was pensive.

"Now, after what my mom told me, I'm thinking something happened to him during the experiment." Ronnie's eyes were wide now. "She was sure he was losing his grip on reality, rambling on during his last night that he'd had a breakthrough. He'd been up all night and was frantically eager to get back to the lab. He'd just come home to shower and eat, then he was going back." She stood up, her foot landing in the small trash can, and she fell forward. He caught her and lifted her back to the counter.

Mike watched her intently. "That would certainly change the whole scenario. We need to get that journal back, don't we?"

"Yes, I didn't have much time to read it. And to be honest, he was so depressed in the beginning it was hard to keep diving into it. It made me so sad. I didn't even know how miserable he was. I was too busy enjoying college."

"You said he had more journals, right?"

She nodded.

"Maybe there will be more information in a different journal."

"Yeah, that's a good idea. Plus, I need to find this Jason Korbin. If he was there that day, he would know what really happened. Maybe he can shed some light on it. My mom never looked into it because she was convinced he was just going mad."

"God, that must be hard to think about your dad having mental health issues." Mike bent low, moving the trash can under her foot again.

Her eyebrows merged. "It's consumed me lately. If he was crazy, maybe I am too. I'd so much rather it be all about his experiment for a lot of reasons. One, maybe it worked, and he reached his lifelong dream. Bittersweet. If his life was cut short, then the experiment was as well. I've been toying with the idea that maybe the experiment had a weird side effect that put him in a coma..." She paused and looked away, then wiped away a tear.

He touched her uninjured knee. "I'll help you sort through this, Ronnie."

"Thank you, Mike. That would be wonderful. I hope the hotel can get that back to me. I think writing helped my dad relax...to write it down each night. My mom wanted me to read this particular journal just after she told me it was her decision to pull the life support plug."

"Really? Why did she tell you now, not when it happened?" A twinge of pain shot through his temple and for a second his vision blurred.

"I think she believes my dad and I share a gene that causes..." She trailed off.

"Causes what?" Mike stopped and looked up at her.

She looked away. "Nothing."

Mike set the tweezers down. "No. Causes what, Ronnie? You were just getting to something important."

She shook her head. "My mom is a social worker and spends every day with the mentally ill." Ronnie looked directly at him.

"And?" he prodded, pulling on her good ankle as if to pull the information out of her.

She looked away again, her mouth turning down.

"Come on, I just spilled my guts about Kelly. It can't be worse than being accused of killing your fiancée."

She exhaled and shook her head. "My mom thinks my dad and I share the crazy gene. That his last day alive he lost it. He was frantic, talking about going somewhere strange. He'd been up all night, as she describes it, in a manic episode." Ronnie wiped away a tear, but her voice was strong. "Something went wrong, and next thing, the lab called and he was in a coma."

"Oh wow, that's horrible."

"Yeah, Mom just told me that last week. I was furious. What if he wasn't crazy? What if he made some significant discovery and the experiment damaged him? Why was she so impatient to remove him from life support?" She was close to tears.

"Ronnie, I'm so sorry." He stood to give her a hug, but she waved him away. Mike sat back down, waiting for her to continue.

It took her a minute to pull herself together enough to talk. Her voice was shaky. "She says my episodes during the storms may be connected to his disease process and my..." Ronnie looked directly into his eyes and panic showed plainly.

"Your what?" he prodded, eager to know more.

"My...dreams...or whatever happens when I'm passed out...sound like his ramblings during his...as she calls it...psychotic breaks."

Mike leaned back in the chair, a swirl of emotions clouding his head. "Psychotic break? What dreams do you have?" He could feel the pulse in his temple increasing and he grabbed his head in pain.

"Mike, are you okay?" She slid off the counter and touched his hands that gripped his head.

"My head is about to explode. I need to stop for now. The focusing on these little dirt pieces is hurting my brain."

"Mike, please don't freak out. My mom sees everything through her mental health lens. My dad was not crazy. I'm not crazy." She sounded panicked.

Mike released his head and folded her into his arms. She sat sideways on his lap, and he rested his head on her shoulder. "Ronnie, I'm here for you no matter what you're going through. You are definitely not psychotic. You are probably the most well-adjusted person I know."

She hugged him fiercely now, making him groan. "Oh, I'm sorry, Mike."

"It's okay."

"It's just that my mom and Jeffrey have been trying to convince me I'm losing my grip on reality, that I'm following my father's footsteps."

"Bullshit. You cannot believe anything Jeffrey says. His words are laced with manipulation. I don't know your mom, but you are *not* crazy. I'm certain of that."

"Thank you. That's what Steph says, too. At least I have you guys."

"I'm here for you, Ronnie. We will get that journal back. I'll do whatever it takes to figure this out. Even if it's a gene and a disease, we will get through it."

She melted into him, and he pulled her tight, pressing his face into the crook of her neck. She smelled of soap and coconuts.

When she pulled away and stood in front of him, he patted the counter. "Let me just rinse off your knee, then we'll bandage it for the night. If my brain cooperates, we can do more in the morning."

Ronnie sat on the counter, quiet now, and he poured the entire bottle of water over her knee, reached for a second bottle, and did the same. He dried it with paper towels, then patted antiseptic on it and reached for the medical tape and gauze. When he was done, he kissed her hand again and pulled her to a standing position, folding her in his arms.

"We will get through this, Ronnie, I promise."

She draped her arms around his neck. "Thank you." She pulled away and looked at him, her brows drawn together, the weight of her father's mysterious death filling her mind.

"I have a plan for our sleeping arrangements." He brought her over to the front of the store. "My dad worked the night shift. I imagine he…" Mike realized he was rambling on about something, but when he stopped talking, he had no idea what he was saying.

"And…?" Ronnie looked at him, puzzled.

"And what?" He tried to grab the thread of what he'd been saying, but it was gone. A twinge of apprehension crossed his mind, interrupting the train of thought.

Ronnie looked worried. "You stopped mid-sentence. You were talking about your dad."

"No, I wasn't. I was talking about where we were going to sleep…" Now he was thoroughly distracted. "My dad, what was I saying?"

Ronnie took his hand. "It doesn't matter. Let's get this mess cleaned up and then get you to sleep." She smiled, but it was forced. Ronnie was disturbed by his lapse too.

Mike had no recollection of the last few minutes. Full on panic flooded his mind. He reached for the rack of towels and pulled off several. Ronnie did the same. "I will…" He lost his train of thought again.

Ronnie grabbed his arm and led him between the shelves, away from the plate-glass window. "Let's get you to bed."

266

His inner animal growled, but he told it to shut up. "Yes'm."

They quietly laid out the towels, making two pallets. Ronnie sat down on one and looked up at him, her t-shirt demurely tucked between her legs. He reached for another towel and covered her legs.

"You okay, Mike?"

"I think I need to shut this brain off for a while." He tried to not sound worried, but he could hear the stress in his voice.

"Yes. So, I wake you in the middle of the night? Is that our plan?"

"No, let me sleep. It's not like you're going to drive me to the hospital in the dark. We're better off just sleeping and seeing what's what in the morning."

"Are you sure?" Worry showed on her face.

"Yeah." He made a pillow of another towel and settled onto the hard floor. He was asleep in a matter of minutes.

Chapter 51

Jason Who?

Steph gripped the steering wheel, dodging the traffic. A flash of lightning up ahead snapped her to attention. She was driving Ian to commit a crime. Her mum would be devastated if she learned that instead of helping Ian stay out of trouble, she'd pulled him directly into the criminal life.

"Och, Ian, what are we doing? We can't just break the law. Nae bother."

"Stephanie, we have a key. We are not breaking in—we are just opening it up. No harm, no foul."

"Tell me again how you're gonna not be seen on the cameras they have outside the storage unit."

Ian shook his head, then pulled the hood up.

"You look ridiculous. It's ninety-five degrees out there and you're wearing a black hoodie. They're gonna know you're up to no good."

"Stop saying shite like that, Stephanie, seriously. You're giving me the heebie-jeebies. You have to assume no one will be watching every second of the film. If Jeffrey grasses us up, our car isn't in view, the video will show a dude in a hoodie—he'll have no idea I did this. Besides, they can't prosecute me for not stealing anything."

"I don't like this." Steph was annoyed that she'd been pulled into Ian's scheme, even if it had been her idea to take him there.

"Imma juss going tae look around and take only pictures, okay?" His accent grew stronger with his frustration. "You're the worst getaway driver in history."

"I know, but this can go wrong so many ways." Steph's worries mounted, fueled by his lack of concern.

Ian shook his head. "I wish I'd brought Billy instead. Text me if anyone is coming and I'll run to our meeting place on the other side of the apartments. It's *no* gonna go south. Fer God's sake, Stephanie, stop going mental."

"Aye, I'll be glad when we are done with this." Steph shook her head and turned into the apartment complex adjacent to the storage unit.

Ian hopped out and strode with confidence across the grassy path.

Steph watched with trepidation, willing everything to go well. "Hail Mary, full of grace."

Ian disappeared out of sight, and in a minute, he texted her. *Come here, you're gonna wanna see this.*

Steph frantically texted back, *I don't have a hood, ya numpty. How can I do that without being seen?* He could be so dense sometimes.

Ian texted back a picture of a gaping hole in the wall. *Come here. I spray-painted the camera.*

"Shite! Ian!" Steph's breath quickened.

Come now, Stephanie, his message read.

"Damnit, Ian." Steph opened the car door and looked around, the heat rising off the pavement. Thunder rumbled in the distance. The parking lot was nearly empty. Most people were at work this time of day. She took a few steps towards the unit and stopped in a panic. Would this be a moment she regretted for the rest of her life?

Ian came around the corner and took her arm. "Get in here."

"What's going on, Ian? We didn't plan for me to get out of the car."

"No, we didn't plan on this either." He walked into the storage unit and pointed at the wall. It matched the picture he'd sent.

"What the hell?"

"I know. It looks like someone broke in from the unit behind." Ian shook his head. "It's pretty weird, don't you think?"

Steph stood still, staring at the gaping hole large enough for a person to crawl through. "Ian, what if they think we did it?"

"They won't. Obviously, we didn't rent that unit. Someone else broke in here."

"Let's get out of here. This whole thing is giving me the creeps. What if the FBI is waiting for someone to show up and arrest them for whatever Jeffrey is hiding in here?"

"You're such a wee kid. Whoever broke in took a lot of his stuff. You can tell from the markings in the dust they moved things around. But there are a few items left behind. Look at this."

He pointed to a framed picture. The protective paper was torn away and clearly it was a diploma. Steph turned the picture towards the light at the open end of the room so she could read it. She tore the paper more. It was a diploma from Princeton University.

Ian prompted, "Look at the name."

Steph read the entire diploma's cursive script. But it confused her. "Who the hell is *Jason Korbin?*"

"Hell if I know. What kind of poufy name is Princeton? Is Jeffrey a prince?"

"Princeton is one of the best schools in the US. Why does Jeffrey have Jason's diploma in here? It doesn't make sense."

Ian glanced at the diploma. "I dinnea ken, but whoever broke in didn't want it. Look, there is a box with more things in it."

Steph knelt on the floor and thumbed through the box. It looked like someone had already pilfered through it. "Yearbooks, papers? This looks like memorabilia from high school. Is this Jeffrey's?" She picked up one of the books and thumbed through it. "1989. That would make him..." Steph did the math in her head. "Thirty-three now." She flipped through the yearbook pictures for each year. "I don't see Jeffrey Brennan in any pages. Whose is this?"

Ian took it from her and thumbed through to the K's. "It's Jason Korbin's. Look, he's a freshman." The picture showed a nerdy boy with glasses, braces, and long, weird hair. "Who the fuck is Jason Korbin?"

"No idea. And why does Jeffrey have it? Did he do something to Jason?" Steph couldn't finish the thought.

Ian was digging in another box and pulled out a pen flashlight. He held it between his teeth as he thumbed through the contents. "Physics books, atmospheric sciences..." Ian stopped. "Jesus, Steph, come look at this. Jason Korbin wrote a doctoral thesis on...what does this mean?"

Steph picked up the binder and read the title. "Thermodynamics of Tropical Cyclogenesis." She flipped open the book and read out loud. "'A hurricane is the ultimate storage of energy. The average tropical cyclone can release over six hundred terawatts of energy. Only a small portion—twenty-five percent—is from the wind of the storm. The remaining energy is in the stored heat that is released as water vapor condenses to rain. In this thesis, I propose harnessing this energy to supply localities with power during severe weather events, whether tropical cyclone, superstorm, or similar cyclogenesis.' Connected to hurricanes? That isn't sketchy at all, now, is it?" Steph shook her head.

"Power of hurricanes. What does power have to do with what happened to Ronnie though?" Ian dug through the rest of the box.

Steph shook her head and handed the binder back to Ian. "You'd probably need a lot of power to send someone back in time, wouldn't you?"

"Yeah, but who is Jason Korbin, and why does Jeffrey have his stuff?" Ian set the box down and walked around the storage unit, looking at the items strewn across the floor. "Hey, hey, what's this?" Ian bent over to pick up a scrap of paper. It was a cut-out newspaper clipping. "It's an obituary."

Steph walked over and read it along with Ian. "Dr. Ronald Andrews, May first, 1999."

Ian's eyebrows knit together. Steph solved the mystery for him. "It's Ronnie's dad, ya numpty. Dr. Andrews."

"Why...?" Ian shook his head.

Steph snatched the clipping from his hands and read it. "He died of heart disease. That's what her mother said, but why on God's green earth does Jeffrey have a clipping of Ronnie's dad in here?"

Ian scowled. "Did Ronnie even know Jeffrey then?"

"I don't think so. This was 1999. They started going out three years after this, I think." Steph tried to remember when but wasn't sure.

Ian inhaled sharply and let it out. "Jesus, this guy is slippery. Who knows what all this means, but I'm going to start looking into the bastard and this Jason Korbin guy."

"Me too. I'm curious about why Jeffrey has his stuff in here. What do you think it means?" Steph put the clipping in one of the nearby boxes.

A bright flash startled her, but she realized Ian was taking pictures of everything. "Hand me that obit, Stephanie, will you?"

Steph pulled it out of the box and held it up for him to snap a picture. "He didn't clean the floor when he moved in. It's a dusty mess, but you can see the outline of something about two and a half feet round here." Ian scraped the floor with his foot to show her where. "And over here was a duffle bag or something soft. You can see the creasing of the material in the dust."

"Where is that stuff now? Nothing in here matches that shape." Steph walked to the corners to be sure nothing was hiding in the dark recesses of the storage unit.

Steph turned around but Ian was gone. She found him crawling through the hole in the wall. The flashing proved what he was doing in there.

Steph peeked through the hole. "Anything in there?"

"Only footprints. I think it was raining when she came in. Small feet too. I think it was that woman that was in the office the other day. Remember, the guy said she wanted a unit near Jeffrey's? An old flame or something like that."

Steph nodded. Ian made a great detective. "Yeah, that's right. Aren't you the smart one?"

"Not as smart as Jason Korbin, eh?" Ian chuckled. "Wish I had a way to find out who our mystery lady is. She was hot as fuck."

Steph was annoyed. "Hot?"

Ian laughed. "I could cozy up to her and find out what she's up to. Get in her pants, ya know."

"Always planning for the sexy times. Ian, you'll never change." Steph playfully pushed Ian as he crawled through the hole.

He fell on his knees and stood up. "Och, Stephanie, you wee darling'." Ian stood up then bent over again. "What's this?"

He held up a strip of paper the size of a bookmark. Ian flipped it over to find a bunch of phone numbers written on it in purple, frilly cursive.

"No dude wrote this. I wonder if it's from our culprit."

"Look at you, Sleuthy McKay!" Steph smacked Ian on the back.

He laughed and slid the paper into his pocket. "I'll be doing a little research on that baby."

Steph's worry returned full force. "Don't be doing anything stupid that will get us caught. Last thing we need is ole Jeffrey coming after us."

"For what, Stephanie? Being nosey?" Ian moved another box and went through the contents.

"For butting into his life and maybe uncovering his sins. Looks like someone beat us to it though." She stepped closer and looked in the box. "What's all this stuff?"

"Looks like tax forms from our ole friend Jason. You know, Stephanie, I wonder if he hid all of this because the FBI is on his tail. He didn't want to be caught with Jason's stuff. Is that because he doesn't want Jason talking to the Feds?"

"Brilliant, Ian. I bet you're right. Jason will hold the key to this whole thing." Steph held up a page for Ian to snap a picture. "I just wish there was something here that gave us more information."

"There is." Ian's white teeth shone in the low light. "Taxes have addresses, and social security numbers. I have all I need to find Jason. The breadcrumbs will lead to what Jeffrey is really hiding."

KJ Waters

"Ochhht, you're right, Ian!" She hugged him from the side. "I wish there was a way to know what she took and why. I sure hope we can find out who she is and what she's up to."

"Same." Ian put the lid on the box and stepped away. "I wish I could see Jeffrey's face when he realizes his stuff is gone."

"Ha! Yeah, me too! Bastard." Steph looked around nervously, remembering her earlier reluctance about coming into the unit. "Let's go, Ian."

Ian dusted off his hands and walked out of the unit and waited as she exited then pulled the door down and locked it.

They walked silently back towards the car. Ian stopped short and put his hand on her arm. "Stephanie, someone is leaning on our car. Please, for the love of God, let me do the talking."

Steph's heart raced. "Who is it?"

"I don't know, but if they mean us harm, I'll handle it. If they want information from us, keep your damn trap shut, okay?"

Chapter 52

Cowboys and Indians

Ronnie startled awake. She listened intently, not altogether certain where she was. The air was stale and smelled of mildew. A smashing sound forced her to a sitting position. Was she back in time again? It was pitch-black and hot, and a repetitive whoosh sound caught her attention. Someone was breathing nearby. Ronnie scrambled to her hands and knees, ready to fight. Pain seared through her body.

Her knee! She shifted positions, and it all came flooding back. This was Puerto Rico, and Mike was sleeping nearby with a concussion. She reached around for the flashlight and clicked it on, her heart thumping out of her chest. The light bounced around the shelves of snacks until she pointed it near Mike. What if his head injury had worsened? If he was unconscious, how the hell would she get help?

Panic drove her to rouse him. Hadn't he asked her to let him sleep? "Mike."

He was dozing on his side, with the battered temple facing up. The injury was gruesome, swollen, and he had significant bruising around the eye.

"Mike, wake up." She shook his shoulder now, panic increasing.

Mike rolled onto his back and groaned, gripping his head. "Oh, damn. Point that flashlight somewhere else. You're breaking me." His voice was deep and gruff, but his words were innocuous.

"Oh gosh, I'm sorry. I just heard a noise and then got worried about you."

"What noise?" Mike sat up and gripped his head. "Oh God."

"Lie back down, Mike. I'm sorry I woke you. I can get you more ibuprofen."

"What was the noise?"

"Crashing."

He stood, gripping the shelf nearby to steady himself. "Flashlight."

Ronnie handed it to him, feeling like a surgical assistant, then stood up, steadying him.

"Where was the sound coming from?"

Ronnie pointed towards the garage. Mike walked away but stopped to grab a pair of flip-flops from the shelf. Ronnie followed suit, relieved Mike was thinking clearly. That was a positive sign.

They strode past the bathroom and stepped over the broken doorframe where the

273

remnants swept into a tidy pile. The roof was leaking in the back corner of the garage near the old Chevy.

"Probably a tree branch poked a hole in the roof. I think we need to move this truck." Mike held up his hand. "Stay here." He moved a bucket under the leak and then walked to the old car. "If the roof caves in, it'll bury the car, blocking our only escape."

"Crap!"

Mike opened the truck's door and sat in the driver's seat. Ronnie jumped when he cranked the engine and it sputtered then caught. "Hey! That's good news!"

She tried to lift the garage door, but the heavy metal wouldn't budge. Mike jumped out of the car and released the latch built into the metal frame on the ceiling. They both lifted the door and a gust of torrential rain whipped in, accompanied by a whiff of earth and pine. Ronnie walked to the second garage door and waited while Mike pulled the cord.

Mike sat back down and drove out into the rain, headlights shining off the slick asphalt. He re-parked it in the second bay, as far away from the leaking roof as he could get. Then Mike shut off the engine and walked towards her. "Nearly a full tank, too. I think we found our escape vehicle."

"That's terrific! I'm so sorry I woke you though. I could have done all of that myself. You look a hot mess, Mike."

He laughed. "Ronnie, I already told you I'm indestructible." They made their way back to the convenience store.

Ronnie stepped gingerly over the broken door that separated the two sides of the building. On the ground was a sticky note that read, *I will pay for the damages, Mike Walsh,* with his phone number scrawled in neat print. "I was worried about your head. You were losing your thoughts last night."

"I'm just glad you saved me from that dream." Mike picked up her hand and kissed it as they walked back to where they'd been sleeping.

"So, you could say I rescued you twice."

"Absolutely. First time from a raging river, second time from snakes and murderous outlaws."

Ronnie stopped short as Mike continued, and she pulled on his hand to stop him. Mike turned to her, worried. "What?"

The air whooshed from her lungs. A flashback of Max beheading the snake and flinging it at Jere Miah blasted through her mind. "What are you talking about, Mike?"

His brows furrowed. "Yeah, my dream. Why are you reacting like that? You okay?"

Ronnie forced herself to breathe. Could it be a coincidence?

"Jeez, Ron, you look like you've seen a ghost. Do you need me to get you some food?"

Ronnie reached out and took his arm. "I need to sit down."

Alarmed, Mike helped her to the pallet of towels they'd slept on. "Here, lie down. How about some crackers?"

Dark stubble and black eyes gave him a menacing expression, but the kindness and worry were evident in his voice. Ronnie lay down, hoping that would quell the dizziness.

He returned with a box of club crackers, ripped it opened, and handed her a sleeve. She took them and shoved one in her mouth.

"You alright?" he said, hovering over her, the flashlight shining on the ceiling, giving it a horror movie vibe.

"Sit. I'm okay. Just a bit woozy." Ronnie's mind was racing. "Mike, tell me more about your dream."

"My dream? Well, okay. That isn't what I expected you to say. I think when daylight arrives, we need to study some of those maps," Mike nodded at the rack of local maps near the checkout counter, "and figure out where we are and if there is a chance we can get to a doctor. I'm worried about you."

"I'm okay, I swear. I'm more concerned about *you*. You may not want to face the mirror." The shadows provided additional ammo for his thug look. "Please, Mike. This is really important. Can you tell me about your dream?" Her voice came out in a squeak.

Mike cocked his head and looked puzzled. "Okay, if that makes you feel better. You woke me just as I was getting shot, so thank you immensely for that."

Ronnie's breath quickened, and the memory of Max's dead body flashed in her mind. "What happened before that?"

"Why? I can tell this is really important to you." Mike squinted in confusion.

Ronnie placed her hand over his. "Please. I'll explain. It's either a weird coincidence or..."

"Yeah. So..." He ran his hands through his hair and twisted his mouth. "Let's see. I guess it started with a..." He watched her carefully as he said the next words. "Buffalo stampede."

Ronnie sucked in her breath and forced her lips to stop quivering. "And?" Just before she'd seen Max, he'd almost been trampled by a herd of bison. "Mike." Ronnie had to catch her breath. "This is going to sound really weird but..." She bit her lips, not sure if she wanted this to be true. "Was there a guy named Max?"

Mike's eyes widened, and he leaned in towards her. "What the hell...? How could you know that?"

Ronnie looked away, rubbed her eyes, and struggled for where to start. "Just tell me more so I can figure this out."

Mike frowned. "Figure what out? Were you dreaming the same thing? Are you psychic?" His tone had shifted to anger laced with confusion.

"Not really. Please, don't be mad. I have to hear more so I can see if it's just..." She bit both of her lips, sealing her mouth shut.

"It made absolutely no sense to me." He shook his head, then snatched a water near him and drained it, bouncing the empty water off the opposite shelf, catching it adroitly. "Yeah, Max was there. Plus, Jere Miah and Ben, but they were really Jesse and Frank James."

Ronnie's mind exploded with shock, and a feeling of terror laced with relief overwhelmed her. "Wait? *Jesse James*?" The faces flashed in her mind as she remembered the men she'd encountered...Jere Miah, Gary, Ben, and Clayton. There was no *Jesse* or *Frank* James. "In your *dream*?"

"In my dream and...well, I'm pretty certain. So many things about these two men screamed it."

"Like what?" Ronnie was astonished out of the million other questions she'd wanted to ask.

"For starters, Jere Miah's nickname was dingus." He glanced at her, studying her face as if he could read her mind. "He blasted off his finger cleaning his gun during the Civil War. Some of the other stories they told fit."

Ronnie stood up and paced down the aisle, her hands over her ears. How could this be true? Her breath caught. This was unbelievable.

Mike stopped her, grabbing her elbows. "You're scaring me. Tell me what is happening."

Ronnie stared into his face, overwhelmed with competing thoughts. *Mike was Max!* He had been back in time with her. Mike was everything Ini had said he was. But what the hell did the Frank and Jesse James part mean?

Mike shook her elbows. "Ronnie, tell me what the goddamned hell is happening."

Ronnie pulled away and took a few steps backward, trying to form words through her complete shock. "I...Mike...oh God." She covered her face, trying to push this new reality away, rejecting everything she thought she knew about the world. A swirl of emotions made her burst into tears. It was Mike, not Max, who had been killed in Maggie and Lawrence's house.

Mike stared down at her, fists clenched, a mixture of annoyance and growing anger showing on his face. "What is happening, Ronnie? What is this about?"

"Mike, I was *Rose*." It was her turn to study his reaction.

He stared at her blankly, his fists relaxing. "Wait, what?"

"Mike, please sit and let me tell you everything." She took his hand, and she was afraid he was going to pull it free from her grasp. She needed to feel his solidness now more than ever.

"Tell me what? That you're a witch or something?"

The words stung. On her first trip back in time, she'd been jailed for being a witch. Was Mathias standing before her in a different time? As Ini had said it, in a different life?

Mike reached out and took her hand, his tone softening. "I'm sorry. You're totally freaking me out here. Ronnie, please, tell me what the *hell* is going on."

Ronnie sat down on the towel and pulled his hand to sit next to her. How could she explain everything to him? "Please don't be mad. I'm as confused as you are."

"Okay. I'm not really mad. I'm watching you struggle with this, but you're not giving me much to go on here. I gather it's something big." The anger edging his face softened.

"I don't even know where to start." Ronnie fought back tears, and when she could speak without it coming out in a squeak, she said, "I'm so glad we are in this together, Mike. Maybe you can help me figure some of this out. I've been losing my mind over this."

Mike's expression softened. "We are in it together, Ronnie."

That calmed her down a notch. "So, remember what I was telling you about my mom thinking I was crazy?"

He nodded.

"This is why. What you dreamed wasn't a dream." Then it occurred to her that maybe for Mike it *was* just a dream. Was he channeling what she'd been through?

"So, I'm crazy too. Is it a disease I've caught from you?" His eyes widened, and he looked scared.

"I don't really know. Did you feel pain? Did you experience everything in excruciating detail?"

"I did. While it was happening, I was certain it wasn't a dream. It lasted for days." Mike inhaled sharply and let it out in a slow exhale, almost a whistle. "Shit, is this what your dad had too?"

"Well, who knows? But you've just given me hope that it's not friggin' mental illness. Let me go back to what happened during Hurricane Charley. But before I do, did you just dream this tonight? Or back at the hotel?"

Mike nodded. "Hotel. And I dreamt it tonight. It hasn't left my mind since then."

"Exactly when did it happen?" A new emotion filled in the crowded space in her tangled thoughts. Hope.

"When you locked yourself in the bathroom, I unlocked the door and saw you passed out on the floor. It was just after that I got dizzy and woke up in a buffalo stampede. Just dumb luck I wasn't killed then."

Ronnie leaned over and kissed his cheek, startling him. Then pulled away. "Oh my God." She smiled. This man was her salvation. He'd just proved his connection to her through time. "Your mind is about to be blown, Michael William Walsh."

"I think it already is."

Ronnie stuffed another cracker in her mouth and washed it down with water. This was going to take a lot out of her. But the buoyancy of knowing Mike was a part of this took the edge off. For the first time, she could explain what she'd been through without having to persuade someone she wasn't nuts.

Mike stretched his legs out and leaned back on straightened arms, watching her carefully. He looked like the rebel Max had been back in the Wild West of Texas—stubbly, angry, bruised, and battered.

"Do you remember when we met at Barnes and Noble after Hurricane Charley?" She settled on a concrete place to start.

"Of course."

"And remember when I freaked out like a complete psycho and had to go to the bathroom while Steph entertained you?" That seemed like a century ago.

"I wouldn't describe it like that, but yeah." Mike squinted as he studied her.

"That was a few hours after I had my first episode. I was still trying to figure out what the hell had happened to me. I felt just like you do now. Totally confused, scared, and traumatized because I had to die to return to this time."

Mike nodded, not taking his eyes off her. "Okay."

"I freaked out because you reminded me so much of the man who helped me through that situation. His name was Mathias."

"Really?" He rubbed his stubbly chin. "Jeez. Tell me more. I mean, you're saying words, but I have no idea what you're talking about."

"Yeah." Ronnie paused. A jumble of thoughts rolled around in her head. Where to start? "Mike, I had the same type of thing happen during Hurricane Frances, but that storm lasted longer, and it happened three different times."

"Holy shit, really?" His mouth crumpled, and he looked sad and alarmed. "So, wait...the coma? Were you somewhere else when you were unconscious during the storm?"

"I was."

Mike's eyes widened. "Ronnie, is that what happens to your body when you go back in time? You are just limp on the floor, helpless?"

"Yeah, I guess."

"Is it possible that your father was somewhere else and was still there when your mother pulled the plug?"

Tears stung Ronnie's eyes. "Yes, damn, you are a quick study. That would mean my mother killed my father, in a way."

Mike shook his head. "Could he have been brought back alive?"

"I don't know. But the thought absolutely guts me." Should she tell him about talking to her father in her travels? She would save that for later.

"Okay, so much makes sense now about how you've been behaving. God, no wonder your mom thinks you're nuts. This *is* nuts."

"It is. But we can be nuts together!" Ronnie smiled.

Chapter 53

Watches and Witches

The memories rushed back, filling Ronnie with competing emotions. Horror, worry, fear, and excitement, knowing she was not batshit crazy. "The first time I traveled, I landed in Regina Ingram's body, just after a carriage hit her. Did your body feel disconnected at first?"

Mike nodded. "I could hear everything but couldn't see."

"That's how it was for me. In the confusion, a man found me and carried me to his house."

"Mathias?"

"No, Jack, Regina's brother. Mike, every time travel episode there is a pattern that repeats. There is bad guy who tries to hurt me, and another man who helps me, like you did as Max."

Mike nodded. "A pattern, that's interesting. Tell me everything you remember. I'll see if I can recognize any more patterns."

Ronnie recounted every detail, even ones that seemed inconsequential. Mike sat still, absorbing every word. Finally, he peppered her with questions. "Ronnie, the watch is significant, right?"

Ronnie nodded. "You're right. I knew it then too. It was the only thing from my own time. It had to be the link to return to Florida. I was devastated when Jack took it off my wrist during the bloodletting."

"What a nightmare! Bloodletting was their cure-all back then, wasn't it?" Mike bared his teeth in a grimace of disgust.

"It was. I bumped my head. How the hell is taking blood going to help a concussion? Ever hear of a scarificator?"

Mike shook his head. "No, sounds awful."

"Yup. A doctor invented it to make the cut for the bleeding. It's a brass cube about this big with little blades inside." Ronnie held her finger and thumb a few inches apart. "I tried to get away. Jack threatened to beat me if I didn't hold still."

"Did you hold still?"

"Not at first. All I could see were the doctor's bloody, rusty instruments. Then Jack demanded to know where the watch came from, and I let it slip it was a birthday present from Jeffrey. Stupid, right?"

Mike kissed her hand. "A few days ago, I might have agreed with you, but I know how overwhelming it is, especially the first hour when you're still trying to figure out if it's a dream or reality. To be honest, I'd be pissed too if a strange man was giving my sister an expensive gift."

"Yeah, but Jack got his revenge. Jack and his wife accused me of being a witch. I don't blame them. I acted nothing like Regina."

"Oh, damn, and I just asked if you were a witch." Mike sat up, shaking his head. "I'm so sorry. What happened to the watch?"

"It's okay. Jack grabbed it." Ronnie shared the horrid experience with Lord Barton, and how Jack instructed her to seduce him into proposing, and when that went sour, Mathias attempted to intervene. "Mike, Jack carted me off to jail, and they tried me as a witch."

"What? Ronnie, in 1752 they no longer had witch trials. Was this in a remote village?"

Ronnie shook her head. "No, in London. I wondered about that too. I looked it up. The last witch trial in England was in 1716 when a mother and daughter were executed. In 1735 a law was passed prohibiting the practice. I was there seventeen years later." Ronnie shook her head. "You know what else was strange? Mathias was so mad when I mentioned America. He was furious that my tutors had failed to teach me of the United French Colonies."

Mike squinted, and his mouth dropped open. "Please tell me France didn't take over the British colonies in America."

"According to Mathias Stohl. He kept correcting my rendition of history. I wonder if we landed in an alternate plane, like those time travel movies where you go sideways in time."

Mike's jaw dropped. "Through the wormhole?"

"Yeah. Oh jeez, what have we gotten into, Mike?"

Mike's eyes were wide. "What happened next?"

"I was in jail until the trial." Ronnie mentioned the water trial and the rats. "I was convicted, and Mathias arranged for a bunch of thugs to break me out right after the trial. Mathias was smart enough to only pay half to ensure my safe return, but when I got out, he was nowhere to be found."

"Did something happen to Mathias?" Mike was leaning forward, soaking in every word.

"Yeah, he was stabbed right after the trial. He told me later Jack hired someone to do it."

"Oh. That is evil."

"Worse, because Mathias was his cousin by marriage. When Mathias didn't show up to collect me and pay the rest of the fee for my release, we went looking for him. We found him in an alley, bleeding out from the stab wound."

"Oh my God. Then what?" Mike bit his lower lip and shook his head.

"Mike, Mathias was dead when I found him. I had to revive him, but by then the police were out looking for me and brought me back to jail. The next day, all the prisoners, including me, were driven to Tyburn for the hanging."

Mike's eyebrows shot up again. "Holy shit, really?"

Ronnie paused, reliving the horror. "Yeah, I watched the lowest of humanity butcher the newly dead. I'll never forget it. Did you know it was lucky to have the severed hand of a freshly hanged criminal?"

Mike's lips curled up in a sneer. "Seriously?"

Ronnie nodded

Mike covered her hand. "Terrifying. How did you get away, Ronnie?"

Ronnie sighed. "I didn't. Mike, they hanged me."

"No! Ronnie, you're serious? They *hanged* you?"

Ronnie picked at a nub of fabric on the towel in front of her. "It's okay. Just at the last second, Mathias showed up. As I was dying, he pressed the watch into my palm, and I came back to Florida. Without it, I may have died there and not returned. But who knows?"

Mike squeezed her hand. "Ronnie, I can't imagine how horrific that was. It's the kind of thing that changes you forever." He pulled her close and hugged her, kissing the top of her head. Then he held her by the shoulders. "So, let me get this straight. You died by hanging, and a few hours later you met me at the bookstore?"

"Yeah, I was a mess, but Steph talked me into going." Ronnie pushed down the putrid smells, the haunting screams, and the gruesome sights. It *had* changed her forever.

"Ronnie, you are a goddamned badass. Let me ask you something. Did time pass differently? Were you there for days but here," he tapped the floor, "it was only an hour?"

Ronnie nodded. "Yes, I was there for days and days, but in our time, it was only an hour and a half."

"We were *stealing time*, Ronnie."

Ronnie chuckled, "Yeah, I guess we were."

He smiled. "Thank God Mathias was there for you. I wonder if that happened to your dad, where he just wasn't able to return without a link to 1999, or if something else happened to him."

Ronnie fought back tears. What had her father gone through? She'd give anything to know what happened that night. Was he connected to this?

Mike shook his head. "How did Mathias find the watch? Do you know where Jack hid it?"

"I'm not sure, but I think Jack locked it in his desk. Why?"

He smoothed down her hair. "It's just weird that he brought it with him."

Ronnie finished her water. "I begged him to bring it to me when I was in jail. I was sure it would take me back."

"Oh, that makes more sense. Where was Jack's house?"

Ronnie was confused. "His *house*? They called it the Ingram Estate, but I think it was Farthington Manor in southeastern London. Why?"

"We can look it up in the historical records. See if we can track down anyone and compare it to your experience." Mike pressed his lips together and shook his head.

Ronnie smiled. Mike was the perfect person to help sort through all of this. Logical to a flaw. "I researched it, but it's been hard with the storms and moving. I've just not had much time or access to the Internet. You know what's weird?"

"Besides everything you've told me so far?" His eyes lit up with mirth.

Ronnie laughed. "When I returned to Jeffrey's lab after the hanging, the watch was gone."

Mike leaned towards her. "That is weird. I thought you'd have it in your hand or on your wrist."

"Me too. If I'd not gone back at all, it should have been on my wrist when I woke up. It's one detail that I've held onto when everyone was saying I'm crazy."

Mike shifted position, bending one knee and resting his arm on it. "How did Jeffrey react? From his perspective, he gave you an expensive gift, and you immediately lost it."

Ronnie rubbed her eyes. The exhaustion was catching up to her. "He was livid and didn't care that I was totally freaked out. All he could focus on was the missing watch." As she said this, a vivid memory flashed through her mind. Just after she'd returned, when Jeffrey was holding her, she'd felt a stab in her thigh. Had Jeffrey drugged her? It would explain her fuzzy memory of how she'd returned to her apartment.

Mike sat expressionless. "What did you tell him?"

"We didn't talk until later. A fire broke out in his lab, and I sat in the lab next door for a bit."

"Whose lab?"

"I'm not sure her name, let me think…Hannah. I have no idea how I got home, Mike."

"How do you explain that?" His eyebrows nearly touched, and he shook his head, looking very menacing. "I mean, when I returned yesterday, I was clear-headed once I landed in my body. It was jarring to go from dying to being back in the hotel. But I remembered everything."

"I dunno. We talked about it later, but he says I was in a fugue state. Mike, Jeffrey may have given me a sedative. Oh, and get this…" Ronnie touched his calf. "He says he found the watch later in his lab. He said I must have taken it off. But I didn't."

Mike cocked his head to the side. "What is a fugue state?"

"It's like sleepwalking, but you're awake. You become aware again when it's over and have no idea how you left your house." She shook her head.

"Ronnie, maybe he had a spare watch. Is Jeffrey behind all of this?"

"Steph is sure Jeffrey is involved. But how the hell is he doing it? During Frances, I traveled a few times with the watch. I took it off at one point, hoping it would make the traveling stop. But I still traveled and returned without it."

"That is so weird. It travelled with you twice? And what happened after you removed it?"

"It didn't seem to make any difference."

He screwed up his face, looking perplexed. "So, you don't really need the watch to travel, do you?"

"I don't know for sure."

"But when you wear it, it goes back with you?" Mike held her hand and played with her fingers.

Ronnie nodded. "Yeah, right now the watch is at Questlabs in Florida. We just both time traveled without it." Ronnie took a deep breath. She'd been so wrapped up in telling Mike everything, she'd forgotten about the last trip.

He looked confused. "Questlabs?"

"Looking for the bubonic plague." Ronnie waited for his reaction.

His jaw dropped open in shock. "The bubonic plague? What the hell?"

"I know, right?" Ronnie scooted closer so she could hold his hand without stretching out. "During Frances, I landed in the body of a girl who had bubonic plague. We were caught in the Great Fire of London. I was trapped as the fire approached, and to keep from burning up, I slit my wrists to speed it up a little. When I returned, the watch was covered in blood."

"Holy shit. You're serious?" Mike's eyes were enormous now.

"I am. I thought the blood would be the only way for me to prove I traveled in time, even if only to myself. If it's positive for the plague, I'll know for certain. Of course, now I have *you* as proof."

"Ronnie, seriously, tell me everything that you've been through, so I can help you figure this shit out."

A wave of relief washed over her. Steph believed her, but there was a wariness too. Maybe Steph's Catholic upbringing and her faith kept her from diving in too deep. Mike had been there too—he was a true believer. Ronnie spent the next hour sharing the strange events over the last few months, explaining all she'd been through. Mike listened intently and asked logical, smart questions.

When they'd exhausted every detail, Ronnie asked, "Mike, what happened to you? You mentioned Jesse James. Are you sure we were both in the same place?"

Mike looked away and then changed positions, clasping his knees and leaning back against the shelf. "I'm sure it was him. I guess I have to share my experience."

"I want to hear everything while it's still fresh."

Mike laughed. "Still *fresh*. How could I ever forget?" He rubbed the stubble on his chin again, making a rasping sound. "Then you have to explain what happened to Rose. I mean you. God, this is confusing."

"Deal. Tell me everything from the second I locked the bathroom door at the National Suites."

Mike pursed his lips and looked up at the ceiling, letting out a long, slow breath.

Chapter 54

Stampede

Mike cracked open another water and handed it to Ronnie. "Drink while I talk." He opened another one for himself and took a swig, gathering his thoughts. His mind was still in a whirlwind, knowing he'd traveled back in time.

He took a deep breath and let it fill his cheeks as he let it out. "When you locked yourself in the bathroom, I broke in and was alarmed to find you on the floor. Scared me to death."

∞

Two days prior.

Mike reached out to Ronnie, horrified by her limp form splayed on the bathroom floor. "Ronnie, wake up!" He gently shook her. "I'm so sorry I lost it." He leaned down to make sure she was breathing, laying his cheek near her mouth, wishing they were this close under different circumstances.

Ronnie's breath was light but regular and the panic subsided a smidge. Mike's first instinct was to get her off the bathroom floor, but a wave of dizziness overwhelmed him. He sat back against the tub and held his head, hoping it would clear so he could help her. Her only instructions had been to keep her comfortable.

Mike willed her to wake up, to tell him it was okay, and to give him a chance to explain the newspaper article. It struck him suddenly that this is exactly what happened with Kelly. He'd lost his temper, punched the wall and...

Interrupting that desperate thought, a strong wave of nausea hit him hard. He held it back as best he could and contemplated his next move. Could he lift the toilet seat and throw up with Ronnie laying on the floor under him? He glanced at the tub and did not relish the thought of cleaning that up. They may not have running water with the storm raging outside.

Without warning, his body jerked upwards, and he felt a violent tearing through his entire being. Mike fought it with all his might, squeezing his eyes shut, but it was to no avail. The dizziness returned, and he opened his eyes to find the room spinning. What he saw shocked him to the core. The view was of his own body, sliding sideways till he rested on the floor, legs perpendicular to the tub, his torso laying along the side. Ronnie's face was as peaceful and beautiful as it had ever been. So close and yet so far. She looked like she had in the hospital, still, settled, yet not truly there.

How could he see this perspective? His logical mind was unable to make sense of it. He'd have to be hovering outside his body. Before he had a chance to come to terms with it, he was jerked upwards, impossibly, towards the sky, with no sign of the hotel, Ronnie, or the storm. Mike's limbs remained limp and unresponsive. He felt like he'd been in a car wreck, left with limited senses, only his vision and hearing operating. His mind was anything but still. Mike knew he was leaving his body on Earth. Was he going to heaven? That would be a shocker. What was his cause of death?

Mike fell into a trance-like state, losing track of time and space for what seemed like hours, days, maybe lifetimes. Until suddenly the momentum shifted, and he was falling now, picking up speed. Terror clouded his mind and retelling this later he would have described it as lasting only a fraction of a second, but at the moment, he recorded every nuance as if it were in slow motion, recalling every millisecond as if it were minutes.

It reminded him of the chemical weapons training in the Marines, where they shoved you in a room with other jarheads and filled it with mustard gas. Everyone was clawing at their eyes, getting sick and disoriented. Once they opened the door, the men were blindly trying to get out the door, pushing, punching, desperate to find fresh air. This time he could breathe, but it was that same wholly unsettling feeling that you have been overwhelmed by something outside your control. He'd had nightmares about it. Not many situations left you feeling completely out of control, with no approach to fix it. Only one other situation had eclipsed that feeling — when he found Kelly dead in the shower.

The descent ended abruptly, and he was sure it had killed him. In any rational world, falling from that distance, whatever it had been, would be enough to kill a man. Pain seared through every fiber of his being, but to his surprise it dissipated, leaving only a loud rumbling in his ears. His vision was murky and didn't seem to be connected to his brain.

If he had any semblance of sanity left after this, it had left him. Nothing in this moment was the way it should be. The sounds were terrifying, almost like thunder, but it carried on *ad infinitum* with angry voices thrown into the mix. The smells were gamey, as if some weird beast was nearby, and the grit registering between each raspy breath had no resemblance to the humid hotel room. The men's cries grew more cohesive, with some speaking in an unfamiliar language that was rough and sporadic. A piercing scream harkening to the war cry of a Native American tore through the fog in his mind. Yup, he'd gone mad.

Mike strained to move, danger of the unknown plucking at his mind to move to safety. He choked on a gritty breath and coughed, struggling to breathe. Slowly his vision cleared, but he could not accept what his eyes were reporting. An endless rampage of enormous animals ran past him with deadly hoof beats. Cows? Their heads were much too broad for it to be any cattle he'd ever seen. One of them nearly trampled him, and he got an uncomfortably close look. A herd of buffalo with their heads down, eyes wild, were running from something. The dirt from their stampede rose in a cloud that was carried away by the wind.

Mike stood now, and felt behind him, grabbing the only reason he was still alive. He clung to the massive boulder that jagged out of the reddish soil and watched the beasts running past him on both sides. Dirt covered every square inch of his unprotected flesh and even crusted on his eyelashes. He squeezed his eyes shut and held his arm over his mouth and nose. Mike was surprised to feel fabric on his arm. A minute ago, he was in a t-shirt. The long-sleeved shirt filtered the dust-filled air, allowing him to get a clean breath, albeit one full of not so fresh linen.

After a few interminable minutes, his eyesight improved enough that he could make out a few men on horseback, dressed like cowboys. "What the fucking hell?" he murmured and regretted the words, for they did not sound like his own. His voice was higher. Was it the dirt choking off his larynx?

Movement on the right caught his eye, and it was even more astounding than what he'd already seen. Natives in full dress sat atop horses. One raised his fist and hollered something at another Native almost parallel to him but blocked off by the stampeding herd. A woman wearing a long beige dress struggled to stand, and the Native struck her. She slumped to the ground and lay still.

Mike yelled out, "Hey leave her alone!" but the words couldn't rise above the sound of the hoof beats. The Native bent down and seized the woman, and in a lithe, remarkably athletic motion, he mounted the horse with her body draped in front of him. He fled with the other Natives in the same direction as the herd.

Mike rubbed the dust from his eyes. He was trapped with the beasts running past him on both sides, preventing him from helping the woman. A gust of wind carried the soil up and behind him in a strange, lifelike cloud. His eyes followed the formation. When he looked back, the stampede was reduced to a trickle of what must have been the back of the herd, with older or more sickly animals as they struggled to keep up. One of the cowboys was heading towards him on horseback, leading another horse.

"Max, good God. Are you alright?" Piercing blue eyes looked him up and down. "I thought you were good as dead." The man had a strong mid-western accent, and lopsided ears stuck out under the bowler hat, fitting tight on his head, and curving up around the edges.

Why was he calling him *Max?* Mike nearly corrected him but thought better of it. Silence was safety from the unknown. Distracted and disoriented, Mike walked towards the man. Before he made it more than a few strides, an angry bison bent low to make use of his short, sharp horns. Blackness engulfed his vision and he passed out.

Chapter 55

Homeland

Ian approached Steph's car, keeping Steph behind him. "May I help you, sir?"

The man was dressed in a black suit, black tie, and crisp, white shirt. He stepped away from the car, lifted his sunglasses, and held out his hand. He towered over Ian and Steph. "Great to meet you both. I'm Agent Jackson with Homeland Security."

Steph caught her breath and was sure the guilt oozed off her.

Ian stepped forward. "Great to meet you, agent. What can we do for you?"

"We are looking into a matter following the storm. Are you familiar with the name Jeffrey Brennan?"

Ian glanced at Steph and bugged his eyes out at her as a reminder to let him talk. "I know *of* him."

"Great, great. Can you tell me how you know him?"

"What is this in relation to, if you don't mind me asking?" Ian said.

Steph was impressed. She'd have spilled the beans about everything with the look the man was giving Ian.

The man tipped is head back and gave a barely perceptible nod, as if Ian had called his bluff. Had he? "It's a matter of national security, and I wish I could divulge the details, but as my hands are tied, I can't share that. But you'd be doing our country a world of good if you help by answering a few questions."

"I'm all ears," Ian said, crossing his arms.

"We saw you leaving Jeffrey Brennan's place a few days ago. We've followed you thinking you were involved in this, but I've concluded that you are unaware of Mr. Brennan's...issues. My partner..." he nodded towards his car, "has a different idea."

Ian turned to Steph. "Good cop, bad cop. Nice one."

The agent stepped closer to Ian. "I detect an accent. Where exactly are you from, Mr. McKay? Do I need to look into your visa?"

"Are you threatening me?" Ian's tone shifted to anger.

"No, just assessing your willingness to help." Agent Jackson smiled calmly.

Steph couldn't keep quiet any longer. "He's legal, a temporary visa."

Ian stepped between Steph and the agent and whispered, "Hush yer whisheet."

Agent Jackson motioned for his partner to join them. When the man walked over, he introduced him as Agent Hernandez.

The new agent nodded his head to the left and spoke directly to Steph. "Why don't we talk over here for a minute?"

Ian grabbed her arm. "No, I think we're done here. If you want to chat more, we can bring our lawyer. You boys won't find anything here with us. We're just going to mosey along now." Ian motioned for Steph to go to the driver's side of the car.

Jackson interceded, "Sir, we can call you down to the station if you'd rather talk there."

"I'm good," Ian said.

"Ma'am, just one question please," Agent Hernandez said. "We aren't interested in either of you. Just one question may be the difference between protecting our nation or allowing something nefarious to escalate." Steph looked at Ian, but the man continued. "How do you know Jeffrey Brennan?"

Steph blurted, "He used to date my best friend."

Ian shot her an alarmed look, but Steph ignored it. There was no way in hell she was going to get her brother deported because of damn Jeffrey.

Hernandez continued, "When is the last time you saw him?"

Steph stepped away from Ian. "A few weeks ago, I believe."

Ian reached out and took her arm. "Stephanie, let's go."

Steph ignored Ian. "He left a few days ago, but I don't know where he went. We are trying to find something my friend left in the storage unit. He said we could look in there."

Ian looked at the sky, shaking his head. "For the love of God, Stephanie."

"What? It's true. Show him the key," Steph blurted, but the look Ian shot at her said it all. She'd said too much.

"So, he gave you permission to look in the unit?" Jackson asked, taking a step closer.

Steph spoke up, knowing it was a lie, but stuck with it. "Yeah, he did."

"Could we just take a quick look in there?" Hernandez asked.

Ian snatched the car keys out of Steph's hand. "No, I don't think that's wise. I mean, it's Jeffrey's stuff. He didn't say we could let the FBI in there."

Jackson laughed. "We aren't the FBI, Ian. Homeland Security." He handed a card to Ian, who shoved it in his pocket. "Just wanting to clear up a few things." He turned to Steph. "Do you know where Jeffrey went?"

"No, he didn't say. I don't talk to him on a regular basis."

"So, when were you going to return the key for this place? When he returns?"

Ian butted in. "He asked us to leave it in his mail slot."

"Oh, that's weird. He doesn't have a mail slot in his condo, does he?" Jackson exchanged a knowing glance with his partner. "Just give us a call if you learn anything new or just want to chat."

Hernandez gave his card to Steph.

"Sure, sure. We will." Steph opened the car door and plopped down in the driver's seat.

Ian walked between the men and got in the car and stayed silent until they were on the highway. "Oh my God, what part of *let me do the talking* didn't you understand?"

"I didn't tell them anything, Ian." Steph felt guilty for not being able to control herself.

Ian shook his head and turned towards her. "You sure as fuck did. You confirmed that we were in Jeffrey's storage unit. They could get a warrant and get in there."

"*I* did that?"

"Yeah, Sherlock. They ask opened-ended questions, hoping idiots like you will give them info they'd not even thought to ask."

"Occccht, no. I *did* that." Steph smacked the steering wheel. "You're the one who lied about the mail slot."

"Damn it, I don't know why I said that. It was stupid. I caught your disease. Mad *coo*."

Steph steamed. "Don't be calling me a cow, Ian. I panicked."

Ian raised his voice. "Precisely why I told you to keep your damn gob shut. Now they'll be following both of us to see where we lead them, like total eejits." Ian looked out the window and crossed his arms.

Steph glanced at him. "Ian, I'm sorry. I'm just not good at this stuff. You shouldn't have called me in there."

"I'm glad I did. They'd have had you to themselves and would have gotten everything out of you. If they approach you, just say you're not comfortable talking to them."

"Ian, I don't know what Jeffrey is up to. Isn't it better to just talk to them so they know I'm not involved in whatever skeezy stuff Jeffrey is doing?"

"No, you're not better off. Who knows what you'll tell them that can interfere with our trying to find out what he's doing or who Jason is? If we tell them anything, they'll shut us down. Maybe even arrest us for something, who the fuck knows? Don't speak to them. Seriously, they'll use me as leverage. They said as much. If they saw me leaving Jeffrey's place, that's breaking and entering. They acted like they didn't see me so they could follow me. They could arrest me on the spot for that alone."

"Oh God, I knew that was a bad idea, Ian. You have to be on the straight and narrow. Talk to them if they threaten you. We really don't know squat about Jeffrey and whatever he is involved in."

"We know he sent Ronnie back in time. That's pretty big, wouldn't you say?"

"Oh, *no*." Steph's cheeks were hot, and she felt nauseous. "Ian, I have a bad feeling about this. Why does everything connected to Jeffrey turn to hell?"

"It's Jeffrey, luv. He's the kind of trouble Ronnie should never have gotten herself into."

Chapter 56

Colt Open Top

Mike slowly grew aware of a gentle rocking that crept into the blackness. It was simultaneously comforting and immensely painful, depending upon what portion of the motion he was in. Before Mike could open his eyes, he struggled with the images of bison stampeding on all sides of him. It must have been a super realistic dream. An uneasy feeling bled into his consciousness that perhaps it wasn't a dream. Unfamiliar voices bounced around in his mind until his eyes opened. Two men were helping him to a grassy bank.

The next moment he was sitting in a pond surrounded by sweaty men and horses. Both man and beast looked like they'd been ridden hard and put up wet. One of the men, with brown hair and an unkempt mustache, angrily reprimanded him, but it was hard to take in his words, for he had no context of who the hell he was or why he would be yelling at him. Why was he wearing old-fashioned clothes?

Not far away, he spotted a woman hiding in the bushes. His befuddled mind couldn't piece together much more than a few words. When he called out to her, the woman stood and straightened her skirts, then approached them wearing a filthy beige dress and looked about as dazed as he felt. She was young, in her early twenties perhaps, and was pretty with blue eyes and light hair. As she approached, a trickle of dried blood was visible on her forehead.

The sandy-haired man called out to her. "Rose, oh my Lord, what a sight to see. Are you okay?"

A ping of recognition needled his conscience. He'd seen her somewhere before, just before he'd been knocked out. Recalling where was something his battered skull was not capable of in this state. It was hard for his scrambled mind to keep up with what was going on, but apparently, there were Natives approaching and they needed to leave. Leave where?

Mike followed the men up a hill and forced his legs to respond, feeling like Frankenstein becoming accustomed to his new limbs. The men disappeared into a tiny dugout, and in a flurry of activity, they packed anything useful. Their apprehension was worn on their faces like a favorite shirt, as if it had been a regular part of their days for some time now. Mike did his best to mimic this aspect and not let the confusion get the better of him.

The woman eyed him and said something, but Mike was too muddled to make much of a response. His head throbbed, and he gripped it. Noticing a half wall just outside the dugout, he sat on it and observed his new surroundings, trying to make sense of it. Small details cried out to him, like the marvelous display of weaponry. Strapped to the horse closest to him was an antique Winchester lever-action and a sawed-off shotgun.

The horses shuffled as the men packed what they could into saddlebags, each animal strapped with a shotgun within easy reach while riding. One man walked past him, and Mike's gaze fastened on the Colt 45 revolver holstered around the man's waist. His vest bulged at the small of his back, giving away a smaller weapon. As the man turned to mount the horse, another holstered Colt was evident on his left side. These men were ready for a fight. A bead of sweat trickled down Mike's temple. These were dangerous men, and he wasn't naïve enough to think that their wrath wouldn't be directed at him, eventually.

Like a very large, woozy kid in a toy store, he let his eyes follow the next man to walk in front of him, holstering what he surmised was a Smith and Wesson Model 3, given the distinct grip. It was dusty but in excellent condition. The other men were similarly outfitted.

Despite the lack of brain cells firing, Mike felt like a little boy at Christmas and patted his hips, half expecting to find the toy guns he'd carried around during his cowboy phase. To his surprise, he felt solid metal and unholstered the weapon, turning it over in his hand. It was a stunning seven-and-a-half-inch Colt Open Top, with six bullets in the chamber. It sparked a memory of shooting antique revolvers with his father. If he remembered correctly, this weapon was the predecessor of the infamous Colt Single Action. Stamped on the frame just below the trigger was the coveted Colt pattern, showing it was an early serial number.

A thrill coursed through his body. In the Marines, Mike had shot a lot of weapons in training but, fortunately, had never seen combat. When he held that big Colt, memories flooded back of his toy revolver and countless imagined gunfights with childhood friends and imagined desperados.

There had to be more ammo somewhere. First chance he'd have to look in the saddlebag. Mike shoved the Open Top back in the holster and wondered what other magnificent antiques were in the group. He felt along his back. Like the other men, he had three handguns. Mike resisted the urge to pull it out and examine it. That would have to wait. He didn't want to draw attention to himself.

As his mind cleared, Mike was able to focus briefly on his own condition. He was fairly certain that he'd suffered a concussion and obviously had lost consciousness. This still didn't explain why he was now surrounded by these rough-looking men. How did he get a concussion? And would that make him hallucinate?

One of the men waved his hand in front of Mike's face. "Max, for heaven's sake, are you comin' with us or fixin' to get pierced with an arrow?" The man stood holding the reins of a tall black stallion that shot him an impatient look with one huge equine eye.

Mike grunted and took a few steps closer. Then he glanced around the group.

Another man turned his horse to face them. "Clayton, leave him if he can't get his mind straight. He'll only slow us down." Did he know this guy? His face looked familiar. It was the first man he'd seen during the stampede. Then the man spurred the horse and took off. A few others followed.

Mike forced his unwieldy limbs to slide his foot into the stirrup and climb aboard the beast, not wanting to be left behind.

"For Christ's sake," Clayton grumbled, "you forget how to ride a horse, Max?" He shook his head as he spurred his animal forward to catch up with the other men as they made their way through the long, dry grass. Mike's horse turned his head, annoyed with his incompetence, and snorted. He'd ridden before, but it had been a long damn time ago. Mike gripped the pommel as the beast galloped to catch up with their motley crew.

The group slowed to a steady pace, with Mike in the last position, giving him time to contemplate his situation. He forced his wandering mind to focus. An hour ago, he'd been in Puerto Rico with Ronnie in the middle of a hurricane. Now he was riding northwest with a wealthy reenactment crew. Somehow that didn't seem right. The fear in their eyes was real. Either way, he wasn't by Ronnie's side. Frustration clouded his already impaired mind.

It made no sense. You couldn't just *will* yourself somewhere else. And to that point, he'd not willed himself anywhere. The only place he wanted to be was next to Ronnie, fulfilling the promise he'd made to take care of her during the storm. Damn, Jeffrey had torn them apart by bringing up his past. From Ronnie's perspective, she had every right to be alarmed. If she'd only known the truth of what happened that night. If she'd listened instead of locking herself in the damn bathroom. Of course, he'd not done much to help her fear by losing his temper.

Mike imagined putting the full force he'd sent to the wall into Jeffrey's face. How he would love to beat the ever-living shit out of that pencil neck for making Ronnie lose faith in him. The irony of the violence-induced rage was not lost on him. If she would just give him a chance to explain everything. How could he? They were not even in the same part of the world. With one speedy Google search, he could show her the newspaper article that cleared his name. Of course, Jeffrey wouldn't share that with her.

Mike glanced at his right hand for evidence of punching the wall. He held it up, examining it in utter disbelief. These were not his hands. Panic tore through his body, making him suddenly feel out of breath. His clothes were not his either. What the hell was happening? He wore a long-sleeved shirt covered in a fine powder, nearly brown on the cuffs, but the rest was almost white, showing partially unsuccessful washings. The mahogany leather vest was open and stiff from its dip in the water. The dark pants he wore were wet and decidedly helpful in preventing overheating from the brilliant late-day sun. How had it taken him so long to notice any of this?

Mike's head spun, this time not from a blow, but from utter shock. How the hell was he here, in someone else's clothes, maybe even someone else's body? That was why his voice seemed odd. It wasn't his! A pounding in his skull drowned out any other sounds, and he saw spots in front of his eyes.

So many odd things coalesced into a panicked idea. Natives were not much of a problem in the twentieth century but had been an issue in the West from the 1500s till then. The pistol in his holster was a hundred fifty years old and it looked damn near perfect. It didn't look more than a year old, and with the rough living of these men, likely less than that.

He pulled out the weapon holstered at his back, holding it carefully, not wanting to lose it with the motion of the horse. The walnut grips were almost new, something unheard of with antique weapons that had seen any action. The nickel finish gleamed in the sunlight and his heart nearly stopped beating with excitement. He examined the revolver, smaller than the Colt, with a three-and-a-half-inch barrel.

He patted his pockets to see if there were any clues there. Nothing. Then Mike patted the vest and felt a circular object. Dipping in the breast pocket on the inside of the vest, he pulled out a small watch on a long chain attached to the top button of the vest. The casing was embossed with an intricate pattern that covered every inch of the shiny brass. He pushed a small lever on the side and the cover popped open, revealing a beautiful watch. The maker was the American Horologe Company, and the date was 1851. The watch was in perfect condition, confirming it was not one hundred fifty-three years old.

Was he dropped back in time? There was no other explanation unless everything was a reproduction, but that seemed highly unlikely. Somehow, someway, he was back in time. His mind wandered back to when he was four, when he wore his toy guns every day. He'd even had his first injury because of it. To a little kid, a bloody thumb was a big deal. He'd caught it on the way down a slide while playing cowboys and Indians. He glanced at the unfamiliar thumb, checking for the scar. It wasn't there.

The effort of staying on the horse made the challenge of sorting through all the information more difficult. It evoked memories of horseback riding on his great-aunt's farm in Schenectady. Mike had not ridden a horse in twenty years but had spent a month every summer on the farm and had become very proficient. He'd ridden through the woods every day and camped out overnight every chance he could with the local boys down the road. It was what had led him to want to be in the Marines, with grander adventures, yet still sleeping out with the boys from the unit.

Strange, he'd always imagined he was a cowboy on horseback, as they were right now, but these men were wearing bowler hats. He plucked the covering off his head and examined it, chuckling. It reminded him of the Lucky Charms guy, although it was black, more of a derby. He clapped it back on his head, pushing it down to keep it on. There was a certain beauty about the curved brim though, allowing the wind to move around while not lifting it. A traditional Stetson would have blown three miles down the path by now. The wind in the open prairie had nothing to block it. It blew at a steady clip, which made him feel like he was on a motorcycle, albeit a sweaty, rocking one.

As they rode, he studied the dynamics among the men and guessed the one they called Ben was the leader. A close second was Jere Miah. Something about how they carried themselves, how they interacted, gave him the impression that they were now, or had been, in the military. Not the modern military that he'd been a part of, obviously. For time period, his best guess was post-Civil War, given the pistols and gear. Landscape was likely Texas or Oklahoma, maybe even eastern New Mexico, but no farther west given the dry flatness of the land.

In Mike's deep thinking, he let the horse set the pace, and he approached Rose and Clayton. Rose smiled and shyly looked away, her blue eyes flashing a reflection of the sky. Rose's cheeks were pink despite the beige dress trying to drown out her fair coloring. A shadow of a black eye was forming, and she had a cut on her forehead, right near the hairline. Something about her seemed familiar, and it hit him. Rose was the woman kidnapped by the Native when he'd first woken up here. The beige dress was the clincher. Distinctive in its outright boringness.

Clayton nodded politely. "You alright, Max?"

Max? Again with the name, but he went with it. If they needed him to be Max, then by God it would be so. "Don't quite feel like myself, but I'm alright," Mike said, not wanting to hear that weird voice again. "How'd you get her from those Natives?"

Rose looked at him in surprise and glanced back at Clayton, waiting for his response.

"Shot 'im dead as he was fixing to scalp her." Clayton shook his head. "Mighty close to being too late. The rest of the gang was on the other side of the stampede. So, I chased him down. He'd taken her a mile or two away. I found her on the ground. Looked like his horse had been caught in a 'dog hole, but it hadn't deterred him."

"Dog hole?" Mike asked.

"Prairie dogs, you know, always digging those burrows," Clayton said. "Horse got its leg caught. You sure you're alright, Max?"

Mike shook his head, eying the ground.

Clayton continued, and Rose's expression shifted to worry. "I supposed he thought she was dead and no good for ransom. Sure looked that way to me, too, but thankfully I got there just in the nick of time to murder the son of a bitch and save her hide."

The harrowing recounting haunted Mike. "Well, thank God you showed up in time. Rose, how do you feel?"

Rose's face drained of all color, making the skin around her mouth an almost translucent blue. "Really, I don't..." She stopped and looked deep into his eyes, linking their thoughts, or so it seemed.

Mike had an eerie feeling she'd had a similar experience, where she wasn't sure how she ended up here, but likely it was just the near-death situation. Must have been the shock of his own confusion making him feel that way. But the intensity of the feeling grew and something deep inside recognized her essence, and the depth of this recognition shocked him to the core. Strange enough he was here, but to have these feelings of utter certainty that he knew this woman... This was a foreign concept. He was logical. This sort of mumbo jumbo feelings crap didn't happen to him. He took people for who they were and that was that.

Rose looked away, breaking the spell, but the thought lingered, and he explored it further. Something about her was familiar, and not just because he'd seen her being taken by the Native.

Jere Miah circled back to check on them. "Everything okay back here?" His piercing blue eyes conveyed impatience.

"Just," quipped Clayton.

Rose spoke up. "Where are we going?"

Jere Miah shot her a look of annoyance. "Takin' you back. We'd not be in this scramble if'n you'd stayed with your man." He barked, "Speed it up, fellas, watering hole ain't far from here."

That ended the conversation, and Clayton nudged the horse so they rode in front of Max again. Rose turned her head to the horizon, and he followed her gaze. Were there Natives following them? One damn good thing about this flat land was the Natives wouldn't be able to sneak up. The line of sight was all the way to the horizon in every direction, save a minor hill or two. The complete lack of any vegetation outside of those bushy green shrubs, maybe mesquite, gave them plenty of warning. They could shoot no arrow or bullet with accuracy from that distance. The bushes were not large enough to hide in ambush.

Mike laughed at that thought. How could he be contemplating a Native attack from a hotel bathroom? It was preposterous. Could this be a dream? His thoughts tumbled around with no suitable answers, but he was grateful he was thinking more clearly now. Soon the watering hole appeared as a clump of greenery and a mixture of grasses and shrubs. A welcome reprieve from the faded green-brown he'd feasted his eyes on since he'd arrived.

Mike's Spidey-Senses were tingling. Something felt wrong. Ben and Jere Miah must have felt it too because they responded precisely as he would have expected trained Marines to react, adding to his suspicion about their background.

Doves spooked by something in the thicket shot out of the trees, making everyone's nerves stand on end. What was lurking by the watering hole?

Chapter 57

Watering Hole

Every nerve in Mike's body was on alert.

"Gary!" Ben called out from where he sat on horseback. Mike watched as the older man came forward. "Rat out whatever is lurking in the watering hole."

Gary dismounted and drew his big Smith and Wesson. Mike heard shuffling, and all the men dismounted, some standing slightly behind their horses. Mike grabbed the rifle and checked the chamber.

Gary must have been point man, and likely lowest man on the food chain, given the charge. It was suicide going into cover like that if someone wanted to do you harm. Gary crouched low and made his way down the slight embankment, disappearing behind tall grasses with another identical pistol drawn, seemingly unperturbed by the danger. A bevy of small game fowl flew up in response to his entry into their peaceful ensconcement.

Rose sat high on the horse, peering to see what Gary was doing. Clayton helped her down, pushing her behind him for cover. Mike dismounted, as did the other men, not wanting to be easy pickings for arrow or bullet, and waited eagerly for shots fired, or the all clear called. He pulled the rifle off the horse and checked the chamber.

A terrible moaning echoed through the air. Clayton's expression shifted from intensity to fear, and he grabbed Rose's arm and pulled her to the back of the group, her eyes huge.

A split second later, an enormous shape burst through the grasses and up the hill. A bison, wounded and bleeding, covered in flies, ran past them. It stopped twenty-five feet away, panting, obviously struggling to stand. Every ounce of its body showed sheer anger, tempered with exhaustion, but it gave one last glorious stand as it pawed the ground.

Jere Miah cocked his rifle and aimed squarely at the great beast's head as it snorted and charged the group. A blast disrupted the quiet skies, and Rose let out a scream. The bison slowed, jerking its enormous head upwards but continued, unperturbed. Mike blasted the beast again, hitting directly between the eyes, filling the air with smoke, acrid in his nostrils.

The animal dropped mid-step, making the ground tremble with the weight. A cloud of flies rose and returned to their quarry.

Ben called out, "Gary, where are you?"

Mike was impressed with Jere Miah's quick handling of the situation. Again, it reminded him of his military brethren, trained to react aggressively and not wait for instructions in battle. He had not faltered, charging directly at him, showing nerves of steel. Jere Miah shot him a look of respect, and Mike returned it.

Gary stepped through the path the bison had taken and waved. "All clear, just that old buffalo injured and dying. Y'all get him?"

Ben nodded, clapping his hat on his thigh. "By God, you scared us! That monster nearly ran us over. Thanks to this good ole boy, here." He clapped Jere Miah on the back, who glanced back at Mike.

Gary approached the bison and pulled out a knife, slitting the animal's throat, allowing it to bleed out into the dry grasses. "Dinner will be a feast tonight!" Gary started the butchering process. "Ben, we got time for me to get the hide on this ole bull? It's worth a fair sum. Or you want vittles? Not sure we have time for both."

Mike wondered if the meat would go bad, but salting would help quash the microbial growth. Still, the heat of the day made him wish for modern conveniences.

Ben eyed the animal and the sun in the sky. "Old bull hide will be impossible. Just make a quick job of it." He led his horse towards the water and called back, "Just get the tongue, tenderloin, and whatever else suits you quickly, until we're ready to go."

Flies frenetically buzzed around the animal's eyes. Rose stared, mouth agape.

Clayton took her arm and moved her to the path. "Let's get some water, Rose. I don't think you want to watch the butchering."

"You got that right." Rose showed the revulsion of someone unaccustomed to the slaughtering of animals. Surely in her daily life she'd seen buffalo shot and skinned before. It would have been impossible not to have witnessed at least cows slaughtered on the ranch.

Mike walked behind Rose through the brush and found a sandy bank. The horses had their muzzles buried, taking long, deep drafts of the fresh spring water. Jere Miah was standing in the spring rinsing out his shirt. Two large scars on his chest marred the otherwise fit body. Bullet wounds from the Civil War? How could he be looking at a living, breathing man who had fought in that war?

Jere Miah splashed water on his face and turned to see who was walking towards them. Ben was rinsing off a small laceration just above his horse's rear hoof. Ben and Jere Miah seemed to have their own language, not so much in words, but in kinship with the identical set of their shoulders, the cock of their head at a question not understood. They were mirror images of each other. Could they be brothers?

Rose lingered nearby, looking shell-shocked.

"Rose." Mike stepped closer to her. "Get yourself cleaned up. Drink if the others do."

She smiled. "Okay." Rose splashed water on her face, scrubbing her cheeks and hands.

Mike led his horse to the water and left him, then meandered to the springhead and drank the clear water unmuddied by the horses and men. Then dunked his head under and basked in the glory of the cool water dripping down his back. After a few minutes, he returned to the animal, who was munching the greenery around the watering hole.

Mike rummaged through his saddlebags and found cartridges not packaged in cardboard boxes like he was used to, but in paper packets with no labels. They looked brand new, but they didn't look like modern ammo.

Mike left his mount, letting it get its fill of the lush, green grass, and sought out Gary's company. He pulled the knife out of the sheath at his waist and knelt near Gary. "What can I do?"

"Max, mighty kind of you. Go on and get the tongue for us. That'll make an easy supper." Gary already had one shoulder removed, packed in salt and wrapped in leather that must have been brought for that purpose. "I'll get the tenderloins. Much else and we'll get scalped by the next band that heads this way."

Mike pulled the animal's tongue and reached in its mouth, slicing as far back as he could. Flies swarmed inside the mouth, revving for the fresh blood as Mike set it down on top of the shoulder. Gary took it and packed it for travel.

"So, was Rose kidnapped by Indians?" Mike knew he was supposed to know what happened to her, but Gary seemed a friendly sort.

Gary didn't glance up from his work at first, giving away that maybe he wasn't so keen on talking about it with the intonation of his voice. "Well, she's run away from her husband, as Jere Miah tells it. If you'd ask ole Jeb, he'd tell you different on account of pride and all. But from what I know, Jeb's beat the tar out of her one time too many and she up and run off." Gary looked at him directly, leaning back on one foot, then nodded at Clayton, who'd come over to help. "I cain't cotton to hitting a woman. I just don't understand why words won't do a better job. Once you raise a hand," he glanced around to be sure no one was behind him listening, "you lose all control. If she has any spunk, you either have to break her spirit to keep her in tow or keep beating her till you do. So much better to just use reason and logic. For that matter, kindness goes a longer way than any of that shinola, if you're really wanting my advice." He winked, probably because he knew Mike hadn't asked for it.

Clayton chimed in. "It's more than that, Gary. Jeb hurt her so bad the last time he got sauced, Rose had a miscarriage and nearly bled to death. When she finally recovered and got up the courage, she grabbed her horse and rode away, hoping to make it to town, but she got turned around in a storm and..." He wiped his forehead with the back of his sleeve. "Next I know I was chasing down an Indian to get her back."

"Now, you just making up stories, Clayton, or did you hear that from her?" Gary smiled good-naturedly.

"Mrs. Swanson saw her riding off, and a short time later a wicked storm hit. Just put the two together, s'all," Clayton said as he took the tenderloin from Gary.

Gary nodded. "Just bad luck."

"What would the Indians have done to her if you hadn't saved her, Clayton?" Mike asked.

"Not sure. Sometimes they ransom 'em. Oftentimes, they just torture or gang rape 'em, sometimes give them to their wives as slaves. The squaws are more brutal than their husbands. You know about Matilda Lockhart?"

Mike shook his head.

"She was captured in the 40s, and when they got her back," Clayton sniffed, "wasn't a place on her body bigger 'n my hand without a burn mark."

Mike shook his head. "Brutal."

Gary continued, "She's the gal they burned the soles of her feet so she wouldn't escape, right?"

Clayton nodded. "Savages. They'll chop off your arms and legs and toss you on the fire to roast a bit. And since you can't run away, all you can do is call out for help and writhe like a damn worm." He read Mike's face showing disgust. "And that ain't no exaggeration, my friend. They actually do that to the white man, and their Native enemies."

"Rose wouldn't have purposefully gone out alone like that. Was she running to a relative for help?" Mike felt for her either way. No woman deserved such treatment.

"I don't know, but believe me, whatever the hell he did to her, it ain't so bad when your alternative is being burned alive as you bleed from four stumps. Not much worse than that, in my opinion." Gary shook his head and plopped another hunk of meat on the leather, flies covering it instantly until he waved them off with the motion of salting, then wrapped it up with the shoulder.

Clayton shook his head and stood, carrying the leather-wrapped meat. "All this talk about injuns, I think we better keep on moving. I don't want to meet any more than we've already done."

Mike held the meat in place on the back of the horse just behind the saddle as Gary fastened it in place, thinking over Rose's predicament. These were terrible choices for any woman who was being abused.

Clayton stood and looked Mike square in the eyes. "Max, I just want to be done with this whole goat rope."

Gary wiped his knife off on a rag and handed it to Mike, who did the same. "I hear ya, Clayton, this has not gone like Jere Miah sold it to us. Just want to be back done with this whole mess."

Mike handed the cloth to Clayton, who tidied his hands and weapon and re-sheathed it, handing the rag back to Gary.

Jere Miah rode close and looked down from his steed, the sun bright behind him. Mike had a flash of why he was so familiar and stepped back in shock. Could it really be the face from the poster from his childhood?

Chapter 58

Jesse James

Ronnie soaked in every word and intently watched Mike's facial expressions and gestures, nearly seeing his story as a movie playing out in her imagination. When he paused, she handed him a cracker, and he shoved it in his mouth. Then he took a sip of water, crumpling the bottle and tossing it in the open trash bag, looking satisfied with the shot. "If you were there, you know the rest."

"I don't know how you returned."

Mike cracked open another water and took a huge drink, then marked its consumption on the list he was keeping of what they'd taken from the convenience store for the owner's reimbursement. "We hear all the romanticized stories of the Wild West. I spent my childhood playing cowboys and Indians from the 1950s Hollywood version of events. Now that we all know more about the Natives' plight, we see them as the victims of westward expansion. There is a middle ground that I'm just beginning to understand from all of this." He met her gaze, then continued. "The Natives are to be respected, not as victims needing our pity, but as their toughness of character to withstand the pressure of our culture and desire to exterminate them. They were incredibly strong."

Ronnie had felt the same way. "Being there, seeing them firsthand, makes this much clearer. They truly were the toughest adversary imaginable. The brutality they showed whites was the same brutality they showed other tribes. They fought to the death. They fought tooth and nail to keep their way of life, to keep the land and traditions they'd always known. It was hardly the Hollywood version of the evil Natives and the cowboys in white hats, or the later version where Natives were to be pitied for what we did to them. They deserve much more respect than either has portrayed them."

Mike studied her then nodded, seeming to agree with every word. "Seeing them in action was a life-changing experience. I didn't like what they were doing to Rose. I mean *you*. Oh God, this is confusing, isn't it?" He ran his hands through his hair.

"It is." Ronnie smiled, thrilled to finally have someone to talk to about the strange experience.

Mike continued, "But they were so athletic, so lithe. I wish we'd been able to see more of them in their natural element. I mean, I didn't want the murderous rage part. But just to see them before their culture was destroyed and their spirit broken. It is so sad to think about how post-Civil War America ended so many magnificent cultures."

"Yeah, living it, seeing actual people who lived and died with the struggle…" She shook her head, thinking of Kwa-na and his party of Natives stealing the horses.

"What they described could have happened to Rose…" he looked at her as if realizing again that she was Rose, "that you would have had to endure if Clayton hadn't chased after you…" His face fell, as if that horrible realization had just hit home. "Ronnie, this time traveling is a wonderful thing on the surface, because we can relive the past. We can experience something that no one on Earth has ever experienced. But the cost." Mike turned away, hiding his emotions. He took a sip of his water. A stalling technique she'd used herself as you pulled yourself together enough to speak. "The cost is too great. What if you…?" He let the emotion show, not trying to control it. "If they had taken you, you would have had to endure that torture. Gang rape? Amputation? Burning?"

Ronnie joined in his tears. "It is horrible, you're right. The cost is too high. Despite the incredible opportunity to live how our ancestors lived for a brief time, the time traveling always ends in a horrible death."

Mike pulled her close and Ronnie let loose a few tears but didn't want to let out the torrent of emotions for fear she'd never stop crying. Mike's compassion was heart-wrenching. He hadn't worried about what could have happened to him but had been upset at *her* possible fate.

"Tell me, please." Mike pulled away and tenderly wiped away her tears. "What happened to you after I left?"

Ronnie spoke through the emotions, her mouth turning down. "Nothing so bad. Definitely not like you're describing. Jeb was rough on me when I left the house, but he'd not had time to really hurt me. He locked me in a woodshed and went back after you."

Mike pulled her close again and hugged her tight. "Thank God. I couldn't live with myself if I'd left you with Jeb, Jesse James, or worse, the Natives to murder you."

Ronnie pulled away. "*Jesse James?* You said that before. Why do you think we were with Jesse James?"

Mike explored her face, perhaps reading her expression. "You didn't know?"

"No." Ronnie's heart was racing a mile a minute.

"I guess you didn't figure it out. Jere Miah was Jesse James."

Ronnie's jaw dropped. He had looked a little familiar. "*The* Jesse James? The actual guy?"

"Oh my God, you didn't realize it. Ben was his brother, Frank. I'm certain of it." Mike shook his head, as if trying to shake that thought from his mind.

"How do you know for sure? I mean, I never picked up on it." Ronnie felt like crying again. This was too much.

"I was always fascinated with the James brothers. We still don't know a lot about them. Most of the stories told were just made up to sell newspapers and books." Mike leaned against the shelves.

Ronnie shook her head. "So, what made you first realize it was *him*?"

"He was familiar right off the bat, but I couldn't place it. There are some distinctive features they always mention about Jesse—lopsided ears, sloping shoulders, one nostril bigger —but none of those things are that noticeable." He took another sip of water. "He rode up on me after we butchered the buffalo with the sun behind him and it hit me. He looked so much like a poster I had of him as a kid. But when they told the story of blowing off his finger and Ben called him dingus, I was certain of it."

"I never heard that story about Jesse James." Ronnie stood and helped herself to a diet Coke from the cooler, bringing one for him as well. He waved it off but marked both on the list anyway. She sat back down and cracked it open, enjoying the bubbles and sweet taste. "I saw your reaction to that story. I just thought you were squeamish."

"I was up most of that night trying to disprove it to myself, but come morning, I knew what I had to do."

"What?" Ronnie's mind was on fire, trying to see what he'd seen. Jesse freaking James!

"Do you remember the snake incident the next day? How I stormed off and left you alone with them?" Mike shifted to leaning on his arms behind him, bunching up his broad shoulders and flexing his triceps.

"Yeah, I did think that was rather weird. Gary and I were talking about it later."

"What did Gary say?"

"How out of character it had been for Max...uh, you, to make enemies with such dangerous men." A memory broke free. "Mike, after you rode off and Jere Miah tried to shoot you, he accidently called Ben another name. He called him *Frank*!"

"He slipped up in a moment of stress. Ha, more proof! How could I make a move to get you out of there without being killed by either of them for trying? Once I realized who I was dealing with, my best option to prevent you from being handed over to Jeb was to separate from the group."

"Smart. It didn't make sense to me at the time, but it did work to a point, didn't it? What else made you think it was the James brothers?"

"First, think about the year. It was no earlier than 1871, right? My pistol was made in 1871. The fact Natives were a problem still that wasn't truly cleared up until early 1900s."

"Yeah, I guess you're right. I didn't notice the weapons bit."

"Jesse had several aliases he went by and one of them was Jere Miah. Frank went by Ben Woodson." He paused for another drink, then continued. "During this time, they were hiding out from Missouri law. The Macy they kept talking about..." Mike paused to make sure she was following along.

Ronnie nodded.

"Jesse and Frank had an Uncle Macy who lived in Texas. They spent some time hiding out there outside of Midland before the next robbery. I knew right off the bat they were ex-military men, given their demeanor and how they led the group. You know they were both in the Confederate Army, right?"

"Yeah, they said that. I didn't know that about Jesse and Frank, though. I'm still so blown away that you went back in time too, Mike. I don't think you understand what a big deal this is."

Mike ran his fingers through his hair and looked somber. "I had no idea you've been through this, and you've gone back several times, Ronnie. I mean, how the hell did you keep your shit together this last month with all of that going on?"

"I barely did, Mike. There is so much I need to tell you. You are the only person who fully understands what I've been through."

The bruising around Mike's right eye was intensifying. "Hardly could say I understand a damn thing about it, but what I do understand is the experience of being yanked to a place and time where you have to use your wits and strength just to make it through the day. Exhilarating, if you can set aside the absolute horror of losing everything important to you. Including your own body, and everyone you ever loved. We did go into someone else's body, right?"

"Yeah, isn't that the weirdest feeling? What do you think happened to Max and Rose when we bumped them out?"

His eyes widened. "Jeez, I never thought about that. Did they die and just leave, or were they transported back in time too? I don't think they came to our time and traded places with us."

"No, they definitely don't come to our time. Steph can confirm that. And you saw me in the hospital during Frances, and in the hotel. I was just lying there."

He shook his head, apparently trying to wrap his mind around it.

"Yeah, you are the only other person who gets what I've been through." Emotions made her face crumple, and she looked away, embarrassed, shifting her position on the hard floor.

"Hang on." Mike stood and grabbed two more fluffy towels, both the bright yellow he'd given Frank. "Stand up. We'll get you more cushion there."

Ronnie stood and watched as he layered the towels over the one she'd been sitting on.

"Thank you." Ronnie stepped towards him and stood face-to-face, feeling the sexual energy coming off him, despite the serious conversation. Mike's hair was curlier and more unruly than usual and his eyes darker in the low light. He motioned for her to sit back down, and she did, this time lying on her side. There was so much more she needed to tell him.

"Was there anything else they revealed about their past after I left?" Mike asked, sitting closer to her now, more intimately, but not in an aggressive way.

"After you left, we were in the restaurant in Sterling City and Gary mentioned a few things." Ronnie could almost hear Gary's Tennessee twang. "He was puzzled why you'd made such an enemy out of the pair of them because they were likely to shoot you on sight."

"I knew that risk as soon as I lifted a hand to Jere Miah. I had to get away from them so I could use my only weapon against them, the element of surprise."

Ronnie furrowed her brows, understanding the full extent of the strategic nature of his exit. "I do remember Gary saying that Jere Miah joined the war effort when he was fifteen years old and that he'd seen the atrocities of war. Oh, and something about the reason he joined." Ronnie tapped her hip, trying to remember what he'd said. "Yes, that the Union soldiers had tried to torture his stepfather and that had spurred him to join up."

Mike's face lit up. "He did? Well, that's even more information than I had. Have you ever heard of William Clarke Quantrill?"

"Maybe, but I have no idea why." Ronnie laid her hand on his, and he looked at her in surprise, then smiled.

"Frank James was in the Missouri State Guard when the Civil War started, and he fought in the first battle of Lexington with Sterling Price and Jackson. They had to retreat because they couldn't hold their position. Frank got sick, eventually surrendered, and decided to accept amnesty that required him to pledge to stop fighting against Union forces."

"Jeez, Mike, how do you know all of this stuff?"

"Civil War buff. I was a huge fan of Jesse James as a kid and spent many days pretending I was in the Wild West. Totally qualifies me as an expert now." He snorted. "Anyway, Frank joined up with Quantrill and his guerrillas and thus violated his parole. They think a lot of the men in that group were responsible for numerous robberies, and Jesse and Frank are lumped in there too." Mike paused and ate a cracker.

"Lumped in there too?" Ronnie asked, wanting to hear more.

"I mean Jesse and Frank were blamed for more robberies than they actually were involved in, but only *they* know for sure which ones. The Union found out about Frank's involvement and came to the James' farm in Missouri and questioned his family to find out where Frank was. Jesse was still living at home as a young teenager and witnessed the Union soldiers hang his stepfather, nearly killing him. Jesse joined up in the Civil War shortly thereafter to get back at the cruelty they showed his family."

Ronnie shook her head. "Wow, I didn't know any of this. We learned about the Civil War in school, but you forget how it affected the people who lived through it."

"It was a terrible time for Americans. They called it the Reconstruction for a good reason. Literally, the social fabric of America had to be stitched back together from 1863 to 1877. Rose and Max got a glimpse of the horrors of post-Civil War, and the James Gang were caught up in the middle of that tumultuous time."

Ronnie squeezed his hand and imagined what life would have been like as he talked.

Mike lifted her hand and laced his fingers in hers. "Hundreds of thousands of soldiers died or were survivors of horrific war injuries. At home, farms in the North and South were marauded by starving troops, some of whom raped or murdered mothers, wives, and daughters of men away at war. I have a lot of sympathy for Frank and Jesse. Since the North won the war, the former Union troops were discriminated against as the government took back the reins of control, picking up the pieces of our governance. It was hard for Union soldiers to find work, to be accepted back into society, especially in places like Missouri, where there was such a mixture of Northern and Southern sympathizers."

"Horrible times." Ronnie drew a pattern in his upturned palm, marveling at how much he knew about the time period they'd just visited.

"You know, it was hard to not just be a fanboy and enjoy the experience, but I was so worried about Rose. I knew that returning her to Jeb was out of the question."

Mike flashed a glance at her. "I mean you. Tell me, Ronnie..." Mike cocked his head.

Ronnie focused on how he said her name, with a little Midwest twang, and imagined him whispering it intimately under difference circumstances.

"When I woke up in the hotel room, you were still out cold. I gotta say, I was totally freaked out." A flash of fear crossed his battered features, his eyes growing wider and mouth slack. "Does that mean I died before you did?"

"Yes. You died. Max died." She grimaced, feeling the horror she'd felt discovering Max's bloody body in the wagon. "This is confusing. But I saw Max's body, so I guess you came back before I did."

Mike's eyes showed compassion and worry. "I'm almost afraid to ask, but how did you return?" Mike laced his fingers in her hand again.

"As I said, Jeb locked me in a smokehouse. When I finally broke out, a band of Natives had heard my struggles and were curious, I guess. They invited me to go with them, but I had to go back and see what happened to you. I have to admit, the thought of traveling with them was so intriguing. But I knew what they might do to me. Mike, I was covered in soot from the ashes. The smokehouse was full of spider webs and I spazzed out a little..." Ronnie felt her cheeks heat up and a smile registered on his face. "Dawn had just broken, and in the low light I guess they thought I was a mistreated slave. I couldn't go with them. I needed to see if you were alive, and if you weren't, I wanted to leave with them. I figured if it got bad, I could just kill myself like I have before."

"What a choice to make." Mike's eyes widened.

"Yeah, I was almost burned to death. I chose to bleed out. Remember the watch? That's why it was covered in blood."

Mike squeezed her hand. "Jesus, Ronnie. We have to find a way to make this stop. You've been through too much."

"Agreed. Mike, tell me what happened after Jeb took me away."

Mike looked down at the floor and let out a long, slow breath. "Yeah, that was bad. You're not going to like it. Are you hungry?"

"A little." Ronnie was trying to ignore the rumbling in her stomach. Mike handed her a box of Pop-Tarts, then marked it on the growing list. They shared the first packet as he continued.

Chapter 59

Silver Dollar

Mike controlled the nausea. Was the head trauma causing this, or was it the prospect of Ronnie enduring the brutality of the Natives?

Ronnie shook her head. "Even if it is just a junky old convenience store, at least we're not going to be captured by Natives and hacked into pieces." She leaned forward and touched his arm. "Mike, before you tell me what happened at the ranch, what happened after the incident with Jere Miah? I mean Jesse. This is confusing. I still can't quite put the two together."

"The whole thing is baffling. I'm still trying to wrap my mind around it." Mike grinned and regretted it.

"Tell me the rest," Ronnie insisted.

"After you fell asleep, when we were out on the plains, I pleaded that they let you respectably be presented to Uncle Macy by allowing you to bathe and get new clothes. I reasoned that it would help Macy more likely pity you, while giving me time to break you free."

"That was smart. Tell me everything, Mike. What happened after you left us after the snake incident?"

∞

Mike focused on his hand pain that throbbed with each movement of the horse, steaming mad at Jere Miah and his thugs. How could they all just go along with returning Rose to her abusive husband? The fear in her eyes haunted him.

He pondered the possibilities of breaking her free and taking her someplace safe. Last night Jere Miah made it clear that Uncle Macy didn't take kindly to outsiders butting in where they were not welcomed. Ben agreed, but at least he'd been able to give them something to chew on. One of them may do the right thing. If Mike had his way, though, she'd never reach Macy's. If they'd allow her to bathe and change her clothes, it would buy him time to swoop in and help her escape. Dusk was an hour out, and this increased their chances of staying in town overnight, giving him a wider window to get her out of there.

Stamped on the horizon was the outline of Western-style buildings, with large facades in the front making the buildings seem larger than they were. It would be easy to see them approaching. Beyond that, Mike had no real plan. Where would he take her? This was their territory, not his.

It was too new for him not to marvel at the old Western town, still in its glory days. Rough men sauntered down the dirt-packed street, sidearms strapped to their hips. Women, demure and shy, walked briskly to their destinations. In his mind, they all feared a shootout. More likely they just wanted to get out of the dirty, dusty street before their dresses were the same reddish brown as their environment.

Mike dismounted and tied up the horse at a nearby saloon. Deep down in the belly of the saddlebags, he discovered a sack of coins and shoved it in his pocket. Smoke wafted out of the saloon's swinging doors, as if crooking a finger to draw him in. The saloon was full of rough-looking men smoking and playing cards. The other evident scent made it abundantly clear deodorant had not yet been invented. Mike approached the bar, ready to ask questions. The bartender beat him to it.

"What can I get for you, sir?" His voice was gruff, and while his shirt was clean, his unkempt mustache completely concealed his mouth.

"Got anything medicinal for this?" Mike hoisted his hand onto the bar. It was beginning to feel like a lead weight attached to his wrist.

The barkeep eyed it and shook his head. "Mighty fine busted up hand you got there. I'd mosey over to Shelly's on the outskirts." He turned and grabbed a bottle of whiskey with one hand as his other slammed a glass on the bar. "This'll sharpen your senses and dull the pain."

"Shelly's?"

The bartender looked up, surprised. "Blacksmith. Shelly can set anything broke, from bones to wagon wheels."

Mike exhaled. "Blacksmith, of course." His stomach turned. A man who heated metal and banged the absolute hell out of it was supposed to delicately repair a broken hand. Hardly seemed reasonable.

"Last building near the stables, just down the road a piece. Can't miss it." The barkeep nodded and walked away to help another patron.

Mike downed the liquor, enjoying the burn in his throat. He needed to keep a balance between being sober enough to rescue Rose, but not so sober that he'd have to feel every damn pulse of pain. When the barkeep was free again, he raised a finger to get his attention.

"I'm eager to get to Shelly's. Anything I can eat pretty quickly?"

"Vittles here are hot and fast, just like our women." The barkeep tossed his head back and laughed, giving Mike a view of what the mustache was attempting to hide. Rotten, brown teeth. Functional fashion. As if his conscious mind had finally assigned a source to the newest foul odor, the sour hot breath wafted towards him. Mike turned away out of self-defense. Liquor was supposed to kill germs, but plainly not those born in your mouth.

Mike forced a laugh. "Hot and fast, it is. I'll be over there in the corner." Mike nodded at an empty table, far away from the colorful ladies, that still offered a view of Rose's approach. His associates would be turning up in the next hour. Mike eyed the women, questioning the hot part of the statement, deciding it meant sweaty instead of good-looking.

"Two bits." The barkeep tapped the bar.

A bit was twelve and a half cents, if his memories of the cowboy stories were right. What the hell did a bit look like? Mike reached in his pocket as the man waited, probably expecting him to not have the money. He drew out the small leather sack and opened the drawstring. He had no idea what to give the man. Mike emptied a few coins on the counter. "Eyes aren't what they used to be."

The barkeep shook his head. "You're too young for that." He grabbed a few coins. "Another shot?"

What Mike really wanted was water. "Mighty parched. What's good for a dry throat other than whiskey?"

"Beer is headache ale here, on account it goes bad pretty quick." He nodded at the tap. "This here's been around for a while. I'd recommend tea. We had lemonade, but it didn't last long."

"Iced tea is great. No liquor in it, right?"

The barkeep cocked his head. "Well, no, but I can add some if you like?"

"No, I just prefer to be hydrated..."

The barkeep squinted and leaned on the counter. "Mighty queer syntax, if you don't mind me saying so."

Mike abandoned trying to get any point across. "Just plain ole iced tea is perfect. How much?"

The man pursed his lips. "It's included in your meal."

Mike felt stupid, but it couldn't be helped. He didn't need any more liquor, and without liquids in his system, things would go downhill fast. "Thank you." Mike shoved the remainder of the coins back in the bag, hoping he'd not been ripped off. His canteen, still on his horse, was full of spring water, and he wanted to keep it that way, hoping to escape this little town as soon as he nabbed Rose.

Mike sat near the window, soaking in every detail of the place. The women at the bar were colorful, flirty, and flamboyantly vying for the attention of any man in the place. He watched a fight break out. The bartender and another man quickly removed the offending patrons, then straightened up the mess.

A teenager delivered a plate of beans, cornbread, and cooked tomatoes. Before he ran off, Mike decided to get what he could from the lad.

"Say, I'm new around here. How far is the next town?"

The boy smiled and seemed to relax a bit. "Oh, sir, it's just a few miles north. It's not much of a town. But you can find plenty of kindly folks to put you up if'n you're going farther north."

"I am. Thank you. I have some friends meeting me here soon, but we didn't know the lay of the land. Is this the only place to get food or...?" Mike shrugged his shoulders.

The boy peered around. "We're the biggest place, uh huh."

"But...?" Mike sensed he wanted to say more.

"Yeah, biggest. I didn't say we were the best. If I were searching for vittles, I'd eat over at the Silver Star." He looked at the bartender and suddenly added, "But don't rat me out, sir. I'ze not supposed to be giving that type of candor, being that I'm employed at this establishment."

"I appreciate that, son. Which side of town is it on?"

"Just a few doors down, sir." The boy pointed to the right.

"Son, tell me something else. If you'd be staying overnight, what kind of place is available here in Sterling City? Other than where the colorful ladies like to, uh…" Mike smiled. "Lay down."

The boy's face reddened, and he glanced at the women giggling and fawning over a man in an expensive-looking suit. "Not here. Nope. My auntie puts people up for the night if you're looking in the back rooms of the Silver Star. They've got a pretty nice setup for overnight guests."

"Well, that sounds perfect."

"Don't get me wrong, frequently these, uh…" he coughed, "ladies, as you call 'em, are over there too. But not quite as many and sometimes they shoo them off during family-type hours. If you know what I mean." His voice broke on the last word, and his face turned beet red.

Mike reached in his pocket and pulled out a coin and handed it to the boy. "Mighty grateful for your advice."

The boy gawked at the coin in his hand. Mike got a glimpse of it, and it looked like a silver dollar. The boy's face reddened further, which didn't seem possible. "Sir, this is too much. It's gonna…"

"No, no, son. I can see you're making ends meet. Go on now, before they question your work ethic." Mike smiled and wondered what kind of tip he'd just given the boy, but at least it hadn't gone to waste.

Mike scarfed down the food, asked for a refill on the iced tea, and stepped out into the evening skies, hoping to see Jesse and company riding into town soon. He was not disappointed. After about fifteen minutes, a cloud of dirt kicked up in the sunset by their approach, adding to the dramatic effect of the perfectly clear skies and deepening colors as night made a fast approach. The silhouettes riding hard into town would have made a great postcard, with reds and oranges lighting up the sky. *Welcome to Sterling City.*

Down the street towards the back of town he found a stable open to the public. Mike left his horse with the old cowboy, asking him to water and feed the animal with instructions to leave the saddle on.

Walking back to the edge of town, he made sure his quarry was still approaching. They were close enough they could spot him if they were looking. Mike stepped between two buildings where he could keep an eye on their approach but wouldn't be seen in the low light of dusk. It was past sundown, but the wide-open horizon reflected just enough light bending over the edge of the earth he could still see them.

As the boy had predicted, they stepped into the Silver Star and spread out, each sitting at different tables. He could plainly see Rose talking to Gary through a side window. Mike would have to wait for the opportunity to retrieve her without rousing the firepower of the James brothers. No use getting himself killed.

His meal sat heavy in his gut and Mike longed for a cup of coffee and some serious pain killers. The wind picked up, cooled by the setting sun, and whipped a steady stream of dirt in his face. Mike shifted positions, letting a building break the assault. When he glanced back again, Rose was no longer in her seat. Mike switched to another window and caught the ire of a man trying to eat his meal in peace. Mike waved and moved along, but not before he caught a glance of Rose walking down a hallway inside the house. Were they getting private rooms already? That was quick.

He followed Rose's progress towards the back of the Silver Star, trying to catch sight of her. To his utter shock, Rose tumbled out of a window, untangled herself from a tumbleweed, and took off between two buildings. A man called out to her and gave chase. Damn it.

Chapter 60

Innocent Casualties

"Well, you experienced the rest." Mike shook his head, still not accepting his own words. How could any of this be true? It defied the logic he'd always relied on to study the world. Now, his grasp on what was real and what wasn't blurred, making him feel discombobulated and skittish. Or was that his concussion muddling the mind again?

A flare of lightning briefly lit up the room. Ronnie squinted and glanced towards the window. A crack of thunder made them both flinch, followed by a prolonged onslaught of wind battering the front of the store.

"I don't know the rest. Tell me what happened at the ranch house with Jere Miah and Ben," Ronnie asked.

Mike took a deep breath and let it out in a whoosh. "Nothing I want to recall."

Ronnie pressed her lips together in a look of determination. "Tell me please, Mike."

"Yeah, that was a bad deal." His mind didn't want to relive the pain of what he'd done. But she deserved to know.

A delicate crease between her brows enhanced the mournful expression in her eyes.

"When Jeb took you away, you warned me they were coming up the stairs. Thank you for that, by the way." Mike glanced down at his hands.

"A lot of good it did." Ronnie forced a hard sigh, and he felt the air on his face.

"No, I appreciated it." Mike hesitated, drawing the tangled thoughts together. "So, this part I'm still trying to piece together. I tried to get downstairs before Jeb rode off with you. I didn't want him to lay a hand on you. I just figured he took you back to his place. You know, he never returned to the ranch house, Ronnie."

"Really? I wonder where he went. He was coming after you when he locked me in the smokehouse." Ronnie hugged her knees. "Have you ever heard of a man called Kwa-na?"

"Quanah Parker?" Mike's inflection was smoother than Ronnie's.

Ronnie stared, wide-eyed. "You have? Who was he?"

Mike leaned towards her, nodding. "Sure, Quanah Parker is legendary. He was the last Comanche chief. Why?"

Ronnie buried her chin in her folded arms and stared, her eyes dark and intense. "Mike, Quanah was at the ranch."

"Holy shit. Jesse James and friggin' Quanah Parker? I had no idea!"

She shook her head. "Why haven't I heard about Quanah before? Who was he?"

Mike smiled and felt a surge of adrenalin. "Probably just forgot. Did you ever hear about Cynthia Ann Parker?"

Ronnie shook her head.

"She was Quanah's mother. Cynthia Ann was captured by the Comanches in a raid on her family ranch when she was eight. She grew up to marry a respected war chief named Peta Nocona and lived with the Comanches for twenty-five years. The army..." Mike made finger quotes, "'saved' her during a surprise attack that massacred Peta and most of their tribe."

"That's awful. Why was he famous? There must have been hundreds of Natives that had similar fates." Ronnie unwrapped another Pop-Tart and passed it to Mike.

He took it and held it between thick fingers while he talked. "Quanah and his brother fled the bloodbath and rode on horseback to another tribe. Quanah became a warrior and raided homesteads and murdered settlers as they expanded into their territory. Years afterward, when the army rounded the Natives up to place on the reservations, Quanah helped the army peaceably bring in more tribes, saving thousands from slaughter."

"Wow, I had no idea. Mike, he was so gentle with me. It's hard to see him as a violent marauder."

"Ronnie!" Mike took her hand. "Seriously, you've experienced something no one, as far as we know, ever has! You met the James brothers and Quanah Parker on the same day. And to think we were born a hundred years from when they shared the same air."

Ronnie smiled and squeezed his hand. "This is unbelievable. I still can't believe you were there too." Ronnie's grin evaporated. "Mike, what happened to Maggie?"

Mike's elation vanished. "I was going to come after you." As he spoke, memories flooded back, clearly as if they'd just happened. "Ronnie, I think I know what happened to Jeb."

**

Mike peered out of the upstairs window. The sun was rising, presenting just enough light to see movement in the shrubbery. A man on horseback rode towards the house. Mike intently watched, hoping it was Gary or Clayton coming to diffuse the situation. Suddenly the horse stopped short, as if tripped by something, throwing the rider and horse to the ground in a loud jumble of equine and human limbs. The animal quickly scrambled to its feet. From the shadows, a man bolted out and seized the reins. A Native! He could clearly see the contour of his long hair sprawled over his bare chest in the sparse light of dawn. *Indian attack!*

An abrupt movement kicked up a cloud of dirt, and when it settled, the rider's head was yanked up and his throat slit, darkening the ground below him. Mike strained to see who it was. The dead man was too young to be the grizzled, gray Lawrence. The dogs noticed the movement and rushed to the scene, sniffing the downed man, ears flattened against their skulls, their cries sounding more alarmed as they gave chase.

A creak on the stairs alerted Mike to movement nearby, drawing him from the window. He sprinted to the hallway, aiming Lawrence's 12-gauge muzzle loading coach gun at the shadowy staircase, watching for movement. His crippled hand screamed out in protest. He ignored it. In the darkness, the distinct sound of a pistol cocking preceded the appearance of Jesse's dirty face. Mike squeezed the right trigger, blasting the darkened stairwell while dodging to the right. Jesse's bullet whizzed past his ear and settled in the wall behind him, too close for comfort. The report echoed through the corridor between the rooms, gunpowder choking his lungs.

Mike cocked the coach gun and rose back to the target, but as he squeezed the left trigger, an already wounded Maggie stumbled past Jesse, intercepting his next shot. The sound of her moans sending alarm bells through his already reverberating skull. Maggie's expression was drawn and panicked as they locked eyes. Before she could speak, her body collapsed on the floor, blood soaking through her apron. The shotgun didn't need accuracy. It hit everything in its path, including Maggie.

"Maggie, no…" Mike wanted to kneel and help her, but his attention was pulled back to a bloody Jesse, lurching towards him like a zombie, determined for the kill. Blood dripped from his hand, gripping the pistol. Jesse's Colt Single Action 45 caliber revolver clattered to the floor, landing in the widening puddle of Maggie's blood. He was wounded, but undeterred, his eyes glaring hatred in the low light.

Mike's heart shattered for what he had done to Maggie, but there wasn't time to get soft. Jesse fucking James was not going down without a fight. Mike tossed the spent coach gun aside and eyed Jesse's pistol on the floor near Maggie's limp form. He had a split second to either rush for the Colt or tackle Jesse. Instinct took over as he rushed Jesse, aiming for the legs as he had so many times on the wrestling mat. The outlaw's expression said it all—frustration, anger, and determination—as he drew his other revolver, aiming at Mike's moving form.

The bullet pierced Mike's vest, but a sound of metal on metal spurred him on. A reverberating pain of bruising flesh in his chest registered before he heard the report, rushing adrenalin through every cell in his body. A bullet must have hit the old pocket watch. Momentum carried him forward, allowing him to reach his target. They fell together on the floor. A clatter nearby caught Mike's attention, confirming the revolver was no longer in Jesse's hand. A whoosh of air exited Jesse's lungs, driven by their collective impact, spraying Mike's face with blood. Mike lifted his fist and pounded Jesse's face, breaking his nose, blood spewing down his already busted lip. Mike collapsed on top of him, pinning Jesse to the floor with the weight of his body. Jesse stretched towards his pistol, just a few feet away.

Mike gripped his arm and dragged it away from the weapon, forcing out, "No, you son of a bitch!" Blood smeared on the wooden floor as they grappled for control.

Using every ounce of fortitude, Mike rolled over and kicked the revolver, skidding it across the floor. It impacted the wall ten feet away. Remembering the pistol strapped to his back, Mike forced an unwieldy arm to free it. He cocked the hammer, pointing it unsteadily at Jesse.

"Tell me the truth. Are you Jesse James?" Mike barked through gasps. It was harder to breathe now.

Jesse wiped the blood from his nose and tried to sit up, but the change of expression from rage to surprise made the claim for him. Mike shoved him back down with his boot, pinning him to the floor while he struggled to stand, supporting his weight on Jesse's chest.

Mike fired the pistol at Jesse's good hand. "Answer me."

Jesse yelled, frantically struggling to get loose. The damage had been done. The hand was splayed open where the bullet entered, and arterial blood kept time with his heart.

"Next bullet is between your damn eyes. Are you *Jesse James*? Is that Frank outside?"

Jesse spat, "Max, you devil, how am I going to work a day in my life with both hands destroyed?"

Mike stepped harder on his chest and noted the blood oozing out under his boot. "I think you have bigger concerns than your hands, Jesse."

Jesse coughed violently. Mike wiped the blood out of his eyes with his sleeve. Jesse's eyes were wide, but not in terror, as he'd expected. He showed the grit of malice. "I *am* Jesse James."

Mike stared, not wanting to believe his childhood hero was bleeding out on the floor from his own bullet. Well, technically Lawrence's. He'd always imagined they ran together. Mike felt a stabbing in his chest and pulled out the pocket watch from the vest pocket. The bullet was wedged in the brass casing. "Damn lucky aim, Jesse. Would you look at that?" Mike held the destroyed pocket watch up for him to see.

Newly minted soldiers were slaughtered in battle because they let the emotions of the moment cloud their training. Mike felt the bullet pierce his heart the same instant he heard the shot. The momentum of the projectile carried him backward to the floor, but not before he saw deep into the soul of Frank James. Struggling to take his last breath, wheezing with the effort, Mike realized his lung had collapsed. In his head, he commended Mr. James for a well-placed shot as everything went dark. Consciousness lingered long enough for Mike to hear Ben—no, Frank—comfort his brother.

"Jesse, I shoulda let you kill him when you had the chance. Now look at what that son of a..." Frank trailed off.

Mike strained to hear a soft reply. "It don't matter, Frank. You got him today."

The voices swirled into oblivion as Mike slipped into a blackness that quickly transformed into space reaching towards infinity.

Terrified, stunned, and broken, Mike succumbed to death's grip. His last thought caught in his mind, rolling around like a marble in a tin can. *This is not how I imagined the end.*

Chapter 61

Sideways in Time

"Holy crap, Mike." Ronnie shook her head, thrilled and terrified at the same time. "What happened when you came back? Where was I?"

Mike twisted his mouth, obviously freaked out. "I don't know. I thought I'd died, but when I woke up in the bathroom next to you, my first thought was to keep my promise and make sure you were comfortable. It never occurred to me that you were back in time with me."

"Wow, that must have been quite a moment. Did you think it was a dream?"

Mike picked at a callus on his hand. "No, it was too real, too lucid. But as time went on, I'd have moments where my mind convinced me it was some hallucination or mind trick. Too realistic, but how do you convince yourself you've left your body and *killed Jesse James?*"

Ronnie's head was spinning. "Oh my God, Mike. How does that make any sense? Jesse James wasn't killed in 1872. Or by a man named Max."

"I know. I can't quite make it fit with reality. Are you sure we actually go back in time? It's not just a psychotic break?" Mike shook his head, looking worried.

Ronnie took his hand. "Do other people share your psychotic breaks? Mike, you see now why my mom thinks I'm nuts. It is crazy."

"No, you're right. People don't share their psychoses. And you're not crazy. That much I know." Mike forced a smile, although it elicited a grimace.

"Remember what I said earlier, that Mathias was mocking my bad tutors? His history of early America didn't match ours. What if we are sent sideways in time?"

"Sideways in time? What didn't match our history?" His face scrunched up, making him wince in pain again.

"I was trying to tell Mathias that bloodletting is dangerous. George Washington died because of it." She waved her hand. "Mathias mentioned the French United Colonies and that there were no Americas. He was mad that my tutor had been so bad at teaching history."

"United French Colonies? You mentioned that before."

Ronnie smiled. "It does, especially in place of the United States. At first, I thought maybe it was a small skirmish that I didn't know about, but I looked it up. There was never any country called the United French Colonies."

Mike slowly shook his head. "So, was he just messing with you?"

"No, I'm convinced I went back to a different timeline where most everything is the same, just a few details don't match."

"What was the same? If France controlled the US landmass, pretty much everything else was screwed up."

"I was sure when Jack and Lord Barton talked about the time shift that it wasn't something that happened in our past. But they were referring to something else. England switched to the Gregorian calendar in 1752, with leap year and the calendar year starting in January instead of March. England refused to convert in the 1500s when the Pope made the change. By the 1700s, England and the rest of Europe were eleven days different. Think of how confusing that must have been."

Mike pursed his lips, maybe avoiding the more natural squint for obvious reasons. "Seriously? Why did England thumb their nose at the Pope?"

"Henry the Eighth changed their religion so he could divorce Catherine of Aragon and marry the hot and not infertile Anne Boleyn. This caused a rift between England and the Pope. Elizabeth, Henry's daughter, was in charge when they came out with the Gregorian calendar, and she wanted nothing to do with the Pope's decree."

Mike laughed and rubbed his eyes. "Why don't we know this stuff?"

Ronnie sighed, adjusting to the shift in her world. Mike was a part of this, just like Ini had said. Her subconscious had been nudging her towards this conclusion—she'd just been distracted by Jeffrey's bullshit. "Ha, I was surprised too." She ran her fingers over his palms, which were covered with thick calluses from years of weightlifting.

Mike opened his hand to let her do as she pleased, then cocked his head to the side. "Like a witch trial? They stopped doing those a few decades before you arrived. Not in London anyway. So, you don't think that a Google search of Jesse James will show some dude named Max killed him in a ranch house north of Sterling City, Texas?"

Ronnie rolled her eyes. "Ha, I don't think so."

Mike shifted positions. "So you think we made a split in time, like adding a new branch starting when we went back? If that's true, then who made the branch split when the United French Colonies timeline happened?"

"Oh my God, that's brilliant!" Ronnie looked up at the ceiling, processing this idea. "Who would that have been? As far as I know, I was the first person who went back...ah, sideways in time."

"Wait!" Mike raised his voice, startling her. "This is multiverse theory!"

Ronnie's heart lurched, "It is? What the heck is multiverse theory?"

"It's a quantum physics theory that fits perfectly." Mike sat up, pulling his hand out of her grasp, and became more animated. "The classic definition is that there are an infinite number of parallel universes out there. Every time you make a choice, like to save me in the river or not, both choices create a daughter universe that actualizes the choice. In this universe, you chose to save me. The other universe exists where you chose not to, but we just don't know because we are here. Maybe there is a third one where you tried to save me but gave up."

Ronnie tried to process what he was saying. "Wait, that's actually a scientific

317

theory? I thought that kind of thing was just in sci-fi movies."

"No. Ever hear of Schrödinger's cat?" Mike's eyes were wide.

"Maybe? Tell me." Hope grew in Ronnie's heart. This was irrefutable proof she was not insane. Science even backed it up.

"A guy named Schrödinger explained a theory with this example. Imagine a box that has a cat in it. We don't know if the cat is alive or dead. At that moment, the cat is *either* alive or dead, but we don't know which state it is in until we open the box."

"Or if the cat meows, then we know," Ronnie added.

"Yes, but the cat doesn't meow in this example. Is he dead or not?"

Ronnie shrugged. "No way to know, I guess."

"Exactly. At that moment, the cat is both dead and alive."

"Not really, he is either one or the other." Ronnie tried to follow along but felt there was much more to this than a cat.

"Multiverse theory says there are two versions of what happens. The moment we open the box, the universe splits. One version we see the alive cat. The other universe has us opening the box and finding a dead cat. In that moment, the two universes diverge. When you saved me in the river is when the universes diverged. This is called many worlds, and both continue to exist—we just can't observe both outcomes because our reality is in only one of them."

"Huh, that sounds much more like some sci-fi creative making this up. This is *real* science, Mike?"

"Yeah, high level physicists came up with this. They were having trouble explaining the full level of quantum physics and had to create string theory, which didn't fully explain it, then multiverse theory was better at explaining everything they'd seen in experiments. With Schrödinger's, the outcome of the experiment was changed by the actual viewing of the cat."

"Because we looked at the cat, we changed the outcome?" Ronnie's mind was sparkling with possibilities. "That's no weirder than killing Jesse James."

Mike laughed. "Exactly. We may have stumbled into another universe, similar to ours but divergent because we interacted with it." He looked down at his hand, then back at her. "What is your working theory on what's making us travel?"

She smiled at their new shared term for what had plagued her for months now. "Steph is convinced that Jeffrey is doing it."

Before Ronnie could finish her thought, Mike cut in, not hiding his frustration. "*Of course* it's Jeffrey."

"How can you be so sure?" Ronnie was alarmed at his conviction that Jeffrey was involved, not at its face value, because that seemed the most likely now, but Jeffrey wasn't here in Puerto Rico. How could he have set all this up from Florida? How and why did he get Mike involved? A chill snaked up her spine, despite the stuffy, hot room, and she felt Jeffrey's grip on her soul from a thousand miles away.

"The watch." He raised his eyebrows and craned his neck towards her, passionate in his response. "You were in *his lab* for Christ's sake."

"I know. It's clearer to me now looking back on it, but at the time I didn't have any idea. You have to understand, Mike, he is ridiculously smart. That coupled with the fact that he has mastered the skill of lying his face off. I didn't see it. I friggin' defended him for a month. Plus, when it happened again, I was not in his lab. The second time I was at my house, and he was at his condo."

Mike cocked his head to the side and raised his eyebrows. "But he was at your house. Couldn't he have set something up ahead of time?"

"He must have. Jeffrey was there until I invited Steph, Ian, and Nick to stay with us. Man, was he furious." A twang of fear stabbed her stomach remembering how mad he'd been.

"Uh huh, he must have been. Ronnie, you ruined his plans. But somehow he succeeded anyway."

"Jeffrey must have done something when he was shoring up my roof in preparation for Hurricane Frances. He was up there several days ahead of the storm." Ronnie's mood shifted back to the helpless feeling she'd been buried in since her birthday, when all of this had started. She crumpled under the crushing feelings of helplessness.

Mike wrapped his arms around her and kissed the top of her head. "Ronnie. I think anyone would be freaked out in this situation. It's not something you ever expect to happen. It's no wonder he's tried so hard to convince you that you're losing it. He probably even recruited your mom to help the cause. I wouldn't put anything past him."

Ronnie nodded but didn't respond for fear it would come out in a squeak.

"Look." Mike pulled her over to sit closer and cradled her in his arms. "You have *me* now." He pushed her hair off her face and pressed his forehead against hers. "I will make sure that asshole never hurts you again."

Ronnie fought back tears, feeling his protectiveness. She'd felt so alone for so long. Finally, she whispered, "Thank you, Mike." Then hugged him. "You know, another thing I need to tell you about."

"You can tell me anything, Ronnie." His voice was soft and coaxing.

"Remember the psychic Steph took me to?"

"No, tell me." He reached out for her hand and rubbed his finger over her palm. The tenderness of his touch melted her, but she focused. "Ini said something fascinating. Every time I go back, there is a pattern. She's right. Each time a man is working against me, and another one helps me. She told me to write everything down. I did, but it's floating down the river right now."

"Wow."

"Every time I go back...or sideways, a man has helped me. Mike, I feel strongly they are connected to you."

Mike's eyes widened in surprise. "Me? How do you know it was me?"

"Remember in the hospital when I woke up screaming?"

His expression fell. "How could I ever forget that horrible moment?"

Ronnie caressed his cheek and let her hand drop. "I had just returned from traveling and you were there by my side. Normally I just come back floating and it's almost like I wake from a dream. That time it was horrible. Both worlds were visible at the same time, shattered in a way, recombined in a horrible but beautiful moment. In the other world, or should I say multiverse, Morris was by my side in 1588 in early America. You both formed the same words, but yours were American and his were

Old English."

"Seriously?" He shook his head, soaking this in.

"In the bookstore after Hurricane Charley, I had the same feeling outside on the patio. You and Mathias merged into one man for a split second. That's why I freaked out."

"I would have too. Now this Jesse James adventure, I was there with you. Even *I* know it this time. So do your analysis on our trip. There were several bad men. Of course, Jesse and Frank. But also Jeb." He looked away, attention caught by a noise just outside the window.

She'd heard it too. Probably just the wind. The sky was not as inky black. The sun was almost up. "The good guys. Let's see. Max for sure. You rescued me."

Mike smiled. "Well, you kind of rescued yourself by climbing out of that window. You little badass, you."

A giddy feeling bubbled up in her stomach. No denying it. She was falling for him. "I've gotten bolder—I take more chances. It's a lot easier when you know you have to die so you can return."

Mike laced his fingers through hers, confirming her feelings that he was an important part of this. "That's a good point. I didn't have any clue that dying would help me get back. I may have just shot Jesse and Frank while they slept that first night and taken a bullet in the process."

"Don't sell yourself short. You took a lot of risks for me." Ronnie leaned in and kissed him softly.

Mike lingered on the kiss, making the butterflies in her stomach go berserk.

Finally, he pulled away. "I didn't know it was for you. I just couldn't stand the thought of letting Rose go back to a man like that. I did feel an uncanny connection to her, um...you. Now I know why."

"I felt it too. I've felt it every time. It just took me a while to listen to that inner voice." Ronnie leaned in for another kiss. Would Mike be as exciting as Morris had been in the sack? She sucked on his lower lip, wanting badly to find out. Her hands wandered over his thick, broad shoulders, squeezing his biceps, and returned to his thick neck. Mike shifted positions, pulling her closer now, and she leaned against him, loving the solidness of his body.

Ronnie pulled away and looked deep into his eyes, wanting to learn everything about him, but savoring every second, not wanting to rush anything. They would have a lifetime to learn it all.

Something wasn't right about his eyes. "Mike, your pupils aren't even. Is that normal?"

The smile left his face. "There is more light on this side." He handed her the flashlight. "Check again with this." His voice carried an urgent tone.

Ronnie shined the beam across both of his eyes. Mike winced when it hit the side with the larger pupil, the side with the injury on his temple. "It's still uneven. This side doesn't react as much. This side is bigger for sure." Ronnie tapped his right hand.

"Shit." Mike gripped his head.

"You okay?" She squeezed his shoulder.

He shook his head but kept his fingers pressing into his eyes. "Ronnie, it means I have a concussion and God only knows what else is going on in there."

Chapter 62

Sunup

Ronnie watched Mike closely. He seemed fine other than his uneven pupils, but they were just sitting and talking. Would it get worse?

"We need to wait until the sun is up. It will be too dangerous to drive in the dark," Mike said still covering his eyes. "I want you looked over as well."

Ronnie glanced out the window. "As luck would have it, the sun is coming up. You okay, Mike?" She gently touched the hand pressing into his eyes.

Mike opened his good eye. "Yeah, just don't shine any more lights at me for a bit." He forced a smile. "I guess we should pack some supplies and try to figure out where the hospital is."

Ronnie stood up, looking around. "There's a whole rack of maps over there. Let me grab one." She walked to the storefront and looked out the window. The sun hadn't come up over the mountain, but it wouldn't be long. She looked over the choices and pulled out a detailed map of Guayama and a larger map of Puerto Rico and returned.

"How far do you suppose we made it from the hotel?" She opened the map and found the National Suites and tapped it.

The relaxed Mike was gone. She could see the tension in his face, making him look more tired and strained. "It took us about…I don't know…a half hour. Then we hit the mountains." He followed the road on the map with his finger until it curved up the mountainside. He tapped a spot where the river and mountain were close to each other. "I think this is where we are."

Ronnie pointed. "Look, here is a gas station."

"Yeah, so I was close. This is the hospital we were heading to." Mike tapped it.

Ronnie calculated it was only fifteen miles or so. "How difficult is it going to be to get there? I sure as hell don't want to be in another accident."

Mike shook his head. "No guarantees that we won't run into trouble. We could just stay put and wait for someone to check on the store. We have supplies." He wasn't convincing.

"I'm really worried about your head. I just don't want anything to happen to you."

Mike let out a long, slow breath. "Let's pack up some supplies and get going soon."

"Okay." Ronnie stood up. "I'll find a bag."

Mike stood slowly, carefully, and that scared her even more. "I'll get some water." The sun was shining in now, lighting up the place. Ronnie looked through the aisles and stopped. "Hey, Mike, look what I found." She held it high over the top of the aisle to show him.

"What is it? I can't tell," he called from near the drink coolers.

"Walkie-talkies!" She tore open the package. "It's waterproof!"

"Oh, that's a great idea. Let's make sure they work."

Ronnie knelt on the ground and broke open the plastic packaging then put in the batteries and walked one set over to Mike. "Let's try it out." She moved to the other side of the store and waited for him.

Over the walkie-talkie she heard Mike's voice in a thick country accent. "Breaker one-nine, breaker one-nine." At least he hadn't lost his sense of humor.

Ronnie pressed the button and responded, "This is Little Red Riding Hood. To whom do I have the pleasure of speakin'?"

She could hear Mike's laugh sail over the distance between them. Then her walkie-talkie crackled. "Smokey, this is Buford T. Justice. I'm comin' after you."

Ronnie laughed and pressed the button again. "I feel like I'm twelve and we're planning a trip with my friends."

In the distance, the distinct sound of a helicopter broke through the storm sounds. Ronnie walked back to Mike. "Did you hear that?"

He glanced out the window. "Yeah, I did. If it gets any closer, I'm running outside and waving my arms."

"Do you think they saw our car? Maybe somebody reported it."

Mike shook his head. "Probably military. I wonder why they'd be over here."

Ronnie searched the sky to see if it was coming near, but tall trees blocked her view. "I'm surprised they're out in the storm. It's still pretty bad out there."

"The winds have died down considerably. Just a lot of rain coming down right now."

Ronnie continued her search for a duffel bag or backpack and found a sparkly purple one with *Puerto Rico* in bold yellow letters. She walked over to Mike, who had filled a small cooler with waters. She held up the bag for his inspection. "Isn't it beautiful?"

"Ha, stunning. Grab food and let's get some breakfast before we head out. I'm starving."

She finished filling the small bag then sat down on the towel where Mike was already preparing something.

Mike smiled. "Let's see. What shall we have today? Pop-Tarts?" He held up the half-empty box.

Ronnie shook her head. "Nope." She shoved the last sleeve in the backpack.

Mike waved a box of Puerto Rican cereal at her. "Unpronounceable sweet crap?"

Ronnie grabbed a box of Raisin Bran and tore open the top. "This works for me."

"Here."

Ronnie took the Styrofoam bowl he proffered and poured the cereal then handed him the box. "Mike, be honest. How are you feeling?"

Mike's face grew serious. "I'm a bit worried. I know that with these types of things you can go from feeling decent then crash pretty fast." He pressed his lips together in a worried smile, raising his eyebrows. "I don't want to be here if that happens."

"Yeah, I'm worried too." She leaned over and kissed his cheek. "Let's eat quickly and get you looked at."

Mike held her arm so she'd stay close, then kissed her gently on the lips, holding it just long enough for the butterflies to start up again. Then he let go and she moved away.

"I'm worried about you, too. You've time traveled, kicked up your Korsakoff's enough to go into shock, watched a man die, got in a car accident, rescued some dumbass in the river, and climbed a mountain."

Ronnie snorted. "Geez, it sounds so much worse when you say it like that." A brief flash of the bloodied doctor splayed on the floor dashed through her mind. That would stay with her forever.

"You never told me how you got back. How did you die, Ronnie?"

Her mood deflated, and she resisted thinking about that moment. She took a deep breath and exhaled. "Ben shot me."

"What? Why did he do that?"

Ronnie shook her head, sorting through the confusing moment. "I mean Frank shot me. I snuck up to see what happened to you and found Ben and Lawrence moving bodies out of the house. Yours first, then Jesse's."

Mike looked alarmed. "Not mine, Ronnie, I'm right here."

"Yeah, it's still hard to tell this part. They both went inside, and I didn't know if it was you for sure, so I climbed on the wagon and looked. They came back outside, and I ran away, but Ben saw me and pursued."

"Oh, shit. What did you do?"

"Quanah rode up and pulled me up onto his horse. Ben yelled out that he was coming to help me, but fired just as the horse turned, and I took the bullet."

"Wow, so you saved Quanah in that timeline." Mike's eyes were wide.

"Maybe I did. Who knows? As I faded away..." She debated about telling him more.

"Wow, we both got shot by Frank James!"

She shook her head. "We did." Ronnie decided to take the plunge. "Mike, I heard my father's voice telling me to trust my gut, to find Jason Korbin."

"What do you mean *your father*?"

"My dad has spoken to me a few other times, right as I'm shifting from one place to another."

"Ronnie, that's huge. What if he is trapped somewhere in the wormhole or whatever? It means maybe, just maybe, we can get him back here in the same timeline with us."

Ronnie's mouth dropped open and she stared numbly. "What! Are you serious?"

He took her free hand. "I mean, who knows? This thing is a total clusterfuck. Sorry." He smiled apologetically. "But it would make sense. If he went back in time and was left there. I didn't mean to interrupt, go ahead. Who is Jason Kinser?"

Ronnie's throat tightened thinking of finding her dad and bringing him back.

"Jason *Korbin*. I have no idea. But I'm going to find out as soon as I can look into it."

"This keeps getting stranger and stranger. Do you know what else this means?" He grabbed her hand and squeezed.

Ronnie shook her head, fighting back tears.

"Your dad might be one of the good guys when you go back."

Ronnie's jaw dropped. "Could he have been Quanah? Oh my God, Mike."

Mike smiled. "Yeah, that is an incredible thought. Could any of the people who helped you in your other travels have been your dad?"

She thought through the people she'd met through the various time travels, but nothing came to mind. "I don't know. Maybe?"

Several simultaneous sounds caught their attention. Mike stood and looked around, likely trying to determine where it had come from.

Ronnie stood too, her heart beating rapidly. "What *was that*?"

Mike held up his hand, hushing her, then bent down and pulled a glass bottle from the trash bin, one of their empties from last night, and smashed the end on the metal aisle shelf. He held it by the neck menacingly.

Ronnie was glad of his protective instincts, but it was alarming.

Mike spread his arms, blocking Ronnie from moving away from him, pressing her to the shelves.

Ronnie whispered, "Somebody coming in?"

Mike held his finger to his lips.

A movement in the back of the convenience store caught her attention. Ronnie grabbed Mike's shoulder. The jostling noises from the back of the store sparked alarm. By the sound of it, there were multiple people coming into the store, and their attempt at silence was unsuccessful as they spread through the aisles.

Ronnie and Mike were in the middle of the aisle, vulnerable from either end. Ronnie bent down and picked up the flashlight and saw the walkie-talkies. She slid one in the backpack and slung it over her shoulder, then handed one to Mike. He absentmindedly slipped it into a Velcro pocket in the back of his trunks. Mike gripped her wrist and mouthed, "Stay behind me."

Chapter 63

Hardball

Mike's pulse steadily thumped in his temple. He braced for a confrontation, expecting the store owner and his compadres to burst around the corner any second now. To his surprise, a deep voice with an American accent called out, "Is there a Ronnie Andrews here? A Veronica Andrews?"

Ronnie stepped closer to the voice. "Hello!"

Mike reached for Ronnie's arm and whispered, "We don't know who they are." To his left, someone chambered a round. Jesus, whoever it was, they were armed.

From the shadows, the same militant voice called out, "Identify yourself, ma'am."

Ronnie pulled free and took several steps towards the voice, turning to him. "That's crazy, Mike, they've come for us." Ronnie called out, "I'm Ronnie. So glad you're here."

Mike pulled her back as a stocky, dark-skinned man stepped out of the darkness towards them.

"Hi, Ronnie. So good to see you're safe. I'm Bailey."

Ronnie pulled her arm free of Mike's grip. "Thank you so much for helping us, Bailey."

Mike lunged to pull Ronnie back behind him. "Please, let's ask some questions first."

Bailey's tone changed from friendly and calm to contentious and commanding. "Sir, please step away from Miss Andrews."

A noise behind them caught Mike's attention. A Hispanic man cautiously walked down the aisle towards them. He wore the same black tactical pants as Bailey and was packing heat. Their black polo shirts had no insignia, ringing alarm bells. This wasn't a local rescue crew. They were hired help. Mike pushed Ronnie against the shelves, and he stood in front of her, arms spread wide.

"Mike, seriously?" Ronnie whispered.

In front of them, Bailey took a few steps closer, hand on his holster. "Sir, please identify yourself."

Mike held up the bottle. "Who sent you? How did you find us?" While Mike's attention was focused on Bailey, the other man moved closer. They were using teamwork to distract and encroach. "Who the *hell* sent you? Let's start with that. And I'd appreciate you backing off." Mike waved the bottle at one man then the other.

Bailey took a cautious step closer and unholstered his weapon, a Kimber .45, pointing it at the floor in front of him. "Sir, identify yourself and release Miss Andrews. We are here to help, but I need your full cooperation so no one gets hurt."

Fear forced his adrenalin to surge. "I'm Mike Walsh. Who the hell sent you?" He was quickly losing control of the situation.

Bailey answered in a nasally Midwestern accent. "Jeffrey Brennan sent us to help. I see you've gotten Miss Andrews in a somewhat difficult situation. Mr. Brennan only wants to bring you both back to safety." He motioned to his left. "Miss Andrews, please step over here so I can make sure you're okay."

Ronnie stepped in front of Mike. "Jeffrey sent them. You're being too protective, Mike."

Mike held her shoulders and whispered in her hair, "Ronnie, please stay with me. I can't protect you if they separate us."

Ronnie turned her head and kept her voice low. "Protect us from what, Mike?"

As if on cue, the other man closed the distance and pointed a Glock 9 mm at them. Closer now, the man's defining feature was clear—an oversized jaw. In the Marines he'd known someone who had a similar look with the nickname Jaws, named after the James Bond villain.

Bailey barked, "Mr. Walsh, drop the bottle and release Miss Andrews."

Ronnie hesitated and glanced back at the Jaws lookalike. "Put that damn gun away. Mike helped me—he isn't dangerous."

Bailey snorted. "Tell that to Kelly Escobar or the doctor at the hotel."

Ronnie's mouth dropped open in shock. Mike held her shoulders. "Ronnie, *think*! How did Jeffrey find us out here in the middle of nowhere? How do they know about the doctor at the National Suites? Something isn't right."

Jaws aimed the Glock at Mike's chest. "Release the woman."

Mike released his grip on her. The last thing he wanted to do was provoke any of these morons into shooting and potentially hitting Ronnie.

Bailey grabbed Ronnie's arm and pulled her behind him. Mike took a step towards her, but Bailey squared off, preventing him from reaching her.

"No, I want to stay with Mike. Let go!" Ronnie tried to pull her arm free, but Bailey shoved her behind him and another man rushed her down the aisle. "Mike!"

Mike looked over Bailey's head and caught a glance of the purple child's backpack moving away. "Ronnie, don't go with them!"

A wiry man whisked Ronnie out of sight and said, "Hi, Ronnie, I'm Russ. I'm just going to look you over."

Panic grew, making the pounding in his head blur his vision on the right side for an instant, sending new waves of fear tearing through his mind. "Ronnie!" Mike yelled and started after her.

Bailey held up the pistol and barked, "I wouldn't do that if I were you."

Mike yelled, "Ronnie, don't go with them." Then he focused his attention on Bailey. "What the *hell* is all of this? How did you find us? I'm unarmed." Mike wished they would relax. Then he realized he was still holding the bottle and dropped it into the trash bag on the floor behind him and held his hands up.

Bailey shook his head. "Walsh, man, you gotta let us control this situation. We've all been briefed on how dangerous you are, so cut the *shit*. You cannot win this battle."

"Dangerous? What bullshit did that pencil neck Brennan tell you?"

Authority carried in Bailey's tone. "We will have a little chat, but first my friend here…" he nodded to a smaller man behind him, "is going to cuff you. Then, I'll have someone see to your wounds." His eyes flicked to Mike's temple. "Please don't give us a reason to hurt you. Seriously, this can go smoothly, or it can go to shit. Your choice." Bailey let the smaller man step forward.

He approached cautiously, his eyes wide, sweat beading along his upper lip. Mike crouched, bracing for a takedown. The man flinched and held up his hands, earning the nickname Nervous Nelly. Nelly for short.

"Cuff me? You're here to rescue us. Why the hell would you handcuff me?" Mike knew as soon as he was bound they could do whatever they wanted to them. With Jeffrey running this shitshow, anything could happen. He planned out his defense. A right hook and kick to the knee. "You're not cuffing me without a fight."

Bailey held one hand up. "You want to know why we came loaded for bear? It's this *attitude,* Walsh. Really, it's not necessary. Mr. Brennan wanted to be sure you were neutralized before he comes in to see his girl."

They were well trained. Mike knew the tactics. Get the subject emotional and off balance so he made a mistake, then take him down. Mike hated to admit it, but it was working. Just the mention of Jeffrey's name made him furious, and the added *his girl* lit the fire. "You're wrong about me. I served my time in the Marines with honor and have been in no trouble as a civilian. None. Kelly's name should not be on your lips, *motherfucker*. She deserves better than that."

Bailey twisted his mouth in an angry snarl. A crackle over a communication device interrupted them. He nodded at Nelly and pulled a comm device off his belt, speaking clearly into it. "No dust-off. Hardball," then returned it to his belt. He cocked his head to the right, and his men glanced in the direction of the front door.

There was no better proof of their military background than their lingo. Bailey had indicated to someone on the outside that they didn't need air rescue—they'd go out by car. They must have been prepared to address a life-threatening scenario. That meant there were more than the four in the building. *Shit.* How much had this little operation cost Jeffrey? And how the hell had he known where they were with such precision to send a little army?

Bailey pointed the gun at him. "Look, asshole, we are going to cuff you. My instructions are immovable. Mr. Brennan is about to arrive, and I will secure the room. Then we can just shoot the shit once he leaves."

"Shoot the *shit*? You just accused me of killing my fiancée and a doctor."

Bailey signaled Jaws with a flick of his hand. "One way or the other we're cuffing you so Mr. Brennan can enter the building. You want me to make your face even uglier than it is?"

Mike turned to see what the order meant and looked down the barrel of the Glock. His standoff was about to end. "Damn it."

Bailey smiled. "Just turn towards me so we can get this over with. Then we'll get you out of here."

Nelly holstered his weapon and reached out to grab Mike's left wrist. With one powerful right hook, Mike sent him backward into the opposite shelf, knocking snacks on the floor. Mike shook out the pain and readied for Bailey and Jaws, who rushed him, knocking all three of them to the ground. As Mike struggled to break free, Nelly leaned into the melee, leaving himself wide open. Mike kicked the rookie in the stomach, knocking him backward on his ass. Then Jaws threw a punch, but Mike saw it coming and rolled away, his fist landing next to Mike's ear on the floor in a loud thud. Jaws stood, grunted in pain, and shook out his hand.

Bailey kicked Mike in the ribs, yelling, "Fuck!"

Shockwaves of pain resounded through Mike's side, but his wrestling training kicked in, and he gripped Bailey's leg, jerking him off balance. Before he could twist and dump *his* ass on the floor, Jaws landed a blow to Mike's left eye, forcing him to let go to protect his face.

Jaws quickly closed the handcuffs on Mike's wrists, and he and Bailey lifted him off the floor onto his feet. In a rush of fury, Bailey gripped Mike's neck, choking him, the force slamming him painfully into the metal shelves.

Bailey hissed in his face, "You're going to hold the *fuck* still now, motherfucker."

Mike locked eyes with him and spat. "Bet."

Bailey squeezed harder and Mike struggled, spots forming in his vision, the pressure of the blood trapped in his head forcing a throbbing in his newly damaged left eye and right temple.

A crackle on the comm device brought Bailey to his senses, and he released Mike. He stepped away and straightened his shirt, then leaned in. "Walsh, why'd you have to be such a fucking dick?"

Mike lunged at Bailey, but Jaws shoved him back against the shelves with one meaty paw. "*Chill*, man."

Mike ignored him and glared at Bailey. "This is bullshit. You can't hold me against my will. This is unlawful arrest."

Bailey barked to Nelly, "Pat him down," then pulled out the comm device and spoke. "Clear."

Nelly, true to form, cautiously stepped closer, eyes wide and panicked. "Walsh, turn around."

Anger flared and Mike barked, "Don't you *fucking* touch me. I lost everything in the river. Do you think I chose this ridiculous bathing suit on purpose?"

Bailey shook his head to abandon the pat down, then picked up the comm device. "Roger that."

Nelly shot Mike an angry glance while rubbing his chin, making it clear he'd not enjoyed the right hook that set off the melee.

Mike leaned towards him. "SITFU, you *fucking* boot." In Marine jargon, it translated to suck it the fuck up.

Bailey smirked, making Nelly's anger blossom. All of Jeffrey's henchmen were twitchy now. Mike's offense was paying off. Jaws shoved Mike down the aisle towards the front of the store. Motion in the parking lot caught their attention, but the window was fogged, disguising the shadowy figures approaching. A tall blond man stepped in through the front door and the atmosphere sparked with a different energy. This was their commander.

Bailey straightened. "Sarge."

Mike studied the new adversary, bracing for more aggravation.

The blond man, Sarge, nodded.

Bailey stood next to Sarge and whispered heatedly as both men eyed Mike. In the broadening daylight, Sarge's features were more visible. His face was pockmarked with acne scars and his blond hair was cut high and tight. The guy was about thirty and he smelled of rain mixed with sweat. Sarge was about his height and broad-shouldered, but slim through the hips and legs. Mike probably outweighed the man by about fifteen pounds. Maybe more. He could take him down, if need be, but it wouldn't be without pain and suffering.

Sarge noticed Mike studying him and took a step closer. "Mike Walsh. Well, well. I see you're causing my men some trouble today."

Mike straightened to his full height and looked Sarge in the eyes, flexing his shoulders that were tightening up from the scuffle. "I'm not fond of random fuckwads interrupting my breakfast and taking my friend away from me." Mike lifted his cuffed hands behind him. "What the hell is all of this? A rescue party with police powers?"

Sarge smiled. "You can call it a citizen's arrest, perhaps. We were informed that you are wanted for questioning. We were also told you were armed and dangerous, so we wanted to be sure no one got hurt."

Mike shook his head. "Do I look like I'm fucking armed?" Was he a Marine too? Sarge's perturbed glare said that he was.

A car door slammed, then another. Was Jeffrey *fucking* Brennan going to join the fun, or would he disdain from the dirty work? A shadow broke the beam of headlights, darkening the window, and Sarge stepped forward to open the door.

Jeffrey stepped into the convenience store, running his hands through his hair, slicking off the rain. He smiled, speaking in a low tone to Sarge while eying Mike. "Where is she?"

Sarge nodded to the back of the store.

Jeffrey stepped closer, a smug smile on his face. "Mike, how are you?" He attempted to look down his nose, which was hard to do since Mike was several inches taller. "I see you're having a little trouble with the law again." He nudged Sarge. "Nice outfit."

Mike stepped forward but Jaws held his arms so he couldn't get too close to Jeffrey. Mike sniffed and looked at Sarge. "Damn, I thought I smelled something. Why did you bring this *sack of shit* with you?"

Jeffrey's smile fell and he bristled. It must have played out differently in his head. "Let him go," he barked and waved the men backward, but Jaws kept ahold of Mike's arm. Jeffrey stopped a few feet away and jabbed a finger in Mike's face. "I know what you did to Kelly. You should be in jail. You are a very sick man!"

Mike stared at Jeffrey then shook his head and looked down, feigning resignation. In a rage, Mike leapt forward, pulled out of Jaws's grip, and plowed Jeffrey down. He landed hard on top of him, pinning him to the ground. Mike headbutted Jeffrey, but with his hands cuffed, he didn't have the control needed to break Jeffrey's nose as he'd intended. Instead, he smashed into his mouth. Sarge and Bailey scrambled to the floor, jerking Mike violently up and on his feet, pulling him backward.

Mike bent over Jeffery, who cowered on the floor, blood oozing out of his split lip. "You better not touch Ronnie, or I will destroy you, you fucking coward."

Jeffrey stood, wiping his mouth with the back of his hand. "You can add battery to the list of crimes, asshole!"

Mike stepped towards Jeffrey, ready to teach the prick a lesson, but Sarge and Bailey pulled him back. This time they held on tight.

Jeffrey waved towards the door. "Get him out of here. I can't stand the sight of him!"

Before Mike could respond, Sarge and Bailey marched him outside, where they were pelted with rain and wind. Bailey barked in his ear, "Now, Walsh, why the *hell* did you do that? Not smart."

Mike ignored him and yelled, "Ronnie! Don't go with them! Stay here! I'll come get you!"

Bailey jerked his arms and barked in his ear, "Quiet!" Then led him towards a nearby black SUV.

Chapter 64

Polaroid Picture (Hey Ya)

Russ led Ronnie to the garage, walking down the narrow hallway. "Ma'am, be careful of the glass here." He pointed to the shattered glass where Mike had broken in.

Mike yelled out to her, "Ronnie, don't go with them!"

Ronnie turned around. "Mike!"

Russ blocked her way. "I'm sorry, ma'am, I really am." He held his hands out to grab her, and Ronnie ducked, almost getting past him.

Russ was a little taller than she was, but muscular and wiry. Before Ronnie could react, he scooped her up and carried her over the broken glass. Ronnie kicked her legs and tried to get free, but Russ was having none of that.

He gently set her down inside the garage, his face neutral. "Ma'am, you have to cooperate with me for your own protection."

Ronnie got a better look at Russ. He was in his early twenties, with dark, bushy eyebrows with mismatched red hair, giving him an angry look.

"Get off of me! What the hell is this? You've obviously been instructed to separate us. Why?"

Russ must have had training in this because he oozed concern. "It's really important we assess you separately. Miss Andrews, in any situation where a man and woman have been alone together, you need to separate them and do an assessment when she isn't under pressure from the man. If you've been coerced and he's standing right nearby, you may not feel safe to..."

Ronnie interrupted him. "What? You think he coerced me? And that somehow gives you the right to manhandle me? What the hell did Jeffrey tell you anyway? The lying sack of shit."

Russ's expression stayed neutral. "No, no, nothing of the kind. Please, just let me ask you a few questions and then I'll take you back to Mike."

Angry voices carried through the door separating the garage from the convenience store.

Ronnie shook her head, not wanting to play this little game. "Damn it, just get on with it. I can hear a lot of noises over there I do not like."

"I need to send a confirmation picture. Do you mind?" Russ held up a Polaroid camera.

Ronnie shook her head, but acquiesced, crossing her arms and accentuating her angriest look. The flash blinded her, forcing to the forefront how utterly helpless she was. None of this made any sense. How had Jeffrey found them, and why the hell would he bring so many armed men?

Russ pulled the picture out of the camera and shook it. Then he spoke into a radio on his shoulder. "Retrieve confirmation." Then he turned to her. "Firstly, are you okay? Do you have any injuries that need attention?" Russ looked her over and obviously noticed her knee covered by a bandage partially soaked through with blood.

"No, I'm fine, just a lot of scratches, but we took care of them last night." Ronnie was losing patience, but without shoes she couldn't even make a run for it.

He peppered Ronnie with a series of questions. "Are you with Mr. Walsh on your own volition?"

"Of course I am." Ronnie crossed her arms and glared at him.

Russ nodded. "Has he harmed you in any way?"

"No, of course not." Ronnie's anger was brewing.

Russ stayed neutral. "Has he made any unwelcome sexual advances?"

"He has not. This is stupid."

Russ rubbed his chin and looked away briefly. "Ma'am, have you had intercourse with Mr. Walsh?"

"What the hell kind of question is that?" Ronnie eyed the back door, planning an escape to run around to the front of the building and see what they were doing to Mike.

Russ stopped her, grabbing her arm. His tone intensified. "You are staying here with me. That is the plan. Do you understand me, Miss Andrews?"

Ronnie's attention was pulled by the angry voices from the next room. "Call me Ronnie, for God's sake. What are they doing to Mike in there?"

He turned his head, listening to the racket. "Sounds like someone isn't cooperating."

"Oh my God, are they hurting him?" Ronnie was on the verge of tears. She knew if she were there with Mike, they'd probably be easier on him. Why hadn't she listened to him?

Russ held his hands up. "Ronnie. I don't know what is going on back there, but they're trying to get some answers about what happened to the doctor at the National Suites."

Ronnie's cheeks burned. His Adam's apple bobbed as he swallowed, and now she couldn't take her eyes off it. It was huge. "I was there when the doctor came to examine me."

"Yes, can you detail what happened?" Russ pulled out a pad of paper and pencil from his pants pocket and waited for her to speak.

"Is that what this whole thing is about? A way to get Mike in prison? This is ridiculous. He didn't do anything wrong." Ronnie felt weak and looked around for a place to sit. There was a rickety old office chair nearby. Ronnie walked over to it and sat down.

"Ronnie." Russ stood nearby and said softly, calmly, "Can you tell me what happened to the doctor?"

The stress was catching up with her, or maybe it was the booze she'd had last night. Her stomach's dissatisfaction was making itself known. "I passed out during the storm and Mike called the front desk to have the doc come up. When he walked to our room, the atrium collapsed, and shards of glass were blown into the hallway."

Russ made a few notes then paused and looked up. "Yes, then what happened?"

"He..." Ronnie fought back tears and forced her voice to work. "The doctor came into the room and bled out right in front of us." She wiped away a tear. "Mike tried to stem the blood from the glass in his calf, but we didn't notice the huge piece of glass in his neck until he'd already lost a lot of blood."

Russ looked up again. "So, Mr. Walsh was helping the doctor when he died?"

"Yes, Mike was trying to save his life. It was just too late. The neck wound..." Ronnie felt nauseous and forced her mind to go blank.

"You know he has a history, Ronnie. Did he tell you about Kelly?" Russ said, kneeling down in front of her, softening his voice.

"I know that she died in the shower...epilepsy," Ronnie said through tears. "Jeffrey sent me an article that accused Mike of killing her, but it was false."

A man rushed in, interrupting them. Russ took a few steps towards him and handed over the Polaroid picture, and he was gone before Ronnie could address him.

Russ continued, "You know that most domestic abusers lie about what happened. They don't want anyone to know what kind of monster they really are."

Tears fell down her face. "If he murdered her, why isn't he in jail then? There are other articles out there that cover the coroner's report."

"Who told you that?" Russ said gently. "Mike? Have you seen the articles yourself? Have you any proof outside of him telling you he isn't a murderer? Good lawyers get monsters off all the time, Ronnie."

Ronnie shook her head. "There wasn't even a legal case against him. The coroner ruled it an accident."

Russ smiled and stood back up. "Again, have you seen this evidence with your own eyes, or is this all from Mr. Walsh? Believe me, I've seen enough men who can lie their faces off, and some are so good at it that everyone comes to their defense."

"That's not what is happening here," Ronnie said, her nausea turning to anger.

Russ flipped the notebook closed. "Did he cry when he told you about it?"

"His fiancée died. Yes, he cried when..." Ronnie's voice was choked off by emotion.

Russ nodded, as if that proved Mike's guilt. "All I'm saying is to find your own evidence. Don't just take his word for it."

"Didn't *you* just take Jeffrey's word for it? Mike's innocence is a matter of public record. I bet you never looked, did you?"

An angry voice echoed through the hallway, announcing someone's arrival. Ronnie stood and took a few steps closer, hoping it was Mike.

Chapter 65

Fat Lip

Jeffrey stormed into the garage followed by a string of curse words. Russ stood straighter and nodded. Blood poured out of his lip, and he tried to protect his button-down Oxford, to no avail.

Ronnie felt a mixture of fear and revulsion. "Jeffrey, what happened?"

Jeffrey ignored her and barked at Russ, "For fuck's sake, help me with this."

Russ opened a small pouch attached to his belt and fished out gauze and an ice pack. He tore open the package of gauze and handed it to Jeffrey, then popped the ice pack and shook it vigorously.

Jeffery snatched the gauze from Russ and pressed it to his lip.

Ronnie shook her head. "Jeffrey, what the hell happened out there? Why are you here?"

Jeffrey pressed the ice pack to his lip then removed it, barking at her, "Fucking Mike Walsh is what happened to me."

Alarmed, Ronnie exchanged a glance with Russ. He twisted his mouth sideways and opened his eyes wide as if to say *I told you so.*

"What do you mean?"

Jeffrey paced across the garage and turned to face her, pointing his finger in her face. "That asshole attacked me." A flash of fear showed in his eyes.

"How the hell did you find us and why did you bring a crew of armed men in here? Someone could have been killed."

"You know why I brought these guys?" Jeffrey stuck his lip out. "Mike is violent. Look what he did to me. He fought all of them. I probably should have had a few more guys here." He looked down his shirt. "I'm pressing charges. We can add it to his other crimes. And he owes me two hundred dollars for this shirt."

Ronnie couldn't control her anger. "What the hell? You bust in here with your little army men and take me away from him? What did you expect him to do? Mike was protecting me."

"I expected him to do like he is told." Jeffrey returned the ice pack to his lip, nursing his wounds.

Ronnie was seething with anger. "Aww, your little ego is hurt because he kicked your sorry ass? Is that it?"

Jeffrey rushed over and raised a hand as if to hit her. Russ stood between them, holding his hands up.

Jeffrey craned his neck towards her in an ugly grimace. "You little, ungrateful bitch."

"Jeffrey." Ronnie softened her tone, not wanting to poke the bear so much he would maul her when Russ left the scene. "I didn't ask you to come here."

"Ronnie, what was I supposed to do? Let you suffer here on the island? I know how storms affect you." Jeffrey glared.

She wanted to yell that her traveling was all his fault. Instead, she tamped down her anger, knowing the only way to deescalate was to be calm. "How the hell did you find us, Jeffrey? We are out in the middle of nowhere."

It was working. Jeffrey's tone softened. "Your cell phone, Ronnie. I had Verizon find your phone."

Ronnie shook her head. "Nope, my phone is halfway down a river right now. I call bullshit on that."

Jeffrey smiled, shaking his head, adopting his usual arrogant tone. "You can be so naïve, Ronnie. Your phone shows the last location it was working, and they can figure out your general location. It was easy enough to see you'd have to end up somewhere on this hill."

The words made sense, but she knew him well enough that this was not the whole truth. "Oh really? That's so generous of Verizon to help you like that. Did they hire a small army to rescue me too?" She glanced at Russ, whose expression remained neutral.

"Did I mention how ungrateful you are? God, Ronnie." Jeffrey took an aggressive step closer, and Ronnie retreated. "Come here," he barked.

Ronnie shook her head and remained near Russ, just in case. Jeffrey had never been violent with her before, but he was incensed.

Jeffrey looked down at her, wrinkling his nose. "Damn, what is that smell? Is that you?"

"Screw you, Jeffrey. You don't even ask me how I am. You don't ask me what we've been through." Ronnie pointed to the convenience store where Mike was. "I have been through hell in the last twenty-four hours. You could at least feign for your friend here that you actually give a shit about me. Instead, you can only comment on how I smell. You are the one who smells, Jeffrey."

Jeffrey looked at her, confused.

"Like an asshole," Ronnie jabbed.

Pain showed in Jeffrey's eyes. He took a step closer. "Look, Ronnie. I am sorry you had to go through all of that. I did tell you not to come here. It's too soon since your hospitalization. But you kicked me out instead of listening." Jeffrey pressed the ice pack back on his lip, which was swelling up now.

Ronnie realized now how petulant he sounded, grating on her every nerve. He spoke like someone who had always gotten what he wanted, like a spoiled child in a toy store. "I kicked you out because you were scaring me then, just like you are now. You're a vile person. You only do things for Jeffrey, never for anyone else." She glanced at Russ and watched his Adam's apple bob.

Jeffrey's tone softened and he played up the hurt feeling dramatics. "What are you talking about? I did this for *you*, Ronnie."

She saw through him now. She'd had a year and a half of his manipulating the facts. Now free of his spell, his motives were clear.

"You did this for *me*? Or was it to make Mike know who really was in charge? We were about to drive to the hospital. We didn't need you to come all the way here with your toy soldiers." She turned to Russ. "Sorry."

Russ shook his head, eyebrows lowering.

Jeffrey scowled. "Right, because he took such good care of you. He insisted you come to Puerto Rico straight out of the hospital. Mike put your life at risk, forcing you to leave the hotel in the worst part of the storm to crash and nearly die." Jeffrey shook his head. "That Mike sounds like a monster to me. He sounds like a man who is capable of killing someone with his bare hands." Jeffrey squared his shoulders, looking at her with wide eyes, jutting his chin out, forcing a trickle of blood out of his fat lip.

Mike had given Jesse James a fat lip too. Ronnie crossed her arms. "He didn't make me come here. I chose to get the hell away from you and your bullshit."

Jeffrey stepped closer, then held his nose dramatically. "God, you stink. Enough of this. I'm taking you to a hotel to clean you up." Then he focused on her clothes. "What the hell are you wearing?"

Ronnie glanced down at the oversized t-shirt. "What am I supposed to wear? My clothes are wet and muddy."

"Don't you have something else to change into?"

"Seriously? All of my stuff is down that river! My wallet, my ID, all of my clothes. EVERYTHING! What the hell kind of a person even thinks that? *Never mind*, can you just take us to the hospital? Mike has a concussion and needs to be looked over."

Jeffrey laughed. "Oh, there is no *us*. Mike is going to talk to the police. He's wanted for murder. *You* are coming with me." He grabbed her arm and led her towards the garage door.

Ronnie jerked out of his grip. "Oh no. Mike did not kill that doctor. That is total bullshit. First that false newspaper article about Kelly, now this? You are the monster Jeffrey."

Jeffrey shook his head and stepped closer. Russ stepped in between them again.

Ronnie glared at both men. "I'm getting my stuff." Ronnie pointed at Russ. "I don't need your help."

"You do that." Jeffrey sneered and threw the ice pack at the garage door, making a loud rumbling noise.

Russ followed her to the small bathroom and blocked the passageway to the convenience store. He watched as she gathered her clothes and filthy Nikes. Where were Mike's things? She returned to the office chair and Russ followed like a lost puppy. Ronnie absently shoved the still damp clothes in the purple backpack, digging through to find the wet socks, then sat on the chair.

The petulance was set aside for now and Jeffrey's arrogance was back in full force. "*Mike* killed Kelly. Ronnie, I have another document I have been meaning to share with you. But that can wait. He murdered a doctor at the hotel. You didn't know *that*?" Jeffrey smirked and walked to the garage door, attempting to lift it. Then gave up.

"That is total bull, Jeffrey. I was there when the doctor came in to help me." Ronnie glanced at Russ. "He was killed by falling glass. Mike and I tried to save him." Ronnie stuck her hand in her shoe. It was still soaking wet. She dropped it on the floor, put on her socks, then slid on the soggy shoes.

Jeffrey stepped closer. "So, you're willing to lie for him too? That's going a little far for that worthless meathead, don't you think? I'll give Mike credit for using the storm as a cover for his criminal behavior." Jeffrey returned and reached out for her wrist. "Ronnie, don't you see the pattern? This weather loosens your grasp on reality. You're delusional. We really need to get you medicated."

Ronnie jerked her arm away. "My mental health is perfectly intact. How dare you push that lame theory on me, after all you've already put me through? You sorry son of a bitch." Ronnie swung at Jeffrey, but he stepped back, dodging the blow.

Jeffery laughed, dramatically putting his hands up for protection, and glanced back at Russ. "She's a wildcat, eh? At least I don't beat my women to death in the shower!"

Ronnie fumed with anger. "Jeffrey, you are repulsive."

Russ gently pulled Ronnie away, releasing her and standing between the two of them.

"Let's go," Jeffrey barked, glancing at Russ.

Russ opened the garage door in one smooth movement. Bright headlights shone in their eyes.

Ronnie rushed over to Russ. "Please, I want to go with Mike. Don't leave him here. He needs a doctor."

Jeffrey laughed. "Seriously, after everything I've told you about Mike, you're still stuck on him?"

Ronnie turned to Jeffrey. "He needs a doctor, Jeffrey. Where is he?"

"He already left. Come on, we are too."

Russ rushed out into the rain to open the door behind the driver. Jeffrey marched her out to the Jeep and Ronnie struggled to pull away, but Jeffrey was ready for her this time. He shoved her in the back seat, and Ronnie sat down hard, pulling the long t-shirt over her legs. The rain cooled her skin in the air-conditioned Jeep, creating goosebumps over her arms.

Another man was already in the back seat and smiled, handing her a bottle of water. "Ma'am."

"Thank you." Ronnie absently opened it and took a sip. Mike had told her not to go with them, but where was he? What choice did she have now? She glanced back towards the store, but everything was quiet. "Where the hell did they take Mike? He has a concussion. He needs to see a doctor."

Russ sat in the driver's seat as Jeffrey turned around from the passenger seat to glare at her. "Mike? All you can ask about is fucking Mike. How about a *thank you, Jeffrey*? Do you have any idea how much time and effort we all went through...?" Jeffrey tapped Russ on the shoulder, who looked away from the road for a second. "Seriously, you are the most ungrateful fucking human on this planet."

"Ungrateful! Jeffrey, I did not ask you to come out here. We were totally fine without your help."

Jeffrey's scowl deepened. "Your idea of fine is a little different than mine. You almost died in the middle of a friggin' hurricane. You should have stayed at your mother's. How can you put your life in Mike's hands? He's bungled this for damn sure. I told you he is dangerous."

Ronnie's fury grew. "Jeffrey, we didn't need your interference..."

Jeffrey interrupted her again. "No, stop this bullshit. He has you brainwashed or something. How can you think you were going to be fine? You left the safety of a hotel. Mike should be brought up on more than just murder charges. He needs to be punished for reckless endangerment, attempted murder, or at the very least criminal negligence."

"Legal charges? For what? For helping me out of a horrible situation? For taking good care of me in a crisis? You have no idea what you're talking about, Jeffrey. He saved my life twice, and Steph's during Frances."

Jeffrey turned to the man sitting next to Ronnie. "You see what I'm talking about. She is batshit crazy. Look at her."

The man glanced at Ronnie. His eyes widened and he blinked rapidly, as if unsure of what else to do. Before Ronnie could defend herself, the car stopped abruptly, and Russ jumped out, slamming the door behind him. He passed her window, drawing her attention to the adjacent field. To her astonishment, there was a helicopter with blades running and lights glowing in the low light of the stormy morning.

"Oh my God. Is it safe to fly that thing?" She glanced to the man next to her, who was unbuckling his seatbelt.

He nodded. "They wouldn't fly if it was unsafe."

Ronnie's anger fell away. Worry replaced it as Jeffrey's accusations ran through her mind. Mike had been carted away like a common criminal. Would they hurt him? Would they get him to a doctor, or were they taking him to jail?

Russ opened her door and offered his hand. He led her to the helicopter, through long, rough grass. Ronnie's tired mind chewed on the doubts about Kelly's death. Part of her believed Mike, but she would need to do her own research, as Russ had said. Just to pacify the doubts.

Chapter 66

Jaws and Nelly

Mike pulled free of Sarge's grip and kicked behind him, catching Bailey in the kneecap, who crumpled to the ground. Mike ran to the back of the building with Sarge in pursuit.

Mike struggled to pick up speed with his hands cuffed behind him. When the pavement ended, he tripped where a puddle concealed a ditch and landed hard in the wet grass. He rolled to his side and struggled to stand. Before he could get his feet under him, Sarge tackled him, knocking him flat on the ground. Mike yelled out in pain as the right side of his face bashed into the muddy ground.

Sarge grabbed Mike and yanked him up to his feet. "Nice try, fuck-face," he barked directly in his ear.

Nelly approached cautiously.

Mike was out of breath and still rocked from jarring his injured temple. "Where are you taking Ronnie?" When Sarge didn't answer he called out again, "Where?"

"We aren't taking her anywhere—Jeffrey is." Sarge and Bailey jerked Mike roughly back to the SUV. Bailey held the back door open, his black tactical pants covered in mud.

Sarge grabbed Mike's neck, pushing his head low, and shoved him in the back seat. Jaws was waiting and drew his weapon, shaking his head. "Damn, man. What the fuck?"

Mike shot him an angry glance and exhaled slowly. He took stock of his body, noting a few new scrapes, but nothing serious. Nelly entered the SUV and sat on his other side.

Sarge climbed in the driver's seat and slammed the door shut. He turned to face Mike. "Look, asshole, if you so much as side-eye one of my men, I will tear off your head and shit down your neck! DO YOU UNDERSTAND ME?" He barked the last bit like a drill sergeant.

Mike smirked, glad he'd caused as much turmoil as possible. *Fuckers.* "Just tell me Ronnie will be okay. He isn't going to hurt her again, right? Do you even give a rat's ass about her?"

Nelly leaned forward and looked over at Jaws. "Speaking of ass, he'll probably fuck her brains out tonight. That's what I'd do if she were my girl." Jaws and Bailey laughed.

Sarge shook his head and started the engine, then turned back around and barked at Nelly, "Put his seatbelt on. Jesus." He made an angry noise, a half groan, half grunt. "God damn, man. Do I have to tell you everything?" He glanced at Bailey and shook his head, then turned on the wipers.

Mike leaned forward so Sarge could hear him. "Where are you taking me?"

When Sarge ignored him, Jaws barked, "Police department. You are wanted for questioning."

Sarge shook his head again, flashing an angry look in the rearview mirror. "You couldn't just get in the *fucking* car like a normal person, could you?"

Mike shook his head. "Would *you* in this situation?"

Sarge held his gaze for a few heartbeats, and in Mike's mind, his answer was clear. He'd do the same to protect someone he loved. So many questions swirled about uncontrolled, but his instinct was to let everyone's adrenalin subside, then get them to reveal some information, working on the two less experienced men on either side of him. He'd already surmised the hierarchy. Sarge was the leader of this goat rope, with Bailey second. Jaws was seasoned, but the weak link was Nelly.

As Mike calmed down, he tried to piece together how Jeffrey had found them. If someone had been following them along that mountain road, they'd have been swept into the river too. That seemed unlikely. Maybe Jeffrey had tracked Ronnie's cell phone, but that would only work if it could connect to the satellite. The last ping reported would have been just before the power went out last night at the hotel, or when the nearby cell tower fell. How did the sneaky bastard find them in the convenience store with enough certainty to bring all of those resources to bear?

Mike sat tight for the next fifteen minutes, marveling at Mother Nature's destructive forces. Twice they had to stop and remove a fallen tree from the road, with Nelly and Bailey on that duty and Jaws holding him at gunpoint to stay put.

Their brotherhood had to be a stronger bond than anything they could have with pencil neck. Money talked. But these were his people.

After everyone seemed to settle into the drive, he tossed out a question. "How did you guys get involved with that fucking twat Jeffery? You are obviously former military, maybe Marines. Cut me loose and I'll forget all about this. I won't press charges."

They ignored him, but Nelly shot him a glance and he took the opening.

Mike glanced at Nelly. "Camp Santiago?"

Nelly gave a nearly imperceptible head shake.

"Mainland, then? You buddies with him from his time in Virginia Beach, yeah?"

Nelly flicked his eyes at Mike in reaction. Bingo!

"Richmond? You Virginia National Guard?"

Jaws nudged him. "Shut it, or I'll shut it for you."

Mike eyed Nelly to see if he could confirm. Nelly looked out the window, then back at Mike, glaring. "Yup."

"Bailey, you National Guard too? Let me guess, enlisted Marine from the Midwest?"

Bailey ignored him, and Sarge didn't even glance in the rearview. Rain was coming down hard and he likely needed to focus.

"I heard the chopper but not your entrance until it was too late. You guys executed that well. The rest was a complete clusterfuck."

Nelly couldn't resist. "You were pretty focused on what you were doing with that blonde. It wasn't very hard." He paused. "Or was *it*?" Laughter echoed around the car.

Mike rolled his eyes. At least they were laughing.

Jaws leaned forward to scold Nelly. He could almost hear what he was thinking. "Don't encourage him."

Mike knew it was changing the dynamic. He wasn't sure if it was helping or hurting his cause, but he'd never be a passive prisoner. "Look, you can let me out of the car. Tell Brennan you dumped me off a bridge."

Jaws cocked his head and made eye contact with him, then glanced at Bailey, who remained immobile.

Sarge glanced in the rearview mirror. "Shut your suck, Walsh. My men are eager for payback for the games you played back there."

Mike was going to push all their buttons until something broke. "C'mon, don't you think this is all a bit dramatic? You do know you are unlawfully detaining me." Mike glanced from Nelly to Jaws. "Maybe even kidnapping."

Sarge looked in the rearview again, this time leaning forward to lock eyes and nod at Jaws. Shit, he'd pushed it too far. Jaws unbuckled his seatbelt, twisting towards Mike. Jaws reached behind him and pulled out his Glock, raising it above his head.

Mike attempted to block it. Jaws pistol-whipped him, landing a solid blow to his injured temple.

"Ooooooohh!" Mike yelled out in pain. His vision blurred and white dots floated by as he caught a glimpse of Bailey's angered face. Warm blood trickled down his cheek, and he tasted it, metallic and coppery. He tried to move, to speak, to yell. Slowly everything just turned black. The only sense that worked in this fog was his hearing. He heard their panicked voices and the squeal of tires. Then it was quiet.

∞

An acrid stench penetrated Mike's senses, forcing him to turn his head away. As consciousness returned, memories flooded back. The distinct odor was familiar, but he couldn't place it. He opened his eyes and immediately regretted it when a painful stabbing assaulted his brain. Mike tried to cover his eyes, but his hands were restrained.

"Mr. Walsh," an older male voice called out, too loud for the proximity. "Can you hear me?" A Puerto Rican accent coated every nuance of the words.

"Ah, fuck." He placed the scent. Smelling salts! "Where am I?"

Mike glanced around the room, squinting even in the low light. Sarge was standing nearby, scowling down at him. It was too dark to see the others in the room, but Mike guessed they were nearby.

An older man smiled back, salt and pepper hair draped over dark eyebrows. Mike forced his mind to register the words he was saying. "...pupils are uneven...subdural hematoma. He needs to go to a hospital immediately. His brain is swelling."

"Fucking Walsh. You had to push it, didn't you?" Sarge barked in his face. "You fucking just couldn't go along for the ride. You had to bust up my men, muddy up my car, and now get yourself damaged to string us all up by our balls."

"Oooh-rah," Mike mumbled weakly.

Sarge stabbed a finger at his chest. "Real fucking funny, Walsh. You will regret this."

"I regret meeting you, that's for damn sure," Mike eked out, surprised at how weak he sounded.

The older man, likely a doctor, pushed Sarge away. "Leave him be. You are not going to antagonize him further." The doctor picked up his phone and dialed a number. "So, what did you do to him?" He hung up the receiver. "Damn phone lines are down."

"We found him this way. We're taking him to the police station because he is wanted for questioning." Sarge shook his head, anger biting at his words.

Mike raised his hand to get their attention. Instead, one finger lifted off the examining table. His hands were cuffed to the railing. "I call bullshit on that."

The doctor ignored him. "You boys don't look like cops. A bit too American."

Sarge ushered the doctor out of the room. From a distance away, he could hear their voices but couldn't make out what they were saying.

Jaws leaned into view and tapped his bicep. "So, this gal, Ronnie. She with you or Mr. Brennan?"

Nelly appeared out of the shadows. "She's gorgeous. I'd have given her a piece of my mind..." Then did a revolting pelvic thrust.

"Your dick does all your thinking?" Mike shook his head and immediately regretted it. "You must be the genius of the bunch."

Nelly, no longer nervous, came a little closer and flashed his light in Mike's eyes, making him wince.

Jaws laughed, then swatted Nelly's arm. "Cut that shit out. He's got a brain injury."

"Yeah, he won't remember this. We can fuck him up a little and no one will know."

Jaws shook his head. "You really do think with that limp dick, don't you?"

Mike chuckled, but any movement was becoming increasingly painful. His head throbbed.

Sarge and the doctor returned. The doctor's demeanor was angry now. Whatever they'd talked about had pissed him off. "I cannot condone what you boys are doing. This man needs a hospital, and I don't give a goddamn who you work for. Get him help now. I'm not going to say it again."

"Hey, doc, my head is really fucked up. Can you give me...?"

Before Mike could finish the sentence, it started deep in his gut. Slowly the shaking took over his entire body. Then he bit his tongue, tasting blood again, and tried to make his body stop shaking.

The doctor called out, "It is beyond what I can do here." He pressed a tongue depressor between Mike's teeth. "He needs a hospital. If he dies..."

Mike's brain continued the doctor's words, making up his own unorganized, shaky version. *Dies. Dies. That rhymes with flies. There will be flies on all the dead guys.* He smiled at how silly they sounded, but realized they were talking about *his* death. A strange buzzing sound drowned out any thoughts.

Chapter 67

Helo Ride

Jeffrey burst out of the Jeep and rushed to the trunk, shielding his eyes from the pounding rain. The driver beat him to it and pulled out the duffel bag and handed it to him. What was his name, Russ?

Jeffrey glanced back to see Russ helping Ronnie out of the Jeep. Anger fumed as he slammed his duffel bag onto the floor of the chopper, then he climbed aboard, shaking the water from his head, saturated not only from the rain, but from the seething hatred for Mike for ruining his moment rescuing Ronnie.

Movement outside the copter caught his eye as Ronnie struggled to climb in. The co-pilot stood and gave her a hand, uncoordinatedly bumping into him. Jeffrey shot the man an angry glance but held his tongue.

Ronnie's hair was plastered against her face and shoulders, and the backpack straps pressed the shirt against her curves. There was no way she was wearing a bra.

Jeffrey lifted his eyes from the wet t-shirt to find Ronnie glowering at him. "Why are you giving me that look, Ronnie?" Jeffrey matched her expression, feeling at the end of his patience.

She sat and shook her head, pushing the unruly hair out of her eyes. "You claim you're here to rescue me, but you don't even help me into this damn machine."

Jeffrey leaned towards her, aggressively pointing his finger in her face. "Do you have any idea the effort this operation took, Ronnie?" He nodded at the pilot. "How self-absorbed can you be?"

Her eyes widened. "*Self-absorbed?* You don't even treat me like a person, Jeffrey. You saw me struggling to get in the helicopter and just watched."

"You never asked me to..."

The pilot tapped Jeffrey on the shoulder and pointed to the headphones in the seat pocket in front of him. He slipped them on and listened to the instructions, handing Ronnie her set. After she adjusted the headphones, she buckled the seatbelt across her chest, but it was crooked.

Jeffrey reached over to straighten it for her. "Oh my God. You smell like dead fish."

Ronnie slapped his hand away and straightened the buckle herself.

The co-pilot handed Ronnie a blanket and she covered up completely, robbing him the view of her long, beautiful legs. The pilot's voice sounded in the headphones as he went through the safety instructions, and they took off. Ronnie turned away and looked out the window. He wanted to share the file he'd gathered on Mike, but it would have to wait. Since basic reason had left her, he'd brought plenty of reading material to help convince her Mike Walsh was a bad dude.

Jeffrey watched Ronnie, hoping to be able to show her he'd calmed down and was ready to be civil, but her eyes were fixed on the dramatic scenery below. He looked out his window and was shocked at the scene—a flooded river strewn with fallen trees and other debris washed down from the mountains. Was that where they'd been? How could this smart woman keep getting herself into such dire situations? And why was Mike always by her side when it happened?

Anger snaked through his usual crisp, logical mind. He touched his lip, reliving the brutality Mike had shown. It was supposed to be *his* moment. Instead, Mike had stolen it, embarrassing him in front of the crew, ruining his big moment with Ronnie. He'd expected her to be excited to see him, grateful that he'd come all the way out there to save her from Mike's terrible mistakes. Instead, she'd seen him whiny, battered, and weak.

His thoughts swirled like the blades of the helicopter, finally settling on a calmer, more generous tone. After all, she'd been stuck with Mike. No wonder she was testy. At least Ronnie was safe. The rescue was a success, and no one was hurt. Mike would be trapped in Puerto Rico's legal system in the middle of a natural disaster. He'd either get charged with something or not. It didn't really matter because no one could process him until power was back, tying him up for days, maybe weeks. By then Ronnie would see the light. The fact that Mike had no ID was just icing on the cake. It would be infinitely more difficult for him to worm his way out of the situation, and he'd have no way to find Ronnie again.

When National Suites had mentioned Mike was wanted for questioning, he'd poked around a little, finding out about the doctor's death. The information had solved several problems. One, it gave him another reason to hype up the rescue team against Mike. Maybe more importantly, it gave him a legitimate reason to separate Ronnie from Mike.

After about twenty minutes, the helicopter landed. Jeffrey nudged Ronnie awake. "We're here." The helicopter may have been unnecessary, but there was no way to know how bad the roads were. Plus, it was important to show Ronnie the power at his fingertips.

Ronnie looked startled, exhausted, and almost childlike, sparking pity inside him. She returned the blanket to the pilot and smoothed down her hair, looking confused. Thankfully, the anger had subsided, for now anyway. Jeffrey stepped off the helicopter and turned to hold her hand as she exited.

Once she had a hot shower and decent food she'd come around and realize what he'd done for her. Then he could soften her up to drop the bomb on Mike and destroy anything that had developed between them. Mike's actions this morning only proved his violent nature.

**

346

Ronnie shivered and pulled the t-shirt down to cover her legs. "Can you put the heat on? I'm freezing."

Jeffrey adjusted the dials of the SUV's heat and glanced over at her. "Can you do something with your hair? We're going to be at the hotel in a few minutes. I can't have you traipsing through the lobby in the middle of the day like that."

Ronnie looked at him sideways. "Like what, Jeffrey? Like someone who crashed into a river in the middle of a hurricane? I bet half the people in there have been rescued from something today."

Jeffrey watched her perfect lips form the words. "First of all, it's only a tropical storm. Can you arrange your hair to not look like you're totally insane?"

Ronnie smiled and let it slide into a grimace. "That's a nice touch. Keep me thinking I'm crazy."

Jeffery glanced over at her, then back at the road, not wanting to miss their exit. "I mean...if the muddy Nike fits..." He laughed.

"Yeah, you're so funny, Jeffrey. The more you push the *Ronnie's crazy* theory, the more pitiful you become."

Pushed beyond his limit, he slammed his hand on the steering wheel, making her jump. "Pitiful?" Bitter anger bubbled up against his will. Pitiful was not how he wanted to be seen. Powerful was more like it. "I don't think this is the time to break into your issues, Ronnie. Like trusting the dipshit who keeps getting you into trouble. This is a nice hotel. Your shirt is wet and completely see-through, you smell horrible, you're covered in bloody bandages. What are people going to think?"

"I don't give a flying frick what I look like. Where are they taking Mike? You need to make sure he sees a doctor."

Jeffrey widened his eyes. "Listen. You are not in a position to tell me what to do, Ronnie."

"Pitiful," she said under her breath.

"What was *that*?" Jeffrey glowered.

Her arms were crossed over her chest, and she looked beaten down.

"Here is our exit. At least fix your hair." Jeffrey flipped down the visor and opened the mirror.

Ronnie looked in the mirror and used the neckline of her t-shirt to wipe away the last vestiges of yesterday's river mud, then flattened her hair, which was curling wildly. "You are getting me a separate room, right?"

"Why would I do that?"

"Jeffrey, you can't make me sleep in the same bed as you. Seriously."

Her words stung. He'd imagined this part of the plan much differently. A flash of her naked curves assaulted his brain, urged on by her nipples poking against the damp t-shirt. "I'm sorry to say there are no available rooms. When you're neck-deep in a sweet bubble bath, you're going to feel much better."

"You have two beds?" Ronnie's eyes were wide.

"It's a suite. I'll sleep on the couch in the living room area if you want me to."

She was quiet as he pulled into a parking spot of the Caribbean Star Luxury Resort. He reached behind to grab his duffel bag, then stepped out into the rain.

Ronnie exited the SUV and walked quickly to the front door, her filthy sneakers splashing in the puddles. In the lobby she made a beeline for the front desk. Before Jeffrey could stop her, she approached the clerk. "Excuse me, sir. Do you have any available rooms?"

The man was well trained, for he didn't bat an eye at her appearance. "No, I'm sorry, ma'am. We are completely booked."

"Shoot." She glanced back at Jeffrey, shaking her head.

Anger flared. He should have expected her to not believe him. Jeffrey took her arm and pulled her towards the stairs, glancing back at the clerk. "Please excuse us. We're having *a day*." Jeffrey turned to her. "Power is out, but they've been great with candles and there is some hot water. I guess they have a generator for some things."

Ronnie slicked the water off her arms. Jeffrey pulled out a flashlight, lighting the stairwell.

When they reached the room, he unlocked the door, and they entered the kitchenette area with the living room just beyond. A separate bedroom was to the left. Ronnie slipped off her shoes and set them on the tile near the door, where they left a muddy puddle.

Jeffrey lit one of the candles and handed it to her. "You go ahead and get in the shower, and I'll order some food." He lit another one and followed her into the bedroom and set it on the desk.

To his surprise, she didn't say a word. She just stepped into the bathroom and shut the door.

Jeffrey scrounged through his bag, looking for something she could wear. He hadn't thought to bring any of her clothes. She would look hot in his light blue button-down shirt, but she better not still have river stench on her when she was done in there. It was an expensive shirt. Jeffrey tore off the bloodied shirt the meathead had already ruined, tossing it on the floor, and grabbed a clean t-shirt from his duffle bag.

Chapter 68

Escape to Rape

Ronnie set the backpack on the counter and pulled out her wet, stinky clothes. Something hit the hard floor, clattering under the sink. It was the walkie-talkie. Did Mike still have his, or had they taken it away from him? She tucked it under a towel on a shelf under the sink. She was tempted to try it out, but it would have to wait until she had complete privacy.

Her plan was to feign exhaustion, which wouldn't be too hard, and lock him out. Thank God there was a bedroom door to give her that option. If the phones weren't out, she'd call Steph and tell her what was happening. It might give her an insurance policy to make sure she or Mike weren't 'lost' in the shuffle. It would make her feel better to let someone know Jeffrey had taken them both.

Ronnie peeled off the wet t-shirt, letting the competing worries spin around in her mind like a tornado, all made more difficult to control with exhaustion tugging at her mind. Mike's life was in Jeffrey's hands, and that didn't bode well for him. His concussion was probably worsening. How would Jeffrey take this out on her? He'd already been so arrogant, expecting gratitude for pulling her and Mike apart, just when they were going to leave to get Mike to a hospital.

The door flung open, startling her. Damn, she'd locked it, but it must not have latched. Ronnie covered her chest and turned away. "Jeffrey, get out of here. Seriously, this is not okay."

A smile spread across his lips as he eyed her nearly naked flesh, the injured lip bunching. He stepped closer then turned away. "God damn, I can't wait for you to be all fresh and clean."

Ronnie was trapped between the shower and sink. "Get the hell out of here, you asshole!"

Jeffrey grabbed her wrist and pulled her close, then caressed her ass. Ronnie swatted his hand away. "What the hell are you doing? Did you forget we broke up?"

"God, look at you. I'd almost forgotten how perfect you are, Ronnie." He gripped her hands and held them away from her body so he could get a good look.

"Get out of here!" Ronnie pulled free and attempted to step into the shower, reaching for the curtain, but he grabbed her arm, pulling her against him.

"Before you get in there..." Jeffrey ran his hands down her hip and around to her ass, holding her against him.

"Get off me!" Ronnie pushed against his chest, trying to get away, but he held her firmly, almost too tightly.

Jeffrey turned her towards the sink and moved quickly, wrapping his arm around her waist to hold her still, then slid an unwelcome hand under the band of her bikini bottoms. His finger slid inside of her. He leaned, aggressively pinning her against the sink, staring at her reflection in the mirror.

Ronnie kicked behind her, but he opened his legs to avoid the blow. Before she could break free, he released her.

"What the goddamned hell do you think you're doing?" Ronnie stepped away, holding her hands up protectively, the towel rack pushing into her back.

Jeffrey washed his hands in the sink and dried them off, pressing his lips together. "Just seeing if you fucked him."

Ronnie crossed her arms. "What the absolute eff, Jeffrey? That is none of your damn business."

"It sure as hell is. I need to know how hard to turn the screws on that asshole."

Ronnie opened the shower curtain and stepped inside, feeling completely violated. "Get the hell out of here, Jeffrey!" She cranked on the shower, as if that would protect her from his groping hands and stepped out of the way of the icy water.

Jeffrey pushed the curtain open, and she immediately closed it, almost hitting his face in the process.

He continued talking through the curtain. "Ronnie, I keep telling you he is dangerous. You should not get involved with him. In fact, I want you to find another job as soon as we get back."

Ronnie peeked around the curtain. "Get OUT OF HERE!"

He held up his hands. "Okay, okay, I'll give you a chance to freshen up, then we can talk about next steps. At least you didn't have sex with him. Thank God for that!"

"Jeffrey, there are no next steps. You are out of MY life. I don't have to be manipulated by you anymore."

"If you can't start making better choices...what the hell were you thinking coming here with fucking Mike Walsh? He is dangerous. He is a..."

Ronnie turned the shower head towards him, hoping to spray him. It wasn't flexible enough to get more than his feet wet. "Get OUT!"

"Jeez, no need to act like a crazy bitch. Okay, get your shower." Jeffrey turned on his heel and left the bathroom. Ronnie stepped out of the shower, slammed the door shut, and locked it, this time making sure the door was fully latched. Then she returned to the shower as fury rose and manifested as it often did, as tears. Ronnie wiped them away aggressively, not wanting to cry. Her exhaustion made it impossible to stop, along with the layered worry over what was happening to Mike. Jeffrey's violation flipped the worry back to anger and she relived the helpless moment where he held her, forcing her to submit to his exploration.

Ronnie let the hot water claim her attention for a millisecond. It rinsed away the top layer of stress but was not made of magic. Mike needed a doctor. Instead, he was probably shoved in a jail cell waiting for power to come on, maybe some thug beating him up, worsening the damage. His brain could be swelling right now, and no one was helping him. A terrible thought broke through. Had Jeffrey ordered his men to get rid of Mike? Surely, he wasn't that horrible of a human being, was he?

Ronnie fervently forced her will on the world, pushing the universe to help Mike, to not allow the pattern to continue. Now it was happening in her real life. Every time someone helped her back in time, they ended up at the vicious mercy of Jeffrey's counterpart. Now Mike was in his crosshairs. Ini had been right—she needed to stop the pattern here in this plane. But how?

"God, please protect Mike. Help him through this, give him strength to fight. Wrap him in your caring caress, keep him safe from evil." The prayer calmed her. She would let God handle it, taking the burden off of her shoulders. He could do more than she ever could. Ronnie kept her eyes closed, soaking in the moment, focusing her mind on the prayer and the connection she felt with her maker.

Bubbling anger pushed at her emotions. Letting God handle the worry about Mike, she focused on her own predicament. First, she had to get the hell away from Jeffrey. Something told her that his aggressive probing was just the beginning of what he had in mind. Then she could focus on finding Mike. Ronnie slid off the bikini bottoms, wishing now she'd kept them dry. She had nothing else to wear. She soaped and rinsed them, hanging them on the shower rack.

Even after she finished scrubbing away the violation, she stayed under the shower, postponing the confrontation with Jeffrey. Reluctantly she turned off the water and grabbed a towel. She swiped the steam-covered mirror, allowing her to get a good look at herself. "Get the hell away from him," Ronnie whispered to her reflection as she wrapped herself in a towel, then grabbed another one for her hair. She opened the door, letting the steam dissipate into the already humid room.

Jeffrey was on his computer and turned towards her. "There she is. I've ordered some food for you. You okay with an omelet and toast?"

"Yeah." She sat on the edge of the bed, glaring at him. "I thought you were going to let me have this room."

"I am." He cocked his head. "Why?"

She nodded at his suitcase in the corner.

"Oh that? I slept here last night, Ron. I'll be happy to move my stuff." But he didn't move. He just watched her carefully. "Oh shoot, you need something to wear, don't you?" Jeffrey stood and pulled a shirt off the back of his chair. "Wish I'd brought you some clothes. I just assumed you'd have your suitcase with you. Why did you leave the hotel? I mean, that was kind of dumb."

"Mike was taking me to the hospital. The hotel was being evacuated and we had to leave anyway." There were no regrets. She and Mike had made the choice together, knowing the risks.

Jeffrey shook his head and tossed her the button-up shirt. "You'll look pretty hot in this."

Ronnie grabbed the shirt. "Don't you fucking touch me again. Do you understand?"

Jeffrey laughed. "I'm sorry about that. I had to know if you'd messed around with him, Ronnie."

She stood clutching the towel to her body. "Jeffrey, you violated me." Tears stung her eyes, and she locked the bathroom door behind her, donning the long button-up shirt. Ronnie dug through his gear and found a comb and ridiculously expensive leave-in conditioner. For a dude, he sure was big on his hair.

Ronnie worried his self-righteous products would infest her mind as they softened her hair. When she'd gathered her strength, she returned to the bedroom.

"So, I have a few questions for you, Jeffrey." Ronnie paused, waiting for his full attention. Her legs were shaking, so she sat on the edge of the bed. When he turned the desk chair towards her, she continued. "How did you find us?" She wanted to share the anger she felt, but she knew him well enough she'd get a lot more out of him if he stayed calm.

"I told you, the phone company shared your location." Jeffrey smiled. "You look amazing in my shirt, by the way."

Ronnie cut him off. "I have no way of disproving that, but I am suspicious. Let me ask you something else."

His eyes glanced down her bare legs and back at her face.

Ronnie squinted. "How did you manage to get a helicopter to fly in the middle of a hurricane?"

Jeffrey's pride showed through the smile. "I've got..." He rubbed two fingers and thumb together. "Money, honey."

Ronnie shook her head and stood. "Where is your suitcase? I need to wear more than this."

"You're just going to sleep. Why do you need to dirty up more of my clothes?" She scanned the room but didn't see a suitcase.

"Ronnie, let me rub your feet. You said it yourself, you've been through a lot. Lie down over here, Ron." He nodded at the bed.

"I'm not here to sex you up, Jeffrey. Those days are over." She glared at him, anger bubbling up.

He stood and took a step towards her. "You know, I need payment from you."

The fear choked her again. "Payment?"

His breathing quickened. "Yeah, you didn't think I'd go through all of this expense and humiliation..." he licked the welt on his lip, "for nothing." He stared at her chest.

She crossed her arms. "Well, you better disabuse yourself of that notion. I didn't ask you to come here. I certainly am not going to give you *payment* for your effort." Ronnie's blood coursed through her veins. He wouldn't *make* her, would he?

"Relax, Ronnie, it won't hurt. I promise, it will be excruciatingly pleasurable."

Ronnie held her hands up. "Stop that. Get those absurd ideas out of your head. I'm not having sex with you, Jeffrey."

He adjusted his pants and stepped closer. "Come on, you can't be that naïve. Don't you think I deserve a little reward for all I've done for you?"

"I never asked you to come here, Jeffrey. We were fine without you. Besides, I dumped you, remember? We are *not* together."

Had her words hit home? The smile left his lips. Jeffrey crossed the space between them quickly. "He didn't touch you, did he?"

Ronnie stood up, walking backward away from him. "You know, the funny thing about that is I don't have to tell you a damn thing. That is what's known as..." Ronnie paused to emphasize her point. "None of your damn business."

His anger flared. He grabbed her arm and shoved her onto the bed face-down. Before she could get her knees under her, Jeffrey leaned all of his weight on her back, pinning her to the bed.

He whispered into her hair, "I can make it my business."

Ronnie panicked. There was nothing she could do if he wanted to take her right there.

Jeffrey pressed against her butt, and she could feel his arousal.

"No! Jeffrey, get the HELL OFF ME!"

He shoved her head down onto the bed and ground against her ass. Then pulled away, fumbling with the fly of his pants, increasing the pressure against her neck.

"What the hell are you doing?" Ronnie yelled and kicked wildly, but her legs were pressed into the bed with his knees digging into her lower back. He returned his full weight on her, spreading her legs with his.

A knock at the door interrupted them and Jeffrey released her. He stood up, tucking his erection awkwardly back into his pant. He laughed. "Had you going, didn't I?"

Ronnie sprang up off the bed and ran into the bathroom, slamming and locking the door behind her. Fear pushed out any logical thoughts. He'd been seconds from raping her.

Jeffrey jiggled the door handle. "If I were into that kind of thing, it would be happening right now. A little gratitude for all I've done would have been nice though."

Ronnie pressed her head against the door, trying to control the shaking deep in her gut. "Fucking asshole." Jeffrey wanted to make sure she knew he was in control here. A month ago, she'd have scoffed at the idea of Jeffrey being a rapist.

Chapter 69

Time Travel Times Two

Ronnie listened carefully, realizing Jeffrey was talking to the room service guy. He could help her! She bolted from the bathroom and found Jeffrey pushing the cart to the living room area.

Jeffrey moved to block the door, leaning against it. "Breakfast is here." Then, seeing her face, he stepped towards her. "Look, Ron. I'm sorry about that."

"Give me more clothes, you manipulating asshole." Ronnie glared at him.

Jeffrey's cocky expression fell away, and the mask dropped. Did his face actually turn red? He knelt on the floor near the door and dug through his duffle bag, then pulled out a pair of basketball shorts and tossed them to her.

Ronnie returned to the bathroom and slid the shorts on, her mind spinning over her options. One way or the other she was getting the hell away from him. Remembering the walkie-talkie, she found it in the towel and shoved it into the shorts pocket.

"Ronnie, please come out. You need to eat. Let's get off on a better footing here. I don't know what came over me. You know I'm not like that."

Ronnie weighed her limited options. Staying in the bathroom all day wasn't much of a choice. The last thing she needed was a relapse, leaving her helpless for his untoward advances. Unsteady legs brought her to the table built into the kitchen counter, and she sat across from Jeffrey, seething with anger, and not more than a little afraid of him. Ronnie bit into a piece of toast, embarrassed that her hand was shaking.

Jeffrey sat in the chair across from her and unfolded the napkin, spreading it over his lap. "Ron, I'm so sorry. It is not like me to do something like that. I'm a fucking animal when I get jealous. I didn't really know that about myself until now. I've never been jealous before Mike showed up."

Ronnie cringed at his words. Then poured cream into her coffee and focused on that small task.

"Ronnie, look at me." He reached out to lift her chin.

She swatted his hand away. "Don't you fucking touch me."

His eyes widened. "Fuck." He threw the napkin down on the plate. "I royally screwed up. I swear to God, Ronnie, I don't know what came over me. You looked so ravishing in my shirt with your hair all sleek and wet."

Ronnie took a bite of the toast, stalling until her voice would be strong enough to speak without wavering.

He filled in the empty space with his own words. "We used to have so much fun in bed. Don't you want that again? We don't have to date, we can just be fuck buddies."

Ronnie looked at him now, fury untamed. "*Fuck buddies?* You were a second from raping me, Jeffrey. You violated me in the bathroom. Do I look like I enjoyed any of that? What makes you think I would ever sleep with you again? What we had is over because of your selfish, evil ways. It could never have worked. As soon as I started seeing the real Jeffrey, not the fake one you share with the world, but the real manipulative, selfish Jeffrey, I knew it was over. Why it took me so damn long I'll never know. I guess that's how good you are. Steph saw through it right away—finally I see it too. We will *never* be together. You are scary." She held her hand out, still shaking from adrenalin. "See what you've done to me?"

Jeffrey inhaled sharply. "I never meant for it to be like this. I swear. I envisioned finding you stranded in the storm and getting you out of a difficult situation. Ron, I wasn't there for you during Frances and that drives me crazy. I wanted to do better this time. I thought you'd realize I'm not so bad given how much trouble I went through to help you." His expression showed defeat. "God, what an arrogant prick."

Ronnie watched him closely, looking for the falsity. She'd never heard him be so honest before. "I just don't understand how you can do that to me after everything between us."

Jeffrey pressed his lips together and the fat lip poked out, making him look like he was pouting. "I don't know what it is about Mike that makes me so angry." He shook his head. "What is the status between you two?" He leaned forward now, eager for her answer. "Like seriously, Ron, don't give me that pat answer that he is your boss. He's more than that now. You two have been through a hellish experience together. At the very least, you're on friendly terms. At the most, you're wanting to start something with him. Maybe you already have?"

Ronnie took a huge bite of her toast, giving her a moment to gather her thoughts. He uncharacteristically waited for her to answer, without being pushy. At least he was trying to listen. "My situation with Mike is between the two of us. You don't get updates on my life now. I don't think I'll ever forgive you for what you just did in there." Ronnie pointed at the bedroom. "You will never ever threaten me like that again." She said it firmly, but neutrally. She'd wanted to scream it in his face but knew that would set off a powder keg of anger and she was definitely not ready to deal with that monster. She'd keep this one talking until she could get answers to her most pressing questions.

Jeffrey took on an angry flush, and he looked away, then tapped his fingers against his thigh. "It will never happen again. Ronnie, I acted like a total fucking asshole. I know we are done. I know that. I just sealed the deal. I have no explanation, except the thought of Mike being with you..."

She watched him closely. Was he blinking away tears?

Jeffrey pressed his lips together. "I will get you off this island, Ronnie, and leave you be. I do want us to remain friends. I mean, we've been through a lot together. There is no reason we can't stay in touch. Be close friends, right?"

"Close friends, are you high?" Ronnie crossed her arms. "You just threatened to rape me. You took Mike away, accusing him of something he didn't do. Can you at least tell me why he gave me a fat lip?"

Jeffrey looked up at the ceiling, scrunching up his face, then looked at her. "My men got a little aggressive with him. Maybe Mike was resisting their efforts to pat him down or something. I don't know, but when I showed up, he exploded at me."

Did they take the walkie-talkie away from him? Damn it. "Exploded at you, just out of the blue?" Ronnie shook her head. "What words preceded the detonation, might I ask? Since we're being so honest about everything now."

He winced. "Something to piss him off. You know me too well, don't you? Don't think for a second that I won't press charges against him for that, though. It's assault."

"What the hell are you talking about? You just carted him off, I'm pretty sure against his will. That seems a little illegal to me. And seriously, did you expect he would let some strangers separate us? He was protecting me from an unknown threat."

"He shouldn't have fought back. I don't think Sarge is going to let him mess around without getting his head bashed in."

"Jeffrey, his head was already bashed in from the accident." Fear crept up again, taking over Ronnie's emotions, the anger set aside for now. "If he suffers permanent brain damage, either by those hired thugs or by lack of medical care, you will be to blame."

The corners of his mouth turned down. "You really are into him, aren't you?"

Ronnie leaned forward and looked him in the eyes. "Jeffrey, you have no idea what we've been through together. We are intertwined in ways you could never imagine."

Jeffrey's mouth twisted in a sardonic smile. "Intertwined? What the hell is that dramatic bullshit?"

Ronnie squinted, trying to read his expression. "You caused it. Apparently you haven't made the connection yet, but damn, you practically pushed us together."

Jeffrey tapped the table to accentuate his point. "I assure you, I've done everything I can to keep you away from him. He's fucking dangerous."

Ronnie shook her head. "Who's the near rapist? Mike would never, in a million years, do that to me."

Jeffrey's face reddened. "How did I push you two together?" His mouth was a thin line, other than the protruding injury.

Ronnie took a bite of her eggs, trying to find the words. Finally, she decided it was too much work to try and be clever. She no longer gave a flying eff about making him mad. She swallowed, gripping the fork. "You sent us back in time together, Jeffrey. Oops! Now we have a bond that cannot be broken." She watched his expression carefully and was surprised when he didn't react at all. "And guess what that means."

Jeffrey didn't guess—he just stared blankly at her.

"I am not crazy. He went back in time, too. That means that this whole bullshit you've been throwing at me...that I'm mentally ill...is a complete lie. Another manipulation tactic to destroy me. Is that how you get off now?" Her anger mounted. "Your entertainment these days is sending me to these horrible places, making me suffer death to return. You're a sadist! Then you try to convince me that I'm nuts, even though we both know you're behind all of this." Ronnie stood now and leaned in towards him, pointed her finger in his face. "You've been trying to destroy me for months now. You're *damn right* we're over. You lost me when you included me in your goddamned experiments. You could have at least told me."

Jeffrey's eyes widened and he opened his mouth to respond.

She held up her hand. "Let me finish, before you start trying to manipulate me again. I know you've been behind it—I just don't know how you did it. Congratulations, genius, you've invented time travel at the expense of your girlfriend's life and nearly her sanity. What a guy!"

Jeffrey shook his head and set his coffee back down. "Roll back a minute on that tirade, Ron." He leaned in, cocking his head to the side, his teeth bared with emotion. "Mike went back too?"

Jeffrey's simple response surprised her. "Yeah, you sent us both back. Why do you look surprised?" Ronnie had mastered reading his expressions now that she was no longer under his spell.

His eyes showed a shift in tactics. "What the hell are you talking about? Are you still on this time travel nonsense?"

Ronnie laughed. He was going to stick to his guns. "Yeah, I mean, you worked your magic, your hocus pocus, and sent us back. Did you think you were going to leave Mike there or something? Leave me alone in the storm to die of Korsakoff's? Be rid of us both?"

Jeffrey tapped the table. "He told you that? Hilarious." He broke out in an unflattering cackle. "Mike is so full of shit. Why the hell did you tell him about your crazy shit, Ronnie? Of course he said he did too. No better way to get close to you than fake your crazy-ass time traveling."

The honest Jeffrey was gone, and in its place returned the arrogant, snarky one. Ronnie shook her head slowly. "Not so funny, because I never told him squat about it. He shared a dream he had last night that completely mirrored the place and time you sent me to."

The smile widened, threatening the split in his lip. "During Frances? He probably got a hold of the notebook you write all this crap down in. Jeez, you are so naïve, Ronnie." He picked the coffee up and slurped it loudly.

"Frances? No, we went back here in Puerto Rico. Just last night." It had seemed like a lifetime ago.

Jeffrey paused mid-sip, covering his expression with the mug. When he lowered it, his face had shifted to something else. He looked spooked. His mouth was turned down, face flushed, and his eyes were wide. Finally, a visceral reaction. Then he sputtered, "You...but... What the fuck are you saying?" There it was—the anger bursting forth. But honest anger, not feigned.

Ronnie watched all of the emotions cross his face. This was news to him! "Don't act like you weren't behind it this time. I mean, God knows you tried your best to pretend I'm crazy. You've even gone so far as to convince my mom of my sanity. But there is no way you can tell me you aren't the central piece to this puzzle."

"Last night? Where? In the convenience store? He is lying to you, Ronnie."

Ronnie's smile faded. "No, Jeffrey, at the National Suites. I guess it was the night before?"

Jeffrey squinted. "So, you and Mike time traveled at the hotel? You have both lost your damn minds!"

"Jeffrey, seriously, you're gonna need to find a new insult. Mike told me things only he could have known if he were back with me. I have never been more certain about anything in my entire life. YOU are the one who is lying. How long have you been in Puerto Rico? A few days, just long enough until everything went to shit, then you swoop in and save us?"

Jeffrey's face was beet red, and he stood up, turned on his heel, and stormed into the bedroom. Ronnie followed behind him, shocked. He was supposed to admit it, or lie his face off more, not walk away from her. He sat at the desk and opened his laptop. Was he reeling from what she'd told him? He was!

Jeffrey turned to her. "He's really good at reading your mind then, and you're both batshit crazy." The fire wasn't behind his words anymore.

Ronnie pressed further. "Jeffrey, I asked you a question. How long have you been in Puerto Rico? After all you've put me through, I deserve an answer."

Jeffrey glared, shaking his head. "I had nothing to do with this, Ronnie. Nothing." She could feel the panic in his words. Jeffrey was not lying. He grabbed the mouse, clicking frantically.

"Nothing to do with this? You are such a liar. You have *everything* to do with this, Jeffrey." He was not supposed to brush her off so easily. How could he be messing around with the computer when she was trying to get answers? The pit of her stomach dropped to the floor. Something was not right. She studied his profile and tried to understand what had shifted with him.

Chapter 70

Lost

Mike slowly became aware of a shaking, deep from within. Another seizure? No, he assessed his body, realizing it was not caused by his own movement. The shaking stopped and it was deadly quiet, but it didn't last. A loud clicking made him jump, and his heartbeat sped up, causing the injury in his head to throb. The blessed relief of being unconscious was out of his grasp, and he longed for it to return.

The noise built into a full on *whomp, whomp*. Followed by a silence. *Whomp, whomp*. Repeating endlessly. Terror seized his thoughts. Was he back in time stuck in some machine? His eyes popped open, and he regretted it, but the sights confirmed he was in fact stuck inside a machine.

Full on panic drove his pulse to new heights, and an uncontrolled, unplanned yell escaped. "Ahhhhh, help, help. Get me out of here!" Mike tried to push his way out of the shiny white metal above him, but he was strapped down, only able to move his hands. "Goddamn it, someone help me!" Mike yelled again.

Was he in the future where the machines had taken over the world? It struck him suddenly he was no longer handcuffed but strapped down now.

A disembodied electronic voice echoed in his ears, making him blink in surprise. "*Señor*, please. Remain still. I will have to re-shoot that entire segment."

"Oh God, you're there! Help me, I'm stuck!" Mike yelled again, relieved someone else was nearby. Panic, and the interminable headache, thrust out any cohesive thoughts.

"Calm down. You are not stuck. You are in an MRI machine. We are trying to scan your brain. Please hold *still*."

Mike's eyes widened, then he laughed. "So, I'm okay?" *What a dope!* That's what happened when you unexpectedly went back in time—you no longer trusted the world as you'd known it.

"I don't know if you're okay or not. Do you need me to give you a break, or can you stay put for another fifteen minutes?"

"I'm good. Keep going," Mike answered, willing his foot to stop shaking. He needed somewhere for the adrenalin to go. He closed his eyes and took a deep breath, focusing on the pain in his head. It was hard to remember anything. Where was he?

Florida? Rochester? *Thud, dump,* responded the pulse beating in his head.

Then it hit him. Why the hell was he getting an MRI? He tried to remember something, anything. Oh, Puerto Rico, right. Thoughts tumbled about but no memory appeared around how he'd ended up here. It was alarming to be so out of it.

The *whomp, whomp* continued and it began to sound like *fuck you, fuck you.* Well, fuck you, too. Surely he wasn't hurt that bad. Right? Then it stopped. The absence of the noise was deafening.

A queasiness made his stomach lurch, just like he'd felt when he was in the bathroom tending to Ronnie. But it was just the table moving him out of the machine. He risked opening his eyes again, hoping his head wouldn't explode. As he emerged from the tunnel, the first thing he saw were the horrible foam ceiling tiles and white metal supports of a public building. Then his eyes focused on a man on his right side who smiled down at him.

"Señor, how are you feeling?" He had a thick Puerto Rican accent and a major five o'clock shadow.

"Lost," Mike managed.

Movement on his left caught his attention, and Sarge's smiling face appeared. Mike's eyebrows nearly touched. "Booooo! I want someone else here, not you. Isn't there a pretty blonde somewhere?"

Sarge shook his head. "I am the only pretty blond you're going to get today."

"Rat bastards," Mike said, but a wave of nausea was building. Sarge and the technician helped move Mike to a gurney by lifting the sheet he was on, adding another symptom to the mix—dizziness. An oxygen mask appeared out of nowhere and the tech strapped it to his face. A transport person pushed Mike out double doors. The motion was buoying his nausea.

Sarge was alone. Where were the other men?

"Hey, shitbag," Mike called out. "Why are you here?"

Sarge recognized his new nickname and leaned over the gurney. "Semper fi." He made eye contact briefly, then looked away. *Semper fi* was the Marine Corps motto, literally translated as *always faithful.* It represented a brotherhood that lasted for life.

Mike responded weakly, "Ooh-rah," and looked away. His mouth had gotten him in this situation, but at least it had paid off enough for the good sergeant to get him some help. *Aaaaand* the ole memory wasn't totally reset. Mike remembered him well enough, and a few elements of the past few hours returned in a flood, like the recap at the beginning of a TV show.

The gurney stopped and Mike's eyes flew open. He was going to be sick. They were wheeling him onto an elevator. The new motion, upwards, was the final straw. There was no stopping it. In a violent upheaval, everything in his stomach lurched out of his body. Sarge tried to move out of the way, but there was nowhere for him to go in the cramped quarters of the elevator.

Mike wiped his mouth and lay back down. "Gooooaaaaaalllllll!"

Sarge held his hands up. "Jesus, man. Did you have to do that?"

"Had no choice. Just glad my aim was true." Mike closed his eyes and felt a little better. He had used his only weapon to his best advantage. The elevator dinged, the door opened, and the motion continued until it abruptly stopped. Mike craned his neck around to see why. The transport guy picked up a phone and spoke in Spanish, probably telling some poor custodian to clean up the mess. *Sorry, Mr. Custodian.*

Mike kept his eyes shut, silently begging for them to stop as they rolled down the hallway. He took deep breaths, hoping to avoid another spew. A horrible odor assaulted his nostrils and that was the last straw. Mike got sick again, waking up an older man lying in a bed nearby.

Mike groaned, "Get me out of this room!" He wiped his mouth on the hospital gown. "Change that man's diaper, for God's sake. Can't you put me somewhere not so funky-smelling?"

The transportation guy was looking exceedingly weary, and so was Sarge. He pushed the gurney out into the hallway and Mike had the luxury of getting an eyeful of the Sarge's black outfit painted nicely with his last meal.

Sarge addressed the transport clerk. "Can you get him a private room? I'm sure he has great insurance."

Finally, he was wheeled into a small private room with a TV, a small chair, and a private bathroom, confirmed by one quick peek.

A nurse, who must have followed them into the room, held his chart. She had a pretty face, bright red lips, and a plump frame. "Mr. Walsh, we will get you taken care of. I am Hortênsia." She eyed Sarge. "Well, what have you gotten yourself into? Phillippe here will get you some fresh clothes." An orderly was standing behind her and led Sarge out of the room. The nurse stepped closer and touched Mike's arm. "Are you still nauseous?"

"I'm good for now," Mike answered.

"Just let me know. I can give you something for that in your IV, Mr. Walsh."

"Call me Mike."

Hortênsia nodded, then deftly removed the soiled hospital gown, efficiently cleaning him up, protecting his modesty with a towel. In some magic trick, she changed the bedsheet with him still in it. The nurse checked his IV and put a blood pressure cuff on his arm.

Mike just wanted to sleep. "When will they have the results back on the MRI?"

"It usually takes an hour or so for the doctor to review it."

"Do you think I'll need surgery?"

"Well, you seem pretty coherent. But that doesn't always mean you're out of danger." She turned his head so she could get a good look at the injury to his temple. "If you have a subdural hematoma, they likely will have to operate and relieve the pressure on your brain. If you don't need surgery, you'll be fine. You might just be a little dumber than you already are." Hortênsia winked.

"Damn, that's not good." A subdural hematoma was a bleed inside the brain that built up pressure, and if not relieved, it could cause permanent brain damage or death. One of his classmates in high school had whacked his head pretty badly in a car accident. What had his name been? Rob something with a K. He and his buddies hadn't even had time to see him in the hospital before they'd whisked him away for surgery.

"Mike, I'm going to clean off that wound. It's pretty nasty. You may have a fracture." She walked to the foot of his bed and picked up his chart. "Why the hell didn't they do an x-ray down there in emergency? I swear they just don't think things through."

"Are the phones working?" Mike asked. If he were going to be gorked, he'd at least want someone to know where he was.

"Yes, go ahead." She moved the phone to the rolling table next to his bed and handed him the receiver.

"How do I dial the US?"

She shook her head. "Only local calls, sir."

Mike looked at the phone and realized the hospital name. He pressed zero and waited for the operator to answer. "Carlos Munoz, please."

Hortênsia's eyes widened as she added a fresh bag to his IV.

Mike waited as the phone rang. A woman spoke rapid Spanish, and "Carlos Munoz" were the only words he understood.

"Yes, hi. May I speak to Mr. Munoz?"

The woman switched to English. "Sir, may I ask who is calling?"

"Mike Walsh. It's an emergency."

"Please hold."

Mike mentally crossed his fingers.

A deep voice came on the line. "Carlos here. Mike, how are you?"

"Been better, Carlos. Look, I'm in a bit of a difficult situation."

"You sound weak. Where are you?"

Mike was relieved he'd taken his call. The last time they'd spoken, Mike had been cussing him out over the situation with Ronnie. "I'm in one of your hospitals." He covered the receiver. "Where am I?"

The nurse held up a pamphlet that was on Mike's table. Mike read the words with terrible Spanish pronunciation.

"Not far from me. I hope you're okay." Carlos sounded worried.

"I've got a head injury. I'm not sure how I got here, but..."

Carlos interrupted him. "Oh no, how is Ronnie?"

"Ronnie, oh God." He'd forgotten so much. "I don't know where she is."

"Mike, sit tight. I'm coming to you. Let me speak to the nurse."

Mike handed the receiver to Hortênsia, and her smile widened. She turned away from him and spoke in rapid bursts of Spanish. After a minute, she hung up and was clearly blushing. "How do you know Mr. Munoz?"

"I work for him, I think." But Mike knew that wasn't quite right.

"So do I," she said, fanning herself.

Mike smiled. "He's your type, eh?"

"Oh God yes, half the women here are in love with him. Charisma on steroids." She smiled and shook her head.

"He'll be here soon." Mike was relieved. Maybe he could at least get Sarge off his back.

"What, seriously?" A glimpse of panic flashed in her eyes.

Another nurse walked in, and Hortênsia handed the chart to her. "Munoz will be here today. Mr. Walsh works with him."

The new nurse's face lit up. "No way."

Hortênsia smiled at Mike and pointed her thumb at her. "See? *In love.*"

Mike shook his head, but it only made it pound worse.

Hortênsia held out her personal cell phone. "Hun, Señor Munoz told me to let you use my cell phone. Is there anyone you'd like to call?"

"He did, really? Thank you so much."

"It's against hospital policy, but if Señor Munoz says to do it, you do it." Hortênsia raised her eyebrows and laughed with the other nurse.

"I have to call the US. Is that doable?"

She smiled. "Yes, it's a US phone. My brother is in New York."

Mike took her phone and tried to remember Billy's number. He punched in the familiar pattern and hoped he wasn't being stupid. It rang several times.

"Come on, Billy. Pick up."

The women spoke to each other in Spanish and arranged his bedding and the room to their highest standards, probably prepping for Munoz's immanent arrival.

Sarge entered the room with a set of scrubs wadded up in his hands. He spoke to the nurses, then disappeared into the small bathroom, adjacent to his bed, to change. The bathroom must have had a shower because the sound of running water emanated forth. Sergeant Barf-Pants must be cleaning himself up.

"Hello?" Billy sounded like he had been asleep.

"Dude, you'll never guess where I am," Mike said, faking exuberance he did not feel.

"Mike, you fucking douchebag. Where are you?" Billy sounded more awake now.

Mike repeated the hospital's name, grateful it had stuck in his short-term memory this time. "I've got to make this quick. Write this number down." He gave Billy his mom's number. "Call my mom and let her know I'm okay, but I may need surgery."

"What? Surgery?" Billy's voice rose, giving away the worry.

"Don't know yet. Hopefully not brain surgery." Mike glanced at Hortênsia, who made the sign of the cross and looked at the ceiling.

Billy let out his booming laugh, and Mike had to pull the phone away from his ear. It caused too much pain.

"Billy, I'm serious."

"Wait, brain surgery? Dude, no! What happened?"

"Car accident during the storm. I think." Mike wasn't completely sure.

"Holy shit! You okay, man? Need me to come out there?"

"I'm not sure how bad it is. I may have a subdural hematoma. If I do, they're going to have to cut my melon open."

"What the hell, man?" Billy sounded like he was still unsure if Mike was messing with him.

"They're waiting for my MRI results."

"Damn, Mike. You're not going to fucking die on me, are you?" Worry laced Billy's words now.

"I'll stay strong just for you, Billy." Mike tried to make it sound like a joke, but it came out much more desperate than he'd intended.

"Mike, I'm coming to get you," Billy insisted.

Mike shook his head and regretted it. "The island is a mess. I'm sure the airports are closed. Look, as soon as I hear something, I'll have someone call you. I don't know if I'll be able to talk to you directly." He paused, then added, "Carlos Munoz runs the hospital. He's why we came here." He struggled now—his words were choppy. "He may call you, or someone else might."

"Wait, how am I going to get ahold of you again?" Billy sounded panicked.

"My hospital room, I guess." He gave Billy the hospital information.

Hortênsia stepped closer. "Tell him to call this number." She called out her cell phone number and Mike repeated it.

Billy's voice was higher, choked off. "I love ya, man. Just be okay. Okay?"

Mike smiled at his big, goofy friend. "Love you too, man."

Chapter 71

Breaker One-Nine

"Jeffrey, I'm trying to talk to you." Ronnie shoved Jeffrey's shoulder so he would face her. But he resisted, and he continued agitatedly typing, banging out his commands on the keyboard.

Ronnie contemplated slamming the computer shut to get his attention. Before she did, the screen came to life and a blinking light flashed on a map of the world.

Jeffrey stood, blocking her view. "Go finish your breakfast. This is urgent." He pushed her out of the room. "Eat your breakfast. Let me do this, Ronnie. It's important."

"What the hell!" As soon as he let her go, she turned around, ready to continue her tirade. The bedroom door slammed in her face. Then he locked it.

Ronnie pounded on the door. "What the hell are you doing? We are talking here." She paused and put her ear to the door. "What are you tracking?"

He still did not answer.

Ronnie pounded on the door. "Jeffrey!"

Then it struck her. There was nothing keeping her here. She could just walk out the door! Ronnie gulped the now cold coffee and grabbed a piece of toast, jamming it between her teeth. On the kitchen counter near the door was his wallet. He must have left it after tipping the room service guy. Rifling through the wallet, she grabbed a wad of cash, slipped it in the chest pocket of the shirt, and opened the door and silently closed it behind her.

Ronnie sprinted to the stairwell, glancing behind her, sure he was giving chase. The hallway was empty. She flung the stairwell door open and ran down the flight of stairs. Ronnie ran from the stairwell to the lobby, not sure what her next steps would be, but she knew for certain that Jeffrey Brennan would not be part of them. He might try to commit her, or worse. God knew she looked the part. Ronnie ran to the ladies' room and pulled out the walkie-talkie, hoping it was designed to carry a distance. Since she'd traveled by helicopter and fallen asleep during the flight, she had no idea if she was a few miles away from wherever Mike was, or a hundred. Ronnie pressed the call button, forgetting all protocol. "Mike, if you can hear this, please answer me!"

The walkie-talkie crackled in response.

"Mike, this is Ronnie. Can you hear me?" She squeezed her eyes shut, praying frantically that he would answer. She tried for several minutes until finally she got a response.

"Hey," a male voice answered.

"Mike, is that you?"

"Yes, I can't believe you still have your walkie-talkie!" His voice was weak. It didn't sound like the man she'd last seen.

"Where are you? I've gotten away from the asshole, what do you call him, pencil neck?"

Mike chuckled. "Yeah, I'm at the hospital. Write down this address."

"You are? Oh God, that is a relief." She had nothing to write with but memorized the name and address of the place. "Mike, I have no way to get there."

"I have an idea but you're not gonna like it, Ronnie. Call Carlos Munoz and have his driver come get you."

"Wait, what? *Carlos?* God, no, Mike!"

"Ronnie, I just spoke to him. He wants to help us."

The device crackled and Ronnie turned down the sound. "Crap, I don't want to see him. Especially not like this." Ronnie glanced down at her ridiculous outfit. She'd been mocked enough for one day.

"Yeah, I don't know what other choices you have. I'm going to need your support."

"Okay. Did they take you to jail, or were you able to talk them out of it?"

"Yeah, well something happened. They, um..."

There was a silence for a second or two and she immediately panicked. Was he gone? The walkie-talkie crackled again.

"Mike, tell me."

"They pistol-whipped me. Right on my already injured melon."

Ronnie's face felt hot. "Are you serious?"

The bathroom door opened, and Ronnie smiled at the lady who entered. She lowered the volume again as she left the bathroom, looking around for Jeffrey. She turned down a corridor towards the hotel offices.

"Mike, sorry. I need to find a phone before Jeffrey finds me. Are you okay?" At the end of the hall, she found a door labeled *Conference Room A*. She tried the handle and was surprised it opened. A large window added light to the space, allowing her to see a door in the back of the room. Hopefully that connected to the hotel offices and she could find a phone.

"Yeah, I think so. They might have to do surgery."

"Oh no, Mike. Brain surgery?"

"To relieve the pressure. It's more like skull surgery. Men with scars are much more desirable, aren't they?"

She knew he was trying to be funny, but it broke her heart. "Mike, I don't care about that. Just hang on, I'll be there as soon as I can."

"Ronnie, be careful out there. Whatever you do, don't let Jeffrey follow you."

"I won't." She hoped that wasn't a lie.

"I'll feel much better when you're here. Wake me if I'm asleep." Mike's voice cracked.

How could she ask for Carlos's help after his atrocious behavior? It would just spark his aggressive advances. Damn it, wasn't there someone else they could call?

Ronnie opened the door to find a darkened kitchen. She felt her way along a long metal prep area. A door at the back let in a smidgen of light from a small square window. Ronnie peeked through it and saw a phone. Bingo! She tried the door, but it was locked. A man walked past on the other side and Ronnie knocked to catch his attention. He turned and opened the door.

The man spoke authoritatively in Spanish, probably admonishing her for poking around where she wasn't meant to be.

Ronnie held up her hands. "This is gonna sound really weird, but I have an abusive ex-boyfriend who will storm down here any second now. Can I use your phone and stay out of sight back here?"

"*Señorita*, please forgive my harsh words." His dark eyes showed compassion. "You will be safe here. I'm not going to let anyone near you." Without hesitation, he whisked her through the door and led her between several cubicles to an office. He closed the door behind them, eyes wide.

"Thank you so much." Ronnie crossed her arms, realizing she had no bra on, and she probably looked a bit ridiculous in Jeffrey's clothes.

He motioned for her to sit at the desk. "Feel free to use the phone. You can stay here as long as you need to. If he asks about you, I'll throw him off the trail."

"I'm so grateful." She'd need a few minutes to gather courage for the phone call.

The man did a slight curtsy and nodded. "I'm Luis. I was at the desk when you came in earlier."

"Oh yes, I remember you. I'm Ronnie. Thank you for helping me."

"Don't worry about it. It's my pleasure." He waved and shut the door behind him.

Ronnie prepared herself for dealing with Carlos. Maybe she'd just be able to talk to his secretary. At least Mike had already spoken to him. She'd not have to tell him how desperate she was.

Chapter 72

Where in the World is TOTO?

Jeffrey closed the door and locked it. How the *hell* had Ronnie and Mike traveled back in time? He'd scarcely had enough power to send one person back during Charley, a strong storm. How could two people travel during such a small storm? It was barely a hurricane. Either she was lying—and his gut debunked that theory—or she'd actually gone back in time. Mike must have convinced her he'd gone back, too. Bastard.

He impatiently tapped his thigh, waiting for the satellite connection to link to his tracking app. Ronnie had to be within ten feet from the time travel machine for it to connect and send her. That was physically impossible. TOTO was in a storage unit in Florida safely tucked away. If the damn connection would fucking link, TOTO's location could be confirmed. After the last fiasco during Hurricane Frances, where he'd lost the power capture disk off the roof of the hospital, he'd added a tracking chip to each of the disks. If TOTO was still in Florida, there was no way Ronnie went back. No way unless…

Ronnie was barking something outside of his door. He tuned her out. If the Feds had somehow gotten into the storage unit, they *could* have his equipment in an FBI lab somewhere near Orlando, or possibly along the East Coast. Could they have accidentally amplified the signal to reach Ronnie? The science didn't support that. It would be impossible to activate the chip he'd implanted between her shoulders from any lab in the States, or even Puerto Rico. TOTO had to be immediately next to the subject, and his launch laptop would have to submit the code to start the sequence.

Pure unadulterated fear choked off his breathing. Everything would be crumbling down around him if the FBI had TOTO. He had lied his face off to protect his experiments. Last he checked, lying to the FBI was a crime, and not having approval for human experimentation would be another quiver in their arrow against him. He steered his mind away from that rabbit hole. Hopefully there was another explanation for Ronnie's claims. Maybe the lesion on her brain was causing hallucinations?

The rabbit poked its head up again and he chased that line of thought, somewhat against his will. The FBI would steal the technology, make a deal to lessen his sentence if he'd help them develop it for clandestine purposes. He'd never get the credit he deserved. The military would keep it a secret and use it against America's enemies. Maybe even bastardize it into a powerful weapon that would change the world. His precious work all for naught. Dr. Andrews's vision destroyed in the blink of an eye.

A message on his screen pulled him out of his panicked thoughts. *Targets found.* Jeffrey zoomed in on the three small dots blinking on the screen. He sat back in shock. "What the *absolute fuck?*"

A new theory clicked into place as he zoomed in, finding the disks' exact location. Fury overwhelmed every thought, but he forced his mind to settle, to focus on the task at hand. Finally, the street address was clear. He scribbled it on a scrap of paper and examined the map more closely. Jeffrey lifted the hotel phone and dialed the number. He waited impatiently for someone to pick up, and finally they did.

After a brief conversation, he slammed the phone down. "Shit, shit, shit." He grabbed the nearest item and threw it across the room. The TV remote shattered against the wall and landed on the carpet in several pieces. If Ronnie *had* gone back in time, the machine would have emitted a pulse and the FBI would know the exact location. Ronnie had been at the National Suites that was currently in disarray, but they'd still have records of her reservation there. Another piece of information connecting her to the pulse, bringing them closer to his doorstep. Now that she suspected he was responsible for her time traveling, she would undoubtedly tell the FBI. Ronnie was a liability now. Everything he'd worked for was in jeopardy.

Jeffrey packed up his laptop and plug and glanced around the room, sorting through his next steps. Then flung the door open, expecting to find Ronnie fuming mad. "Ronnie, where are you? RONNIE!" The seething anger returned. His wallet lay open on the counter near the door. "Shit!" She'd cleaned out his cash but left his credit cards.

Jeffrey grabbed the car keys and stormed out of the room. Where the hell would she go in the middle of the storm with no car, no ID, and only the cash from his wallet?

He rushed down the stairs to the lobby and approached the front desk. "Hey, have you seen a blonde down here, long legs, wet hair?"

The clerk eyed Jeffrey. "No, *señor.*"

"Are you sure? Think!" Jeffrey asked, losing patience and glancing at his name tag, and added for good measure, "Luis."

The clerk smiled. "Hard to miss long-legged blondes. I am sure."

Jeffrey slammed his hand on the counter. "She had to come through here about ten minutes ago. Where is she?"

The man jumped and stepped away from the counter. "Sir, please. This is not your office. You can't just yell at me and slam the counter until I obey."

Jeffrey calmed his tone. "I'm sorry. I just need to know where she went. Please, it's really important."

"I didn't have the pleasure of her company," the clerk said curtly, closing the conversation.

Jeffrey looked around the lobby, debating his next steps. First, he needed to retrieve TOTO, then he could track Ronnie and find out where she was. She would be easy to recapture. She was alone and Mike was in custody. If he couldn't retrieve TOTO, everything would be lost. Choice made, he stepped out into the rain that soaked him to the skin in the short time it took to find the car.

The wipers could hardly keep up with the deluge dropping from the sky. The roads were slick and littered with leaves, branches, and God knew what else. Luckily, he didn't have far to go. He parked the car and entered the hotel. A friendly Puerto Rican woman was at the front desk. Jeffrey approached her. "I'm here to drop off something for one of your guests. Can you tell me what room number she is in?"

The woman shook her head. "*Señor*, my computer is down. But I do have a list of who is here. If you give me a minute to look it up, I can call the room and inquire."

"I can wait, thank you."

The clerk flipped through some handwritten papers, then lifted the receiver and called. "*Señorita*, there is a gentleman here. *Sí*." She hung up and looked at him. "Room 407. You will need to use the stairs. I apologize, the elevators are not working due to the storm."

Jeffrey thanked the clerk and climbed the four flights, gathering his thoughts as he did.

He knocked on room 407 and waited. The door opened and a curvy brunette answered. "I'll be ready in a minute..." She left the door open and walked into the candlelit room, retrieving something from the bed.

Jeffrey walked into the room and shut the door, locking it behind him.

Hannah Volpe stared in surprise. "Oh my God. Jeffrey, how did you find me?"

Chapter 73

Charisma on Steroids

After a few minutes of calming her nerves, Ronnie picked up the phone and dialed zero. A woman answered, and she asked to be connected to the hospital. The phone rang and Ronnie panicked. Did she want to talk to friggin' Carlos Munoz? The last she'd time seen him, he'd offered a key to his apartment for a rendezvous. Damn it, he was the last person she wanted to see...other than Jeffrey.

Before she could hang up, a woman answered the phone, speaking rapidly in Spanish. She mustered up the courage. "Carlos Munoz, please."

"May I ask who is calling?" the woman asked in perfect English.

"It's Ronnie Andrews."

The phone shuffled and she heard voices in the background. Then a man's voice came on the line. "Ronnie, are you okay?" It was Carlos and he sounded flustered.

"Yes, but I need to get out of here. Mike said you could help me. I'm trying to get to the hospital."

"Yes, yes. I spoke with him. Where are you? I will send my driver."

Ronnie gave him the name of the hotel. "Thank you, Carlos."

"Anything for you and Mike. Ronnie, are you hurt?"

"No, just a little banged up."

His voice lowered and he almost whispered, "Oh, such a shame, your beautiful self should never be marred."

Ronnie shifted the phone to her other ear, cringing at his words. "Thank you, Carlos. How long before your driver can come and get me?"

Carlos must have covered the phone because all Ronnie could hear were muffled voices. "Fifteen minutes at the soonest. The storm, you know, is making it difficult to get around the island. You are not far."

"Oh, thank goodness. I just need to be with Mike."

"Ronnie, are you in danger? I will come myself if you need me."

"No, no. I'm in a safe place right now."

"Okay, stay there. Don't take any risks. How will my driver find you?"

"Just ask at the front desk. The clerk Luis knows I'm here."

"Perfect."

Ronnie didn't want to talk to him any more than necessary but needed to know one more thing. "How did Mike sound when you talked to him?"

"Mike?" Carlos sounded surprised at the question. "He was...what is the English word? Oh, um...shattered."

"Shattered?" That was an alarming choice of words.

"Yes, he was broken and weak." Carlos was using words to diminish Mike. Was this his machismo version of reality? What was the truth though?

Ronnie felt like crying. "That is not comforting."

"No, I suppose not. He sounded like he was afraid, Ronnie. I think he's not in great shape. I talked to the nurse. He has a serious head injury, and they're waiting for the MRI results. It could go one of two ways. One, he heals and is fine. Or..." He paused dramatically. "He could suffer a major brain injury or stroke from the bleeding in his temple."

Ronnie gasped. "Oh no. Oh no." Tears rolled down her face and she looked around for a Kleenex box. Not finding one, she used Jeffrey's shirt.

"I will visit him soon to see how I can help. Mike is a good friend. I will offer the best of care to help him recover."

"I'm so grateful, Carlos. Thank you for helping us both."

"Sure, sure. It is nothing. But just know my offer still stands."

Ronnie covered her mouth, fighting an anxious feeling that crept up her spine. "Carlos, that is not an offer I will accept. I do appreciate your interest, and I mean no disrespect by refusing you. I only have to say that it makes me really uncomfortable. Please understand."

"I do understand. I do not want to interfere with our working relationship, or new friendship. I just want to be clear, so you may feel free to take me up on my offer, or as you wish, refuse it. Either way, I am happy to help you...and Mike, and be as comforting as possible."

"Good, as long as we understand each other. I want to keep things as they are...just friends." She hoped she was navigating the waters here carefully. From what Frank had said, Carlos's actions were very Latin. It would be best to protect his pride.

"I completely understand. You cannot blame me for making a move on you. You are a delightful woman...quite irresistible. But if you are not feeling it too, I will *lay low*. Is that how you Americans say it?"

She was relieved he'd given her a chance to address his behavior. "Yes, lay low is a perfect description of what I need right now."

"I aim to please, Ronnie." She could hear the smile in his voice. "Please, accept my sincerest apologies for my boorish behavior in the stairwell. I must have misread your cues. It was an honest mistake."

Ronnie exhaled. It had not been honest or a mistake, but at least he was apologizing. "Yes, Carlos, from your perspective, it is. From mine it was frightening."

Carlos hesitated, then cleared his throat. "Frightening? I never intended to frighten you. I merely wanted to convey my feelings towards you."

"Well, we are past that now, aren't we? I know what you're offering but I cannot accept. Carlos, you are, I'm sure, everything a woman could want in a man. My life is just very complicated right now. I'm glad you understand."

"I do. And I'm here for you in any way you may need me, or my apartment, or driver. No strings attached. I honestly want to help a friend in need. No matter how seductive she is."

Ronnie smiled, appreciating his honesty and most especially the promise of no strings attached. "I don't think you'd find me seductive right now. I'm in men's clothes, looking pretty pitiful."

"Men's clothes? A suit?"

Ronnie laughed. "No. Gym shorts and a dress shirt. I borrowed it. The rest of my clothes were lost in the accident."

"*Accident?* Mike didn't say what happened."

"Yeah, we were caught in a mudslide on the way to the hospital and it pushed us into the river. Mike bashed his head." And Jeffrey's men may have roughed him up, but she didn't want to share that part.

"How unfortunate. So, you need to be seen as well. I will arrange a doctor to attend to your injuries."

"Oh no, I'm fine, Carlos. Honestly, I just need some rest."

"I insist. We will make sure there is nothing wrong with that beautiful body and mind of yours."

"Okay."

"Bye for now, Ronnie. I will see you soon. Please do let me know if there is anything...*anything* I can do for you."

"So grateful for your help, Carlos." Ronnie hung up and stepped out of the office to tell the clerk a driver was coming for her. A familiar voice was barking something angrily nearby. It was Jeffrey! Ronnie listened to the hotel clerk lie his butt off to protect her. Thank goodness for him!

When Jeffrey left, she called out to him, "Pssssssst!"

The clerk left the desk and joined her in the office. "Oh, hey, was that him?"

"Yeah, thank you for covering for me."

"*Girl*, he is yummy. You didn't tell me he was so..." He paused and mocked grabbing his shoulders. "Ummm."

"He looks good on the outside, but the inside is nothing but crap."

The man wrinkled up his nose and shook his head. "Nope, not attractive anymore!"

"Luis, someone is coming to pick me up and take me to the hospital. Can I stay back here until he arrives?"

"Yes, you can. Just make yourself comfortable." He smiled and waved, then shut the door and returned to the front desk.

Ronnie paced the room. Tears flowed down her face against her will. Carlos had been very clear. Mike was in trouble, and it could go downhill fast. She had to get to the hospital while he was still conscious. Would he be okay? Damn, this was not how it was supposed to go.

Mike was taking on the same role as Mathias, Morris, and Max. His involvement had cost him dearly. Would this end the same way as it had for those men? Would Mike survive his injuries?

"Damn it, Jeffrey, why did you have to take Mike away from me? Why did your men have to hurt him?" Ronnie laid her head down on her folded arms and closed her eyes. She focused with all of her remaining energy absorbing the new reality with Mike at the center of her prayers. *Please make him be okay!* She replayed all they had shared over the past twenty-four hours. Mike had to be there to help her sort through everything they'd been through together. *Please, God, don't take him from me. I finally found him.*

After about an hour, Luis opened the door. "Your driver is here. Oh, *pequeña querida.*" He came over and hugged her.

Ronnie hugged him.

"Be right back." He stepped out of the room and returned with a box of Kleenex. She blew her nose and wiped her eyes. "Thank you so much for your help."

"Anytime. You take care of yourself, okay?"

Ronnie nodded.

"Wait." Luis arranged her hair, moving a piece to the side. "There. Much better. Come this way." He held the door open for her and she followed him out to the counter.

A man dressed in a black suit and tie stepped forward. "Ronnie Andrews?"

"Yes, I'm Ronnie. Who sent you?"

The man looked her up and down, but politely didn't comment on her strange appearance. "Mr. Munoz asked me to bring you to the hospital." He smiled. "Where is your luggage?"

"In a river." Ronnie waved to the clerk and walked to the car waiting under the portico.

"In a river?" the driver asked as he opened the passenger door.

"Long story." Ronnie sat down and he shut the door.

The driver started the car. "It should only be a short drive. Carlos sent some food for you. He wasn't sure if you'd had a chance to eat."

Ronnie's face lit up as he handed her a paper bag. She opened it, and the smell of fresh cinnamon made her stomach growl. She pulled out a spiral-shaped roll covered in powdered sugar and a bottle of water. "So nice, thank you."

"Troubles are always helped by a full stomach."

Ronnie smiled, then wiped the sugar off her face as the driver moved out into the deluge of water pouring out of the sky. Worries crowded in and she was glad for the quiet space the driver offered as they drove.

∞

When they arrived at the hospital, the driver asked her to wait in the lobby while he parked the car. Ronnie walked on wobbly legs through the emergency room door. The antiseptic air hit her hard, bringing back memories of sad times in the hospital, when her grandmother was dying, and when her mother had surgery. The waiting room was full of wet, miserable-looking people. Finally, the driver appeared, and he took her down a hallway, unlocking a door marked private. Ronnie calmed her nerves, anxious to see Mike, but also afraid of what shape he might be in.

The driver took her up a service elevator, where they came through another door and onto a patient floor. He waved to the nurses at the desk, and one handed him a slip of paper. He glanced at it and stopped outside a room. "Mr. Walsh is in this room. Please let the nurses know if you should need anything."

Ronnie smiled. "Thank you so much for your help."

"Anytime."

Ronnie steeled herself for what she may find and opened the door.

There was no bed in the room. Had something happened to Mike? She burst through the doors to the nursing station. "Where is he? Where is Mike Walsh?"

The nurse smiled. "Oh, he's not there?" She spoke in Spanish to another nurse. "He is in a procedure. It shouldn't be more than an hour."

"A procedure? What are they doing to him? What happened?" Ronnie's heart was in her throat.

"Ma'am. As you're not his next of kin, we cannot give you that information. Mr. Munoz has allowed you to be in his room, so be satisfied with that. Everyone else must wait in the family room during procedures."

"Can you just tell me if he is okay? Please?"

The nurse took pity on her and stepped out from behind the counter. "Here, let me get you settled."

Ronnie bit her lips and fought back tears. She wasn't going out on a limb to tell her he was going to be okay. Did that mean he had worsened? Mike had to be okay.

Chapter 74

Seduction

Hannah Volpe stepped back in astonishment. Adrenalin coursed through her veins. That's just the effect Jeffrey had on her. "Well, well, what brings you to my door on a dark and stormy evening?" She smiled, taking in all that was Jeffrey Brennan. His hair, curlier than usual, was wet and dark. His eyes were intense, and in her mind, she was sure it was because he shared her passion.

"I hear you've been having a little fun here on the island." Jeffrey's voice had an edge she'd not heard before, adding to the beating of her heart.

A twang of panic forced an uncomfortable laugh. "I'm so happy to see you. I didn't expect you so soon. And may I say, you're looking as handsome as ever."

Jeffrey's smile slid to a grimace. Did he have a split lip? "Dr. Vasu would be impressed with your work. Does he know about your successful storm seeding?"

Hannah laughed over-exuberantly and ran her finger down his arm. "Yes, of course he does. You scared me. I thought you were my driver. I had no idea you were on the island. Can you believe this stinker of a storm?"

Jeffrey sneered. "Cut the crap, Hannah. Did you start this storm knowing Ronnie was here?"

She smiled. Was he mad about *that*? It was the least of the things he should be tweaked off about. "You're damn right I did."

"I mean, you could have gone to any island in the Caribbean."

"Sweetie." Hannah took a step closer then walked around Jeffrey. "I started this in the *Virgin* Islands, but they rejected me."

Jeffrey watched her, his eyes raking her body. "Virgin Islands couldn't handle you? I'm sure that's true." His tone shifted to something scarier. "Tell me something else..." He pulled his eyes from her cleavage. "Did you take something of *mine*?"

Hannah cocked a hip, then tipped her head back and laughed. "Jeffrey, you tossed me under the bus with those FBI geeks. Did you think I'd just let you get away with that?"

Jeffrey's eyebrows lowered and his mouth scrunched up. "Where is my gear, Hannah?"

"All safely in this room. I took great care of it. In fact, I made some improvements you're really going to like."

Jeffrey glanced at the piles of luggage near the door. "I gotta hand it to you, you're a lot smarter than you look."

Hannah scrunched up her nose. "No need to be insulting, baby. I merely wanted to get your attention." She turned and walked away, then sat seductively on the edge of the bed, patting the spot next to her. "Come sit next to me and let's talk."

Jeffrey watched her warily and didn't join her on the bed.

Hannah lowered the zipper on her silk jacket. "I have a lot to offer you." Jeffrey's eyes were exactly where she wanted them. Hannah pushed her breasts together, accentuating the deep groove. "I'm not only flexible, experimental, and slutty, I'm also one smart, bad bitch." Hannah laughed, feeling her power.

Jeffrey stepped closer and helped the zipper down further. "You're at least one of those things. Tell me, how did you manage to send back both Mike and Ronnie?"

Hannah threw her shoulders back, sticking out her chest towards him, revealing creamy white lace against her tan skin. "I sent Mike a shot at the bar laced with your magical pellets. Thank you for leaving such thorough instructions. They were super helpful."

Jeffrey's eyes flashed anger and his mouth tightened. She'd better tread carefully.

"Mike downed it and looked around for the hot babe who sent it. Men are so easy to manipulate, I swear. Ronnie was a bit trickier."

Jeffrey shook his head. "Not all men. Just the dumb ones." He inhaled sharply and let his breath out slowly, as if forcing patience he didn't have. "How did you manage the power elements of that challenge?"

God, what Jeffrey did to her body was ridiculous. Her panties were already wet. "It wasn't hard...oh wait, I take that back." Hannah reached out to grab Jeffrey's cock. He swatted her hand away. "You don't know this about me because you only talk about yourself, but I studied under a genius in the quantum power field."

"*Quantum* power? That doesn't exist."

"It sure as hell does. Just because you don't know about it doesn't mean it isn't being developed." Finally, she had his attention for more than just her sexuality. She debated about dropping to her knees, but she had a lot more to say and that would be difficult to do simultaneously.

Jeffrey stepped away, adjusting his pants. "If you're telling the truth, you succeeded in tackling a problem I've been working on for a few years. Show me how you did it."

Pride welled up. Her original plan was to insulate herself from an FBI probe. Once she realized what she'd stolen from the storage unit, her goal had morphed to inserting herself directly in his secret project to show how useful she could be.

"Do you think you're the only genius at the lab? Are you like most men who assume pretty females are beneath you, couldn't possibly be worth more than the fun bags and good lay you use them for?" She pretended to sneeze out her boss's name, "Dr. Vasu."

"Bless you." Jeffrey looked at her intently. "Show me, Hannah."

Hannah smiled seductively and unzipped her jacket, leaving it completely open, showing off her white silk bra, nipples protruding enticingly from the lace.

Jeffrey's eyes widened and he knelt in front of her. "I didn't mean that, but hello gorgeous!" He reached out with both hands and caressed the material, then covered one protrusion with his mouth, playfully teasing through the material.

Hannah leaned into him, letting her head fall backward, feeling the passion rise in her. "Mmmmm, you were always so good with your mouth."

Jeffrey stood, eyes still glued to her bra, the right side completely see-through now. "Show me the battery pack. Prove your brains despite your beauty."

She stood and grazed his pants, running her hand across his erection as she walked past him to one of the pieces of luggage by the door. "This is the magic I created for you, Jeffrey." Hannah bent over and stuck her butt out a little extra, arching her back, knowing his eyes were engrossed in her every movement. She lifted the small black case and walked to the bed. He helped her lift it and set it down. Hannah unhooked the clasps and nodded. "Do the honors."

Jeffrey sat on the bed and opened the case. His face lit up. "They're so small. Tell me how it works."

Hannah, not wanting to miss an opportunity to get his body and mind going, sat on the bed and laid her hand in his lap. "It is not small, don't ever say that again."

Jeffrey gently removed her hand and gripped it tight. "Tell me how this works, *Hannah*." A harsher edge crept into his voice.

She'd pushed it too far, and heat burned up her cheeks. Hannah reached over and gently removed one of the sixteen black triangular prisms. It was a foot long and three inches thick. She held it up for Jeffrey to inspect. "This beauty is a marvel of underground scientific research. It's a prototype that won't be ready for the world for at least five years."

Jeffrey gently took it out of her hands and turned it over. "Incredible. It's a quantum battery?"

Hannah nodded.

Jeffrey nodded eagerly. "So, when you say you studied *under* a genius, you meant you were fucking his brains out, right?"

Hannah laughed. "You know me too well. He taught me more than quantum physics. Shall I show you?" She glanced at his crotch.

"In a minute. How does this work with TOTO?" Jeffrey nodded at the battery case. TOTO was the name he'd given the keg-sized time travel device.

"Let me show you." Excitement brimmed and she giggled as she sashayed over to TOTO. She unzipped the padded bag she'd purchased to protect it for the flight and tilted the machine, angling the bottom edge up to reveal a newly added input port. "I made a very small adjustment. I hope you don't mind, but I needed a connection."

For a millisecond, anger flashed across Jeffrey's face, but a look of interest filled in the harsh lines. Had she looked away, she'd have missed it.

"I'm sure you're a bit furious that I broke into your storage unit and stole your prized invention." Hannah landed the confession of her misdeeds by sliding the jacket down, revealing one shoulder.

Jeffrey slowly dragged his hand across his forehead. He let his hand drop and spat, "Show me how this all works, Hannah, and we will deal with that later."

Hannah sucked in her breath, not wanting the seduction to fade so quickly to anger. "Sure." She adjusted the jacket to cover her nearly naked torso, then walked back to the bed and lifted the battery case, flipping it over. On the back side there was a zippered compartment, and she pulled out the cord then returned to TOTO. "Just like any battery pack." She plugged the cord into the socket on TOTO and held the other end up. "Voila. Easy, simple solution."

"You could have destroyed TOTO with your meddling," Jeffrey spat, then lifted TOTO out of the case, inspecting the changes.

A stab of fear tamped down the sexy thoughts. "Have a little trust, baby. TOTO has never been better."

He peppered her with questions. "How volatile are the batteries? Do you need to use them all at once? Aren't these supposed to be encased in a protective shield?"

Hannah addressed his questions in succession, eager to get to the acceptance phase and her reward afterward. "Don't get in a wreck with the batteries, they may explode. Yes, you need to use all of them to have enough power for two people. In a lab, protection is important. Out in the field, things change a bit."

"Hmmmm, genius."

Hannah brimmed with pride, happy to finally share her work with him. "Thank you for noticing." She let the jacket open again and leaned back on the bed, supporting herself on her elbows and crossing her legs. Jeffrey's eyes noticed her efforts and she smiled, wanting to take back the power and push aside his anger.

"So how do you know TOTO didn't misfire? Were you able to send both Ronnie and Mike back? Where were you when you sent them?"

"I booked a room right next to Ronnie at the National Suites, sent Mike a shot at the bar with your magical pellets, and mixed some in Ronnie's food. The room service guy took some convincing, but let's just say I worked it out." she winked, "Because Hannah knows how to use her assets to get what she wants." Hannah paused to read his expression, but he was getting better at hiding it. The shock must be wearing off. "Then when everything was sorted, I seeded the storm right off the coast near our hotel."

Jeffrey shook his head slowly, maintaining eye contact. "You're a clever, conniving witch, aren't you?"

"I am. Man, they were loud that night. Lots of yelling. I'm not sure which way they were going at it, but...either way, they both shut up quick when I powered up your baby." She glanced at TOTO.

Jeffrey glowered. "Going at it?"

"Jeffrey, I'm kidding. They were definitely fighting. Ronnie was furious at Mike over something, which made him punch the wall. It reverberated nicely on my side."

"I wish you'd left her out of it."

"Why? If this whole thing went belly-up, we'd be rid of them both and we could happily join forces." Hannah leaned forward, squishing her boobs together beguilingly.

His eyes drank it in. Jeffrey shook his head and looked away then returned with an angry squint. "If she is fucked up because of your careless power play...there will be investigations."

"Why would she be fucked up?" A moment of panic forced its way through the sexy fog.

"Yeah, a lesion in her brain formed after the second round of experiments." Jeffrey looked away and shook his head, "Plus, now you've given her a reason to know she's not crazy. She and Mike have this intense new bond. Damn it, Hannah. I can't believe you did all of this behind my back. Why didn't you just tell me you had a power source? You knew I'd been working on this for years."

"I had my own plans for it." She felt defensive. She had anticipated his resistance around Ronnie but hadn't expected this. "Jeffrey, you know as well as I do, you'd never let me in. Don't you see I've done you a favor? If Ronnie is with Mike, you won't have to worry about her interfering with the research or discovering something she shouldn't." Hannah covered his hand with hers.

Jeffrey jerked his hand away. "You did this to push them together? I just spent a big chunk of change to keep them apart. Hannah, who the hell do you think you are to interfere in my work, my personal life, and...?" He looked away, lips pressing into a thin line. He tapped his fingers on his leg. "My inventions."

"Jeffrey, I wanted to show you how much I can match your brilliance. I'm your perfect partner." She held up one of the quantum batteries. "I made enormous strides in your work. In just a few days I solved your power problem. I just wanted to solve your personal problem as well. If I failed, Mike and Ronnie would be gone. GONE, out of our hair. And the storm would cover my tracks. I could have you to myself and stop sharing with that goddamned supermodel you're dating."

"Hannah, we broke up. Don't you get it? Your meddling made me come out here to save her." Jeffrey looked up at the ceiling, completely exasperated. "Do you know how much that cost me?"

"You could have just let fate take care of her! She'd either die or be fine, but now you've become her savior. She's never going to let you go now."

A dark look crossed his face. "Savior? Nope. Ronnie hates me even more than she did before." He shook his head and bowed it. "I lost my temper and did something..."

Hannah put her arm around his shoulder, elated at what he was confessing. "What did you do?"

Jeffrey wrapped his arm around her waist. "Nothing. I'm just an asshole."

Hannah pulled him close, grabbing his chiseled shoulder and thinking of the rest of his hard, muscular body. "Look, maybe that is for the best. She can only bring you down. We..." She turned his face towards her. "We are what matters. Let's work together on this, Jeffrey. Please."

He glanced at TOTO and frowned but didn't share his thoughts with her.

Chapter 75

Procedure

Ronnie followed the nurse into a small hospital room. She gestured for Ronnie to sit in a chair near the door. "Have a seat. I'll just make up the cot for you. I'm Hortênsia. You are?"

"I'm Ronnie. Mike and I are..." It wasn't something they'd defined yet. "Together. He's my boss, but there's more."

Hortênsia's eyebrows rose. "I understand the attraction to powerful men. I don't blame you. He's very handsome."

And then some.

Hortênsia pressed on the clunky pleather chair and miraculously it separated and pulled out into a bed. "You look exhausted."

"I am," Ronnie confessed.

"If you want, I can make sure they bring up the meal. I don't think Mr. Walsh will be eating today, but there is no reason you can't have a tray delivered."

"That would be great, thank you."

She cocked her head at Ronnie, probably feeling sorry for her. "Mr. Walsh is getting an angiogram."

Ronnie's eyes widened. "Oh, thank you for telling me. What is that?"

"Just another way to find out what is going on in his brain. They're debating about surgery but want to avoid it if they can."

Ronnie was glad she was sitting down. Her stomach did a flip. "Oh God. Is he going to be okay?"

"We shall see. Brain injuries are very unpredictable. I've seen miracles here, and tragedies." She crossed herself, then covered the cot with a sheet and offered Ronnie a pillow. "I'm not sure when Mr. Walsh will return. You'd be wise to get some rest now, while you can."

Ronnie nodded, numb from everything that had happened the last few days. She looked up a few minutes later after having spaced out for a bit and realized she was alone in the room. The cot was looking very inviting, and she succumbed to the nurse's advice. Rest would do her good. The emotional toll was adding up. She lay on the cot and pulled the sheet and blanket up to her shoulders and closed her eyes.

A minute later someone opened the door and entered. Ronnie stood up and smoothed down her hair. Carlos Munoz entered the room, his presence wafting in along with his cologne, consuming her full attention.

"Ronnie..." Carlos said. "Let's talk outside." He ushered her out the door. In the hallway he strode past the nurses' station, and a hush fell upon the nurses as they watched him pass. They all eyed Ronnie suspiciously.

He led her to one of the offices and shut the door. "You okay, Ronnie?" He stepped closer to her with his arms outstretched, but she waved him off. He smiled and motioned towards one of the chairs.

Carlos made his way around the desk to sit in the power seat.

Ronnie sat down, smoothing the shorts to cover more of her legs. "Good, just worried sick about Mike. Do you know anything more?"

"No, I've been in meetings. I just got away to check on him." Carlos picked up the phone and spoke in Spanish. "I brought you this." He reached in his pocket and pulled out a cell phone.

Ronnie reached out, and his hand brushed hers, making fear creep up her spine. She tamped it down.

Carlos watched her face closely.

"Wow, that is so kind of you, Mr. Munoz." Ronnie flipped open the phone and it showed the time. 12:45 p.m.

"Please dispense with the formality. Call me Carlos. It's for you to call home. To find comfort with friends, maybe call Mike's family." Carlos smiled, leaning back in his chair, looking over his steepled fingers.

"Carlos, Mike and I will never forget your kindness. Thank you for sending your driver." Carlos had come through. Creepy or not, he'd taken very good care of them.

Someone knocked on the door and Carlos looked up. "Come in."

A woman entered wearing a white lab coat with a stethoscope around her neck. She spoke to Carlos in Spanish. He responded in English and waved for her to sit next to Ronnie.

"Miss Andrews," the doctor said, "I'm Dr. Castillo. I'm the attending."

"Great to meet you, doctor," Ronnie eked out.

"Mr. Walsh is stable. The testing we've done so far shows he has a brain injury called a subdural hematoma. Essentially a collection of blood under the skull."

Fear poked around the edges, but Ronnie stayed outwardly calm, willing her tired logical brain to take over. She could be a mush blob later. "Will he need surgery?"

"We are not sure. Right now, he needs rest, steroids, and monitoring."

The doctor glanced at Carlos, who nodded and asked, "Do you know how he acquired the injury?"

Ronnie nodded. "I was there with him. We were in a car accident." She glanced at Carlos. "He was too busy protecting my head to protect his own." At the time she'd felt smothered, but now she realized what a selfless act it had been. "After the accident, someone hit him in the same spot as the injury."

The doctor's eyebrows met, and she looked at Carlos.

She debated about how much to tell them. "Yes, we were stranded at a gas station and some men came to rescue us."

Carlos's eyebrows rose, approaching his hairline. "What men?"

Ronnie glanced at the doctor. "My ex-boyfriend was there, so I guess he hired some guys to find us. Mike went with the men, and I went with my ex-boyfriend. Mike was trying to protect me and got in a scuffle. That's when the men pistol-whipped him."

Carlos leaned forward, his hands resting on the desk. "Ronnie, these men were armed?"

Ronnie shook her head. "Yes, they all had guns. I don't know who they were or why they were all armed. They looked like military guys but were not in uniform."

Carlos looked angry. "Where is your ex-boyfriend? We need to find him and ask questions. Press charges on the man who assaulted Mike, perhaps."

The doctor held up her hand. "Let me finish, Señor Munoz, if you don't mind."

Carlos raised his hands in surrender and the doctor continued.

"So, two separate injuries. How far apart do you suppose they were?"

Ronnie looked away, running through the dramatic events of the last few days. "The car accident happened yesterday about three or four o'clock in the afternoon. The pistol-whipping happened just a few hours ago. What are your next steps?"

The doctor nodded. "What about his left eye? Do you know how he got that injury?"

Ronnie shook her head. "When I saw him last, that eye wasn't black." *Was it Jeffrey?*

"We inserted a sensor into Mr. Walsh's skull to monitor the pressure. We have administered some medications. In a few hours we will do another quick scan and see if there is any change in the size of the swelling."

"And if there is?" Ronnie asked, afraid to hear the answer.

"Surgery. We will have no choice. If the pressure gets too high, he will risk permanent injury if we do not act."

Ronnie bit her lip and fought back tears.

The doctor continued, "If the pressure stabilizes, we will just monitor him and let the medicine work. That is all we can do right now."

"Okay. Thank you, doctor." Ronnie smiled. "I appreciate you giving me the information."

"Miss Andrews, you are welcome. That is why we are here. Does Mr. Walsh have any health conditions we should know about?"

"Not that I know of."

"He's healthy, and strong. He should pull through, but what damage this may have caused his brain we cannot be sure. His nausea, seizure, and pupil size all point to major changes in his brain due to the swelling. Was he coherent after the accident?"

Ronnie nodded. "He was unconscious for about fifteen minutes right after it. But then he seemed fine until bedtime when he said it was hard to focus. That's when I noticed the uneven pupils. When we woke up, he was worse, and we decided to go to the hospital. Before we could leave, the men broke in."

"Thank you, doctor." Carlos stood. "You are so kind to stop in and update us."

The doctor stood, knowing she was being dismissed.

Ronnie stood too. "Thank you, Dr. Costillo."

The doctor nodded and left the room.

Carlos leaned towards her. "I need to understand what happened. Who are these men that broke in and took you to separate places?"

Ronnie took a deep breath, not wanting to pull Carlos into the fray. Ronnie plucked the shirt away from her chest, and she felt self-conscious without a bra. "My ex, Jeffrey Brennan. He came to rescue us but took Mike away."

"Why? And how did he find you? Did you call for him?"

Ronnie shook her head. "No, that's the weird part. He couldn't know where we were." She paused, and he waited for her to answer the rest of his questions. "I didn't call him. We were in a mudslide when we were trying to get to the hospital. Our car crashed in a river, and we climbed the mountain and found a convenience store to take refuge in."

"Where is this man, Jeffrey, now?" Carlos demanded, anger lacing his words.

"Carlos, I don't need a champion. I just want Mike to be okay."

"No, you said you were in a safe place at the hotel. Did he threaten you? He certainly did not treat Mike well, as you have described the events."

"He..." Ronnie covered her mouth, not wanting to start crying, but she was still shaken from Jeffrey's threats.

Carlos covered her hand with his, and Ronnie pulled it free.

"He threatened to rape me, to get payment for rescuing me!" She looked him dead in the eyes, and he sat back against the chair. "So, I'd be very grateful if you'd have a little sensitivity now. I don't want any close contact. *Please*, Carlos." She bit her lips, not wanting him to see her cry.

He held up his hands in surrender. "Oh, I am so sorry. I abhor men who take advantage of women like that. Where is Jeffrey? At the hotel where my driver picked you up?"

Ronnie stared at him open-mouthed, but hushed her angry thoughts, then shook her head. "No, Carlos, don't get involved." Out of nowhere, Ronnie coughed and had trouble catching her breath. Finally, it passed.

Carlos shook his head. "Have you seen a doctor yet?"

Ronnie shook her head.

"You don't look well. I will have you examined at once." Carlos added, "I will have words with this Jeffrey character. We cannot have armed men just roaming around our island assaulting people. Especially not my friends."

Ronnie looked down at her hands in her lap. "Carlos, please. He is not worth your time."

Carlos did not try to hide his anger. "The man mistreated you. I sure as hell will, at the very least, have words with him."

"Carlos, please don't give him a reason to take his anger out on me. I've had enough of that."

Carlos's expression shifted rapidly from fierce defender to compassionate friend. "Oh, I see. I must be careful of the consequences to you. Perhaps we shall deal with Mike's issues and then we shall see how things play out."

"That would be best." Ronnie let out a deep breath.

"First, just so I have the information, could you write down Jeffrey's name and address? I will look into his background just to get a sense of who he is."

A wave of exhausted fear drained her energy. "Carlos, really, I can't have you involved. It will just make it worse for me."

Carlos looked away, shaking his head. "Ronnie, I have contacts here on the island. You have to understand the kind of sway I can have in preventing this man from leaving without our knowledge. I prefer to know where he is, and to be able to assess his ability to interfere with either of you again." Carlos smoothed down his thick mustache. "If I commit to not making a move unless you have given me permission? Is that, as you American's say, *doable?*"

Ronnie crossed her arms. On one hand it would be good for someone to detain Jeffrey, keep him from leaving without having to at least answer for what he'd done to them. "Let me think about it, Carlos. I'm too overwhelmed to know the best way to proceed." She knew if she told him Jeffrey was dangerous and could hurt him too, he'd bristle and insist. She needed to think through the consequences before sharing Jeffrey's information, and she was far too tired to make that call right now.

"Let's get you looked over." Carlos stood and opened the door. He waved to the nursing station and a nurse nearly ran over to him.

"Señor Munoz, how are you today? You're looking..."

Carlos cut her off. "Please, if you could look over Miss Andrews for me. She and Mr. Walsh have been in an accident. I want to be sure she is well cared for." Carlos turned to leave.

Ronnie grabbed his arm. "Carlos."

He turned and smiled.

"Thank you for all your help. I'll think about what you suggested and let you know."

He smiled and kissed the top of her head. "My number is in the phone I gave you. Do not hesitate to call me for any reason." Carlos turned and walked away, with multiple pairs of eyes following his progress down the hall.

The nurse eyed Ronnie, jutting her chin out. "*Phone?* He gave you a phone?" Her tone was almost accusatory.

"I lost everything in an accident."

Her look persisted and Ronnie felt defensive.

"Don't get any ideas. He hired my company to help with a new healthcare software installation for the island. That's it."

The nurse shook her head. "I see how he looks at you. It is more than that." The nurse turned and walked briskly away.

Ronnie rolled her eyes. "Then you also saw how I look at him. It is less than that. *Much less.*" Ronnie followed her, rushing to keep up. She stopped near the nursing station.

The nurse swiped a thermometer across her forehead. "Your temperature is elevated. Are you feeling ill?"

"A little, but I think I'm just tired." It was no wonder. She'd been cold and wet most of yesterday.

She took her vitals and asked her a series of questions, then confirmed she was in good shape, handed her a packet of Tylenol, and grabbed an apple juice from the fridge. "Please, let me know if there is anything else you need."

Ronnie shook her head. "No, I'm good. I'll sleep a bit. Thank you." Ronnie felt like a broken record, thanking everyone, but she was grateful to be here, and not in the river, the convenience store, or Jeffrey's room. She wondered if Carlos was making inquiries about Mr. Brennan's whereabouts. Part of her wanted Carlos to decimate him and put him in jail. The rest of her knew better than to poke the bear. Plus, she'd had enough of men expecting payment for helping her. She definitely did NOT want to owe Carlos anything else. Ronnie quietly entered the room and watched Mike's sleeping form, then lay next to him in the cot and covered his hand with hers. She fell asleep, feeling completely exhausted.

Chapter 76

Bullet

Jeffrey allowed Hannah to feel like she was in control. She kissed his face, and he turned towards her, pulling her to his lap, kissing her as he slid off her jacket, tossing it to the floor. He unclasped her bra and pushed her to lie on the bed, tossing it aside.

"Wait!" She jumped up, returned the battery to the case, and closed it. "Safety first." Hannah set the case by the door, then lay on the bed next to him.

Jeffrey caressed her breasts, pinching each nipple with sensual attentiveness. When he paused to kiss her, she removed his shirt. Her hands ran over each ripple of abs down to grip him through the fabric.

Jeffrey nodded to her pants. "Take those off."

Hannah obeyed, batting her eyes, then unbuttoned her jeans and slid them off. Jeffrey took both of her hands and kissed her, pressing his chest to hers. Jeffrey pushed her to lie flat on the mattress and he covered her with his body, pinning her hips to the bed, grinding against her, kissing her deeply, then dragged his lips down her body.

"Oh God, please, Jeffrey. Please."

Jeffrey pressed his mouth into her, and she moaned.

"Yes, baby, you know what I like." Hannah opened her legs and Jeffrey settled between them, forcing them to open wider, then teased her inner thigh with his tongue. He pressed into her panties, tasting her wetness through the fabric, then slid the fabric aside, nibbling on her most sensitive flesh.

"Oh my God, I'd forgotten how good you are at this." Her hips pressed up towards him. "No, I lied, I never forgot... Why do you think I went to all this trouble...? Oh God..."

Jeffrey stopped. "Are the quantum batteries fully charged?"

Hannah's smile fell. "*What?* Oh, yeah, they retain their charge indefinitely until they're disturbed."

Jeffrey forced her legs up to her chest and continued his thorough exploration, then stopped just before she climaxed. "Did you use your real name to check into National Suites?"

The question caught her by surprise. "No." She shoved his face back and he got to work.

Inside Jeffrey fumed with anger, but he didn't let it show. No one inserted themselves in his work. No one invaded his privacy and stole from him. His tongue worked his magic, something he'd perfected over the years, and it never failed to make the woman's logical mind turn off. She'd get an oxytocin rush, fostering feelings of trust, making her significantly more malleable. Nipple stimulation was the key to start this process, and coincidentally exceedingly pleasant to administer. Orgasms triggered the brain to pump out streams of exquisite hormones in a flood of chemical manipulation. Science was a beautiful thing.

Hannah quickly climaxed again with the help of his fingers, and he continued to slide over her, coaxing a few multiples out of her as well.

Her face was flushed, and she was out of breath. "Be right back." Hannah sashayed to the bathroom, her body jiggling in all the right places.

Jeffrey reached into his pocket and pulled out a small bottle. He added a few drops to the glass by her bed and poured the remainder of a nearby bottled water into it. When she returned, being the gentleman that he was, he handed her the water.

She took it. "So kind of you, Jeffrey baby." Hannah gulped the water down, her throat probably dry from all the noises she enjoyed making.

Jeffrey watched her face muscles relax and she lay back against the bed.

"Let me at youuuu..." Her words slurred and her eyes closed briefly. The medicine was working.

Jeffrey grabbed her legs and flipped her over, smacking her ass.

Hannah laughed, "Fuck me, Jeffrey. Do it. I've been dreaming of this since we were together last."

Jeffrey smiled, enjoying the view of her nakedness. He caressed her thighs and ass and slid two fingers inside her, making her rhythmically bounce. "Hannah, darling. The Feds have figured out how to pinpoint the pulse. They're going to know you were behind this."

Hannah grunted with pleasure. She was trying to form words, but they were too slurred to make out. Did she understand how bad she'd screwed this up for herself? Her movements slowed, then stopped.

"The good news is, they'll put the whole pulse thing on you, and I'll be off scot-free." Jeffrey removed his fingers and turned her face towards him. "Hannah, you okay?"

Her only response was a slight mumble, then her body completely relaxed. She was out.

Jeffrey shoved her shoulder, and still she gave no response. He left her on the bed and rummaged around for his things. In the outer pocket of her bag, he found one of his most precious possessions—Dr. Andrews's journal. He caressed the embossed leather and held it close to his body, then flipped through the pages until he found her dramatic, loopy handwriting. Snagged from the storage unit along with TOTO and the laptop. *What else did she take?*

"Damn you, Hannah." Anger coursed through his body, but he shoved it aside, needing his mind to be calm to finish this, once and for all. That was the final straw. He'd been on the fence until now. "Purple pen? Damn your ass, Hannah!"

Jeffrey walked to the sink and washed his face and looked into the mirror. "Should I?" He watched the reflection tilt his head and smirk. "Fuck yeah." Jeffrey dug through the pile of luggage near the door and retrieved the bag that held his launch computer, the one he used to run TOTO, cringing at the thought of her sparkly fingernails playing along the keys. In the outer pocket, he pulled out a small foam-insulated case. Inside was a plastic vial he carefully uncorked. Two syringes were still safely protected. He pulled one out and returned to Hannah's still form. Jeffrey uncapped the syringe, then debated where to put it. He usually placed it between the shoulder blades, but this time caution was crucial. Jeffrey held the syringe in his teeth while he positioned her body. Then carefully stabbed the needle deep in a place no one would find it, releasing the chip. She moaned and tried to roll over, but she fell back asleep before she could.

"Hannah, darling. The pellets are so last year." He quickly recapped the syringe and placed it back in the case and returned it to the outer pocket.

Adrenalin coursed through his veins, fueled by her helpless, naked form. The things he could do to her now! His eyes lingered on the wetness making a puddle on the bed under her, and his mind snapped back to attention. There was work to do.

Looking around the room, he found her purse on the desk. Jeffrey pulled out a paperback and turned it over. "*Jesse and Frank James*. Interesting." He returned it and scanned through the luggage near the door. In the small rolling suitcase, he pulled out a few random items and tossed them onto the floor setting the scene—a shirt, underwear, socks, and a black silk negligee. It had to look like she had decided to stay.

Then he searched the bag thoroughly, looking for any hidden gems. Bingo! A small, hard object was wrapped up in her underwear. He held it up and examined it. It was a small metal oval with a tiny switch. A bullet, and not the deadly kind, but a small vibrator. He turned it on, and it buzzed happily in his hand, then he switched it off and kept digging.

An overstuffed, flowered bag looked promising. He unzipped it and dug through the pounds of makeup and finally found what he was looking for. Sleeping pills. "Yes, please."

Jeffrey snagged the glass she used and washed it carefully with soap and a washcloth, then refilled it and set it next to her bed. Then he pulled down the covers, lifted Hannah, and placed her in the middle of the bed.

Carefully wiping away any fingerprints, he turned the bullet on and spread her legs, then gently inserted it using part of the sheet, marveling at how wet she was. At least she would go out with a bang. Damn, what a wasted opportunity, but he needed to be like a Boy Scout and leave no trace.

She moaned, "Oh God, yes, baby!"

Jeffrey grabbed her hand and pressed it between her legs, and her busy fingers went to work. "Good girl, Hannah. Come for me, you sexy minx."

Her eyes opened briefly, her fingers pressed the bullet deeper. Mesmerized, Jeffrey watched for a minute, then continued with his preparations. Mesmerized, Jeffrey watched for a minute, then continued with his preparations.

Jeffrey pulled TOTO out of the custom padded bag and set it in the middle of the room. The power cord was already connected from her demonstration. Why had she set the input port at the bottom of the machine? If there was any water on the floor, that's the first place it would enter. *Idiot.*

Glancing at the journal, he read the instructions and pulled each battery out of the case, finding the small connections that linked them all together, marveling at the design. Each stacked neatly on top of the other, oriented to form a single, larger, solid triangular prism, four on the bottom row, then three stacked on top, then two, and the remaining one clicking neatly into the others below it. He flipped back to her hideous wide-looped script and reread the instructions, checking and rechecking to be sure he'd followed each step properly.

When everything was set, he took her toiletry bag and set it on the bathroom counter, carefully removing a few items with his washcloth-clad fingers, laying them out randomly on the counter. Then he returned to the bedside. Using the sheet, he rubbed the container clean, opened the sleeping pills, and set it on the bedside table.

Jeffrey stood over Hannah, surprised how young and innocent she looked. "Hannah, baby." He shook her shoulder.

"Mmmmm, Jeffrey, it feels so good."

"Hannah." Jeffrey sat next to her on the bed. "Please take your medicine." He helped her sit upright.

Hannah's eyes opened and she mumbled, "What medicine?"

Jeffrey revealed a handful of her sleeping pills. "It's time to take these."

She dutifully picked up a few and put them in her mouth, then took the proffered cup and swallowed.

"Good girl. Get the rest in there, sweetie," Jeffrey coaxed, offering more pills.

Hannah obeyed, draining the glass. He guided her hand to returning the glass to the bedside table, pressing her fingers tightly onto the glass, leaving definitive fingerprints. Then she rolled over, hugging the pillow. The bullet buzzed on the sheets under her.

"Bye, Hannah, thank you for all your help with my project. I don't appreciate you writing in Dr. Andrews's journal, though. That was uncalled for."

She mumbled, "Sorry."

Jeffrey smiled. "All is forgiven. Remember that, Hannah. I could have just let you die. Instead, I'm rewarding you with a trip to a marvelous location."

Jeffrey debated on the time period but settled on something interesting, perhaps fitting, and then returned to his laptop, grimacing again at the thought of her fingers touching the keys. He plugged the laptop directly into TOTO and began the startup protocol, watching the prism closely. A small green light glowed on each segment to show it was powering up. It was strange to operate TOTO without the disks he'd created to pull power from the storms. Would this be a new, fresh tool, lither, easier to use without relying on a hurricane?

Jeffrey's fingers moved over the keyboard like a pianist, overwriting her keystrokes. Finally, pressing the launch key, he turned to Hannah.

"Hannah, can you hear me?"

She groaned a little.

"How did you crack my password?"

"Smart bad bitch?" she managed.

"Not smart enough. Here, let me ease your trip." Jeffrey picked up the washcloth and maneuvered the bullet, holding it in place.

"Mmmmmm," she moaned as he pressed the washcloth against her in rhythmic circles. She convulsed against the assault until, like a switch was flicked, she was gone.

The laptop confirmed the transfer was complete. Jeffrey pulled the sheet up to her chin and packed the gear. He dug through the bags to collect her cloud seeding research and scanned every page, making sure nothing was mentioned about him or his work, then left one notebook open to the proper notes from the night she'd seeded this storm.

Jeffrey made a quick sweep of the room, carefully wiping down anything he may have touched, then waved. "That will teach you to fuck with my stuff, Hannah."

Jeffrey gathered TOTO, the battery case, his laptop, and Dr. Andrews's journal, carting them out to his Jeep and packing them carefully in the back seat. Anger flowed and ebbed. Hannah had put his entire project at risk.

Mission accomplished. The authorities would find her and make the leap that she'd committed suicide or accidentally overdosed. With any luck the FBI would finely pinpoint the pulse, find her research, and pin the entire thing on Hannah.

Chapter 77

Make Your Own Miracles

Ronnie returned to Mike's room and was surprised to find several people in the doorway. She cautiously entered, expecting Carlos to be in there making a big deal with the nurses or something equally obnoxious.

Mike smiled weakly, looking tired and bruised. "Hey, you."

A wave of relief washed over her. He was awake and making sense! "How are you feeling?"

Mike winced. "Been better, but you're here so now I'm almost cured."

Ronnie took his hand, noticing the swelling around his left eye, now turning a bluish color. "What did they just do to you? Did they find anything out?"

He closed his eyes and exhaled. "I don't even know."

Ronnie looked to the nurses. One was reading in his chart, and the other was connecting him to the monitors.

Hortênsia turned to her. "Angiogram." Then glanced at Mike. "Mr. Walsh, we were checking out your big brain. Looking good!" She gave him a thumbs-up.

"Really?" Ronnie asked, her hopes rising.

"Yes, no aneurysm. Veins looked good, just a lot of swelling. He may still need surgery, but we will watch him closely." She leaned in closer to Mike. "Don't you let this pretty lady get your heart rate going. You need to rest. Sleep if you can." She eyed Ronnie. "Do *not* get him excited, you hear?"

Ronnie smiled. "Nope. I'll be so quiet you won't even know I'm here."

Mike blinked sleepily. "I'll know. And it makes all the difference."

Ronnie sat down on the cot, now almost touching the bed. She reached out and took Mike's hand again. "I'm here. Can I get you anything?"

"No. I'm going to sleep."

Ronnie watched the tightening around his mouth and eyes relax. His breathing was even and slow. It broke her heart to see the strong and protective Mike so battered, so worn out. She bent over his sleeping form, praying for a full recovery, praying to ease his pain.

His numbers looked good. Blood oxygen was ninety-eight percent. She marveled at his long, dark eyelashes gently brushing against his swollen eyes. As helpless as he looked lying there sleeping, Mike's strength was visible too, pressing against the hospital gown, giving Ronnie hope it would pull him through this.

The words from Dr. Costillo rolled around in her mind. Mike may never be the same. He could be damaged forever, or worse. Tears stung her eyes. Ronnie covered Mike's hand with hers, hoping she'd not wake him. He did not stir. She was both relieved and disturbed by this. Overwhelming feelings of affection bubbled up from deep inside. He had done so much to protect her. The sacrifice he'd made during the accident brought her to tears. He'd proffered the same protection in the convenience store, taking a beating to protect her. No one had ever sacrificed so much to keep her safe.

Jeffrey would have saved himself, saved his ego, saved his precious things before helping her. The contrast between Mike and Jeffrey had never been so stark. Anger, fear, and tears flowed out of her. What would have happened if the room service guy hadn't shown up when he had? Would Jeffrey have raped her? Ronnie snagged a Kleenex out of the box and dabbed at her eyes. "Damn it."

Mike shifted in his bed but didn't wake. Ronnie tiptoed to the bathroom and blew her nose. The floor was wet, and she looked around for evidence that someone had used the bathroom. It hadn't been Mike—he'd just returned from the angiogram. A towel was hanging on the hook behind the door. What the hell?

Ronnie quietly opened the bathroom door and left, heading to the nurse's station. "Excuse me."

A nurse set down a patient file and looked up at her. "*Si.*"

"Was the bathroom in Mike Walsh's room cleaned? There is a wet towel hanging up in there."

The nurse looked at Ronnie blankly. Hortênsia came from another patient's room and the two nurses spoke in Spanish for a minute. Hortênsia answered, "*Si, Señor* Walsh vomited on the man who came in with him. The man showered and changed clothes."

Ronnie nodded. "Do you know where this man is now?"

Hortênsia shook her head. "No. He was in there before you showed up."

"I'd like to speak with him if he comes back. Can you let me know if you see him again?" Ronnie did not like the thought of the man lurking around the hospital with Mike in such a weakened state.

"I will if I see him." Hortênsia looked surprised.

"Thank you. Is there somewhere I can make a call? I don't want to disturb Mike."

"*Si.*" Hortênsia nodded to the left.

Ronnie pointed to an unmarked door.

"You can use this room." Hortênsia brought a key and unlocked the door. It was a small office, with a desk and chair, like the one Carlos had taken her to.

"Thank you." Ronnie shut the door, then opened the flip phone and called her mom.

She answered on the first ring. "Hello?"

"Mom, it's me."

"Ronnie! Are you okay?"

"Yeah."

Her mom sounded stressed. "I got your message and then turned on the news… It's showing Puerto Rico with major damage and…" Her voice shook.

"It's a mess here. But I'm fine. Don't worry about me. I'm at the hospital with Mike. He's hurt."

"Who is Mike?" her mom sniffed.

"My boss. But he's grown into so much more than that, Mom."

"Oh, I didn't know. What about Jeffrey? You know, he's called me twice in the last month. What is going on with you two? It spooked me the first time. I thought he was calling to tell me something happened to you."

"Mom, I broke it off with Jeffrey. He is not good for me." She hadn't the energy to update her on everything.

"Oh, why is that, hun? I always liked him."

"Long story. Look, Mom, I don't have long. I just wanted to let you know I am okay and to ask you something."

"I'm so glad you called. I've been worried sick. David called me too, and once we hadn't heard back, I called Steph. She told me she hadn't heard from you either, except before the storm hit."

"Yeah, I've not had a chance till now. Mom, do you know who Jason Korbin is?"

"Jason…" Her mom trailed off. "It rings a bell. Where did you hear this name? Maybe that will jog my memory."

Ronnie stalled, not sure if she wanted to bring her mother's scorn down on her. The exhaustion spoke for her, spilling it out uncoordinatedly. "I hear Dad's voice when I time travel. He told me that Jason Korbin could give me answers to what is going on with me."

The line was silent.

"*Mom?*"

"Yeah, I think you know what I'm going to say about that, honey." Her mom's tone shifted to skeptical professionalism.

"I do. What about the name, though? Did Dad ever mention it to you?"

She was quiet for a few seconds. "I'm not sure, but I think that was the name of your dad's intern."

"Really? Are you sure?"

"No, Veronica. But I could look through your dad's desk. Or call the lab where Ron worked. They would know for sure. Is it important?"

"Very. Thanks, Mom. Can you call Steph with the info? I have borrowed someone's phone and may not have it for very long. Here is my number in case you can get it soon." Ronnie rattled off the cell number. "Either way, it would be good to know. I really want to talk to this guy and see if he can fill me in on what Dad was working on. Maybe even give me more info on what happened that day."

"Veronica, how is your boss? You said you were at the hospital."

Ronnie struggled to keep her voice from squeaking. "Not great. He has a head injury, but I think he'll be okay."

"I'm sorry."

"Mom, don't talk to Jeffrey anymore if he calls you. Just hang up. We are not on good terms. Please don't tell him where we are. Don't talk to him, okay?"

"Okay. I won't."

"Thanks. I'll tell you everything when I'm home. I need to call Steph now. Tell David I'm okay. I'll call him soon."

"I will. Be safe and let me know if there is anything I can do to help."

"Thanks, Mom."

"Veronica."

"Yes."

"Mike needs to have hope. Give him that and he will fight harder. Sometimes people can create their own miracles when they have hope."

"I love that. I'll help him create his own miracle, Mom. Thank you. Love you."

"Love you too, hun. Talk soon."

Ronnie hung up the phone and fought back tears. Her mom's words were exactly what she needed to hear. Create your own miracle. She could do that for Mike. He'd done so much for her already. He had to be okay.

Chapter 78

Killing Time

When she had her voice under control, she called Steph.

"Hello?" her best friend answered.

"Oh my gosh, Steph!" Ronnie lost the battle with her emotions.

"Ronnie? Where are you? Are you safe?" Worry laced Steph's words. The phone shuffled and Steph called out, "Ian, Ronnie is on the phone."

"Hi, guys. Yeah, things are falling apart, Steph." Ronnie dabbed her eyes with the Kleenex she still clutched in her hand.

"Oh, luv, tell me everything."

Ian broke in, "Hey, Ronnie, what'cha wearing?"

Steph spewed out a string of Scottish reprimands.

Ronnie shook her head. Ian was so predictable. "I'm wearing an expensive, pretentious dress shirt and even more pretentious gym shorts."

Ian laughed. "See? She's no offended, Stephanie."

Ronnie could almost hear the glare protruding out of Steph's eyes.

Ian said, "I'm sorry, lass. I didn't know..."

"Ian, hush. Let her talk," Steph said. Ronnie imagined her smacking Ian's arm. "What's going on there? What's falling apart?"

Ronnie let out a long breath and decided which disaster to tell her about first. "Mike's in trouble." She paused to get her voice under control.

"In trouble? What happened?"

"We left the hotel trying to get to a hospital. A mudslide washed us down a friggin' mountain into a river. He hurt his head in the accident." It still seemed unreal. "He was protecting me when we crashed."

"No! Oh, luv, how bad is he?"

Ronnie shook her head. "Not sure but he's being monitored. They put a sensor in his head. If the pressure goes up, they'll need to do surgery."

"Ronnie, I'm so sorry."

"And worse," Ronnie continued, "Jeffrey broke in and took him to jail, except they never made it."

Steph paused, not understanding her jumbled story. "Broke in where? *Jeffrey?* Did

I hear you right?"

"Yeah, let me back up. After the accident we walked up a mountain and found a convenience store to shelter in. The storm is still raging outside. Well, it was. Now it's just raining." Ronnie knew she was rambling, and her unorganized thoughts just plopped out on the table for Steph to untangle.

"Luv, what were you saying about a convenience store? I'm not sure I followed that." Steph sounded worried and confused.

Ian added, "Wait, Jeffrey?"

"We walked up the mountain and found somewhere to stay. We were getting ready to drive to the hospital to have Mike checked out..." Steph didn't even know Mike had gone back in time. There was so much to tell her. "Anyway, Jeffrey and a team of soldiers broke in with guns."

"Soldiers with guns? Are you sure it was Jeffrey?" Steph said, talking over Ian.

"Yeah, Steph, he accused Mike of killing a doctor. So, they took him to the cops."

"What...?" Steph started.

Ronnie felt sorry for her—she was not telling any of this well. "Shoot, this is such a mess. Jeffrey's men took Mike to the police, but according to Mike, they pistol-whipped his temple in the same place he was hurt from the accident, and now he may need surgery."

"Oh, luv, I'm so sorry. So, he is in jail? What can we do from here?" Steph asked, compassion filling her voice.

"No. I'm sorry, guys, I'm not telling this well. I'm so tired. So much has happened and I'm rushing to tell it all at once." Ronnie repeated her story, this time taking care to not jumble everything up.

Steph sounded clearer. She must have taken her phone off speaker. "Wow, Ronnie, I sure hope Mike is going to be okay."

"You guys, there is something else I need to tell you. Something monumental."

Steph stayed silent, probably bracing for more convoluted mess.

"I went back in time again. And get this...so did Mike." Ronnie was hopped up now. Her face felt hot.

"What the hell!" Steph must have put Ronnie back on speaker because she sounded farther away. "Ronnie, repeat that for Ian."

"Ian, Mike and I both traveled back in time."

There was dead silence.

Ronnie looked at the phone to see if they were still on the line. "Steph?"

Ian broke in, "Mike went back too? Holy friggin' hell."

Ronnie nodded. "I know. We didn't figure it out until later when Mike told me about it. You're not going to believe what happened to us..." Ronnie paused, trying to slow it down so she didn't confuse her friends. "Mike killed Jesse James. And Frank and Jesse James killed Mike."

Ronnie was met with dead silence again and she pictured them staring open-mouthed at each other.

"No, I'm serious, guys."

Ian spoke first. "I don't even have words. Are you shitting me, Ronnie? Mike, your boss Mike?"

"Yes. I had no idea they were the James brothers, because they used aliases. I will tell you all about it when I come back. I don't have the energy right now. But it's crazy, right?"

Steph jumped in. "No! Mike going back proves you're *not* crazy. Ronnie, this is huge!"

"Yeah, it is."

"Luv, how are you feeling? The doctors were pretty clear that you shouldn't risk going back again."

"I'm good now. When I first came back, I felt pretty out of it."

"Get someone to look you over, Ronnie. Promise me," Steph said.

"I did. I have all my limbs and most of my senses. I feel good now, just tired."

Ian's deeper voice interrupted Steph's. "That explains where Jeffrey has been the last few days."

"How did you know he was gone? Are you spying on him?" Ronnie said it jokingly, but then a twang of panic hit her. What had Ian gotten himself into?

"Well..." Ian started but Steph cut in.

"You're not gonna like this, luv."

Adrenalin coursed through Ronnie's body, making her head pound. "What am I not gonna like?"

Steph said, "Yeah, we...um...we followed Jeffrey last week to a storage unit about an hour north of here. This wee eejit broke into Jeffrey's condo and found a key. Then..."

Ronnie shook her head. "What the hell?"

"We went back to the storage unit and opened it up. If anyone asks you, we were looking to see if he stole any of your things."

"Steph, I can't believe you guys did that. Ian could be arrested and sent back!"

Ian cut in. "Don't be mad, Ronnie. I made her do it. Did you know about this storage place? It's in Sanford."

"No, he never mentioned it." All the blood rushed out of Ronnie's head, and she saw spots in her vision. She sat back in the chair and stared up at the ceiling. Ian was talking again, but Ronnie couldn't focus. She put her head down on the desk, hoping the spots would subside. "What did you find in there? Did anyone see you guys?"

Steph spoke fast and nervously. "It looked like he'd had a bunch of stuff stored in there and then moved it out. But we poked around a bit. There was a huge hole in the wall, Ronnie, and we think some lady broke in there."

"What lady? I don't understand."

"Ian, what was her name?" Steph asked.

"Hannah Volpe, I think. Does that ring a bell?"

"Steph," Ronnie said. "That is the chick who works in the lab next to Jeffrey."

Steph answered, "Shut up! Apparently, she told the clerk she was his ex and wanted to be in the unit next to him."

Ronnie sat up. "Why would she do that? Steph, remember when Jeffrey first moved down to Florida, you saw him out with someone. Did it look like the same woman?"

There was a pause, and Steph finally said, "Oh my God. Ian, remember I said she looked familiar, but I couldn't place her? It might have been her."

Ronnie shook her head. "Jeffrey brought her up a few times and acted really weird."

"Oh God, I wonder what she was after," Steph said. "Ronnie, I'm pretty sure Hannah is involved in this. What could she be after?"

"I have no idea. Maybe she was suspicious of Jeffrey and what he was doing. Maybe she is in love with him. Whenever Jeffrey mentioned her, it always creeped me out a little, like there was something more between them than just the lab."

Ian leaned in close—his voice was clearer. "I'm going to snoop around and see what I can find out about her."

"Ian, I don't want you breaking in anywhere else. It won't be worth it if you're in jail."

Ronnie felt a wave of nausea at the realization that everyone around her was being dragged into her troubles. Ini had warned her about this. She had brought Wahab's evil back with her into her own life, her own time. In her time travels, almost everyone connected to her was destroyed when she went sideways in time—Morris and his entire village, Max, Maggie, Jeb, and even Jesse James. They would still be alive if she'd not shown up in their world. Now it had leached into her own time, with Mike's life hanging in the balance and Ian and Steph taking huge risks to help her.

"Lass, I can take care of myself," Ian said with pride.

His words rang in her head. She'd thought she could take care of herself too. Had her father thought the same thing? He'd paid the ultimate price. She was the central figure connecting all these strands together, like a black hole sucking them into the evil from the past. She had to find a way to make this stop.

Chapter 79

Jason Korbin Strikes Again

Steph made that distinctive Scottish sound. "Och, Ian, that's why you're here. You cannae take care of yourself. Don't break any laws—just find out where she lives and maybe follow her. See if she's up to something."

"Damn that Jeffrey. Stephanie, tell her about the guy's stuff," Ian chimed in, rapidly changing topics, putting Ronnie completely off track.

"Oh right, I forgot about that. We found a bunch of papers in the storage unit from Jason Korbin. Do you know who that is?"

The blood left Ronnie's face and she leaned back in the chair. "What? *Jason Korbin*, are you serious?"

"Why? Who is that?" Ian asked.

Ronnie let out a deep breath. "Oh my God, seriously, this gets weirder and weirder. Guys, you know how I can talk to my dad when I'm in between this world and the next?"

"Noooooo!" Steph said.

Ian asked, "Really?"

Ronnie's mind jumbled again, and she pulled on the thread, focusing on her father's voice and Quanah Parker's face. "My dad said I was gaining strength in the sphere and in my own life. He told me to trust my gut and I would wander into the right realm and undo what has been set askew. 'Find Jason Korbin. He will have the answers you are seeking'." Ronnie bit her lips, forcing back the emotions that were choking off her voice. "I just talked to my mom. She said she thinks that's the name of the guy who my dad hired as an intern in his lab."

Steph yelled, "Noooooo!"

Ronnie's stomach turned sour. She was feeling rather nauseous now.

Ian stammered, "Who? I'm not following."

"Ian, my dad told me to find Jason Korbin, that he could answer some of this for me. I think he's the guy my dad hired as an intern on the project that put my dad in a coma. I'd really like to find him and ask what my dad was working on the night he died. Now I want to know how he knows Jeffrey."

The phone shuffled and Ian was loud and clear. "Well, unfortunately you cannae. Jason Korbin died in a car accident years ago."

Ronnie shook her head. "What the hell are you talking about, Ian?"

He repeated, "Jason is dead."

Ronnie's head was spinning. "He is dead? Ian, how can you possibly know *that*?"

"In Jeffrey's storage unit was a newspaper clipping about Jason's death. Ronnie, why would Jeffrey have his stuff?" Ian asked.

Steph interceded, "He died in a car accident, Ronnie. Why would Jeffrey have Jason's diploma and other papers?"

"I have no idea. Who was Jason? What is the connection between my dad, Jason, and Jeffrey? It makes no sense."

Ian pronounced dramatically, "Ronnie, I have a sneaking suspicion that Jeffrey *murdered* him."

Steph cut in, "Ian, we have absolutely zero evidence of that. I have no idea how he got his stuff, but that doesn't prove Jeffrey killed him."

"Wow, this is a lot to take in." Ronnie's mind was a swirling mass of confusion and raw emotions. "I can't believe he is dead. He was the one person who could shed some light on what my dad was working on. It would have helped answer why I'm going back in time."

"Your dad?" Ian asked. "How is he part of this? I thought he died in 1999."

Steph cut in, "Yeah, remember Ini the psychic said her dad was at the center of her time travels?"

"But what were your dad and Jason working on?" Ian asked.

Ronnie fought back tears. "That is what I was going to ask Jason. Now I may never know."

"Your mom has other journals. We can have her look through them." Steph's voice cracked. She was getting emotional too.

"Steph, I need to tell you something else without Ian on the line." Ronnie was close to tears.

The phone clicked and Ronnie was off speaker. She heard a door shut and Ian protesting in the background. "Yes, I'm here, Ronnie."

She'd have to just spit it out, no time to nuance her words. "When Jeffrey took me from the convenience store where Mike and I stayed, he made me shower, then tried to rape me, saying I owed him for all the trouble he went through to get me."

"Noooooo. The bastard! Ronnie, are you away from him now?"

Ronnie fought back tears. "Yeah, thank God he didn't. Room service interrupted us. Then he kind of freaked out when I told him Mike went back in time with me. He locked me out of the bedroom while he was messing with something on his computer."

Steph's voice was strong now. "I can't believe he did that. He is such a friggin' monster."

"One more thing, Steph. Then I need to get back to Mike."

"Yes, I'm here."

"Jeffrey accused Mike of not only killing Kelly, but when we were at the National Suites, a doctor came up to my room to help me after the time travelling. I was going into shock and Mike wanted someone to help me."

"Yeah?" Steph kept her questions at bay so she could get this out.

"I think the hotel was hit by a tornado. When the doctor came to the room, a chunk of glass from the atrium punctured his neck. Because he bled out right in my hotel room, it looked like a murder scene. Mike tried to save him from a fatal injury. Only Jeffrey would try to manipulate that into a murder just to get at Mike."

"Oh, Blessed Mary. God rest his soul."

Ronnie inhaled deeply and sent up a prayer for Dr. Acosta. "Here is what is really weird. How could Jeffrey have possibly known about the doctor's death? We left the hotel when everyone else was about to be evacuated, and the place was in total chaos."

"That is really strange. How did he find you at the convenience store? What the hell, Ronnie? Is he an evil genius with superpowers?"

"He is evil, and he has the time travel thing, so in a way yes," Ronnie said, shaking her head, imagining a cartoon figure with an egg-shaped forehead.

"Ronnie, however he found out about that and the Kelly situation, Jeffrey is just using that to keep you away from Mike. He sure has spent a lot of money and energy trying to keep you two apart. Is it just an emotional attachment to you, or are you important in some other way?"

"Like what?"

"Like an important part of his science experiment? That would give him more reason to rescue you and then keep you two apart. Mike would find a way to end Jeffrey's experiments, to protect you from him. I bet Jeffrey is afraid of Mike. You said he brought in armed men. Why else would he do that? You two were stranded, not at a fort full of weapons making a last stand or anything."

"You're right. A bunch of military guys in a helicopter is overkill. Something really sketchy is going on with Jeffrey. I have no idea how he found us. We were literally dumped off the road and down into a river. We had to climb up a mountain on the opposite bank out in the middle of nowhere during the storm. All our stuff floated down the river, including the car, our luggage, wallets, phones—everything. There is no way he could have found us. And yet he did."

"Don't trust a thing he says," Steph said. "He is full of crap."

"I know. I am finally to the point where I can ignore his words and just read his body language. His lies are obvious when you can do that. Steph, I should have listened to you from the start. Why didn't I see it?"

Steph sniffed again. "I don't have any idea, Ronnie. I guess you were into him. I've seen through him for years. Luv, let me write down your new number." A shuffling noise and muffled voices interrupted them. "Hold on, Ian is banging on the door." She heard the door open, and Steph put her back on speaker.

Ian said, "I just rang Billy. I'll just put his phone up to yours, Stephanie."

Ronnie heard shuffling and then Billy's voice. "Hey, Ronnie."

"Hi, Billy! You know about Mike, right?"

"Yeah, he called me not too long ago. Any change?" Billy sounded much different without his exuberance leading the conversation.

"They did an angiogram and found pressure but are just monitoring him for now."

"Keep me posted, Ronnie. Ian, give her my number when we're done."

"Aye."

"Ronnie," Billy continued, "Mike is as good of a guy as you're ever going to find. I've shown Ian the article posted about Kelly's cause of death after the coroner's report came out. She died because of her epilepsy. Must have come on while she was in the shower. Mike was completely cleared but that fucking snake Brennan didn't bother to tell you that, did he?"

"No, Jeffrey wanted me to stay away from Mike."

"Mike has the full coroner's report. I can show it to you when you get back. It's all legit. Mike didn't lay a hand on her. He'd never do anything to hurt you either. As I said, Mike is as good as they get. He's not gone out with anyone since she died. It hurt him so bad to lose her. And everyone believed the damn cop at the scene. He was sure Mike had beaten her. But she got banged up and drowned during a seizure. That's it. Tragedy, but not something Mike caused."

"Thank you, Billy. Mike said the same thing when we talked about it. I would like to see the report when I get back."

"Let's get our boy better," Billy said, sadness seeping into his voice.

Ian's Scottish brogue broke into the conversation. "I knew something was up with that. I just couldn't fit it in my head that Mike would do something like that to a lass."

"Billy, what else did Mike say about what's going on here?" Ronnie asked.

"Just that he may need surgery to fix his head. The bastards that took him away from you pistol-whipped him. He didn't sound too good. I thought he was kidding me at first."

Steph said, "I'm so sorry, guys. Ian and I will be praying for you and Mike."

"Thank you, Steph," Ronnie said. "Is anyone near a computer?"

There was a pause, then Billy's voice cut in. "I am. Why?"

"Can you tell me how Jesse James died?" she asked.

Billy laughed. "All this going on and you need a history lesson? Okay. I'm not even going to ask. Give me a minute."

Ian laughed. "You're no gonna believe her anyway, Billy. Ask your mate when he can talk about it."

"Okay." Ronnie could hear the sound of Billy typing on his keyboard. "Okay, here it is. Jesse James was shot by Robert Ford while he was straightening a picture."

Ronnie and Ian spoke in unison. "What year?"

Billy laughed. "There has to be a good story here somewhere. Let's see. On April third, 1882, in St. Joseph's, Missouri."

"Are you sure it wasn't in Texas? No mention of a guy named Max?" Ronnie asked.

"It says Missouri and there is no mention of a Max. Wait…"

"You sure?" Steph asked.

"Let me click on this article." Billy clicked the keys. "Nope, they're all the same. Except some dude named J. Frank Dalton claimed to be the real Jesse James when he was ninety years old back in 1949."

"Thank you, Billy. What year was he born?" Ronnie asked.

"1847," Billy responded. "Someone owes me a beer and a long-ass story when this is all over."

"Guys, I want to get back to Mike. Steph, my mom may call you with some info on Jason. Call me if you learn anything else."

"I will, luv."

They said their goodbyes and Ronnie slipped the phone in her pocket. She sat at the desk for a minute, gathering herself. Jesse would have been twenty-three when Mike shot him. Maybe Mike was right about the multiverse theory. Her dad had said if she could slip into the right realm—was that the word he'd used? —she could make this stop happening to her. Unfortunately, the one person on this planet who might know how to do that was gone! Maybe her dad's journals would reveal some of the answers she was looking for, but her dad would not have written about his last day alive, would he?

She felt like an important piece of the puzzle was missing forever with Jason's death. She slammed her hand on the desk. "Dad's journal!" Ronnie rushed out the door and stopped, then did an about-face. Could Carlos's driver get the journal from the bedside table in her hotel room? How far away was that? Her face felt hot. Would she have to call Carlos again and ask? Would he be creepy again?

Chapter 80

Lost Puzzle Pieces

Ronnie reached in her pocket and pulled out a slip of paper. "Yes!" The driver had left his number. She dialed it and he answered right away. Ronnie glanced at the nursing station and two nurses she didn't recognize exchanged a glance, then they laughed. Ronnie smiled, knowing she looked a bit unstable with her clothes and behavior.

"*Señorita, hola*. What can I do for you?"

"Hi, I do have something. Do you know how far away the National Suites is? Is there any way to retrieve something from there for me?" A pang of guilt coursed through her veins. What if something happened to him while driving there?

"*Si*, not far. What do you need? Señor Munoz has instructed me to help in any way I can."

"Thank you so much. I left an important journal in the bedside table of room 527. It's leather. It's from my father who passed away."

"*Si, señorita*. I will call you at this number if I need further instructions. You say it's in room 527?"

"Yes. There's a little table between the beds."

The driver asked, "Are you still at the hospital with Señor Walsh?"

"Yes, I'm there with him. Can you bring it to me?"

"As soon as I am able."

Ronnie felt a wave of relief. "I cannot thank you enough. Be careful out there."

"I will be there in a few hours, if not sooner." The driver hung up.

Ronnie released a long exhale. Maybe if her father mentioned Jason, that would answer some of these pressing questions.

Hortênsia waved Ronnie over. She was standing at the entrance to Mike's room. Panic tore through her. Had something happened to Mike? Ronnie rushed over.

Hortênsia whispered, "He's awake and asking about you. I was about to get you."

"Is he okay?"

"See for yourself." Hortênsia held the door open for Ronnie and smiled.

Mike was sitting on the edge of the bed. "There you are."

"Mike, hey, should you be doing that?"

Mike smiled. "What? Sitting? Jesus, I'm not so far gone that I can't even sit up, am I?"

Ronnie rushed over to him. Mike opened his arms and folded her in a hefty embrace. "Oooooffft. You're squishing me."

"Sorry. I was worried that I only dreamt you were here. I was a bit wasted when I got out of that angiogram." Mike released her. "Oh, what a weird-ass outfit. Where did you get this?" Mike plucked at the sleeve of the dress shirt that hung on her loosely.

"One guess."

"Pencil neck. Damn. Hey, Hortênsia. Is there any way to get her something else to wear? These are rich, snobby clothes. I mean…" He held her at arm's length. "Seriously? Gym shorts too? Are those Armani? I didn't even know they made gym shorts."

Ronnie glanced down at the logo near her knee. "I don't know. I wasn't expecting you to be so perky. God, you look horrible, Mike. Two black eyes and a scrape every other inch on your skin. But you're feeling better?" She rested her hands on his thick shoulders, enjoying how alive he felt.

Hortênsia left the room and returned a minute later. "I have scrubs. What are you, a small?"

Ronnie took them from her and smiled. "Thank you. Wow, it would be nice to take these off."

Mike raised his eyebrows. "Yeah, it would. We need to remove any thoughts of that…" He glanced at Hortênsia and skipped the rest.

Ronnie looked at her too. "He seems much better. Do you agree?"

Hortênsia stepped over to his monitors. "Steroids can do that. Perk you right up. We still have to be careful, though. Sometimes it's a false high. Lie back down. Let's keep you still the rest of the day just to be sure."

Mike started to protest, but Ronnie jumped in. "Lie down, Mr. Bossman."

Mike broke out into a smile, then he winced. "Yes, ma'am." He lifted his feet back onto the bed and lay back, grabbing her hand and pressing it to his chest. "You'll have to hold me here. I'm eager to pull off every damn wire stuck on me." He glanced at the machines.

Ronnie pressed into his chest, pushing him flatter on the bed, enjoying the groove where his pectoral muscles met. He was firm and solid. And alive. Mischief shone in his eyes. Ronnie leaned in and kissed him.

"Mmmmm." He moaned into her lips. "I love your kisses. But I'll love 'em more without you dressed in *his* clothes."

Ronnie laughed and grabbed the navy scrubs and went into the bathroom. She shut the door and remembered about the wet towel. Mike could tell her more about the man who'd brought him here. Ronnie quickly changed into the scrubs and pulled out Jeffrey's money, the driver's number, and the walkie-talkie and slipped them into the scrubs' chest pocket.

Mike smiled as she walked towards him. "How about now?" She leaned in and kissed him again, savoring the firm, alive feel of him.

Mike wrapped an arm around her and pulled her closer, then glanced at Hortênsia, who held out a plastic cup of medicine. "Mr. Walsh, since you're awake and feeling better, I'll give these to you orally."

Ronnie smirked, and Mike caught her look and his face pinkened, just a smidge. Was he thinking the same dirty thoughts?

Hortênsia handed Mike the Styrofoam cup of ice water on the table, and he swallowed the pills. "Antibiotics. Are you feeling up to dinner? I can send up two trays."

Mike peeled his eyes from Ronnie's and turned to Hortênsia. "Yes, I'm ravenous."

"Hmmmm," Ronnie said. An overwhelming relief washed over her. She'd not expected him to even be awake, much less playful and teasing.

Hortênsia rolled her eyes dramatically. "Get a room, you two." Then strolled out, turning back to them before opening the door. "In about an hour the meals will arrive. Don't embarrass the candy striper, for God's sake." She winked and walked out.

"An hour..." Mike said, reaching out and rubbing her arm.

Ronnie laughed and bent over him for another kiss. "Mike, I have so much to tell you. I don't know if that smarty-pants brain is up for some sleuthing, but I could use your help."

His eyes sparkled. "Hit me with it."

"Where is the guy who brought you here?"

Mike looked around the room. "Oh God. I totally forgot about him. Last I remember I threw up on him."

"Which guy was it?"

"Ron, they all used aliases, but I don't think you saw him. Sarge? He came in with Jeffrey then took me away."

"Sarge? No. What did he look like?"

He shook his head. "A dude. I don't know. Tall as me, but slighter build."

"Hair, eye color?"

Mike pressed his lips together and shook his head. "I wasn't trying to date him, Ronnie."

"Seriously, you don't know what he looked like?"

"He's a white guy. Muscular, but not bigger than me. Sorry, I'm a dude, that's how we see other men."

Ronnie shook her head and updated him on all she'd learned through her mom, Steph, Ian, and Billy. "I have my dad's journal showing up soon. I'm hoping my dad wrote something about Jason. Anything to help us figure out who he was, and maybe that will help us figure out how his stuff got in Jeffrey's secret storage unit."

Mike reached across to the rolling table and grabbed a cell phone. He held up a finger while he dialed. "Billy, you big, goofy dumbass."

He held the phone away from his ear. Billy's over-exuberant, "Miiiiiikeeeeyyy," carried loud and clear.

Mike smiled and answered Billy's questions about how he was doing then asked, "Hey, man, look up Jason Korbin in your database." Mike held the phone back up to his ear and locked eyes with her. "I'll wait." Mike smiled and kissed her hand while he waited. Then Billy's voice came on and Mike said, "Okay, first Google this. Car crash, Jason Korbin." He smiled. "Bingo. Okay, take his date of birth…"

Mike winced as Billy yelled something in the phone. "Dude, I'm not deaf, my brain hurts, and your damn yelling isn't helping… I know you're not stupid... Yes…" Mike rolled his eyes. "I know you can figure out how to research someone. Yes. I'll wait. Touchy." Mike caressed her hand and smiled. "You feeling alright, Ron?"

Ronnie nodded. She was eager to see what Billy's database pulled up. "What database is he using?"

"Billy's a realtor. Not sure what it's called but he can look up Jason's info and see where he's owned houses before." Mike adjusted the phone on his left side. "Yes. Okay, good." He looked at her again. "He's found Jason Korbin. He lived in Manhattan. Then moved out to Virginia. What years?" He lifted his chin towards her. "Ronnie, when was your dad looking for an intern?"

"1998."

"Yeah? Okay. Email me that. Ronnie too. What's your email?"

Ronnie struggled to decipher when Mike was speaking to her versus Billy. Ronnie rattled off her email address, knowing she'd not be on there until she got home, but at least she'd have the information.

Mike continued, "Thanks, man. What else can you see about him?" He smiled and nodded at Ronnie.

Her heart skipped a beat to see Mike so alive, so on the ball. He was much better than he'd been last night before they'd gone to bed.

"Great. Okay, send me whatever you find in text. Thanks, man, you are the best." Mike handed her the cell phone and she set it on the table next to her.

"What did he say?"

Mike took her hand and smiled. His phone buzzed and she handed it back to him. Mike talked to Billy for a few minutes then hung up.

"Damn, he is good. Billy says Jason moved to a Norfolk, Virginia address about the time your dad was looking for an intern. That's pretty close to Virginia Beach, right?"

Ronnie nodded.

Mike's eyes were lit with excitement. "Jason went to Princeton undergrad, then graduate school at MIT for his PhD. Where did Jeffrey go?"

"He got his PhD at MIT."

"Jeez, I wonder if they were roommates or classmates or something. That could be the connection."

Ronnie shook her head. "Yeah, could easily be. Why the hell would Jeffrey have Jason's old papers and diploma and stuff?"

"I have no idea. But at least there is a possible link. They both were at MIT. They both lived in the Virginia Beach area at the same time. Billy is finding out more and will let us know. I bet they were buddies and maybe Jeffrey got the research from Jason, or maybe stole it from him. Who knows? Could he have stolen Jason's papers to find out more about the work your dad was doing?"

"Jeffrey never mentioned my dad. Wouldn't he have said something to me over the last year and a half?" An unsettled feeling crept over her. Jeffrey never talked much about his past. Just that he had *money, honey*. A shiver ran up her spine. Had Jeffrey sought her out after her father had died? Or had they met by chance? Had her father ever spoken to Jeffrey? What was the connection?

Chapter 81

Lies upon Lies

Ronnie suppressed thoughts of utter betrayal. It couldn't be true. She hadn't been that naïve. Why would Jeffrey lie to her about who he was? Her gut told her there were a lot more lies from Jeffrey.

Mike's expression hardened. "That sneaky son of a bitch!"

"That's what I wanted to ask Jason about. What were they working on the day my dad died? After what Steph told me today, I want to know if he knew Jeffrey."

"I'm sorry, Ronnie. I wish Jason was around to answer those questions. Maybe the journal will give us more information." His phone buzzed in his hand again. He read Billy's text out loud. "Dead end around the time Jason died. He owned property but there is no information after that. If he'd sold the house in Norfolk, there would be a record of it. It's still held by someone in his family, maybe?"

Ronnie grabbed Mike's arm, wanting to feel his strength, even if it was waning. Something much bigger was developing and it made her feel queasy, and completely unsettled. "Can Billy send the details of Jason's accident to your email too? I'd like to see if he died under mysterious circumstances. Ian thinks Jeffrey killed Jason. No idea why, but it would be worth looking into it."

Mike slowly typed a response, then handed Ronnie the phone. "Please, can you type it out? My eyes hurt."

Ronnie typed out his message. A text came back, and Ronnie read it to Mike. "Ian has a picture of the article. He's sending it."

Mike's phone dinged and she received the text. It took a minute for the full picture to show up. Eventually the whole thing appeared, and she read it out loud.

"Manhattan man dies in fiery crash. Jason Korbin died in an automobile accident off the pier on…" Ronnie couldn't read the outer edge of the article. Ian's flashlight had only lit up part of it. "Something. Police suspect driving under the influence was a factor." She skimmed the rest of the article but gleaned nothing new.

Mike twisted his mouth to the side then said, "Shame. He would have been very helpful."

"Yeah. Poor guy, that is a bad way to go."

Mike leaned in for another kiss and was interrupted by the cell phone buzzing in

Ronnie's hand.

She answered. "Billy, hey, man. Thanks for all your help."

Billy's voice took on an edge she'd not heard before. "Hey, put Mike on."

Ronnie shook her head. "He's okay. I just wanted to hear what is going on."

"Ronnie, I'm a bit pissed at you. Mike's never been injured on my watch. Now he's interested in you and all this bullshit happens to him. He could have been killed."

Ronnie's mouth dropped open. She had not expected this from good-natured Billy. "I know. I feel horrible about everything he's been through for me."

Mike snatched the phone out of her hand. "Dude, what the hell are you doing?" He held the phone away from his ear for a second as Billy's angry voice carried through. "Right, right...okay." Mike rolled his eyes, then covered them, massaging with his fingers. "You done with your childish tirade?" He glanced at her. "Don't you ever talk to her like that again. That woman you are badmouthing saved my damn life. You don't know what we've been through." Mike shot her an apologetic look. "Billy, *I* was driving when we got in the accident. *I* insisted we leave the hotel. *She* is the one who pulled my unconscious body out of our wrecked Jeep, swam me in a swirl of hurricane debris, and saved my damn life."

Billy talked for a full minute and Mike's eyes were glassy with tears. Then Mike handed her the phone.

Ronnie took it out of his hand. "Hello?"

The line was silent for a second, then Billy cleared his throat. "Ronnie, Mike is my best friend in the whole world. I know you're starting to be his breast friend." He chuckled. "But we've been through a ridiculous amount of shit together."

"I know, Billy." Ronnie glanced at Mike, who was wiping away tears. What had Billy said to him?

Billy cut her off. "No, let me say this. I don't want him hurt. Do you understand me? He's been through hell. Absolute fucking hell."

"I know, he told me some of it."

"You don't know the half of it. Anyway, please forgive me if I'm a tad protective of my boy. I know he can take care of himself and all, but I just can't have anyone breaking his heart, or taking him away from me. If you go out with him, you will not, under any circumstances, hurt him. Or keep us apart. You are not allowed to do that stupid chick shit where you keep your man away from his friends. Do you understand?"

"I understand. I promise I won't keep you two knuckleheads apart." Ronnie smiled. It was touching how much Billy loved Mike. The giant, goofy dude was as protective as a German shepherd.

Mike took the phone from her. "This doesn't sound like an apology, Billy." Mike handed the phone back to Ronnie.

Billy's voice cracked. "I'm sorry for what I said. You didn't cause this. Mike explained it to me. You saved his life? You really did that?"

"I did. He was a huge, unconscious blob, but thank God I managed to pull him out through the back window and float his fat ass downriver to safety."

Billy let out his booming laugh. "You are awesome, Ronnie. I'm sorry I doubted you. Just take care of him and keep that promise."

"I will." Ronnie smiled at Mike, who shook his head angrily.

Billy said in her ear, "Oh, damn, I'm an idiot. I called because I found something big. Does your phone have speaker? I want Mike to hear this too."

Ronnie pressed the speaker button on Carlos's loaner phone.

Mike said, "Go ahead, you jackass."

Billy laughed again. "I looked up Jeffrey Brennan in my database. Guess what I found."

Ronnie and Mike exchanged a glance.

Billy answered for them. "He didn't exist before 1999. At least according to my database. So, I looked up all his information. I found Jeffrey's name on the condo in Florida but nothing else. Not a single damn thing. Except one small notation. Guess what it was."

"No games, Billy, just tell us," Mike said. His expression showed alarm.

"Okay, fair enough. There was a transfer of Jason Korbin's house in Norfolk to…get this, Jeffrey *fucking* Brennan."

Mike's eyes widened. "What the hell does that mean?"

Ronnie felt the bottom fall out of her world.

"My best guess is Jason changed his name to Jeffrey. You can't transfer a deed unless you are close family. Even with that, the state usually wants you to sell the property to a new owner if the original owner is dead. They probate the will and fix all the paperwork. That is not what happened here. It was a transfer."

"A transfer?" Mike lay back against the pillow, looking more exhausted.

Billy spoke excitedly, making Ronnie revise the image to a golden retriever. "Dudes, they do that with a name change. If Jason Korbin legally changed his name to Jeffrey Brennan, they'd fix the paperwork. It was probably triggered when he tried to buy the condo in Florida. Without the connection to his old life as Jason, Jeffrey Brennan would have no credit. No one would sell a condo to a thirty-something-year-old dude with no credit history—no car purchase, no apartment lease, no electric bill, no cell phone. As far as the credit lending world was concerned, Jeffrey Brennan didn't exist."

Mike looked alarmed and took her hand. "So, you're saying you have evidence that Jeffrey Brennan is *Jason Korbin*?"

Billy laughed. This time it reverberated in the speaker. "I sure as shit do. Ronnie, did you know he changed his name? You were seeing him when he bought the condo in Florida, weren't you?"

"I…I was. That explains why he didn't want me to move in with him. He's a lying sack of shit. Mike." Ronnie fought tears and he pulled her close. "He's been lying to me all this time? Billy, what year did Jeffrey Brennan's name show up?"

"1999. No wait. After that…" They heard clicking. "Jason bought the Norfolk property in 1999. The transfer happened in January of 2004." He paused and there was more clicking. "Here it is! I have the name change paperwork. It's attached to his deed. He changed his name to Jeffrey on January twenty-seventh, 2003."

Ronnie had trouble catching her breath. They'd started dating in the spring of 2003. He'd changed his name *just* before they'd met. Their entire relationship was a big fat lie. "If he were Jason in 1998, that means he was working for my dad…"

Mike's eyes widened. "He ran the experiment the day your dad went into the coma!"

Ronnie's mind completely stopped for a few seconds as this information soaked into her soul. Steph had been right from the very beginning. Jeffrey was up to something. But what? "Did he seek me out after my father died? He changed his name a few months before we started dating. Did he do this so there would be no connection from him to my dad?" Ronnie exhaled, feeling like she'd let go of the world she'd known the past year and a half with Jeffrey. As she inhaled, her world reset on a different axis, and she felt that nothing would ever be the same again. How could she ever trust anyone again?

Chapter 82

Semper Fi

Jeffrey drove back to his hotel, reliving the *coup de grâce* with Hannah. It was the perfect sendoff for such a sex-craved bitch. Definitely not something he would have prearranged, but there was a certain symmetry to how things had unfolded. She had screwed him over, and he'd repaid her with the slap in the ass she deserved. Well, more like a prick in the ass. Jeffrey chuckled.

The wipers were barely keeping up with the rain, and he slowed to make sure he'd not run into something on the road.

When he'd taken Hannah out to dinner for the first time, she wouldn't shut up about the Oneida Community, and how they'd taught their members about Jesus's Millennial Kingdom, or some other crazy shit. Now she'd get to meet her hero, John Noyes. Would she know him on sight? He'd been the leader of the little community in upstate New York, circa 1850. She'd fit in nicely with their free-love culture and group marriage philosophy. Hannah had been fascinated with their traditions of male sexual continence, where the man would control his ejaculation and maintain the plateau phase of intercourse for as long as possible.

"You're welcome, Hannah. You can be in your favorite weird sex cult with all the men you can handle." Now that was a weird bit of history. The silverware manufacturer Oneida had begun as a commune based on a sex cult. Maybe Hannah would become famous for designing cheap stainless 'silverware' in her new life. And, if not, she would at least enjoy the polyandrous, never-ending, never-climaxing sex.

He'd have to call his fixer, Rick Harris, to plant a few retroactive MySpace posts, or some other crap to tie Ronnie's weird experiences to Hannah. Maybe Rick could unearth a few emails confessing Hannah's hatred of "the damn supermodel" Ronnie. Rick would know what to do. Either way, with Hannah's storm seeding research and the final pulse tracked to her hotel room, it should be enough evidence to connect the phenomenon to Hannah, and they'd put the investigation to bed. Hannah's final act, death by suicide, would tie a neat bow on the entire probe. It would be a relief to have the Feds off his tail. He would be cleared. After all, according to his passport and a few witnesses, he'd been in Virginia Beach handling a personal emergency. Dr. Vasu could back that up.

Jeffrey turned into the parking lot and parked the car and ran to the front door. Next on the list was to touch base with Sarge and see how Mike's visit to the police station turned out. Hopefully, he'd stew in a dark prison cell for a few days, maybe even be killed by a cellmate while awaiting his arraignment. There were possibilities still with that. Mike had deserved that and much more. He'd have to give Sarge and his team a bonus for all the crap Mike had put them through. Bastard. What did he think he was, Rambo or something?

At some point he'd have to track down Ronnie. In his rush to retrieve the equipment Hannah had stolen, he had to let her go. What would she do without Mike? He was in a jail with no way to reach out to her. Ronnie needed to be managed while helping her get back to Florida. After all, she had no money, no ID. She *needed* him. She needed another round of hypnosis to change her feelings about him. It had worked before.

Jeffrey returned to his hotel and climbed the stairs. It would be worth tossing his clothes in the trash. You could never be too careful if anyone decided to look into Hannah's suicide.

Jeffrey entered the room. Their breakfast was still there, reminding him of the shock Ronnie had delivered. God damned Mike Walsh.

Jeffrey changed his clothes, choosing a bamboo jersey t-shirt in a light green tone—Armani, of course. He'd not brought too many changes of clothes and had lost another shirt when Ronnie had left. She had his gym shorts too, damn her. He'd have to get back soon or buy more clothes. He chose a pair of white shorts and paired it with his deck shoes, then dug in his duffle bag for the burn phone to call Sarge.

The phone rang a few times, then Sarge picked up. "Yo."

"Sarge. Update me."

Sarge cleared his throat. "There has been a situation."

Jeffrey walked to the table and picked up a cold piece of toast, realizing how hungry he was. Murdering people was hard work, as it turned out. "I don't like the sound of that. Was Walsh the cause of this situation?"

"Dead on, sir."

"Are you going to tell me what happened, Sarge?" Jeffrey would have to rethink that bonus if they fucked this thing up. "And use plain English. I'm sick of all the military jargon. You know I'm a civilian."

Sarge obliged and kept it in simple terms. "When we left the convenience store, Walsh tried to escape, but we recaptured him. Then we were in the process of transporting the ornery son of a bitch when we had an unfortunate mishap."

Jeffrey's mind toiled with the possibilities. "He's dead?"

"No, not as far as I know."

"Get to the point, Sarge. I don't have all day."

"Mr. Brennan, one of my men had to discipline him. Walsh was damaged in the process."

"Damaged? Fatally?"

Sarge grunted. "No, stop doing that. Walsh is alive as far as I know. He sustained a head wound. Well, he already had one, but let's just say a member of the team exacted a bit of revenge for being such a huge PIA."

"PIA? Explain please." Jeffrey chewed the last bit of toast and swallowed the cold coffee.

"Pain in the ass." Sarge cleared his throat again. "Let me cut to the chase for you. Walsh was unconscious and we tried to get help from a local physician, but he insisted I take him to the hospital. So that's where I left him."

Jeffrey set the coffee cup down and turned around, stabbing the air with his finger. "You took him to the hospital? Do you remember Plan A, Plan B, and Plan C?"

"I do." Sarge's tone was apologetic.

"Did any of those contingency plans involve saving Walsh if something should go wrong?"

"No, sir. They did not."

"Please tell me you dumped him off at the door. Or better yet, in a fucking river." Jeffrey slammed the coffee cup on the table.

"No, sir. *I* brought him to the hospital."

"Can you explain your deviation from our plans? Please, for fuck's sake."

Sarge didn't respond.

"Just tell me what happened, Sarge, for God's sake! What were you thinking?"

"Mostly I was thinking about something that Walsh said to me. To us."

Jeffrey sat in the chair in front of the food. "What the fuck did he say, Sarge?"

"*Semper fi*. Do you know what that means?"

Jeffrey gritted his teeth. "Always faithful, or some bullshit like that?"

Sarge cleared his throat again. "I wouldn't expect you to understand the full breadth of it."

Jeffrey shoveled cold eggs into his mouth and chewed. "I sure as shit do not. Who else went?"

"Just me, sir. The team is at the hotel awaiting instructions. Do I need to move them to another location? Or are we…at ease?"

Jeffery pressed his hand into his forehead. "I want to know how badly injured Mike is so I can decide how to best proceed."

"Walsh has a head injury. He was in pretty bad shape when I left him."

"You should have dumped him on the side of a road. Or better yet, run the sorry asshole over with the Yukon."

"That's a felony. I do recall laying out what the team was willing to do. Rescuing your girlfriend from a murderer. Check. Extracting them back to safety. Check."

Jeffrey seethed with anger. "Making sure *Mike* is in jail at least for a few weeks. That was the plan. And if he got mortally injured in some freak accident, I was totally okay with that."

"I know, sir."

"I'm not sure if there is more we need to do. I was going to give you a bonus for all the trouble Mike caused you. Damn it! Can't you stop being a damn grunt and call him Mike like a normal person? But seeing as you didn't even accomplish the full mission, I can't even say that you failed by no fault of your own, because you made the choice to take him to the hospital."

"Mr. Brennan. The choice was made by the doctor. Walsh was in a bad way. He was having a seizure and the doctor made it clear if we…"

Jeffrey cut him off. "The doctor made it clear? Is the doctor paying for your time on this godforsaken island? Is he?"

"No, sir."

"God damn, fucking Sarge. This is not what I wanted."

Sarge cleared his throat again. It was his way of showing discomfort. "How did things go with your girlfriend? Was she as happy to see you as Walsh had been?"

"Who, Ronnie?" For a panicked second he thought Sarge meant Hannah. "I don't even know where Ronnie is. She ran off, and I've not had a chance to find her yet."

"Sir, ran off? How did she manage to do that?"

Jeffrey stood up and paced the room. "Long story. Look, I'm going to sort through that. I'm going to call this mission concluded. You and your team can head back in the morning. I'll wire payment when I get back."

"Roger that," Sarge said. "Have a safe trip back. And call me if you need anything else down the road. I'm always ready for some fuckery."

"Sarge."

"Yes, sir."

"I might need you later if they ask where I've been the last few days. Just tell anyone asking that I was with you, we got wasted at the beach. Okay?"

"Absolutely. We should do that sometime, Mr. Brennan. I could show you around the bars there."

"Thank your team for me. Let me know if there are any incidentals." Jeffrey hung up the phone and tucked it back in his duffle bag.

Chapter 83

Betrayal

Ronnie crawled into bed with Mike, and he had held her close, kissing her head and whispering that it was going to be okay. He'd fallen asleep shortly after. A wave of nausea washed over her, but she quelled it.

How could Jeffrey not even be Jeffrey? Every single thing about him had been a lie. She pictured his face and focused on his real name, *Jason Korbin*. It just didn't fit. Jeffrey, or Jason, had betrayed her on every level. Ronnie had always been careful who she let in her life. She'd never had a one-night stand, never slept with a guy unless she was in love with him and knew he was trustworthy. It shook her to the core Jeffrey had been able to invade the place she'd tried so hard to protect. He had totally and completely fooled her...for almost two years.

Ronnie closed her eyes and tried to summon her father. *Dad. Please, tell me what Jeffrey is up to. Why did he seek me out of all the people on the planet?* Another insidious thought sprouted and grew dangerous tendrils, further unseating her foundations of trust. Had Jeffrey caused the accident in the lab so he could steal her father's life's work?

She felt hot now, realizing the depth of the betrayal. Her dad had taken Jeffrey under his wing, to share his knowledge, his prized invention, his life's work. What had Jeffrey done with that? Had he killed her father, or at the very least set his demise in motion, choosing to not share anything with her mother before she pulled the plug? He could have saved her dad. Would her dad be here today if Jeffrey hadn't been his intern? Would they have found his heart issue before it killed him?

Tears flowed down her face, against her will. There was no greater betrayal than what Jeffrey had put her through. Lies to manipulate her into unwittingly be part of her dead father's time travel experiments.

Ronnie pressed her lips together and fumed, her emotions turning from sadness at the loss of her father to the urge for revenge. She had to get back at Jeffrey for the abuse he'd put her through. The final straw, when he digitally raped her, and threatened more as payment for his unwelcome rescue. And equally vile, hiring a private army to kidnap and accost Mike, setting him up for a crime he did not commit and in the process, damaging him further in their botched attempt at putting him in jail.

She'd been sleeping with the enemy. Why had it been so important for him to seek her out? Why had he put her through all of this? Was he acting out of revenge for something her father had done to him? Where was he now? He must be furious that she'd left the hotel.

Mike stirred and she held still, not wanting to disturb him.

"Hey." He woke up and pulled her closer. "You okay?"

Ronnie sniffed. "Just upset. I just want to know why Jeffrey did all this. Why did he change his name? Why did he let my father die?"

Mike kissed her hair. "It has to be pretty damn upsetting. I mean, who does that? He is a sick bastard. I just can't believe he did all of that to your family."

"He is sick. Why did he do this to me? Why is he trying so hard to hurt us?"

Someone knocked on the door. Ronnie climbed out of bed and padded over to it, wondering who would be knocking. She opened the door and Carlos's driver stood there, damp from the rain.

"Please come in." Ronnie stepped out of the way. "Thank you again for retrieving that for me."

Mike nodded. "Hello, who are you?"

The driver stood awkwardly in the middle of the room, dripping on the floor, holding a plastic garbage back with something inside. He nodded at Mike.

Ronnie introduced them, then asked, "Is that my dad's journal?"

"I am hoping. It was the only thing in that bedside table." He gently unfurled the trash bag and handed her the leather journal. "Is this what you were looking for?"

Ronnie clutched the precious cargo to her chest. "Yes, thank you so much. How bad was the room? Was it hard to get in there?"

"Emergency crews were there evacuating the last guests. Apparently, the hotel was hit by a tornado. I'm glad they let me pass. They were worried about the structure. That bedroom window had crashed in. Putting it in the drawer saved it."

Tears gathered in Ronnie's eyelashes. "I'm so grateful for you." Ronnie was overwhelmed with gratitude and hugged the man. He stood stiffly, not sure how to react to her exuberance. Finally, she let him go and he stood back, eyes blinking in shock. He must not have been used to people hugging him. "Please, can you write down your address? I'd like to send you something for doing this for me."

The man stepped backward, eying the door. "Oh, no, no. This is just a service I provide for Carlos. He pays me well, I assure you. Is there anything else I can do for you? Carlos was very clear. I'm here to help you two." He glanced at Mike and bowed slightly.

Ronnie followed his gaze. "Mike, do we want to get the name and address of the owner of the convenience store? I don't want him to be out the money for what we used."

"Yes, that's a great idea. Plus, Jeffrey's men damaged more of the things on the shelves."

"They did?"

"Well, not on purpose. Let's just say we had a scuffle or two." An angry look passed through Mike's features. "I insist you write down your name and address for us. I want to compensate you taking the risk on her dad's journal, and if there is way to find the owner of that store we took refuge in."

The driver shook his head. "No, it would be very uncomfortable for me if you did that. Please, what is the information to find the store?" He shook his head and held up his hands, one still clutching the trash bag. "I insist."

Ronnie turned to Mike. "How do we tell him where we were?" She was eager to crack open the journal and to see if her father mentioned Jason.

Mike explained the roads they'd taken before the crash and where the convenience store was located. His mind was firing on all cylinders now. He remembered more than she did. When he was done, the driver excused himself and left.

"That makes me feel so much better. I want to repay the owner for repairs to the two doors I messed up. Somewhere in there is the list of food and drinks we took. I'll have to throw in some money for the wrecked stuff Jeffrey's men helped ruin." Mike nodded to the journal in her arms. "Come here and let's see what your father said about his intern."

Ronnie handed Mike the journal and she climbed back in the bed with him. Mike adjusted the head of the bed to a sitting position and tried to move over more.

There wasn't much room in the narrow hospital bed, but Ronnie relished being so close to him. He handed the book back to her. "Mike, I can't believe it's safe. If I'd had my act together when we were packing, it would have gone down that river with the rest of our luggage." She didn't want to say it out loud, but a little part of her believed her dad had helped save the book.

They spent the next hour combing through the pages. Ronnie was proud to share her father's genius with Mike. It was like they were meeting for the first time, and she badly wanted Mike to like her dad. Her dad would have loved Mike—it was a shame they'd never get to meet.

When Mike had dozed off, Ronnie sat back on the cot and continued reading her father's words, soaking in his thoughts, his trials and tribulations, and his victories. By all accounts, the intern…Jeffrey, had worked out well, adding the fresh new thinking needed to provide success.

Chapter 84

The Intern

Mike opened his eyes, dreaming of kicking asses and taking names. He glanced over at Ronnie's still form in the cot next to him. She was engrossed in the journal, flipping pages and making notes on a pad of paper one of the nurses must have brought. Ronnie's hair spilled over her shoulders and splashed down the navy scrubs.

The stress of outside forces had forged their bond, turning their initial spark of attraction to tempered steel. She had proven her strength, even in her weakest moment, giving him her all without question in the face of danger. The way Ronnie had laid down the law with Billy, like she intended to be there for the long haul, and her graciousness with Carlos's driver, even something as small as that, made him want more. It almost felt like he'd always loved her, on a level way deeper than sexual attraction alone.

Ronnie noticed he was awake. Her face lit up and she leaned over the bed to kiss him. "Wakey wakey." Then she giggled.

"What?"

The dimples were showing. He could get used to seeing that every time he woke up.

"You said *wakey wakey* to me when you woke me up at camp with Jesse and his gang. It seemed so out of character for someone in 1872."

"It was. Nothing I did back there was in character. I was a bumbling idiot." He stretched and sat up.

"No, you weren't." She took his hand. "You were brave, strong, and sexy. Even in Max's body."

"Can you say that to me every morning we wake up together?" He squeezed her hand.

"Deal. Want to know what I found out?" Ronnie picked up the pad of paper.

"Absolutely."

"My dad did hire someone named Jason Korbin. He didn't give a description of his physical attributes, but confirmed he was in his last year of getting a PhD at MIT." Mike nodded. "That fits."

She continued. "My father did make a note that one day he walked into the lab and Jeffery was staring at my high school graduation picture. It was odd enough for him to bother to write it in the journal."

"Creepy bastard." Mike tamped down the anger that threatened to crush his buoyant mood.

"Yeah. He doesn't go into much detail, but every mention of the intern after that confirms he was involved in my dad's project. There is a formula I wanted to ask you about." She flipped the page. "Here it is. Do you recognize this?" Ronnie held up her notes and showed him the handwritten formula. It showed two capitol letter Rs with a bar over top, covering both letters. "He called it double R bar magic."

"Double R bar?" Mike searched the recesses of his memory of college physics, mathematics, and economics. "No, I don't think there is a capitol R in any formula I can remember, unless you're talking about real numbers and that is a funky-looking R. A lowercase r can mean radius, rate of interest, or growth rate. In physics a lowercase r in bold means vector."

"Someone's brain is working pretty well, I see."

Mike smiled and tapped his head. "I didn't invent new mathematics though, so don't be too impressed."

Ronnie laughed. "*Sucks for you.*" Then Ronnie glanced at her notes and the smile fell. "Apparently, Jeffery was invaluable in helping my dad create the formula." Ronnie sniffed.

"What? Are you crying?" Mike touched her arm and she smiled.

"No. It disgusts me that the one person I hate the most in the world was an integral part of making my dad's experiment work. From my dad's own admission, he had been doing the math wrong. The experiment—he doesn't say what it was, but I think we both know." She cocked her head to the side. "It was finally successful because of the new formula they created together. Jeffrey's math fixed it. His life's work was successful only because of Jeffrey's intelligence." She shook her head. "How screwed up is that?"

Mike shook his head. "I can't believe such a horrible asshole could be smart enough to do anything but fill a toilet. My question is why did Jeffrey…? We're sure the intern was Jeffrey?"

"Yeah, the housing stuff proves it." She glanced back at her notes.

Mike continued, "Why did Jeffrey let your father die the day the experiment sent him back? Why didn't he tell your mom what happened so she could keep him alive until they could retrieve him?"

"I don't know. I wish I could find out exactly what happened that night. I wonder if my mom has any papers from that day. Would he have time to write up what happened?" She dabbed at her eyes. "Mike, my dad named the formula after me. Double R bar. The first R is for Ronald. The second one was for me."

"You're kidding? Really? What an honor." Mike smiled.

"Yeah, it's wonderful. My dad and I were so close. He called it the double R bar magic."

"Do you think there was something about you specifically that had him name it for you? And why not V for Veronica?"

"The letter V is velocity, isn't it?" Ronnie answered.

"Oh duh. You're right. He'd not use that."

"My dad called me Ronnie. My mom preferred Veronica. I switched to Ronnie in college because I hated my name. Stuffy Veronica. You asked if there was something about me specifically that would have them naming it after me. Like what would that be?"

"Blood type. Do you share the same blood type as your dad?"

"Oh my God, I do. We're both O positive. My mom and brother are A."

"Maybe that's it. Is that why Jeffery would come find you? Were your genes similar to your dad's, making you crucial to continuing the experiments?"

"Maybe." She sounded sad.

"Maybe the asshole Jeffery figured out what glitched and caused your dad to not return. Maybe he fixed that glitch and came back to find you, changed his name so he could get close to you. He sought you out and started dating you while he was finishing up the research."

Ronnie shivered and rubbed her arms. "Holy crap, Mike. You might be right. Jeffrey was studying power. That's why he moved to Florida, to work at the weather lab and see if he could store the power of the big storms to use later."

"Jeez, you're *kidding*. I bet he moved to that lab to find enough power to continue the experiment. Too bad your dad had to be sacrificed." Mike shook his head. "But I went back too. Do you think Jeffrey intended to send me back?"

Her eyes widened, and she leaned forward towards him. "Mike, he was completely shocked when I told him you went back too. He looked like he'd been touched by a ghost. That's when I got away from him. He ran into the bedroom and got on his computer right away. Then he locked me out of the room and that's when I left."

"You didn't tell me about this, Ronnie. What happened when they took you away from me?" Fear and anger blocked the thread of logic. Now all he could think about was choking the pencil neck. Had he hurt Ronnie?

Ronnie sighed and let out a long, slow breath. "Mike…" She covered her mouth.

He sat up and grabbed her hand. "What…? Please tell me." The monitor beeped in time to his accelerating heartbeat.

She shook her head and looked into his eyes. "They took us off the mountain in a helicopter and then Jeffrey drove me to a hotel. He kept complaining about how much I smelled and how ungrateful I was since I didn't grovel and thank him for separating us. I was so worried about you, Mike."

Her eyes were tearing up, and he knew there was something he'd not like in what she was about to tell him. "Helicopter. That's what we heard in the convenience store. How much did he spend on this little rescue mission?"

"I have no idea. A lot. Anyway, at the hotel I showered but he said I owed him." Ronnie looked down at her hands and bent a corner of the pad of paper.

"And…?" Mike set aside the anger. She needed to get this out without his interrupting. He squeezed her hand. "I'm not going to punch a wall this time, I promise."

Ronnie looked up at him and gave him a sad smile. "Good, because this might be worse than Jeffrey lying about Kelly."

"Shit. Please just tell me, babe. I swear I'll handle it better this time." Fear stoked his pulse higher.

"Mike, he pushed me to the bed and said he was going to get payment. I tried to fight him off. The asshole may have finished the deed if the room service man hadn't shown up."

"The deed? You mean he almost raped *you*?"

She met his glare and nodded, biting her lips.

Mike looked away, swallowing the vicious hatred, the desire to murder evil geniuses. "Fucking fucker." He tried to say it calmly, but it came out in a bark. The heart monitor bleeped louder as his heart blasted away the anger. "He didn't hurt you, did he?"

Ronnie shook her head. "No, he didn't." She shot a glance at the monitor and shook her head. "Maybe it's better to let it out?" She cocked her head to the side. "Here punch this." She offered the pad of paper.

Mike turned away and let out a long, slow exhale. "When I saw him at the convenience store, I tackled him to the floor and busted open his lip. Then warned him that I'd destroy him if he laid a hand on you."

"You do have a bit of a temper." Ronnie scrunched up her nose adorably.

"Ronnie, he has to pay for what he's done to you. The attempted rape is probably the ultimate violation. But it's not the only thing he's done to you."

"I know. I'd be happy if he'd just go away forever. I think he'll leave me alone. We know what he's up to. He can't expect to get away with it anymore. And I have you now to protect me."

He shook his head, fighting a tumultuous array of emotions, none of them good for head injuries. "I promised I'd keep you safe and I didn't. I'm so sorry, Ronnie. Will you ever forgive me?"

Ronnie looked shocked, then climbed in the bed with him.

He pulled her close.

"Mike, no one has ever done so much to protect me. When we crashed into the river, you pulled me tight, cradling my head. I'm convinced I came out of that with very little damage because of your instincts to protect me. You got us up that mountain, diving into my deep-rooted, yet unknown, fear of chupacabras to spur me on."

Mike chuckled, then kissed her head. "I would do a lot more for you, Ronnie."

She kissed him on the lips. "You already did. You fought how many dudes to try to keep me away from Jeffrey?"

"A couple of guys. It was no big deal. And it didn't do anything but get me in the hospital." In his head he counted four: Sarge, Jaws, Nelly, and Bailey.

Ronnie sat up and stared at him. "No big deal? They were trained soldiers with guns."

"Marines, babe. You don't call Marines soldiers."

"Oh really? How do you know they were Marines?"

He smiled. "They're easy to spot. I spent four years surrounded by them." He touched her face. "I just wish I could have kept you safe from Jeffrey—from all the bullshit he's thrown at you."

Hortênsia busted into the room, followed by two doctors.

"Mr. Walsh, great to meet you." Dr. Costillo walked closer holding a clipboard. "I'm Dr. Costillo. Hello again, Miss Andrews."

Ronnie nodded.

The doctor continued, "Mr. Walsh, please meet Dr. Vasquez." The man nodded and Mike waved, eager to get past the formalities and onto his diagnosis.

"We are here to give you some good news." Dr. Costillo smiled.

Ronnie crawled back to the cot and grabbed his hand.

"Your MRI results have come back. You're going to be okay. As long as you take it easy for a few days here with us. You do have a hematoma, but given your latest test results, I'm willing to say you're going to make a complete recovery."

"Thank you, doctor." Mike turned to Ronnie, who beamed back at him.

"The MRI shows some damage, but not enough that we need to perform surgery. The monitor we placed in your head is showing the medications are working to bring down the swelling. Your pressure has dramatically improved."

"That is great news, doc. How long will you keep me here?" Mike asked, not able to stifle a smile.

"A few days. There is the outside possibility that the swelling could return, but as long as you're resting, not doing anything physically exerting..." Dr. Costillo turned her attention from Mike to glance at Ronnie.

Ronnie feigned innocence, making her eyes huge and smiling guiltily. "I swear, I didn't just make his heart rate blow up a few minutes ago."

Hortênsia laughed. "Likely story."

Mike turned to the doc. "So, what, a few days if I'm a good boy? Is there any possibility of us getting back to Florida in the next few days?"

The doctors exchanged a glance. "Mr. Walsh, let's not get ahead of ourselves. I don't want you making any plans until we clear you. The head injury you suffered is a very serious matter. I'm just telling you that we don't need to do surgery. I'm not telling you that you are healed, though."

"Gotcha. But you think I'm not going to have any permanent damage from this?" he asked.

"Doctors stay away from two words. *Always* and *never*." Costillo smiled. "But you're looking good right now. I do think there won't be any lasting damage, but only time will tell. You may have headaches for quite some time. How is your vision? Do you see double? Are you having any vision changes?"

Mike shook his head. "No. I see fine."

Dr. Vasquez reached out to turn Mike's head and examine his temple. "You must have a very hard head. I was surprised you didn't have a fracture."

"I've been told I'm hardheaded on multiple occasions." Mike let both doctors poke around and flash a light in his eyes. "Just for the record, I'm not a fan of bright lights."

Vasquez nodded. "Sensitivity to light is a common symptom for this type of injury. Just lie low for a few days."

"I will, doc. Thank you."

"Do you have any more questions for us?" Dr. Costillo asked.

Ronnie raised a finger. "Can Mike eat dinner tonight? Is he on any other restrictions?"

Costillo addressed Mike. "I'd like you to be on bed rest. No running around. Get up to use the bathroom. Sit up to eat. Then lie back down. It will help lower that pressure in your head if you just rest."

"I'll make sure he does, doctors." Ronnie smiled at him.

The doctors left and Hortênsia checked his vitals then left them alone.

"Mike, this is great news. You're not going to be a bumbling idiot forever. Just a few more days!"

Mike pulled her towards him, kissing her passionately. "Ronnie, baby, I love you." He hadn't meant to say it. Good news and the thrill of having her close made him do it. That was something he'd known for at least a week now.

She pulled back and stared into his eyes. "Mike, you meant that?"

"I do. I promise to never let Jeffrey hurt you again. Just give me the chance to be the man you deserve. I can't wait to get back home and just have a happy, normal life. Can we do that?"

Ronnie blinked away tears. "I've never wanted anything more, Mike. My summer has been a total disaster. Moving, hurricanes, *time travel*. Let's just be boring and skip all that drama!"

"Deal." Mike kissed her until the beeping of the heart monitor made them both laugh.

"I love you, too, Mike." Ronnie shoved him to the bed and kissed him like she had along the river, with wild abandon. Mike thought about the doctor's prescription to lie down. He was complying with those orders.

Epilogue

Watching the Plague

The Next Day

Nick was in the kitchen when Steph and Ian got home from the grocery store. Music blared in the speaker next to the stove. Steph walked up behind Nick and wrapped her arms around his waist then cupped his perfect pectoral muscles.

He set down the spatula and turned to kiss her. "There is my Scottish beauty. How was your day?"

"Hell. But better now that you're here. I'm worried sick about Mike and Ronnie."

"Babe, you need to stop worrying. There is nothing you can do from here but wait until they call."

"I know."

"Good, save yourself the worry." He slid his hands around her waist. "Dinner is almost ready. I've made your favorite...haggis!"

Steph peeked over his shoulder at the stove. Steam rose from the frying pan full of chicken stir fry. "Oh, you lie!" His playfulness was in such contrast to the stress of the last few days.

"No, babe, I tease. I promise I will never make you haggis. It is not in my repertoire, nor will it ever be, I suspect." Nick laughed.

Steph chuckled. He was so good at making her forget her troubles, or at least put them aside for small moments. "You'd probably butcher it anyway."

"Isn't it already about as butchered as it possibly could be? It's the internal organs of a sheep chopped up and served inside its stomach, for God's sake."

Ian strode into the kitchen. "Don't knock it till you've tried it, Nick."

It was her duty as a Scot to defend haggis. It was part of Scots' law. Ian led the charge and the men playfully bantered back and forth.

Steph poured white wine and set the table, lighting the candles, enjoying the tradition she'd recently created with the three of them sitting down for meals.

"Steph, I picked up Ronnie's mail on the way home. It's by the door."

"Oh, right, I almost forgot."

Ian snagged a carrot from the pan and Nick swatted him. "Get your dirty paws out of my food, you wee brat."

Steph sat down at the table, ignoring the men, and sorted through Ronnie's mail, passing by everything but a notice from a lab. She opened it. It read:

> At MagLab we take our role seriously as an important part of patient care. Because of the findings of this lab sample, the CDC has been notified that the blood sample supplied to us for testing was found to have *Yersinia pestis* bacteria.
>
> This is a serious infection that can be spread and lead to severe illness or death. You are urged to seek immediate medical attention. Our attempts to contact you via your provided contact information have failed.

Steph stood, knocking the chair down with the movement. "Nick!"

Nick rushed from the kitchen. "What? What's wrong?"

Ian followed behind her. She handed him the letter. "Is this about Ronnie's watch?"

"Yes, what the hell is *Yersinia pestis* bacteria?"

Nick righted the chair and looked over at the letter. "Bubonic plague."

Steph sat down hard as all the air escaped her lungs.

Ian's face was ashen. "So... wait...are you telling me that Ronnie was right? That the blood on the watch actually did have the disease from her time traveling?"

Steph nodded as a deep, dark panic crept up her spine.

Nick answered for her, "Yeah, Ronnie just proved beyond a shadow of a doubt that she did time travel. I can't believe it."

Ian whooped.

Nick continued. "I mean, I believed you about her travels, but this is irrefutable proof." He read the rest of the letter and the attached sheet detailing the disease, his expression changing to likely match her own. "Oh my God, Steph, we've all been exposed. We were here in the house when she came back." He pulled up the chair next to her. "What if Ronnie ends up sick in Puerto Rico? She really needs to get treated."

Steph burst into tears, and he reached over to hug her. "I knew it! I felt something bad was going to happen! Oh my God, Nick." She hugged him again, squeezing him tight, then pulled away. "What else does it say?"

Nick read the rest. "It's a pamphlet from the CDC."

> Symptoms and Treatment
>
> Persons exposed to *Yersinia pestis bacteria* should seek immediate medical attention, regardless of symptoms, for a possible post-exposure prophylaxis. Any persons experiencing fever, cough, and labored breathing, or producing sputum that is bloody, watery, or visible pus, should seek immediate treatment. Prominent gastrointestinal symptoms may also be present. Pneumonic plague may be present if severe, rapidly progressing chest pain, labored breathing...

The End

Look for *Fracturing Time*, Book 4 in the Stealing Time series. Out in spring of 2023.

Enjoyed the Book? Leave a Review!

One of the best ways to show your support is to leave a review on Amazon, Goodreads, BookBub, Barnes and Noble or wherever you purchase your books. Don't know what to say? Just leave a sentence or two about what you liked. To make it easy, I've included the link to the review page on Amazon here: www.geni.us/KTEndMatter.

Sign up for my newsletter here:www.kjwaters.com/newsletter. Be the first to receive exclusive previews, special deals and contests.

Letter to My Readers

I cannot thank you enough for being here by my side as I share my stories with you. It has been an immense thrill to let you inside my imaginary world to different times and places through the eye of a hurricane. I know I've put Ronnie through a lot, and I hope you see how much I really love her…and love torturing her, too. My instincts drive me to be much sweeter to her, but the elements of a compelling story do not allow characters to go to bed happy.

Thank you for spending all this time inside my head. I know this book was much longer than my others, but I hope you are as excited as I am with the story and all the sparkling possibilities of where it could go next. It is such a thrill to hear from you. If you'd like to share your thoughts, I'd be so grateful! Please visit the contact form on my website here, www.kjwaters.com/contact-me, where you can share ideas, comments, and whatever you like. I love hearing from you.

Killing Time took a substantial measure of research, as all my books do, but I love bringing history to life. One of my favorite pastimes is to visit living museums and tour old homes, providing a snapshot of the lives of people from diverse cultures and time periods. I soak it in and imagine the lives of those who lived in that house. I've woven that feeling into my writing, taking it a step further by dropping my character from modern times (albeit 2004) to unique challenges our ancestors had to face.

I wanted to keep the time travel portion of the story in the United States and focused on an iconic part of history to take you to. I chose the Wild West because it is such a rich area for storytelling. I poked around at what was happening in 1872, which seemed about the right year for a new adventure. Lo and behold, I found Jesse James hiding in Texas to get away from the Missouri law. Not much is written during that period of his life, which made it ripe for me to imagine what he was up to then.

What I realized in my hours of inquiry is a lot of the James brothers' account is contradicted. The newspapers and books of later decades romanticized much of their exploits. I found suggestions that the James brothers were, in fact, several cousins with the same or similar names, and their transgressions were spread out among them. I have no sense if this is true, but it is intriguing to ponder about, don't you think?

When I realized another Western legend was there too—Quanah Parker, lauded as the last Comanche Chief—I toured his Star House in Cache, Oklahoma. In the 1980s, a local family had acquired the Star House and was in the process of acquiring other historic homes to create a living village to include in their amusement park. Sadly, the uprising of bigger amusement parks put this little one out of business, and they have left the entire property to decay for decades. On that tour, I was totally shocked when the guide pointed to a shabby house about twenty feet from the Star House and proclaimed it was owned by Frank James! I could tell you for hours about this trip, but instead, I'll be writing a blog post that illustrates the adventure. Check out my blog at kjwatersauthor.blogspot.com and look for the one labeled "Star House." I've not written it as publication date, but I will soon.

The inception of the *Stealing Time* series was provoked by experiencing the 2004 hurricane season with a front-row seat. We (my husband and I, and two young children) moved to Florida just three days before Hurricane Charley struck. I was in Orlando and everyone there told us not to worry. They'd not had a direct hit by a major hurricane in sixty years. Great timing, huh?

We were lucky and only sustained damage to our roof during the last hour of the last storm (Jeanne) when a branch from a pine tree dropped about forty feet into our Florida room. The missile was from the tree we almost cut down after the first storm, Hurricane Charley, except an eagle landed in it just before the crew was to remove it. The neighbors all came out and were in a tizzy about cutting that tree down, so we left it, hoping to not disturb their world. Bad luck, huh?

In 2005, inspired by the *Outlander* series, I started the story while driving from Florida to Maine on a family vacation. Little did I know it would end up being three books, and now I've imagined at least one more after *Killing Time*.

I hope to have *Fracturing Time* out in the next year or so. In this story, you will learn what happened to Ronnie's father during that fateful night of his failed experiment. I'm also going to bring back Mathias (from *Stealing Time)* and I cannot wait to share his time travel adventures with you. My developmental editor, Cameron Chandler, has thrown a giant monkey wrench in the idea of wrapping up the series by throwing a huge plot twist idea into a Book 5. Stay tuned to see how that develops. At some point, I want to pitch this series to the streaming services. I'd love to see it in a longer format than a movie, so it can keep all the twists and turns.

I hope you enjoyed this book, and if you've not checked out the first two books in the series, I hope you dive right into them. *Stealing Time* covers the first hurricane (Charley) and takes Ronnie back to 1752 London during a shift in time. *Shattering Time* is the second book and finds Ronnie during Hurricane Frances, which was the size of Texas, lasting an entire weekend. She is sent back to multiple timelines as Jeffery tries out the equipment. She sees the Fire of London and the Lost Colony of Roanoke Island. I also have a short story called "Blow."

Writing *Killing Time* has been a labor of love. It took me almost four years to finish the manuscript. Along the way, I've quit a (horrible) job and now dedicate the first part of my day to putting words on the page. My next book will be along a lot sooner, I promise! I'm also working on a new series that I hope to have out next year.

Acknowledgements

I have had a lot of help putting this story together. I am so grateful for their generous gift of their time and talent to make *Killing Time* sparkle. It's hard to know where to start, but the one person who has helped me the most has to be **Suzanne Kelman**. We meet almost every week to talk story, book marketing, and life. Thank you, Suzanne for always being there for me. Visit her website to see the magical stories she creates at suzannekelmanauthor.com.

My family has put up with a lot as I craft my stories, so a huge thank you has to go out to my husband and kids. My husband knows weapons and has kept my cluelessness from showing (for the most part), and also with the Marine jargon, dude point of view, and other story elements. My mom, sister, and stepsister are huge supporters and extremely helpful in getting me to the finish line. My father is an antique clock buff (and repairer) and always gives me great advice to keep the covers on track, and he and my stepmother are wonderful encouragers.

One difficult element of my stories is the physics of time travel. I happen to have an in-house science expert, as my son is studying physics in college. He has helped me develop Jeffrey's time travel elements, and the double R bar magic was his idea. I loved it and ran with it. He has been one of my biggest supporters in my writing and I'm hoping he has caught the writing bug. The boy is brilliant enough to be an amazing writer, we just need to see where he ends up in his career and if that lends itself to storytelling. I will be twisting his arm.

I don't even have the words to thank Cameron Chandler for taking on this giant story and helping me keep all the pieces together to finish the book. He has been an incredible support and become a dear friend along the way. You have been a godsend in helping me wrangle the best out of *Killing Time*. Thank you, Suzanne, for recommending him!

When my previous editor dropped her business to teach, I struggled for a while to find an editor who was fast, accurate and didn't totally break my bank. I'm so grateful to have found Audrey Mackaman. She's been amazing how quickly she worked her magic.

One way I enjoy spicing up my stories is adding colorful characters from other cultures. This takes extra work and the thoughtful guidance from people who know far better than I do how these folks would really behave outside my head. Ini was brought to life by KT Bond, you can find her at Author KT Bond on Facebook. KT is a native Jamaican, a wonderful writer, and a generous supporter. Thank you KT!

Ian and Steph's delightful Scottishness rolls around in my head so much now as I run around in my daily life. It's not always proper Scots though, so I've had Simon Dick set me straight correcting my sad attempts at Glaswegian. He has been with me since the first book. His corrections are hilarious and always come with delightful

Scottishisms that make me love the Scots even more. Every Scot I've met has been self-deprecating, clever, and funny as hell. Simon has all those qualities with the added bonus of being smart. Thank you, Simon, for making me not feel like a total numpty.

Ben Coleman has breathed life into Jesse and Frank James and the other western elements of the story, especially the historical nuance of post-Civil War struggles. He's also been an amazing support of my writing and story craft.

I have an amazing group of folks over on my Street Team and newsletter group. A huge thank you for your mass outpouring of support with this latest installment. If you'd like to join either, you can do that here: www.kjwaters.com/newsletter and Street Team on Facebook here: www.facebook.com/groups/950502348401864

Stay in Touch

The best way to keep up to date on my new releases and projects is to sign up for my newsletter here: www.kjwaters.com/newsletter. Please check out my website: www.kjwaters.com.

You can find my author social media accounts:
Twitter: @KJWatersAuthor,
Facebook: KJ Waters, KJ Waters Author
Pinterest: kamajowa,
Instagram: @kamajowa,
BookBub: KJ Waters,
Goodreads: KJ Waters

I am also an author consultant helping authors write, publish, and market one book at a time. Website: www.kjwConsultancy.com.

In October 2015, I started a podcast called Blondie and the Brit with Suzanne Kelman. It is an author podcast with interviews, social media tips and more. Check it out here on podbean at Blondie and the Brit and iTunes.